Capturing Her Heart

NINA BRUHNS
CARIDAD PIÑEIRO
KATHLEEN CREIGHTON

All the characters in this book have no existence outside the imagination of the author, and have no relation whatsoever to anyone bearing the same name or names. They are not even distantly inspired by any individual known or unknown to the author, and all the incidents are pure invention.

All Rights Reserved including the right of reproduction in whole or in part in any form. This edition is published by arrangement with Harlequin Enterprises II B.V./S.à.r.l. The text of this publication or any part thereof may not be reproduced or transmitted in any form or by any means, electronic or mechanical, including photocopying, recording, storage in an information retrieval system, or otherwise, without the written permission of the publisher.

This book is sold subject to the condition that it shall not, by way of trade or otherwise, be lent, resold, hired out or otherwise circulated without the prior consent of the publisher in any form of binding or cover other than that in which it is published and without a similar condition including this condition being imposed on the subsequent purchaser.

® and ™ are trademarks owned and used by the trademark owner and/or its licensee. Trademarks marked with ® are registered with the United Kingdom Patent Office and/or the Office for Harmonisation in the Internal Market and in other countries.

First published in Great Britain 2012
by Mills & Boon, an imprint of Harlequin (UK) Limited,
Eton House, 18-24 Paradise Road, Richmond, Surrey TW9 1SR

CAPTURING HER HEART © by Harlequin Enterprises II B.V./S.à.r.l 2012

Royal Betrayal, *More than a Mission* and *The Rebel King* were first published in Great Britain by Harlequin (UK) Limited in separate, single volumes.

Royal Betrayal © Harlequin Books S.A. 2006
More than a Mission © Harlequin Books S.A. 2006
The Rebel King © Harlequin Books S.A. 2006

Special thanks and acknowledgement are given to Nina Bruhns, Caridad Piñeiro and Kathleen Creighton for their contribution to the Capturing the Crown series.

ISBN: 978 0 263 89686 2
ebook ISBN: 978 1 408 97048 5

05-0412

Printed and bound in Spain
by Blackprint CPI, Barcelona

ROYAL BETRAYAL

BY
NINA BRUHNS

OLDHAM METRO LIBRARY SERVICE	
A33604146	
Bertrams	25/03/2012
ROM	£5.99

Dear Reader,

Royal Betrayal is a bit of a departure from my usual edgy stories, but one that I thoroughly enjoyed writing. I'll bet you never guessed that I'm a closet historical writer…but it's true. I've always loved reading historical romances, with their lords and ladies and luxurious aristocratic settings. Finally I got to write a book with all that, and a dynamite mystery, too! What more could a lady…er, author, ask for?

It was such fun working with the other talented authors on these contemporary fairy tales! It's not every day you get to invent a whole new country, complete with princes and dukes, lords and ladies, and a dastardly villain or two thrown in for some spine-tingling action.

So get ready to be swept away once again to the Kingdom of Silvershire as my hero, Dr Walker Shaw, and heroine, Lady Zara Smith, continue the quest to find the true royal prince, and along the way find something even better—true love.

Nina (who dedicates this book to my wonderful editors, Julie Barrett, Melissa Endlich, Patience Smith and Jessica Alvarez. You are a true joy to work with, ladies!)

Nina Bruhns credits her Gypsy great-grandfather for her great love of adventure. She has lived and traveled all over the world, including a six-year stint in Sweden. She has been on scientific expeditions from California to Spain to Egypt and the Sudan, and has two graduate degrees in archaeology (with a specialty in Egyptology). She speaks four languages and writes a mean hieroglyphic!

But Nina's first love has always been writing. For her, writing is the ultimate adventure. Drawing on her many experiences gives her stories a colorful dimension and allows her to create settings and characters out of the ordinary. She has won numerous awards for her previous titles, including the prestigious National Readers Choice Award, two Daphne Du Maurier Awards of Excellence for Overall Best Romantic Suspense of the year, five Dorothy Parker Awards and two Golden Heart Awards, among many others.

A native of Canada, Nina grew up in California and currently resides in Charleston, South Carolina, with her husband and three children. She loves to hear from her readers, and can be reached at PO Box 2216, Summerville, SC 29484-2216 or by e-mail via her website at www.ninabruhns.com or via the Harlequin website at www.eharlequin.com.

Prologue

The Royal Palace, Silverton
In the country of Silvershire
July

The king was dying.

And there was nothing she could do about it.

Panic crawled deep within Dr. Zara Smith. Gently grasping the old man's hand, Zara willed King Weston to regain consciousness and once again shine his wise, kind smile upon her. The smile she'd worked so hard over the past month to put back on his face.

All for nothing.

Why wouldn't he wake up? She'd removed the tumor ravaging his brain days ago. The surgery had gone perfectly. There was no reason the king should still be in a coma.

Not again, she prayed. *Please, not again.*

"Any change?" asked Emily, the day nurse, sending both of them a worried glance.

Zara shook her head, turning away from the trace of pity she saw in the other woman's eyes. She knew exactly what the nurse was thinking. If King Weston died, the country would lose a much-beloved monarch…and Zara would lose her future. Between this and the child's death last year, no amount of medical brilliance or even Lady Zara's aristocratic title would be able to save her career as a doctor. The tabloids would have a field day—again. She'd be forced to go crawling back to her father's estate in disgrace, her plans shattered, her goals crushed. Lord Daneby would never forgive her for besmirching the family name by allowing the king to die on his daughter's watch.

God, Zara would never forgive herself.

Maybe if she—

Suddenly, a deafening roar ripped through the room like the boom of thunder. Glass and wood and metal exploded all around her, sending deadly shards in every direction. Screaming for help, she instinctively launched herself over the old king, shielding his body as a wall of flaming instruments from behind his bed collapsed over them.

Again she screamed, this time from the pain stabbing through her shoulder and side. Something hard and sharp cracked over her skull, and a red-hot shower of pain detonated through her head.

Then all went black.

Chapter 1

Late afternoon, one week later

Dr. Walker Shaw tried to look somber and professional while accompanying His Grace, Russell, Duke of Carrington, the acting regent of the tiny country of Silvershire, as they strolled through the imposing halls of the palace toward the medical wing. After all, he was here on official business. Walker's appearance might be a tad disreputable, and his accent slow and lazy as molasses, but his credentials as a consultant with the elite Lazlo Group were sterling enough to allow him regular admittance to places mere mortals rarely visited. Places such as this.

It was not appropriate to be wearing the roguish grin of a man with nothin' but romance on his mind.

But he simply couldn't help himself. He'd been fantasizing about coming to the quaint island kingdom for seven years now, to track down and charm the exquisitely sexy and mysterious Lady Sarah—with any luck right into his bed—as he'd done so memorably all those years ago at that medical conference in Italy.

Lord willing, she was still living in her native land. And single.

"I understand your specialty is memory loss," Lord Carrington said, yanking Walker from a particularly vivid memory of Lady Sarah's delicious behind bending over a breakfast tray.

"That's right," Walker answered, shifting smoothly into his professional persona. "Mainly as it relates to advancing age and dementia."

As a doctor of psychiatry, Walker had spent the better part of his adult life researching the affliction in the elderly. In his flourishing practice, he had treated patients with all kinds of memory loss resulting from everything from psychological trauma to physical accident to Alzheimer's. Medical research hadn't been his job, it had been his calling.

Well. Until the ugly scandal that had tanked his meteoric career three years earlier put an end to all that.

"I trust it won't matter," Lord Carrington said, "if your patient here is all of thirty-four?"

Walker hardly registered the quick churl of regret at the word patient. He certainly didn't bother to correct it. What the hell. He had moved on. And the life he had now was far more relaxed than the one he'd had as an overworked doctor. He was even doing much of the same kind of work—minus the research, of course. With the Lazlo Group, he consulted on fascinating cases by day and had lots of free time by night. He'd be a fool to miss his old life.

"Not at all," Walker said, turning his attention to his newest assignment. "I understand she was injured in the assassination attempt on King Weston."

"The palace bombing, yes."

"A terrible thing. She's a doctor, isn't she?"

Lord Carrington nodded. "Dr. Zara Smith."

"The renowned neurosurgeon?" Walker asked, vaguely surprised. Though they'd never met, he'd read a couple of her papers in the journals. Intelligent woman.

"She's been treating the king's brain tumor. She sustained her head injury saving his life during the blast."

"How did it happen, exactly?"

"Under the plaster, the palace walls are made of stone," Carrington said. "Several dislodged in the explosion, and one of them caught her in the temple. She remembers nothing. Not even her own name."

Walker thought about the relative merits of being able to forget one's past so completely. There had been days over the past three years he'd have gladly traded places with her. But no more. He'd made peace with his demons.

Besides, not for anything would he give up the memory of a certain auburn-haired young lady stretching across an elaborately carved feather bed, bathed in the glow of the magical Italian dawn. If he couldn't remember her, how could he find her?

"Has Dr. Smith regained consciousness?" he asked, getting back to the point. The sooner he dealt with this, the sooner he could start looking. And hopefully fill some of those free nights he had…

"She woke the next day. Her physical injuries are nearly healed now. It's just her memory that is lacking." The duke's long-legged stride slowed. "That's why we need your help. We're anxious to have her remember as quickly as possible, so she'll be able to tell us more about the bombing. We're

hoping she saw something. Perhaps even the perpetrators."
The future king's eyes sought his. The weight of grave
concern and heavy responsibility were clearly etched in his
young face. "We need to catch these traitors. Silvershire is
already in an uproar over the death of Prince Reginald. And
now this vile attempt on the life of our king. The stability of
my country could very well depend upon the information Dr.
Smith might give us."

Walker returned his gaze steadily. "I understand."

Corbett Lazlo, Walker's boss, had given him a bit of background on the situation before sending him in. Crown Prince
Reginald had been found murdered at his lavish country estate—poisoned by cocaine spiked with digitalis—and there
had been all sorts of speculation in the press about who might
have killed Reginald, and why. At the moment the leading
contenders were the Union for Democracy, a radical anti-
monarchy group that had been steadily gaining political clout
over the past decades, and Lord Carrington himself.

In addition to clout, the UD had also been increasingly accepting of violence as a vehicle for political change. On the
other hand, before the murder, Lord Carrington, although un-
related to the present king, had been second in line for the
monarchy. Now he'd not only moved up to number one, he'd
also hastily married the crown prince's fiancée and then
become acting regent when King Weston collapsed. Two
months from now, due to an ancient, quirky law that mandated
the ascension of the heir to the throne upon his thirtieth
birthday, Carrington would be crowned King of Silvershire.

It all seemed a little too convenient to the country's rumor-
mongers and particularly the local weekly tabloid, *The Inquisitor*, popularly dubbed the *Quiz*.

Still, the Lazlo Group's money was on the UD and not the

duke, who seemed sincerely reluctant to become king. It was he who'd hired them to investigate both the prince's murder and the attempt on King Weston's life. But it would be nice to have proof of his innocence in the tangled intrigue. Walker could see why Carrington was anxious for Dr. Smith to recover her memory if he was indeed innocent.

"How long has it been since the bombing?" he asked.

"Just over a week."

Walker pursed his lips consideringly as they passed through a magnificent gilded hall filled with mirrors and tapestries, huge paintings and windows overlooking a formal courtyard garden. A week wasn't all that long. He'd seen cases where it took a year or more for the memories to return. "She's remembered nothing at all?"

"Nothing."

"And your physicians have ruled out any lingering physical injury?"

"Their examinations have been meticulous. Can you help her, Dr. Shaw?"

"I'll certainly try," he said, knowing better than to promise anything. The mind was as unpredictable as the weather in a South Carolina springtime. As they approached the palace medical wing, Walker added, "But there's one thing I need to insist on."

"Anything. Just name it."

"The way I work requires that the subject not be told anything about their former life other than what's strictly necessary. Has anyone talked to Dr. Smith about her background?"

Carrington shook his head. "Just her name, nothing else. Corbett Lazlo already made that recommendation. She hasn't been allowed to watch the news or read the papers, since she has been all over both since the blast. I even managed to dissuade her family from visiting her yet, though it wasn't easy. Her father is the Marquis of Daneby, one of the most influential men and highest ranking nobles in the country."

"I appreciate his cooperation. The reason for the precaution is to prevent false memories. It can be hard for amnesia victims to distinguish between something they are told and a true memory. We don't want to influence Dr. Smith's recollections in any way."

"No, of course not."

They'd arrived in the medical wing, and Walker glanced around at the compact facility, modern and crisply white. The nurses' station was manned by a rosy-cheeked matron named Emily, whose smile lines indicated she was usually a lot more cheerful than she appeared today. There was a short bank of blinking monitors, cozy furniture and a couple of framed paintings of flowers. No signs of fire or debris.

"You've already made repairs from the explosion?" he asked, surprised Corbett would have allowed that.

"Good God, no," Carrington said, indicating a hallway to their right. "The room where the bomb went off is down at the end. We haven't touched anything, since the investigation is ongoing." He swept a hand in an all-encompassing gesture. "Damage was pretty much confined to King Weston's recovery room and Dr. Smith's connecting office and lab. The stone walls are over three feet thick."

"Is that a fact?" Walker hid a smile, recalling a similar comment by the nubile Lady Sarah concerning the walls of the Florence palazzo where they had been staying. And they'd been grateful for every sound-dampening inch. "I'm surprised anyone even heard the explosion."

They arrived at a closed door and Carrington halted. "This is Dr. Smith's room. Would you like me to go in with you?"

"I'm sure your schedule is more than full, Your Grace, so I won't keep you any longer. Thank you for meeting with me."

With a formal nod and an offer of any further assistance, Carrington strode purposefully back down the hall.

Walker watched him round the corner, then he turned to the door in front of him and took a deep breath. After a quick knock, he entered the room and stood in the doorway, his eyes adjusting to the dimness. The lace curtains were drawn, but the sun was setting on the other side of the palace, throwing the interior of the room into a misty sort of soft focus.

On the tidy bed lay a woman, her long, loose auburn hair spreading across the pillow.

His body gave a jolt of surprise. Or maybe of primal recognition. There was something about that hair….

His mind was still working in slow motion when she turned her face toward him.

He froze, welded to the spot, his entire being shocked to the core.

Sweet merciful heaven.

It was *her*.

There on the sterile hospital bed lay his delectable Lady Sarah. No longer a young ingenue, but all grown up and sexier than ever, her mouthwateringly curvy body ill-concealed under the thin white sheet, her beautiful face pale and fragile, her sensual eyes wide with apprehension.

She gazed right at him.

Without an ounce of recognition.

Another stranger.

Lord, who was she kidding? *Everyone* was a stranger to her. Including herself.

She stared back at the handsome man standing in the

doorway watching her with an appalled expression. As though he'd seen a ghost.

Did she really look that awful?

"Sarah?" he whispered. Or rather, croaked.

She swallowed, resisting the urge to pull her unruly hair back in a twist at her nape. "They tell me my name is Zara. Zara Smith. And you are…?"

His startlingly blue eyes skittered up from her body. "You don't remember?"

Something in the way he said it made her think she should. She clutched at the sheet covering her and pulled it a smidgen higher, to the base of her throat. Then shook her head.

"No," she said through a trickle of panic that was beginning to seep through her veins. "Not a thing."

Panic? Or was it embarrassment, over the sudden sexual awareness that engulfed her…?

"Who are you?" she repeated. Then a startling thought occurred. "Are you my…gentleman friend, or—" *surely they would have told her!* "—or my husband?"

The stranger's square jaw dropped. It was *definitely* panic that flew across his face, accompanied by a low curse. "No. I'm not— I'm your— That is, I'm a—" He clamped his teeth together, said, "Excuse me," through them, then turned on a toe and disappeared back through the door. It closed behind him with a soft whoosh.

"Well," she whispered aloud, feeling uncomfortably like Alice at the Mad Hatter's tea party. "That was very curious. But then, everything's curious these days."

Not the least of which was that she could quote passages from Lewis Carroll but not remember her own name.

She squeezed her eyes shut, wondering who the stranger

was. And why he'd seemed so upset. Was he the consultant Dr. Landon had mentioned? She was certain he'd recognized her. Why hadn't he said anything? And why had he called her Sarah, when everyone insisted her name was Zara? What was this all about?

Her nerves hummed with tension. She wasn't afraid, exactly. Not for her safety. Everyone had been very kind, especially Dr. Landon and Emily. But nobody would tell her a flipping thing. She wasn't even allowed the morning papers.

She despaired of ever knowing who she was.

Fighting the hot tears she felt just below the surface, she focused her mind instead on the stranger. He was American. He hadn't said much, but she'd recognized his accent, slow and smooth, like spun honey. *Southern*. How did she know that? Had she been to the US? She tried to think, but nothing came to her. Except the face of the man.

He even looked American. Though very nicely tailored, his gray wool suit had a rebellious cut to it and his white shirt was defiantly cotton, rather than silk. And despite his too-long wheaten hair, his shadowed, angular jaw and those piercing blue eyes that looked like they'd seen more than most men cared to, his face had an open, sincere quality to it that European men's lacked, especially the blasé, sophisticated men with whom she came in contact.

Her eyes sprang open at that little insight. It was the very first personal revelation she'd had since waking up a week ago with bandages wrapped around her head. She smiled. A small triumph, but huge nonetheless. Could this be the beginning of remembering?

Suddenly, there was another knock and the door swung open. It was the American again. He stood there in his James Dean suit, hands on lean hips, a muscle popping in his jaw.

"I'm Dr. Walker Shaw," he said, almost angrily. "I'll be treating your amnesia."

She sucked in a breath. "You?" The word just jumped out. She hadn't meant to sound so incredulous. Or so disconcerted.

"Yes, ma'am," he responded. "And there're going to be a few rules." He raised his hand to tick off fingers. "First—"

"You're a doctor?" she interrupted, sitting up on the bed. She tried for authority, but it wasn't easy with her hair falling down about her shoulders and the rest of her covered only by a lace dressing gown.

To which his eyes immediately dropped. His mouth worked for a second before he jerked them up again.

"I'm a psychiatrist," he said. "Specializing in memory loss. You should know I'm not licensed to practice in Silvershire, so I'm here only as a consultant, at the request of…your government. If you have any objections to working with me, please say so now and I'll—"

"Can you get my memory back?" she cut in, filing away his hesitation over who'd requested his services, to think about later.

"I don't know," he said, and glanced away. The muscle in his jaw popped again. "There are a lot of factors—"

"Yes, yes, I know all about the factors." She waved away his speech irritably. She'd heard it at least a dozen times a day for the past week. At least he'd been honest. All of the others had bent over backwards to reassure her the memories would return. Sooner or later…

She sank back on the bed, pressing her temples between her fingers, rubbing at the beginnings of a headache. The pain in her head had been ferocious for the first several days, but had slowly receded as her wound healed. She'd barely felt it today. Until now.

"What's your methodology?" she asked through the throbbing.

His brow raised slightly. "I was about to get to that when you questioned my credentials."

"I'm sorry," she murmured. "I didn't mean to—"

"Don't apologize. You have every right. The fact is I'm not allowed to practice medicine here, and you should run anything you're uncomfortable with by your regular physician, Dr. Landon. I'm only here to suggest a possible course of treatment. Anytime you want out, just say the word and I'm gone."

"I appreciate your candor," she assured him. "But what I want is to remember my life. If you can help, I'm willing to do whatever you ask."

His bald gaze held hers, and for some unfathomable reason she felt herself blush.

He cleared his throat and looked away. "Yes, well, as to how I work…I'd say fairly casually. The only thing I'm adamant about is that you must remember everything on your own. You'll get no help, or hints, that could just as easily throw you off."

She closed her eyes and rubbed her throbbing forehead. "Ah. That explains it." Why no one would tell her anything.

"Do yourself a favor and don't try to cheat. It'll only hurt your recovery in the long run. And you'll never know if those memories are real or fantasy."

"I understand."

"Meanwhile, if you feel well enough, in the morning we'll walk around a little and hope that something clicks. Oftentimes you'll see something, or hear something, or smell something, that triggers your mind and suddenly all your memories come flooding back."

"Smell?" she asked, her lip quirking.

"The sense of smell is the most powerful one we have. A particular smell can bring back things you've forgotten for years, or even decades. A long-ago holiday, the scent of your mother, a different country you've visited…" his deep voice paused infinitesimally "…a favorite lover."

Her fingers stilled on her temples as the word hung in the air between them like one of the evocative scents he'd described. The hairs on the back of her neck prickled, and she reached deep into her mind, searching, searching. For a favorite lover, for his unique scent, for the brush of his hand over her skin. A shiver traced through her body. But the memory eluded her.

She turned to him and his gaze lingered on her, questioning, encouraging. He remained silent, though, until she gave a nervous laugh.

"You've quite a bedside manner, Dr. Shaw."

After a second of surprise his eyes suddenly shuttered, and the spell was broken. "Whatever works," he said gruffly. He reached for the door handle. "I'd like to start tomorrow. You up for it?"

"Absolutely," she said.

"Get as much sleep as possible. If this is your first time out of bed, it'll be a tiring day."

"I'll look forward to a breakthrough," she said with a weak smile, letting her eyes drift closed against the throbbing in her head. When she heard the whisper of the door opening she added, "Thank you, Dr. Shaw."

"See you tomorrow, Zara," he murmured before it closed again.

Or had he said Sarah? Darn, she thought as sleep wafted

over her, she'd meant to ask him about that. Never mind. She'd see him in the morning. She could ask then.

She sighed happily. And for the first time in a week, felt real anticipation for waking up to a new day.

Pounding.

Her head was pounding, pounding. Like a heavy hammer on metal. Great shifting sheets of metal. She was screaming. Screaming and screaming from the pain in her head and the loud screeching of metal sheets grinding and snapping together.

No. It was not her screaming. It was a baby! No. Two babies! Screaming at the tops of their lungs. Hungry. Wet. Confused. Where was their mother? Gone.

Was she their mother? Desperately, she searched her memory. Why couldn't she remember? She felt warm tears on her cheeks, long muddy grass beneath her bare feet. She was running. Running toward the babies.

They disappeared in a blinding flash of purple. Purple and red, with swirling gold symbols spinning down at her from every direction. Crazy symbols. Meaningless. A kaleidoscope? Purple with gold. Red with Gold. Spinning, spinning. Crashing into her. Crushing her. Pounding.

Smothering her. Suffocating.

Suddenly, everything went black.

She screamed again, desperate, clawing at the darkness, and this time she knew it was her own screams. The babies were gone. Gone.

It was just her, screaming in the dark.

Calling out. For someone. Someone... Who?

And where were the babies?

"Help us!" *someone screamed, and she bolted awake.*

* * *

Zara sat panting on the disheveled bed, sweat beading on her aching brow. "Good lord," she whispered into the silence of the black night. What was happening to her? She'd never had a dream like that before. Haunting. Terrifying.

She gave a strangled laugh. At least she didn't think she had. Who knew? Talk about falling down the rabbit hole.

She slid out of bed and padded to the porcelain sink in the compact but well-appointed WC attached to her room, then changed her mind. Slipping off her uncomfortable night-dress—she hated wearing anything to bed, it made her feel hot and confined—she stepped into the shower.

The pulsing stream of warm water felt heavenly on her ragged body; it soothed her nerves, easing the residual tension in her muscles and the trembling in her limbs. Soon, even the strange throbbing in her head disappeared.

What an odd dream.

She thought about the babies in it, and what it could have meant. Were they hers?

Could she have children? That was something she'd never even considered before now. Surely, if she had children the doctors would not have kept her from them. That would be too cruel.

As she dried herself, she tried to plumb the depths of her mind, searching for a hint. She didn't feel as though she had children. She glanced in the mirror. Her body didn't look like she'd had them. Her breasts were still high and firm, her waist narrow, her stomach flat. Fairly flat. She frowned. She didn't even know how old she was.

With a huff of frustration, she debated for a moment, then gave up and pulled on a fresh nightdress. The nurses wouldn't care if she left it off, but the new guy might.

Speaking of whom, tomorrow she wanted answers. Lots of answers. She'd tell Dr. Dreamy American exactly what she thought of his ridiculous methods. Keeping her ignorant would not improve her memory. It would only make her more irritable.

And frankly, there were other emotions she'd far rather explore around a man like that. She didn't need to know who she was to know how attracted she was to the good doctor. Bad temper and all. The man was a stunner, if a bit of rough.

But first things first. In the morning she'd confront him. Demand to know some basics about herself. So she could stop worrying about whether or not she had children. Or a husband. So she could move on to more important things. Such as strolling around with Dr. Shaw, dredging up her old memories.

And maybe, maybe even making some new ones.

Chapter 2

"Corbett, listen to me. I'm serious. You've got to take me off this case."

"Wish I could, lad. But you know that's impossible."

Walker held his cell phone and listened impatiently as his boss expounded on all the reasons why Walker Shaw was the only person on earth for this job.

"Corbett, that's bull and you know it. There are a dozen or more legitimate doctors who could do this just as well as I can."

"But they don't work for me. That's really the only reason that counts, isn't it? Besides, you're being too modest. You are still a legitimate doctor, even if presently unlicensed. You're also one of the world's leading authorities on memory loss."

Walker snorted. "Yeah. And that and a five-dollar bill will buy me a cup of coffee."

"Do I detect a trace of bitterness?" Corbett's voice was laced with humor. His boss knew damn well Walker was more than happy with his present employment, but that it irked the hell out of him how he'd been unfairly dismissed from his former one.

"What do you think?" he asked dryly. Then sighed. "Boss, please, have pity on me. I'm telling you, this woman and I have a history. A hot and steamy history. For crying out loud, ninety-five percent of the time we spent with each other we were naked."

"Spare me the sordid details, my boy," Corbett interrupted, laughing. "I'm sorry about that. Honestly I am. But—"

"I'm begging, here, Corbett. Don't do this to me. I won't be able to keep my hands off her. You know what happened to my medical career because of a woman. Except this time it'll all be true." He groaned.

"Does Dr. Smith remember you?"

"No," he admitted. Undecided whether to be relieved or offended. That weekend he'd been—

"Brilliant. My advice is to keep your hands in your bloody pockets and concentrate on getting her memory back. Once she does, you're off the case. And I might even be persuaded to give you some time off for good behavior. Or whatever."

Walker could see he was getting nowhere. An unholy stubbornness was one of the many traits that had helped Corbett Lazlo build the most exclusive, sought-after investigative agency in the world. Once he had his mind set on something, God help the man who disagreed.

Up until now Walker hadn't. He'd also never, ever gotten personally involved in a case in any way, shape or form. Because of his past, he'd been scrupulous about that. Hell, he'd never even been tempted. If anything, the opposite. Once burned, and all.

But Zara Smith was…different.

There was something about her that appealed to him deep inside, in a primal, carnal way. It had knocked the air from his lungs the first time he'd seen her sitting eagerly in the front row at the paper he was giving at the World Medical Conference in Florence. It had given him the balls to approach her afterward and boldly ask her back to his hotel room, and had kept him hard and lusting after her the entire weekend. Then it had kept the memory of her alive and smoldering within him for all this time, waiting for a chance to break away from his hectic schedule and track her down, drag her back with him to the States, if necessary, and continue where they'd left off.

He let out a long breath. "All right. Fine. It's not like my reputation can get any more blackened than it is."

"Walker—" Corbett began.

"No, it's okay," he cut him off. "Frustration is good, my mama always tells me. Builds character in a man."

Corbett laughed. "Call me if you need to talk."

"In a pig's eye," he said, and hung up.

Damn, damn, good goddamn.

Walker strode down the medical wing's stark white hallway, heading for Zara's room. Preparing himself to see her again. He'd put it off as long as he could. It was almost eleven, and he had said he'd be by in the morning, not the afternoon.

He would be cool and distant, he told himself. Ultra professional. Not a single personal thing would pass his lips. And his lips would stay firmly on his own mouth. Not hers.

He almost groaned aloud at that particular image.

No.

Distance.

No lips. No hands.

Doctor-patient, he reminded himself. He wasn't about to fall into that trap. Not even for the luscious Lady Sa—Zara. He had more self-respect than that. Despite Ramona Burdette's accusations. Despite what the tabloid headlines back home had blared.

"Dr. Shaw." A soft female voice sounded from off to the side. He jerked around to see Zara hailing him from a small round table in a sunny room behind the nurse's station.

"Dr. Smith," he responded, scrabbling for neutral professionalism in his nodded greeting.

Her brows shot up and her mouth curved. "*Doctor* Smith?"

He closed his eyes briefly at his unwitting mistake and growled a low curse.

"I should have known that's why I've felt so at home here. I'm a doctor!"

Good job, Shaw. No point trying to put that horse back into the barn. "You can't always trust your feelings," he said, "but sometimes they do turn out to be right."

"Thank you," she said with a grin. "This is starting out considerably better than I expected. Coffee, Dr. Shaw?"

"No, thanks," he gritted out. "Let's get going."

"By all means." Zara rose and trailed him out of the room. "Don't feel too bad. I was going to make you tell me anyway. This just saves us time and probably a lot of arguing."

"I wouldn't have told you," he groused, then stalked down the hall toward her room. But he realized that was the last place he wanted to be with her. He turned abruptly. She almost ran into his chest, and he barely resisted grabbing her. To steady her.

"Yes, you would have," she said quietly. She was wearing some soft, silky thing the color of ripe peaches, which made her amber eyes mellow, like leaves in a Shiloh autumn. She reached for him. Almost had her hand on his arm.

He stepped back.

Her chin went up. "And there's one other question you'll answer for me," she continued.

"Oh?"

"Family. I want to know if I have any. A husband. Children… It's just not fair to keep that kind of information from a person." She narrowed her eyes mutinously. "And I don't care about your damned methodology."

At the moment, he didn't, either. He was tempted to tell her everything she wanted to know, and more that she probably didn't. He told himself she wasn't asking about a husband because of him…because, however unconsciously, she still wanted him.

"Very well," he said, making a decision that went against all his own firm rules. And told himself he wasn't doing it because he desperately wanted her to still want him, any way he could get it. "No husband. No children." *Talk about being in denial.* "You do have other family. But they've agreed to stay away for the time being."

"What's the time being?"

He held up his hands. "Enough, now. That's all you'll get from me. No more questions."

"Grump," she huffed.

"I'm not a grump. I'm doing what's best for you." He glanced at her but she didn't look annoyed. She actually looked pleased.

His chest squeezed, remembering the comfortable banter they'd shared in bed. From the start it had been like they'd known each other, been lovers forever. It was one of the things that had kept him thinking about her for so long afterward. How comfortable they'd been together, even as they'd gotten to know each other's bodies.

Hell. He had to stop torturing himself. She didn't remember him, and even if she did, she probably wouldn't want anything to do with him. A professional with her reputation wouldn't associate with a dishonored doctor. And no, she wasn't married, but she undoubtedly had a boyfriend. Carrington hadn't mentioned anyone, but it would be strange if a woman like her didn't have men swarming after her.

She hadn't come looking for him after their lost weekend in Florence, had she? Though she knew very well who he was and where to find him.

"Are you all right?"

He jerked back to the present and found her regarding him with concern.

"Just a bit tired. Jet lag," he lied.

"Mmm. I didn't get much sleep last night, either."

He peered at her face, seeing for the first time the taut lines around her pretty eyes and the corners of her luscious mouth. "Why not? Is there something I should know about?"

She seemed to hesitate for a split second, then shook her head. "No. Just excited to start. I want so badly to remember. It's truly awful not knowing anything about myself."

"In that case, we better get going."

The next hour or so Zara and Walker spent talking to the resident and two nurses on duty, and the medical student who took care of the minimalist but ultra-modern lab. Then they went down and checked out the large, basement-level emergency room, which was also used, albeit rarely, as a private morgue.

She recognized nothing and no one from before this week. Every minute that went by, she got more and more discouraged.

By the way Walker directed the casual conversations, it dawned on her she must be one of the doctors in charge of this facility, working regularly with these people. And yet, they appeared awkward speaking with her. It was obvious what Walker was doing. Showing her familiar places and faces, drawing out facts and bits of personal information from everyone, hoping something would trigger a specific memory in her.

But the only thing it succeeded in doing was convincing her she seldom spoke to her staff about anything other than work. For some reason that depressed her.

"What did I do here? What kind of a doctor was I?" she asked him. Realizing, belatedly, that she'd used the past tense. That depressed her even more.

He shook his head. "Sorry. No dice."

They were standing at a window, gazing out over a gorgeous lawn and garden. An endless expanse of lush green flowed out from the butterscotch-yellow building they were in, canted and bordered in a riot of yellow and white roses, dollops of purple violets and mounds of white carnations. She could almost smell the old-rose and sweet-spicy clove scents.

A memory hovered, so close she could almost taste it. Then it vanished.

With a sigh she pressed her forehead to the pane and glanced sideways at the ornate facade of the building.

She turned to him, puzzled. "Is this the Royal Palace?"

She could see the cogs turning in his head, but he nodded. "Yeah. Do you remember, or is that a guess?"

"A deduction," she said.

A wry smile lifted his mouth. "You're one smart lady. But be careful not to make any assumptions about anything. They could land you in trouble."

"Would I get into trouble if I assumed you'd rather be somewhere else?"

During their time together she couldn't help noticing everything about him. The way his raffish trousers hugged his killer backside and athletic thighs, the way he'd casually rolled up the sleeves on his collarless dress shirt to show off his tanned forearms—and the way he avoided looking at her whenever possible, and always kept a good distance between them.

He cleared his throat and for once met her gaze head-on. "I can say without reservation there's nowhere I'd rather be than with you."

Once again, she found herself blushing like a schoolgirl without exactly knowing why. Except maybe that the intensity in his glittering blue eyes made her weak in the knees. And perhaps that he knew it…

"You *are* my boyfriend," she whispered before she could stop herself. Which made her blush even more furiously.

That muscle in his jaw popped. "No. I'm not."

"We know each other well, though, don't we?" she demanded in a hushed voice. "Close colleagues, or—lovers." She slapped a hand over her mouth, mortified. What if they weren't? If there was any doubt about her attraction to him before, there was none now.

The muscle popped twice more. "Of course we're colleagues. I'm aware of your work, and I imagine you've heard of mine. But you live in Silvershire and up until recently I was in the States. Those distances would hardly be conducive to…a relationship. As appealing as the thought might be."

The hand on her mouth shook slightly as she stared at him, sifting through the wealth of information contained in his denial. Except, it wasn't a denial at all. And she didn't believe him anyway.

They'd been lovers. She was sure of it.

If only she could remember.

She turned away. "I'm sorry. I didn't mean to make you uncomfortable."

"Zara." His hands gripped her shoulders. Turned her back

to face him. She caught a whiff of something in the air…musky and masculine. He dropped his hands and took a step backward. "You're my patient."

"You said you were only a consultant," she reasoned.

"And you're splitting hairs. We'll talk about it again when you have your memory back. If you still want to." With that he walked away, glancing over his shoulder. "Coming?"

"Do I have a choice?" This was too frustrating. "Isn't it lunchtime soon?"

"Almost. There's one more stop I want to make first."

Reluctantly, she tagged along after him until they came to a room with two guards at the entrance. They seemed to know who she and Walker were, and one knocked on the door. They entered a room occupied by a phalanx of beeping instruments that surrounded a single large bed upon which an old man was lying. Next to the bed sat Emily, one of the nurses they'd spoken to earlier. She rose as they came in.

"Any change?" Walker asked.

"I'm afraid not." She tucked the book she'd been reading under her arm, checked the monitors, and stepped aside.

Walker silently motioned Zara to the bedside.

She came closer, looking curiously at the man attached to the wires and tubes. "The king!" she exclaimed softly. "My God, it's King Weston!"

Walker's face wreathed in a smile. "You recognized him."

"Yes!" Joy surged through her, followed quickly by distress. "What has happened to him? Why is the king here in the medical wing?"

Some of the brilliance went out of Walker's smile. "I can't tell you that. Well, at least you recognized him. That's something. Why don't you sit down for a moment and talk to him."

She shot him a troubled glance. "He looks unconscious."

"He is. But he might well be able to hear you. You know that. Right?"

She nodded uncertainly. "Yes. I do. But…do I know him? Personally, I mean?"

"Yes. Go on. Tell him what's happened to you. It may do you both some good."

It dawned on her that perhaps the king had been injured at the same time she had. Only he hadn't woken up yet. A wretched thought.

"All right." She took a seat, and unconsciously reached for the old king's hand. It felt frail and cool as it lay in hers. Lifeless, except for a thready pulse barely discernible in his wrist. Inexplicably, tears filled her eyes.

She blew out a steadying breath and started talking. Awkwardly at first. But soon all the terror, the fears and the hopes she hadn't dared let herself feel for the past week came pouring out.

How she'd awakened to a world she couldn't remember and been frightened out of her wits, how she couldn't hear for two days, and how her whole body had ached but especially her head. How she'd fought the despair, feeling instinctively she was among good people. And how, now, she had someone taking special care of her, helping her to remember. That she was certain everything would come back to her soon.

Then she whispered to the king that he must try very hard to get better now, too. His subjects needed him. The country needed him.

When she finally fell silent, she glanced around, a little embarrassed at everything that had come out of her mouth. The nurse stood off to one side, dabbing her reddened eyes. Zara realized her own cheeks were moist, too. Walker handed her a tissue and came to stand next to her, squeezing her shoulder as she composed herself.

"I don't know about you," he said after a few moments, "but I'm starving. Let's go find some lunch."

Zara smiled as she popped the last French fry from her plate into her mouth. "If nothing else, my appetite has returned."

Walker chuckled, recalling the endless room service she'd insisted on during their weekend together. "Hunger is always a good sign. Feeling better?"

"Immensely."

At the time, he'd been surprised she didn't weigh a ton, the way she packed it in. Then again, despite the rounds of heaping plates, they'd probably burned three times the calories they'd taken in during those forty-eight glorious hours.

Besides, he liked her soft curves. A lot.

"Feel like a nap? Or do you want to continue the tour?" he asked, mindful of her tiredness. His own had miraculously vanished.

"Continue, please."

With his cell phone, he called Lord Carrington's secretary, who had promised to send a docent when Walker was ready to show Zara around the rest of the palace, since he was unfamiliar with it.

The place was gigantic. And like something right out of a fairy tale. Naturally he'd been in many castles and palaces in the course of his work with the Lazlo Group. Two of the group's specialties were locating and rescuing kidnapped royals and investigating high-level political deaths, such as that of Prince Reginald. But this place was incredible, even by royal standards.

Room after room was filled with the finest antiques, the

most beautiful tapestries and oriental rugs, the most intricate inlaid floors and plaster reliefs he'd ever seen. The docent droned on about the history of each room, the paintings and the architecture.

Zara listened politely, and he watched her face and her reactions. Interested, but no recognition.

Patience, he told himself. He better than anyone knew you couldn't rush these things. The brutal fact was, she might never regain her memory.

God, what would he do if she didn't? Carrington would have a cow, and Walker— Walker would be right back to square one with her.

"This leads to the oldest section of the palace," the docent said as they came to a dark stone archway that had been roped off. "Originally, the palace was built on the site of an old abbey. Parts of the abbey still remain, integrated into the architecture."

"Looks spooky," Zara said, peering into the dimness.

"I don't recommend going in there. The rooms are in a terrible state of disrepair and it is very easy to get lost. It's like an ancient honeycomb, twisting and full of false doors. There's nothing much to see, either, except for the old Bourbon rose garden located in the abbey courtyard tucked into the east side of the wing. But you can get there by walking around the outside. It is worth seeing if you get a chance. No one tends them any more, but the antique roses are still incredible."

"Sounds nice," Walker said. "Do you like roses?" he asked Zara.

"I love them," she said without hesitation, then grinned and poked him in the arm. "You tricked me."

He shrugged unrepentantly. "Like I said, whatever works."

Of course he knew she liked roses. There'd been a cascade of musky-scented ochre-yellow roses surrounding his tiny balcony in Florence, and she'd been enchanted with them. She'd picked an armful, then plucked the petals off and strewn them artfully over the bed that first afternoon as he opened the champagne.

He hadn't smelled a rose since that didn't remind him of sliding into her, surrounded by that sweet-musky scent.

"We should go see the rose garden," she urged, giving him a smile that told him she had no idea. "Maybe I'll remember something."

He smiled back, doing his best to hide the direction of his thoughts. "Maybe. Maybe tomorrow. I think you've had enough for today."

She took his arm and they accompanied the docent back through the stately rooms and regal halls. He kept his free hand firmly in his pocket and did his damnedest to hide the arousal the erotic memory had given him. He wanted nothing more than to sweep her into his arms and kiss her to within an inch of her life. Instead, he endured her warm hands on his arm and made small talk with the docent until they were deposited back at the medical wing.

"Will you have dinner with me?" she asked as he walked her to her room. "The food's actually not bad. For a hospital," she said wryly.

"Sounds tempting," he said. *Way too tempting.* "But Lord Carrington has invited me to dine with him. No doubt he wants an update."

"No doubt," she agreed, sounding disappointed. "Well—" Suddenly, she stepped close and gave him a hug. "Thank you. For trying."

"No prob—" The banality died and he swallowed heavily when she didn't let go.

Her body was warm and soft and the scent of her hair

filled his nostrils. She'd changed shampoos, but he could still smell her own rare scent under the flowery drift.

"Zara…"

"I know," she whispered. "But I had to see. If I'd remember your body."

He slammed his eyes shut, using every ounce of willpower not to hug her back. Not to respond to the feel of her. "I can't do this. You know I can't."

"Yes," she said, and stepped away. "But you didn't. *I* did."

He turned his head so she wouldn't see the hunger in his eyes. "Good night," he said. "I'll see you tomorrow."

With that he strode straight out the door without looking back. He couldn't. Because if he did and saw a matching hunger in her eyes, he wouldn't be responsible for his actions.

Or rather, he *would* be responsible.

And that was the one thing the world would never excuse.

"Did she remember anything?" Nurse Emily asked as he walked past her station at the hub of the medical wing.

He shook his head. "Nothing meaningful. Just some general stuff."

"Such a shame. She really is a very talented surgeon. I hope she recovers."

"Yeah," he said, and leaned a hip against the reception desk. "Tell me about her."

Emily considered. "I don't really know her all that well. None of us do. I think she's what you'd call…driven…in her work. Doesn't socialize much."

"No, huh? Any close friends? Or…someone special in her life, romantically?"

"She occasionally had lunch with some doctors from the Royal Medical University. No gentleman friend that I know of."

Walker tried not to feel too pleased about that as he strolled down the hall. But failed. He wanted her all to himself.

Why the hell had he waited so long to come look for her? That was the biggest mystery of all.

Okay, not really. She was in her last year of residency in Cambridge, Massachusetts, when they'd met, and had made it clear she had no time for a long-distance relationship. He'd been nearly six years her senior, teaching at Duke, in North Carolina. He'd taken her at her word, but when he'd tried to get in touch after the academic year she'd already moved back home to Silvershire. His schedule was insane, with no time for a European vacation. One year turned into two, then three, and so on, and then— Well, then he lost interest in pretty much everything…especially women.

Until this assignment reminded him how much he missed having a woman in his bed. And maybe even his life.

He glanced around and realized he must have taken a wrong turn somewhere. The corridor he found himself in was cold and deserted, the walls coated with a filmy black substance. With a start he recognized the place Carrington had indicated as the site of the bombing—the assassination attempt on King Weston during which Zara had been injured.

Since he was here, he might as well take a look around. There might be some pictures or some other personal effects left that he could show Zara.

Careful to avoid touching anything, Walker entered the bombed-out suite and frowned in shock. It was a total wreck. Burned husks of monitors and instruments littered the floor, along with bent, upended furniture and giant pieces of stone block. Black, sodden bits of drywall and fabric dangled from everything.

With growing anger, he made his way to the double doors

that led to the room where Zara'd had her office and lab. It was in even worse shape. There was nothing at all recognizable in the space, just a jumble of metal, stone and shredded books in various shades of greasy black and gray.

Holy hell. No one had told him it was *this* bad!

It hit him like a two-by-four in the gut that Zara would surely have died in this room if she hadn't been with the King next door.

With a clenched jaw he turned back through the adjoining door and sought out the bed where Weston had been lying at the time of the blast, where Zara had flung herself over the old king. The explosion had hurled it to the far end of the room, flipping it over in the process, possibly saving both their lives. It'd been a miracle either had survived. If the bed had been just a few yards closer to the origin of the blast—

Suddenly, Walker stood stock still. A gnawing, horrible certainty slowly crawled through him like a pack of rodents.

The blast origin was plain as day, even to someone whose only training was a weekend course in explosives required by Corbett for all Lazlo Group members. The origin of the blast was in Zara's office. That placement made no sense at all. Not if King Weston was meant to be killed by it. And the amount of explosives made no sense if it had not been meant as a killing blast. It was meant to be fatal. But… Oh, God.

The target of this assassination was not King Weston.

The target had been Zara Smith.

Chapter 3

Lord Carrington's eyes flared with incredulity. "You can't be serious. Who would want to harm Dr. Smith?"

Walker kept a tight rein on his emotions and sipped the excellent burgundy being served with supper. "I have no idea. But it makes no sense to plant a bomb in Dr. Smith's office if the intended target is unconscious in the next room and unable to move. Why not plant it right under the king's bed?"

Carrington didn't have an answer. "The National Police are investigating. Surely, they would have checked that possibility."

Walker forced himself to take another bite of the five-star lamb in tarragon, but didn't taste it. "How many bombings have there been in Silvershire in the past year? Or two? Or even five?"

"Well," Carrington hedged. "None, actually."

"Does your National Police even have a bomb expert?"

"No," he admitted. "They've sent the recovered pieces of the device to New Scotland Yard in London for analysis."

"So they're just assuming the king was the intended victim?"

"*Everyone* assumed so."

"Until now. Your Grace, may I suggest you call Corbett Lazlo and have him send someone immediately? I know there are at least two bomb specialists on the group's payroll. I am certainly not one of them. But if even I can spot a discrepancy…"

"I see your point." Carrington sat back in his slender Heppelwhite chair. "I can't imagine you are correct in your theory, but absolutely, it must be investigated."

"Thank you, Your Grace. In the meantime, I recommend Dr. Smith be moved somewhere else. Somewhere safe. I saw signs today that she is beginning to remember things. Her memory should return any minute. There's really no need for me to continue—"

Carrington held up a hand to halt Walker's stab at extricating himself from this damnable situation. "Out of the question. I don't want assurances. I want her memory back completely. Your job is not finished until that happens. Understood?"

He was going to make one hell of a king, Walker thought sardonically. He definitely had that whole ring-of-royal-authority thing down cold. "Yes, Your Grace," he said.

"Please continue your treatment as planned. But if you think it prudent, I could assign her a bodyguard…."

"That won't be necessary. The Lazlo Group puts all of its agents through rigorous arms and defense training. I believe I'm capable of keeping her safe. However…I'm planning to take her around town tomorrow. It's necessary for her treatment, so I can't cancel. But I'll call Corbett and have someone assigned to tail us. Just in case."

"Good Lord!" Zara exclaimed.

It was midmorning and she and Walker had just ambled past the twin telephone-box-sized guard posts at the end of the footpath leading from the back of the palace out onto the main thoroughfare. Walker had recommended a leisurely stroll around town, hoping to jog something loose from her memory. They'd taken the rear footpath in order to avoid the herd of paparazzi that always hung about the official front drive. The press was a constant presence, most often a menace, even if at the moment they wrote about Zara as though she were a hero, having saved the life of Silvershire's beloved king in the bombing.

The colorfully dressed guards saluted them smartly with a snap to attention, gripping their upturned rifles.

Zara gasped. She recognized them! Not the men themselves, but their uniforms and ritual. The whole setting.

"What?"

She spun around and took in the busy street, looking left to the Royal Medical University located two blocks south, and right to the Ministry Complex, several blocks to the north.

"I recognize it! Everything! I know exactly where I am!" She spun back and launched herself at Walker in a big hug, whirling them around in pure joy. "I can't believe it! I remember!"

He laughed with her, his smile lighting up his face. "That's great!" His arms tightened around her. "I'm so glad." Then he pulled away a little, looking down at her, a shadow of uncertainty in his eyes. "Everything?" he asked. And waited for her answer.

She'd been so busy celebrating the overwhelming sense of knowing *where* she was that she'd missed the more important point. She still didn't remember *who* she was.

Her happiness took a crash dive. "Damn. No," she said cheerlessly. "*Not* everything." She shook her head. "Nothing about me. Just the city."

"Ah." Walker released her, leaving her feeling oddly abandoned. "But that's good. Definitely progress," he said, his voice filled with an optimism that sounded slightly forced. He smiled again. "I predict very soon it'll all come back."

She let out a long sigh. "God, I hope so. I can't tell you how strange this is, remembering just bits and pieces of one's life. Like my brain is made of Swiss cheese."

He chuckled, looking at her with sympathy and understanding. "Try and use that. You're a doctor. Store up those feelings of frustration so you can relate better to what your patients go through. When you get back to work."

She felt her own smile return, if weakly. "I appreciate your confidence."

"You'll get there. It's already started. Just relax and give it time."

Something at the edge of her vision caught her attention, and she turned. But nothing was there. Just the traffic and the chin-up guards. Wonderful. Now she was seeing things.

Walker looked at her expectantly, but she shook her head. "Just a shadow."

"Maybe not. I arranged for an agent to tail us today. In case anyone shows undue interest."

"Is that really necessary?"

"Just a precaution. Everyone closely involved with the royal family is getting extra security."

"I understand." She rubbed a shiver that went through her arms.

As they started walking again, her shoulder brushed against him and she felt a jolt of pleasure. At his powerful presence next to her, at the nearness of his body. She could feel his steady strength in the fleeting contact before he moved away.

How she wanted him to pull her back in his arms and hold her! Somehow she knew she hadn't had that in her life—a strong, comforting presence. From what she'd learned yesterday she had few friends, and no man. What a dull and lonely life she must lead!

At least she had family.

Somewhere.

But what about Walker? What was their relationship? Had they once been lovers, as she suspected? What had happened to them? Had they parted friends, or had one of them dumped the other? That would explain the distance he always kept between them, both physically and emotionally. Especially physically. While she longed to pull him close, he avoided touching her.

And yet, his eyes… When they sought her out, she felt the heat of his regard radiate from them like a furnace.

Did he still want her?

"Where would you like to go?" Walker asked, drawing her from her *outré* thoughts.

She gathered herself. "Why not the historic district, Silverton-upon-Kairn, across the river? Have you seen it yet?"

"By historic," he drawled, "you mean older than the two-hundred-fifty years the Palace has been around?"

"Oh, that's right." She grinned. "You're a Yank. Anything built before the last century is ancient to you."

He wrinkled his nose at her. "Very funny. And for your information," he said, feigning indignation, "I'm *not* a Yank. I'm a Reb. Born and bred in South Carolina."

"I thought you sounded Southern. Tell me about your home."

He held up a hand. "Another time. Right now we're concentrating on you. So, what about this old town you're taking us to?"

"It's a bit touristy, but wonderfully quaint and quirky. Full of small boutiques and antique shops and scrumptious tea rooms with sinful pastries."

He gave her a teasing smile. "Sinful's good."

Lord, how she loved his smile. It brightened the whole morning. With his deep blue eyes and his bad-boy hair, the combination was simply deadly.

"We could stop for lunch," she said, looping her arm through his so she wouldn't reach up to touch that dazzling smile. Or worse, kiss it. "I know a place that serves the best pasta this side of Florence."

Abruptly, he halted on the sidewalk so she was forced to stop, too. "You've been to Florence?" he asked, peering down at her intently.

She licked her lips, sensing a sudden tension in the air. "Um…" She wracked her brain. Why had she said that? Did Florence mean something to him? To them…? Her heart took off at a gallop. "Have we been there? Together?"

His gaze didn't waver. "You tell me. *Have* we?"

"I—" She gave her head a frustrated shake and looked away. "I don't know. Please, Walker, can't you tell me? This is driving me mad."

Indecision tortured his expression, but he finally said, "No. I can't do that. Aside from possibly hindering your recovery, it would be a major breach of ethics."

"But how?" she protested. "It's not like you're trying to seduce me! You've been nothing but professional!"

"Think about it. I'm your doctor, and you trust me, right?"

"Of course I do."

"So I could tell you anything, and you'd believe me."

Her mouth opened, but she couldn't truthfully deny it. "I suppose."

"I could lie and say we were lovers, even if we'd never met before yesterday. You'd be vulnerable to me."

"You wouldn't do that."

"How do you know?"

"I just do. Lord Carrington would never have hired you—"

"What if I wanted you so much I was willing to lie about the past to have you now?"

Her mouth dropped further. "Do you?" she whispered. "Want me that much?"

He grasped her shoulders in his powerful hands. "Zara, what if we were lovers in the past," he said, ignoring her question, "but you'd left me for some reason? Maybe I was cruel to you, or had cheated on you, or been accused of doing something awful so you didn't want anything to do with me. But you don't remember. I could be telling the truth, but it could still be a terrible lie, to lead you on."

"You wouldn't," she repeated.

His eyes softened, and he dropped his hands from her shoulders with a gentle sigh. "But you don't *know* that. Not for sure. And until you remember for yourself, I can't talk about us. Not in the present, not in the past."

She stared up at him in sublime frustration. He was right, of course. He was doing exactly what he should be doing to protect both of them. So why did that just make her want to scream?

Apparently patience was not among her virtues.

She took a deep breath. "Fine. But if I still haven't remembered in a week, you're telling me whether you want to or not."

"A year," he countered. She looked up at him aghast. "Okay, six months," he conceded.

"One month," she said firmly. "Non-negotiable. If you refuse, I'll get Lord Carrington to order you." His brow rose, and she lifted her chin. "Don't think he won't. He likes me, you know. The duke is an old family friend." Walker's brow rose even higher. Her head wobbled. "At least I'm pretty sure he is."

He chuckled. "Whatever you say, sugar."

She stared up at him. His words echoed in her mind, low

and sweet, filled with laughter, like the tinkling of a bell from far, far away. *Whatever you say, sugar*.

She tried to latch on to it, but it was already gone.

Behind her, a woman passing them on the sidewalk bumped her, then muttered under her breath. An apology, but it sounded harsh and ugly compared to the sweet wisps of memory.

"Something wrong?" Walker asked.

She forced a smile. "No. But if that's our tail she wasn't very polite," she said as a shudder went through her.

Walker let her set the pace as they threaded their way through the impatient morning crowd of the modern glass-and-concrete business district toward the bridge over the Kairn that would take them to the old town. To be honest, she felt strangely at home in the hurry-up hustle and bustle of the designer-dressed throng. But today she wanted to escape it. Lemon-polished antiques and spice-scented tea houses called to her.

"Wow." Walker whistled as they approached the ornate Golden Bridge over the Kairn River. "That is something else."

The bridge spanned the sparkling blue water in graceful arches, each gilded loop topped by a flickering crystal gaslight crowning a fancy golden lamppost. Iron lace scrollwork, painted gold, made up the railings. At either end of the bridge, two sphinx-like red porphyry lions sat regally on the low granite walls guarding the entrance, their once-golden patina worn away by two centuries of weather. The whole thing was incredibly elegant.

"More than one guidebook calls it the prettiest bridge in the world," she said, the information coming out of nowhere as they strolled to the other side. "It was built by King Theodore in the seventeen-hundreds at the same time as the new palace was constructed. The lions are from the Temple of Luxor, in Egypt. A gift from Napoleon."

Walker winked at her. "Nothing wrong with that part of your memory."

She rolled her eyes. "Yes, a veritable font of trivia about everything save myself."

"Some men would consider that an advantage in a woman."

She punched him in the arm, smothering a smile. "Cheeky git."

He jumped out of range, laughing. "So, was there an old palace? What happened to it?"

"An old castle. It's a museum now. A dark and spooky-looking bit of work, full of hidden rooms and secret tunnels. Very gothic. You can just see the towers, there on the hill, poking above the rooftops."

She pointed to a rise in the jumble of ancient buildings and verdigris copper roofs spreading out in a confusion at the other end of the bridge. Three conical turrets ringed by crenellated parapets were clearly visible.

"Towers, hidden rooms and secret tunnels, eh? Sounds fun."

She gave a shiver. "Until you get lost in one of them. No thanks. I've always been terrified of close, dark places."

He swung a glance at her. "Yeah?"

"The house where I grew up had secret rooms."

"Where was that?" he prompted casually.

She gasped in realization. Another personal memory! *Where had she grown up? Think!* But the heavy feeling of moldering darkness evaporated like mist. The creeping unease, however, lingered. She glanced around and rubbed her arms, feeling as though…as though she were being watched. *Good Lord*. She really must get hold of herself.

"Can't remember." She sighed. "Damn, I hate this."

"Never mind," he said. "Don't think about it. You seem to do much better just talking about whatever pops into your head."

At least they'd started trickling in, the memories. As elusive as they were. "I suppose you're right."

So she did her best to put the reason for their excursion right out of her mind and simply enjoy the scenery, the glorious morning and Walker's company. The warm summer sun felt wonderful on her face after being cooped up in her antiseptic hospital bed all week, and Walker's warm smile heated her insides even more. His easy banter made her laugh, and the admiring glances of the women they passed made her proud to be the only one he looked at.

They explored the narrow, winding cobblestone streets, pausing at every curiosity shop and bohemian art gallery on the way, bought sweet-salty pretzels and taffy to snack on and fed cracked corn from converted gumball machines to the swans floating in postage-stamp ponds in envelope parks squashed between quaint timbered town houses dripping with geranium-filled window boxes.

When the sun was high in the cloudless sky and they finally ambled into the square in front of the old castle, she said, "Thank you for helping me like this." For three hours she'd actually forgotten all about wanting her past back, and only thought about the present. "This morning has been so fun. I can't remember when I've enjoyed myself so much." She darted him a wide-eyed look, then burst out laughing. "Oh, my God. I'm so pathetic."

He laughed, and swept her into his arms. "No. You're adorable."

Surprise cascaded through her body, followed closely by a shiver of pleasure. In his embrace, surrounded by the warmth and strength of his arms, at last she was where she wanted to be. Where it felt so very right to be. She wrapped her arms around him and held him close.

And felt exactly when he realized what he was doing. His body stiffened, just a little, and he murmured a soft curse.

"Please," she whispered before he could move away, "don't leave yet. Just hold me for a moment."

She felt him take in a deep breath and let it out slowly. "This is so wrong in every way," he whispered back. "I shouldn't. We shouldn't."

"I know. It's just…"

What could she say? That he made her feel safe and secure for the first time since she'd woken up from the accident? That she was so attracted to him her limbs nearly melted just looking at him? That she felt a connection with him far beyond doctor-patient, beyond friendship even, to a down-to-the-very-core intimacy—despite the fact they'd barely touched each other—that would have scared her if he weren't so honorable, so above reproach in his principles and conduct.

She had a feeling none of those insights would help her case one bit. He would say all of that was due to her vulnerability. Misplaced feelings of gratitude, and sublimated fear and dependency. She knew all the medical arguments against getting involved. But they were all wrong. She just…really liked him.

And judging by the silent battle waging in his muscles as he held her, he liked her, too.

Unable to help herself, she moved her hand up, slid her fingers into his long, thick hair. And pulled him down for a kiss.

Their lips met with a low moan. Hers. And his. Harmonizing in a soft exhale of longing.

He opened his mouth, teased her tongue with his. The taste

of him flowed through her, spiced with pretzel, sweetened with taffy. And under it, achingly sensual, the warm, rich flavor of desire. *He wanted her*.

All too quickly, he retreated.

"Zara," he breathed. "We can't do this. We're being watched."

He was aroused. Small consolation when he took her arms and peeled her from his chest.

Thank God he didn't let her go completely. She would have dissolved onto the cobbles at his feet.

"I know," she said. "But it's so unfair."

"There'll be plenty of time for kisses after you remember. If you still want to."

Something in the way he said the last part sent a prickle over her scalp. "Of course I'll want to. Will you?"

His gaze filled with a slow certainty, overlaid by another emotion…something…wistful? "Sugar, that's a guarantee."

She took a cleansing breath and shook off her disappointment and yearning. "All right. I can wait. But when I get my memory back, better watch out."

His mouth curved up as he let her go. "I'll look forward to that."

She had to fight not to launch herself back into his arms. Instead, she turned purposefully away and set her attention on the shops and cafés lining the square. The old castle loomed above their heads, dark and menacing like a storm cloud against the pristine blue sky. She ignored the creeps it gave her and took Walker's hand, leading him to the closest shop window, threading through a crowd of tourists.

"The restaurant where I want to take you to lunch is just ahead. The Dog and Fiddle. But let's check out these antique dealers along the way first. Okay?"

"Sure," he agreed. She'd noticed he enjoyed poking around

old things as much as she did. That was good. Something they could do in the future. In between kissing…

If they were still together, a little voice in her head whispered. The way he kept doubting whether she'd want him made her uneasy. Like maybe there was something he was hiding. Something big.

She told the voice to go jump in the lake.

"Oh, look at that!" She pressed a hand to the window they were strolling past. "An old dental cabinet."

It was gorgeous. Dark, rich solid wood, with a zillion little narrow drawers marching down the front in two rows.

"Let's go in." Bells on the door tinkled as Walker opened it and held it for her.

They oohed and aahed over the cabinet and several other outstanding pieces, then wandered through the rest of the shop, which was filled to the rafters with beautiful, curious and odd things. Each wall overflowed with paintings of all kinds. Oils and pastels, watercolors and lithos.

Walker stopped to admire one particularly large oil as she ran her fingers over a damask silk love seat in front of it.

"Man, can you imagine living in a place like that?" he murmured, his voice tinged with amazement. "There's got to be a hundred rooms in it."

"Hmm?" She glanced up at the painting.

And froze.

Her heart stopped. Then zoomed into hyperspeed.

"One hundred and thirty-seven," she whispered hoarsely.

"Huh?"

She clutched at the damask of the love seat she suddenly found herself sitting on. Memories flooded through her in a blinding flash of colors and shapes. "A hundred and thirty-seven rooms. Not counting the secret ones…"

He was sitting next to her in an instant, grasping her hand. "Zara. Baby, are you all right?"

Just then, the store proprietor came over, smiling. "Aye, that's quite the estate. Up in the north country, it is. As ancient and noble a house as ye'll find in all Silvershire. They call it—"

"Danehus," Zara said, making the three-syllable name rhyme with noose. "Danehus Hall."

"Ah! I see the lady's familiar with it," the man said, obviously pleased he had a knowledgeable customer.

"I should be," she said, shock and wonder fueling her words with the breathiness of momentary disbelief. "I grew up there." She met Walker's wary gaze. "My God, Walker. I'm Lady Zara. Daughter of the twelfth Marquis of Daneby."

Chapter 4

Walker swallowed, keeping his excitement at bay, doing his best to maintain a professional facade while inside he was doing cartwheels.

"Good. You remember," he said. Praying this wasn't just another false alarm.

She nodded.

"How much?"

"I—I'm not sure."

He stood, putting his hand on the antique dealer's shoulder. "We'll take the painting. Wrap it up for us, if you will? We'll come back for it after lunch." With that, he pulled Zara to her feet, banded an arm around her waist and hustled her out of the shop. They needed to talk. In depth. "Where's that restaurant?" he asked, scanning up the street.

She pointed. "Half a block that way."

"Let's get something to eat. We could both use it."

She looked pale, like she'd seen a ghost. Hell, she probably had. No doubt more than one. People's pasts usually contained as many unpleasant memories as good ones. Something that was easy to forget while in the panic mode of amnesia.

"I could definitely use a drink," she said.

"That bad, eh?"

Her lips twisted sardonically. "You might have warned me."

He leaned over and placed a kiss on her hair as they walked. "I honestly don't know a thing about your background, other than your father's title."

She looped her arm around his elbow. "Walker?"

"Yeah?"

"I still don't remember about you. Should I?"

A vise of disappointment squeezed his chest. She wasn't the only one who hated this. He evaded her question by asking, "Do you remember your job? Where you went to school?"

Several tense seconds passed. Then she shook her head. "No."

He pressed his mouth into a thin line. *Damn.* "But your family? Your childhood?"

"Yes. All of that."

She didn't sound overly pleased to have discovered she was a titled, presumably rich, aristocrat. He wondered what that was all about. But they'd arrived at the restaurant, so he banked his curiosity until they'd been seated, gotten their drinks and ordered. Pasta, of course.

She took a deep sip of her red wine and gave him a long, wry look. "So is this memory thing reversible? I mean, can I go back to not remembering?"

She looked so pained as she said it, he laughed out loud. "Come on, it can't be that terrible."

"Says you."

"All right, tell me about Lady Zara. Everything you remember."

She groaned and held her head in her hands. "Where to begin. I am the oldest child of the Marquis of Daneby. Our lands lie on a bay just under the northernmost tip of Silvershire. My ancestors were marauding Viking warriors who were given the most remote region of the island as a bribe to leave the rest alone."

He chuckled. "A very sensible arrangement."

"I've apparently inherited most of my blood from those marauding warriors. Or so my father keeps telling me. I've been a fighter from day one."

"That I can believe."

"Because I'm a woman, I cannot inherit his title, even though I'm the oldest. I always thought that was unfair."

"Well, it is," he agreed. He leaned more toward an equal split himself, but he could see how that might get messy when a title and family lands were involved. The American founding fathers had been smart to avoid that whole can of worms.

"At the ripe old age of seven, I made it my life's ambition to change that old-fashioned arrangement. I fought to be better at everything than my little brother, who is in line for the title, thinking I could change my father's mind. But, of course, it's not my father's choice, it's set out in the entailment. Been that way for a thousand years. The oldest boy inherits, regardless of which child is better suited."

Walker could see the veiled pain of a lifetime of disappointment in her eyes, the impossible dreams of an outraged little girl who has been cheated out of that which she holds dearest.

"Life sucks," he muttered. He knew all about being cheated out of one's dreams. He clicked his glass to hers in tacit commiseration. "Go on."

She let out a long sigh. "The men in my family are all doctors. From way back. Kind and nurturing men—at least to their people, the villagers and farmers who work their lands. The Lord-Physician. Healing his flock. Everyone loves my father."

Walker could see just where this was going. *Christ.* "So you decided to become a doctor, too."

"Brilliant idea, yes? Around that time, the king made a proclamation saying the royal succession could pass to any royal child, regardless of gender. Naturally I thought it should apply to all of Silvershire's nobility." She shrugged. "It didn't. But I thought I could change that, too. In the meantime, I'd gotten the bug to become a doctor. So I announced my intentions to the family."

"What happened?"

"Relations have been a bit strained ever since."

"Surely, they couldn't object to that. I mean, what's wrong with becoming a doctor?"

She tilted her head. "Have you known many aristocrats?"

"Well, yeah. The Lazlo Group works with royalty and noble families all the time."

"And what is the preferred occupation of the women?"

He considered. "Charity work. And…well…"

She nodded. "Shopping. Parties. Society functions. Anything but a real job. That's how my sisters live. Why spend years pursuing a career you don't need?"

"I see your point. But if you *wanted* to do it…?"

"As the oldest girl, I was supposed to make a brilliant match and settle down to care for my husband's estates. Solidify political ties. Strengthen the family coffers. That sort of thing."

"But you were a fighter."

A smile, if self-deprecating, finally broke through. "That,

and the fact that the noblemen I've met are either inbred idiots, gay or already married."

Though he grinned, his pulse kicked up slightly at the thought of her marrying. "So… You went off to the university and became a brilliant doctor instead."

She lifted a shoulder. "So you say. But that's where the memories stop."

Damn.

Disappointment tumbled through Walker once again. Would she *ever* remember him? The feel of their brief kiss still sizzled on his tongue and lips. He didn't know how much longer he could resist dragging her to him and kissing her until she recalled every vivid detail of their affair.

Their food came and he dug in, grateful for something to do with his hands besides reach for her. Luckily, the pasta was superb, as promised.

"I'm tired of talking about me," she said between mouthfuls. "Tell me about South Carolina and your family."

He smiled, always cheered by thoughts of his parents and siblings. "Typical middle class. My dad's a teacher, my mom runs a garden center. I have a baby sister and two brothers, all younger. One's married with a kid. The other's a flake."

She chuckled. "Are you close?"

His insides warmed with love. Followed quickly by a flash of anger that he'd been forced to leave them because of the threats of a lying psychotic female sicko. He shut down the anger and concentrated on the love. "Yeah. We are. I miss them, living over here."

Surprise widened Zara's eyes. "You live over here? In Silvershire?"

"On the continent. France. That's where the Lazlo Group is headquartered."

"Oh." She studied him, and he wished like hell he knew what was going through her head. Then her brow beetled slightly and her gaze dropped to her plate.

"Zara?" he asked.

"Yeah?" She didn't look up. *What was she thinking?*

"Do you still want to become the Marchioness of Daneby?"

Her eyes raised back to his and her face took on a proud, serene mien. "Yes," she said with a certainty that pierced his heart. "I do."

And in that instant, he knew why she'd never tried to find him again after their affair. Why he'd never stood a chance with her, even as they'd spent the most incredible weekend of his life together.

He wasn't good enough for her.

A commoner, a middle-class American man with a school-teacher dad would never fit into her glitzy, aristocratic world. Especially not a man who'd been kicked out of his profession for ethical misconduct.

No matter how great their chemistry, a future marchioness didn't marry a lowborn man in disgrace.

Walker had suddenly gotten quiet.

Zara was worried. So worried, her stomach started a slow roil. What had happened to his smiles and his quips, his heated sidelong looks? As they finished up their lunch, he seemed to withdraw, once again becoming the impassive doctor who had first greeted her in her hospital room.

She wanted her friend back.

"Is something wrong?" she finally asked as he opened the door for her after picking up the oil painting of Danehus from the antique dealer down the block. He'd insisted on paying for the painting, but hadn't met her gaze during the transaction.

In answer, a smile appeared on his lips, but the crinkles around his eyes didn't shift. "Nothing's wrong. Shall we take a cab back to the palace?"

He was keeping something from her. But what?

A pain shot from her stomach to her chest thinking about what it might be. She grasped his arm to steady herself. "I am feeling a bit knackered," she admitted.

His brow creased. "You look a little pinched. Didn't the pasta agree with you?"

"No, I—" A wave of nausea hit her square in the gut. Okay, she was concerned about his sudden chilliness, but this was ridiculous. She rubbed her chest, which burned like the devil. "I'm not sure. I—"

"Come on, let's find somewhere to sit down. You're really not looking so good."

"No, I'm fine, really. I just—" Suddenly, her whole body clenched so violently she cried out. "Oh, God! Walker, my stomach! I think I'm—"

And for the second time in a week, the blackness reached out to grab her with sharp, ugly talons, dragging her down into the spinning depths of nothingness.

"I don't *know* what's wrong with her," Walker snapped into the cell phone as he paced the Royal Medical University Hospital emergency room floor. "I'm a freaking psychiatrist, not a—"

"Walker, calm down." Corbett's order was sharp and direct. "Take a breath."

Fighting panic, Walker tried his best to do so. "Okay. Okay. I'm sorry, boss."

"Start at the beginning."

There wasn't much to tell, and what there was took about

three seconds to relate. "And then she collapsed. Thank God I caught her."

"Could it be food poisoning?"

He forced himself to think, dredging symptoms from his med school days and comparing them to Zara's attack. "Seemed too violent for that. Unless it was something really nasty. But we ate the same thing. I should be sick, too."

"Heart attack? Stroke?"

"Maybe. She did grab her chest. But she said it was her stomach."

There was a long silence. He knew they were both thinking the same thing. The unthinkable.

"Sounds like she's been poisoned," Corbett said at last.

Just like the crown prince two months earlier.

Walker swore a violent oath. "This is my fault. I should never have taken her out of the palace."

"Don't be absurd. None of us foresaw this development."

"Hey. It was *my* theory she was the real target of the bombing, remember?"

"Yes, but—"

"I should have *protected* her. Instead I led her right out into the open where anyone could get to her. And they did." He swore again. The weight of guilt was crushing. *If she died…*

"Have the hospital overnight a sample of her stomach contents to our lab. Meanwhile—"

"Why the hell would anyone want to poison her?" Walker demanded. "Or plant a bomb in her office? I don't understand. Corbett, is there something going on here I don't know about?"

"I assure you, we're as much in the dark as you are." Walker could plainly hear the anger in Lazlo's voice. His boss hated being blindsided. "We need to find out what's happening. Quickly."

The call to action made him pull himself together. "Right. I'll—"

"No." Corbett cut him off. "You already have a job. It's more important than ever that Dr. Smith regain her memory now. *All* of it. I'll send von Kreus to investigate the attempts on her life. He just came off another job."

"But—"

"No buts. You're too close to this. Stay with Zara. Finish what you started. Let me know when she comes round."

The phone clicked off just as the admitting doctor strode around the corner looking for Walker.

He hurried over. "Is she all right?"

The doctor nodded. "Thanks to your quick work. Getting her here in record time made all the difference. We pumped her stomach and stabilized her heartbeat."

"Was she poisoned?"

The doctor's brows shot into his scalp. "*Poisoned?* Well, in a matter of speaking. It looked to me like an overdose of some sort. Her heart rate was through the roof."

"Not food poisoning?"

"Definitely ingested, but not the food. It was something chemical."

"Such as?"

"Impossible to say for sure until the tox screen comes back. But my guess would be some kind of heart medication."

Walker could feel the blood drain from his face. "Like digitalis?"

"A definite possibility."

The same drug used to poison Prince Reginald.

His head was spinning as he thanked the doctor and asked when he could see Zara. The answer was not what he wanted to hear. She'd be sleeping for a few hours and wasn't to be disturbed. On the other hand, it did give him some badly needed time to think.

What the hell was going on?

Someone really was trying to kill her. But why?

What had his little fighter gotten herself into—or seen—that she shouldn't have?

Pounding.

Something was pounding, pounding on her chest. Like a hammer on her heart. Ripping into her stomach. She was screaming. Screaming and screaming from the pain in her chest and stomach, and the weight of metal sheets grinding into her body.

She tried to turn, but something held her down. She heard voices. Arguing voices. Life and death voices. You won't get away with this. The hell I won't! *Then laughter. Laughter fading into a baby's cry.*

And suddenly the darkness. The long, eerie darkness. Clawing at her. Suffocating her. Panic. Panic! *Wait… There's a light! A pinprick of yellow light, morphing into a symbol. A strange, exotic symbol. Writing? More lines and symbols and weird drawings, dozens, all swirling around her crazily, as though caught in the vortex of a tornado. So dizzy! Her stomach hurt so much, and her chest.*

Someone was coming. She had to get away! Away!

She struggled. Fighting to move. Fighting to escape.

Strong arms held her firmly. Held her down, calling…

Zara. Zara!

She opened her eyes and gasped.

Walker saw the terror in Zara's eyes and fury roared over him. Whoever had done this to her was a dead man.

"It's me, honey. Shhh. You're all right."

Her wild eyes focused on him and slowly the fear fled. "Walker?"

Thank God. "I'm here, sugar. Wake up. You're having a bad dream."

Her breath soughed out. "Just a dream," she whispered hoarsely. Then her eyes darted around the hospital room. "Where am I? What happened?"

Walker made a snap decision. She had enough stress just trying to remember who she was. She didn't need to know someone might be trying to kill her. "Must have been something bad in the pasta," he said evasively. "Don't worry, they pumped your stomach and the doc says you'll be just fine."

Her hand went to her throat. "No wonder it feels like sandpaper. What the hell, Walker. Bad pasta? Has anyone heard of that?"

Smiling, he smoothed a lock of hair from her face. "Who knows? The important thing is you're okay."

She sighed. "At least I didn't lose my memory again."

"You'll have to stay here overnight, I'm afraid." He glanced around the stark room. "Not exactly as glamorous as the Royal Palace."

Her lips curved. "I'll live. I hope."

He scowled. "Jeezus, Zara. Don't even joke. You scared me to death."

"Did I? Really?" She looked at him balefully. "Last I remember, you were hardly speaking to me."

He sat on the edge of her bed and took her hand. "Yeah, sorry about that. Just got hit by a dose of reality, I guess." He said it lightly, attempting to disguise the acute disappointment ripping through him at the reminder of today's depressing insight. "Nothing to worry about. I'll get over it."

"What kind of reality?" she persisted.

"Zara, now is not the time to go into all that."

"All what?"

He closed his eyes for a moment, then opened them. "Okay, fine. After we talked I realized it didn't really matter whether or not we'd met before yesterday. With your background and ambitions, I'm not the kind of man you could ever get seriously involved with, anyway. I'm not…suitable for you."

Her jaw dropped. "Don't be ridiculous. What could be more suitable than a doctor?"

"A duke. A prince. An earl. Not a poor Carolina boy."

She let out a soft laugh. "Honestly, Walker. The ideas you have. Obviously, you've never read Cinderella. As if any of that mattered. Besides, you're hardly poor. You wear Dries van Noten, for crying out loud."

He glanced down at his open-necked, sleeve-ruched shirt and rumpled pants, amazed she didn't think they came from a thrift store. "You can dress the boy up…" he said with a shrug.

"Is that why you broke up with me before? Because of some outdated bourgeois notion of how the aristocracy behaves?"

Like he'd ever break up with her. He wagged a finger at her and stood, unwilling to be drawn further into this conversation. When she regained her memory she'd be singing a completely different tune.

"You're fishing again." He gave her a peck on the forehead. "Get some sleep. I'll see you in the morning."

He pointed his feet to the door and got out of there quick, before her tempting eyes and tempting lips could tempt him into having any kind of hope for any kind of future with tempting Lady Zara.

"It's just a title, Walker," came her parting shot.

"Night, sugar."

Good thing all he had was a case of monumental lust for

her, and nothing deeper. What he'd been feeling for Zara was *not* love. How could it possibly be? They'd spent a sum total of forty-eight, okay, now maybe sixty, hours together. A man didn't fall in love in three days. It just didn't happen.

So he'd be fine. As soon as she got her memory back, he'd be out of there. Then he'd be A-okay. He had a good job and plenty of offers for female company. Who needed the complication of keeping a fickle, high-maintenance aristo in his bed?

Not that she seemed all that fickle.

Still, he'd been right not to pursue her all those years ago. He must have known instinctively it could only end badly. For him, anyway.

And now, of course, it would be downright impossible. Not with the scandal of Ramona Burdette's accusations still clinging to him like static-charged laundry.

Unless Zara was only after another quick roll in the feather bed, he was just not destined to be her man. Not now. Not ever.

Cinderella. Yeah, right.

Chapter 5

"Lady Zara." Lord Carrington extended his hands and took hers warmly when she arrived at his private office along with Walker.

"Your Grace." She returned his air kisses with just the right deference for a future king. She couldn't believe the little rascal who'd regularly chased her and her brother around Danehus with water balloons when his parents came to visit had grown up to be this tall, imposing man. And married to a princess, nonetheless. "I hope your beautiful bride is well."

"She's doing fine. The morning sickness has nearly passed."

"Oh! A baby? Congratulations, Russell. That's wonderful news!"

Carrington hesitated, flicking a glance at Walker, who shook his head slightly. She flushed, understanding at once she must have been aware of this before.

"Please tell me I didn't attend the announcement dinner," she said with a groan.

"You were in surgery, I believe," he said smiling, a hint of the mischievous boy she'd known shining through.

"Thank God for small favors. Forgive me. My memory is still a bit murky."

"So I hear." His smile turned more serious. "How are you? You gave us all quite a turn yesterday."

"Leave it to me to get food poisoning along with amnesia. I'm fine, though. And slowly getting the memories back."

A hint of citrus drifted through the room. Russell's cologne? Furniture polish?

"Good." He ushered them to a set of elegant visitor chairs. Taking a seat behind his inlaid mahogany desk, he glanced again at Walker. "The thing is, Zara…"

Suddenly, it dawned on her this was not a social call. She straightened. "What is it Russell?"

"I don't want to alarm you, but…we need to talk."

"About what?"

"There is evidence that seems to indicate…well, that you might be the target of a bit of foul play."

She blinked. "Foul play? Whatever do you mean?"

The duke turned to Walker in appeal.

"What His Grace means," Walker said, clearing his throat, "is that yesterday's poisoning may have been deliberate. And the accident where you lost your memory might not have happened exactly as we—"

Deliberate? Alarm trickled through her limbs. "How can food poisoning be deliberate? And you never told me what kind of accident I had," she added, her concern rising even more. "Did it have something to do with the king? Is that why you took me to see him?"

The two men looked at each other. Walker sighed. "I told you she'd figure it out."

"Always has been too smart for her own good," Russell agreed resignedly.

"What's going on?" She was becoming genuinely anxious.

"We think someone may be trying to kill you," Walker said.

"You mean the king."

"No. You."

An incredulous laugh escaped her. Then another. And another, until she was laughing outright. "Why would anyone want to kill *me*?"

They weren't even smiling. "We rather hoped you could tell us," Russell said. "If that damnable memory of yours would only come back we might have a clue."

"Good lord, you're serious."

"Deadly, I'm afraid." Her old childhood friend folded his hands over his desk and leaned forward. "Zara, Dr. Shaw thinks you're ready to see the scene of your accident. I'm worried you're not strong enough after yesterday."

She looked from one to the other. This was absurd. They had to be wrong. "I feel fine," she said, standing. "Will seeing the accident scene bring my memory back quicker?"

"The shock just might do the trick," Walker said, also getting to his feet.

"Then what are we waiting for?"

Shock was an understatement. When Walker opened the door to the dark, cold suite at the end of the corridor, disbelief slammed Zara square in the chest. She stood and stared at the destruction, her jaw nearly hitting the rubble-strewn floor.

"*Good Lord*. What hap—" Suddenly, lights flashed in her

head, and an explosion sounded in her ears so thunderous she covered them with her hands.

And just like that, the memories were back. All of them. Like they'd never been gone.

She felt Walker's hands on her arms. "Zara?"

"Bloody hell," she whispered, moving her fingers to her mouth as he pulled her to his chest. "A *bomb?*" She felt him nod. "Have they found out who did it?"

"Not yet. Do you remember something, anything, that might help the investigation?"

She searched the newly resurrected memories, probed into the hours, even the minutes, before it had happened. And shook her head. "I can't think of anything even remotely suspicious. I was with the king, holding his hand and talking to him, worried because he still hadn't emerged from his coma, from the surgery. No one went in or out that I noticed."

"Well, keep mulling it over. Something may come to you later."

Her mind reeled. Someone had tried to *kill* the king. What sick mind would want to murder such a sweet old man just to make a political statement?

The king.

Suddenly, all her concern and fear over King Weston's recovery returned, like an avalanche crashing over her.

Oh, God, she needed to get to him.

She straightened out of Walker's arms. "The king! I must go to him. I can't believe I forgot I'm his doctor! His brain tumor—" She jerked away. "Has he regained consciousness yet?"

"No." Walker grasped her arm as she was about to rush out of the room. "Zara, listen. Dr. Landon is taking care of the king now. Until you are cleared to resume your practice, you can't—"

Dr. Landon, the doctor who had also been officially treating her. She knew him. He was brilliant, but—

"I remember everything, Walker." *Including the guilt. Lord, especially the guilt.* "It's been over a week," she said, her voice rising with each word. "I have to run tests. Make sure the king's tumor hasn't—"

"Dr. Landon is doing everything—"

"No! Don't you see? *I* have to do it! If I don't check everything myself, something might—"

She halted at Walker's concerned frown, battling to stop the flood of raw emotion bubbling up from deep within her. Irrational emotion she knew stemmed from the unnecessary death of a child two years ago. When she'd trusted the nurse to administer the correct dosage of—

She squeezed her eyes shut. Used pure willpower to calm herself. As she'd done every time the crippling guilt nearly overwhelmed her, making her second-guess her every move since that awful day. It didn't happen very often any more. Logically she knew it hadn't been her fault. Despite what the child's mother, Mrs. Lloyd, thought. All doctors, including her, lost patients. Nurses sometimes misread charts.

If she'd only checked the dosage personally…

Yes, accidents happened. *But not on her watch.* Not ever again.

All at once, she remembered what Walker had said in Russell's office about the bombing. *Had that been her fault, too?* Sickened by the very thought, she took in the twisted debris of the room. *Because of her?* No, that was insane.

She turned to Walker desperately. "You said earlier that

someone is trying to kill me. But…surely this was an assassination attempt on the king by the Union for Democracy? They've been threatening to disrupt the upcoming coronation for months now. What better way than this?"

Walker's firm hands guided her out into the hall, closing the door after them, then propelled her slowly down the corridor. "I don't think so. Lord Carrington met with Nikolas Donovan yesterday."

"The leader of the UD?"

"Yes. Donovan swears they had nothing to do with the bombing. However, he did warn that a faction is growing stronger within the Union that condones violence."

"There you are, then. It must have been them."

"Zara—" Walker's expression turned grave. "We have Lazlo agents, including a bomb specialist, investigating every angle. We'll soon know the truth. Until then—"

"I need to be with King Weston."

"Naturally you can visit. But until you're given a health clearance and a specialist has extensively tested your medical knowledge to be sure it's completely intact…"

He didn't need to finish. "Of course," she said, contrite. No one more than she wanted to be absolutely certain of her competency. "I wasn't thinking. How quickly can the recertification be done?"

"Under the circumstances probably within a day."

He regarded her oddly. Then stopped to lean his back against the corridor wall. They were nearly to the empty nurses' station. Soft laughter reached them from the lounge behind it.

"Which I guess means my job here is done." He continued to watch her with that strangeness in his eyes. A kind of wary expectancy.

"Just like that?"

It hit her then. *She still didn't remember him.*

He looked at her as though she should.

She licked her lips. Where did she have to be, again? It was singular how when Walker looked at her everything else flew from her mind. Everything but him.

"Unless…there's something else…?"

Why couldn't she remember him?

Perhaps there was nothing to remember?

His eyes said there was.

She took a step toward him. "Does that mean I'm no longer your patient?"

"As soon as I sign off on the job."

She licked her lips again, dropping her gaze to his mouth. Maybe if she kissed him—a real kiss this time— she'd remember….

"Today?" She took another step, bringing her to within touching distance. "Right now?"

"Zara, do you—"

She kissed him. Before he could ask the one question that would make him stop her.

Her lips met his and opened, inviting him in with a soft moan. He hesitated for a split second, then took her mouth fiercely, scooping her up in his arms, pulling her close. He groaned as his tongue swept in, the taste of him bursting through her, the smell of him surrounding her. His mouth covered, took, demanded.

He swung them around, pressing her back against the cool wall. She shivered. Shaking with the sudden need to give him everything he wanted. Everything she wanted.

"Walker," she whispered on a moan.

Her whole life had been ordered and regimented toward

a specific goal. All logic, all reason. But this man made her want to *feel*. For the first time since college she wanted to let herself go, and just fall into the dark velvet sea of the impulsive unknown.

"Ah, sugar," he murmured between kisses. "You have no idea how much I've wanted to do this. It's been torture, ever since I saw you lying in that hospital bed. But…are you sure?"

"Oh, yes." Her bones were slowly dissolving, her blood deliciously thick in her veins. When was the last time she'd felt like this? Maybe never… "It's been a long time since you held me," she whispered, taking a chance.

"A lot has happened in those years."

"You'll have to tell me everything."

Suddenly his tongue and lips stilled. "Zara?" he asked, his voice gravelly. "You don't know? Or you don't remember?" His chest rose and fell against hers as he waited for her answer. One she couldn't give.

"It doesn't matter," she whispered. "Whatever it is, I don't give a flip."

He swore under his breath. "Damn it, Zara! I thought you said you remembered everything!"

"I do! Everything except—" She clung to him when he would set her away.

"Except me?" His brow rose. "Or is your whole love life gone?"

She gave an unladylike snort. "Assuming I had such a thing. Which I don't."

"Great." He pulled free and paced away from her, thrusting his hands in his pockets. "Just damn great," he said disgustedly. "I guess we're not done here after all. And so exactly the damn memories I want to be working with you on."

She pulled the ends of her hair together and twisted them

into a knot at the back of her neck. "There are sod-all memories to work on! I'm telling you, Walker, I haven't a clue why I've blanked you out, but I do remember how I live my life. Men are not a part of it."

He propped a hand on the wall and gazed at her, his expression mildly disbelieving. "You gay, or what?"

She managed, just barely, to rein in her outrage and find a tone of sarcasm. "Lord, no. Here I thought *you* were gay."

He raised a finger and shook it at her.

"I've kissed you twice now. You've yet to return the favor, so I assumed…" She waved a hand. "Whatever. There's no shame in being gay. Some of my—"

He strode right into her face and said, very calmly, "I. Am. Not. Gay. And you know perfectly well why I haven't returned the favor. Now, tell me why the hell there aren't a dozen damn men in your life, dying to return your kisses and a whole lot more."

"Because…" She jerked away from the temptation of his hard-edged stance and quivering muscles and crossed her arms over her soft silk blouse. A reminder to soften her expression.

"I told you yesterday. I have a thing about being the best at what I do. I have goals. All of that takes dedication and commitment. Men in my social circle tend not to like being interrupted by a woman's pager every time they're just getting to the good bits."

He looked away, his jaw working. "The good bits. Cute. I guess that figures. Stupid. I plumb forgot about your whole social circle thing." He blew out a breath. "Johnny Reb at the Court of the Marchioness of Daneby. Whooee," he mimicked, making a mockery of his beautiful accent. "I suppose that explains why I disappeared so resolutely into the quicksand of your mind."

"Walker!" She grabbed his arm when he turned to storm down the hallway. "Don't."

"Sugar, believe you me, you're better off this way."

"No. I don't believe it and you don't, either."

"I'm seriously not the kind of man a woman like you would knowingly get involved with."

"Why do you keep saying that? I know you, and—"

"That's where you're wrong, baby," he interrupted, and eased his arm from her grip. "The damn truth is, you don't know me at all."

Walker swore at himself the whole time he was instructing Nurse Emily to make sure Zara got in bed and stayed there for the rest of the day. The betrayed look on Zara's face as he stalked off was almost enough to crack his resolve. Almost.

"I'm not tired!" she yelled after him.

"You've had a shock," he answered without looking back. "You need rest if you expect to pass your medical recert tomorrow."

He had to get out of there. To somewhere quiet where he could regroup. Lifting his cell phone from his pocket, he thought about the Bourbon rose garden the docent had described yesterday. That had sounded real quiet.

But first he called Lord Carrington and let him know the strategy had worked. Lady Zara's memory had returned and she was chomping at the bit to be tested and get back to work.

"You don't think it's too soon?"

"That's for Dr. Landon to decide. If her medical knowledge checks out, I see no reason to hold her back. This kind of amnesia doesn't relapse."

"Excellent. I've arranged for her to take a full board examination so there'll be no doubt."

Next he called Corbett for a progress report on the investigation into the bombing and poisoning.

"The tox screen's not in yet, but the explosives expert has confirmed your suspicions about the placement of the bomb. It was planted in Dr. Smith's office, in an unlocked file drawer. He's flown up to London to take a look at the reconstructed device at New Scotland Yard."

There wasn't a better bomb team than the guys who worked for the Lazlo Group. By the time they were finished, they'd know where every part of the thing had come from, how it had been put together and in what order, what the bomber had eaten for breakfast the day of the blast and the color of the shirt he was wearing.

Instead of being reassured, Walker hung up feeling even more angry.

He definitely needed to find a quiet place and calm down.

But it wouldn't stop eating away at him. The burning question. Who the hell was messing with Zara Smith, and why?

Not that it was his job to find out; that was up to von Kreus. Walker had done his part. He was out of it now. Walker Shaw was not a criminal investigator, he was just a doctor. A psychiatrist.

Correction: a *former* doctor. *Former* psychiatrist. Just a consultant.

And a lover good and gone from Zara's life.

Former lover.

He brooded over that as he exited through a set of French doors and made his way around the outside of the palace. The gardens were as opulent and showy as the rooms inside. A precise riot of bloom in coordinated beds of carefully planned casual disarray. Perfect cozy English gardens within a strict grid of French symmetry.

Not unlike his own life. Outwardly casual and devil-may-care, but inside walking a razor-thin line between a stolen past and a future he resented.

No. He didn't resent his future. He loved working for Corbett. He just resented like hell that the choice of what he could and could not do had been taken from him.

Still and all, the flowers along the brick walkway were pretty and smelled nearly as good as the ones back home. Normally they'd work just fine for a spell of relaxation, but not today. Today he longed for the dissolute splendor of a decaying Southern plantation in which to soothe his righteous frustration.

The abandoned rose garden was more Keats than Tennessee Williams, but it would have to do.

He barely noticed the tangle of creepers, heavy with sweet-smelling blossoms, that covered the crumbling brick walls of the courtyard. He homed in on a small patch of green grass that militantly guarded the center of the crumbling square, surrounded by fragrantly overgrown bushes dotted with white and butter-yellow buds. Dropping onto the grass, he pulled off his shirt and tossed it aside.

It was hard to stay mad surrounded by all this beauty, but somehow he managed it. Damn, he could use a drink.

He propped his arms under his head and gave in to a scowl. For the first time since turning his back on his old home and familiar life, he wondered if he'd made a mistake walking away from the scandal. Should he have ignored the threats, stayed and fought it? Denied the accusations, demanded a fair hearing?

Would anyone have listened?

Probably not. He was only the wonder boy, the handsome but penniless young doctor of psychiatry who'd had the devil's own timing, managing to study just the right thing and meet just the right people and get just the right grants to ensure an early stardom in his chosen field, and what's more, to help a whole lot of folks along the way. There'd been no down side to his life. Everyone admired him. Everyone loved him.

Including, unfortunately, one of his patients.

She was the daughter of the state senator, brought in after a car wreck. She'd lost her memory and her daddy wanted the best his considerable fortune could buy. Daddy's daughter wanted Walker. He did not share her ambitions. She was his patient. She didn't care.

When he refused her advances, she turned ugly and accused him of all sorts of improprieties, none of which were true. Other than, perhaps, that first surprised kiss.

But who did the tabloids and gossip rags believe? A bad-boy head doctor who came from nothing, or the innocent daughter of an illustrious senator? But what the press didn't know, and he soon learned to his everlasting sorrow and fury, was that the woman was unstable. When he said he would set the record straight, she threatened his family—his parents, sister and brothers. When his daddy had found his favorite hunting hound with a slashed throat, Walker had started to take her seriously. He didn't say a word to the press. The woman was genuinely insane. But her father was a senator....

His old employers had known the truth of his innocence, and yet, because he couldn't defend himself, they had shown him the door. Perception was far more important than truth, they'd told him. Everyone knew that. No one would send their daughters or fathers or grandmothers to a medical facility with any whisper of sexual scandal attached to it, not in the conservative South. They were certain Walker understood why they couldn't stand by him...not against the senator who controlled their funding.

Walker understood, all right. When all was said and done, skill, brains, dedication all meant squat. All that mattered in their world was who your people were. If it came down to a choice, there was no contest.

Just as there'd be no contest when Lady Zara found out exactly who he was and what sordid secrets lay pressed between the pages of those forgotten memories. If she'd just been plain Dr. Jane Smith, he might have stood a chance if he laid it all out for her. But an aristocrat, one of a handful of privileged European nobility? No way. There'd be no more kisses for him from that quarter. Oh, no. That little future marchioness would not be trolling in his waters again, not once she knew the truth.

That was for damn sure.

And that was one, pure, damn shame.

His cell phone chirped, rousing him out of his even greater frustration. He wasn't one for a pity party. Normally he took his licks like a man and moved on. But Zara had him twisting in the wind.

He flipped open the phone and checked the name scrolling across the screen. Corbett.

"Yeah, boss?"

"Where's Zara? Is she with you?"

"She's in bed resting. She had a rough—"

"Is there someone guarding her?"

Instantly alert, Walker sat up and reached for his shirt. "Estevez, the agent assigned to shadow us yesterday, is keeping an eye on the medical wing. Why? What's going on?"

"You were right. She was poisoned."

He swore roundly. "You got the tox screen back?"

"Just this minute. The prelim definitely shows digitalis. Garden variety, not pharmaceutical grade."

Walker was already on his feet. "Just like the stuff that killed Prince Reginald."

"Except this time the pasta was spiked, not a line of cocaine. I'm sending von Kreus to question the restaurant staff."

Besides being a top-notch investigator, von Kreus was the group's information extraction specialist. The best interrogator on the planet. "He'll put the fear of God into them if anyone can," Walker said, hurrying toward the medical wing entrance.

"I'll let you know what he comes up with. Meanwhile, get Estevez on Zara's door. You'll have to take the night shift unless I can find a rent-a-cop. The Group is spread pretty thin right now. I've got three other cases going besides this mess in Silvershire."

"Already on it," Walker said, thinking of a thousand problems with that scenario. But he had no choice. "I'm fine with temporary babysitting duty. Unless you've got another job lined up for me…?"

"You signing off on Dr. Smith's recovery, then?"

His boss didn't need to know the only gap left in her memory was Walker himself. Because he didn't signify. "I've done everything I can do. There may be some holes, but as long as Dr. Landon gives her the okay on the medical stuff, I'm officially signing off."

"All right. Relieve Estevez tonight. Until we figure out her role in the crazy palace intrigue playing out in that country, I don't want her left alone for a minute."

"She'll object, you know. She thinks we're barking up the wrong tree."

"Not her call."

"She's not going to like us on her ass."

"Walker?"

"Yeah, boss?"

There was a slight pause. "Then make her like it."

Chapter 6

*P*ounding.

Something was pounding, pounding like a drum. Like a fist. A fist on the door.

Awoken from a deep sleep, she gasped as the door was flung open.

Walker!

The room was dark, black dark, midnight dark, and he was standing in a wedge of dim light shining in from the corridor, the corridor that was always lit, always eye-blindingly bright. But now it was in a dim glow, as if by candlelight. Or the golden dawn of Italy…

Walker's blond hair shimmered as though wet, too long and quiveringly untamed and…caveman-sexy. He wore soft blue jeans and a long-sleeved shirt, open, that billowed out from his skin in a warm gentle breeze. She could see his chest, broad and muscular and coarse-haired, with small flat nipples that beckoned to her tongue.

She shivered.

"What do you want?" she asked, though she knew the answer. She could read it in his eyes. She'd read it there the first time she'd seen him, and in each moment that had passed since.

"You."

She licked her lips. And realized she was completely naked. Lying on a cloud-soft bed that smelled of…roses.

"Scared?"

"I've never done anything like this before," she whispered. "Ever."

Sex with a stranger was dangerous. In every way possible. But she wanted him.

And he wasn't a stranger. He was Walker.

She spread her legs, very slightly. His didn't miss the movement. He stepped into the room and closed the door. Instant blackness. She heard the snick of a lock. Her heartbeat zinged.

"You are a very naughty little girl." His lazy Southern accent was smooth and sinful, reaching out to her from the absolute darkness.

She spread her legs wider. Dizzy with anticipation.

"Yes," she said in a small voice, the tips of her breasts tightening to hard, aching points. Her body so ready for him she would surely die if he didn't come to her soon.

"I do like that in a woman," he purred.

She felt the bed dip. Smelled his cologne. Spicy, rugged, American. So different from what she was used to a man smelling like—refined, elegant…boring. Walker was different from any man she'd ever met.

"You know what I want, Dr. Shaw?" Shy. Demure. Teasing. So unlike her.

The bed dipped again and the edges of his open shirt brushed over her breasts. A cascade of goose bumps. Strong legs in rough denim forced her thighs far apart. The smell of crushed rose petals. The whisper of warm breath.

"What does my lady want?"

Him. *She wanted him so badly her whole body trembled beneath the weight of his erotic appeal.*

She put her mouth to his ear. Told him exactly what she wanted. In words she'd never uttered aloud.

He chuckled. Full and wicked, laden with a rogue's promise. "Whatever you say, sugar. Your wish is my command."

Then his tongue was on her breasts. Her body lifted, bowed. Blinding pleasure. Endlessly blinding pleasure. His tongue…his tongue. Oh, yes. Oh, yes.

"Walker!" she cried.

He tried to stay in the chair. Honest to God, he did.

Three times Walker had risen to his feet, and three times he'd made himself sit back down in the overstuffed armchair by Zara's bedside. She hadn't awoken when he'd slipped into her room, relieving Estevez just before midnight. Estevez had stayed in the corridor. Walker preferred being inside, with visual contact. He hadn't known she'd be naked, tangled in the sheets….

Now she was dreaming. And it was obvious what she was dreaming about. Christ, he felt like a voyeur.

He didn't dare get any closer to her. Hell, he should have marched right out of the room at her first whimpered sigh. Made himself sit in the molded plastic chair outside her door. Like a gentleman.

But he was no gentleman. Ask anyone.

So, in guilty fascination, he watched. And listened. And sweated. And ached.

But at the sound of his name on her lips, cried out with such passion, such surrender, his willpower crumbled. He vaulted to his feet, overcome by the sheer stunning temptation of it.

Sweet holy Jeezus.

How much could a man endure?

Yet he stood there, stock-still as his lover's body quivered with pleasure at the hand of his own incubus, glued to the spot by his perpetually inconvenient sense of honor.

She was gorgeous in her unconscious abandon, a living, moaning portrait of how every man dreams of making his woman feel. The irony of the situation was not lost on him.

He watched until she stilled on the disheveled sheets with one long, final exhale. He exhaled, too. Far less contently.

"Walker?" she whispered, eyes opening at some silent signal, disoriented by the potent morphia of sleep and satiety. Her hand reached for him. "What are you doing out of bed?"

He swallowed heavily. Naturally, he would not be let off so easily.

"Zara. Wake up. You've been dreaming, sugar."

Her slumberous eyes took in his finger-mussed hair, his unbuttoned shirt, his enormous arousal.

"No," she whispered. "I've been remembering." Her hand remained raised, her fingers poised in invitation. "Italy. Rose petals. And the touch of a man who truly wanted me."

His gut clenched. A war raged within. "A man who'll always want you," he quietly admitted.

Her lips curved up, softly sensual, and he knew he'd lost the battle before it had begun.

"Come back to me."

He took her hand. Allowed her to strip him of his clothes

and draw him down on top of her. Sighed with need as he sank into the cradle of her embrace, even as his conscience made one last stab at making sure she was fully aware.

"Zara—"

"Shh. I remember, Walker. Now, make love to me the way you did in Florence."

He groaned. Unable to resist her. All the while knowing the whole affair was doomed; they were not meant for each other and never would be. She didn't know about him. Couldn't. He didn't care. He wanted her too badly.

He covered her mouth and her body and took what she offered. Took every beautiful inch, every whispered entreaty, every sweet moan. And in return gave her everything he had.

For this night she was his again. And he was hers. Completely. Until morning intruded, there was no outside world. No princes and ladies, no scandals and ruined chances. No perceptions.

Just two minds and bodies intertwining in perfect union.

He would forget everything else and concentrate on that. On tonight. While he still had the fantasy within his grasp. Tonight would have to last a lifetime.

Because tomorrow…

Well, tomorrow was another day.

When Walker awoke, the sun was shining through the mullioned windows, filling the room with the clean, crisp light of morning. Zara was draped across his chest, yawning and starting to stretch muscles that must be as tasked as his own. His arms were around her, loosely, her hip just grazing the evidence of his continued want of her.

He felt the moment she became conscious of his presence under her, of their nakedness, of his arousal, of all they had done the night before. She gave a soft gasp, then glanced up at his face and smiled.

Suddenly, though, it faltered. Her sleepy eyes became questioning, wary. And his heart sank.

So soon, his reprieve was up.

She opened her mouth, but he carefully laid his thumb over her lips.

"Hush, now. I was afraid you hadn't recalled everything last night. But now you do. I understand that you have to take it all back and let me go. But please, sugar, don't think badly of me. I couldn't stand it if you did."

Her head gave a little shake. Uncertain. It broke his heart.

He wanted to spin her under him again, beg her to let him take her one more time. One last time fill her with his length, and know what it was to possess her.

But he didn't have the courage. Her rejection would shatter him. And reject him she surely would. She had to, if there was a hint of doubt in her mind that he had slept with that girl back home. Last night was too soon after Zara had officially ceased being his patient—or whatever she was—to be a convincing argument in his favor. He knew that. He had known that when he'd made the choice in the throes of temptation.

Still, she would believe in him, or she would not. He prayed she would. But in the end it would not matter. It was those ubiquitous perceptions that would prevail if she remained true to her lifelong dream.

She slid off him, eyes cast down, hurrying into the bathroom.

Damn, he thought. Damn, damn, damn.

He rolled out of bed, swiped up his clothes and threw them on, then paced back and forth at the foot of the bed. When he heard the shower turn on and the curtain move, he knocked and opened the door.

Just getting under the water, she turned to him guardedly. He leaned a hip against the door frame and folded his arms across his abdomen, trying not to react when she whipped the opaque plastic across the rod, shutting him out.

"Your medical board with Dr. Landon is set for nine o'clock," he said.

"I'll be there."

Well, at least she was still speaking to him. A good sign?

He glanced at his watch. The second hand advanced slowly. The sound of water hitting flesh was driving him crazy. "Estevez will be back to start his shift in about twenty minutes."

"I don't need a bodyguard, Walker. I don't like it."

He sighed. Stubborn woman. "In case you hadn't noticed, someone may be trying to kill you, Zara."

"I'm not convinced—"

"Doesn't matter." He cut her off. "Lord Carrington's orders."

Long, awkward moments ticked by, filled with hot steam and the scent of floral soap and shampoo. He stuck his hands under his armpits against the urge to pull back the curtain.

"Fine, whatever," she finally said. "Hand me a towel, would you please?"

"No," he said. Perversely petulant. He wanted to see her lush curves again. All of them. She could get her own damn towel.

There was a brief pause, a jetted breath, then the curtain yanked back. She regarded him, doing nothing to hide her nudity. Then she jerked a towel off the rack. "Walker, I don't regret what happened between us, if that's what you think."

"Good. Because Corbett put me on guard duty with Estevez. I've got your back every night until this thing is solved."

Her eyes went wide and she forgot about the towel.

He didn't. He shifted his stance, leaning his back against the jamb, and crossed his ankles, wishing he could do something about it. "Don't worry. I'll stick to a chair in the corridor from now on." Like a proper gentleman.

"No need for you to put yourself out."

"Zara—"

"I'm moving home today."

"What?" He almost fell backwards in his haste to straighten off the door frame. "When was this decided?"

"Just now."

"No. No damn way. Corbett'll have a hissy fit and I—" his gaze slid over her water-slick body, making her pull the towel around herself "—I'm not comfortable with that arrangement."

Her chin rose. "As I said, there's no need. If Russell insists I have a bodyguard, I'll hire someone else."

It was as though she'd slapped him full on the face.

Hurt and fury swirled through him. He stared at her in disbelief.

Hell.

He didn't deserve this. He'd maintained his honor and integrity throughout this whole painful ordeal, succumbing to his true feelings only *after* she was no longer his patient. When *she'd* invited him in. He'd cut it close, true, but he had waited. Unlike her, who'd repeatedly thrown herself at him.

"You don't give a good goddamn about my side of the story, do you?" he growled.

At least she had the grace to look embarrassed. She started to speak but he slashed his hand in a gesture for silence.

"Never mind," he said, spun on his heel and stalked out.

"Walker!" she called after him, but it was too late. He was done.

He slammed the door behind him, the bang echoing off the three-foot-thick stone walls like a gunshot. Juvenile, but gratifying.

He stormed down the hallway, almost running into Estevez. The other man's brows hiked. "Hey, what's up, buddy?"

"Not a damn thing," he gritted out. "She's all yours."

And he was welcome to her.

Oh, God.

What had she done?

Zara groaned out loud.

Walker was right. She'd been brutally unfair to him. Like the imperious Queen of Hearts shouting "Off with his head!" Condemning him without a trial because of her own fear.

She'd been gutted by the brilliant memory of what they'd shared in Italy. Gutted by their incredible night of lovemaking. And even more gutted by the subsequent recollection of his very public fall into professional disgrace—and the reason why.

Because that fall made all the rest impossible.

Just as he'd said all along.

He'd known. And when she'd realized she couldn't have him, she'd resented him for it. For not warning her.

Except he had. Repeatedly. And she hadn't listened. She'd listened only to her own foolish fantasies. Turning a long-ago schoolgirl crush into something it wasn't. Something real. Making a charismatic scoundrel into something he wasn't. An honorable man. The whole academic community involved in neurology had been abuzz with the scandal involving their golden boy. His lack of denial had shocked everyone, condemning him in absentia.

She straightened her spine. But even a scoundrel deserved a fair hearing. She hadn't given him a chance to give his side of things. Maybe there were mitigating circumstances. Lord knew, she herself had thrown professional ethics to the wind easily enough when it came to Dr. Walker Shaw.

She was of the nobility, the daughter of one of the most respected men in the country, and she was supposed to set an example for the people of Silvershire. Use wisdom and reason in all things. Make decisions founded on facts, not rumor. With Walker, she'd acted on pure, base emotion. She of all people should know better.

And she did. She took a deep, cleansing breath. After she was finished with the medical recertification, she'd go to him and apologize. Listen to his side.

Then maybe she could forgive herself this particular guilt. So she could get back to her life. To her work. Because that was all that mattered now. Now that Walker was lost to her.

Meeting with Russell and Dr. Landon in one of the intimate palace salons, Zara was somehow able to push Walker to the back of her mind and concentrate on answering their questions. After the obligatory tea and biscuits had been served, Russell went first, quizzing her gently about friends and family.

"They've been very worried about you," he told her. "It's been hard on your parents to stay away all this time. They'd like to see you, now you've recovered."

She smiled. Her father had probably been a royal pain in Russell's backside with his phone calls. She and the Marquis had their considerable differences, but he took his duties as a father seriously. Despite her heretical opinions about the succession of his title and her ambitions in that direction, he would see her to rights.

"Are they here in Silverton?" she asked.

"They want you home at Danehus."

"Ah." The warm-fuzzies dimmed slightly. "I'll give them a call this afternoon. I don't like leaving King Weston while he's still critical." She gave Dr. Landon an apologetic look. "I know you're doing everything in your power—"

The distinguished doctor waved her off. "It will be a relief having you back on the team. Perhaps together we can figure out what is keeping him in his coma."

With that segue, Russell excused himself, and Dr. Landon settled into his questioning, starting by asking her about her health in general, and if anything at all had changed since the accident, other than her memory.

She stifled a sigh. *What hadn't?*

But she wasn't about to go there.

She picked up the Royal Copenhagen teapot from a silver tray at her elbow and refilled their cups, avoiding his gaze. "I've had some rather bizarre dreams," she admitted, endeavoring not to blush at the one she'd had last night. The one that had directly led to this morning's fiasco. She wasn't going *there,* either. "But I suppose that's to be expected with a head injury."

To be honest, she was a little concerned about the two other, really strange dreams she'd had. They'd been so extraordinary and yet so…lifelike, they almost hadn't seemed like dreams at all. More like hallucinations. No, like *visions.*

"Are you still having them?"

She added milk to their tea. Regardless, she had no intention of letting a couple of silly dreams prevent her from going back to work. "I really only had two or three," she evaded. "I'll let you know if I have any more."

Thank goodness that satisfied him, and he brought out a National Medical Board exam booklet and the real test began. She was able to answer each question to the degree that they actually started debating theory together and comparing notes on the various procedures they'd done in common. Instead of being the chore she had anticipated, it was so exhilarating that several hours later they both looked up in surprise to see Russell walking in followed by two liveried manservants carrying loaded lunch trays.

"I say, is it so late?" Dr. Landon asked with a laugh.

Russell gave him a dry look. "It's after three. I thought you both might have passed out from hunger, so I took the liberty."

Zara grinned. "No sardine sandwiches, I trust." Russell had been an infamous prankster growing up. One of his specialties had been making sardine sandwiches for their picnics—using fish bait instead of the traditional ingredient.

The future king feigned a wounded look. "Certainly not." Then they burst out in laughter.

The country of Silvershire didn't know what it was in for with him as head of state.

As they ate and chatted, she thought about how much he'd changed from that carefree young rapscallion. Though he didn't exactly have the stolid, serious demeanor of most reigning monarchs, he had taken on the heavy responsibility without protest, putting his all into the job, even though he had stated publicly he really didn't want to be king.

On the other hand, she had stayed much the same.... Ever the serious, driven perfectionist. Even as a girl, she'd always been the epitome of propriety and aristocratic decorum. Yet here he was destined to be king, and she…would she ever achieve her goal of becoming the first Marchioness of Daneby…?

Russell supported her quest to change the ancient laws, even going as far as to say he'd bring it up for discussion with the Privy Council when the time came. So there was finally some real hope on the horizon.

But not unless King Weston recovered. If he didn't, no one

would ever speak her name again at court. So it was time to put her whole focus on work.

Which meant she had to clear up one last lingering problem....

"Your Grace," she said after Dr. Landon had taken his leave, "There's something we need to discuss."

Russell glanced up at her use of formal address. His mouth assumed a determined line. "It's not up for discussion."

"But you haven't even heard—"

"I know exactly what you're about to say. Dr. Shaw has informed me of your intention to hire some outside bodyguard. I'm afraid it's out of the question."

She opened her mouth to argue.

He raised a finger to stop her. "No. I've appointed the Lazlo Group to take care of this whole painful situation, and I trust Corbett Lazlo's judgment implicitly. If he has assigned Shaw to be your bodyguard, your bodyguard he shall be. Also," Russell continued, taking the wind completely out of her sails, "Shaw mentioned something about you wanting to move back home. That I may consider, though my instincts are against it."

She flopped back in her chair with a scowl. "You've really gotten quite bossy in your old age, Russell," she said peevishly.

He had the nerve to grin. "I do rather like being king of the world." He looked at her sympathetically. "So. What's going on between you two?"

She held her expression perfectly neutral. "Whatever do you mean?"

"Don't even try, Zara. I recognize all the signs. Having been there myself. Very recently." He steepled his fingers. "Dr. Shaw is a good man. However…" He paused. "Be careful. He does come with a certain amount of unpleasant baggage. You'd do well to be discreet, given your position in society."

She had no idea what *signs* he was talking about, but she'd heard enough. She didn't need Lord Russell Carrington's advice. He had been the very height of indiscretion, carrying on with the late crown prince's fiancée practically on the eve of the royal wedding! Their hasty marriage after the prince's untimely demise had been nothing less than a scandal. But Amelia was a princess, so that made everything all right….

Shocked at her uncharitable thoughts, Zara was nevertheless unable to stop a subtle rebuke. Rising from her chair, she used every ounce of aristocratic bearing she could muster, and said, "You know me better than that, Your Grace. What I cannot do openly, I won't do at all."

With a sigh, Russell came to his feet as well. "Yes. I do know. Come, darling. I didn't mean to insult you. I only meant, once in a while you should let yourself do something really reckless. Just be smart about it."

He sounded so sincere, she was unable to stay angry with him. "Like you, you mean?" she softly chided.

There was that grin again, the unrepentantly mischievous one that said he'd do precisely the same things all over again, and more, given the chance. "Yes. Exactly like me."

"Well," she said, allowing him to pull her into a brotherly hug and kiss her on the forehead, "I'll think about it."

And undoubtedly she would. For a long, long time to come. But that was all she'd do. Because anything more would be…reckless.

Chapter 7

"**W**hat the hell happened?"

Fearing the worst, Walker rushed into the emergency room at the Royal Medical University Hospital. After running the gamut of reporters and tabloid photographers and a line of cops, he headed straight for the white curtain surrounding the only occupied bed in the ER.

The urgent message he'd gotten from the Lazlo Group secretary had been garbled by bad cell reception, but he'd heard the words *Zara*, *hospital* and *hurt* loud and clear.

He scanned the small enclosure after hurriedly pulling back the curtain. Zara stood by the headboard with her arms wrapped around herself, looking shaken. Estevez was lying in the bed grimacing as a doctor fussed with his arm.

Walker let out a whoosh of relief that their positions weren't reversed. Breaking the speed limits to get here, his only thought had been…too awful to contemplate. He was still mad as hell at Zara, but that didn't mean his heart hadn't almost stopped beating, thinking about her injured, or worse.

"Jeezus, what happened?" he repeated, his pulse lowering a bit.

They both looked up. "Just a broken arm," Estevez said, giving him a pained smile. "Nothing serious."

"Nothing serious! He was sideswiped by a car!" Zara exclaimed, her voice a couple of octaves higher than normal. "The blighter didn't even stop. I'm so angry!"

Walker looked from Zara to Estevez, his pulse kicking right back up. He didn't say a word, but his expression must have asked the question for him. Estevez lifted his shoulders almost imperceptibly, his eyes saying he wished he had a better answer.

"How did it happen?" Walker asked Zara.

She paused for a second, then said, "I spent the afternoon with King Weston and planned to go back this evening, but I wanted to move my things home to my apartment before it got too late. Mr. Estevez and I had done that, and were walking across the street to a deli to grab a bite of dinner." She took a deep breath. "Neither of us saw the car. I think it must have been parked and didn't see us as it came out into traffic."

Estevez remained impassive as he added, "I saw it first and pushed Dr. Smith back onto the sidewalk, but couldn't get out of the way fast enough. He just clipped me, but I landed badly."

"Was it intentional?" Walker asked, deliberately keeping his voice even.

"What do you mean?" Zara asked, frowning. "Of course it—" The words halted as her eyes widened. She glanced at Estevez tentatively. "It was an accident...wasn't it?"

"Under the circumstances I'd definitely treat it as suspicious," he responded, then said to Walker, "Didn't get the plates, but I gave the cops a pretty good description of the car."

"I assume you called Corbett?"

"On the way to the hospital. He said not to let Dr. Smith out of my sight until you got here. Obviously I'm out of commission for guard duty. You're supposed to stay with her until he can find someone to take over for me."

"*Me?*" Walker stiffened, turning to Zara. Now that he knew she was unhurt, all his previous fury with her returned. "I thought you hired someone else."

Her gaze skittered away. "Lord Carrington nixed that idea. He wants you with me."

Oh, wasn't that just peachy. And just what Walker wanted, too—to spend another night in her immediate vicinity. Not. He slashed a hand through his hair and shot Estevez a look. "You going to be okay, buddy?"

The other man nodded. "No sweat."

"Call me tomorrow," Walker said, and started out through the curtain, holding it open for Zara. "Let's go."

She still didn't look at him as she ducked past. "I know a way out that won't take us past the media circus outside."

They didn't talk as she led the way through a series of busy passageways then up a flight of stairs, eventually emerging into the parking structure.

"You've used this escape route before," he said, unlocking the passenger door of his rental car.

"Being the daughter of a marquis has its advantages, but also its downsides. Paparazzi being the worst."

"Tell me about it," he said disgustedly. "A bunch of vultures." The response had been automatic. Visceral. Stupidly revealing.

"Were they very bad to you?"

He didn't need to ask what she was referring to. Not that he wanted to talk about it. She'd had her chance. "Bad enough. Get in, please." She hesitated, then did as she was told. "Where to?" he asked, buckling himself in. She hesitated again.

He made a concerted effort not to snap. "Look. I'm no happier about this situation than you are. But unless I quit my job we're stuck with each other until morning. And I'm not about to quit my job."

"That's not… Walker, I want to apologize," she said, finally meeting his gaze. "For this morning."

"No need," he said, voice gruff. He *so* did not want to have this conversation. "Last night was my fault. I knew better." God, did he ever.

"Oh, and I didn't?" she said dryly.

"No. You didn't have all the facts." He spun the car toward the rear exit, away from the hoopla out front.

"I still don't. Why don't you enlighten me?"

What was the point? It wouldn't make any difference, even if she believed every word. She was trapped by her circumstances, just as he was by his. "Why don't we just drop it, and you tell me where we're going."

She folded her hands in her lap. He figured it was to keep from strangling him. When he was calmer he'd appreciate her efforts. But right now he didn't.

"Fine." She gave him directions to where she lived. It wasn't far. A stylized nineteen-thirties building of about a dozen floors, it was situated on a prime piece of real estate overlooking the River Kairn, with views of the Golden Bridge and the historic district across the water. She obviously had some serious bucks. Or maybe her influential family owned the thing. Maybe both. Must be nice.

When the tires squealed into her assigned spot in the building's underground garage, he looked around, suddenly remembering the reason he was with her. He was supposed to be protecting her.

For the first time in his life Walker wished he owned a gun. Corbett had tried to give him one on several occasions, saying, "Take it. You never know when you'll need a little persuasion," but he had always refused. He was a doctor, not an agent. Sure, he was a Southerner, had hunted deer and ducks with his daddy all through his youth, and could handle a gun better than most—at least a shotgun and hunting rifle—but he didn't like the things. Doctors saved lives; they didn't take them.

"Is something wrong?" Zara asked.

"Just checking the scene."

Something didn't feel right. He backed the car out of the narrow slot and headed for the opposite end of the garage. "I think we'll skip your usual spot for now. Are there any unassigned spaces?"

She frowned. "Is this really necessary?"

"I'm not taking any chances," he said. "But I think you need to know, I'm unarmed and I don't do daring rescues."

"Doesn't matter. I'm used to doing my own rescuing."

For some reason, the firmly stated pronouncement tugged at his gut. That was just plain wrong. His mama would agree with Zara, but his daddy would have a thing or two to say about it. Daddy was from Alabama and believed that a man should take care of his woman. In every way.

But Walker wasn't his daddy, in any way, and Zara sure as hell wasn't his woman. So he didn't comment.

"Here, put this over your shoulders," he ordered after getting her door for her. He slipped out of his suit jacket and held it out. When she stared at him uncomprehendingly, he slid it around her, flipping up the collar. Then he put his arm around her waist, tugged her close and started for the elevator.

"What are you doing?" she demanded, attempting to pull away.

He didn't let her. "If it wasn't an accident this afternoon, someone may be hiding down here, watching for you. They won't be looking for a romantic couple."

Her steps faltered for a split second before she melted into his side. "The garage is gated."

"Yeah. That'll stop them. No, don't look around," he told her when she started to.

He heard her swallow. He followed suit. But for a totally different reason. He hated being this close to her. He could smell her scent, the scent with which he'd reacquainted himself so intimately last night. The warmth of her body as it rubbed against his ribs was the final straw.

He felt himself harden, unable to stop the images of their lovemaking, or his body's reaction to them.

"Walker?"

"Yeah."

"Thank you."

He turned to her, startled. "For what?"

"For doing this. I'm not exactly sure what your job description is with the Lazlo Group, but I'm pretty sure bodyguard isn't it."

"I do a lot of things for Mr. Lazlo," he said as the elevator arrived and they got in. The second the door whooshed closed he let her go and stepped as far away from her as the tiny cubicle allowed.

Holding the lapels of his jacket in her fingers, she pulled it tighter and leaned back against the elegant mirrored wall. "I'd like to hear about them."

He leaned his butt against the opposite wall and regarded her, wanting to hit something when she unconsciously closed her eyes and brushed her nose over his jacket collar, obviously smelling him on it. Her almost imperceptible smile made his already hard arousal lurch.

"No you wouldn't," he growled, and her eyes blinked open. "What floor?" he asked in the same harsh tone.

"Top," she said.

The penthouse. Figured. He punched the button with a little too much vehemence.

The elevator was insufferably slow. It crawled up the twelve floors like an overdressed snail, fluid and silent. She watched him the whole time. He wouldn't give her the satisfaction of looking away, but kept his eyes steadily on hers. As annoying as it was, it impressed him when she didn't look away, either.

As the car crept past the eleventh floor, she said, "Russell thinks I should have an affair with you."

He didn't even move an eyelash for shock. *What was that supposed to mean?* They reached the penthouse and the door opened to a gorgeous marble foyer. They continued to stare at each other until he finally said, "Remind me to tell Carrington to mind his own damn business."

She lowered her eyes and walked out. He followed, acutely uncomfortable on so many levels he lost count. She got her key from her purse and he took it from her.

He pointed off to one side. "Stand there and don't move until I say you can come in."

She opened her mouth. He glowered at her and she closed it again.

Cautiously, he unlocked and cracked the door, sticking his head in before entering. Damn, he was no good at this stuff. What did he know from clearing a scene? Still, he figured it was mostly common sense—turn on all the lights and don't put your nose where you can't see.

Which was exactly how he proceeded—as soon as he re-covered from his first glimpse of her apartment.

In keeping with the building, the massive living room was done in high Art-Deco style, with muted colors and graceful curving furniture of burled walnut. Crystal vases, bowls and other arty pieces of frosted pink, clear and sea-green glass dotted the tables and glass bookshelves, some containing dead flower arrangements. A long, low, gray sofa grouping mean-dered around an incredible inlaid stone Art-Deco fireplace.

Everything in the room oozed of style and class. He was almost afraid to move for fear of breaking something.

Snapping himself out of it, he quickly searched though the rest of the rooms, until he got to one that contained a huge bed with richly carved head and footboards, covered with a pink satin comforter and lace pillows. It smelled of Zara.

He stood paralyzed for a moment on the threshold of his lover's bedroom in a sudden agony of desire, battling against the overwhelming need to go out to the foyer and grab her, throw her onto this seductive bed and thrust himself deep inside her. Fisting his hands at his sides, he counted to ten, twice, and made himself skirt the suitcase sitting by the door and walk in.

He held his breath as he checked the closet.

When he turned to get out of there, she was standing in the doorway. Watching him. Looking like she wanted to say something but was afraid to do so.

He raised a warning palm—*don't*—and swept past her, out of the room. "I thought I told you to stay in the corridor," he gritted out.

"And I told you, I do my own rescuing." She walked after him, the sound of her fashionable high heels on the carpet all but disappearing into the deep pile. "I thought you might need—" she blanched at his expression as he whipped his head around "—a drink. I certainly do." Her voice tried to be resolute but he detected a slight waver.

She went directly to a sleek bar cabinet in the living room. When she lifted the lid it lit up inside, and the front automatically opened down to a flat surface, like a writing desk.

She fetched up a glass from inside, and a bottle with a fancy label. "I'm having a vermouth. If you want something mixed, you'll have to fix it yourself. All I can manage right now is ice." The bottle clinked against her glass and a few drops spilled. "Blast."

He wondered what the chances were of her having a beer in that contraption, and decided slim to none. "Bourbon's fine. No ice."

To his everlasting amazement, she actually pulled an excellent Kentucky brand from deep in the bowels of the cabinet. "It says twelve-year-old, but I imagine it's at least fifteen by now." She tried to smile, but failed miserably. Picking up a squat glass, her hands shook so much he took pity on the bourbon, strode over and relieved her of it.

"Thank you," she murmured, and slid away from him as he poured his drink. She left her heels half way to the sofa, letting them lie where they fell in an artful arrangement.

Damn the woman. She even made taking off her shoes a sensual experience.

He threw back the finger of bourbon he'd poured.

Suddenly, he decided the last thing on earth he should be doing was drinking. After a moment's vacillation and a silent curse, he poured himself another. A double. But made himself walk away from the bottle.

Strolling over to the mantel, he propped himself against it, sipping. She was sitting on the sofa, shapely legs crossed, her head tilted back on the cushions and her eyes closed. In her hand, her glass was empty. He debated filling it for her.

Instead, he decided to let the angry gator out of the pen. "What made you say that? About Russell Carrington?"

Her tongue peeked out from between her lips and swiped over them. An endless moment later, her lashes lifted. "Because every time I see you, all I can think about is taking your clothes off. I wanted you to be as miserable as I am." Her eyes studied him for a moment, then drifted closed again.

He took a long time easing out the breath that had instantly backed up in his lungs at that little tease.

What the goddamn *hell* did she expect him to say to that? "Why don't you, then?" he wanted to shout, but stopped himself. Just.

He tossed back the rest of his drink. "Believe me, sugar, I am," he said.

That little wisp of a smile appeared again at the corner of her mouth, and his balls started to ache.

"Good," she whispered. "Now if you would just accept my apology, I might be able to sleep tonight."

"You're a real piece of work, you know that?"

The smile spread. "Surely, you can do better than that? I've been called much worse."

"I can believe it," he muttered.

She lifted her head and tilted it somberly. "Walker, I am sorry. I had no right to judge you. If you don't want to talk about it, I understand. But I really would like to hear your side of the story."

"Why? So you can assuage your embarrassment over seducing me?"

She grimaced. "Ouch."

He was being unfair and a royal bastard. He knew that. Regardless of who seduced whom, he was the culpable party. He was just so goddamned angry with her because she *had* judged him.

But before he could say anything, she rose, went over and carefully set her glass on the bar, then turned to him.

"I'm not embarrassed. I'm glad. I just wish…" She stopped, sighed and shook her head. "Never mind. The guest room is the first on the right. You should find everything you need. I'll see you in the morning."

Frustration swept through him as he watched her walk down the hall without looking back. Should he go after *her*? Turn the tables and seduce her? Get his piece of revenge by showing the perfect Lady Zara exactly what she'd be missing here in her cool, perfect penthouse without a man to warm her bed? Specifically, him.

Tempting.

But no. He'd never met a woman with a stronger backbone than Zara Smith. She'd kick him out of her bedroom in a hot minute if he went sniffing in there.

Besides, his daddy's words were ringing in his ears…the ones recited as Daddy'd let him borrow the keys to the farm truck on his sixteenth birthday. "Remember, boy, never drive drunk," he'd said with the devil's warning on his usually temperate face, "and don't drive mad. They'll both git you in trouble faster 'n a snake'll bite your ass."

Tonight he was two for two. Drunk—not on bourbon but on lust, egged on by an imagination intoxicated by the bliss they'd shared last night. And definitely mad. Mad enough to know better than to go within fifty feet of the woman while she was sleeping.

Nope, going for a ride tonight would be plumb stupid.

Which left what? Sleep? Not in this lifetime. More bourbon? Not a bad idea, but…he was on duty tonight. He'd already had more than he should.

So he triple-checked the locks on the front door, humored himself by checking under all the furniture and in all the drawers for explosive devices and settled down on the sofa to a long, sleepless night. Trying desperately not to think about how much he wanted to walk to the end of the hall and crawl under that pink satin comforter.

Pounding.

Something was pounding, slowly, like a drum. A timbal. Like a timbal in a funeral procession.

The king's funeral.

She clutched her head, her heart. Massive guilt descended, down, down, pressing her down into the depths of despair.

The king was dead! All her fault.

Suddenly she was in a meadow. A forest meadow, filled with birds and flowers and…no, not flowers, symbols. Strange symbols and letters in gold. Dancing mockingly across the waving grass toward—

Two men. Young men. Fighting. Like two wolves, snapping, tearing, two bears swinging angry fists.

A gun!

The two men stopped, the deadly weapon between them. Pointing. A death knell for…

King Weston! It was the king! Younger, stronger, healthy. But not for long. The other man—who was he?—pulled the trigger. Slowly. Agonizingly. The king's face. Sad. Questioning.

Why?

The sound of the gun exploded in her ears.

No!

* * *

Zara woke up screaming.

"No! Stop! Not the king!"

Two powerful arms came around her. "Zara!"

She had to get away! She fought against him. "*No!*"

"Zara it's me. Walker. Wake up. You're having a nightmare."

She stilled, scraped the cobwebs of terror from her mind and struggled to emerge from the blackness.

"Walker," she whispered. "Oh, God. It was awful. The king. He was trying to kill the king."

A strong hand stroked soothingly down her back. "Who, baby?"

"I—I don't know."

"Tell me what he looked like," Walker's deep, smooth voice urged.

She clung to him, the remnant images of this dream merging with the others she'd had, forming a trio of horrible, frightening visions. *What was wrong with her?*

His warm breath whispered over her temple. *Baby.*

"Tell me. Tell me about it."

She hated weakness. Hated when she felt needy and out of control. But she'd never needed anything in her life more than she needed his arms around her right now.

"Hold me," she murmured. "I'll tell you, but I need—" She didn't finish, ashamed and mortified over her own vulnerability, yet unable to resist the comfort his presence would lend. "Hold me. Please."

Four long heartbeats went by before he moved. Through his clothes she could feel the reluctance in his muscles as he slid into bed beside her and took her into his arms. He froze for a second when he realized she was naked; she was terrified he would vault out of bed again and leave her. She tightened her arms around his waist. It wasn't intended as an invitation, exactly, but if he took it as such, so be it. She needed him there that much.

"Thank you," she whispered, then nestled up against him and told him what he wanted to know. She described the young man with the gun, and at his urging, the rest of the dream as well. Then she told him about the other two. How similar they were. How vivid and lifelike. And frightening.

"What could they mean?" she asked when she'd related everything, down to the tiniest detail. He'd been quiet throughout, except for an occasional probing question.

"They could mean anything. Or nothing," he said after a thoughtful moment. "The mind is an incredible instrument. You don't think you remember anything from the bombing, but maybe you do and the dreams are its way of coming out."

"I suppose…although these really don't feel like memories. They feel more like…visions. Like some kind of a warning. About the king."

"You mean, for the future? I thought you said he was young in the dream."

"Yes, but— Oh, I don't know. The whole thing sounds absurd, even to me."

He was silent a while as his fingers slid unconsciously over her skin. Her body moved instinctively under them, making slow, involuntary undulations as they trailed down her back and over her hip.

"No. Not absurd," he finally said. "I'm sure these dreams are somehow meaningful to you. The question is what they're trying to reveal, what they're all about. You are a highly educated woman and the symbolism could come from anywhere your mind has been. Despite the appearance of the king, they may not be about him at all, but some other man. Or situation."

"Like what?"

"You tell me."

She smiled against the smooth cloth of his shirt. "You're starting to sound like a psychiatrist. Always questions. Shall I get on your couch?"

He made a choking noise and his fingers stopped. "I think you're already quite comfortable enough." His breath shuddered out. "Do you always sleep in the nude, Dr. Smith?"

"My one guilty pleasure, I'm afraid. I love the feel of cool, smooth sheets on my bare skin."

His fingers moved a fraction, and suddenly tension hung in the air as thick as the morning fog over the Kairn.

"Zara?" he whispered.

"Yes?"

"I should go."

Chapter 8

"Stay."

The word slipped out of Zara's mouth before she could stop it.

A soft groan rumbled in Walker's chest. "Baby, this is not going to solve anything."

"I know."

"It'll just make things worse."

"Undoubtedly."

"A glutton for punishment, are you?"

"Only with you."

Pushing his fingers through her hair, he gathered her closer, letting her feel which side of this argument his body was on. "Is this just sex?"

She wasn't sure which answer he wanted. Yes, or no? Most men would prefer the former. But Walker wasn't most men.

"If you want it to be," she whispered.

"And if I don't?"

"Then we're both in trouble."

He swore lightly and canted over her, the weight of him putting a sigh on her lips and a race to her heartbeat. His fingertips glided slowly from her hip to her breast and back. Her breath caught in her throat, along with an ache of desire.

"I'm furious with you, you know that," he said, almost conversationally, as his fingers wreaked havoc over her trembling body.

"Yes," she said. "I noticed. I did try to—" she sucked in air as his knuckles grazed her nipple "—apologize."

He looked down at her, his face barely visible in the dim light of the moon that shone through the window. He was so deadly handsome in his rough-edged, bad-boy way, sexy enough to suck the willpower right out of her. As he had from the first moment she'd seen him, back when she was too young and too filled with blind ambition to appreciate what she had found. Why hadn't she ever answered his calls that final year in the States? What a fool she was.

"I'm not interested in apologies," he said. "I want you to believe me. To believe in me." His fingers caught her nipple. Squeezed. "Do you believe *in* me, Zara?"

She was panting. Squirming. His fingers were slowly, systematically killing her. She started to speak. But his lips came down on hers.

"No. Don't answer," he whispered into her mouth. "I don't want lies. Don't ever lie to me, Zara. Even if it hurts."

"I won't," she promised as his mouth covered hers and he kissed her. Wondering if she had been about to do that very thing…

Pushing away the thought, she opened to him, relished the taste of him, the feel of his cotton shirt scraping over her breasts and the wool of his trousers tickling her thighs, the smell of their desire musky in her nostrils.

When he reached for his buttons, she stopped his hand. "No. I want to."

He let her roll them so she was on top, straddling him. He looked so incongruous—his disreputable hair and two-day stubble jarring against the feminine pink satin and white lace of her bed linens.

He was so wrong for her. So inappropriate. A disaster surely waiting to happen.

But she'd never wanted anyone or anything more. And he was all hers.

For tonight, at any rate.

One by one she undid his buttons, kissing and licking his sweat-spicy skin as she went. He protested mildly when she broke off to peel his shirt from his arms, but the protest ended on a moan when she worked his zipper down and parted his fly. Like everything else about him, his arousal was flagrant and demanding, pulsing hungrily beneath a thin veil of cotton.

"Don't stop now," he murmured, rough and low.

"Not for anything."

She pushed both layers of clothing down his hips, and took him in her mouth.

His reaction was powerful and instantaneous. He bowed up, swore harshly, and held her head still with an iron grip. "Sweet mercy, woman."

She could taste his passion, salty and potent, and smell the earthiness of his fever. She licked around him, circling his iron-hard thickness with her tongue.

A second later she was on her back and he was on top of her. Then he was inside her. Moving. Thrusting. *Pounding*.

She wound her arms around his neck. Giving herself up to

it. To him. And she knew with desperate certainty that if she weren't careful, this man could spell the end to her life as she knew it, to all her dreams.

To have this…this incredible feeling, could she throw it all away?

How could she choose?

He took her without mercy, without quarter, without sweet words or promises. But without questions, either. Which was good, because she wasn't sure she could answer them truthfully.

Except for one. The only question she could think of as he scythed into her over and over, bringing them both to the glittering edge of sanity.

Did she want him, always?

Tumbling over the other side, she called out her answer. "Yes! Oh, Walker, yes!"

The next morning could have been awkward. Should have been awkward. Their differences and impossibilities still lay over them like a shroud, nothing having been solved and everything hopelessly muddled by indulging in another night of lovemaking.

Except that Zara awoke to Walker's formidable length sliding into her from behind.

She smiled, coming awake by delicious degrees. "I could get used to this," she said on a soft moan.

"Definitely." He lifted her hair to kiss the back of her neck. "A surefire way to have a good morning."

He held her and thrusted, making her toes curl. *So good.* How could you push away a man who felt so extraordinarily right inside you?

She couldn't. Closing her eyes, she allowed him to set the pace and bring them both to a leisurely but earth-shaking climax.

After last night's tumult of dream-visions and then the carnal excesses of Walker's lovemaking throughout the intervening hours, she felt spent and boneless. But oh, so wonderful. The imprint of his body was on hers permanently; she could still feel him hot and hard between her legs even when he finally withdrew to slide from the bed.

"What are you planning for the day?" he called from the loo.

She stretched luxuriantly. "Back to work. I need to be with King Weston."

She heard the shower start. "Wow. This bathroom is something else. I thought you said your only sinful indulgence was sleeping in the nude." He appeared in the doorway with a grin. "Four heads? A fireplace?"

She grinned back as she got out of bed. "A woman has to take her pleasure where she can get it."

His brow hiked roguishly. "Yeah? Tell me more."

"You are incorrigible." She gave him a quick kiss that somehow turned into a long one. "Lord, Walker, even you must have a limit."

"Haven't found one yet. There an extra toothbrush in that guest bedroom?" She nodded, and he said, "I'll be right back."

By the time he returned she was in the shower. He joined her without asking, and immediately plastered her against the cold marble wall for a quickie she didn't think she had in her.

Afterward, she laughed, grabbing his shoulders when her knees threatened to dissolve under her. "Darling, when you asked if this was just sex, I thought that proposition included things like breathing and eating in between."

"Can't keep up, eh?"

"I'm shocked you can. We're not teenagers."

He winked. "I've had a bit of a dry spell. Besides, we have a lot of time to make up for. Seven years' worth."

She mock groaned. "I'll need crutches."

He gathered her in his arms. "You complainin', Dr. Smith?"

After another long kiss, she sighed dreamily. "Definitely not, Dr. Shaw."

They finished getting ready, and Walker grimaced at putting the same clothes back on again. "Since I haven't heard from Corbett about Estevez's replacement, when we get to the medical wing I'll arrange for a couple of the palace guards to take over for a while. I need to go to the hotel and collect my things." He glanced up at her. "I assume it's okay if I move in here?"

The question threw her for a loop. She hadn't really considered that aspect of their relationship.

If Walker showed up at her apartment with his luggage in hand, the tabloids would have a field day. She knew Edwards, the doorman, must have an arrangement with the *Quiz* to keep an eye on her comings and goings. They always seemed to know everything she was up to, complete with photos. Even now, she was sure they had a photographer downstairs to catch them as they left the building.

A bodyguard she could explain, after the bombing. But not one with a suitcase and a sated smile on his face. They'd want to know everything about him. And they'd find out, too. The *Quiz* was fickle and relentless.

Her hesitation caused his smile to disappear. "Zara?"

"Walker, I'm not sure that's such a good idea."

As her meaning became clear, his mouth thinned to a flat line and his beautiful blue eyes shuttered to a hard gray. "I see," he drawled. "Forgive me. I seem to have forgotten my place, milady." He made a mocking bow and strode from the bedroom.

"Walker, wait!" She hurried after him, grabbing her jacket on the way. "I didn't mean we can't—" The words congealed in her mouth at the stony look he gave her.

He took a pair of silver reflector sunglasses from his pocket and slid them on, effectively cutting her off. "I'll be waiting in the foyer when you're ready, Lady Zara. As befitting my station as your bodyguard. Even one providing stud service."

She reeled back as he whisked through the door and closed it behind him with a definitive snick.

Stud service?

Oh! Of all the impudent, rude, arrogant—

For the first time since she was a girl she wanted to stomp her foot and growl, then smack the man but good. The bloody *nerve!*

Moving in together after a couple of nights in bed might be what one did in America, but it certainly *wasn't* what one did in Silvershire. Especially if one was a public figure. Everything she did reflected on her family name; not to mention her chances of convincing an old-fashioned public and a hopelessly calcified Privy Council into changing the ancient entailment laws.

Walker would have to understand. Making love to her was like making love to a thousand years of tradition.

Except, of course, they *hadn't* made love. They'd had sex. Complicated sex, but just sex. They'd agreed...hadn't they?

He'd even warned her himself about getting involved with a man like him. Implying that the scandal surrounding him would rub off on her. Did he think because she'd slept with him she was willing to take that risk?

Apparently he did.

Oh, God, she had made a terrible mistake!

As selfish as she was, she *wasn't* willing to take the risk. His reputation *would* rub off on her and she'd be tainted, her childhood dream shattered. And now, of all times, when it was so close to coming true. When Russell had promised...

With a frustrated huff, she finished getting ready and sailed out the front door to join her recalcitrant lover.

"Allow me, milady," he said, and smoothly took the key from her hands to lock up.

"Stop it, Walker," she snapped. "Just bloody stop it."

He turned the deadbolt key belligerently and handed it back to her. "Sorry if my service displeases—"

"Don't be a snot." She closed in toe-to-toe and poked him in the chest. She could be as intimidating as any man she knew, despite her lack of inches. "You know damn well how I feel about you. I couldn't have made it any clearer. I've never been as foolish with any man as I've been with you." Sentiment aside, she was dangerously close to being on a tear. And Dr. Zara Smith on a tear was a force to be reckoned with. "But just because I've been foolish doesn't mean I'm a fool. I have to live in this country long after you've gone. I want to be with you, Walker, but I must use a little discretion."

She refused to back up when he looked down his rebellious nose at her with a raptor's stare. "Is that what Lord Carrington told you?"

"What?"

"To use discretion. When he advised you to have an affair with me."

Her mouth gaped. "This has nothing to do with what Lord Carrington did or didn't say! I have a reputation to maintain. And you—" She halted. Laying it out in black and white was unnecessary. He knew all this already.

"And I," he pronounced carefully in his slow, honeyed drawl, "am a major liability." His mien was flinty and his eyes tried hard to be cold, but the chill disguised the barest shadow of hurt. "Here's the thing, sugar. I don't do boy toy. Which is why I told you all along to keep your hands off me." His mouth thinned. "I have no interest in being Lady Zara's dirty little secret."

With that, he sidestepped her and went to the elevator, holding the door that opened right on cue.

She stared at him for a moment, uncertain whether to feel chastised or insulted. A little of both, she imagined. And more than a little chagrined that he had pinned the situation so unequivocally. Not that she had thought of it in exactly those terms…but the truth of it was undeniable. If they were to continue, she would have to hide him from public view.

She got into the elevator and after he punched the button, she went over to him, again standing toe-to-toe. But this time she lifted her lips to his cheek, brushing them over his skin, absorbing the scent of him, shivering at the prickle of stubble on her chin.

"I'm sorry," she whispered.

And since that said it all, she stepped back and turned away, steeling herself for the long ride to the ground floor, and whatever lay beyond.

Walker kept his mouth shut and was careful to stay a step or two behind Zara, as befitted a hired watchdog. He'd worn his reflector shades and deliberately not shaved since starting this gig, to make himself less recognizable to the *Quiz* paparazzi. He kept his face away from the phalanx of cameras as the car emerged from the parking garage, and again while walking into the Royal Palace.

He was being a prick to Zara, he knew that. But he just couldn't help himself. He didn't like being treated like a servant. He was used to calling the shots, being the head honcho, the star talent on the team and basking in the limelight. Not the rent-a-grunt hidden in the back room. He *hated* that.

For the first time since joining the Lazlo Group, he felt

renewed anger over his lost career and furious frustration at the circumstances under which it had been taken from him.

And for the first time ever, he considered calling Ramona Burdette's bluff. He should have reported her to the police and told the press the truth, even if they didn't believe it. For his honor, if nothing else.

Doing that might not have helped this situation any, but at least he wouldn't feel dirty and ashamed. He could hold his head high when Zara refused to acknowledge him publicly, and know she was dead wrong.

But as things stood now, who could blame her? She had no way of knowing about the threats to his family, and he was not about to tell her, or anyone.

Damn, what a mess he'd made of his life.

How had that happened?

All he'd ever wanted was to help people, to do his medical research, making the world a little better for his being in it.

He had definitely hit bottom when the woman he was falling in love with wouldn't even admit to the world they were dating, much less in a relationship. If that's what it was.

Nope. Until he figured things out, it was far better to keep some distance between them. Letting his emotions run wild was the very worst thing he could do. All that would accomplish was landing himself in a world of hurt. And that was something he could live without.

"Sorry, old thing," Corbett said on the phone a few minutes after Walker had delivered Zara to King Weston's bedside. There were already two guards posted at the king's door, so Walker felt safe leaving her there for a few minutes to call Lazlo.

"What do you mean, you can't find anybody?" Walker fumed. "There's got to be someone who can fill in for Estevez!"

"Afraid not. Everyone's on assignment. We're stretched to the limit."

"What about Carrington? Can't he lend you a couple of palace guards, or pull someone from the National Police?"

Corbett cleared his throat. "Lord Carrington seemed to think… That is, he implied that it wouldn't be a problem for you to stay with her 24/7."

"And what the hell gave him that idea?" Walker demanded. Unless Zara had called him in the middle of the night—which he knew for a fact she hadn't—there was no way Carrington could know about them.

"Didn't say. I just assumed you two had taken a stroll down memory lane. As it were." Corbett chuckled at his own joke.

Walker gritted his teeth. "I'd just as soon skip being smeared all over the European tabloids and dragging her along with me. Which you know will happen if they think we're an item and find out who I am."

"Lad," Corbett said more somberly, "Work with the aristocracy long enough over here and it's bound to happen sooner or later. May as well get it over with."

"I won't take Zara down, too."

"Ah." Corbett sighed. "Well, in any case, we've no choice. She needs protection, and you're the only one who can do it right now. I'll call as soon as anyone frees up."

Shutting off the phone, Walker let out a string of curses. Damn, damn, damn. He was so screwed. And he had a sinking feeling Zara was, too. All because of him.

"Lord Carrington has invited us to lunch."

Walker glanced up from the book he'd been pretending to read in a wingback chair across from the nurses' station. Carrington? Just the meddling son of a gun he didn't want to see. "No thanks."

Zara's brows furrowed reprovingly. "One cannot refuse the acting monarch his generous hospitality."

"I can." He lifted his book again and ignored her.

Her pretty flowered pump swung back and kicked him neatly in the shin, almost surprising him into a smile. "Stop acting like a petulant child, Walker. Honestly, you'd think I'd refused your advances instead of practically dragging you into my bed."

He couldn't stop his lip from curling at her description. Yeah, he'd been kicking and screaming, too. He leaned back and regarded her. "Not a petulant child, baby, a wounded lover."

Her little chin went up. "I can't help the world I was born into, Walker. God knows I wish things were different. But they aren't. Can't we at least be friends?"

"Friends?" he asked, incredulous. "Are you insane?"

She huffed. "All right, civilized, then."

He gave a humorless bark of laughter. "You forget, I am an untamed savage from the colonies. A Southern bad boy with manners to match. I don't do civilized."

"Silvershire never had colonies," she said archly, and crossed her arms over her breasts. "And I'm growing a bit weary of all the things you don't 'do.'"

"You didn't have any complaints last night," he said evenly. Goadingly. It infuriated him that even now, after all that had been said between them, he still wanted her. His body pulsed with need just from her nearness and the slight drift of her scent that reached him from where she stood.

"No," she said just as evenly. "Only this morning. Come on. Russell is waiting."

She looked so expectant and imperious that he almost continued to refuse. He was dead sure no one dared refuse her anything when she used that look. She must have studied it for years in front of a mirror to get it just right. He'd love to see her reaction if he really put on his mule and dug in.

But he was her bodyguard and shouldn't let her out of his sight. Life sucked.

"Well, in that case—" he stood resignedly and swept a hand for her to lead on "—it wouldn't do to keep His Grace waiting."

Walking three paces behind her down the ornate hall of mirrors and portraits, he decided the view might be worth the concession. She had on some kind of couture suit the color of a Caribbean sea, very tailored and very flattering to her auburn hair—even stuck up in a confining twist the way it was. The pencil skirt fitted her like a kid glove, showcasing all the right curves in all the right places. Her killer high heels were the perfect height to show off her slim, shapely legs. And the whole package was even better because she knew how to walk like a samba. Hell, she was so sexy she made his mouth water.

What was wrong with the men of this country that they'd let a woman like her remain single for so long?

Then he remembered who she was. There probably weren't a lot of men who measured up to the standards she set for herself. Hadn't she said something about that? About a duke, a prince, an earl, being a suitable match for her? No wait, that had been him talking.

Why didn't he ever listen to himself?

"Darling, you look lovely," Carrington said to Zara as they entered the small salon where the noonday meal was being served. He kissed each cheek, glancing smugly over her shoulder at Walker, who was doing his best not to react to the sight. Or flatten the bastard.

Hell, Carrington was a duke, soon to be a frigging king.

Had she had designs on him before he'd run off and married a princess? A sobering thought.

"Dr. Shaw, so glad you could join us."

Walker politely refrained from pointing out he'd had no choice. You see? He could be a gentleman when he had to.

For the Lazlo Group's sake he continued to exhibit exemplary manners that would make his mama proud, though they were damn difficult to maintain while Carrington oozed continental charm all over Zara and fairly ignored him throughout most of the meal. Especially when the duke turned to him and said, "So, Shaw, I trust you are keeping our Lady Zara safe…and happy?"

"Safe, yes," he replied with a hint of challenge in his tone. "Anything else is none of your business." At Zara's gasp, he added, "Your Grace," with an incline of his head.

Instead of being furious at the affront, Carrington gave a roar of laughter. "I see you've finally met your match, darling," he said to her with a grin. "I had a feeling that might be the case."

"*Really*, Russell," she admonished, an unreadable look on her pinkened face.

The grin stayed firmly in place, but Carrington's eyes were deadly when he turned back to Walker and said, "See that she stays safe, Shaw. I would be very unhappy if she were hurt— in any way."

"As would I," Walker said with equal gravity, and seized his opportunity to get out of this untenable situation. "Which is why I'd like to ask you to find someone else to watch Dr. Smith's back. Someone who actually knows something about security."

Carrington's brows shot into his scalp. "Indeed? You don't feel competent to guard her?"

"I'm a doctor. I've had weapons training, but not much else. I don't even have a gun."

"Well, that is easily rectified. But I'll admit you've taken

me by surprise. I hadn't foreseen a request for a replacement."
He glanced at Zara, who was studying her dessert plate with
an inscrutable expression. "I'm afraid, though, that I'm
inclined to leave the decision to Lady Zara. After all, it's her
life we're talking about."

"Dr. Smith is hardly the right person to—"

But Carrington waved off his protest. "Zara? Is that your
wish, too? Shall I place your care in someone else's hands?
Or…do you still want Dr. Shaw?"

Chapter 9

Walker didn't cotton to having his future decided by others. He liked even less the feeling that the use of his body was being negotiated as though he were some kind of male courtesan. "Do you still want Dr. Shaw," had nothing to do with guarding her safety, and all three of them knew it.

Walker swept to his feet, but before he could spit the protest from his tongue, her eyes met his and she calmly answered, "Yes. I still want him."

His outrage was tempered only by the gratification that she was willing to humble herself to the ruler of the land to keep him in her bed.

Faint recompense for the sting of her not believing in him.

Carrington smiled. "Well, then, it's settled. I'll notify the captain of my guard, Dr. Shaw, and you will be issued your weapon of choice."

His weapon of choice would be dueling pistols at dawn.

But that wasn't likely to happen. Besides, he wasn't sure who should be holding the other pistol. As appealing as the thought of Carrington was, the duke was only trying to run his country by protecting a possible witness to treason. By comparison, his own concerns didn't amount to a hill of beans, as an equally cornered man once said.

Walker was plenty Southern enough to know when to stand tough and when to retreat to fight another day.

Loosening his grip on the back of the Louis XV dining chair, he sketched a half bow. "Your Grace." But he wasn't going down without some concession. "I'll need my things," he stated. At Carrington's questioning look, he said, "My luggage. I'll want it delivered to Dr. Smith's apartment."

"I'll see to it at once," the duke said, and signaled to a servant standing by the door. As quickly as that, it was done.

Zara was watching the exchange, those inscrutable eyes still peering at him from above blushed cheeks. He gave her a take-that look and her spine straightened even more than it already was. He didn't know why that subtle gesture made him want to sweep aside the porcelain and crystal from the table, push her onto it and—

Lord have mercy.

Where the *hell* was this coming from? Time to get out of here.

"Thank you, Your Grace. If you'll excuse me, I think I'll go see about a weapon right now, while you two finish up."

With that, he strode toward the door.

But Zara's voice stopped him. "Dr. Shaw, when you're free, would you please join me in the medical wing? I'd like your help with a project this afternoon."

He turned, shocked to feel heat creeping up his neck. But no. Even *she* couldn't be that bold. "A project?"

"I assume you can use the Internet?"

It took a good five seconds for him to drag his mind back north from where it had wandered. "I know what Google is."

"Good. Then bring your reading glasses. If you need them."

He regarded her for a long moment before wordlessly turning on a toe and striding out the door.

She knew damned well he needed reading glasses.

In Florence they'd spent a highly memorable hour or so putting words into actions from a small volume of nineteenth-century erotic Italian poetry she'd had in her purse from an earlier shopping expedition. She'd made him read as she translated the Italian onto his body until they'd been so distracted they'd forgotten all about the poems—and his wire-framed reading glasses, which he'd found later, bent all out of recognition.

The little witch.

What exactly, he wondered with an unwelcome mix of arousal and aggravation, was she planning?

Zara couldn't miss the amusement on Russell's face after Walker's temperamental exit from the dining room.

"Are you sure you want to play with that fire, darling?" he asked with a grin.

"I'm sure I don't know what you mean," she said, carefully placing her fork back on her plate at just the right angle, tines downward, signaling she was finished with the mouth-watering chocolate dessert.

As the servant swept the plates away, Russell leaned back in his chair, still grinning like a hyena. Sometimes he could be so infuriatingly adolescent. "I mean, anyone can see the man is way out of your league."

"Thank you very much, indeed, Your Grace."

Russell had the nerve to laugh. "Face it, Zara, you may be at the top of your game professionally, but you're still a novice when it comes to the opposite sex."

"Oh, and you're Mr. Experience, I suppose." She cringed at his knowing smile. Of course he was. And he was right about her, too, the wanker.

"He'll have you for breakfast if you're not careful."

"He already has," she informed him primly. "So I may as well enjoy myself. Wasn't it you who recommended that?"

His amused expression turned gentle. "I was being a twit. I never thought my practical, no-nonsense Lady Zara would actually fall for a rogue in wolf's clothing."

"It wasn't exactly his clothing I fell for," she muttered, making his eyes widen.

He choked on a laugh. "Good lord, now you're making me blush."

She snorted. "Unlikely."

"As unlikely as you and Walker Shaw. Am I making a mistake letting this fire burn uncontrolled?"

She pushed out a breath. "Russell, I know you like to think of yourself as emperor of the known universe, but there are some things even you can't control."

She, neither, it seemed. Unfortunately.

She was fairly certain she had just made the biggest mistake of her life, insisting on keeping Walker in it. What was it about the man that had her treading on ice so thin she could see right through it to the treacherous depths below, and still keep right on going?

She could already clearly hear the ice cracking. But she was powerless to stay away from the pond. She just prayed when the plunge came, she remembered how to swim.

* * *

"Where the hell is he?" Zara mumbled to herself, checking her watch for the umpteenth time.

She slammed the book in her lap closed, then glanced up guiltily at King Weston. But seeing his slack face only reminded her how ecstatic she would be if he actually did wake up from the sharp sound. He was still in a coma, and she was growing more desperate for each hour that went by without him regaining consciousness.

Guilt weighed so heavily on her she wanted to scream. Had she done something wrong in surgery when she removed his brain tumor? Or was it the residual effects of the bomb explosion? Either way, it was Zara's fault he wasn't waking up.

With unbidden images of the dead little Lloyd girl doing a macabre dance in the back of her mind and the sound of Mrs. Lloyd's shrill accusations ringing in her ears, this morning Zara had gone over the king's thick chart again and again, searching for something, anything, that would explain the coma. But there was nothing.

It was probably the stress of the past week's events, the threats on her life, the unsettling dream-visions and the out-of-control situation with Walker that had stretched her nerves to the snapping point. But she couldn't shake the growing feeling there was some important bit of information she was missing. Something she could still do to help save the king.

But the only thing she could think to try was to find some meaning in the strange letters and symbols that kept recurring in the nightmare visions in which he had appeared. The ones that felt like warnings.

It seemed woefully inadequate, but anything was better

than sitting and watching King Weston slowly slip away. So she'd sent to the library for a stack of books on Silvershire archaeology. The ruins and artifacts of ancient Silvershire were rich in symbols. Maybe she could find a clue there.

She'd wanted Walker to check the Internet for symbols used in psychology, such Jungian dream symbology, that her subconscious might be drawing on. But Walker was late.

Too late for it not to be deliberate. It shouldn't take three hours to have a gun issued. Had he stopped at the palace guards' shooting range for some target practice? Looking for a reason to delay seeing her again, no doubt.

She definitely shouldn't have mentioned those reading glasses. That had just been asking for trouble. But she'd been so infuriated with him for the way he'd aired their private affair to Lord Carrington that she hadn't been able to help herself. Just to remind the bloody beast what he was so determined to walk away from.

Sighing at her serious lack of judgment, she dropped the richly illustrated hundred-year-old book onto a pile on the floor and reached for another. So far, she'd found exactly nothing in her reading to help her interpret her visions.

"Dr. Smith?" Nurse Emily opened the door, her round face filled with concern. "Someone just brought this in. I thought you should see it right away."

"Yes? What is it?"

The nurse handed her a newspaper. "This morning's issue of the *Quiz*. Center page."

A prickle of foreboding shivered over Zara's arms as she took the newspaper and opened it to the middle page.

Horrified, she stared at the headlines. "Oh, my God," she whispered.

The entire two-page spread was filled with pictures of her

and Walker taken over the past two days, accompanied by text and headlines blaring out Walker's identity, the scandal from his past, and a thick, black question regarding the exact nature of the Marquis of Daneby's daughter's relationship with her black-sheep bodyguard.

The byline was that of Paul Seacrist, the most tenacious reporter at the *Quiz*. He must have spotted them on their excursion to the old town. Some of the pictures in the article were almost intimate, showing them laughing together, or with Walker's arm around her. There was even one of him carrying her from the taxi into the emergency room after she was poisoned, with a look on his face that clearly conveyed his feelings for the woman in his arms.

"Oh, my God," she repeated. Her dirty little secret was secret no more.

With every muckraking word she read, the angrier she became. *How could they get away with this?* The things they said about Walker, the awful veiled and not-so-veiled accusations, were simply not true! He would never have seduced that girl! *Never!* She knew firsthand how honorable the man was. Especially about that sort of thing. Why, just to get him to kiss her, Zara'd had to—

All at once she jumped to her feet. She had to do something to quell this slander!

Damn it, he was *innocent* of those charges. Every one of them! She knew that now with every fiber of her being. And anyone who'd bother to get to know him would, too. Why he hadn't denied them back then she had no idea, but Walker Shaw was *not* guilty of professional misconduct. She didn't need to hear his side of the story to know that much was true. It was obvious from every action he'd ever taken with her.

Every verbal caution. Every physical stepping away when she'd tried to get closer.

And this article was exactly what he'd been warning her about.

Had he seen it? It would destroy him. Especially if ill-willed reporters caught up to him before he'd had a chance to formulate answers to their nasty, insinuating questions.

She must find him. Warn him.

And tell him she believed him.

That was what he was asking of her last night. The thing she hadn't understood because she was too wrapped up in her own selfish needs to see his.

She realized now she did believe in him. Whatever else stood in the way of their relationship, that wasn't it.

Hurrying from the room, she asked Emily to sit with the king. "Get me on my mobile if there's any change in him," she called over her shoulder as she rushed down the hall for—

For where?

After trying Walker's mobile and getting the answering service, she rang the captain of the palace guard and asked if he was still there. He wasn't, but the captain put out a page and reported back, "He was last seen heading for the old section of the palace, where the abbey is. He asked one of the guards how to find the Bourbon rose garden from inside the palace, so I expect that's where you'll find him."

The Bourbon rose garden. She'd never been there herself, but remembered the docent describing it on their tour the other day. Walker had asked her if she liked roses, knowing all along she adored them.

She smiled, remembering her reaction to the canopy of yellow blossoms hanging over the balcony of his palazzo room in Florence. The first time they'd made love was on a rose-fragrant, petal-strewn feather bed.

It was so romantic she wanted to weep.

What had happened to her since that starry-eyed girl had a crush on Walker so achingly sweet it still filled her with longing? Why had she never felt anything like that before or since? Was her life so empty of emotion?

Or was Walker that special?

She had a sinking feeling she knew the answer.

At the velvet ropes cordoning off the oldest part of the palace, she lifted the soft barrier and ducked under it, hurrying down the increasingly dark and dusty corridors toward the courtyard nestled in the middle of the ancient abbey.

She'd spoken to the same guard Walker had, and received the same directions. It seemed easy enough. Two rights, a left, to the end of the passage, another left, then a short flight of steps down. The thick wooden courtyard door was off the vestibule at the bottom of the stone stairway.

She got as far as the other left, but didn't see any stairs, stone or otherwise. Had she remembered wrong? Was she supposed to take a right? Hopelessly muddled, she tried to retrace her steps, but got turned around and ended up in a maze of interconnected rooms with no hallways at all and very little light.

Despite the stale, chilly air in the uneven, neglected passageways, she felt a trickle of sweat glide down her spine.

No reason to panic.

She was *not* lost. She knew the trick for getting out of mazes—always keep your fingers touching the left wall and simply walk until you wend your way around all the barriers. It might take a while, but eventually you'll get out. Besides, this was the palace. How lost could a person get inside a building?

More minutes later she'd still not found her way out. Her heartbeat started to speed. Memories of the moldy, dark tunnels of Danehus sent goose bumps cascading down her arms. She'd always hated tight spaces, and her brother had mercilessly dared her to go exploring with him, knowing she would do anything to prove she was braver than he. Invariably they'd gotten lost, stuck in the bowels of seemingly miles of "secret" underground passages under the estate, until a footman was finally sent to retrieve them. Her brother had thought their expeditions a great adventure. She could hardly breathe when they'd finally emerge into the light of day.

"Don't be a ninny," she told herself firmly. It was July, the middle of summer. The sun would be up for a good four hours yet, and there wasn't a tunnel in sight. She had nothing to fear.

Nothing at all.

She stopped and closed her eyes to clear her head of nonsense. When she opened them again, she was calmer. There wasn't much light, but there was some. Which meant there had to be windows somewhere. Examining her surroundings, she saw that one doorway was brighter than the others. Pulse pounding, she went through it and kept following the light until at last she emerged into a grand hallway with arched windows along the top. At the other end was the gothic doorway of a chapel entrance.

Easing out her breath that had stalled in her lungs, she sent up a silent prayer of thanks and walked to the tiny chapel. The wooden door had long ago disappeared, leaving the entry open to the pillared hall.

She gave a gasp of delight when she stepped inside. There at the end of the shadowy, narrow chapel was a stained-glass window, a beautiful red rosette centered in another gothic arch of purple. Gorgeous fractal light was thrown in all directions by the sun filtering in through the colored glass. Four dark wooden pews, worn smooth by the silks and satins of bygone worshippers, still stood sentinel before the raised stone altar gracing the sanctuary.

A sudden stab of pain made her grab her temples and cry out. Flashes of red and purple assailed her for a split second, swirling with gold, then disappeared as quickly as they came. Just like her first vision.

Grasping the cool wood of the nearest pew, she sank into it, rubbing her forehead. Catching her breath. Forcing herself to calmness.

She thought of Walker. He must be so close, yet she couldn't find him. *Where was he?* Again the panic started to rise. Just as it had in the vision.

No! Desperately, she looked around, battling the fear that struggled to break through her levee of determination.

Along one wall she saw a wrought-iron stand filled with the remnants of candles. A candle. Yes, she would light a candle. Jumping up, she hurried to the stand and searched between the stubs for matches.

She found none. Inexplicably, her eyes wanted to fill.

She sucked down a hiccup. This was ridiculous. She refused to cry over something this silly. Suddenly, she noticed a sparkling glint of light above the stand of unlit candles. She stumbled backward in stunned surprise.

It was a framed icon. The bronze relief-work shone like gold in the beams of light tunneling through the darkness from the stained-glass rosette. She rubbed her eyes and stared.

Instead of the usual grouping of saints, it depicted a landscape containing an odd building. A series of symbols crowded the outer edge of the relief.

The same gold symbols as in her vision.

It was déjà vu.

Walker wanted to skin someone alive. Slowly. With his dull, rusty Boy Scout knife. Starting with Paul Seacrist, the bastard who had written this newspaper article.

Lying on the grass in the ancient palace courtyard was supposed to be calming his anger. Instead, it was growing with every breath he took.

He tossed the newspaper aside, not caring that it fluttered away in a breeze, catching on the thorns of the old rose vines covering crumbling stone walls. He stacked his hands under his head.

Well. He'd wanted to be reassigned. This great publicity ought to do the trick. He was just sorry Zara had been caught up in the dirt, too. As exasperating as she was, she didn't deserve having her world blown out from under her like this. Because of him.

If he were any kind of gentleman, he would tell the press they were right. She was innocent. He'd deliberately seduced her. And everything else they'd written about him was true.

His curse echoed through the rose-scented courtyard.

If he were a gentleman.

"Walker? Are you all right?"

He didn't bother to open his eyes. He knew who it was. Would have known it if she hadn't said a word. "Just peachy. And you?"

"Been better." There was a pause. "You saw?"

"Oh, yeah."

"I'm sorry."

He slitted his eyes and peered up at her. "What the hell do you have to be sorry about?"

She didn't answer, just sighed, so he closed his eyes again. He didn't want to see her. Didn't want to look at her beautiful, expressive face. Didn't want to see her adoration turn to suspicion, as it had yesterday. Or doubt, like this morning. What variety of knife blade would she use now, after the *Quiz's* meticulous exposé? Simple hatred? He didn't think he could take that one.

He heard the rustle of cloth, two soft thuds, and suddenly she was lying next to him. He lifted his head in surprise. She'd taken off her jacket and shoes and flung them on the grass by the newspaper. Stray auburn hairs tickled the underside of his bent elbow, her body tucked so close to his they were almost touching. Almost. He laced his fingers together under his head to keep himself from lowering his arm to close the gap.

"I'm sorry I got you into this whole sordid mess," she murmured.

She could save her pity for someone who needed it. "You didn't."

"If it weren't for me you wouldn't be here. They'd never have written that story."

"Then it would have happened somewhere else."

"Why didn't you fight it, Walker? When they first accused you?"

He gave a humorless laugh. "Why? What would have been the point?" Even without the threat to his family, it was a losing proposition.

"Because you're innocent."

Her three simple words floated in the air around them like the sound of birdsong so poignant he didn't quite believe it was real. "And how would you know that?"

She rolled to her side, fisted her hand on his chest and rested her chin on it. "Because you've always behaved honorably with me. I don't believe you have it in you to behave any other way. Neither does Corbett Lazlo or he wouldn't have hired you. Neither does Lord Carrington or he wouldn't be trusting you with me. That's a lot of evidence in your favor, Walker."

He let these words settle over him, welcoming them into his soul like a much-needed balm. Wanting to believe them so badly.

"You might be a bit biased," he suggested.

"Maybe. But that doesn't make it any less true."

He felt a great weight lift from his chest. In its place he felt the warmth of her body canted over his, the press of her breasts into his ribs, the slide of her thigh against his leg.

Making what he had to do all that much harder.

"It means a lot to me to hear you say that, sugar. Unfortunately, it makes no difference to what's happening."

"Darling, you have to fight it. Tell them the truth."

"And dredge all that stuff up again? No thanks. I have no desire to see my name dragged through the mud again. And this time they'd drag yours right along with it. What would that do to your chances of having Silvershire's entailment laws changed? Even ol' Russ couldn't help you then."

She was silent for several moments, then she sighed again and rolled off his chest, resuming her place next to him. Not touching. He felt the absence of her warmth like a physical blow.

"It's not fair," she whispered.

"Life's a bitch and then you die," he agreed, feeling the truth of the old cliché down to his bones. In his peripheral vision the newspaper fluttered against the tangle of blossoming rose vines, resurrecting his impotent fury.

She'd said she believed in him.

But there was still no way they could be together. Even though so far the press was casting her as his innocent victim, they'd be dogging her like bloodhounds. And there was no way for him to defend her without putting his family in danger from a crazy woman. No, Corbett would have to find Zara a new bodyguard, and Walker wouldn't even be able to see her from a distance, let alone…

He drove his fingers through his hair, letting out a swear word he seldom used.

She looked up. "What?"

Jetting out a long breath, he did his best to contain the rage in his heart.

He knew what he had to do. It was the hardest thing he'd ever done. Harder than losing the job of his heart, harder than losing his honorable reputation, harder than walking away from the family he loved to start a new life thousands of miles apart from them because of a lie.

"I can't stay," he said. "I have to get out of Silvershire so they won't create a scandal around you."

She would keep her dreams, even if he couldn't. He'd known all along it had to be this way. It would be too selfish to stay, just because he'd found the woman he wanted to share the rest of his life with.

She spun back over him, grasping his arms. "But, Walker—"

He gripped her shoulders, holding her firmly above him. "We have no choice, Zara. I have to leave you."

Chapter 10

Zara's eyes misted over. "Why are you so damned stubborn?"

"Guess I inherited my daddy's 'Bama pride,'" he said, holding her away from his body, though it was killing him to do so.

"If that were true, you wouldn't be letting them kick you while you're down," she said, her pretty mouth in a downward curve.

Walker winced. "Ow, baby. Have a little mercy, here. I'm doing this for your sake."

"The hell you are. If you really wanted me you'd be out there clearing your name so we might have a chance to be together."

"Dammit, it's not that simple—"

"Simple? Do you think it's *simple* to change attitudes and laws that have been in place for over a thousand years? Do you see me giving up just because it would be easier that way?"

His temper spiked. She didn't understand. He had no option. "Zara, listen to me—"

"If I'm going to be a marchioness, I need a man my people can respect. How could they ever respect a coward?"

He jerked back, cut to the quick. "There's a difference between being a coward and being *realistic*. You know, realistic. As opposed to foolishly naive wishful thinking."

She gasped, wide-eyed with outrage. She tried to yank herself out of his grasp.

He didn't let her go.

"Zara, sugar—"

"Don't you sugar me, you bloody—"

Ah, hell. This was not working.

He pulled her down on top of him, drove his fingers into the twist of hair at the back of her head and brought her lips to his. Her quick intake of breath opened her for his taking.

She struggled at first, until his tongue persuaded her to delay her ire for a more convenient time. She made a noise that could have been a protest. Or it could have been a moan. He didn't stop to find out.

Honorable? Not this time.

He rolled her under him. Tipped his head for a better angle and plundered her mouth. She moaned again, opened wider and slid her arms around him.

"That's right, baby. We're no good for each other, except for this part."

He wanted her to deny it, to tell him he was wrong. That they were good in so many other ways.

But all she said was, "I hate you, Walker Shaw," and deepened the kiss.

He stripped her of her aqua skirt and pale yellow blouse, her pantyhose and lacy underwear, then made quick work of his own clothes. When he slid between her thighs, she started to speak again, so he kissed her. Hard.

He didn't want to talk. He only wanted to enjoy her one last time. Feel her body wrapped around his. Feel her sweet response to his loving. Feel the rightness of being one with her.

He buried himself deep inside her. Spread her legs wide and thrust as far into her as he could get. She sobbed out a moan, clinging to him.

They stilled, locked together in love's most ancient puzzle. Around them the courtyard buzzed with life, insects humming, birds twittering and a warm breeze riffling through the trees. The smell of crushed grass filled his nose and the taste of his lover lingered on his tongue as he pulled back and looked into her eyes.

"You know it's impossible. We're impossible," he said softly. Angrily.

"Yes," she said, eyes reflecting his own pain. "I know."

"You deserve better than me."

She gazed up at him wordlessly for a moment. Then, "No. And I shouldn't have to choose."

"But you do."

"It's not fair. I've always had to choose."

He gave her a sad smile. "Keep your eye on the prize, baby."

Under him, her body moved. A tiny undulation, like the last remnant of a wave reaching shore. Pushing him even deeper in. "What if I don't want the prize?"

"But you do."

She licked her lips. "I don't know what I want anymore."

"Yes, you do." He kissed her gently. Swallowed. And lied. "This is just sex, Zara."

"It isn't," she whispered.

He took a deep breath. "It has to be."

She bit her lip, and he kissed it, kissing away the sting of the nip, kissing away the sting of his words. Kissing away the agony of losing her before she was even his.

He pulled out of her and pushed back in again. Pulled out and pushed in. Numbing the hurt and uncertainty in the lush response of her body to his physical possession. At least he could have that much. Until they had to leave this secluded courtyard and face the world apart.

She never wanted to leave.

Zara held Walker close long after they'd floated back to earth from the almost desperate ecstasy they'd shared.

He trailed his fingers down her cheek. "We should go back. They'll wonder where we are."

"They know where we are."

"I need to call Corbett."

"For your replacement?" she asked, trying not to sound snippy. But she felt the waspishness swell within her.

"Yes," he said calmly. "Though I hope he won't replace me in all ways."

"I guess you'll never know." She met his furrowed brow with a tipped-up chin. "Since you insist on slinking away into the sunset."

They were still joined, his relaxed body reposing within hers. She could feel the sticky wetness between her thighs, an apt analogy for the sticky relationship between her and her lover.

"Baby, don't start. I'm the one they're trashing in front of millions," he reminded her. "You wanna trade places?"

She released a petulant breath. "No."

"All right, then." He pulled out and rolled off her, and she had to grit her teeth against screaming in frustration.

Again. The man had a preternatural ability to get her ire going. One minute furious, the next panting with desire. Made even more maddening because usually she was so composed.

"Come on, your ladyship. Better put your clothes back on before they start taking pictures over the wall."

He was joking, but she cast a worried glance around them as she sat up. Her gaze snagged on the large sheet of rolled-up paper she'd brought with her to show him. "Good Lord. I completely forgot!"

Earlier, when she'd found the bronze icon, she'd taken it from the wall and rushed back with it to the temporary office that had been set up for her after the bombing. Using a large sheet of exam paper and a thick, soft pencil, she'd made a meticulous rubbing of the scene and the symbols depicted on it.

"What?" he asked, pulling on his trousers.

"The rubbing!"

His grin told her he'd totally misinterpreted her remark. He started to unzip his fly again. "Well, if you—"

"Oh, be serious," she said, and crawled the few feet to the tube of paper on the grass. "You are not going to believe what I found."

Legs stretched out in front of him, he leaned back on his hands and watched her with interest. Of course, she wasn't exactly sure if it was what she was fetching that interested him, or her on her hands and knees doing so.

She snatched up the tube from the grass and carefully undid the tie around it, unrolling the paper to show him the drawing. "Look."

His face was blank as he examined her handiwork. "Uh…"

"Around the edge, they're the symbols from my visions. And this landscape…it looks familiar. I think it was also in one of the visions."

He frowned. "Where did you get this?"

"I was coming to find you, here, and got lost in the old

abbey. There was a chapel, and this was hanging on its wall. I mean, the bronze icon I took the rubbing from was."

He stood, swatted the grass from his butt and swiped up his shirt. "Where? Show me."

"It's in my office, hidden behind a bookcase. I needed paper and pencils to copy it with, so I took it there. But—"

"Let's go take a look."

"There's more. When I lifted the icon from the hook in the chapel, there was a small niche hidden behind it. Inside was a lever attached to the wall, like a handle of some sort."

"A handle? For what?"

"I think it may unlatch a secret door."

He shot her a skeptical look as he took the paper from her hands. "A secret door."

"It's not as strange as you might think. Not all of Silver-shire's history was peaceful. Old castles and manor houses here are riddled with secret doors and underground passages." She shivered involuntarily and told him briefly about her adventures with her brother at Danehus. "I've also heard rumors of tunnels under the Royal Palace, but the docents all insist they don't exist anymore."

He looked over the rubbing, then thoughtfully watched her as she put her clothes back on. When she was slipping into her skirt, he asked, "Have you been in the old abbey before?"

She shook her head. "Never."

"Any idea what the symbols mean? Or this weird building in the landscape?"

"Unfortunately not."

"Maybe you've seen something else by the same artist. In a different castle or a museum."

She put her shoes on. "Perhaps." But she didn't think so.

"I want to go back to the chapel and take another look at that handle. Find out what it opens."

"Not a good idea," he said, shaking his head. "Let's just report it to Lord Carrington and let him decide if he thinks it's worth investigating."

"And say what?"

"Well, exactly my point. I don't really think a handle in some old chapel means anything at all. It has nothing to do with the bombing or the attempts on your life."

"I think it does."

"Such as…?"

"I…I don't know. I just have this…feeling. That it's important to the king's safety. I've had a strong feeling all day that I was missing an important clue, that the visions are a warning. I don't want to leave any stone unturned, no matter how improbable."

He regarded her as he slowly rolled up the rubbing. "You know I've taken you seriously about these strange dreams of yours. But baby, this is starting to sound a little *X-Files*, don't you think?"

She drew herself up. "If you don't want to help, that's fine. I'll go by myself. I'm sure I can find the way—"

"Now, sugar, don't get all prim on me. I'll go anywhere you want."

Seeing him standing there with an indulgent smile on his face, too handsome for his own good in his incongruously tailored trousers, his collarless shirt casually unbuttoned, with shirtsleeves rolled up, she suddenly remembered she was peeved at him. "That's not what you said earlier today, at lunch."

Before she knew what he was doing he had caught her around the waist. "You think this is easy for me? I'm trying to do you a favor."

"By leaving me?"

He pulled her tight to his body, still warm and musky from their lovemaking. "Yes. Zara, I can't keep my hands off you. It was only a matter of time before the press started noticing. I thought I could spare you the scandal. I'm furious with myself for not leaving sooner." He gave her a grim look.

"Well, I'm glad." She slipped her arms around his neck. Wanting him again, desperate that he *would* leave her, regardless of her wishes. "I'm not ready to let you go yet."

His blue eyes softened. "Keep looking at me like that and I won't ever have the strength to leave." He kissed her. "Come on. Let's go see that secret door handle of yours before I land you in an even bigger scandal than I already have."

She clung to him for a second more, then let him go.

Why was this so hard? Because of her lofty goals, she'd sacrificed her personal whims and desires all her life. She'd never had trouble giving up those foolish things before. He was right; even if he was innocent, they were impossible as a couple. The harm to his reputation was done, and would take a miracle to reverse. The press knew it. That's why they smelled blood now. The blood of yet another of her sacrifices. But this one was tearing her heart out.

Banking her depressing feelings, she followed him out of the rose garden into the ancient part of the palace through the side door that had eluded her earlier. With only a few wrong turns she was able to find the chapel again.

"We'd better make it quick," Walker said as she led him through the gargoyled arch into the darkening interior. "There's only about half an hour before the sun sets."

"And I never thought to bring a torch. Darn." The light from the rosette window was muted, but even more beautiful for that. The chapel air sparkled with violet and scarlet dust motes, the shadowed walls painted in the same dusky hues.

They approached the niche in the side wall, a square black hole that whispered to her of secrets and furtive danger. The musty, clammy odor of damp stone filled her nostrils and she held her breath as a tense, mysterious hush fell over them both. She could hear nothing but the beating of her own heart.

Walker reached up and ran his fingers along the handle, which she realized was also made of bronze.

"Shall I try it?" he asked quietly.

"Yes," she whispered, her pulse speeding.

Taking a firm grip, he gave it a tug. His face registered surprise when it easily slid a half turn. He glanced at her, and they both waited in palpable anticipation.

Nothing happened.

They turned away from the wall, searching the nearly dark interior of the chapel for any change—an open panel, a hidden door, a sliding reliquary.

Nothing.

"Well," she said in disappointment. "What do you make of that?"

"The thing it's controlling must be somewhere else."

She glanced at him, brightening. "Of course. The other side of the wall!"

She hurried out and searched the corridor for a door to an adjoining room. It didn't take her long to find it.

She wrestled open the solid wooden door and was about to plunge into the windowless space when she felt a firm grip on her arm. "I'll go first," Walker said. He had his gun in his hand.

Startled, she eyed the weapon warily. "Is that really necessary?"

"I hope not."

He went in. She followed at his back, hooking a finger in his belt loop because she was getting more nervous by the second. It was much darker in here than in the chapel.

"I can't see a thing," she whispered. But she could feel something. A cold, stale breeze.

"There's an opening," he said, going closer to the side that adjoined the chapel. "There."

"Oh!" she said, and stopped abruptly, peering down at the floor in front of where Walker had come to a halt. At his feet lay a gaping black rectangle that discharged a steady draught of cold, dank air smelling of fetid earth and ancient decay. She shivered violently and clung to him. "This is too creepy."

"I'll say."

"It looks like a tunnel."

He nodded. "One of your secret escape tunnels, I imagine."

"Supposedly they dated from the time of the original abbey, but historians insist nearly all of them collapsed yonks ago, and the few remaining were walled up during World War II, according to the docents."

"Obviously, they've been misinformed."

She stood for a moment, staring down into the blackness, her pulse racing, swamped with an overpowering sensation that she must descend into its depths. "I don't think I can," she whispered.

"Can what?" he asked.

"Go down there."

He turned to her and even in the barely existent light she saw the incredulity in his expression. "What, are you nuts? There's no way you're going down in that tunnel. Me, neither, for that matter. Come on. Let's turn the handle back and get out of here. I can hardly see."

She resisted his urging hand. "But—"

"Forget it, Zara. I mean it."

She knew his order was only prudent. It would be madness to set one foot into that horrible abyss without a torch—and a big bag of crumbs to lay down so they could find their way out again. Not that *that* story had ended all that well.

But the compulsion was so strong it nearly overwhelmed her common sense. She felt to the marrow of her bones that this place, this secret passage, was important. A sickening dread filled her at the prospect of even crossing the threshold of the yawning void. The last thing she ever wanted was to feel the confining darkness and close airless space of an underground tunnel again. It was suffocating just to think about. And yet…

"I know you're right. But…maybe we can come back tomorrow, when there's more light. Take a quick peek. Just to see where it leads."

His shadowed expression became indecipherable. "You know damned well I'm not going to be here tomorrow. You've got to swear to me you won't go down there, Zara. I don't care what your damned visions are telling you. *I'm* telling you not to."

She yanked her wrist from his hand. "Why should I listen to you?" she quietly demanded. "Since you won't be here to stop me?"

She marched out of the room and back to the chapel, wrenching the handle back to its original position. She could feel him watching her, could sense the black scowl on his face, hear the frustration in his swift breath. Sod him. What about *her* frustration?

Wordlessly they made their way back to the medical wing.

"Show me the damned icon," Walker growled when they got to the nurses' station.

"I should check on King Weston."

If Walker was going to leave her, she wanted to get it over

with. She hated this. Hated feeling vulnerable and helpless against the emotions roiling inside her. Hated having to choose between the man she was falling in love with and her lifelong dream.

He nodded, but instead of taking the hint he followed her past the guards and into the king's room, leaning moodily against the wall as she went through her routine of checking the old monarch's pulse, blood pressure and other vitals, searching for subtle signs of a difference from last time. She lingered over the task, hoping he'd leave her in peace, at least for a few minutes, so she could collect herself.

Instead, he took her arm and jerked his head toward the door. "You're done. Now," he said in a hushed but firm voice.

Reluctantly, she left the king to Emily's excellent care and let Walker steer her toward her office.

"I don't know why you're bothering," she muttered. "You didn't recognize anything on the drawing, so why would the icon—"

Her words cut off in mid sentence as he opened the door.

They both halted in shock at the sight that greeted them when it swung wide.

The room was in shambles, the bookcase lying broken on the floor.

And the icon was nowhere in sight.

Chapter 11

The room was a wreck.

Walker swore and grabbed Zara, yanking her away from the doorway and shoving her behind his body. From his waistband he whipped out his gun and aimed it into the chaos of her office.

Gingerly, he switched on the overhead light. In the brightness the mess looked even worse. But no one seemed to be lurking in the room.

"Stay here," he ordered, and stepped in to make sure. "Is there a closet or a powder room?" he asked.

"No. Just what you see."

He poked around in the debris for a minute, then stuck the gun back in his waistband. "Okay. It's clear."

Zara rushed to the bookcase and checked behind it. "The icon! It *is* gone." She turned to him in dismay. "Why would someone take it? It had to have been in that chapel for ages, why wait until now?"

Unfortunately, the answer seemed pretty clear to him. "The more pertinent question is, how did they know you had it? And so soon? You only moved it a few hours ago."

For a second she looked spooked. Then she shook her head. "It has to be a coincidence. They must have been after something else, like drugs, and found it instead. It's valuable, so they probably thought—"

"Zara," he interrupted. "Get real. Nobody wanting to steal drugs is going to choose the Royal Palace to break into. They'd never get past the guards. Which leads to the next question. How *did* they get into the medical wing—and then out again, with the icon?"

"Oh, God. You don't think…?"

"It must be someone working inside the palace. No one else can get past security. Especially now, after the bombing."

Her eyes widened. "Oh, yes, they can."

"What are you saying?"

"The tunnel. They could have used the tunnel. Oh! Maybe there's even…" She swallowed and glanced around, her expression fearful.

Ah, hell. "A secret entrance somewhere close, like there is in the chapel…"

He cursed again and went for his cell phone, punching the speed dial for Lord Carrington's direct line. When he came on, Walker quickly ran down the afternoon's developments and requested he send the Lazlo Group forensics team to investigate both the break-in and the tunnel.

"I'll notify them immediately," Carrington said, clearly alarmed by what Walker had told him. "You're absolutely certain it's a tunnel you found?"

"Dr. Smith is pretty sure."

Carrington let loose a very unregal swearword. "I had no

idea any of the ancient tunnels were still viable. God knows who could be using it, and to what purpose. It could even be one of the palace staff…."

Walker was just as worried. He asked the duke about old architectural plans of the palace. Maybe they could find more tunnel openings.

"I'll check to see if the royal archives has anything useful. Meanwhile, I'll put palace security on high alert." Carrington's voice grew even more serious. "I trust you are armed and won't let Lady Zara out of your sight? I want her kept safe." The warning in his tone was clear.

As if Walker needed to be told. "You can count on it."

"I understand you've already seen this morning's *Quiz,*" Carrington said after a short hesitation.

Walker's teeth clenched. *Here it comes.* "Yes, I have. I'm sorry Dr. Smith got dragged into my sordid past." But he felt no need to explain himself to anyone, let alone to an aristocrat who'd never in a million years understand how the world worked for someone who came from the wrong side of the tracks, regardless of his accomplishments. "Naturally, as soon as my replacement arrives I'll be leaving Silvershire."

Again there was a slight pause. "I'm sorry to hear that. Lady Zara knows?"

"She knows."

"Well, it's your decision," Carrington said, voice heavy with disapproval, but to Walker's relief he dropped the subject. "In any case, the forensics team should be there shortly."

Walker hung up feeling agitated and annoyed. Would the man never stop meddling in his life?

"You're still leaving?" Zara demanded from behind him.

He counted to ten before answering. "It's not like I have

a choice, Zara. You know that. We already decided it's best this way."

"That was before. You *can't* go now. You're the only person I trust."

He tried to be pleased by her declaration, but felt only an unbearable frustration. The last thing he wanted was to leave Zara in some other guy's hands. He needed to keep her safe himself. But under the circumstances that would be selfish.

"Baby, I promise, the Lazlo Group people are the best in the world at what they do. They'll take good care of you."

For the first time, real worry broke through her expression. "How do you expect me to trust a stranger if I can't even trust the people I know and work with in the palace?"

"But how can I stay," he countered, "and be the cause of your ruined reputation, and possibly the end of your dreams?"

"It doesn't have to be that way. We could—"

"Stop." He shook his head. He was doing the right thing; he knew he was. He knew all about having one's dreams shredded by the actions of others, and he wasn't about to do it to someone else. Especially Zara. No matter how much it would kill him to leave her.

He opened his cell phone with a frustrated snap. "We'll talk about this later. Right now I have to call Corbett."

"Walker, don't you dare dismiss me like—"

He held up a hand when his boss came on the line. "We have a problem," he said into the phone, ignoring Zara's indignation at being cut off. "There's been a break-in in Zara's office."

"Is she all right?" Corbett asked sharply.

"She's fine. She was with me when it happened."

"Anything taken?"

He told Corbett about the icon, and then explained how they'd discovered the tunnel.

"You think there's a connection?"

"The tunnel to the break-in? Yeah, I do. Maybe even to the bombing. Is Aidan Spaulding checking that possibility?"

Aidan was the Lazlo Group investigator heading up the entire Silvershire case. Corbett said he'd been told the same thing as Zara, any remaining palace tunnels were supposed to have been bricked up during World War II, so the investigators had not considered it.

"Well, this one has obviously been unbricked," Walker said. "The mechanism works smoothly, as though it's been in use lately."

"Did you go inside?"

"At the time it didn't seem important. But better get Spaulding and Forensics here right away. They should go over both Zara's office and this tunnel with a fine-tooth comb."

Corbett clucked his tongue. "Unfortunately, Aidan won't be back until late tomorrow. He's chasing down a lead in Leonia, up on the northern coast. Meanwhile, I want you to take a quick peek in the tunnel. If it looks like a viable lead, I'll call Aidan back here at once."

Him? Whoa! "Corbett, I'm not a criminal investigator. I wouldn't know what to look for."

"You're a trained research scientist, fully capable of a preliminary assessment. Look for footprints and other traces of recent use. Look for anomalies. Hell, look for bad guys," his boss added wryly.

"Funny," Walker muttered. "You don't pay me enough for this, boss. What am I supposed to do with Zara?" He avoided her sharp scowl at the mention of her name. "When's my replacement going to be here?"

Corbett cleared his throat.

Oh, great. "You *are* sending another bodyguard, aren't

you? Do I have to remind you that after that flaming tabloid article I shouldn't be seen within a mile of her?"

"I'm working on it," Corbett said placatingly. "Sit tight for a while longer. The security checks should come through any minute now on the new guy I hired. In the interim, I've arranged for a limo with tinted windows."

Walker made a deprecating noise. "Like that's going to fool the press for a nanosecond. Paul Seacrist is a bloodhound, and he's probably camped out at her apartment."

"Seacrist is the least of your worries, if this break-in is any indication. Under no circumstances should Dr. Smith stay in the palace tonight. What about family? Can't you take her to visit her parents for a while?"

"You're kidding, right? You'd need a crowbar to pry her loose from King Weston's side for more than a few hours."

"Do whatever it takes to get her out of there. I'll have Carrington beef up security at her apartment building. You should be safe there for now—the press might even act as a deterrent."

"Listen, I don't—"

"I know I'm putting you in a tight spot, Walker. But Dr. Smith seems to be a key player in whatever's going on, and my gut tells me you'll watch her better than anyone else I could assign. I'm relying on you, lad."

Before he could protest further, Lazlo hung up.

Walker swore out loud. Things had gone from bad to worse, and he was so far out of his comfort zone on every level it wasn't even funny.

"Well?" Zara asked, her scowl firmly in place.

"Looks like I'll be your bodyguard for a while longer."

"Sorry I'm such an inconvenience."

He wasn't about to play that game. With a grimace, he

pulled her stiff body into his arms. "Baby, don't. What happened in the rose garden should tell you exactly how I feel about leaving."

After a second he felt her resistance melt slightly. But only a little. "What happened in the rose garden was just sex," she retorted, using his own words against him.

"Ah, Zara." He sighed, and kissed her forehead. "I'm going to pretend it was, so we can both get through this." He tipped her face up for a real kiss. When he pulled away, he said, "I need you to sit with King Weston for a while."

"Where will you be?"

This was the part he dreaded. No doubt he'd have to handcuff her to the king's bed. Which might work if he actually owned handcuffs.

"Corbett wants me to take a look in the tunnel tonight."

She blinked. "*You?*"

"Extra guards have been posted to the medical wing. But I don't want you to set foot outside King Weston's room while I'm gone."

Her expression froze as she realized what he was saying. "Oh, no. Not a flipping chance. You are *not* going in that tunnel without me, Walker."

He took her arm and tried to guide her down the hall. "You'll be safer here."

She didn't budge, yanking her arm from his grip. "I don't care. I'm going with you."

He didn't like that idea one bit. His instincts screamed not to let her within a mile of the old tunnels. "Baby, Carrington will skin me alive if I put you in any kind of danger," he reasoned.

She fisted her hands on her hips and glowered. "You aren't hearing me. *I'm going with you.*"

Closing his eyes, he mentally debated the relative merits

of being slowly and painfully filleted by Carrington versus what Zara might do to him if he continued to refuse. There was no contest. If he told her no, she'd just go on her own later and he wouldn't be there to protect her. She'd already stated that intention.

He recognized the determination in her every move and gesture. He could fight her, but he'd lose. Against his better judgment, he decided to take his chances with the duke.

He told himself even if the tunnel had been used by the culprits, they'd be long gone by now. He wouldn't be going in there at all if he thought he'd find anything more menacing than fingerprints…despite the niggling feeling of impending doom.

"You'll stay right with me and do exactly as I say?"

Her eyes narrowed. "I'm just as smart as you are, Walker."

"Yeah, but I've got the gun."

She ground her teeth. "You really are an obnoxious bully, you know that?"

He gave a halfhearted smile. "I knew you'd see it my way."

She answered with a withering glare. "Come on. Let's get some torches from the supply cabinet."

Reluctantly, he followed her down the hall. And prayed his instincts were, for once, dead wrong.

Zara held her breath as Walker turned the handle in the niche. It barely made a sound as it easily rotated the gears behind the wall. The musty smell of dust and beeswax candles coated her throat with a tickle of anxiety. For some reason she'd thought the mechanism might somehow have been disabled, but it worked as well now as it had this afternoon.

Nervously, she trailed Walker around to the adjacent room, stopping at the edge of the gaping hole in the floor.

"We should bring a guard with us," Walker said, shining

his torch down into the darkness. "But I'm worried about destroying evidence with another set of hands and feet. I shouldn't even be bringing you."

The idea of having another strong man with a weapon along held definite appeal, but she saw his point. "I promise to be careful. I'll only touch what you touch."

She didn't want to give him any excuse to leave her behind. As terrifying as the prospect was of descending into the black unknown, the thought of being separated from Walker was even more disturbing. The uncanny resemblance to her dream-visions of the symbols on the icon had unnerved her even before the break-in. But the disappearance of the bronze icon had started a slow drip of fear steadily into her bloodstream. Something was definitely going on.

She had a bad feeling about what they'd find in the tunnel. But if the visions had pointed her here, she must find out why. The king's safety could depend on it.

Walker didn't look happy about her being there. In fact, he looked exceedingly unhappy.

"We have the walkie-talkie," she reminded him. She'd almost kissed the guard who'd insisted on giving them his two-way radio when they'd passed him at the velvet cordon. "If anything happens, we can call for help."

"Yeah," Walker said, but she could hear the extreme reluctance in his voice. "Are you absolutely sure you want to do this?"

She was sure she *didn't* want to challenge this particular childhood phobia. But if he was going down there, so was she. "Yes," she assured him, doing her best to sound far braver than she felt.

She stared down at the crude stone staircase that ended in a yawning black abyss. Oh, God, what was she about to do?

"All right. Give me your hand."

She grabbed it and held on for dear life. And together they stepped over the threshold.

Zara kept close behind Walker as he slowly descended the stairs.

"Keep to one side," he admonished, "where there aren't any footprints in the dust. And try not to touch the wall."

"No problem." She had no desire to put her fingers on the clammy stone, dark with the grime and mold of disuse.

At the foot of the stairs, they halted and took stock. They'd entered a good-sized room, only a bit smaller than the chapel above. It contained some old wooden crates, a few statues and two crypts. She shivered, wondering if the marble sarcophagi contained bodies. Two thick wooden gothic doors that had probably once graced the chapel entrance lay broken in large bits on the ground, an iron lock still attached to the ancient hammered latch.

There was nothing else to be seen.

Disappointment lurched through her, in spite of her nervousness. "Is this all?" she murmured.

"I doubt it," Walker said, examining the dust-covered stone floor more closely. "These footprints seem to lead—" his torch skimmed over the far side of the room "—hmm. Into a wall."

Her pulse kicked up. "There must be another secret door."

Together they searched for anything that might open it.

"Here!" she said, pointing her torch beam at an iron lever protruding from the floor, mostly hidden behind a squat wooden crate. "This must be it."

They approached, but Walker prevented her from pulling it. "Watch out for fingerprints."

Using the lining of his jacket, he knelt and grasped the lever below the middle, then awkwardly pushed. Gradually it eased over, and a few seconds later a section of the stone wall swung open to reveal a second secret entrance, through which the footprints disappeared. Her pulse sped even faster.

"Another staircase," he said, peering down.

One that went even deeper underground. Even grimier and moldier than the first. The fetid odor of dank earth hit her square in the stomach, nearly making her gag. Sharp, terrifying memories of crawling through tight, cobweb-filled spaces assailed her. She slapped her hand over her mouth to keep from crying out.

Suddenly, she found herself wrapped in Walker's strong arms, her cheek pressed to his shoulder, breathing in his comforting, familiar smell.

"You okay?" he whispered in her ear.

She nodded. "Just give me a minute."

"Remind me to beat your little brother to a pulp someday for doing this to you," he muttered, bringing an unwilling smile to her lips at the image of her excruciatingly respectable and polished younger brother being brought to heel by the wickedly disreputable Walker Shaw.

"He's actually not so little anymore. Over six foot," she whispered, scandalized by the certainty of who she'd be cheering for.

"I can take him." Walker's mouth brushed over her hair. "Just say the word."

Smiling, she tipped her face up and found his lips in the darkness. The reassuring taste of him filled her senses, banishing the fear. At least, mostly.

"Want to go back?" he asked.

She was sorely tempted, but shook her head. "No. Let's go on a little further."

He kept an arm around her as they cautiously went through the new opening and down the stairs. At the bottom, the stone floor stopped abruptly, turning to dirt. Above their heads, the tunnel ceiling narrowed to a vaulted shape, made up of bricks instead of stone. Almost immediately, they came to a fork where the passage split into two branches.

"Which one should we take?" she whispered, her low voice echoing off the brick, sounding loud enough to wake the dead.

"Wherever the footprints go."

They shone their torches at the ground, revealing prints leading in both directions.

"Great," he muttered, bending to take a closer look. "Seems like there might be more traces going this way." He pointed to the right.

"Right." She took his hand again and led on, her heart pounding in her throat. A rat scampered across their path and she let out a squeal.

"Baby," he chided, yet his arm went around her waist and he pulled her closer as they crept along the wall. His warm breath came in calm, steady drafts that tickled her ear in the chilly air of the tunnel. She couldn't believe how undaunted he seemed by their ghoulish surroundings. The man's nerves must be made of cold steel.

Which probably explained how he could remain so unflinchingly indifferent to the false accusations which had ended his brilliant career. Then again, perhaps it wasn't indifference at all, but the fact that nobody had stood up for him except his loyal but powerless family. Perhaps it was disappointment—or disillusion—that had led him to walk away.

As he guided her through the stale, pitch blackness, his warm body serving as a steady anchor against the fear clamoring to take over, she knew she had to take a stand for him. He was willing to leave Silvershire to protect her reputation. Was she willing to put her reputation on the line for him in return?

There was no question.

When they got out of this bloody tunnel, she would call Chase Savage, the Royal Publicist. He'd done such a good job spinning the recent palace scandals. He could always use a good story. And he could be relied upon to be impartial until he had all the facts. He'd investigate Walker's background thoroughly and fairly. If anyone could clear Walker's name, it was Savage. It might not be enough to clear the way for her to have a relationship with Walker, but it could be a start. A start she badly wanted.

She was beginning to realize her growing feelings for Walker were not just residual hearts and flowers from a long-ago affair, or based on their present incredible physical chemistry. They ran much deeper than that. Walker made her feel safe and wanted, and soft and vulnerable. And loved. All the things she'd been unconscious of lacking in her life up until now. Up until Walker.

She didn't want to lose those feelings.

She didn't want to lose him.

They came to a bend in the passage and he halted. The walls narrowed and the ceiling sloped down precipitously, so they'd have to hunch over to continue around the turn.

"Want to go back?" he murmured.

Though her knees were liquid with terror, she shook her head. "No. I want to follow it all the way," she whispered. "I need to know how it ends."

She felt his fingers sift through her hair, lifting it from her neck as he placed a tender kiss above her ear. Almost as though he knew what she was thinking.

"Not a good idea," he murmured.

"Probably not," she said. "But it's what I want."

"You could get hurt. Badly."

"I have you to protect me."

He laid his cheek against her forehead. "To the death," he whispered.

They stood there for a second, holding each other, pretending they were still talking about the tunnel.

Or maybe he was, and she was indulging in the worst kind of romantic self-delusion.

"Ready?" he asked softly.

"As ever," she said, and let him go.

She found his hand in the dark and he laced his fingers through hers. Crouching down, she hammered back the terror and followed him into the narrowing passage and around the bend.

They nudged around the sharp turn, then navigated another one going the other way. After several more feet, they came to a third turn, which opened into a wider area.

Suddenly there was a loud shout. A dark figure lunged out at them from the darkness.

Zara screamed, and Walker yelled an oath as his torch flew from his hand, the light cutting off as it smashed against the wall. A loud crack split the air and he hit the ground with a frightening, groaning "oof."

"Walker!"

She looped her light beam wildly about, desperately trying to find him. Their attacker jumped at her, shoving her mercilessly to the dirt floor. She screamed again as he stomped her torch under his boot, and all went black.

But this time she was still conscious.

Chapter 12

Walker groaned, grabbing the back of his head. It hurt like a fiery bastard. The air around him was black as a witch's cauldron, and stank of foul things.

Zara's terrified voice cut through the black vortex of pain and tingly sightlessness. "Walker? Darling, please say something! Are you hurt?"

A hand bumped into his leg and clutched at it, the other joining in as she groped up to his chest and finally found his face. He blinked his eyes anxiously.

"I can't see," he said with another groan when she accidentally shifted his head on the hard ground. "Ow! Hell."

"Sorry," she whispered, sounding close to tears. "He smashed the torches. Are you hurt?"

With a whoosh, he remembered where he was and what had happened.

"Only when I breathe," Walker said, gingerly sitting up,

clenching his jaw against the explosion in his head. As he sat, his hip sang out in pain, too. "Did you get a look at him?"

Zara's fingers slid tenderly over his face, touching his cheeks and eyebrows and lips. "Not really. It happened too quickly. I think he had on a hood or something. Where did he hit you?"

"Back of the head." He grasped her hands before she could test his battered flesh. "How long was I out? Did he touch you?" he demanded, irrationally fearful of what might have happened while he was unconscious.

"I'm fine," she said, her breath shuddering. "Really. He just pushed me down."

Walker put his arms around her and held her close in the absolute darkness. She was trembling badly. "Shhh. He's gone now."

She hitched out a tiny breath as she returned his embrace almost desperately. "How are we going to get out of here?"

"Same way we got in," he said, not looking forward to the prospect without flashlights.

"You still have the walkie-talkie?" she asked, her voice tinged with renewed hope.

That's when he realized why his hip was bruised.

"Damn. I must have landed on it when I fell." He fumbled in his back pocket for the small radio and came up with a handful of plastic bits. But at least he still felt the gun stuck in his waistband. And he had his cell phone. He pulled it out and flipped it open, waiting pensively as it searched for a signal. And found none. "Check yours," he told her.

She did, and it was useless, too.

"We must be too far underground," he said in disgust.

"Oh, God, we'll never find our way out!" The panic rose in her voice with every word.

"Sure we will. How hard can it be?" He put their phones

away and gave her a kiss for confidence. "There was only one fork in the tunnel, and we know which way we came. Come on." He helped her to her feet, blinking in the darkness and grimacing against the pain still throbbing in his head, made worse by the fact that they couldn't walk upright.

Holding her hand firmly, he put his other hand on the slimy, clammy bricks of the tunnel wall. "All we have to do is reach those three sharp bends and find where the bricks turn back into stone. Piece of cake."

"But how do we know which direction we're going? We might have gotten turned around."

"Well, there is that." He exhaled, closed his eyes and thought. "If it's not one way, it's got to be the other, right? See if you can touch the far wall."

She stepped away from him, and he could feel her stretching her other arm out to find the opposite side of the tunnel. "Oh! It feels like… Oh, God, it's another branch."

It turned out they were standing right in the middle of the intersection between four different tunnels, with no way of telling which way led back to the palace.

This was getting complicated.

Zara's hand in his was nearly as cold and damp as the brick walls around them. Was she going into shock?

"I should never have brought you," he growled, anger rising swiftly over his stupidity and spinelessness at allowing her to talk him into this insanity. He knew better.

He heard her take a deep breath. "Nonsense. They know where we are," she said, surprising him with the evenness of her words, though her voice trembled slightly. "If we're not back soon they'll send down a couple of footmen…I mean guards, after us."

His admiration for her went up another several notches.

Those childhood memories couldn't be easy to overcome. "You're being mighty brave, sugar."

"I'm not as frightened since you're here with me," she said softly.

He wasn't sure about the logic or wisdom of that sentiment, but it pleased him nonetheless. He couldn't resist dropping to his knees, pulling her along with him and giving her a long kiss.

For a time the pain and darkness was forgotten in the warmth and succor of her welcoming mouth. He didn't care about the sting of gravel on his knees or the fact that their clothing would probably be unsalvageable. He needed to feel her. To know she was his, if only for a short time in the dark.

The absence of light made her scent sweeter, the feel of her arms around him and her tongue against his more sensual. The pounding of his heart for her louder in his chest.

"Walker?" she whispered when their lips finally parted.

"Hmm?" he asked, changing angles. Wanting one more taste of her before coming back to reality.

"I feel a breeze."

It took them another half hour of stumbling forward in the total darkness, following the barely discernible draft but at last, Zara felt the warm, sultry night air of the outside world caress her skin. The earthy smells of the River Kairn filled her with a sense of profound relief. They'd made it!

As they cautiously emerged from the tunnel, past a tangle of bushes and vines and out into the open, her pulse still pounded with adrenaline. But oddly, the full-blown terror had long since ebbed. Walker's influence? Probably. With him by her side she could face even her worst fears.

She glanced around the starlit landscape, seeing the stately, glittering waters of the river just before them. Above glowed the shimmery yellow gaslights of the Golden Bridge, and beyond, the twinkle of Silverton city. Behind them lay the well-concealed mouth of the tunnel, disguised by a jumble of piquant vegetation, a rusted storm-drain grate discarded in the shadows next to it. This must be how their attacker had entered.

"Think he's out there?" she whispered with a shiver, imagining someone lurking nearby, lying in wait for them.

"He's long gone," Walker said reassuringly, but pulled the gun from his waistband just the same. "Let's hike up to the bridge and flag down a taxi."

A taxi.

And just like that, reality reared its ugly head.

He started up the slope, but when she hesitated he turned back to her questioningly. Something in her face must have given her away, because his mouth thinned and his eyes shuttered.

"Ah. Nearly forgot. I can't be seen with you in public."

She had to think. "Darling—" What had happened to her resolve to stand by him?

"Now, that could be a problem," he interrupted, "because I'm also responsible for your safety. I really can't let you go anywhere alone."

She'd lived most of her life in the limelight and had always handled the press—even the paparazzi—with manners and patience. They were only doing their jobs, after all. But at this moment she wanted to line them all up and shoot them. Or at least their bloody cameras and computers. God *damn* them for making things so difficult.

Wordlessly, she took out her mobile—which functioned fine now they were above ground—and dialed Russell's number.

Shocked and concerned, he promised to send the Lazlo forensics team immediately.

"Come straight to my study when you get to the palace,"

he ordered. "I'll have the police and the Captain of the Guard here to take your statements and begin an immediate inquiry. This is outrageous!"

When she hung up, Walker was staring out across the river with his arms crossed tightly over his chest. Above the murmur of the water and the faint sounds of traffic she heard the distinct popping of his jaw.

She'd hurt him. Again.

She sighed, and for the first time in her life started to question the validity of the dream she'd held dear since childhood.

Did she really want to be the Marchioness of Daneby? Or was it, rather, the unfairness of being denied the chance that was driving her to seek to change the laws? A strike for female equality?

Was being a marchioness really worth having to hurt those she cared about? Was it even worth all the sacrifice and heart-ache she'd already gone through to see it become a reality? Was the fight for women's equality in something so inherently in-equitable simply absurd, and meaningless to society as a whole?

Was her struggle really one of pure, selfish vanity?

Shouldn't her highly satisfying career as a surgeon be enough for her?

She wanted to throw her arms around Walker and tell him it was, that she didn't care about his past or his reputation. That being a marchioness didn't matter. That *he* was what she wanted, more than anything else in her life.

But old habits died hard. She was nothing if not cautious about decisions affecting her life goals. And who said Walker was even interested in anything long-term? Sex with him was astounding, but maybe that was all he wanted. He'd never said he loved her. And despite their silent, possibly one-sided, communication in the tunnel, he'd never spoken of a future together beyond bed.

Though, instinctively, she felt that given half a chance he would.

Which scared the hell out of her.

Enough to keep her mouth shut about the whole subject. Because she just wasn't sure how *she* felt.

"Carrington is sending the limo. It should be here any minute," she said, stepping up to his back and resting her cheek against his stiff shoulder blade. "He wants us at the Palace right away."

Walker nodded. "Tinted windows. I remember."

"Will you spend the night with me, afterward?" She ducked her heated face at her boldness. But she didn't want there to be any doubt in his mind what she wanted. At least for now…

"I don't believe I have a choice."

A sting of hurt lanced through her at his cutting tone. "Would you anyway, if you did?"

He turned, gazed down at her. Golden specks from the lights of the bridge reflected in the deep blue of his eyes. "No," he said. "I'd be on my way out of here. For both our sakes."

She looked away, nodding. But didn't speak. She couldn't, for the huge lump in her throat.

He was really leaving. He didn't want her.

What would she do without him in her life?

And that's when she knew she loved him.

She had to do something. Say something to let him know. Maybe there was a way to keep him and have her dreams, too. Together they might be able to figure something out.

But unfortunately, the police and forensics teams chose precisely that moment to show up.

Forcing down her aching need to talk to him, she let Walker

handle them, showing them the tunnel entrance, explaining the situation and what had happened. After several minutes of questioning, she and Walker were released.

An officer led them up the steep slope of the riverbank to the road where the limo waited. Her heeled pumps slipped in the damp grass and mud, and Walker put his arm around her to keep her from falling. She couldn't resist returning the gesture. A small comfort in the turbulence of her mind.

As soon as they crested the hill, the officer gave a loud shout. "Hey! You there! Don't even—"

But it was too late. Suddenly, she was blinded by a multitude of camera flashes, and Paul Seacrist's familiarly irritating voice shouted, "Lady Zara! What kind of trouble did your womanizing psychiatrist get you into this time?"

What a flaming nightmare.

Zara had barely managed to keep from slapping the smug smile right off the little weasel reporter's face. Walker, on the other hand, had given Seacrist a bloody earful. Zara was thankful he'd forgotten about the gun in his waistband.

But for a brief, blinding moment as Walker had ferociously defended her honor with all the verbal fury of a modern-day St. George, she'd been so in love with him that it actually hurt.

Unfortunately, by defending her he had only dug himself deeper into the tabloid quagmire, focusing the cameras and rapid-fire questions on himself. She'd had literally to drag him into the limo so they could escape to the Palace, where they were now sitting with Carrington and Chase Savage, the royal publicist, who had been called in for some much-needed damage control. Better late than never.

She groaned out loud and in one gulp downed the second

glass of sherry Russell had poured for her. "Really, Carrington. Don't you have anything stronger?"

Russell raised a brow, then strolled to the sideboard and mixed her up a double martini, which she accepted gratefully. Walker shook his head at Russell's silent offer, as did Chase Savage.

"I suggest we take the offensive," Chase said. "After the *Quiz*'s spread this morning, and the pictures and quotes they got tonight, everyone will want to know everything there is to know about the notorious Dr. Walker Shaw."

"I say tell them to mind their own bloody business," Zara muttered, picking at the holes in the knees of her tights.

"A novel approach," Chase said with a half smile, casting a glance at Walker, who was standing with his hands jammed in the pockets of his dirt-stained trousers, pretending to study the fireplace ornaments. "But hardly practical. Before the next issue of the *Quiz* comes out, the Royal Palace needs to make him into a hero."

Walker snorted softly, but didn't comment.

"Play up the angle that he restored Lady Zara's memory and has now taken on the job of guarding her safety, foiling two attempts on her life."

"That could be tricky. The Lazlo Group cannot be mentioned," Russell reminded him. "Otherwise the inquiries into Prince Reginald's death, as well as the other incidents, could be compromised. No one can know a private firm has been brought in to investigate."

"I understand," Chase said, then pursed his lips. "I've heard a rumor that Zara and Dr. Shaw had already met several years ago. Perhaps we could use—"

"How did you find that out?" Walker demanded, coming to attention.

"So it's true." Chase nodded thoughtfully. "Good. Yes, I might be able to salvage the situation."

"I want Walker cleared." At her words, the three men turned as one to her. "He's innocent of those charges of impropriety. That's what you should be writing about."

"No!" Walker's clipped refusal cut through the civilized atmosphere of Carrington's study like a swift sword. "I don't want all that dug up," he growled. "Leave it be."

"But, darling—"

"No. It's not an option. Spin me however you like, but leave ancient history out of it."

"Walker, be reasonable. Why on earth—"

"God *damn* it, Zara!" He stalked to her chair and bent over her, nearly knocking the martini glass from her hand. "I know you aristocrats are used to treating commoners like pawns on a chessboard. But I'm sick to death of you lot trying to run my life for me! This is *my* decision, and I've made it. No discussion!"

She stared at him in shock at his outburst, absolute silence reigning in the room. Good Lord, what was he on about?

Suddenly he straightened and backed up a step. Turning to Carrington, he inclined his head. "I apologize, Your Grace. Mama would tan my hide for displaying such bad manners. If you'll excuse me, I'll just wait outside."

With that, Walker strode out of the room.

"Well." Carrington ambled over and took the martini glass from her hand, which was in imminent danger of tipping its contents onto her lap, and set it on the end table. "That was interesting. Wonder what he's hiding?"

"What makes you say that?" she asked in surprise.

"Doesn't seem natural that a man won't clear his own name."

"Hmmm," Chase said. "He could be protecting someone.

I believe I may just do a little digging and find out. You're absolutely sure he's not guilty?"

"Impossible," she blurted out, then felt herself blush when the two men glanced at her indulgently. "I may be biased, but I know he'd never seduce a patient. He's completely honorable."

"Then I'll see what I can come up with," Chase said, his photogenic smile back in place. "Meanwhile, I'll put out daily press releases touting his previous accomplishments and his unqualified success with your amnesia, as well as his heroics in rescuing you from the attempts on your life."

"Chase is right," Russell said. "If the palace treats him as a hero and ignores his supposed disgrace, people will at least question the dirt the *Quiz* is slinging at him."

"Business as usual, Lady Zara," Chase advised. "Treat him no differently than you would any bodyguard. Put him and his gun out there front and center so everyone knows he's doing his job. Show everyone you don't believe a word of the slanderous gossip."

"That will be easy, since I don't."

A few minutes later, their strategy had been set and Zara took her leave.

It was as if a weight had been lifted from her shoulders. She'd hated the whole dirty-little-secret atmosphere that had surrounded her and Walker's relationship, and now that would be gone. Thank God! At least with Carrington and the Palace behind Walker, her reputation wouldn't suffer from associating with him.

She just wondered why he wouldn't let her defend him the way he'd done her. He was being dead cagey about his reasons, immediately deflecting the subject every time she'd brought it up.

Was he hiding something?

She found Walker outside the salon, pacing the grand hallway. When he spotted her he stopped, hands loose at his sides like an old-time gunslinger, looking as handsome and rebellious as ever, despite the deplorable state of his clothes.

Her heart fluttered. God, he was magnificent.

"So, have y'all decided my fate?" he inquired with a slight edge to his voice, though he no longer appeared angry, as he'd been earlier.

"Don't be an ass, Walker," she said levelly, and swept past him. "We're only trying to help."

"I don't need or want your help. Not with this." It didn't take him more than a second to catch up, matching his stride to hers.

"Yes. You've made that abundantly clear. One can't help but wonder why."

His eyes narrowed as they swung to her. "What is that supposed to mean?"

"It means you're acting like a guilty man, when we both know you're not. Is there anything you'd like to tell me?"

There was that shuttered look again. "No."

She pushed out a breath. She couldn't force him to trust her. But it hurt nonetheless that he wouldn't. "Very well."

"Where are we going?"

She made the turn toward the side porte cochere. "My flat. It's after midnight and I desperately need a bath. We'll take your car."

"No tinted windows," he reminded her dryly.

"Doesn't matter."

"No? Since when?"

She nodded to the footman at the porte's foyer. "Dr. Shaw's vehicle, please." Then turned to look at Walker. "Since I decided I don't care what people think. I want to be with you, and they can go to hell if they don't like it."

For a second he looked gobsmacked, disbelieving, as though she'd just pulled out a gun and shot him. Then a painful longing shadowed his eyes and he turned away from her. "You know that's not possible," he finally said. "For a million reasons."

"I don't agree," she said. "But if tonight is all we have left, I don't want to waste it arguing."

Seacrist was standing at the palace gates when they drove out together, Walker behind the wheel of his compact sports car. Zara took particular delight in giving the open-mouthed reporter a sweet smile and a finger-wave. The pillock had obviously thought he'd had Walker on the run, and she could see she'd shocked him by daring to associate openly with her as-of-this-morning-infamous bodyguard. She didn't even mind the chain lightning of camera flashes.

"I can't believe I let you talk me into this lunacy," Walker muttered as he sped expertly past them.

"Royal command," she said. "Carrington was very clear about following Chase's orders that you be highly visible." She'd had to explain this three times before he'd finally agreed to forgo the anonymous limo in favor of his easily identifiable hired car.

"I hope you know what you're letting yourself in for," Walker muttered. "If you think that mob will swallow me as any kind of hero, you're dead wrong."

"True, it would help if you were a little more forthcoming with your heroic qualities…."

He shifted gears with a lurch. "You are a persistent little thing, I'll give you that."

She turned her sweet smile on him. "You have no idea."

"If I didn't like you so much, I'd be damned worried."

Hope brushed velvet-soft through her heart. "Do you? Like me?"

"Baby, you know I do. But you and I—we're not going to happen. We both have to accept the fact that when my replacement gets here, we say goodbye."

For someone who claimed to like her so much, he seemed stone-set on leaving her.

"Do we?" she asked rhetorically. "Anyway, there isn't going to be a replacement," she added, to vex him as he was vexing her. They'd already discussed it, and his opinion was that Corbett would listen to him, rather than Carrington. Obviously delusional.

He glanced at her, mouth turned down. "We'll see."

Unfortunately, that part was right. She just wished there weren't so much riding on the outcome. Or that, either way it went, she would be the loser.

She wondered just how far he was willing to go to avoid further entanglement.

Would he want to share her bed tonight? Or would he avoid that, too?

Chapter 13

There was a cluster of paparazzi waiting at Zara's apartment building, but Carrington had arranged for a National Police guard at the entrance to the underground garage, so Walker and Zara were safe from being accosted beyond the gate.

Despite the police presence, Walker again slid the car into a spot well away from Zara's assigned slot. He hadn't forgotten why he was there. Twice now she'd come close to dying, and twice more had close calls. He wasn't about to let anything happen again. After parking, he came around and opened her door, helping her from the car as he scanned the silent cement cavern for danger.

Something was bothering him. Something that had occurred to him as he'd paced back and forth along the grand hallway earlier, waiting for her to emerge from the meeting with Carrington and Savage.

If the attempts on her life—the bombing, the poisoning and

possibly the car incident where Estevez was injured—were related to the ransacking of her office and the disappearance of the mysterious icon, then why hadn't the man in the tunnel tonight tried to kill her, too? Their attacker had barely touched her—Walker had been the one injured.

And that made no sense at all.

Wracking his brain, he tried to figure out what it all meant as they rode the private elevator up to the penthouse. He had plenty of time; a glance at the lighted buttons reminded him how excruciatingly slow the damned elevator was.

Zara was watching him, a strange, cheerless look on her face. Dirt streaked her cheek, her pretty designer suit was stained and filthy, and the knees of her hose blown out. But she had never looked so beautiful. So incredibly beautiful.

And sad. Because of him? No doubt. She'd barely batted an eye at the rest of the week's stressful events. She'd been stronger than anyone he knew as she'd dealt with one blow after another with grace and poise.

Until *he* had gone and complicated things.

He hated himself for taking the bright smile from her lips, extinguishing the joyous sparkle from her eyes. He'd come to reclaim the carefree girl from Italy, but instead…he'd added to her burden by turning her world upside down. And his, as well.

"You're a million miles away," she said quietly.

"Not really." He jingled the change in his pockets. "Just thinking what a jerk I am."

The very corners of her mouth curved, but she didn't comment.

He leaned back against the mirrored wall. Tilted his head. *God, how he wanted her.* Even now. Even after everything that had happened. After everything he'd told himself about the impossibility of their situation.

"I suppose sex is out of the question?" he said philosophically. Not wanting to give away how desperately he wanted her in his arms. He might have to do the right thing by her, but that didn't mean he had to like it.

She blinked. Then laughed. "Christ, Walker. You really do skip the foreplay and get right to it, don't you?"

He shrugged. Caught her gaze. "Well?"

They arrived with a soft thud at the top floor, and the elevator whooshed open. She went out without replying. At her door she fished her keys from her purse.

He took them from her and stepped close, into her space, standing over her, silently waiting for an answer.

"Yes," she finally said. "Sex is out of the question." She took the key back, turned away and unlocked the deadbolt. "However, I may let you make love to me, if you'd like to give that a try."

Before she could open the door, he grabbed her around the waist, and said, "No." She stiffened. "No, I mean, don't turn that knob. Let me."

He set her away from the door, shooing her farther across the foyer when she stopped too close, then repeated his ritual from the night before, cautiously entering and checking all the rooms, the closets and under the furniture. By the time he was finished, she had come into the living room and was standing next to his suitcase, which had been left in the middle of the floor.

"Please tell me Carrington doesn't have a key to your apartment," he said, looking at it with a frown. And for a crazy moment he reevaluated the duke's place on the Lazlo Group suspect list for this crazy palace intrigue.

"What? Oh, no, of course not. The building manager must have let them in."

Rationality and jealousy fought within him; rationality

won. He made a mental note to see if the building manager had let anyone else in recently. Though, von Kreus would certainly have covered that base in his investigations of Zara's poisoning.

Zara was still standing there next to his suitcase, looking for all the world like a homeless waif amid the bustle of a train station, wondering where to go. His heart melted.

"You look like you could use a slow, sweet loving," he said, aching with the need to reach for her. Knowing it would only make their parting more difficult.

Not that it wasn't already. Already he'd spend the rest of his life getting over her.

Again.

She gave him a half smile. "Is that an offer, Dr. Shaw?"

"Yes, ma'am, if you'll let me."

Her eyes softened. "I'd like that."

And so, after they'd thrown away their ruined clothes and taken a hot shower to scrub the dank tunnel from their skin, he picked her up, carried her to her bed, and made long, sweet love to her until they both fell to sleep, exhausted by the trials of the day and the blissful joining of their bodies.

And that, he decided as he pulled her close with a sigh, was far better than sex.

Walker should have known when he awoke feeling irrepressibly optimistic and lighthearted that the feeling wouldn't last.

But for the moment he just relaxed and enjoyed it, stroking his hand over Zara's hip and waist as she slumbered in his arms. He was hungry for her—as always—but contented himself with tactile indulgence rather than losing himself inside her. He'd done that last night, enough to satisfy any normal man. But when it came to Zara, he'd long since accepted that his cravings were anything but normal. He wanted to bury himself in her, curl up and stay there forever.

But that was not to be. He didn't even get the chance to make love to her again. The insistent bleat of an intercom blasted the peace of the morning and jarred her to wakefulness before he could reach over and tell the idiot, whoever it was, to shut the hell up—if he could figure out where the damn thing was.

She unfurled her body from his and pushed a button on a pink Art-Deco-style box sitting on the nightstand. "Yes?" she asked, her voice soft and sexy from sleep. "What is it, Edwards?"

"Good God, girl, are you still in bed?" a thunderous voice boomed over the surprisingly clear speaker. "It's after nine. Get yourself up at once! Your mother and I are here to see you."

A host of emotions flashed through Zara's eyes before she closed them and, for the first time in Walker's memory, said a colorful swearword.

He would have grinned, except for the obviously awkward situation he was about to find himself in.

"I'll be in the guest room," he said, and slid from the bed.

She grasped his arm. "Oh, no you don't." Her chin went up in that way that never failed to stir his loins. "I'm thirty-four years old, for God's sake. My brother keeps a robe in the guest loo. Put it on and join me in the living room." She shot him a warning glance. "Or I'll come and get you. I'm not facing my father alone."

Hell of a way to meet the Marquis of Daneby: newly mucked by the *Quiz*, fresh from his daughter's bed and wearing his son's bathrobe.

Lord have mercy.

Good thing Walker had been born a Southerner. If all else failed, at least he still had his sense of humor.

He just hoped he lived long enough to use it again.

He found the robe, a hunter-green silk number with the Daneby heraldic crest embroidered on the breast—*that should go over well*. He donned it and went to do his gentlemanly duty.

Zara seemed to find some kind of perverse comfort from his suitcase, because she was again standing right next to it. When the door buzzed he held up his hand to her and went to answer.

Doing his best imitation of a tough, unsmiling bodyguard, he swung open the door.

A tall, formidable-looking iron-gray man, equally unsmiling, waited on the other side. Beside him was an elegant woman in a stylish dress. They stared at him, the woman in apparent shock. The man's expression altered not a fraction, even as it swept over Walker's state of undress. Walker stared back, feeling himself being measured, weighed, catalogued and dismissed.

The thing about being a Southerner—other than the sense of humor—was that in the South there reigned an aristocracy and class structure every bit as formal and rigid as that in Europe. Walker had grown up with it, struggled under the crushing weight of its politesse, and had eventually learned to turn it to his favor.

He waited. Silently.

"Lord Harald Smith, twelfth Marquis of Daneby, and Lady Daneby," the man finally said, voice rigid with irritated formality, "here to see Lady Zara, *if* you please."

Walker pursed his lips.

He didn't mean to be a prick, he really didn't, but he suddenly understood a whole lot about Zara and her drive. A fierce, visceral need to protect her rose up in him. Not only against the threats to her life, but also against the cold hardheartedness of this unsmiling man who was her father.

"Step back, please," Walker said. Drawing his weapon from where he'd tucked it into his belt, he leaned out into the foyer and made a show of checking the blind spots along the wall for anyone who might be hiding there. Satisfied, he moved aside and allowed them to enter.

"So it's true, then," Lord Daneby clipped out as he came to a parade halt before Zara, treating Walker like the Invisible Man.

"Hullo, Father, Mum," she said, giving her mother a quick hug and air kisses. "Walker, I'd like you to meet my parents, Lord and Lady Daneby. And this is Dr. Walker Shaw."

Walker smiled inwardly. His little fighter was definitely alive and kicking.

"Charmed, to be sure," Walker replied in a thick drawl he reserved for just such occasions. "Well, I'm hardly fit for callers," he said, coming to stand by Zara's side. "Sugar, I think I'll mosey on in and put some clothes on."

If possible, Lord Daneby's stance became even more rigid. A blush colored Lady Daneby's cheeks as her gaze flitted over Walker, robe and all, bending down to pick up his suitcase.

Zara's fingers found his and squeezed, making him pause in his escape long enough to give her a kiss on the forehead. Except her face tilted up and it landed on her lips. He smiled, and kissed her again. Very chaste. But potent as an atomic bomb.

"Come right back," his little fighter whispered for all to hear.

As soon as he closed the bedroom door behind him, he heard Lord Daneby's voice start to boom again. "I hope you're proud of yourself, young lady…."

Walker ignored the words, not wanting to hear any more lest he be forced to stalk out there and flatten the old bugger.

After a speed-shower, he shook out his favorite Helmut Lang suit and put it on. Modern-day armor. Oh, yes, this was definitely a battle to the death.

He walked back into the living room just as the words, "The man will be your ruin!" echoed loudly off the plaster, marble and walnut surfaces of the living room.

"Well, then, I'll just make some coffee, shall I?" he drawled into the sudden hush.

"That would be lovely, darling," Zara said warmly, looking up from the sofa with a surprising sparkle in her eye.

He wanted to sweep her up in his arms and hug her. He wanted to grab her and shake her until her teeth rattled. She *shouldn't* be taking his side. Lord Daneby was family, and Walker would soon be gone. He didn't want to be the cause of a deeper rift between father and daughter.

But it warmed his heart to the furthest reaches that she was willing. How could he not love her to distraction?

He went through to the kitchen and filled the strange bulbous vacuum coffee brewer everyone seemed to use in this country, putting in an extra scoop of the gourmet Costa Rican blend Zara preferred. He needed the caffeine.

When he turned, Zara's mother was standing in the kitchen doorway. "How is she?" she asked.

Walker figured she didn't mean in bed. "Her amnesia is gone," he said, "and there are no residual effects of the bombing. You can rest easy. She's back to her old self."

Lady Daneby regarded him with a shade of what could be skepticism. "Is she?"

The fact that Zara's mother was even talking to him—seeking his opinion nonetheless—and seemed genuinely concerned about her daughter's well-being sent her stock way up in his estimation. Which is why he didn't take offense at the question.

He leaned against the counter, crossing his arms over his waist. "Yes. Her personality and judgment are the same as before her injury, if that's what you are asking." It wasn't, but close enough.

Lady Daneby went to the cupboard and started assembling cups and saucers on an antique silver tray, and therefore wasn't looking at him when she said, "You'll pardon me for observing, it's not like Zara to become involved with…"

"A scoundrel like me?" he helpfully supplied with a dry smile.

Their eyes met and he found himself, much to his surprise, liking Lady Daneby. He admired her self-possession and her willingness to shoot from the hip. Concerning her daughter, at any rate. It was obvious which parent Zara took after.

"I assume you've been told of the attempts on her life?" he asked. Lady Daneby nodded, eyes becoming worried. "Well, now that she has her memory back, my job is to protect her. Nothing more."

Frowning anxiously, Lady Daneby opened the bag of breakfast pastries he and Zara had picked up on the way home last night and arranged them on a delicate plate. "I can't think who would want to hurt Zara. She's always been so dedicated and careful in her work, despite what that child's mother claimed a few years back. Are you sure there's no mistake?"

He shook his head recalling the story nurse Emily had told him about the young patient Zara had lost through no fault of her own. "No mistake."

"Then it must have something to do with the king. Or

the coronation. Lord Carrington is a dear friend of ours. That horrible Union for Democracy is somehow behind this, I'm sure of it. Trying to upset the monarchy any way they can."

"We have top investigators working day and night to find out who's responsible," he assured her. "It'll break soon. In the meantime, I'm not letting Zara out of my sight. No one will get the chance to hurt her again, that I guarantee."

Lady Daneby gave him a considering look, then plucked a long sprig of fragrant purple lavender from a vase in the window and laid it on the tray next to the silver sugar bowl.

"My daughter has always had a very level head on her shoulders," she finally said. "I assume if she's…fond of you, there's more to you than meets the eye—or the headlines."

That was as big a compliment as he would likely ever get.

"Thanks," he said. "I'd like to think that's true. But—" he took the full coffee carafe from the brewer and poured the contents into the sterling-silver pot she had set out "—however much I wish things were different, and believe me I do, I understand the difficulties in this situation. I won't be staying in Silvershire beyond the end of the case. So you needn't worry on that account, either."

She didn't say anything, so he picked up the tray and carried it into the living room.

He knew better than to think Lady Daneby was remotely on his side, but he was glad they'd cleared the air. She was one classy lady.

Zara gave him a nervous look when he set the tray down on the coffee table in front of her. He winked, and the tension left her face. She patted the sofa next to her so he took a seat there as she poured coffee all around. Lord Daneby glowered from his place propping up the mantle, but Zara's mother took the chair across from Walker as though it were just another in a long succession of Saturday breakfasts together.

He had to admit, the whole morning had a kind of surreal quality to it.

"Looks lovely, darling," Zara said. She didn't kiss him, or even touch him other than on the fingers passing him a cup. She didn't have to. The way she looked at him said it all. His heart squeezed.

She'd dressed while he and her mom had had their conversation, and was now wearing a silky jade-colored top with a light skirt that rode sexily up her thighs.

"So do you, sugar," he said. "But Lady Daneby put the tray together, so she should get the credit."

Before anyone could respond to that, the phone rang. Not his cell phone, but the phone tucked into Zara's bookcase.

Walker managed as politely as possible to down three cups of coffee—Lady Daneby's brow rose fractionally as she filled the third for him—while Zara talked on the phone for a few minutes, and then spun back to them, her eyes alight with excitement.

"He's awake!" She practically jumped up and down, hanging up the receiver with a clatter. "Thank God, King Weston has regained consciousness!"

"Don't fuss over me, girl! You know how I hate that."

Zara was trying not to hover over the king as the nurses attended to him, but with little success. She was too ecstatic to see his eyes open and a smile on his face not to stick like glue to his bedside, holding his hand. And she checked every single thing the nurses did.

Nothing was going to mar this moment.

"How are you feeling?" she asked, bursting to question

him about everything at once. "Do you hurt anywhere? Your head?"

She would have gone on asking about every place on his body, but for the deep chuckle that the king let out at her worried inquisition.

"Dr. Smith, I am tired, but immensely happy to find I'm still alive. Thanks to you." He squeezed her hand.

Her eyes brimmed with tears. She wouldn't tell him about the bombing yet, not until he was stronger. But guilt over it nearly gutted her. "No, Your Majesty, I'm the one who's immensely happy to see you awake." More than he would ever know. "We all are."

The nurses murmured their agreement as they worked, broad smiles lighting their faces as they busily took his vitals and washed his face and changed his gown.

"How long have I been unconscious?" he asked, letting his eyes drift closed.

"I'm afraid you've been in a coma for quite some time," she said gently. "Around two months."

His eyes popped open. "Two bloody months? Good Lord!" Immediately, grief suffused his expression. "My son, Reginald. He was buried, then?"

Her eyes filled again. She hadn't particularly liked the crown prince, but she knew King Weston had doted on him. It was impossible not to share his pain. "Yes, Your Majesty. The ceremony was beautiful."

"Have they caught the bastards who killed him?"

She glanced over at Walker, who was standing by the door quietly observing. He shook his head. "Not yet, sire," she said, turning back. "But I'm sure they're getting close. The inquiry is everyone's top priority."

"And the other?" he asked, his voice dipping low.

She frowned, unsure. "The other…what, Your Majesty?"

"The one they told me about just before I collapsed," he whispered so she had to bend close to hear. "Have they found the true prince? My other son?"

Chapter 14

Zara nearly fell over, stunned. She had to have heard wrong. *The true prince?* King Weston had another son?

She shot a frantic look at Walker but he was too far away to have heard. "I—I—I don't know," she stammered.

Suddenly her ears were filled with the piercing sound of babies crying. Two babies. *The babies from her first vision.* Slamming her hands over her ears, she ground her jaw and glanced around. It was obvious no one heard them but her.

Walker came to attention. "Zara, what is it?" He started toward her, but she waved him back, taking a cleansing breath. The crying had stopped as suddenly as it began. He frowned, but stayed where he was.

The king had closed his eyes again, his whole face showing his fatigue and emotional upset. The nurses had finished their tasks, so Zara dismissed them for now with a thank you. When she and Walker were alone with the king, she went to fetch her purse and pulled from it the folded rubbing she'd taken of the icon yesterday.

She knew she shouldn't be pressing him in his present condition, but she was more certain than ever that her visions were meant as a warning. King Weston's life could depend on whatever they were trying to tell her. Especially if what he'd said about another son was true. Perhaps it was even his son's life that was in danger....

Now, the assassination attempt on the king made much more sense. Another crown prince! The events of the past weeks were coming together in a frightening way.

She smoothed the rubbing open and held it up before him. "Your Majesty, I wonder if you could look at this drawing and tell me…" She waited for his eyes to flutter open and focus on the rubbing. "Do you recognize it? Or any of the symbols on it?"

He looked at the paper for a long moment, his brows drawn together, then glanced at her. "I think I— What is it?"

She explained briefly where she'd found it, but didn't mention her visions. "Does it mean anything to you, anything at all?"

"Perhaps…seen something like it, somewhere. But…can't recall where."

Disappointed, she refolded the paper.

"There's someone who would know," he said, his voice fading. "Take it to Merlin. He can tell you."

"Merlin. You're kidding me." Walker made a face.

"That's what he said." Zara also thought the old king might be losing it. But it was the only lead she had, so she was determined to run it down. Unfortunately, he'd fallen asleep before she could question him further. "I suppose we could try the phone book."

Walker chortled. "Yeah. Why the hell not?"

After sending one of the nurses back to sit with the king, checking the guards and calling Carrington to give an update on Weston's progress, she and Walker went to the staff lounge and grabbed a phone book.

"Yellow pages?" Walker asked with a grin.

She rolled her eyes. "What do we look under? Fifth-century magicians?"

"Right. White it is. Business or residential?"

"Oh, do be serious." She swiped the book from him and looked up Merlin in the business section. "Good grief. There's a listing! Merlin, Argott, Professor of History."

"How about that," Walker said, peering over her shoulder. "Give him a call."

It turned out Professor Argott Merlin was one of King Weston's good friends, and an expert on all things Silvershirean. After a short conversation, Zara arranged that they should go right over and show him the rubbing. His office was in Silverton-upon-Kairn, in the oldest section of the historic district.

"Hmm, very interesting," Merlin said, clearing a spot for the paper on an acre-sized wooden desk cluttered with ancient books, artifacts, writing instruments and manuscript pages. He got out a loupe and examined the symbols first. "They remind me of the writings of an old, secret, mystical society from years ago. Along the order of the Freemasons. Very hush-hush and ritualistic. I'm afraid I can't help you with the meaning, if there is any. But sometimes these things are just for show."

"More of a decoration, you mean?"

"It's possible. However, I *can* tell you about this landscape," he said with a triumphant smile, examining the center relief. "Why, that's easy. It's the old Oriental Pavilion at Castle Perth."

"Where's that?" Walker asked.

Zara's mind was suddenly in a whirl. "On Perthegon Estate, the ancestral lands of Lord Benton Vladimir, Duke of Perthegon. Thirty years ago he was the heir apparent to the throne, until suddenly, old King Dunford chose Weston, Duke of Chamberlain, to become king instead."

Walker gave a whistle. "A succession intrigue? Dunford had no children of his own?"

She shook her head.

"There was quite an uproar at the time," Professor Merlin said. "The country was very divided over who was better suited to rule. Perthegon was the elder by a few months, and thus was entitled to the throne. No one really found out why he was passed over in Weston's favor."

Walker gave a low curse. "Where is this Lord Perthegon now?"

"That's just the thing," Zara said, a bad feeling growing in the pit of her stomach. "No one knows. He disappeared, and hasn't been heard from since."

"We have to go to Castle Perth," Zara stated firmly as Walker followed her down the narrow alley in old town where they'd parked his car.

"Watch out!" he yelled, grabbing her from behind and slamming her into a recessed doorway as a blue compact car barely scraped by them going way too fast. "That driver's going to get the surprise of his life," he growled, scribbling down the plate number on a receipt from his pocket, "when he gets a two-hundred-quid speeding ticket."

Suddenly, he whipped his gaze to Zara, whose eyes were wide as saucers, watching the car race away. "*My God*. Was that the same car that hit Estevan?"

Zara just nodded.

He speed-dialed Corbett Lazlo. "A car just tried to mow us down. Yeah, same one as Estevan. This time I got the plate." He hung up a minute later, adrenaline surging through his veins. "Corbett's sending von Kreus with the SWAT team to pay the driver a little visit."

Zara licked her lips. "You think he was really trying to…?"

He pulled her into his arms. "Von Kreus will find out the truth. Let's hope getting that plate is the break we've been waiting for. Come on. Let's get you back to the palace."

She pulled away. "Walker, no! We *must* go to Perthegon."

"Baby, that's crazy. Let someone else—"

"No. It has to be me. Why else would I be having these visions?"

Exasperated to the max, he slashed a hand through his hair and counted to ten. He was as open-minded as the next guy about this woo-woo stuff, but Zara's whole vision obsession was beginning to be a severe pain in the butt.

"I'm supposed to be *protecting* you," he said, striving desperately for calm. "Not letting you gallivant all over the country chasing down imaginary clues to imaginary threats of imaginary dangers! God, Zara, this is insane!"

So much for calm. He'd practically shouted that last part.

Predictably, Zara's chin reached for the sky. Without a word, she launched herself out of the recess that had possibly saved their lives, and stalked toward his rental car.

He cursed again, and followed.

"At least let me phone for police backup!" he called after her.

Tapping her foot, she waited for him at the car. "We can call the local plod when we get there, if we find anything. Come on, we're wasting time."

He touched the gun in his jacket pocket, debating whether

he should use it on the bad guys or on Dr. Zara Smith. She had that look again. The one that said he was destined to lose this argument, and if he refused to take her to Perthegon she'd just escape custody and go on her own.

He *really* wished he'd checked out a pair of handcuffs along with the gun.

"All right, fine," he ground out. "But at the first sign of anything suspicious, we're out of there. And I do mean *anything*."

"Fair enough," she said reasonably. Now that she'd won.

Even with two wrong turns, it took just half an hour to reach Perthegon Estate, which lay east and north of the capital city. Silvershire really was tiny, only one hundred eighty-two miles long and fifty-eight miles at its widest point. There were counties back home bigger than this whole country.

County Perthegon was quaintly bucolic compared to the capital city. Farms and hedgerows dotted the rolling hills, cozy cottages and small, quaint villages huddled in the valleys. Occasional patches of woodlands canted lazy streams amid the steeper slopes, becoming more plentiful as they drove north. By the time they reached the estate boundary, the trees were tall and ancient, the forest looming dark and mysterious above them.

Driving up the overgrown road to Castle Perth, Walker's unease increased exponentially. An air of acute neglect hung over the place like a pall.

"Doesn't anyone live here?" he asked.

"No. The duke had no heir, but King Weston refused to confiscate the lands for the crown. He kept hoping Perthegon would turn up. The estate has been abandoned since he disappeared thirty years ago."

The dense, claustrophobic forest canopy nearly blocked out the morning sun. Long fingernails of branches scraped at the roof of the car and tall weeds clogged the dirt road, making it difficult to follow.

"It's like something out of the Brothers Grimm," Walker muttered.

Zara shivered. "Where's the white rabbit when you need him?"

They drove on through the lightless forest at a snail's pace for another fifteen minutes until, suddenly, the trees abruptly stopped at the edge of acres and acres of green meadow filled with dollops of bright red poppies. On a slight rise in the center of it all stood a castle.

"Wow," Walker said, bringing the car to a halt. "Not exactly what I was expecting."

Built of sparkling white stone, ornamented with round turrets and Palladian windows, the tall, cheery edifice looked more like a fairy castle than the Dracula's estate he'd assumed they'd find lurking at the end of the driveway.

"I've seen pictures, but it's so much prettier in reality," Zara agreed, smiling with admiration. "I can't imagine anyone abandoning a gorgeous place like this."

"Tells me the man is guilty of something, that's for damn sure."

Walker let out the clutch and eased the car forward until their path was blocked by a huge set of black iron gates.

"I'll see if I can open them," Zara said.

She jumped out of the car and waded through the weeds to the gate. Walker joined her. The design of the iron lace was delicate and intricate, the ground beneath their feet littered with large flecks of gold paint that had peeled off the black iron.

"Must have been really something in its day," he said admiringly.

"A shame it's all been left to ruin," she agreed.

He yanked on the fist-sized iron lock holding the gates closed. "Locked. Now what?"

A low brick wall connected with the outer edges of the gates, topped by twisting iron spikes, preventing them from climbing over that way. Before he could stop her, she'd slipped through the narrow bars of the gate.

"Come on," she urged. "Suck it in and you can make it."

He did, just barely, but was left with a nasty tear in his favorite Helmut Lang shirt. "You're getting me a new one," he grumbled.

"I'll pick one up while I'm buying myself new shoes," she said, making a face at her mud-covered pumps.

"Which way?"

"Professor Merlin said the pavilion should be in a small grove of pear trees somewhere at the edge of the lawns."

"Lawns?" He looked around. After thirty years any lawns were now indistinguishable from the surrounding meadows, and small clumps of trees had sprung up all over the place; at a distance it was impossible to tell if they were pear or persimmon.

"This could take a while."

Two hours later they'd still not found anything that remotely resembled the strange structure on the rubbing. A barn, a gazebo, a hunting blind, a bandstand, a gardener's cottage, a greenhouse and a pump house, but no pavilion.

"We've circled the bloody castle twice," Zara muttered, rubbing her feet. They were sitting on a huge fallen log taking a break from the search to regroup.

Walker grimaced at the blisters on her heels. He'd tried to talk her into abandoning the search an hour ago when he'd noticed her starting to limp in those ridiculous heels, but she'd have none of it.

They'd even called Professor Merlin on Walker's cell

phone to ask if he knew what direction from the castle the
pavilion stood. He didn't recall.

The only place they hadn't thoroughly searched was an
area of meadow close to the river which had over the years
turned into soggy wetlands.

"We have to check the marsh," Zara said. "It's the only
place left."

"You stay here," he said. He was loathe to leave her, but
the area was like a swamp and he didn't want her sinking into
mud up to her knees. He'd been brought up in the swamplands
and was used to it. "I'll go in and check it out."

"Fat chance," she said, springing to her feet with a wince.
"I'm going, too."

Suddenly, there was a loud crack, like a heavy branch splitting from a tree. It took Walker the amount of time for another
crack to ring out to realize it was a gunshot.

"Jeezus, get down!" he hissed, launching himself at Zara
and tackling her onto the ground. They both hit the mud
with a spatter, and he rolled her under him, covering her body
with his.

"What the bloody hell—"

"*Shhh!*"

He cocked his head and listened. Another shot exploded.
Her eyes widened. She whispered, "*Gun*shots?"

He swore, and nodded. "Now would be a good time to call
in the local plod."

A fourth shot echoed across the meadow. He heard a tiny
thwack as it hit about twenty feet away.

He swore and scanned the area again. "That was too damn
close. You roll as tight into that log over there as you can get,
and call the police. I'll work myself around and try to surprise
him from behind."

"Walker, no! It's too dangerous."

He drew his weapon. "Baby, I'm getting a little sick of this shitbag messing with my woman. Where I come from that's license to kill."

Her mouth dropped open in shock.

He sent her a grin and a wink. "Jus' kidding. I only mean to shoot off the bastard's kneecaps."

He gave her a push and waited until she'd tucked herself under the log and fished her cell phone from her pocket. Then he started crawling.

"Walker!"

He turned his head back at her urgent whisper.

"Please be careful." The terrified look on her face as she said those words fueled his determination as nothing else could have. She was scared to death. *For him.*

She wasn't the only one.

He'd never been quite so thankful for his redneck upbringing as he was in the next few tense minutes. Growing up, he, his brothers and their friends had played stalking games all the time in the woods behind their neighborhood. He knew all about sneaking up on things. What it took was patience and a willingness to get dirty and bitten by anything that was down there crawling with you.

He heard a soft thump in the opposite direction from him, which was quickly followed by a shot. He listened anxiously. Had Zara moved against his orders?

There was another thud, and another shot.

Suddenly, he realized she must be throwing rocks to divert attention from him. He swore under his breath, his feelings waffling between gratitude and fury. The shooter would see through that ploy in about five seconds, and Zara's cover would be blown.

Galvanized, he scooted on his belly through the tall weeds, making no sound, slowly closing in on the enemy.

After what seemed like hours, he'd circled around far enough to reach the edge of the woods. Now came the tricky part.

Using the trunk of a tree to shield himself, he rose to his feet. Closing his eyes, he just stood there and listened. For several long moments he hugged the trunk with his backside, paying close attention to the sounds of the forest. The birds, the insects, the light rustle of leaves and undergrowth. Slowly, a pattern emerged. And a hole formed in the sounds.

That was where he would find his quarry.

He caught the very tail end of a scent. At first he couldn't place it, just sensed a note that wasn't quite right in the piney, boggy, wild-flowery mix of the smells of the marsh. Something…artificial.

Cologne? Perfume?

His eyes flew open.

It smelled like…citrus. Not his or Zara's scent.

But then it was gone. Could he have imagined it?

Crouching low, he darted through the brush, heading for the target area, hoping to catch another drift of the smell that had seemed out of place.

All at once he came upon a small clearing near the edge of the wood. The grass was trampled, and the jarring scent of sweet citrus lingered in the air.

This was where the shooter had stood.

Walker swung around, gun poised in front of him. Searching frantically. But whoever had been there had fled.

Scanning the forest floor, he saw half footprints leading into the trees, spaced far apart as though the shooter had been running away, just touching down with his toes. Running shoes, by the look of it.

He took off at a jog, following the trail. It appeared the guy was heading for the road.

Gotcha.

Walker knew it was stupid to pursue. He should just stop and call the cops. But he was so damned angry he sped up instead of slowing down.

He was so going to get this guy.

Bursting from the forest, he sprinted onto the road, hurriedly checking in both directions.

There!

About a hundred yards away, a dark-clad figure was diving into the front seat of a blue compact. *The same car.*

"Stop right there, you bastard!" he yelled, fury spiking.

Using every bit of strength he had, he took off running after the car.

But he was too far away. Still sprinting, he watched as it careened away, jouncing over the rutted road.

"Sonofabitch!" he yelled after it.

Raising his gun, he aimed at the tires and squeezed off four or five rounds, missing wildly except for one that pierced the back end.

"Sonofafreakingbitch!"

He couldn't believe it. The bastard had gotten away *again*.

By the time Walker had hiked back and fetched Zara, the local police arrived at the gate with lights flashing.

"Thank God," she said when the two officers emerged from their radio car. "Did you arrest him?"

"Who?" they asked, looking clueless.

Walker's heart sank. This guy was almost supernatural in his ability to elude capture.

"The dispatch call was a bit garbled," the younger of the constables said. "What exactly happened?"

Walker let Zara explain, then answered their questions about his role, particularly the shooting part. Handguns were illegal in Silvershire, except for certain law enforcement officers, so he produced his special permit from the Captain of the Palace Guard. The constables were impressed. Even *they* didn't carry guns.

They were also pretty impressed with Lady Zara. Since Castle Perth was unoccupied, County Perthegon had few genuine aristocrats living within its borders.

"What on earth were you two doing here?" they asked her, glancing skeptically around at the sadly neglected property. "Planning t'buy the place?"

She laughed, also looking around. "It could be a lovely estate with a little work. But no. We were searching for an old pavilion that is supposed to be on the property somewhere." She fished the rubbing from her purse and showed them. "You don't, by any chance, know where this strange structure is?"

The older of the two men lit up. "Why, that's t'old pleasure house. The Oriental Pavilion, they called it. Saw't once when I were a nipper. T'young duke's twenty-first birthday party. Aye, now, *that* were a feast if ever there was one."

Walker interrupted before he could go off down memory lane. "Where is this pavilion?" he asked.

"Oh, well, now…" the constable tugged off his hat and scratched his head, glancing around again. "I believe…aye, t'were over yonder. Spot in t'middle of that little wood there." He pointed in the direction of the marshland which they hadn't gotten a chance to properly search.

"I knew it!" Zara said. "Well, if we're finished here, we'll just—"

"Ack, I'm sorry, your ladyship, but we have to ask you two t'come down to the nick with us," the older constable said.

"There'll be paperwork," the younger confirmed.

Walker's cell phone rang. It was Corbett.

"What the hell's going on?" his boss demanded. "I'm getting reports of you out in the geography and shots being fired."

"We're fine," Walker said, and quickly rattled off the morning's events.

"Damn. I'll send von Kreus with one of the forensics guys to recover the bullets and footprints. Meanwhile get yourselves back to the Palace and report to Lord Carrington. There's something he needs to discuss with you and Zara."

"What about the pavilion?"

"This is more important. Besides, you've been used as target practice enough for one day, don't you think?"

Walker and Zara filed their report, in triplicate, at the local police station, where von Kreus also stopped in on his way to Castle Perth to interrogate them politely regarding the shooting. He took sample shoe and tire prints from them, as well. By that time they'd missed lunch by a couple of hours so they stopped in at a local pub for a bite, then headed back to the capital.

"I'm afraid Lord Carrington just went into a meeting," his secretary told them when they arrived at the palace, taking only time for a quick shower and change first. "Perhaps you can come back in an hour?"

"Well, pish, if we'd known that we could have checked out the pavilion," Zara grumbled as they headed back to the medical wing.

"We can do it tomorrow," Walker said.

She glanced over at him and smiled. She didn't ask, but he could almost read her mind. He was staying another night?

To be honest, Walker was finding it harder and harder even to think about leaving Silvershire. *But he had to.* Didn't he?

Yes. He'd promised Zara's mother, and her father would blow a gasket if Walker hung around his daughter one minute longer than necessary. This morning's phone call about the king had come in the very nick of time. Their precipitous departure from the awkward breakfast at Zara's apartment had saved everyone one hell of a nasty conversation, he was dead certain.

Anyway, they weren't the only reason Walker had to leave. He was still a commoner, and still in professional disgrace. None of that had changed, nor was it likely to, despite Royal Publicist Chase Savages's best intentions. Neither had Walker's reason for refusing to clear his name. And Zara was still an aristocrat with a lofty goal, which would not survive her being personally associated with him unless he did so. For her sake, he couldn't stay. The most he could hope for was to be her bodyguard until her life was no longer in danger, sharing what precious few moments were left to them. And then go.

Which was so depressing he refused to think about it.

When they got to the medical wing, they went straight to the king's room.

"Hello, my dear!" King Weston's face lit up when Zara entered. Then he noticed Walker. "I don't believe I've been introduced to your young man yet," he said with a friendly smile.

"Your Majesty," Walker said with a formal bow, and stepped forward. "I'm Walker Shaw, Dr. Smith's bodyguard."

The king blinked. "Bodyguard? What the devil for? Has someone been threatening Lady Zara?" he demanded.

"I'm afraid so, Your Highness." Walker knew Zara hadn't

told Weston about the bombing yet, or her amnesia, so he was limited in what he could say about why he was there.

"Some madman has taken it into his head to kill me," Zara said, bailing him out. "Walker saved my life. Several times now."

The king's face grew angry. "First my son and now my doctor," he growled. "Do these Union for Democracy fanatics not see they are harming their cause rather than helping it? What's being done to stop them?"

"We're not sure it is the UD," Walker said. "Lord Carrington has spoken with their leader, Nikolas Donovan, who has assured him they aren't behind any of the recent incidents. Every resource is being used to locate who really is responsible."

"I want you to keep her safe, Mr. Shaw. She means a great deal to me, for she saved *my* life."

"I plan to, Your Majesty."

"*Dr.* Shaw," Zara corrected, turning to fuss with some kind of monitor beeping behind the king's bed. "Walker is really a doctor of psychiatry. Bodyguarding is just a recent sideline."

The king's eyes went from him to Zara and back. "I see."

The hall door opened and a nurse appeared, holding a tray with a covered plate on it. "Tea time," she said cheerily, and sailed in. Walker didn't recognize her. His nose twitched. *Citrus…?*

Standing next to him, Zara turned back from the monitor and froze. "Mrs. Lloyd! What on earth are you—"

Her words cut off in a gasp when the nurse lifted the lid from the plate and threw it onto the floor. And grabbed a gun under it.

She aimed the gun right at Zara.

"You there!" one of the corridor guards shouted.

The nurse's finger started to squeeze the trigger.

Walker's world went into slow motion as the trigger eased

home. He shouldered Zara forcefully aside. And realized the king was right in the path of the bullet meant for her.

He swore fiercely and dove onto Weston, spreading his body over him like a shield.

And gritted his teeth as the bullet slammed into his back.

Chapter 15

Zara screamed, paralyzed with terror as everything around her erupted in chaos. All she saw was Walker sprawled across the king, blood blooming from a gaping wound in his back.

She thudded against the wall with an *oof*, then the two corridor guards threw themselves at Mrs. Lloyd, wrestling the gun from her. The woman cursed and clawed. Everyone else was yelling. Except Walker. He didn't move.

The king was trying to tell her something, beckoning her, but Zara couldn't get her legs to work. Couldn't get her mind to stop screaming, *My God, he's dead. My God, he's dead….*

Emily rushed in with another nurse and the lab tech, took one look at Zara and began issuing orders. They lifted Walker off King Weston and onto a gurney that had suddenly appeared. He grimaced in pain at being moved, and Zara almost wept with relief.

He was alive!

Her gaze darted to the king, who was waving them away from him and back to Walker.

"Are you hurt, Your Majesty?" Zara managed to croak, the lead weights in her limbs easing enough to take a step toward him.

"I'm fine. Go at once and tend to Dr. Shaw," he ordered brusquely. "I want him *alive* when I reward him for saving my life!"

An hour later, Zara peeled off her surgical gown, grabbed her purse and hurried after Emily, who was wheeling Walker out of the basement emergency room to the covered ambulance bay. Although the operation to remove the bullet lodged between Walker's ribs had been successful, Zara had decided to transfer him to the Royal Medical University Hospital. The palace medical wing was top-notch, but their first priority was King Weston, now that he was awake.

"Sugar?" Walker whispered from the gurney, sounding groggy and disoriented as they loaded him onto the ambulance.

"I'm here, darling," she said, climbing in after him and reaching to take his hand. "You're okay. I got the bullet out. No complications." He'd been extremely lucky. The bullet hadn't pierced any major organs and had only broken one rib—the one that had stopped it.

The siren blared and red lights flashed.

"You?"

She swallowed around the lump that had been lodged in her throat for the past hour, and blinked back the tears she'd been holding at bay the whole time she was operating. She leaned over and kissed his cheek, his temple. "You don't think I'd let anyone else touch you, do you?"

Was that a smile?

"King?"

"Unhurt." She stroked her fingers down the curve of his neck. "Thanks to you."

"Thank God," he whispered, and his face went slack as he slipped back into unconsciousness.

She put a knuckle to her mouth and pressed hard.

"We're almost there," the ambulance tech said gently, nodding at the large modern building they were fast approaching.

She sucked in a breath and blew it out again, struggling to get her emotions under control. *Everything was all right.* Walker would soon be good as new, the king was unharmed, and they'd finally caught the person trying to kill her.

Mrs. Lloyd. She couldn't believe it. The mother of the child who'd died two years ago. As the guards had dragged her away, she'd been screaming all sorts of awful, ugly things at her.

Zara's feelings of guilt must have been obvious because during Walker's surgery Emily had told her, "It's not your fault. None of this is your fault. That girl's death, either. You have to know that."

Zara wanted to believe it with all her heart. Maybe in time she would.

They checked Walker in as her personal patient, and settled him into a private room overlooking the River Kairn and the Golden Bridge.

She was sitting in an easy chair pulled up right next to his bedside when he awoke a few hours later.

"I suppose sex is out of the question," he said in a raspy voice, drawing her gaze from the window to where he was lying, stomach down on the narrow hospital bed, cheek resting on the fluffy pillow.

She smiled, her heart leaping at the loving way his eyes

caressed her. "As your physician I'd advise against any vigorous exercise until that rib has healed."

"Hmm. Then can I turn over?" he asked with a wink. "Maybe you could…"

"No," she stated with mock sternness. "Not until at least tomorrow. Wouldn't want to pull your stitches."

"Spoilsport," he said, but his lips curved up.

"Sorry," she said, and suddenly felt her own smile fade. She leaned forward and threaded her fingers tenderly through his long hair, touched his dear face. *Almost taken from her.* "Oh, Walker, I'm so sorry. That bullet was meant for me, not you."

He reached for her hand. "*Baby, don't.* It's a damn good thing it hit me, because if it had hit you or the king, I'd have had to kill that crazy woman and I'd be in jail right now instead of kissing you." He brushed his lips over her knuckles. "Who was she, anyway?"

Zara sighed and recounted the whole depressing story of which he'd heard bits and pieces. "I knew Mrs. Lloyd had gone a bit over the edge at the loss of her child, but I never suspected just how far."

"But why now? Why not back then?"

"Agent von Kreus came by earlier to check on you. He told me it was a newspaper article that had set her off. She saw a picture in the *Quiz* of me caring for the king and she snapped. Was certain I would kill him, too. In her mind, she was helping the king by getting rid of me."

"My God. That's nuts!"

Zara had to agree. She shivered, and Walker rubbed the goose bumps from her arms.

"She confessed to everything," she continued. "The bombing, hitting Estevez, the poisoning at the restaurant, trying to run us down. When none of that worked, she followed us to Perthegon. By that time she'd lost it completely."

"So she didn't care if she was caught."

"She probably wanted to be. She's not a bad person at heart. Grief can do terrible things."

He grimaced as he changed positions, turning slightly onto his good side. Zara went and got an extra pillow from the closet, tucking it under his arm to help prop him up those few inches. Then she held his hand again. She needed to touch him, to know for certain he was alive and safe.

"What I want to know is how the hell she found out about the tunnel," he said.

She traced her finger up his thumb. "Well, that's the strange thing. She says the tunnel's not how she got in."

He frowned. "Then how?"

"Apparently she worked at the Medical University Hospital for a while and still had her ID. She dressed in a nurse's uniform and told the palace guards she'd been sent to help because one of the regular nurses in the medical wing was ill. They let her through."

He briefly squeezed his eyes shut. "Idiots. So you're telling me our attacker in the tunnel *wasn't* this Lloyd woman?"

Zara shook her head. "Probably just some kid exploring who we scared to death."

He was silent for a moment, then said, "Well, I guess that would explain why he didn't try to hurt you. What about the icon?"

She shook her head again. "She claims she didn't steal it."

He swore softly. "Then who the hell did?"

"I still think it was someone after drugs. There's no other reasonable explanation."

"What does von Kreus think?"

"He didn't say."

Walker tugged her closer. "Zara. Can you get me a room with a bigger bed? I want you to stay with me tonight."

She smiled. "Darling, this is a hospital. There are no bigger beds. Besides, I warned you about that sex thing…."

His little-boy smile broke through for a second, then vanished. "As nice as that sounds, it's not why I want you to stay. I'm still your bodyguard." He made a frustrated face. "I need you where I can see you."

Her heart melted at the concern in his voice. "Walker, they caught the maniac trying to kill me, remember? I'll be fine. Honestly."

"Still—"

"However," she soothed, "I'm not going anywhere. I plan to sleep right here." She patted the easy chair. "Because I need to be where I can see you, too."

He squeezed her hand and closed his eyes with a tired smile. "Promise?" he asked.

"Promise," she said, and wished to the depths of her soul she could always be where she could see him. Forever and always, for the rest of their lives.

It took Walker two damned uncomfortable days to get out of the damned uncomfortable hospital. He could walk, slowly and at an even pace, without his rib or the bullet wound in his back hurting too much. The painkillers helped a lot.

Which was why, when Zara announced she was going back to Perthegon to find the Oriental Pavilion, he insisted on going with her.

He thought she was out of her mind.

But she had that look on her face again. He didn't even argue.

He had to be out of *his* mind.

Either that or the painkillers were affecting his judgment.

In any case, he found himself in the passenger seat, gritting his teeth as they jolted over the endless pitted dirt road to Castle Perth.

"Sex would be easier on my aching rib than this," he groused.

She gave him a dry glance. "You *had* sex. Not two hours ago."

He smiled at the blissful memory of just lying back and letting her have her wicked way with him. "Yeah, but you made us stop. To come here and torture me."

"I told you, you shouldn't have come."

"As if."

They finally made it to the gate, and suddenly it occurred to him there was no way he'd ever be able to squeeze through the iron bars with his bandaged wound.

She wiggled her eyebrows, producing a small box that rattled when she shook it.

"What's that?"

"Keys. I called the guy at the antique shop where we bought the painting, and he let me borrow his whole stock of historic gate keys. He said one of them is bound to fit because they were all of about the same design, just different sizes."

Walker smiled. It was just like Zara to remember about the gate and solve the problem before it had even occurred to him. "You know what? You're pretty amazing."

She smiled back. "I am, aren't I?"

She jumped out, and by the time he'd made it to the gate she had it unlocked. "Open sesame!" she said and shoved the gate open. Well, sort of. One of the sides wouldn't budge at all and the other squealed like a banshee, grudgingly creaking open only a foot or two before sticking fast.

But it was enough. Together they slid through and slowly

made their way to the marshy area. Today they'd come prepared, wearing shorts, T-shirts and sneakers that had seen better days. So they waded into the muck. It wasn't too bad. Once you got used to the sucking sounds coming from the soles of your feet. And then there was the view.

"This is truly disgusting," Zara said, but Walker was too engrossed in watching her backside in those sexy shorts to notice.

As the cop had promised, they found the Oriental Pavilion tucked away in a small grove in the middle of the marsh.

"It looks like a Bedouin tent," he said, tearing his attention from her legs to examine the rusting, creaking structure. Shaped like a fancy tent some sheikh would live in, the walls were wavy like cloth and bore traces of paint that had once been bright purple-and-red stripes. "I was thinking Chinese or Japanese."

"In the eighteen-hundreds Oriental meant from the Middle East. Must have been built back then."

"It definitely looks rickety enough to be a hundred and fifty years old," he said.

A gentle breeze wafted through the trees, rustling leaves and branches. A lone grasshopper fiddled a tune behind the pavilion.

Suddenly Walker felt uneasy. He glanced around nervously, without knowing exactly why. Something was giving him the creeps.

"Why…it's made of metal!" Zara said in surprise.

"Yeah. Is that significant?" He scanned the outer edges of the grove, but nothing seemed out of place. Except he could no longer hear the grasshopper.

She peered up at him and bit her lip. "It's just…in my visions…I remember something about big sheets of metal."

He really wished she hadn't mentioned her damned visions. Thinking about them only increased his growing sense of…being watched.

"All right," he said briskly. "Now we've seen it. Let's get the hell out of here."

She resisted his urging hand and turned back to the pavilion with a strange expression. "Not yet. We have to go inside."

He grabbed her before she could move, wincing at the pull to his rib. "Oh no. I don't think so. The freaking thing looks like it could fall down any second."

"We *have* to go in. Whatever these visions have been leading me to, it's here…inside."

He drove his fingers through his hair in frustration. If the thing started crashing down around their ears, he was in no condition to hold it up long enough for them to get out. "Baby, please. Can we just open the door and look in from the outside?"

She hesitated, glancing at his torso, which she herself had wrapped in tight swaths of bandages to keep his cracked rib in place. "Okay," she conceded, to his immense relief. "We can start by just looking in, and go from there."

Naturally, she forgot all about her promise when they gingerly teased open the wobbly, broken-hinged door and she caught sight of the inside.

"Oh, my God," she breathed, and darted in before he could stop her.

"God *damn* it, Zara!"

He had no choice but to follow. Which, after one more thorough scan of the surrounding woods, he did.

"Do you see that border?"

She pointed up to where the walls met the undulating peaked roof. Inside, the paint had been protected from the elements and was still fairly crisp, the pattern easy to see despite the dimly lit interior. The border was purple, about a foot wide, filled with gold squiggly symbols and indecipherable writing.

"The same symbols and writing as on the icon."

"And in my visions."

He muttered a curse. "So, what is it all supposed to mean?"

Her gaze met his and held. She looked as spooked as he felt. "I have no idea."

All at once the pavilion started to sway, creaking and groaning as the roof threatened to split apart above them. The back wall *did* split apart. Blinding sunshine poured through the gash into the dimness. Walker shaded his eyes against the glare, but could swear he saw…a man pushing against it!

"Hey you! *Stop!*"

Just then, with a huge squealing crash, the whole pavilion started to collapse on top of them. "Zara, get out!" he yelled above the sickening screech of metal, giving her a firm push toward the door. *"Now!"*

A giant section of the roof fell, catching an edge in his T-shirt. "Damn it!" He struggled to free himself, but couldn't.

"Walker! Watch out!" Zara screamed as a piece of wall collapsed inward, coming straight at him.

He had just enough time to drop to the ground and cover his head before a heavy slab of metal crashed over him. He bit back a cry when it landed on his wound. But miraculously, it stopped short of crushing him flat, giving him enough room to breathe, but not much more.

"Walker!" Zara screamed as another wall came down.

"Zara! Are you okay? Get the hell out of here!"

"Where are you?" Her voice was high with panic.

The rest of the walls and roof landed around him with a metallic thunder Walker would never forget as long as he lived. But somehow his cocoon of air had survived intact, and him along with it.

"Baby, talk to me! Are you hurt?" he called.

"It knocked me over, but I'm fine," she finally said, voice wobbly. "I can see the outside. Oh, my God! There's someone out there! He's running away!"

Thank God, was all Walker could think.

Chapter 16

The fact that the structure had been made of large sheets of wavy moulded metal worked in their favor; big gaps of space had been left between the fallen bits. It took a bit of doing, but Walker was able to wriggle his way out from under the roof section that had pinned him down.

"You doing okay, baby?" he called. Zara had been silent for a while now, though he could hear a constant scraping noise coming from where she was stuck. "I'm almost to you I think."

"Walker…"

"Yeah, sugar?" He grunted in pain as he struggled to move one last wall section. The painkiller was wearing off and his rib hurt like a bastard.

"You aren't going to believe this."

He paused. He really hated when she said stuff like that. It was never good news. "What?"

"I found something."

"Yeah?"

"Buried."

Ah, hell. He prayed it wasn't a body. "What is it?"

"A chest of some sort."

He sent up a quick thank you to the powers that be. "Like a box?"

"I think this is *it*," she said excitedly. "What I was sent to find."

He was about to object to the term *sent,* but figured he didn't have a lot to argue with. It really was as though she'd been guided here by some unseen hand.

With a heave, he shoved the wall section a few feet aside and he could finally see her. Legs sticking out from under the rubble, she lay on her stomach digging with her hands, a pile of soggy earth growing by her side. She glanced up.

"Look!"

In the center of the hole she'd dug was the vaulted top of a wooden chest. It looked old.

"Pirate's treasure?" he asked with a hopeful smile to mask his uncertainty over how to react. This was so weird.

She broke out in a grin. "Gold, you mean? Or pieces of eight? Wouldn't that be cool." But she didn't sound like she believed it.

"What do *you* think it is?"

She shook her head, scraping a stray lock from her eyes with grubby fingers, leaving a streak of mud through her eyebrow. "I don't know. But whatever it is, it must be important. That guy out there…"

"Crashed this thing on purpose," Walker finished.

"Trying to prevent us from finding it."

A charitable interpretation. "I just hope he's not still hanging around." *With a gun,* he amended silently. His own gun was tucked into his waistband, but he didn't relish another shootout.

"I'm sorry I doubted your instincts about the gun," she said contritely.

She'd argued against the need to bring it, repeating they'd already caught the person trying to kill her. But Walker couldn't dismiss the icon and the tunnel incident as easily as she did. It just didn't fit.

"Ditto, sugar." But he had to admit, her visions had been eerily on target. "Let's dig this thing up and get back to the palace with it as fast as we can."

Walker stood next to Zara, who was waiting anxiously for Lord Carrington to say something. They were in Carrington's private study, the odd vaulted chest shedding dirt on a newspaper on his desk. Zara looked as though she was ready to burst from curiosity.

"Well. It's certainly not heavy enough to be gold," Carrington observed, taking hold of the side handles and shaking it. Something inside rattled around.

"Sounds like there are several things in there. Maybe in smaller containers," Walker said. He'd shaken it a couple of times himself on the way back from Perthegon.

"Can we open it?" Zara asked. "Please? I just know it's important."

"Because of the visions?"

She'd just told Carrington about them, how he and Zara had traced the icon symbols and found the pavilion. And how a man had tried to stop them.

"Yes, and…" She hesitated, seeming undecided for a moment. Then said, "And because of something the king said yesterday."

Carrington looked up sharply. "What was that?"

Zara took a deep breath. "Something about having another son."

Carrington froze. "He *told* you?"

"Excuse me?" Walker was sure he'd heard incorrectly. "What the hell are you talking about?"

She glanced at him apologetically.

Walker turned to Carrington in pure disbelief. "Are you saying King Weston has *another son out there somewhere?* That there's another crown prince of Silvershire? Still alive?"

The duke cleared his throat. "We aren't exactly sure. It came as much of a surprise to King Weston as it was to everyone else. It appears that—" His mouth turned down. "—and I assume I don't have to say this information is not to leave this room…?" Zara and Walker both nodded. "It appears that Prince Reginald was not the king and queen's natural child. That somehow the babies were switched and the true prince was, as incredible as it sounds, given to someone else. Naturally, we have every resource possible trying to trace the child…well, man, really, since he would be thirty years old by now."

"Including the Lazlo Group?" Walker asked. Was he the *only* one who didn't know?

Carrington nodded. "Yes. Your assignment was Zara, and this information was strictly need-to-know. We had no idea it could involve you, or Zara." He still looked unconvinced that it did.

"How long have you known?" she asked the duke.

"Since April."

"And it's now July. Well, Carrington, that certainly explains your sangfroid about becoming king. You never expected to be crowned!"

"Guilty, I'm afraid."

"And here I'd been so admiring your sudden maturity," she said, making a face at him.

Carrington laughed and put his hand on the vaulted lid of the chest. Under the liberal coating of dirt, Walker thought it was quite beautiful. Some type of hardwood, probably cedar, had been hand-hewn and keyed together like a Chinese cabinet, bound with strips of brass at the joints, and held together with brass pins. The lock was also brass, of an elaborate design he'd never seen before.

"I wonder what secrets you hold," the duke murmured.

"Russell," Zara said seriously, "I think whatever is in here has to do with the true prince. I have no evidence whatsoever of that, just a strong…feeling."

Walker could see him evaluate her words, as he himself was. He was weighing the obvious outlandishness of the idea of visions leading her to this important discovery versus cold hard facts: the icon had been stolen and someone had tried to scare them away from finding the chest.

"What do you think, Shaw?"

Walker shrugged. "I think whatever has been going on in Zara's head this past week has been pretty damn strange, but it can't be denied she was right at every turn."

"I'm inclined to agree," Carrington said at last. "So, instead of breaking the lock right now, I'm going to turn the chest over to the forensics team to examine the whole thing very carefully before opening. I hope either that or what's inside will provide us with a clue as to the true crown prince's whereabouts, if not his identity."

Suddenly Zara gave a small gasp. "That woman, Mrs. Lloyd, did she also confess to poisoning Prince Reginald? It was the same kind of poison as she used on me, wasn't it?"

Carrington clasped his hands behind his back. "Digitalis was used both times. But she denies killing the prince. And the tox report confirms her story. The compound in your stomach was of a different type and strength than that which killed the prince."

"I knew it," Walker said, gratified at last to hear support for his own conclusions. "I'd be willing to bet whoever stole that icon and pushed over the pavilion today was responsible for Reginald's death."

"You're no doubt right," Russell said. "Lazlo Group investigator Aidan Spaulding has just uncovered evidence that an international female assassin known as the Sparrow was hired to kill the prince. If this chest you found has anything to do with the true prince's identity, the man you saw today was probably the man who hired the Sparrow."

"Which makes it more important than ever to open it very carefully," Zara said, eyeing the chest with regret. "You will tell us what's in it?" she asked the duke. "I'm dying of curiosity."

Walker choked. "Baby, please don't use that word."

Carrington regarded them both. "Well, the good news is, you should be safe now, Zara. There's no reason anyone should want to harm you now that the chest has been discovered and is out of your hands." He cleared his throat. "Which I guess means…"

Walker's job here was done.

He suddenly couldn't move. He wanted to shout, *No! Wait! That guy could still* be *after Zara! I'm still needed here!* But he knew it wasn't true. Carrington was right.

"It means I'll be leaving Silvershire," he managed to say fairly evenly.

Zara's gaze sought his, looking wounded and stunned. "But—"

Then her mouth shut and thinned, and she turned her head away.

He had no desire to discuss their personal business in front of Carrington, and assumed she didn't, either.

"No need to hurry off," the duke said with an affable smile. "I'd be delighted to have you stay as my guest. In fact, I could use a right-hand man to help keep track of all these infernal investigations. I'm afraid my royal duties have been sadly neglected over the past weeks because my attention has been spread so thin. And now with the king awake again… What do you say?"

Slightly taken aback at the other man's offer, which actually seemed sincere, Walker didn't know quite how to answer. He desperately wanted to stay. But would it simply be delaying the inevitable? Unfortunately, yes.

He gave a slight bow. "Thank you very much, Your Grace. I appreciate all you've done for me, but it would probably be best for everyone if I left."

Zara gave a small, unladylike snort, but didn't speak.

Frustrated anger welled up inside him. "Zara, the press are still hounding you over me. Dragging your name—"

"Don't you *dare* use the press as an excuse," she snapped. Then gave a huff and marched out of the room.

"Zara!"

He appealed to Carrington, who gave him a commiserating look. "Better go after her. Seemed a bit peeved to me."

Clenching his teeth, he said, "Yeah," then headed after her.

"Walker!" Carrington said as he reached the door. "The king would like a word with you. Be sure to stop by and see him."

With a nod, he hurried out into the grand hall to catch up with Zara, who was walking at the speed of light toward the medical wing, high heels clicking angrily on the marble tiles.

"Now who's running away?" he called after her.

She stopped on a dime and spun an about-face, hands on her hips.

God, she was sexy.

It was all he could do to keep himself from grabbing her and kissing her madly, falling to his knees and begging her to come with him. Somewhere. Anywhere. To a place where no one knew his name and they could live together in peaceful anonymity. Somewhere his background wouldn't catch up to him and he wouldn't have to worry about Ramona Burdette's threats.

He'd trade everything he had for that chance. Every penny and every single dream, for the chance to be with Zara, to love her and have a family together and spend their days growing old together.

But that wasn't going to happen. There was no such place.

And even if there were, Zara had her own dreams, dreams she'd spent her whole life working to make into reality. Who was he to ask her to give them up?

"No, Walker," she said. "You're the one leaving, not me."

"And what do you suggest I do?" he shot back, coming up to her, grasping her arms.

"Stay!"

"And do what? Work for Carrington, where I'd be tortured every damned day, seeing you and knowing I can never really have you? That I can never live with you openly, never ask you to marry me?"

She stared at him with glistening eyes. "Try me."

He let out a long breath, fighting like mad not to give in to the plea. Fighting like mad to resist the overwhelming need to take her in his arms. "I'm a commoner. I can't work in my profession, and I can never clear my name. *Never,* Zara. You said it yourself. You need a husband your people will look up to. I'm the furthest thing from that."

"Why?" she demanded as she had once before. "Why can't you clear your name?"

He ground his jaw, wavering only a moment. He trusted her and she deserved to know. "Because if I'm cleared, the woman who made those accusations against me will be branded a liar. If that happens, she has sworn retribution. She has threatened my family. The lives of my parents, brothers and sister depend on my silence. She's rich *and* crazy, Zara. Crazier than Mrs. Lloyd. I'm terrified she'll hurt them. I'm certain she will if I say one word against her."

Zara looked horrified. "There must be something you can do! The police—"

"Have their hands tied unless she actually does something illegal. I'm not willing to take the chance."

"That's so unfair."

"Yeah. Life truly does suck. Especially today." He took a deep breath, brushed his palms down her arms, taking her hands in his, lacing their fingers. "I can't stay in Silvershire and not have you. I wouldn't survive that. But if I stay, the press will continue to crucify you."

"I don't care. Walker, please—"

"Jeezus, Zara. I know what it's like to have your dreams taken away. Everything you've worked for ripped out from under you. Don't you understand? I could *never* do that to you."

A couple of guards strolled by, glancing at them curiously as they stood there with fingers twined and hearts breaking. The bright gilded chandeliers glittered in Zara's liquid eyes, then a tear spilled over her lashes.

"Oh, baby," he whispered, and enfolded her in his arms, holding her tight. The pain in his rib was nothing compared to that in his heart and his soul.

He tilted her stubborn little chin up with his fingers and gently kissed her lips. "I love you, Zara Smith," he said softly. "I'll always love you, as long as I live. But I have to go."

* * *

Zara had thought the moment Walker would first say those precious words to her would be the happiest in her life.

Tears spilled down her cheeks, but instead of tears of joy, they were tears of sadness.

How could he love her, and still leave?

She clung to him fiercely, unwilling to let him go. She *wouldn't* let him go.

"Darling, you have to listen to me," she said between hitched breaths. "I'm telling you I don't *want* to be the Marchioness of Daneby any more. It's just an empty title. It would mean nothing at all without the man I love to share it."

He squeezed his eyes shut. "Oh, hell, Zara," he whispered. "Don't do this."

"It's you I want, Walker. I don't care about your past or what the press says, or what anyone else thinks. If they have any kind of brains they'll love you as much as I do."

His beautiful blue eyes opened and he gazed down at her. The depth of feeling she saw in them took her breath away.

"Yeah?" he whispered.

"Yeah."

"You're willing to give all that up for me?" Quiet wonder filled his voice.

"It's you I love."

He searched her face. "You're sure?"

"Absolutely certain."

His mouth curved up in a smile and he studied her for a long, long time, as though waiting for her to change her mind. She didn't.

"Well, in that case, I've been wanting to do this for seven years…."

She covered her mouth as he dropped to one knee, and took her right hand in his.

"Lady Zara Smith, would you do me the very great honor of becoming my wife?"

She blinked, a sudden rush of joy sweeping through her heart, into her whole body. She felt her fingers tremble on her lips. "Marry you? Really?"

"If you'll have me."

"Of course I— Oh, Walker! Yes! Yes, I'll marry you!" She dropped to her own knees and threw her arms around him, hugging him, rocking with him, laughing and crying with happiness.

All around them applause erupted. The guards, the footman, the maids were scattered about with silly grins on their faces, clapping.

"Ow, baby, have mercy, I'm a wounded man," Walker said, kissing her over and over between laughs and winces.

"Oh!" She dropped her arms contritely, but he put them right back.

"Don't stop. I'll live."

The crowd cheered.

"I assume you have the king's permission?" Carrington said, leaning negligently against his study door with a big smile and that mischievous glint in his gaze.

Walker stopped in mid kiss. "King's permission?" His eyes widened and sought hers. "He's kidding, right?"

She resisted a grin. "I'm afraid not. Daughter of a marquis, and all. A somewhat antiquated law, admittedly, but…" She lifted a shoulder.

Walker actually looked worried. "He can't say no, can he?"

"Well, theoretically…"

He muttered a curse. "Great. I'm s—" she shot him a warning look "—uh, sure he'll say yes."

"Why don't you find out right now?" Carrington suggested, far too keenly, she thought.

So they did.

On the way to the medical wing to see King Weston, suddenly Zara got worried. What did Russell know that she didn't? Even now he was tagging along behind her and Walker, looking cagey and mysterious beneath his pleasant smile.

"Ah, there you are!" King Weston said as they knocked and entered the luxurious private suite he'd been moved to since coming out of his coma. He was making excellent progress, his recovery nearly complete. "Come in! Come in!"

"Your Majesty," they said together, Walker making the obligatory bow. Zara even curtsied, though in her official capacity as his doctor it wasn't strictly required. Russell had knocked her so off-kilter she was running on automatic.

The king was sitting in a chair by the window, wearing an elegant, thick silk dressing gown and slippers. He beckoned. "Come over here, Dr. Shaw. I have something I must say to you."

Zara sensed more than saw Walker hesitate, but he went forward. "Your Highness, I also have something I'd like to say. Or, rather, ask."

Weston held up a finger. "I'm king, I get to go first." He chuckled, and Zara smiled. He really was feeling his old self again.

She could see Walker's shoulders notch down a fraction. "Of course."

"Help me up, lad," Weston said, reaching up to grab Walker's hand.

Zara rushed forward to help, too, but the old man was surprisingly steady on his feet and barely needed it. Still, he kept hold of her hand as he regarded Walker, his expression turning solemn. To her shock, he bowed to Walker. Not just an inclined head, but an honest-to-goodness bow. Walker shot her a panicked what-do-I-do-now? look. She had no clue. Behind her, Carrington leaned against his ubiquitous door frame and looked inscrutable.

The king drew himself up formally. "I thank you, Dr. Shaw, for saving my life. You took a bullet that surely would have killed Dr. Smith if it had hit her, and most probably would have been the end of me or some of my favorite bits, had it hit me." He bowed again.

"Thanks are not necessary, Your Majesty," Walker said graciously, his face flushed with embarrassment. "Really. Anyone would have done the same in my position."

"I'm not so sure," the king responded. "But in any case, I shall reward you generously for your selfless service to the crown."

Walker brightened. "Well, sire, if that is your intention, there is something I was hoping to ask you for."

Weston's brows rose at Walker's charming American brashness. "Indeed?"

"Yes." Walker reached for her. "I'd like to ask your permission to wed Lady Zara."

Weston's brows went even further up. *"Indeed?"*

Walker smiled at her and she beamed back. "We'd very much like to marry."

The king looked from one to the other. "I see." He pursed his lips. "I did have a different sort of reward in mind. Perhaps you'd care to hear it?"

"Not necessary, Your Majesty. Lady Zara is all I want."

"I think I'll tell you, anyway. You can choose which you'd rather have, is that fair?"

Walker nodded, giving her hand a squeeze.

"The reward I'd planned was to make you a Knight of the Realm of Silvershire." He pronounced every word distinctly.

Zara gasped. "Oh, Your Majesty!"

Being made a Knight of the Realm was the highest honor a person could achieve in her country. It happened rarely, maybe once a generation, given only for the most extraordinary service. She grabbed Walker's shoulders. "You can't turn this down. You mustn't!"

The king continued, "It carries the title of Baron, of course. You would be Lord Shaw."

Utterly gobsmacked, Walker swallowed a few times. "I, uh, I'm—I…" He threw a glance for aid at Carrington, who winked, the rat. "I thank you, profoundly, Your Majesty. But as I said, Lady Zara is all I really want."

Weston indicated he wanted to sit down again, so they helped him. As they did, a war raged within her. She desperately wanted to marry Walker, but if it meant he must turn down this incredible honor—and the chance for him to redeem his good name, in Silvershire, at least—she had to change his mind. Somehow.

"Sire, you don't really mean he must choose between being a baron and being my husband?" she pleaded. He couldn't be serious. She knew that the King had a mischievous streak, but still…

Weston waved a hand. "That would be up to the new king," he said with a little smile at Carrington. "He could still grant you permission to marry. If he were so inclined."

She whirled to Russell. "You wouldn't dare refuse! Would you?"

He shrugged expansively. "It might not be up to me, Zara, remember? The true crown prince may be found soon, and he would make that decision if he were king."

Oh, God, she'd completely forgotten about that! It could take ages....

Walker was shaking his head. "Not necessary. My choice stands."

Weston tilted his head slyly. "Perhaps you'll change your mind when I tell you there's more? A baron needs a castle to live in. So I've attached a lifetime entailment of Castle Perth to the barony. It's a beautiful piece of architecture, and it should be lived in."

"But not by me," Walker said firmly, bringing tears to Zara's eyes.

"Oh, darling," she sighed, and wrapped her arms around him. "I do love you so much."

"I love you, too, baby." He kissed her then, long and warm, and only stopped when the king cleared his throat.

"Well, then. If that's your final word, your marriage has my blessing," he said, smiling. Then he frowned and poked the air with his finger. "I don't see a ring."

Again, Walker turned red. "No, uh, this all happened a bit suddenly. I haven't had a chance—"

"Perhaps you'd like to use this?" The king drew an elaborate signet ring from his finger and beckoned Walker for his right hand. When he reached out, Weston took it and slid the ring onto his finger, holding him fast. "I had a feeling you'd choose Lady Zara. But I'm an ornery old man and don't like taking no for an answer...*Baron* Shaw."

Zara pressed her hands to her mouth to keep from crying out. The carved ruby signet that crowned the glittering gold ring was unmistakable—the official seal of a Knight of the Realm.

"Oh! Your Highness! Oh, my lord, I can't believe it!" She was babbling, but she didn't care. She was so happy for

Walker she didn't know what to do with herself. She was actually jumping up and down.

Walker stared at the ring, obviously overcome.

"Better put it on her finger, lad. Before she gets away."

"No! No, seriously." She warded off Walker, making him keep the ring on his own hand. "That's yours. Only yours."

He smiled, his eyes going soft. "And what about you, sugar?"

Sliding her arms around his neck, she said, "I'm yours, too, my lord," and her heart overflowed with love for this incredible man, the man who had stolen her heart seven years ago and had finally come to claim the rest of her. Her own knight in shining armor. "Only yours, for the rest of time."

Epilogue

Silverton, Silvershire
October

The proclamation read: "By the King—A Proclamation," but everyone knew it had been the queen's doing. Her idea, her effort, her success. Not that the king disagreed, mind you, because he was as fair-minded and...well, if you really wanted to put a fine point on it, democratic...as she.

Still, it caused quite a stir, regardless of who was behind it. But after the dust settled, the decree was viewed by the common folk as a positive sign of what was to come from their new king, recently installed on the throne. It read:

Declaring His Majesty's Pleasure concerning the Succession of Titles of Nobility and the Dispensation of Land Entailments:

WHEREAS We have taken note of an inequity of gender in the matter of historical Land and Title Entailments in Our Nation, as it was the practice in times past.

We do hereby, by and with the advice of Our Privy Council, change and declare that the traditional practice of male primogeniture in the inheritance of Titles of Nobility and the Entailment of Estates, such as exist now or in the future in the Country of Silvershire, shall cease immediately, and furthermore a new tradition which does not take account of an heir's gender shall henceforth be used.

Given at Our Court at Silverton Royal Palace, this twenty-first day of October, in the year of Our Lord, two thousand and six, and in the first year of Our Reign.

God Save the King and the People

A wide smile came to Zara's lips as she read the heavy, engraved parchment announcement that had arrived at Castle Perth by special liveried messenger directly from the Royal Palace.

She'd done it! Zara could scarcely believe it, but the new queen had kept her word and talked her husband into changing one of the most ancient laws of the land. Actually, she could believe it. Their new queen was an amazing woman.

The young messenger still stood at attention amid the chaos of renovation debris that currently littered the castle's main salon, feathered hat in hand, along with another large scroll. He'd insisted on staying until everyone in the household had read and understood the proclamation.

"Shaw!" Zara called to her husband, who was busy with dinner in the kitchen. "You must come and see this, my lord!"

Walker strolled in, wiping his hands on a towel. "You've

really got to stop calling me that," he said, rolling his eyes. "At least when we're not in bed."

She winked at the messenger. Walker hadn't quite gotten used to his new title yet, but he had found some interesting uses for it. "Now, darling, behave," she said, handing him the parchment scroll. "And read."

The messenger bowed. "Lord Shaw. The king and queen send their greetings."

"What's this all about?" He scanned the thick parchment in his hand, said, "Wow," and read it again, more carefully. Then he broke out in a grin and gave Zara a big hug, lifting her off her feet. "Way to go, baby. You did it! Congratulations."

She hugged him back and laughed, thinking what a difference a few months made. "I'd better call father at once and tell him I plan to abdicate in favor of remaining a baron's wife."

"Can you do that?" She sent him a wry look, which he mirrored back at her. "Never mind. You can do anything you set your mind to."

"Thank you, darling." She accepted a kiss.

"Lady Zara, Lord Shaw," the messenger said, offering her the other scroll he'd been holding. "This was also sent to you by the king and queen." Then he bowed again. "My lady, my lord, I'll take my leave."

"Now I am curious," she said, and unrolled the parchment eagerly. As she began to read, her jaw dropped.

"Good God."

Declaring His Majesty's Pleasure concerning the Dispensation of the Duchy of Perthegon and its Entailments

We do hereby, by and with the advice of Our Privy Council, declare that Lady Zara, daughter of the Marquis and Marchioness of Daneby and wife of Lord

Shaw, for special service to her King and the people of Silvershire, shall inherit the Duchy of Perthegon along with all its properties and privileges, including such leases and entailments as exist upon it, which she shall immediately exercise authority over.

Our Will and Pleasure further is that Lady Zara, renouncing any other Titles of Nobility, shall henceforth be known to all as Zara, Duchess of Perthegon.

Given at Our Court at Silverton Royal Palace, this twenty-first day of October, in the year of Our Lord, two thousand and six, and in the first year of Our Reign.

God Save the King and the People

Zara was speechless. Unable to utter a single word.

"What the hell…" Walker took the scroll and read it three times, looking as astonished as she felt.

Just two months ago, they'd gone through an incredible ceremony where Walker's knighthood had been bestowed, complete with sword taps on the shoulder and all the pomp befitting the honor. Then there'd been their wedding, held in the palace gardens with King Weston presiding in his final formal act as king. Finally, there'd been the coronation itself, where they'd been among the honored guests of the crown.

Her life had been a literal fairy tale for the past three months.

Even the fickle press had changed their tune and done a complete turnaround on Walker. The *Quiz* had dubbed Walker "Lord Shaw, the Cinderella Knight," making him into the darling of all of Silvershire because of his bravery in saving the king's life. And also for his decision to turn a whole wing of Castle Perth into a state-of-the-art facility for treating Alzheimers and dementia in the elderly, with the financial support of the retired king.

And now this! Duchess of Perthegon!

Walker beamed at her, his gaze full of love and his lips curved in an adoring smile. "I'm so proud of you, Zara. No one deserves this honor more than you."

She shook her head and launched herself into his arms. "My God, Walker, It's all a dream, isn't it? I know I'm going to wake up tomorrow and it'll all be a dream. Like Alice in Wonderland."

He laughed with her, stroking his fingers through her hair. "Now you know how *I've* been feeling for the past three months. Like I've fallen down some incredible rabbit hole into a crazy land where all your dreams come true."

"Just promise me one thing," she said, brushing his darling face with her fingertips…his cheek, his mouth, his square jaw. Amazed that he was real. Amazed that he was really hers.

"What's that, sugar?"

She kissed him tenderly on his smiling lips. "When I wake up from this extraordinary dream, please be there with me."

His smile turned gentle, his eyes shining with more love than she'd ever known possible. "Count on it, baby," he said, kissing her back. "Who needs dreams when we have each other?"

* * * * *

MORE THAN
A MISSION

BY
CARIDAD PIÑEIRO

Caridad Piñeiro attended Villanova University on a Presidential Scholarship and earned her Juris Doctor from St. John's University. Caridad is the first female partner of an Intellectual Property firm in Manhattan. Caridad is a multipublished and award-winning author whose love of writing developed when her fifth grade teacher assigned a project—to write a book for a class lending library. She has been hooked ever since. When not writing, Caridad is a wife, mom and attorney! You can contact Caridad by visiting www.caridad.com.

To my mother-in-law, Mary Scordato, who opened
her heart to me and has always been there when
I needed her! I couldn't ask for a more
loving and wonderful mother-in-law.

Chapter 1

She's to be taken alive, Aidan Spaulding reminded himself as he walked the streets of Leonia, trying to become familiar with the lay of the land before heading to his latest assignment—identifying the killer of Prince Reginald, the man who would have been king of Silvershire.

Corbett Lazlo, Aidan's boss, had received information that a world-renowned female assassin was behind the killing. The Sparrow, as she was known, was believed to have poisoned the prince. Aidan was to confirm that and try to capture the elusive gun for hire.

Aidan had more personal reasons for wanting the Sparrow caught. Two years earlier, he and his best friend, Mitchell Lama, had been on the trail of a suspected terrorist as part of another Lazlo Group detail. They had been about to close in on their suspect, unaware that the man they were seeking was also being sought by the Sparrow.

Mitch and he had split up in the narrow and twisting alleyways of Rome's Trastevere section, communicating via walkie-talkie as they attempted to corner their man.

When the walkie-talkie in his hand had gone dead, Aidan had realized his friend was in trouble. After years in the military together, Mitch knew better than to go incommunicado without signaling his partner. The nature of the mission had changed suddenly as Aidan raced through the alleyways, now trying to locate Mitch. He had finally found the friend who was almost like a brother sprawled on the ancient cobblestones of a back alley.

Mitch had been nearly gutted and was barely alive. Somehow, though, his friend had managed one last word before he died in Aidan's arms—*Sparrow.*

He had been looking for her ever since, intent on avenging Mitch's death. Now here she was, being handed to him on a silver platter. The only problem was, he could do nothing about it until after the Lazlo Group had all the answers it needed regarding Prince Reginald's murder. But after that…

Nothing would keep him from giving the Sparrow just what she deserved.

The young woman they suspected of being the Sparrow— Elizabeth Moore, aka Elizabeth Cavanaugh—ran a restaurant in this modest seaside town. The restaurant—apparently a cover for her real occupation—had become quite well-known for its seafood and Silvershire-inspired cuisine.

He had seen the help wanted sign go up late yesterday morning in her restaurant's front window, so it was the perfect time to see about applying for the bartending position.

Pulling his PDA off his belt as he approached the Sparrow's restaurant, he used the walkie-talkie adapter he had built into the unit to cue Lucia, the Lazlo group's top computer specialist, to see if she was picking up the signal from the earpiece he was wearing.

"Mixmaster to Red Rover. Come in Red Rover. I'm about to go in."

Lucia's chuckle crackled across the airwaves a moment

before she said, "Mixmaster… Do we really have to do this stupid name thing?"

Aidan smiled. Lucia was never one for clandestine shenanigans. Shutting off his walkie-talkie, he replied, "No problema, Lucia. Can you hear me?"

"Loud and clear, Blender Boy," she responded.

He immediately asked, "Kir Royale?"

There was a barely noticeable pause before Lucia said, "One part creme de cassis to five parts champagne."

Satisfied that the wire was working, he started walking toward the restaurant and said, "Let's get this show on the road."

The sun was warm on her back as she tended the garden at the front of the restaurant. Wildly spreading nasturtiums lapped over onto the large granite slabs that made up the patio where guests shared drinks while they waited for a table inside the ivy-covered stone building that housed her restaurant.

Carefully she deadheaded older blossoms and picked others for inclusion in one of the seasonal salads she was offering on this week's menu. She was just about finished when she heard a footfall behind her. A man walked through the opening of the low stone wall that separated her property from the main road. A very attractive man.

Slipping the basket holding her gatherings onto her arm, she strolled toward him, easing off her gardening gloves as she did so.

"May I help you?" Elizabeth asked as she met him by the path leading to the restaurant. She realized she had to look up slightly to meet his gaze. He was about half a foot taller than her with a lean athletic build that accentuated the long lines of his body.

He motioned to her front window with one hand and replied, "I noticed the sign. I'm here to apply for the bartender's position."

She examined him more carefully, from the faded and

sinfully tight jeans to his logo T-shirt and black leather jacket. He looked more like a tourist on vacation than someone interested in permanent employment. "I'm sorry. I didn't quite catch your name."

He held out his hand with a brisk, almost military snap. "Aidan Rawlings. Are you the owner?"

With a quick glance at her hand to make sure it wasn't too dirty from her gardening, she shook his hand and said, "Elizabeth Moore. Chief cook and bottle washer. Literally."

He smiled with teeth too white and too perfect for normal humans. They seemed apropos with his shaggy and sunstreaked blond hair and eyes so blue she couldn't believe he wasn't wearing colored contacts. His smile broadened as he noticed her perusal of him and that she was still busily shaking his hand.

Yanking it away, she wiped her hand down on the gardening apron she wore, realizing her palm had gotten sweaty from the brief contact. "I'm sorry. You said you were here for the bartender's job?"

He nodded and tucked his hands into his jeans pockets. Or maybe it was better to say, tucked the tips of his fingers into those pockets, since the jeans were so tight they didn't really leave a lot of room for anything else besides his long lean legs and...

She stopped herself from proceeding with the perusal.

"Is the job still available?" He rocked back and forth on his heels as he asked, apparently growing uncomfortable, but then again, so was she. Not much of a surprise considering she generally avoided strangers, in particular, men like this one.

Handsome, danger-to-your-common-sense kind of men.

"Do you have experience?" After she asked, she began to walk toward the door of the restaurant and he followed beside her, keeping his paces small to accommodate her shorter legs.

"I've worked in a number of bars," he replied with a careless shrug.

She supposed that he had, but not as a bartender. There was something about him. Something in the way he moved and in the slight swagger that screamed Bad Boy. She could picture him as either a bouncer—he had an air that said he could take care of himself—or an exotic dancer, but not a bartender.

As she reached the door, she faced him. "I'm sorry, Mr....Rawlings was it?"

"How about you just call me Aidan?" he said with a practiced smile that had probably swept more than one woman off her feet. Aidan, however, was going to get a swift lesson in the art of Just Say No!

"I appreciate you coming by, but the position—"

"Is still available, right?"

She responded to his statement with a subtle drop of her head as if she didn't want to acknowledge it. "Quite frankly, my restaurant isn't the kind of place for a Tom Cruise *Cocktail* redux."

He actually jerked back as if slapped and a stain of color came to his sharply defined cheeks. "Excuse me?"

"I just don't think you're the right type." And he definitely was not used to being turned down by a woman.

Surprise appeared once more on his face, followed by what she would possibly call admiration until he carefully schooled his expression.

"And what type are you looking for exactly?" he asked and placed his hands on his hips.

"Someone more...professional. This is a four-star restaurant and my patrons expect—"

"Uptight and pompous? Fair enough." With that, he turned and walked away, but she couldn't help but notice just how nice a derriere he had. Not that it would change her mind.

She needed someone who wouldn't cause trouble and, although pleasant to look at, Aidan Rawlings was trouble with a capital *T*.

Chapter 2

"Crash and burn."

Lucia's words cut rudely across the airways and into the earpiece as he hurried from the Sparrow's restaurant. He was at the edge of the property when something compelled him to look back.

She was standing at the door, still watching him, and when their gazes collided from across the distance, a becoming blush stained her cheeks before she escaped into the building.

Aidan smiled. Good. The lady was not as unaffected as she let on.

"Shut up, Cordez," he whispered beneath his breath.

"All bad moody are we? What do you plan on doing now?" Lucia asked while he continued on to the hotel at which the team was staying, only a few blocks from the restaurant.

"If she wants someone a little more professional, that's what she'll get."

He was already at the door of the hotel when Lucia quipped, "That may take a lot of work."

He ignored her dig and headed up to their suite. Inside, Lucia was busily working on her laptop.

Not that they'd needed it today, Aidan thought as he walked over and stood behind her, watching as she entered a date onto a list she was compiling.

"What's that?" he said and motioned to the screen.

Lucia looked up over her shoulder. "Corbett's contacts—"

"So it's Corbett now is it?" he teased, well aware that Lucia had a crush on the mysterious head of their group.

"His contact at MI6 provided a list of kills that they attribute to the Sparrow. That's in this column." She pointed to one list and Aidan scrutinized the schedule, which comprised nearly a dozen incidents in the last six years. The Sparrow had been busy. There was just one glaring error.

"Mitch's name is not on the list."

Concern flashed across Lucia's face a moment before she said, "MI6 can't connect Mitch to the Sparrow."

"Well, they're wrong. I know what Mitch said to me." He sat on the edge of the desk and crossed his arms.

Lucia laid a hand on his forearm as if to comfort him. "Maybe Mitch was trying to tell you something else about her."

He thought about it, but what kinds of things did a dying man think important enough to say? In his book, first was the name of his killer. "The Sparrow did it. End of discussion."

Seeing that he had gotten his defenses up, Lucia said nothing else, but instead began entering another set of dates onto the list. A number of the dates and locations matched those for the Sparrow's kills. "What are you doing now?"

"More than you are, clearly," she teased, but then added, "Whoever spilled the beans to Corbett about Elizabeth being the Sparrow wasn't completely sure. So I did a search to see where she might have gone. Contests, expos, vacations and…"

Fingers tapping away on the computer keys, she finished her entries. Beside a number of the dates that had already been there courtesy of MI6, there were now four entries for Chef Elizabeth Moore that matched.

"Seems like we have a pretty good candidate for the Sparrow," he said.

"It appears that way. There's just too much coincidence, including this weekend here." Lucia motioned to one entry on her list. "She was at a cooking expo in the town next to the prince's estate. He was found dead that weekend."

"Poisoned, which seems to be a favorite method for our assassin." Which could be why MI6 hadn't listed Mitch, although some of the Sparrow's other kills had been the plain old get-up-close-and-kill-them type. Which made him wonder just what motivated her. Sticking a knife in someone... Seeing that look of surprise fade to a lifeless stare...

He knew it well, having had to kill more than once on his assignments as an army Ranger. It wasn't easy even if you told yourself that you had to do it. That it was either you and your men, or the man whose life you had just taken. But that look never left you. Not even when you slept.

Like the final expression on Mitch's face. One of surprise and possibly even regret. For months after Mitch's death, that image had chased him through his nightmares.

"Aidan?" Lucia asked, apparently sensing that she had lost him.

"I'm going to review the Elizabeth Moore file. Do you think you could give me a copy of that when you're done? And can you add Mitch to the list and see if she was in Rome then?"

"You got it."

He went to his room, slipped out the earpiece and placed it on a mahogany desk that held an assortment of other electronic gadgets he had designed. Grabbing the file on Elizabeth Moore once more, he plopped down onto the bed and began to review the facts.

Elizabeth was an only child whose parents had been local

merchants. When she was fourteen, her parents had been found murdered in their fish shop. The murder had never been solved. The file hinted at possible involvement by members of the Royal Family's ministers to quash parts of the investigation.

He paused, wondering if that was what had set the Sparrow on the path she had chosen? He was still lucky enough to have his parents and couldn't imagine what it might have been like to lose them at such a young age, especially to an act of violence, and then find justice denied.

The photo of the Sparrow stared at him from the left side of the file. No hint of the wide and engaging smile he had seen earlier today. The photo had apparently been taken in Prague when an MI6 operative on another mission had noticed her standing in a square. The serious-looking young woman had fit the description of the Sparrow that MI6 had gleaned over years of investigations. With the renowned assassin suspected of being in town, the operative had decided to take the picture just in case.

It might not even be her, he thought. There must be millions of women who matched the general description—five foot six, brown hair, brown eyes and a slim build.

Not that he would have called her hair just brown. As she had stood in the sun, he'd noticed the vibrant melange of reds, browns and even hints of blond. And her eyes—they had been more like the color of a rich sherry. As for the slim build, definitely slender but with curves in all the right places.

Losin' it, he chastised himself. The lady might be attractive, but that did nothing to change the fact that she was suspected of killing nearly a dozen people. Including Mitch.

It was up to him to get close to her, to confirm whether or not she was the Sparrow and whether she had murdered King Weston's heir, and then she could be punished for her crimes.

Which meant he had to attempt yet again to get her to hire him for the bartending position that was now vacant since Corbett Lazlo had arranged for a friend in London to hire away Elizabeth's bartender.

Lazlo's connections were part of what made the Lazlo Group tops in what they did—handling delicate and often-times dangerous investigations, like this one involving Prince Reginald's murder.

Pampered and spoiled royals like Prince Reginald held little appeal for Aidan. From what he had read in the dossier provided to him, Prince Reginald had been a selfish dilettante who probably would have made a hell of a bad leader for the centuries-old island kingdom.

Not that he involved himself in politics, since his nomadic life rarely gave him reason to grow attached to any particular place, and he had no interest in what happened in this tiny little town. At least, not in anything that wasn't related to this mission.

As for the Sparrow, he thought, she wanted professional? He would give it to her.

The bartending part was under control thanks to the earpiece and the program he had loaded on his and Lucia's PDAs. He'd resorted to that after his best attempts at memo-rizing an assortment of drink recipes had failed. He was a magna cum laude grad of MIT in a number of majors, none of which included Mixology 101.

But now he had to deal with his other dilemma—getting the Sparrow to hire him. He walked to the closet. Inside were an assortment of jeans, but also a few suits. He wasn't normally a suit-and-tie kind of guy. In some ways, he found them too much like the uniform he'd had to wear for so many years in the military. Now that he was in the private sector, he preferred his clothes to be casual. It suited his rebellious nature better.

In fact, the last time he had worn a suit had been to Mitch's funeral two years ago. It was one of the suits in the closet. Somehow apropos, he thought, as he reached for it and pulled it out. The suit was dark charcoal-gray and designer—Hel-mut Lang. Mitch, who had always insisted that his clothes and women be top-drawer, had forced him to buy it, claiming that his friend was never going to meet the right kind of woman if he looked like a Hell's Angels reject or a derelict surf dude.

Aidan had to admit the suit was gorgeous. Maybe it was just what the Sparrow had had in mind when she'd said that her type was someone more professional.

Watch out, Sparrow, 'cause here I come.

Elizabeth was running late. After doing all her shopping and advising her sous chef and assistants as to what to prep for inclusion in that night's dinner specials, she'd decided to tackle the slightly overgrown flowerbeds in the back of the restaurant during her afternoon break. In this backyard garden, which faced the shore, she had created an area for alfresco dining and dancing beneath the stars.

She was rounding the corner of the building on the way to the front door when she smacked into someone heading toward the back patio. Hard hands grabbed hold of her to keep her from falling. "I'm sorry," she said, noticing not just the strength in the hands clutching her, but the fine fabric of the suit jacket as she grabbed tight.

She finally looked up and the familiar blue of his eyes gazed down at her, nearly laughing. "No, *I'm* sorry. Your sous chef said you were out back."

He released her and took a step away, which allowed her to get a complete picture of his total transformation. A suit the color of deep slate—definitely expensive—accented his lean muscular build and broad shoulders. His shirt was a pale gray and he was wearing a silk tie that had a stylish Keith Haring kind of pattern in maroon on a dark blue-gray background. His shaggy hair was brushed off his face, the longish strands secured somehow, exposing the sharp lines of his cheeks and jaw.

He cleaned up well, she thought, although a part of her was remembering yesterday's bad-boy look and regretting the change.

"Mr. Rawlings," she said with a polite nod of her head. "I must confess that I wasn't expecting to see you again."

He offered his arm and she looped hers around his, slightly

surprised by the gallant gesture. She walked with him around the side of the building and to the front door.

"I'm not a man who's easily dissuaded, Ms. Moore," he said as they stopped at the entrance to the restaurant.

"And what if I told you the position had been filled?" she asked with an upward arch of her brow.

"A gentleman such as myself wouldn't dare call a lady a liar, but…" He pointed to the help wanted sign that was still posted in the front window.

Heat rose to her cheeks, much as it had yesterday when he had caught her appreciating his backside. Definitely not good. The last thing she needed around here was someone who would be distracting her from all that she had to do. "Mr. Rawlings—"

He stepped to stand in front of her, held out his arms and said, "You wanted professional. So here I am."

"I did say that, only—"

"I know my way around a bar," he jumped in.

"I suspected as much, but—"

"What have you got to lose?" he interrupted yet again.

Elizabeth gripped the handle of her gathering basket tightly and examined him once more. Dressed like this, she could definitely see him preparing drinks for her patrons. Heck, he was dressed nicely enough to be one of her patrons. But could he mix a mean cocktail?

"A martini," she said out loud.

"Excuse me?" he asked, clearly confused.

"How do you make a martini?" she clarified and nervously swung the basket back and forth a bit, hoping for failure on his part.

He raised one sunbleached eyebrow as if to say, Aw, come on. Try something harder. Then he rattled off, "One and a half ounces of gin. Dash of dry vermouth." He paused, smiled and said, "Shaken, not stirred."

She had to chuckle at his imitation of Sean Connery because it was dead-on. "Too easy. How about a…" She hesitated, trying to think of one of the more unusual drinks with which she was familiar. "A B-52," she finally said and watched him squirm, but not for long.

"The drink, right, and not the alternative band from Athens, Georgia?"

Smiling, she confirmed, "Right. The drink."

"One ounce each of Bailey's Irish Cream, Kahlua and Grand Marnier." He picked up his hands, mimicked the shaking, and she got the rest of the recipe. Not to mention getting the very appealing way the man could move his hips.

Fresh heat came to her face. She gave it one last try to attempt to convince herself it was insane to consider him for the job. "You'll never get this one—Mexican Sunset."

He grinned. It was an appealing little-boy kind of grin. A gotcha grin. "Too easy. Bottle of beer, preferably Corona, garnished with a slice of lime and less a sip so you can add the sloe gin. I'm assuming the sloe gin is homemade. I understand there's a great abundance after the fall harvest of the local blackthorn bushes."

He knew his stuff. She had to give him that. "You don't strike me as the type that will stay for long," she said, firing the last salvo she had held in reserve.

He hesitated since she had scored a direct hit and the grin ran away from his face as he grew serious. "You're right. Dad was an army man so I'm used to a wandering kind of life."

"I know the type," she interjected, thinking of her sister Dani and all her travels.

"So you understand, then. But the way I see it, you need a bartender and I'm here. Not going anywhere for a while and I promise that when I do decide to go, because it *will* happen, that I'll give you plenty of time to find someone else before I run."

Promises. She knew just how often they got broken. But he had a point—she needed a bartender. The past few nights had been horrendous as she tried to cook while at the same time helping out the wait staff with the drinks. "It doesn't pay much, but tips are generally good. If you get here by five, dinner's included. You can start tomorrow."

He smiled and held out his hand to seal the deal. She hesitated before she shook it, and he said, "To new adventures."

"I'm not the adventurous type, Mr. Rawlings," she replied, hoping to make it clear that she had no interest in anything he might propose.

His grin broadened. "Aidan, please. And, Ms. Moore—"

"Elizabeth. All my employees call me Elizabeth," she corrected and pulled her hand from his since it was starting to feel rather warm. Again.

"Elizabeth," he said and took a step toward her. "I think it's going to be quite an experience working together."

She suspected he was right. "See you at five, Aidan. And while the suit is…nice, a white shirt and dark slacks will do."

With that, she turned and walked into the building.

"Score one for the Mixmaster," Aidan heard in the earpiece as he headed for the street.

"Told you she couldn't resist my charm," he replied and hurried back to the hotel, eager now that it looked like the investigation might finally get under way.

"And here I thought it was those drink recipes I was feeding you, only… How did you know about the sloe gin?" Lucia asked.

"You never go into unknown territory without doing your research, Cordez. So I did a little fact-gathering on this town. Did you know that…" As he walked, he recited the details that he remembered, being careful not to be noticed whenever he walked by someone.

He was back at the hotel within ten minutes and found that besides Lucia, Walker Shaw, the Lazlo group's psychiatrist, waited for him in the suite, as well. "What brings you here?" he asked and patted the other man on the back in greeting.

"Snazzy," Walker said as he perused Aidan's clothing.

Aidan held out his hands. "The lady fell for it."

"Well, that's good. At least there's some progress going on here." The frustration was apparent in Walker's demeanor. "We haven't been able to do anything yet with the information Zara and I found. So for now, we're relying on whatever details the two of you manage to get."

"Not too much pressure," Lucia quipped and handed Walker a piece of paper.

It was a copy of the list she had provided to Aidan yesterday. Walker examined it and then looked up at him. "Seems like we're on the right track. It's just too much coincidence that Elizabeth Moore turns up in a lot of the same spots as the Sparrow."

"Including Rome," Lucia added nervously, shooting a half glance at Aidan after she said it.

"What?" He ripped the list from Walker's hands and quickly read until he came to the date and location of Mitch's death. Beside it was a new entry indicating that Elizabeth had been in Rome as part of a contingent for the Silvershire Tourist Board.

"When did you find this out?" He jabbed the air in Lucia's direction with the paper.

"Late last night."

"What?" he repeated, his voice a little louder than before. "Why didn't you say something *before* I went to see her?"

Lucia shook her head. "Duh. I didn't think it would accomplish anything besides getting you angry."

"Angry? You're right that I'm angry. You're part of *my* team and you withheld vital information," he nearly screamed at her.

"Because you're totally capable of compartmentalizing your emotions to maintain neutrality about this job?" Walker said facetiously. He, more than any of them, knew how hard Mitch's death had been on Aidan, who blamed himself for making the decision that the two of them should split up. He had been as responsible for Mitch's death as the Sparrow.

"Cut the psychobabble bullshit, Walker. I understand the nature of the assignment."

"Which is to find Prince Reginald's killer. Period." The other man's tone brooked no disagreement.

Aidan knew that on one level, Walker was right. They had been hired to identify Prince Reginald's murderer, not Mitch's. Taking a deep breath and relaxing his hands—he hadn't even realized he'd made them into tight fists—he let his anger flow out of him. Anger was a distraction. There was no room for distractions with a killer as savvy as the Sparrow.

"I understand and I'm sorry. It's just tough at times, but…I've only failed once at an assignment." He didn't need to mention that Mitch had died as a result of that failure. "I won't fail this time."

Walker stood and laid a hand on Aidan's shoulder. "We all understand, Aidan. And we're here for you."

"Together we will figure this out," Aidan reassured Walker and Lucia, but then excused himself.

Tomorrow he started working for the Sparrow. He had to be alert and ready to handle any kind of situation that presented itself. Which meant that he needed to do some additional research, and prepare a few gadgets that would allow him to keep a close watch on Elizabeth Moore.

He also needed to get a better sense of the town. With that in mind, he quickly reviewed a map of the area that had been included in his dossier and then headed out again.

Leaving the hotel, he walked briskly to the furthest edge of the town where the docks were located. He stepped from the main street onto the large and very old granite slabs that led to the docks. Although it was late in the day, fisherman were hauling boxes and bushels with their catches onto the docks to be transported to the nearby fish market.

The scene reminded him of one of the seaside towns he had lived in briefly before his father's army career had demanded they move somewhere else. Although he didn't consider himself a settling-down kind of guy, it occurred to him that if he ever did decide to let some moss grow under his feet, it might be in a town like this one.

Mitch and he had always loved to go surfing, sailing or fishing whenever their assignments gave them a break. His best friend who was dead. Murdered by the woman who had hired him earlier that morning.

With that thought in mind, Aidan hastened his pace, familiarizing himself with the area around the Sparrow's restaurant. He noticed the clean and tidy homes along the streets, a combination of older stone buildings and slightly more modern stucco-and-wood edifices.

Nearing the edge of the village, which was not all that far from the wharf, mom-and-pop-type stores appeared here and there, interspersed with the residences. Eventually, he was within sight of the restaurant once more.

He couldn't help but admire the carefully kept gardens and manicured lawns surrounding the central building. As he slowly strolled past, he noticed a cottage way in the back, close to the shore. It was similar in style to the restaurant building, made of stone with a slate roof, but with two stories. Colorful blossoms graced the front of the cottage while in back, tall sea grasses waved with the ocean breeze.

If he recalled correctly from his files, the cottage was the Sparrow's home. Her nest.

In time, he would get in there and locate the information he needed. He was sure about that. He would do whatever he had to in order to complete this mission since it was more than a mission to him. It was long-denied payback for his friend's death.

He only hoped that once the mission was completed, he would finally have the peace of mind that had eluded him for the past two years.

With that thought in mind, he hurried back to the hotel to prepare for his first day of work for the Sparrow.

Chapter 3

The early-morning hours at the markets were the ones Elizabeth liked the best. She enjoyed investigating the stalls to search out ingredients for something new and playfully haggling with the vendors over the prices. As she walked past one merchant or another, they shouted their greetings. Most of them had known her since she was a child.

Sometimes, if she finished with the shopping early enough, she would walk down to the water's edge and take the long way back home. If the tide was just right, she could skirt the edges of the tidal pools lingering along the shore and find what the ocean had left behind. Small crabs, seashells and even some lobsters every now and then.

From the shore just past her cottage, she could see the mile or more to where fisherman harvested mussels from the pilings of an ancient stone bridge. The Romans had built the bridge centuries earlier to join Leonia to the smaller seaside town of Tiberia across the narrowest part of the harbor. She served those fresh mussels every day in a garlic-and-white-wine-infused broth. Her parents used to sell them in the fish shop they had owned at the time of their deaths.

She could understand why her sister, Dani, found it so hard to be in Leonia. Everywhere she went there were reminders of their parents.

Elizabeth continued walking along the shore, the bag filled with her purchases dragging at her arm. Memories dragging at her heart as she recalled her mother, father and Dani strolling together along the beach. At times, she felt totally alone with all of them gone. Forcing such thoughts away on what had started out as a delightful day, she trudged onward, trying to enjoy the warmth of the sun and the caress of an ocean breeze sweeping along the coast.

At the beach behind her cottage, she detoured up a rocky path until she was at the edge of the back patio to the restaurant. She paused but a moment to appreciate all that she had built with her hard work. Then she was striding across the yard and to a side door by the vegetable garden. As she neared the entrance, the sounds of activity welcomed her. Walking into the kitchen, she greeted Natalie, her friend and sous chef, who inclined her head in the direction of the front of the restaurant. "Someone's up there for you. Says he's the new bartender."

Elizabeth placed her bag on a prep table and shook a cramp out of one arm. "If you could unpack, I'll see what he needs."

Elizabeth walked to the bar tucked into a far corner at the front of the restaurant. The driving rhythm of the B-52s' "Love Shack" greeted her—Aidan had a boombox on the polished surface of the mahogany bar and was rocking along, his arms and hips moving to the beat. She couldn't help admiring his grace and the sexy shift of his body to the music. It reminded her of her earlier observation that exotic dancer might well have been his previous employment.

When he realized he had been caught in mid–hip grind, he stopped dead. "In honor of the day you hired me," he explained, but quickly added, "It's not too loud, is it?" Hot color rode on his defined cheeks as he crammed his finger-tips into those tight jeans' pockets and shot her an embarrassed grin.

"Not at all. It's just a little different from our usual musical fare," she said and motioned to the sound system tucked onto a low shelf behind the bar.

With a quick look at the stereo, Aidan shrugged. "Didn't want to mess with anything until I was familiar with things. It's okay that I came early to get acquainted, right?"

Getting acquainted, huh? Elizabeth told herself not to read too much into his choice of words. He was, after all, someone who would eventually leave, and getting acquainted with him could cause nothing but problems. "Feel free to familiarize yourself with the liquor stock and other supplies. The music selection is generally a bit more sedate. When you're ready, I'll show you the wine cellar."

Great, Aidan thought. A wine cellar meant another list with which he would have to deal. In his ear, Lucia advised, "I'm on it. Make sure to bring home copies of the wine list and menu."

"I'll let you know when I'm ready for the wines," he said to Elizabeth, and then continued. "In the meantime, I'll see if we're low on anything." After he finished, he examined Elizabeth's face, trying to gauge whether she had overheard Lucia. There was nothing there but interest of a different kind.

Or at least that's what his guy radar was telling him. He hoped it wasn't wrong because it might make the task of getting close to the Sparrow that much easier, although he was a little disconcerted about how someone supposedly as elusive as the Sparrow was apparently so easy to read.

Unless she's a very good actress and is stringing you along?

"Thanks," she replied and pointed with one finger to the back of the restaurant. He noticed then that she wore just clear polish on short, blunt-cut nails. No rings or jewelry of any kind. The hands of someone who used their hands to earn a living. Either chef or assassin.

She continued. "I'll be in the kitchen. If you need limes, cream or anything else, it's in the large fridges. Jeremy, the old bartender, would keep some supplies handy in the fridge beneath the bar."

"Got it," he replied with a quick salute and his most engaging smile as a way to see if his earlier read had been wrong.

Elizabeth delayed briefly, seemingly unsure of whether to go or stay. Then with a shy wavering smile, she bolted from the bar and to the kitchen.

Aidan waited until he was sure she was gone and not returning, and then went to work.

From a well-worn knapsack he had tucked beneath the bar, he pulled out what looked like four fat sewing needles and slipped them into the back pocket of his jeans. Stepping from behind the bar, he scoped out where he could hide one of them, but still get a clear shot from the fiberoptic cameras built into the ends of the thick needles.

He settled on easing one into the stopper on a commemorative liquor flask sitting on the top shelf behind the bar. The empty flask was obviously kept for decoration and would not be moved often. That camera should give Lucia a clear shot of anyone in the anterior part of the building.

"Are you reading this signal?" he said softly and when Lucia confirmed the view was good, he moved to the other side of the dining room. On an end table tucked into a corner, a candlestick, flower basket and brass lamp in keeping with the restaurant's traditional-style décor had been placed.

Dark woods and floral wallpaper graced the walls of the room. Landscapes of the Silvershire countryside were scattered here and there, and at one end of the room, a large stone fireplace held logs ready to be lit if the weather called for it. The curtains at the windows were sheer, offering gorgeous views of the gardens and the shore beyond.

The flowers on the end table were fresh and sure to be discarded shortly and while the candle was newer, it, too, would be subject to regular handling and replacement. He settled on working the camera into the top edge of the ivory-colored lampshade, focusing it on the dining area.

Lucia confirmed that the signal was clear, and, satisfied with what he'd done, Aidan paused for a moment to consider how to approach bugging the kitchen. That area was busier than most and usually occupied. Plus, he really had little cause to go in there, except for those supplies Elizabeth had mentioned earlier. Deciding to use that as an excuse to inspect the area, he hurried back to the bar and was thankful that the fridge Elizabeth had mentioned was empty of anything other than an old-fashioned glass bottle of cream.

Quickly striding to the kitchen, he pushed through the door to find Elizabeth and another young woman standing before a table, glumly looking down at something.

"It's okay, Natalie. It just takes practice," Elizabeth said, laid a hand on the other woman's shoulders and gave a comforting pat.

He moved behind them and with his greater height, peered over their shoulders to examine the dish sitting before them. Whatever it had once been, now it was a pile of stuff colored a muddy shade of brown. Blackened edges tenaciously gripped the sides of a white cooking dish. The center had sunk down, creating a network of cracks in the surface that revealed something gooey and unappealing beneath. "What is that?"

With a sniff and a quavery voice, Natalie replied, "My final exam."

"Oh."

"It's a chocolate soufflé," Elizabeth corrected with a glare over her shoulder and once again patted Natalie's back in a reassuring gesture. "We'll work through it together, Nat. By tomorrow, you'll be an expert and ready for the test."

Natalie sniffed one last time as she picked up the dish with oven-mitted hands. "Let me dispose of this mess."

When she walked away, Elizabeth faced him, clearly annoyed. "She's just learning," she explained, defending the younger woman.

Aidan held up his hands to ward off further comment. "I didn't mean anything by it. I just came for some supplies."

Elizabeth accepted his apology and gracefully motioned with her hands to the spacious and orderly kitchen. "Well while you're here, I may as well lay out the rules for this area. One—don't annoy the chefs and two—don't touch the chefs' knives. You've already broken rule one."

Great. He'd pissed her off. As for her knives... "Your knives being—"

She slipped past him to go to one of the work tables. On its surface was a cylindrical leather pouch tied with a ribbon of leather. He followed Elizabeth and watched as she nimbly undid the tie, grabbed one side of the pouch and with a quick toss, unfurled it to reveal a collection of about a dozen different blades. "*My* knives," she said and held her hand out to emphasize the point.

Before he could say anything else, she whipped one large knife from its holder and with a batonlike twirl of the handle through her fingers, she then slipped the blade into a holder on the belt riding low on her hips. A practiced move done with ease. Too much ease, he thought, replaying in his mind how quickly she had taken the knife—one that was easily about eight inches long—and gracefully maneuvered it onto her belt.

Had she gutted Mitch with as much skill?

He bit back his anger and said, "Neat trick. Where did you learn it?" Even as he said that, he was reaching for another knife, but she slapped his hand away.

"Remember— Don't touch the knives. As for where—in cooking school," she explained, one hand resting on the table near the pouch, the other just above the knife at her belt. Her hip was cocked to one side, like a gunslinger ready to draw. He wondered if she was getting ready to use the knife on him. If he had pushed too far.

When he met her gaze—that sherry-colored, drown-in-me gaze—he realized she was almost testing him. Seeing if he'd follow the rules she'd laid down, as if thinking he wouldn't or that maybe he was the kind of guy who liked to touch—and not just knives. Her jaw was set in a determined little jut, confirming his read wasn't all that wrong. "I get it, Elizabeth. Don't touch."

Elizabeth nodded and realized that Aidan had gotten the dual message in her words. It both pleased and disappointed, but she told herself not to be disappointed since Aidan was just passing through.

"Glad you get it. It will keep things simpler. Do you want to see where the wines are kept?" She motioned to an old wooden door, made from a few hand-hewn planks, at the far side of the kitchen.

He gave her the go-ahead curtly. "May as well get it over with. I can collect my supplies later."

Elizabeth walked to the door, which led down into the cellar, Aidan close behind her. She opened it, flipped a switch on the wall, and then went down the flight of stairs to a large space that ran beneath the entire restaurant. As she reached the bottom step, she pointed to the far wall where a series of racks held her collection of wines. "We keep the stock first by color and then by region. Whites closest to the floor where it's cooler. Reds along the top."

She continued walking, too conscious of Aidan behind her, but as they moved to the racks, it wasn't the wine that seemed to get his attention.

"What's that?" he asked and as she turned to look at him, she realized he was looking at the far side of the cellar, where there was a home gym, boxing bag, mat, lockers and a safe.

"A gym. You're welcome to use it during the hours the restaurant isn't serving meals. The equipment is too noisy otherwise."

A hard look came to his face, but he schooled it and gestured with his hand to the racks of wine. "Anything I can't touch down here?"

Elizabeth shook her head. "While all the wines are excellent vintages, they're generally moderately priced. No sense gouging the customers."

He walked to one of the racks, ran a finger along the bottles as he seemingly inspected the labels. He moved from one rack to the next in that fashion, perusing them intently.

She walked to stand by the end of one rack and clarified, "Italians and local wines are in the first two racks, Californian in the middle, some Australian, Chilean and French in the final section."

Pausing by the rack of Italian vintages and removing one bottle for a closer inspection, he said, "How do you choose which wines you'll carry?"

Elizabeth joined him, took the bottle from his hands and examined the label. With a nonchalant shrug, she said, "Tasting trips. Some are recommended to me by others. Like this one." She returned the bottle to him and continued. "I was in Rome a few years back and someone said I might like it."

This time his reaction to her statement was quite physical. His shoulders tensed and a muscle ticked ominously along his jaw. "Rome, huh?" he asked as, with almost exaggerated care, he placed the bottle back onto the wooden rack.

"Yes. A beautiful city. Have you ever been there?" she asked, wondering if there was something about that city that bothered him.

He faced her, the hard set of his jaw relaxing a little, and shrugged. "No. I tend to stay to the coasts since I like the water."

"Surf much?" Her question coaxed back that little-boy smile.

"Surf. Swim. Fish. I'm an ocean kind of guy."

"Leonia's a good place for all of that," she said and headed for the stairs once more, needing to get to work.

"I'll keep that in mind while I'm here, as well as the gym," Aidan said and followed the attractive sway of her hips all the way up to the kitchen level. The lady had a nice ass and being a guy, he wasn't about to ignore the view.

Once they were back in the kitchen, she made a beeline for the prep table, where Natalie and another young woman were busily laying out a variety of ingredients. Elizabeth joined them, suggesting one thing or another and giving instructions. Her tone with them was patient and friendly. Despite her easy demeanor, however, her mind now seemed totally on the work that needed to be done.

Which was perfect for him. He strolled to the large refrigerators in the kitchen, checking out the surroundings to see where he could place a camera. A speaker up at one side of the kitchen caught his eye after he had removed some limes and lemons from the fridge and was returning to the bar.

Perfect, he thought. He'd have to wait for a lull in activity in the kitchen first, but since they were all so busy there now, it gave him a perfect opportunity in the cellar. Grabbing a menu and a pad of paper as if to take notes, he went back down to the cellar unnoticed and once there, walked to the farthest part of the room, near the safe and lockers.

The lockers were like those you would find in a gym or a school. He opened the first few to find some empty and some holding assorted clothes and bags, possibly belonging to Elizabeth's staff. The last one had an ordinary combination lock that might not take much time to pick. He noted the make, model and serial number to see if there was a way to get a master key to simplify things.

Next, he turned his attention to the safe. Big, gray and old. A bit of rust along the edges, likely as a result of the sea air and dampness in the cellar. Despite that, the lock spun freely and the safe was in generally good condition. Again, he noted the information on the safe in the hopes of getting inside next time he could.

He suspected the safe would hold what most businesses would safeguard—important papers, cash and the like. But he wondered what else it and the locker might hold that wasn't related to the restaurant. The Sparrow's records and weapons?

A noise from above reminded him he had to get moving. Shifting back to the first locker, he found a spot for the camera.

"Lucia, come in Lucia," he said after he had finished positioning the surveillance equipment.

"Perfect shot. I can see the entire cellar."

"Did you see the label on the wine?" he asked and walked back over to the racks, where he once again pulled out the bottle he had been inspecting earlier.

"A little unclear," Lucia advised.

A harsh sigh escaped him before he said, "It's clear to me. This was one of Mitch's favorites."

Chapter 4

Elizabeth stretched a kink out of her back. Just a few hours to go until the start of the dinner service and everything was in order and ready. Which meant that she'd better take her afternoon break.

Natalie and Susanna, another of her assistants, had already left for some rest. Both young women lived nearby, as did most of the staff she employed. Which made her question where Aidan would drift?

She ambled toward the front of the building, but he had already departed. Not out of the ordinary, but she got a sense of something not right with him. It made her wonder if he was in trouble. If that was the reason he moved from place to place, never putting down roots. She made a mental note to ask him for some references if he survived his first night on the job.

Closing up, she went to her cottage, changed into jogging clothes and checked out the tide. Low enough still that she could run along the shore instead of the hard asphalt road toward the center of town.

Even though she stayed on the wetter hard-packed sand, her heels dug deep with the force of her strides and so she pushed a little harder. Her arms pumped as she ran, passing behind the main buildings in town and the public access ramps to the beach. As she skirted a protective stone jetty close to the old Roman bridge before turning around, a fine sweat glistened on her bare arms and legs from her exertions.

"Elvis has left the building," Lucia called out from the central area of the suite.

Aidan put down the microchip he had been laboring over and walked out to view the now-empty rooms of the restaurant from the monitors Lucia had set up in the common space of their quarters.

Grabbing a set of binoculars, he rushed to the corner of the hotel room, grateful that Corbett Lazlo had thought to rent a space with windows that faced the shore and the restaurant. Scoping out the area with the high-powered binoculars, he tried to locate the Sparrow, but couldn't.

"Damn. I'll have to get something in the cottage so we can monitor her better."

Lucia joined him at the windows, another pair of binoculars in hand. "Is that where you think she is?"

Aidan looked at his watch. "It's only three, so she's got a bit of time until she needs to get dinner going. She could be anywhere, but my money is on the cottage. She strikes me as a homebody."

"When she isn't busy being an assassin?" Lucia tossed out.

"So you're finally convinced it's her?" he asked and glanced over at his colleague.

Lucia shook her head before bringing up the binoculars once again. "Either that or there's a hell of a lot of coincidences."

"Hmm." He turned his attention to searching out the grounds of the restaurant and the cottage, but he could see nothing.

A moment later, however, Lucia chuckled loudly. "A homebody, huh?"

Aidan stepped to her side and tracked the line of sight of Lucia's binoculars. He caught the blur of movement along the shore. Training his binoculars on the area, he increased the magnification until he could finally identify Elizabeth.

She was running. He couldn't call it jogging since the pace was too fast. Almost punishing. Her arms pumped smoothly while the hair swept up in a pony tail bounced in rhythm to her long and graceful strides. A cropped dark-maroon T-shirt was plastered to her body by a combination of sweat and a breeze.

She was cold.

He grew increasingly interested as he noticed even more about her. The firm muscles at her midriff and legs shifting and bunching. The running shorts she wore weren't scant, but her legs were long for her height. Very long, which brought disturbing visions of what she could do with those legs.

He groaned.

"Aidan?" he heard from beside him and realized Lucia had been talking to him.

"What? I'm sorry. I was concentrating."

"You are such a guy," she teased with a wide smile.

He had to shake his head and laugh. There was just something refreshing about Lucia's forthrightness when you were used to dealing with people who were generally deceptive.

Like the woman running along the shore, he reminded himself, fighting her sexual pull.

"Okay, so she's…cute," he confessed.

Lucia laughed and let her binoculars drop down on the strap hanging around her neck. "I hope you're a more convincing liar when you're around her."

"You'll find out soon enough," he said and headed to his room, intent on testing the waters in more ways than one.

Elizabeth was nearly back to the cottage when she noticed first the lone swimmer moving toward her from the docks and then the pile of clothes and towel sitting on the beach just behind her home.

Finishing her jog, she paused by the towel and placed her hands on her hips, took a few deep breaths as she watched the swimmer head into shore. His strokes were sure and even. They propelled him through the water elegantly as his head turned from side to side in a rhythmic breathing pattern.

She recognized that head, she realized—Aidan. This was confirmed as he reached the shallows and got caught up in a surge of water. He body-surfed the wave in before he rose up out of the wash of the breakers.

Elizabeth gulped and this time, had to force herself to breathe. He was all lean muscle and athletic grace. As he headed toward shore, he picked up his arms to slick back the longer strands of his hair from his face and all that muscle rippled beneath smooth tanned skin. He wasn't wearing the loose shorts that so many American men wore, but a sinfully slinky Speedo that barely covered him. Barely being the operative word.

Breathe, girl. Breathe. She fanned her face and blamed the hot flash on her jog.

He smiled as he noticed her and hurried from the water, jumping over one wave and then battling the backward pull of the wash until he was standing before her. "You were right about how great the waters are. Although a little rough in spots."

"The swimming and surfing beaches are up more toward town. It's a little rocky here. You've cut yourself," she said and motioned to a raw scrape along his collarbone. "Let's get that cleaned."

Aidan looked down to where a bit of blood mingled with the salt water and ran down his chest. He hadn't planned it that way, but he wouldn't waste a prime opportunity. Especially since he had noticed how she was checking him out as he had come onto shore. "I'll be fine," he said and met her gaze directly.

She blushed and stammered, "W-we really should clean it. You wouldn't want it to get infected."

Again it occurred to him that she was too easy to read, but then again, he hadn't been all that obscure up in the hotel room with Lucia. Was it a cosmic joke that they should both obviously find themselves attracted to one another? Spy *v.* Spy Sexcapades before they had to do each other in?

"Thanks," he said, bending to pick up his clothes and looping the towel over his shoulders. She walked toward the cottage but didn't offer to let him in as he had expected. As he had hoped, since in the pocket of his pants, he had another set of cameras ready to install. Instead, she pointed to a rustic outdoor shower by the back door.

"Rinse off over there while I get some first aid stuff."

Elizabeth walked into the cottage and he waited for her to return before he stepped beneath the shower and turned on the water. He wanted an audience for his show. When he was certain she was observing him, he made a point of getting good and wet. Slick. Then, he ran his hands all along his body, as if wiping away some dirt, and as he did so, he could feel her gaze on him, tracking his every movement.

Knowing she was a voyeur to his little act brought an immediate and unwanted reaction. The upside of it was that in turn, his rather obvious excitement created a riot of color along Elizabeth's cheeks. She ripped her gaze from him then and nervously fingered the plastic box in her hands—the first aid kit.

He stopped and shut off the water, grabbed his towel and dried himself as he walked toward her. He toyed with the idea of wrapping the towel around his waist, but decided against it. In this game, you used every advantage available.

She had put the kit on a low stone wall by the shower and was fumbling with opening it as he approached.

"Here, let me," he said and took the kit from her hands, opened it and laid it back on top of the wall. He removed a tube of antiseptic cream, squeezed a little onto his finger. Working it into the scrape, he made sure to skip a section so that it might require her further attention.

"There." He was closing the tube when she reached out and took it from his hands.

"You missed a spot."

Bingo, he thought.

She placed a dot of the cream on her index finger and after, rubbed that finger along the top portion of the scrape. The action brought her close and he lowered his head, got into her personal space. Despite her run, she still smelled fresh. Feminine, although there was no hint of any perfume. An assassin couldn't afford to leave even something as simple as a scent behind, Aidan realized, but then turned his attention back to her, putting himself where she couldn't avoid him.

Elizabeth stroked the cream into the scrape. His skin was warm beneath her finger. As she skipped her gaze up to his face, she finally realized how close they were. And that she had to reach past him and brush even closer to remove a bandage from the kit. She didn't hesitate leaning toward him, even though her breast brushed his chest as she did so.

Her nipple, already peaked from the chill of the ocean breeze, tightened even more and she shivered.

"Cold?" he asked and rubbed his hands across her bare arms to warm her. It only brought another shiver. One that came from another place she didn't want to acknowledge, so she pulled away from him and shot him a glare. He was obviously used to playing this game quite well, but she didn't intend to be another notch acquired in his wanderings.

"Don't touch, remember?"

Aidan didn't push, although she could see that he was tempted to find out just how far he could.

Stepping away from her, he held his hands up as if in surrender. "I get it. Thanks for the help." With that, he grabbed his clothes, walked back to the beachfront and turned toward town.

Elizabeth watched him go and wondered whether hiring him had been a mistake. She'd hoped getting a bartender would solve her problem, but this guy…

As she watched his Speedo-clad backside saunter away, it

confirmed her original impression that he would be nothing but trouble. When he turned, caught her observing him… again…and winked, she knew she was right.

Aidan was going to give her nothing but grief. She had to keep a close eye on him. She couldn't afford to let him get close or to work his way into her heart. The price to be paid for that was just too great.

Chapter 5

*F*rustration.

That was the only word Aidan could use to describe his feelings on so many levels.

A few days had gone by and he had yet to be able to charm his way into her cottage.

Forget charming his way into her pants. The lady might as well have on a cast-iron chastity belt given how effectively she countered his every attempt to get close. She was a master, he'd give her that.

Not to mention that in the days that he'd been in the restaurant, he'd seen a woman who was patient and kind and all-so-nice that it was hard to imagine a side of her that could kill a man in cold blood.

Frustration. Again.

On a positive note, he had actually managed to fake being a halfway decent bartender the first few days with Lucia's help via the earpiece. Luckily, tastes in Leonia were rather pedestrian. By the end of the week, he had memorized the most commonly requested libations and discovered the many attributes of the restaurant's favorite wine. It was from a local vineyard along the coast and not all that far from Prince Reginald's country estate. He wondered if the Sparrow had bought the wine before or after killing the prince.

He and Lucia were partaking a glass of that vintage as they monitored Elizabeth's activities thanks to the strategically placed cameras. Although the restaurant had closed nearly an hour earlier and all of the staff had gone home, Elizabeth continued to work.

She finally gave a little nod of her head and seemingly satisfied, went back through the kitchen and out the rear door. Once in the backyard, another camera that he had set up in a hanging flower pot on the patio picked up her movement toward the cottage. She entered, closed the door and lights snapped on inside.

"The Sparrow's in her nest for the night," he muttered and took another sip of the wine. He sat there, watching the silent screens, still pondering how he would get into the cottage to plant the other surveillance equipment.

There was generally too much activity during working hours. Every night for the past few days, Elizabeth had gone straight home after work, making it impossible for him to sneak in.

About half an hour later, he was still considering whether he could break in tomorrow between when he left the restaurant for the night and Elizabeth finally closing up, when he noticed the lights in the cottage snap off. The Sparrow was ready for bed.

Surprisingly, however, Elizabeth walked out of the cottage a second later, clearly not dressed for sleep. She had on a black form-fitting cocktail dress. Strapless, it exposed the paler skin of her shoulders and arms, and dropped down to only mid-thigh, gracing him with a view of those sinfully long and lusciously toned legs.

Aidan bolted upright in his chair. "It's eleven-thirty. Where could she be going?"

"Homebody, huh?" Lucia quipped again, but Aidan glared at her.

"We need to track her."

"Time for *you* to track her. Time for me to plant some cameras," Lucia said and rose from the table.

Aidan grabbed the binoculars, turned on the infrared sighting and rushed to the windows. He immediately picked up her body heat moving down the walk leading from the restaurant to the street. Increasing the magnification, he could make out Elizabeth's body shape turning onto the road before the building. "She's coming into town."

"It *is* Friday night, Aidan," Lucia said.

When he faced her, he realized she had changed into all-black clothes.

"You'll bug the cottage?"

She confirmed that she would with a nod of her head. "You'll follow our little bird?"

Glancing at his watch, he realized he only had a few minutes before Elizabeth walked past the hotel. No time to change from the jeans and T-shirt he had donned upon returning to the suite. So he just slipped his earpiece back in and grabbed his leather jacket.

"Keep me advised of what's going on," he instructed and Lucia picked up one of the walkie-talkies set to the same frequency as the earpiece.

"I'll need about half an hour," she advised and he raised an eyebrow at her comment.

"Don't think I can keep her occupied for that long?"

Lucia laughed and shook her head. "Come on, Aidan. So far you're batting zero in that department."

He was annoyed that she was right, but he had his reasons for not pushing too hard. If Elizabeth was the Sparrow, and there was little so far to contradict that possibility except his malfunctioning intuition, he couldn't let himself rush things and maybe make a mistake. He had done that once before and Mitch had paid the price.

"I'm a patient man, Lucia. Some women can't be rushed," he responded.

"Whatever," she replied with a flip of her hand. "Just give me half an hour."

With that, she left the suite and he hurried after her, but took the elevator while she went to the stairs so as to remain inconspicuous.

He stood there, impatient, tapping his foot while he waited, hoping he wouldn't miss Elizabeth as she passed by the building. Not that she would be all that hard to find. There weren't that many places she could go on a Friday night at nearly midnight.

As the elevator arrived and he stepped in, he made a mental list of the dozen or so establishments he had noticed on one of his earlier walks, imagining which of those someone like Elizabeth might favor.

A nice quiet pub somewhere? Then he recalled what she was wearing. Not what you wore to hoist a pint with the locals. As he reached the ground floor, he hurried through the lobby and paused by the entrance to the hotel. Peering out, he caught sight of her about a block up, just turning onto one of the side streets, and smiled.

The Sparrow was about to find out just how persuasive he could be.

The Women's Artists' Cooperative was one of those places that became whatever you needed it to be. During the week the site hosted various literary events, displays of local art and the Wednesday Wing Woman social for women over sixty-five. On Friday and Saturday nights, it transformed into a club featuring local female bands of differing persuasions.

For the women of Leonia, there was no better place to be on a Friday night than the WAC as it was affectionately known by the female population. For the men, the term WAC had a whole different meaning. Not necessarily a positive one.

Most men in town knew to stay away on the weekends since the women at the WAC went there to be free of the pressures of man/woman mating rituals. It was a way that women could bond and enjoy themselves without any inhibitions.

Elizabeth loved that about the WAC. Within its walls, she could spend time with the few women she counted as friends.

Tonight they were meeting at the WAC to celebrate Natalie successfully passing her final exam. With her help, Natalie had learned the secrets to a scrumptious chocolate souffle. She smiled, thinking of the young woman's excitement as she had told her.

As she stepped through the door, she spotted her friends seated at a table near the dance floor and rushed over. On stage, a band of women barely past their teens energetically played a No Doubt tune. The singer was doing a passable imitation of Gwen Stefani and had even styled her dress and hairstyle to mimic the celebrity.

At the table, she hugged all her friends and once she sat, they ordered another round of drinks and toasted Natalie's success. Talk came quickly and easily with the other women as did the desire to dance as the band launched into their own version of "Cruel to be Kind."

Inclining her head in the direction of the dance floor, she said, "Anyone care to join me?"

Natalie and Samantha, a designer with her own clothing shop in town, jumped at her suggestion. The last woman at the table—Kate, the owner of an upscale bath and body store—shook her head. "I'll hold our spot."

Together, the three women eased onto a free spot at the edge of the dance floor and Elizabeth gave herself over to the beat, moving in time to the bass line of the song. Smiling and feeling relaxed for the first time in days, she danced through the song and then stayed on the floor when the band began another tune with a similar beat.

She was enjoying the music and her friends until Natalie leaned over and said, "Check out what just walked in."

Elizabeth followed the direction of Natalie's gaze. Aidan. He was sauntering past a score of women near the long runway from the club's entrance to the main section of the WAC. As he passed and made his way to the bar, heads turned to watch him go by.

She felt only a tiny bit of vindication that she wasn't alone in her attraction to his physical attributes. That feeling was chased by an emotion she normally didn't experience—jealousy.

And then that unsettling feeling that had been plaguing her for the last few days resurfaced. She finally realized the cause of it—Aidan.

Looking away from him, she moved until her back was to the bar and tried to rededicate herself to the music and the fun she had been having just moments earlier. A difficult thing to do with Aidan sitting at the bar. She told herself just to relax, but it was impossible.

Returning to the table, she grabbed her glass to quench the thirst she had worked up while dancing, only to find it empty. Looking around, she realized there wasn't a waitress in sight. She had only one choice—head to the bar or suffer being parched.

As she glanced toward where Aidan was sitting barely twenty feet away, she noted his broad shoulders filling out the black leather of his jacket. Remembering the strength of them when he had been swimming the other day, she cursed beneath her breath.

She would be damned if she let him wreck her night.

Chapter 6

He was drowning in a sea of estrogen, Aidan thought as he sipped on the beer he had ordered. Picking up the long-neck bottle, he took another slug as he tried not to look stupid surrounded by the dozens of women packed into the club. He'd obviously made a major gaffe.

Either Elizabeth was gay—and he couldn't believe that his radar was that off—or he'd stumbled into what was clearly intended to be a ladies'-only club.

No wonder the bouncer, a rather burly woman he recalled seeing on the docks, had given him an odd and unfriendly glance as he had paid the admission fee.

He shook his head at his own stupidity and his failure to reconnoiter the location. He also wondered how he would ever approach Elizabeth without seeming all stalkery. Best that he not—

"Following me?" she said and leaned one elbow on the surface of the bar as she signaled with a wave of her hand for the bartender.

Busted. He looked up at her and faked disinterest. With a shrug, he said, "Heard the band from out on the street. They sounded pretty good. Decided to see what was up."

A furrow appeared between her brows as she considered him. "Judging from your choice of music the other day, female bands of the indie persuasion are possibly your type. Although the black biker jacket screams hard-rock guy to me."

He gave another indifferent shrug and tossed back a slug of the beer again. "I'm a man of eclectic tastes. And you?"

She crossed her arms after finally sliding onto the bar stool beside him. Signals definitely mixed, he thought. "The same. Men generally stay away on Friday and Saturday nights. It's an unwritten rule."

Chuckling, he swiveled his head back and forth as if to check her statement and teased, "Well, color me stupid. I hadn't noticed."

She surprised him by laughing. When the waiter brought her drink—a glass of red wine—she laid some money on the bar and said, "Gotta go."

With a cool nod and another sip of his beer, he replied, "See ya."

Elizabeth strolled back to her table, making sure to add what she hoped was an enticing little sway to her walk, certain that he was watching no matter his attempts to seem disinterested.

Or maybe it was totally egotistical of her to think Aidan was here because of her. Maybe he really had just been looking for some good music, although there were a few other clubs in Leonia that offered entertainment on the weekends. Some of them were probably more suitable for someone like Aidan.

As she sat at the table with her friends, Natalie inclined her head in the direction of the bar. "Brave man."

Elizabeth settled into her seat and picked up her glass of merlot. Peering over the edge of it at her friend, she replied, "Either brave or stupid."

Natalie narrowed her eyes as she considered Aidan once again. "Doesn't strike me as the stupid type."

"He's yummy," added Samantha, shooting a glance over her shoulder.

Wanting to downplay his presence, Elizabeth tried to act cool. "If you like that kind of man."

"Girl, what woman doesn't go for that whole bad-boy routine?" Kate hooted with a nudge to Elizabeth's shoulder.

She held up her hand as if to be counted. "Me, for one. Bad boys don't linger and I've had enough of people leaving in my life."

Her comment cast a pall over what had been a fun gathering. She immediately regretted it, heartfelt as the comment had been. Attempting to regain that earlier lightheartedness, she said, "Although I have seen him in a bathing suit. A rather brief Speedo to be exact. There's not an inch of him that needs manscaping."

Natalie nearly spat out her drink. As it was, she gave a noisy snort. "You're not kidding, are you?"

Elizabeth looked over to where Aidan was sitting, arms spread across the bar, long-neck bottle dangling lazily from one hand. As their gazes met, he smiled and picked up his bottle as if in a toast.

She mimicked his actions, earning a round of snickers from all her friends.

"Right, not interested. Tell us another one, Lizzy Bee," Natalie joked, using Dani's nickname for her.

"So what are you doing here, when Tall, Blond and Dangerous is over there?" Kate chimed in and pointed to Aidan.

"Why, I'm dancing, of course. Anyone care to join me?" She rose from the table.

All three of her friends looked from her to Aidan before Samantha finally stood. "I'm game."

With a glare at Kate and Natalie, Elizabeth quipped, "Cowards," before working her way through the crowd and back to the dance floor.

The band had switched to a classic Bangles tune. Definitely danceable, she thought and once again gave herself over to the energetic beats, trying not to think about the man sitting at the bar, possibly watching her. Every now and then, as her dancing and the crowd shifted her into a different position on the floor, she would catch a peek of him. Still lounging there, sipping his beer.

She wondered if it was his second bottle or if he was still nursing the first. Then she wondered why she cared. She wasn't one for meaningless involvements of any kind, especially with someone like Aidan who wasn't the kind to linger for long.

Faltering to the beat, she forced her mind away from thoughts of Aidan and back to the playfulness of the music. She was just loosening up a bit when the song ended and the band announced that they had a request.

Suddenly, Aidan was at her side, holding out his hand. Samantha was moving back to the table where Kate and Natalie sat, watching with extreme fascination.

The lead singer crooned the opening bars of Gloria Estefan's "Words Get in the Way."

"I'm not interested," she said, glancing down at his hand before shooting her gaze up to his face.

"It's just a dance," he replied, the tone of his voice low. A bedroom voice, perfect for whispering endearments. Lush with sensual promise. A well-rehearsed voice that had likely worked for him on many an occasion.

"I'm your boss," she hissed back and peered around to realize they were starting to attract attention, which was the last thing she needed. She liked her privacy and didn't need the village gossips wagging their tongues over her.

"I promise I won't claim harassment." He grinned and wiggled his fingers, again urging her to dance and rather than risk a scene, she snared his hand and joined him in the slow dance.

Bad boy that he was, he took advantage of the opportunity

to come close. Inclining his head, he whispered in her ear, "Relax."

Hard to do when she was so aware of him physically. Close, but not as close as he maybe wanted. She would give him credit for that. He wasn't a total cad.

His chivalry didn't stop him from keeping his hands at her waist for the longest time while she slipped both of her hands to his shoulders—those broad, leanly muscled shoulders she remembered from the other day.

Finally, he exerted just the tiniest bit of pressure to urge her closer until she barely brushed his chest as they moved to the music.

An annoying tingle of awareness awoke again. A little shiver danced through her when he bent his head and asked, "It's not so bad, is it?"

No, it wasn't. If anything, it was a bit too good. She found herself pressing her cheek to his and moving an inch closer. Which brought a shudder and made her fight her way back from him to avoid her attraction.

She hated how she responded to him and took to mentally counting the seconds that passed in an effort to distract herself.

"Relax," he urged again, smoothing his hands up and down her back. Pressed her to shift nearer.

Reluctantly she went, still counting. Finding that ineffective, she opted for another tack. "Gloria doesn't strike me as your type, either."

He chuckled. "Eclectic, remember? Besides, her music soothes me."

She jerked away and eyed him dubiously. "Soothes you?"

Aidan smiled and cradled the side of her face. "Yes, soothes. As in, to relax. To let yourself go." As he said that, he stroked the side of her face and then eased that hand to the nape of her neck and pressed her close once more.

Once there, he continued, gently whispering in her ear. "Listen to the words. What she's trying to say."

Despite her best efforts, she found herself doing as he

asked. She let the words slip into her, let herself finally relax against him, moving her body to those sensuous beats, and he did the same.

When the song ended and the band abruptly resumed with a loud and fast number, it yanked her from the mood.

"That was—"

"Nice?" he filled in for her, a hopeful look on his face as she realized he was still holding her hand.

Too nice. "I've got to go."

He released her and with a nod, she returned to her table of friends.

Instead of going to the bar, however, he followed her, his hand at the small of her back, as if to remind her of his presence. Not that she could drive away her awareness of him no matter how she tried.

At the table, she glared at him, hoping to make it clear that she wanted him gone, but he obviously either didn't get her hint, or more than likely, the rebel chose to ignore it. "Mind if I join you ladies?"

Her three friends, or maybe it was better to say three ex-friends, shifted to make room for a chair he secured from another table with an irresistible smile.

Elizabeth stood there, reluctant to stay, but unwilling to let Aidan spoil her night. For that matter, she was unwilling to acknowledge that she was attracted to him. He was probably used to women falling all over him constantly. And she suspected he was All-Access Aidan to anyone who was willing.

Which she wasn't.

Hesitantly, she took a seat next to Aidan and allowed her friends to engage him in conversation while she sat back, trying to gauge whether he was as he appeared—a happy-go-lucky guy, intent on just having fun as he drifted from place to place.

But when he leaned away from the table and their gazes locked, there was something else there. Something painful. She noted it as his glance fell on her, as if he, too, was trying to decide just what she was.

She realized then that he wasn't what he appeared to be. Which was fine. She wasn't as she appeared to be, either.

The WAC closed its doors at two, Aidan discovered.

What amazed him was that after a long day of work, none of the women at the table seemed inclined to leave until that hour.

And so he stayed until the announcement was made for last call, and, after, he walked out of the club surrounded by Natalie, Samantha and Kate. Elizabeth was directly behind them as they ambled up the block.

Samantha and Kate lived along the town's central road. He bid each woman goodnight at their doors. That just left Natalie, her arm looped through his, and Elizabeth, who had finally moved up to walk beside them. At a street directly in front of the hotel, Natalie paused.

"This is my stop," she teased and gave him a playful kiss on the cheek. "See you later."

Aidan waved as Natalie crossed the street, and then faced Elizabeth. "Guess it's just the two of us."

Elizabeth immediately protested. "There's no need for you—"

"A gentleman always walks a lady home," he said and offered his arm.

Ignoring him, she walked in the direction of the restaurant, but Aidan followed, matching his paces so that they were side by side. He was silent, since he knew that to say anything would just drive her further away, something he didn't want to do given that he had made some inroads this evening.

Although he had watched her tonight much as he had watched her all week, he was still uncertain. Maybe even troubled by what he had seen. The Elizabeth he was getting to know didn't jibe with what he knew her to be—a ruthless killer.

The Elizabeth he had discovered had been kind. Patient with the staff and the sometimes demanding patrons. Determined, but at times—and he didn't want to admit that those times had been around him—decidedly insecure.

But of course, in his line of work, deception was a way of life.

Elizabeth had to be very very good at it, he thought, as they continued walking onward silently, moving closer and closer to the restaurant. When they reached the low stone wall marking the boundary between her property and the main road, Elizabeth stopped and faced him.

"Although I didn't ask you to, thanks for walking me home."

He shrugged, the buckles on his black leather biker jacket jangling with the action. "It's the least I could do."

She arched one eyebrow, half in question, half in challenge. "Really? And you expected nothing in return?"

Aidan chuckled and smiled at the audacious tone behind her words. "Well, maybe one thing."

That perfectly shaped brow curved ever upward. "And what would that be?"

Chapter 7

She had tossed down the gauntlet and should have known better than to think he wouldn't pick it up.

One side of his mouth quirked as he slowly leaned toward her until he was barely an inch away. He surprised her then by saying, "Last chance."

His breath was warm against her lips. She imagined just how much warmer his mouth would be on hers. The voice of her daring side screamed, "Stop running, girl! Go get him!"

And so she did, closing that last little distance and covering his mouth with hers. Experiencing the warmth over and over again as he answered her kiss. Tasting him when she opened her mouth and he did the same, slipped his tongue in to dance with hers.

Their lips were the only points connecting them and she found herself reaching up, laying her hand on his leather-clad shoulder to ground her since her head was beginning to spin. And then suddenly, he yanked away.

"I'm sorry," he stammered, although he wasn't quite sure why he was apologizing. After all, this was what he'd been after all week long—a way to get closer.

Even in the dark, the rush of color to her cheeks was painfully obvious. "Sorry? You're sorry?"

Again she was throwing him for a loop. "Yes, I mean, no. I mean, I know you didn't want it to go that far," he offered as an excuse.

She crossed her arms and cocked her hip. That eyebrow crept upward again as her sherry-colored eyes burned with annoyance. "Already running, Aidan?"

"I think we'll probably both be thankful in the morning that we stopped when we did."

With a nod, and without waiting for her reply, he hurried away.

He rushed into the suite eager to see what Elizabeth would do once she was within range of the cameras Lucia had set up in her cottage.

A purely professional interest, he reminded himself, but as he caught sight of Elizabeth in her bedroom, he knew it for the lie it was.

Sitting beside Lucia, he watched as Elizabeth reached behind her and undid the zipper on the back of the basic little black dress that hugged her slim curves. The fabric loosened, and then with a dip of her shoulders, the dress slipped off and pooled at her feet on the floor, leaving her standing in nothing but lacy black underwear. Very feminine, highly revealing underwear.

He swallowed hard.

"A woman doesn't wear black unless she wants someone to see it. Especially black like that." Lucia nudged him with an elbow.

"She didn't know I'd be there." He continued watching, waiting for the undergarments to drop, as well, but then Elizabeth grabbed something from the edge of the bed.

She headed to a door at the far end of the room and Aidan

reached for the monitor controls to switch the view, only Lucia batted away his hand.

"I didn't bug the bathroom. There's no way out of that room besides the window."

Chagrined, he replied, "You're right."

Lucia punched a few buttons at that point and a view of the back of the cottage popped into place on one monitor. The light from the bathroom window was visible, a bright beacon against the dark stone of the cottage, but not much else.

"She can't go out that way without us knowing," Lucia explained, and then yawned.

"Maybe we should take turns the rest of the night?" Aidan suggested. "I'll take the first watch."

With a knowing grin, Lucia bid him goodnight.

Aidan settled in, anxious to see Elizabeth again while he replayed over and over that enticing kiss and the confusion surrounding it. He was embarrassed that he had lost his objectivity, forgetting why it was that he was kissing her and actually enjoying it.

Maybe he just wasn't as cut out for this part of the spy business as he thought. He could handle the surveillance and fighting after his many years as an army Ranger, but the rest…

That had been Mitch's specialty. He had been the kind who could charm even a snake-oil salesman. Not that his friend's charisma had been enough to save his life. The Sparrow was apparently immune to it, although tonight…

Had it been his imagination that Elizabeth had responded?

Had she fooled Mitch in much the same way before plunging the knife into his gut?

His mood different, he looked at his watch, wondering what she could be doing in the bathroom for so long. And then he caught a glimpse of motion in another of the monitors at the furthest end of the table. He squinted at the picture; it was so dark, he was barely able to discern much beside the general height and body shape of the individual.

Cursing, he grabbed the monitor controls and flipped a switch that turned on the night vision for that camera. The picture improved, not that he would be able to get much information about the suspect. At first glance, the black-clad figure was built much like Elizabeth, but the identity would be impossible to confirm thanks to the ski mask covering the suspect's face.

The Sparrow? he wondered and glanced back to the monitor in the bedroom where there was still no sign of Elizabeth.

How had she gotten from the cottage to the cellar of the restaurant? A tunnel between the two buildings?

His gaze fixed on the black-clad figure, he watched her move to the safe. With a few quick spins of the dial, she opened it and removed a moderate-sized foot locker from the bottom shelf. Placing the foot locker on the floor, she undid yet another lock and flipped open the top of the locker. The angle on the camera made it possible to see what was inside— an assortment of knives and bottles.

Don't touch the knives, he repeated Elizabeth's warning.

Elizabeth—the Sparrow—reached into the bottom of the foot locker and extracted a holster and gun. She took the time to check the clip and firing mechanism on the gun—a Heckler & Koch Mark 23. He recognized the weapon immediately.

The HK Mark 23 had been specially commissioned by the Pentagon for its Special Operations Command. A friend within SOCOM had raved about the gun and insisted both he and Mitch should check it out. Their friend been right. Both he and Mitch had loved the double-action .45-caliber gun that could be fitted with a silencer. His friend's pistol had disappeared on the night he'd been killed.

More and more evidence was piling up against the Sparrow in Mitch's murder. He had to remind himself that his friend's death was not the reason for this assignment. His goal was to find Prince Reginald's murderer. But maybe one of those bottles in the foot locker held a poison similar to the one that had killed the prince.

Aidan observed the Sparrow holster the gun and slip on the holster, quickly get the foot locker back in the safe and close it once again.

She turned, glanced over her shoulder as if sensing that she was being watched. Pausing, she examined the room, then moved to the one locker closest to the safe. Again with a few quick turns she opened the combination lock.

He wondered what she was up to and was surprised when she pushed aside some clothes hanging in the locker, stepped inside, and then closed the door behind her, disappearing from sight.

Shit. Standing, he rushed to Lucia's room and pounded on the door. "Lucia! The Sparrow's flown the nest!"

As Lucia opened her door, she grumbled, "This better be good, Aidan."

He motioned to the monitors. "The Sparrow is armed and dressed to kill. She headed out of the cellar through some kind of hidden passage in one of the lockers."

"Then you better arm yourself, as well," she said, but he bent and picked up the hem of his jeans leg to reveal the mini six-shot Glock 36 tucked into an ankle holster.

Lucia let out a disbelieving chuckle. "If it's the Sparrow, you'll need more than that pea shooter." She reached into the pocket of her robe, extracted her larger Glock 34 and held it out to him.

Aidan snagged the weapon from her grasp and, as he headed for the door, called out, "Keep an eye on the cellar. Call me if there's any activity."

"Where do you think you're headed?"

"To the beach. It's the most likely place for the tunnel to end. I should be able to see where she's going from there."

He'd raced off the main street and down to the shore, running along what little was left of the beach thanks to the high tide. By the time he got behind the cottage, his shoes and the bottoms of his pants were soaked all the way up to the knee.

The light in her bathroom still spilled into the night.

He pulled out Lucia's Glock, crept up the rocky path from the beach and scoped out the dunes and gardens adjacent to the cottage. No activity besides the movement of the marsh grasses in the dunes from a slight ocean breeze. Crouching down, he kept to the edge of the garden that Elizabeth had crafted behind the restaurant.

Still no sign of anyone.

Moving to the side yard, he examined that area, and then paused, glancing down at the luminous face of his watch. Nearly fifteen minutes had passed since the Sparrow had slipped into the locker. He recollected her pace as she'd run the other day. If she had escaped into an open area and decided to run, she could be a good distance away already.

Cursing beneath his breath that he might have lost her, he pressed toward the opposite side of the yard, but could see nothing in the backyards of the neighboring shops and homes. A dog's bark caught his attention.

He squinted through the night in the direction of the noise.

That was when he thought he saw something moving down at the water's edge, close to the old stone building that was Leonia's fish market. Concentrating, he focused on where he had seen the motion.

Was that something moving in the shadows behind the fish market?

"Come in, Blender Boy. The Sparrow's in her nest," Lucia advised over his earpiece.

He ignored Lucia and peered down to the market.

Definitely something, he thought. Maybe even two people behind the building. "Red Rover, confirm, Red Rover. I think I've got something here."

"Sparrow just came out of the bathroom. What do you have?"

Aidan squinted and cursed that he had forgotten to bring his binoculars. But Lucia had a pair up in the suite. "Red Rover. Focus on the back of the fish market. At about two o'clock."

Some noise came over the wire and in his mind, Aidan

counted the seconds of delay as Lucia grabbed the binoculars, headed to the window and monitored the area he had pointed out. Moving nearer, he tried to confirm what he'd seen earlier, but the closer he got, it seemed to him that he might have imagined it. Or maybe it was two fisherman making an early delivery.

"Nothing in sight. Are you sure you saw her there?"

He wasn't certain and he should have been. He had been one of the army's best and here he was, being led around in circles by a slip of a woman. "Not sure, Red Rover. Returning to base," he advised, then slipped the gun back into his pocket and walked through Elizabeth's gardens to the road.

Once there, he raced back to the hotel and to the suite where Lucia was seated in front of the monitors. In one picture, Elizabeth slept soundly in her bed.

He walked up behind his colleague. "I don't get it. I saw someone preparing for a job. I saw her leave the cellar."

Lucia looked over her shoulder at him. "I'm not saying you didn't. But if she did all that, she wasn't gone for long. Or maybe it was someone else."

"Maybe," was all he could admit. Plopping down into the chair beside her, he returned her weapon and moved his feet, which squished noisily.

Lucia finally examined him and shook her head. "Maybe it's time for you to get clean and get some rest. You need to be back on the job—"

"At ten. The restaurant opens for brunch at eleven."

"I'll take over your watch. Plus, I'll fill Walker in later this morning." She tucked her gun back into the pocket of her robe.

Right, fill in Walker, he thought. But there was one thing he needed to tell her before he went to sleep. "The weapon she had—"

"A Sigma SW9F? That's what ballistics said about her two pistol kills," Lucia interrupted.

Aidan met her gaze squarely and shook his head. "She had an HK Mark 23."

"Mitch's gun." She reached out, laid a hand on his arm. "I'm sorry, Aidan."

"I'm not. Whoever was in that cellar did it. Chances are that it was the Sparrow. I plan on proving that she killed the prince, as well. When you call Walker, make sure and find out if he has any new info."

"Will do," she acknowledged and turned her attention back to the monitor, not that there was much going on. Just Elizabeth still in her bed. Peacefully at rest.

Aidan wondered how she could sleep so soundly. Didn't all her kills haunt her the way Mitch's murder haunted him?

But then again, sociopaths didn't have the same kinds of reactions that normal people did, he thought. Walker would be the first to tell him that. Yet her behavior earlier that night and her kiss…

She had been just a normal woman, enjoying a night out with friends. Friends who might be able to give him more information on the real Elizabeth. Although he had to be at the restaurant by ten, that still left him an hour or so in the morning to visit both Kate and Samantha's stores and talk to the women.

Maybe they would give him some insight on what made the Sparrow tick, because, so far, she had him totally confused.

Chapter 8

Elizabeth was awake long before the alarm went off, chirping stridently to remind her she couldn't linger in bed.

Saturdays and Sundays were always the busiest days of the week thanks to the brunch the restaurant served, but they were also the most profitable. Well worth the extra effort.

She was in the kitchen with time to spare before Natalie and her other assistants appeared. She fixed herself a large mug of coffee, and took a moment for a stroll through the back garden, pausing to pick a dead flower here and there.

In about four hours, her patrons would begin to arrive, but for now, she grabbed a seat on the low edge of the stone wall between her cottage and the beach. As she sipped her coffee, she gazed out at the ocean and observed the fisherman put out to sea.

She had often sat in the early-morning hours in her parents' fish shop near the docks and seen a similar sight. Her mother would sometimes make her a special breakfast of eggs and kippers, while her twin sister Dani—ever the more adventur-

ous one—would tag along with their Da to greet those fisherman who were already inbound with their catch.

She hadn't been able to reach Dani in days and wondered
what exotic part of the world her sister was visiting. She only
hoped that Dani's busy schedule would soon allow time for
a call home for news of when they might be able to get
together again.

With her coffee becoming lukewarm and the growing heat
from the rising sun reminding her that time was short this
morning, Elizabeth headed to the kitchen. She was still the
only one there. She used the time to experiment with a new
dessert recipe she wanted to enter in the annual Silvershire
Cooking Contest at the end of the month—a trifle doused with
a sour cherry liqueur that a local distillery was making.

Concentrating, she selected a recipe for the cake portion
of the trifle that would be firm enough, but not too heavy. She
hoped that when the competition came in a few weeks, she
would be able to place in the contest once more.

Not that she needed the glory. But the awards had brought
her work to the attention of editors at magazines like *Gourmet*
and *Bon Appetit,* resulting in invitations to other cooking
expos and contests. They had given her a chance to see more
of the world.

She smiled and thought that maybe she wasn't all that different from her wandering sister. Easing two pans with the
cake batter into the oven, Elizabeth was turning her attention
to the filling and sauce for the trifle when Natalie popped into
the kitchen.

"G'mornin', Nat," she called out and wiped her hands free
of some cake batter with the towel tucked into her apron strings.

Natalie walked over and slipped an arm over her shoulders.
"Is it a good morning, Lizzy Bee?" she teased with a too-
obvious wiggle of her eyebrows.

Elizabeth rolled her eyes upward. "Nat, even if it were a good
morning that way, do I strike you as the type to kiss and tell?"

Natalie pointed her index finger in Elizabeth's face. "So

you did kiss. You don't need to tell me since it's obvious from the look on your face."

Elizabeth raised her hands to her cheeks as if to hide what Natalie had seen, but then dropped them back down as the guilt behind that action registered. "You absolutely cannot know that from just one look at my face."

Chuckling, Natalie headed to the door to the cellar, but paused before going down. "You're right. I can't. But you haven't denied it, so I guess I'm not so far off base."

With that, the younger woman flounced down the stairs, leaving Elizabeth to wonder what she would do when Aidan showed up for work. *If* he showed up for work. He had seemed conflicted last night.

Join the club, she thought, admitting that she had been just as puzzled by their rather pleasant, but equally awkward interlude.

But she was here this morning and ready to face him. She had to be here. Plus, she couldn't let him get the wrong idea about what was happening and how much he affected her.

She wondered again what he would do this morning if he came to work. She got the sense that whenever things got too complicated or didn't go his way, Aidan was the kind who left.

She only hoped that if he did decide to go, he would honor his promise and not leave her in a lurch. Especially not over the weekend when things would be crazier than ever.

With that thought in mind, she returned her attention to the dessert, the day's menu and a last-minute trip to the markets for ingredients to complete the chef's specials for the day.

A footfall close by made him bolt from bed, gun in hand. Whenever he was on assignment, he slept with his weapon within easy reach, tucked beneath the mattress with the handle sticking out for a quick draw.

Lucia held up her hands in surrender. "I'm sorry I woke you, but Walker's here. He's got some news."

Aidan lowered the gun. "Give me a few minutes, please."

Once dressed, Aidan stepped out into the main area of the suite where Walker Shaw sat on one of the couches, a shuttered look on his face.

"I gather there's problems," he said and took a seat opposite Walker.

"You look like hell," his colleague said. "Rough night?"

"Late night with the Sparrow. First at a local club and then after, when she went for an early-morning stroll," Lucia advised and brought over a tray with a pot of coffee and some cups. "I had room service bring this up. Figured you could use the jolt, Aidan."

"Thanks, Lucia," Aidan said.

Walker added his own thanks and then asked, "Were you able to see where she went? MI6 says there's been a lot of chatter on the wires lately about the Sparrow. She may be on another assignment here."

Aidan shook his head while filling up a cup with the heavenly smelling brew. He loaded it up with a few sugars, but kept it black since as Lucia had guessed, he needed a jump start this morning. "Someone slipped out through a secret passage in the cellar of the restaurant. Definitely dressed for a covert op and she was armed...with Mitch's gun."

Walker paused with his coffee cup halfway to his mouth. "How do you know that?"

"Although earlier ballistics had the Sparrow carrying a Sigma SW9F, she tucked an HK Mark 23 into her holster. Mitch's gun was the same make and has been missing since his murder. Plus, it's not that common a weapon," Aidan advised.

"Connect the dots, huh? But what about connecting the dots to Prince Reginald's murder?" Walker challenged and shifted his gaze to Lucia.

"Nothing yet."

Walker cursed beneath his breath. "Not good, guys. Corbett called this morning. A friend has warned him that the local tabloid—"

"The *Quiz?*" Lucia asked.

Walker nodded. "The *Silvershire Inquisitor,* or, as you noted, the *Quiz.* Seems one of the reporters has a lead on Prince Reginald's last night alive."

"If this *Quiz* is a gossip rag, why the worry?" Aidan wondered out loud as he sipped on the hot sugar-laced coffee.

"Because unfortunately, the story seems to have some truth behind it," Walker advised.

As Lucia fixed herself a cup of coffee, she asked, "So what is the story?"

"It seems the prince met an attractive young lady earlier in the day—slim athletic build, dark-haired."

"The Sparrow?" both Aidan and Lucia said in unison.

Walker shrugged. "Fits the description, doesn't it? Anyway, rumor has it that the prince locked himself in the room with this lady for a night of pleasure."

Aidan laughed harshly. "From what I saw in the file about the prince, that seems to be pretty routine behavior. So why the worry about this magazine's article?"

"Cocaine and murder," Walker answered quickly. "There had been some hint of drug use before with the Prince. A few months ago, immediately after the prince's death, the *Quiz* ran an article claiming that the prince had overdosed. No respectable news service would touch the piece."

"And now?" Lucia pressed.

"The paper claims to have proof positive that the prince was not only using drugs on his last night, but that he was murdered."

"Do the results of the toxicology reports confirm the drug use?" Lucia questioned and at that, Walker leaned down and extracted some papers from his briefcase. Laying them out on the coffee table between them, he motioned to the results.

"I've reviewed them myself and it seems clear. The prince had cocaine in his system along with a poison. The drugs are embarrassing to the royal family and the murder—that may add more fuel to the political fire the Union for Democracy keeps stoking."

Aidan leaned over, grabbed one of the papers and turned

it so he could get a better view. Examining the results, he said, "So the prince got his coke and in addition, a little something extra—digitalis."

"Not a hell of a lot, but enough to stop his heart," Walker explained, and then continued. "The thing is, it wasn't pharmaceutical-grade digitalis."

Lucia peered at the documents, obviously unsure, and inclined her head toward the papers. "How do you know?"

Walker flipped through a few pages of the report until he got to one page. He offered that to Lucia who took it and read while he explained further. "When digitalis is sold commercially, whether for injection or as a pill, it's generally mixed with other ingredients. The analysis of the chemical breakdown solely showed the basic components of digitalis and cocaine."

"And one gets close to unadulterated digitalis how?" Aidan jumped in.

This time it was Lucia who offered up the explanation. "According to this report, digitalis can be extracted from the leaves of a relatively common plant—*digitalis purpurea*—otherwise known as foxglove."

"Foxglove?"

At his question, Lucia handed him the report, which included a picture of a plant.

Aidan read aloud some of the description of the plant. "'The common foxglove can be found widely throughout Europe and the British Isles. Foxgloves have hairy leaves and spiky purple flowers in July. The leaves and seeds can be used for medicinal purposes as they contain cardiac stimulants.'

"Elizabeth's gardens are full of all kinds of plants, but I don't recollect seeing anything tall and purple."

There was silence for a moment as both Lucia and Walker considered his statement. Then Lucia said, "It's August. That description mentioned that the plant flowers in July."

"So it's possible the plant looks very little like this picture right now. Do you think you can get some more information on the Net while I talk to Elizabeth's friends this morning?"

"Don't you think that might make Ms. Moore suspicious?" Walker asked and began collecting the assorted papers he had laid out for inspection.

Aidan took a last gulp of his coffee and rose from the table. "It might, but it doesn't seem like we have much choice. If the *Quiz* knew about the cocaine and the murder, what's to say they won't find out about the Lazlo Group and blow our cover?"

"Aidan's right. We need to act quickly to get more information," Lucia added.

Walker hesitated, clearly uncertain about their plans, but he finally relented. With a nod, he said, "I'll have to trust your judgment. Especially since it seems from past info that someone is feeding the *Quiz* news in order to discredit the royal family. In the meantime, do you have anything to definitively identify Elizabeth Moore as the Sparrow?"

"Like someone with her body type sneaking through the cellar of her restaurant with Mitch's gun?" Aidan said facetiously, growing irritated with the other man's reticence regarding that part of the investigation.

Walker held up his hands as if in surrender. "Okay, I get it. Too many coincidences that can only point to our chef being the Sparrow and Mitch's killer. What we need to do is connect the Sparrow to the prince's murder," Walker reminded. "First, we have Elizabeth being near the estate at the time of the murder."

Lucia counted down another reason. "And a woman matching her description was seen with the prince."

"If the prince died with a smile on his face, Walker, do we have any DNA at the scene?" Aidan questioned.

The other man shook his head. "Not yet. I've brought in our own team to go over the area and reprocess the prince's body. If the prince and the Sparrow engaged in sexual activity, there will be fluids. We should also try to find any DNA evidence that may tie the killer to the digitalis. If it is from a plant, maybe the DNA can provide a signature to its origins."

"Maybe I can find something similar in Elizabeth's assorted gardens," he tacked on.

Walker glanced at his watch and then at Aidan. "You're on at ten this morning and finished at eleven tonight?"

Aidan smiled suggestively. "Unless I can entertain the lady the way I did last night. If I can…" He pointed to Lucia. "There's a special fiberoptic camera I've been working on. I think you can use it to help pick the locks on the safe and locker since we haven't been able to track down a master key due to their age."

"Not without backup," Walker advised. "I'll be back by ten this morning so that you can prep, Lucia. We'll play it by ear after that."

"Sounds like a plan," she confirmed.

With a nod, Aidan grabbed his jacket and walked out the door. He had a little over an hour left before Elizabeth expected him for work and a lot to do.

He was optimistic, however, that the information from her friends might help seal the deal on Elizabeth being the Sparrow. It might also help him drive away his attraction to the enigmatic woman he'd come to know in the past few days.

Chapter 9

Nothing could have prepared him for what was going on in Samantha's shop. A multitude of women, some of them familiar from last night at the WAC, jockeyed for position around the merchandise, cramming every inch of the store looking for bargains. The young fashion designer was apparently running an immense clearance sale.

Samantha and one of her associates were very busy behind the counter, ringing up and packaging purchases. Clearly the likelihood of talking with Samantha was nil, and when one particularly aggressive woman shoved past him with a shoulder an NHL hockey player would envy, he decided to turn his attention to the other young woman he had met last night.

Kate's shop, which was just a block away from Samantha's, was very much like the woman he had met at the WAC. Quiet. Subdued. Elegant. Everything in her shop sat neatly in order on the shelves and display tables scattered throughout the intimate store.

He browsed around the store while Kate helped a customer. There were an assortment of lotions, salts, perfumes and soaps. Aidan paused at one table and eased the stopper off a bottle. A heavy and rather cloying floral fragrance immediately filled the air before he could replace the top. He wrinkled his nose and quickly put the bottle down.

Moving to the next table, he took note of the assorted flowers being used in the preparations. Plumeria. Peony. Lavender. Lily of the Valley. No foxglove.

He wondered who prepared the floral essences for Kate or whether she did them herself. If it was the latter, it occurred to him that maybe she had been an unwitting accomplice to the Sparrow's kills. Maybe Elizabeth had asked her friend for something of a medicinal nature.

Or maybe Kate had managed to pull off a grand charade, he thought, as he examined her while she worked behind the counter. She was gift wrapping the customer's purchase. Her hands were nimble as she worked. Quick and sure with the scissors, he noted.

Kate was about the right height, although not slim. Definitely more voluptuous and of a slightly larger, but arguably medium build. Her hair leaned toward black more than brown, but of course, a woman's hair color could easily be changed.

As Kate finished and walked over, he gave her his best smile, but like Elizabeth, the lady seemed unaffected.

"You don't strike me as the gardenia type," Kate said and motioned to the bottle he held.

He shot the label a quick glance. "I was looking for something for Elizabeth. Do you know what she might like?"

Kate narrowed her eyes and took a long moment to scrutinize him. "Lizzy Bee doesn't strike me as your type, Aidan."

"Lizzy Bee?" he repeated and recollected her friends calling her by that nickname last night. "Cute," he added.

Kate adopted what some might consider a wary stance, arms across her midsection, head cocked to one side. "What do you want from Lizzy?"

Smiling, he put down the bottle of gardenia oil and moved to another table, Kate trailing behind him. "How about this? Do you think Lizzy Bee would like this?" he asked as he picked up another bottle.

Kate gently removed the fragrance from his hands and put it back in place. "Only her friends call her Lizzy Bee."

He wasn't winning any points by being nice, so maybe some shock factor would help this conversation move along in a more helpful direction. "Well, I'd definitely say that what happened last night could be called friendly."

She surprised him then by getting right in his face, her early wariness brewing into anger. As she poked a finger in his chest, he took a moment to examine her roots—all the same color as the rest of her black hair. Either recently colored or her natural shade.

Kate jabbed him once with her finger as she said, "Look, Mr. Travellin' Man. Lizzy has had enough grief in her life. She doesn't need the likes of you causing any more. Get it?"

Recalling the information in the file about her parents and hoping to elicit further explanation from the now prickly Kate, he urged, "What about Lizzy's family?"

Kate's look turned even harder and her poke this time actually registered on his pain meter. "You'll probably hear it anyway if you linger—Lizzy's mom and dad were killed a long time ago. Best you don't bring that up around her."

"I'm sorry to hear that. Accident?" he asked, his tone conciliatory and finally, a break appeared in Kate's armor.

"Murdered," she replied in soft tones and a telltale sheen erupted in her eyes.

With a slight incline of his head both in recognition of her statement and in deference to the deaths, he said, "I hope they got the bastard who did it."

"Unfortunately not, although if there is such a thing as karma, the prince got what he deserved." She spun away from him, heading back to the counter.

Aidan grabbed a bottle from a table along the way as he

followed her. Once she was there, he placed the bottle on the glass top of the counter holding an antique brass cash register. "Care to explain?"

Kate considered him carefully, as if deciding whether or not his interest was sincere. Apparently he passed muster, because she sighed and picked up the bottle, toying with it nervously as she explained herself. "Rumor had it that Lizzy's parents were accidentally delivered a load of fish stuffed with drugs. Whoever was bringing in the load must have found out and gone to retrieve the drugs."

"And Lizzy's parents were in the way?"

"Or maybe they had already found the hidden drugs and needed to be eliminated. Who knows? A suit from some ministry decided to use his pull to quash the investigation."

"Because the prince was involved in the murders?" Aidan pressed, needing to know because on some level, it justified to him what the Sparrow had done to the prince.

Kate shrugged. "Probably not directly. He was too young. But rumor has it he was a party animal. People like him are as responsible as the dealers who killed Lizzy's parents."

She finally looked down at the bottle in her hands. "Lizzy doesn't wear any perfume. You're better off buying her something she'll use."

She took the bottle with her as she walked away from the counter, placed the oil back on the shelf, paused by another table to pick up a small round jar and returned to where he stood. "Here. This is her favorite hand lotion. Slight hint of plumeria. Her hands get chapped."

That she used something on her hands was good, he thought. It might have left a residue on something at the prince's retreat that would help connect Lizzy—the Sparrow he forced himself to remember—to the murder.

"Thanks. Could you gift wrap it, please?" He dug into his jeans pocket for cash. While he was counting out the money for the lotion, he asked, "So who helps you create the formulas for everything?"

Kate punched up the sale on the antique register. With a loud clang and kachunk, the drawer opened and she finally responded to his question. "Most of them I do myself. Every now and then I ask Lizzy. She's a whiz with plants."

Elizabeth had been prepared to keep her cool around him, wanting to create some distance after what had happened on Friday night. Despite her desire to do so, she found herself surprisingly annoyed when it was Aidan who kept his distance.

He had shown up for work the next day, surprising her. She had been prepared for him to run.

He'd been courteous and respectful. No subtle mentions of Friday night's make-out session. No hint that it had left any kind of impression on him or even that he was inclined for a repeat performance.

Color her annoyed. Saturday and Sunday night had come and gone without any kind of move on his part and as for her—she'd be damned if she'd throw herself at him. Lord knew he'd probably had his share of women doing that, what with those blond good looks and that amazing body. Not to mention that whole swagger thing.

Elizabeth paused in the midst of her workout on the boxing bag as she considered that she was just losing focus about Aidan Rawlings.

A light sweat covered her body from her workout. She grabbed hold of the bag, which was rocking a bit from her last blow, and steadied it, considering as she did so that she'd done just fine in her life without a man. She definitely didn't need one to mess up her life right now.

Punch, punch. Jab followed by a drop kick.

The bag swung away again from the force of the blow and she timed its return arc, swung out with a roundhouse kick, imagining as she did so that it was Aidan's head.

From behind her came the sound of someone approaching. In her peripheral vision, a man's arm came into sight, reaching for her.

She grabbed the arm, high up close to the elbow, and with a shift of her hip, sent him flying over her shoulder and onto the mat face down. Once he was there, she twisted the arm she still held and placed her knee smack in the center of his back, pinning him forcefully to the mat.

Aidan, she thought from the familiar sight of his shoulders and that shaggy mane of sun-bleached hair. She was tempted to release him, but there was a bit of anger there, so she maintained her hold and warned, "Don't sneak up on me."

He turned his face to the side, the only movement he was capable of without dislocating a key body part. "Good mornin', love. I thought I'd drop by and see if you wanted to have breakfast. I guess not."

She released her hold a little. A mistake she quickly realized as he reversed their positions and nailed her to the ground. He had her wrists pinned to the mat in a tight grip. She was breathing a little roughly from her workout, and the motion seemed to drag his attention to her breasts.

Typical man, she thought as he loosened his hold much as she had earlier, giving her enough slack to roll and assume the upper position with Aidan now trapped below her. "We're closed Mondays. I wasn't expecting anyone."

He flexed his hips beneath her, right where she was busy straddling him in a very intimate position, she suddenly realized. "And a very good morning it is. Now," he teased.

"You're no gentleman," she said, freed him and rose, grabbing a towel from inside an open locker.

He was reaching out for her again, but she batted his arm away, disliking his assumption that one kiss gave him the right to touch. "Don't," she warned.

"Like to play rough?" he questioned playfully and as if to test how far he could push, extended his hand toward her once more.

As she had done before, she batted it away, but he teasingly repeated the gesture. Tossing down the towel with which she had been drying off, she once again flung away his arm and took a step toward him. "Mister, if you want to learn about rough, I'm game."

"Oooh. Big tough chef—"

He didn't get a chance to finish the statement as she dropped and swept his legs out from under him. He went down onto the mat in an ignominious sprawl.

He leaned up on his elbows and grinned at her. Damn him, she thought, but stayed out of his reach since she suspected he would be more than capable of taking her down. "Pretty nice moves. Where did you learn them?"

He was just full of questions, it seemed. Kate had told her that he had been by her shop on Saturday, prying into her private life. She wasn't about to satisfy his curiosity. She didn't trust him enough yet to tell him anything. "Let's just say a girl needs to know how to defend herself."

A moment of hesitation played across his face, which afterward, grew serious. "On account of what happened to your parents?"

She knew Kate had spilled the beans about her family history. Despite that, she had not been prepared for him to raise the subject. There wasn't anything really personal going on between them. Yet, the daring little voice in her head tacked on.

Walking back to the locker, she picked up the towel from the floor and began collecting her things, intent on going ahead with her normal Monday routine.

Out of the corner of her eye, she watched as Aidan stood and dusted himself off. He took a step toward her, then seemed to reconsider the wisdom of that. Grasping his hands in front of him tightly, he said, "Could we start over?"

Juggling her bag and towel in her hand, she half turned and said, "Meaning?"

"Good morning, Elizabeth. Would you care to have breakfast?" he asked in that husky bedroom voice of his.

She picked up her chin a defiant notch, determined not to let his charm affect her. "Sorry, but breakfast was two hours ago."

He glanced at his watch and with a carefree tone said, "How about lunch then?"

Determined, she would give him that. Smiling, she replied, "That's not for another three hours. Maybe four since I had a nice big breakfast."

In response, his stomach growled. He rubbed his hand over his midsection to silence it. "So what do you plan to do in the meantime? It is your day off after all."

"There's never a day off," she replied and walked to the stairs.

Aidan was immediately there, following her. Was it her imagination that he shot an inquisitive look at the safe and lockers? she wondered, but then realized that his gaze was securely fixed to her Lycra-clad backside.

With a roll of her eyes, and a little extra swing to her hips, she went up the stairs, advising him as she did so, "I plan on shopping."

"Shopping?" he croaked and shot a glance up at her face to see if she was serious. When he realized that she was, he said, "Shopping, huh. Well, I guess I'm game if it includes taking you to lunch."

She paused on the top step and examined his face. He was clearly sincere with his response. She told herself not to be too flattered that he'd risk shopping in exchange for lunch with her. Some men would do anything to impress a girl and Aidan definitely seemed to be that kind of man. Despite her awareness of that, she didn't feel like turning him down. He intrigued her too much, as dangerous as she knew that might be.

"It's a deal. Come back in half an hour. I need to shower."

"I'll just hang in the garden," he replied and once they were on the ground floor, she walked to her cottage while Aidan sat on the stone wall by the cottage path, perusing the various plants.

It occurred to her that there was something odd about his behavior since the other night. Maybe their little excursion would be just the thing to find out what he was really up to.

Her intuition told her Mr. Rawlings was interested in something she might not like.

Chapter 10

Aidan turned his attention to the assorted flowers in the restaurant's backyard and alongside the cottage. He didn't have a clue what most of the plants were and didn't care. His mind was focused on looking for the tall, spiky, purple-flowered plant that would put the final nails in the Sparrow's coffin.

As he searched and snapped photos with his PDA for good measure, cautiously walking along the edge of the garden, it occurred to him that today's little display of martial arts had almost iced it for him. What he couldn't understand is why that bothered him? For two years he'd been searching for the Sparrow and now that she was almost in his grasp, he was actually almost regretting it.

It wasn't because of the fact that she was attractive. He'd had his share of beautiful women to enjoy.

Was it because she was basically a really nice person from what he had seen of her behavior? Possibly. It definitely wasn't because of their kisses, or how good it had been with her riding him during their little physical interlude that morning.

He cursed when excitement awoke at the recollection of her above him, pressed tight, rousing him.

Shooting a glance at the cottage, he realized she was already inside. He switched the functions on his PDA just to confirm it. He had rigged his equipment last night to accept the signal from the assorted cameras and with a few swipes of his stylus, he got to the video feed from her bedroom.

She was undressing for the shower, her back to the camera. Totally unaware that anyone was keeping an eye on her.

He swallowed hard as she tossed aside her workout pants and eased off her panties. Her ass was perfection—and those legs…

He swiped at the sweat that popped out on his forehead and blamed the sun and leather jacket he was wearing, but he couldn't pull his gaze from the PDA.

"Mixmaster. Come in, Mixmaster," Lucia called out over the earpiece.

"What is it, Red Rover?" he snapped as Elizabeth slipped her fingers under the band of her sports bra and eased it up and over her head, displaying the long sweet line of her back, the flare of her breast as she bent to toss the bra and T-shirt on her bed.

"Bad, bad boy, Aidan. You're supposed to be looking at the flowers."

Cursing beneath his breath again as he realized Lucia was observing him, he shut off the video feed on the PDA and returned to camera mode so he could snap off a few photos for additional review. He would send them in via the satellite uplink in his PDA. "Copy, Red Rover. Prep yourself. In half an hour you can try and pick the locks if you've got the backup."

"Walker should be here shortly," she advised and Aidan extended his search for the foxglove to the front yard. Like the gardens in the back, this was a riot of colorful flowers mixed with green leaves and accented with foliage of burgundy, white and gold.

Nothing resembled the foxglove, and Elizabeth would be down shortly.

He strode across the front yard and was stalking around

the corner of the building when he noticed a patch of plants with little spikelets of flowers that weren't quite purple in his book. More a deep rose color, but the blooms were bell-shaped. As he bent and examined the leaves, he realized they were fuzzy. Fuzzy probably passed for hairy in the plant world and foxglove was supposed to be hairy.

Upon closer examination, he realized that the plants had at one time had another larger, central stalk. It prompted a recollection from the materials Lucia had downloaded for him—it was common to cut down the main flower spike after it was past its prime to produce a secondary flowering.

Bending, he took a plastic evidence bag from his pocket and, careful to use the bag to safeguard the integrity of the sample, snipped off leaves from a few different plants. He also took a moment to snap a picture.

"Find something?" Lucia questioned.

Aidan nodded, aware that she would see him via the garden camera. "You might say the mother lode. Let Walker know. I'm e-mailing you all the pictures now for someone to examine."

He placed the bag back into his pocket, quickly dispatched an e-mail with the digital photos, and returned to the backyard, settling himself on the low stone wall to wait for Elizabeth.

When she emerged, she nearly took his breath away. White capri pants emphasized those amazing legs and slim lines. A white crop top with pink polka dots left most of her sculpted midriff exposed. Her thick mass of hair was tied back with a pale-pink scarf, pulling his attention to her amazing eyes and the full lips he had liked kissing so much the other night.

Damn. She was dressed to kill and as her gaze met his, he realized it was not by accident.

She didn't know why she had chosen this particular outfit, but the flare of heat in Aidan's eyes proved she had made a good choice. That is, if she wanted whatever was happening between them to progress to the next level. Which her daring side was thinking she might, immediately before her more repressed side argued that it was totally insane. Daring side being ahead two to nothing at this point.

Reaching into the denim drawstring bag she was using as a purse, she pulled out her keys and dangled them before him. "We need to get the car. It's garaged a few blocks down."

He fell into step beside her as they walked to the main street and then toward the docks. They had gone only a short distance when she stopped by the garage next to the fish shop her parents had used to own.

Aidan seemed quick to pick up on that, for he asked, "Your parents' old store?"

With a nod, she slipped the key into the lock on the garage door. "After they died, a cousin took over running the shop in exchange for buying it out. It helped pay some of the bills."

"But not all?" he questioned.

"Not all," she answered truthfully. If Aidan was after something other than time with her, best he know now that money wasn't necessarily something of which she had a lot. The restaurant turned a profit, but only enough for her to be comfortable.

When she reached for the handle to lift the door, he said, "Let me."

She stepped aside and he grabbed hold of the garage door handle and lifted the door to reveal her father's prized roadster.

Aidan let out a low whistle. "That's a beauty. What is it?"

She walked into the garage and ran her hand lovingly over the hood. "A 1962 Gaston convertible. It was my Da's."

Sleek and sporty, the car screamed speed, she thought, and lovingly ran a hand over the smooth line of the driver's-side fender.

Aidan walked around the car, smiling. "This is a classic. Eight-cylinder engine. Chrome fenders, exhaust and spoke-wire wheels. Even the racing stripe," he said with the unadulterated glee of a boy on Christmas morning.

"Da's pride and joy. Silvershire's finest, he said. I even bought one of the Gaston new hybrids a few years back, but gave it up to keep this one."

"I can see why," he replied and ran his hand along the buttery-smooth leather of the passenger seat.

"Help me put the top down," she replied after Aidan had finished his inspection of the roadster.

He did as she asked and once the top was down and secured, eased into the passenger seat. She started the car and even with its age, the engine was as smooth as ever. She made it a point to have the car regularly serviced as her father might have if he was still alive.

Wheeling the low-slung roadster out of the garage, she turned onto the road leading away from town and Aidan looked at her quizzically. "Where are we headed?"

"Everywhere and anywhere. Just trust me," she said, smiling as the sun shone down on them and the wind blew into the cab of the car as she picked up speed.

Aidan's gaze met hers, and for a moment it seemed as if he was wondering if he could trust her. As quickly as that emotion came it fled, and he was grinning at her, his blue eyes even more startling in color in the bright sun and clear, cloudless day. He settled back into the leather seat of the Gaston, and she turned inland, deciding to save the coast road for the afternoon trip home.

Besides, they were going to have to do their shopping if she was to have fresh things for the restaurant and something they could eat for lunch. Maybe even dinner together if the day turned out right. She wouldn't consider that breakfast was a possibility. She had not met a man special enough to stay overnight in quite some time.

She drove along the woodland country roads for a quarter of an hour or so until they neared the prince's retreat. As they passed the tall wrought-iron gates that marked off part of the grounds, Aidan asked, "Is that private property?"

Peering toward the gates, she said, "It belonged to the prince, God rest his soul."

"Funny thing for you to say," Aidan quickly replied.

"Why do you think that?" she wondered, but kept her attention to the road. Deer were quite common in these woods as no hunting was permitted on the royal estate.

"According to Kate, you believe he's responsible for what happened to your mother and father," Aidan said, his tone almost…condemning.

She finally shot him a glance out of the corner of her eye, trying to understand where he was coming from. Wanting him to know just where she stood on the topic of the late prince. "People like him…don't care that their fun might hurt others. So that makes him responsible in a way."

With a shake of his head, he stressed, "But the royals don't get treated like you and me. If he did drugs, he and his friends were never going to pay for what harm they caused with that."

He was almost baiting her, wanting her to admit she had wanted the prince dead. When her parents had first died and the investigation had apparently been shut down by the royal family's minions, she had wanted to understand why and she wanted retribution. Had been prepared to seek it out herself. But then reason had replaced her anger and she had realized that eventually whoever was responsible would get what he deserved. If Reginald's drug habit had started that early, his life had probably been hell anyway.

"Whether on this plane or another, Reginald was eventually going to face the consequences of his actions," she finally answered, but her response did little to appease Aidan, she realized as she shot another quick glance at him. If anything, his face grew harder and a muscle clenched along his jaw.

When he spoke, his words were curt and filled with pain. "If it was someone I cared about, I'd want him punished. Now, and not in some afterlife."

The emotion was so intense, it compelled her to stop the car. After she did so, she faced him and laid her hand over his clenched fist where it rested on his thigh. "You lost someone like I lost my parents?"

Aidan knew he was close to blowing it, but her calm acceptance that the prince would get his punishment flew in the face of what he suspected she had done. And not just to the prince. But as she placed her smooth palm over his hand and her gaze met his, it was hard to believe she could commit those acts.

Her touch was gentle. The empathy in her gaze nearly undid him. *Nearly* being the operative word. He reined in his desire to test her reaction to Mitch's name and instead, decided to use her own ploy against her.

"My best friend."

"I'm sorry," she said and rubbed her hand over his in a gesture meant to soothe.

Aidan pressed. "If I knew who did it, I would kill them."

Her hand stilled. Her eyebrows knitted together as she contemplated his words. Finally, in a tone so soft he barely heard her, she said, "Then that would end two lives instead of one, wouldn't it? Your's and the killer's."

She met his gaze then, dead on, her chin in a slightly defiant tilt. Her sherry-colored eyes had deepened to the color of a fine aged cognac. He was hard pressed to know whether she was challenging him or troubled by the prospect of what he had claimed he would do.

Given the Sparrow's track record, he couldn't imagine that she would be worried about his coming after her. She'd proven herself too worthy an opponent already. As for the possibility that she was challenging him, that would mean that he had maybe blown his cover, and she knew he was referring to her and Mitch.

If he had done the latter, there was possibly one way to know for sure. "His name was Mitch," he said and waited for her reaction.

"Mitch? Was he the friend who was killed?" she asked, no hint of any recognition on her face.

He went for broke. "Someone knifed him in an alleyway in Rome."

No hint again of anything on her face or in her tone indicated she had a clue what he was talking about. "Was it a robbery? Or a fight over something?"

"Does it matter?" he replied and finally her face reflected some emotion—pain.

"No, it doesn't. Dead is dead. Out of your life. Never to hold you again. Or laugh with you."

She whirled in her seat, then started up the car and pulled onto the road again. As she drove, she occasionally swiped at her eyes, but said nothing else.

Great. He had made her cry. He hated to see women cry. Call him a sucker, but the waterworks always did him in.

And somehow, he couldn't imagine the Sparrow allowing herself the luxury of tears. Which just confused him even more. Elizabeth's words and actions contradicted what he had expected.

Again he told himself to remember that the Sparrow was likely a sociopath and perfectly capable of such a deception. Walker would remind him of that. He suspected the earpiece he still wore had exceeded the range for transmission back to the hotel. A shame. If Walker had been listening in, he might have been able to get a better read on Elizabeth.

Elizabeth, he thought and examined her again. The pale-pink scarf securing her hair matched the polka dots in her shirt. The color brought out the hints of red in her lush hair. The wind was tossing about the few strands that had escaped the scarf. She must have sensed him watching her for she glanced his way for a moment before returning her attention to the road.

"What's so interesting?" she asked, seemingly uncomfortable with his perusal.

"You. You're beautiful," he said, wanting to change the

mood that had taken over since their earlier discussion. Hoping that change would lead to other things. He told himself that was what was necessary for him to break down her barriers and really determine what was going on with her.

But it wasn't a lie that he found her…*attractive* wasn't quite the right word. She was…stunning. Interesting. A woman with multiple layers he wanted to peel back. He suspected that so far he had only managed to scrape the first few layers.

She smiled and a touch of pink in a shade darker than her scarf stained her cheeks. Sparing him yet another glance, she said, "I bet you say that to all the girls."

Grinning, he replied, "Only the pretty ones."

Chapter 11

Elizabeth drove around a bend in the road that led out of the woods and to the first of her regular stops. Up ahead, another car was already parked at one side of the road while along the other, a fence kept an assortment of goats and cows in an emerald-colored pasture thick with summer grass.

She slowed as she pulled up behind the other car, and Aidan asked, "Is this where we're shopping?"

"We call it 'hedge veg,'" she explained and parked the Gaston along the side of the road.

"'Hedge veg?'" Aidan repeated and cocked his head to the side in question. "Is that like the Silvershire version of green markets?"

She shook her head and tucked a few loose strands of hair back. "It's not just greens and typically, we don't stop at markets. Come with me and you'll see."

Not waiting for his reply, since at this point he was basically her captive audience, she slipped from the car and walked to meet him where he waited by the chromed front bumper of the Gaston. As she approached, he offered his arm and touched by the chivalrous gesture, she eased her arm through his. They strolled past the other parked auto and toward a modest covered stand by the side of the road and in front of a well-kept farmhouse. A man who had apparently just made a purchase strolled past them, bag in hand.

"Hi, Addy," she called out once they were closer to the stand.

The older gray-haired woman behind the counter smiled broadly and walked around to give her an enthusiastic hug and Aidan an inquisitive look.

"And this would be?" Addy asked as she shook Aidan's hand.

"Aidan. I'm Elizabeth's new bartender."

Once again, Addy's look was speculative as it passed from Aidan and back to her, but she ignored it. "What do you have for me today?"

Addy grabbed her hand and nearly dragged her over to the counter. "The goat cheese is out of this world today and the husband just finished up a batch of mozzarella," she said and motioned to the samples spread out on the table.

Elizabeth first tasted the goat cheese. Creamy, with a full-bodied flavor. She scooped up another bit on a cracker and offered it up to Aidan, who had come to stand beside her.

He opened his mouth and she popped it in. After chewing, he nodded emphatically. "That's good."

Next, they sampled the mozzarella. Still warm from the vats where it was prepared, the cheese had a rich creamy flavor, milder than the goat cheese and with a firmer consistency. She smiled at Addy to show her approval and said, "I'll take a dozen each of both these cheeses if you have that many. Only, I'm not headed straight back to town. I could pick them up tomorrow...."

Addy waved off her suggestion. "Not to worry, luv. My George has to pop into town during the morning, so he can drop them off."

"Thanks so much. In the meantime, we'll need something

for a picnic lunch. How about the…" She glanced over at Aidan and waited for him to make the selection.

He shrugged, seemingly unsure at first, but then he pointed to the goat cheese.

"Great choice," she confirmed, and Addy quickly wrapped up a round of the cheese in some grape leaves, dropped it into a bag, and passed it to Aidan to carry.

"You two have a nice day now," the older woman called out as they returned to the car.

Aidan tucked the bag into the space behind the front seats that arguably passed for a back seat. It brought a memory to Elizabeth of her and Dani crammed onto that narrow leather bench as young girls while her family did the hedge veg together.

She was smiling as she eased behind the wheel and Aidan must have noticed it, for he said, "Penny for your thoughts."

"Only a penny?" she teased, starting up the car and steering it back onto the main road.

Aidan examined her face carefully, wondering what had put that enigmatic smile there. It was a smile filled with pleasure, but also with a hint of…nostalgia. Surprisingly, he knew the thought wasn't one about him, although how he could read her that well, he didn't know.

Or maybe she was just acting once again. She *was* the Sparrow after all. Or at least, that's what he forced himself to remember.

The next stop was barely a few miles away: a farmhouse where the yeasty aromas of fresh-baked bread wafted all the way to the roadside. As before, there was a stand and this time, a few other patrons were already lined up for the homemade wares.

Just as at the other location, the older woman behind the counter was clearly pleased to see Elizabeth, but then again he told himself, why wouldn't she be glad to see someone who was probably a good customer? Although, as with Addy, there appeared to be something more personal there, which was confirmed when at one point, the two women stepped to the side and Elizabeth eased her arm over the older women's shoulders.

A more serious discussion obviously ensued. Definitely one that wasn't about the assortment of breads and rolls the woman had for sale. At the end of the conversation, the two exchanged an emotion-packed hug before returning to the stand where the woman placed a number of different rolls in a brown paper bag.

Elizabeth paid her, grabbed the bag and handed it to him. "So I'm the bag man, is that it?"

She grinned at him playfully and nudged his shoulder with a closed fist. "You've got to earn your lunch somehow."

He bit back a rather risque comment on how he could earn that lunch.

With a nod, he followed her back to the car, tucked away their purchase and they were off to another stop and then another and another. It took hours to run from one roadside stand to another, sampling the assorted items available for sale. At one small farm that barely looked inhabited, a rough-hewn ramshackle table held a meager sampling of thumb-sized pear-shaped tomatoes. Beside what was left of the tomatoes, a basket contained some money, obviously payment for prior purchases.

Elizabeth perused the tomatoes, selected a few dozen, and deposited some bills into the basket.

"How do you know that's not too much money?" he asked, and then quickly added, "And how does the farmer know people will pay?"

"Dan, the farmer, he's a bit shy. But he knows people will pay for what they take. It's the honor system."

"The honor system," he repeated, but unfortunately couldn't keep the tone of disbelief from his voice.

Elizabeth smiled and shook her head. "Mr. Rawlings, you've clearly seen your share of places where things are…different. In Silvershire, we are simpler. Some things, like honor, still exist."

With that, she walked back to the car, her bag of tomatoes in hand.

He watched her go, intrigued. Perplexed. From their earlier conversation to this one, from the way everyone they met interacted with her, Elizabeth was clearly well-liked and respected, trusted and, last but not least, honorable.

Aidan forced himself to remember that even amongst thieves honor existed.

Back in the car, Elizabeth advised they would make one more stop before heading to a special place for a quick bite. That last location was a vineyard within sight of the water. "Hector makes a wicked collection of pinots. It has to do with the way the coastal fog covers the grapes in the morning and the way the blackthorn and other wild berry bushes surround the vineyard," Elizabeth explained as she drove.

"Is this the ever-requested Lionshead wine?" he asked and Elizabeth nodded as she steered down a short winding road lined by brambly bushes—probably the berries Elizabeth had mentioned.

At the end of the road was a stone building, similar in size and construction to Elizabeth's restaurant—a one-story building made of stone and covered by vines in spots. After they parked the car in the crushed-seashell-covered lot, they walked to the open door of the building.

Inside there were two long counters with some smaller tables and chairs before them—a tasting room from the looks of it, he thought, recalling one Mitch had dragged them to many years earlier during a layover in California's Napa Valley.

"Hector? Are you open?" Elizabeth called out and walked toward the counters.

A man immediately popped out of the back room. Once he realized it was Elizabeth, a broad smile came to his face. *"Mi amiga,"* he said, arms opened wide as he strode toward her.

"Como estas, Hector?" She embraced the handsome man. He was maybe in his mid thirties and attractive if you liked the dark swarthy types, he thought and bit back the little pang of jealousy.

Hector shot a glance at him. An unfriendly one confirming to Aidan that maybe the feeling was mutual. "And this is?" Hector asked after releasing Elizabeth and walking to one of the long counters, where he picked up a bottle and opened it, removing first the foil seal at the top and after, the cork.

Elizabeth held her hand out to Aidan. He slipped his hand into hers and sat next to her at the counter as she said, "This is Aidan. My new bartender."

"Oh," Hector said, but made no effort to take the introduction beyond that. Instead, he placed a glass before each of them and said, "Try my new vintage."

Pouring a bit of wine into each glass, he waited for Elizabeth to offer her comments.

Aidan just picked up the wineglass and took a large sip, earning a murderous glare from Hector. Elizabeth on the other hand, held the glass up to the light, then tilted it on its side. "Good color and tone."

Placing the glass on the counter, she grabbed the stem and rotated it to swirl the wine. Once the wine had settled down, she picked up the glass and sniffed the wine. "Wonderful robust bouquet."

With more of a slurp than a sip, she finally sampled it. "Exceptional, Hector. You can really taste the berries. Mostly…blackberry?" she questioned.

Hector enthusiastically confirmed her guess. "So, you like?"

Nodding, she said, "I like, a lot. Can I get a case delivered to the restaurant and one bottle for now?"

Glancing in Aidan's direction as he realized he would likely be the imbiber of the single bottle of wine, Hector glared at him again, but Aidan merely smiled at the man.

With a grumble beneath his breath about wine heathens, Hector stalked into the back room and a few seconds later, emerged with the single bottle, which he lovingly entrusted to Elizabeth. "Enjoy it, *amiga,*" he said, but all the time he scowled at Aidan.

Elizabeth leaned over the counter and gave Hector a friendly kiss, seemingly unaware of what was going on between him and Aidan. As they exited the tasting room, she met his gaze and smiled. "Ready for that late lunch?"

Aidan shot a quick peek at his watch and realized it was nearly four. "A very late lunch. Possibly early dinner."

She stopped and checked her own watch. "I'm sorry. Time just seemed to fly. Would you rather return to town?"

He stood before her. She looked so troubled that he needed to ease her discomfort. Cupping her cheek, he ran his finger along the smooth skin there, which had a touch of color—the kiss of the sun from their drive. "I've had a great time so far. It's been…enlightening."

An odd choice of words, Elizabeth thought as she examined him. He seemed sincere enough about having enjoyed the day so far, and so she said, "All right, then. We're off to lunch."

Back behind the wheel of the car, she continued onward to the coast road and turned in the direction of Leonia. As she drove, she alternated glances between the coastline to her right, the road before her and Aidan in the passenger seat. He was looking toward her and then past her to the rugged shoreline.

It took another fifteen minutes or so to reach the spot. Her spot. One free of ghosts.

She had discovered it one day many years back during one of her hedge-veg runs. Pulling the car over to a switchback along the coast side of the road, she parked the Gaston and faced Aidan. "Ready?"

He confirmed, "Ready."

She leaned into the back of the car and grabbed just a few of the packages stored there and handed them to Aidan. "I just need to get something from the back," she said.

They both stepped out of the car, but he waited by the front fender while she went to the back. Opening the trunk, she removed the blanket and picnic basket her mother had always kept there for an impromptu stop. She slipped the blanket under one arm and grabbed the basket with that hand. Walking toward Aidan, she offered him her other hand and he took hold of it.

Hand in hand they walked down the grass-covered slope until they were at its rocky edge. Once there, they paused for a moment to appreciate the view. To the left were the imposing palisades and rugged shoreline of Silvershire's North Coast. To the right, Leonia Bay with the sister towns of Leonia and Tiberia nestled at its foot. In the bay, sailboats and fishermen's boats travelled to and fro, or put out to sea.

"Beautiful," he said, but as their gazes met, it was clear he wasn't referring to the view.

The intensity of his interest created a funny little feeling inside her. Bolstered by that feeling, she smiled at him, took a step closer and cradled his cheek. Beneath her palm there was the rasp of his evening beard and the warmth of his skin. She ran her finger along that beard and then to the edge of his lips, fascinated by them. By him.

She dragged her gaze from his lips and up to his eyes. Against the backdrop of sky and sea, they seemed even more blue than before. "Are you hungry?" she asked, but the question suddenly had little to do with food.

Aidan placed his hand on her waist, on the bare piece of skin exposed by the crop top. His hand was hot. His palm rough against the soft skin of her midsection. "Famished," he replied and closed the last little bit of distance between them.

She had to look up at him with his greater height. She watched as he bent his head until his lips were almost on hers. "Is this crazy?" he asked and again, she was puzzled by his choice of words.

Brushing her lips against his in the barest of kisses, she said, "Is it because I'm your boss?"

He pulled away then and his face mirrored his bewilderment and withdrawal. "Let's eat," he said and held the basket so she could lay out the blanket.

She hesitated for a moment, equally confused and…hurt.

She wasn't normally one to just throw herself at a man and now that she almost had…

Denied, her repressed side almost gloated. It stung a bit, but she wasn't going to let that ruin what had been a wonderful day.

Spreading out the blanket on the prickly grass by the rocky bluff, she then took the picnic basket from him and placed it to one side. Then she accepted the remaining items from him, including the bottle of wine, and worked on creating a spur-of-the-moment meal.

The goat cheese went on one plate and she surrounded it with the pear tomatoes, drizzling them with the fresh-pressed virgin olive oil she had bought. She took a bit of sea salt and, with her fingers, sprinkled it all over the cheese and tomatoes.

She placed that plate in the space between her and Aidan, who had taken a spot on the opposite side of the blanket.

On another plate, she placed the rolls and slices of a dry-aged ham similar to a prosciutto purchased at one of their stops. That plate joined the other, and then she handed Aidan the bottle of wine, a corkscrew and some glasses.

"Are you always this prepared?" he asked and took the items from her.

"We always picnicked," she explained. "Sometimes it was after a shopping expedition or a hike. Sometimes a day at the beach."

"It sounds like your family had fun," he said and she nodded, but battled the mix of sadness and happiness the memory brought.

"Yes, we did. I miss them a lot."

Her voice had a tight feel to it. As he looked at her again, he could see the glint of unshed tears. He picked up his hand and moved it toward her, wanting to comfort her once again, but then quickly let it drop back down. This was crazy, he thought, much as he had told himself earlier. Crazy because there were too many secrets between them. Too many doubts.

So instead, he concentrated on opening the wine and

pouring glasses for each of them while she put out the final plate—a dish piled high with an assortment of summer berries.

He handed her a glass filled with Hector's wine, and offered up a silent toast. He waited for her to take a roll, break off a piece and then scoop up a bit of the oil-drizzled cheese. She popped the snack into her mouth and smiled. "Delicious." After, she reached for one of the tomatoes and did the same.

Aidan joined her, ate some of the bread and cheese. The flavors were…amazing. The tang of the cheese and fruitiness of the oil. The creaminess of it all against the crustiness and yeasty taste of the bread. He reached for a tomato and like the bread and cheese, the flavor was intense. Earthy and sweet. "Really, really good."

"Try this," she said and offered a bit of the ham that she had wrapped around a chunk of the bread. He let her feed him the morsel. Again, the tastes and textures were alive in his mouth.

"Hmm," he replied and washed down the bite with a sip of the wine. It was, as she'd noted in the tasting room, quite good. And he could taste the hint of berries.

Or maybe it was his imagination, since from beyond the rim of the glass he was busy watching Elizabeth toss back a bit of the wine and eat a strawberry. As he brought the glass down, their gazes collided and he realized that no matter what he thought she might be, he found her incredibly interesting. Complex. Desirable.

And the feeling, it occurred to him as her gaze travelled over his face and settled on his lips, was apparently decidedly mutual.

Take it slow, he told himself. He needed to explore all the nuances of the woman sitting across from him, just as he could with the wine in the glass. Maybe he could uncover other things about her, as well, during this little…interlude.

He reached for a strawberry—a big, red ripe one. Picking it up, he brought it to her lips.

She covered his hand with hers, as if to steady it. A sweet touch. Gentle.

She took a bite of the berry and the juice from it escaped onto her lips, reddening them. She licked the juice away with her tongue.

He nearly groaned as he imagined that tongue licking other things. As it was, he had to shift his position on the blanket to ease the pressure of his erection against his jeans.

Men were sometimes too easy, Elizabeth thought. But as she took note of other things, her mouth suddenly went dry and she realized, maybe men and women weren't all that different, as parts of her suddenly became…ready.

Physical response notwithstanding, she knew nothing about Aidan other than he would leave, and he in turn knew little about her. Not who or what she was. Not what she wanted from life.

But then again, maybe this didn't have anything to do with any of that. Maybe this was one of those carpe diem times. Time to seize and be seized in return without any thought as to where that would lead. When the voice of common sense rose up to tell her it would lead to nothing good, she batted it way, tired of being sensible.

Grabbing another bit of bread and cheese, she once again offered it up to him. A little smidge of cheese remained on his lips and he must have sensed it for he was reaching up to wipe it away when she said, "Let me."

He stopped, his gaze on her face as she shifted on the blanket to move closer and then, flicked her tongue over his lips to remove that one errant piece of cheese.

He moaned then. Or at least she thought he did, but he made no move to take it any further.

So maybe he wasn't as easy as she had thought. It wasn't going to stop her from doing the seizing. She was a modern woman after all.

Aidan took a deep breath to control himself since he wanted nothing more than to kiss her and lay her down on that blanket and take off every last piece of…

He gritted his jaw and told himself to maintain perspective. He was investigating her. She was likely a renowned assassin who would gut him quite easily with that little knife she was using to remove the skin from a pear she had pulled out of another bag.

With the pear peeled, she made slices which she placed on the plate beside the strawberries. Once she was done, she sipped her wine, grabbed a little more of the bread, cheese and ham. Another tomato.

He watched her enjoy the food with such gusto. He wanted to join her in that sensation and so he did the same, eating more of their purchases. He reached for a slice of pear but was waylaid as she offered her slice to him; he, in turn, offered her his slice.

The pear was sweet and so ripe that the juices dripped onto his fingers and downward. His gaze was locked with hers as they brought the slices of fruit to each other's mouths. Their eyes never wavered from each other as they both bit down and ate the pear slices.

But when nothing was left and he would have reached for another piece, she did the unexpected.

She grabbed hold of his hand and brought it close to her mouth. Slowly, she licked the pear juice from each of his fingers and then finally, slipped his index finger into her mouth to lick it some more.

It was his undoing; he nearly burst the seams on his jeans.

He grasped her head in his hands, but some last little crumb of chivalry reared its head as he asked, "Are you sure about this?"

"No," she said, and he had to smile at her honesty.

Thieves, he reminded himself as he closed the distance between them and said, "Me, neither," just a moment before he finally kissed her as he had wanted to all day long.

Chapter 12

The other night hadn't been an aberration, she thought. He really was an amazing kisser. His mouth was hard and soft. Gentle and rough. Warm.

Unbelievably delicious, she thought, as she licked his lips and tasted the pear and berries and cheese, and, beneath it all, the elusive but heady taste of Aidan.

She whimpered. Or, at least, she thought she did, which made him back away for a second until he realized it was a good kind of sound and he smiled.

She could feel that smile against her lips which in turn, made her chuckle.

He seized the opportunity then and dipped his tongue into her mouth, increased the pressure of his hand on the back of her head. She met his tongue with hers, tasting him. Exploring the different sensations of his mouth, tongue and lips. Of his warm breath coming roughly against her mouth as he expelled a ragged groan.

"Lizzy Bee," he said, but she pulled away from him then, afraid of the intimacy in his tone.

"Don't call me that." She added hastily, "Please."

The warmth in his eyes grew cold. "I guess only your friends call you that," he said and withdrew from her.

Talk about ruining the moment, she thought and plucked at the fabric of her pants. "I'm sorry. I didn't—"

He cut her off with the curt motion of his hand. "It's okay, Elizabeth. Really. I remember the rules—don't touch."

She struggled for the right words. "It's not that. It's just… You're right that only my friends call me that. And my family. And you're—"

"Neither," he quickly shot out and peered at her, his gaze condemning.

"Neither," she repeated lamely. "But I'm…attracted to you and…"

Her hands searched in the air as if she might pluck her explanation from there, but could find nothing better than, "I like you. I want to get to know you. I thought I could do this right now, only—"

She didn't get to finish as he suddenly resumed where they'd left off—kissing her with his lips and tongue until she moaned, and he finally eased away. "We need to take this a little slower, right?"

"Definitely," she confirmed and smiled. "Sometimes you can't rush things."

"Right," he said and picked up his glass. "Like a good wine—"

"It takes patience and…nurturing," she finished for him.

"Caring," he surprised her by saying, and, for a moment, it seemed as if he'd surprised himself by admitting it, so much so that there was almost a physical reaction on his part as his body tensed and he sat up straighter.

"Aidan?" she asked and he forced a smile.

"This is…new for me," Aidan replied. It wasn't a lie. It was new for him on so many levels. He had never lost control with another woman before as he had with Elizabeth. He had never lost his perspective while on an assignment, but here he was, clearly in jeopardy of doing so. Or maybe he had already, since he found himself reviewing over and over again all the things he'd learned about her in the past few days, trying to weigh them against the evidence that he knew pointed to her being the Sparrow.

When she gave him a shy smile and the blush of the sun's kiss deepened on her face, it became even harder thinking of her as an assassin.

"It's new for me, too," she said.

He nodded in resignation, uncomfortable with where this was leading. "Let's finish up and head back."

"Let's," she said as if sensing that to push more right now would only cause problems. "The coast road is beautiful during the day, but at night it can be a little difficult."

He had been so distracted by her, he hadn't realized how much time had gone by and how quickly dusk was coming upon them. Perusing the shoreline, he caught glimpses of the road they would take back to town. It wound wickedly along the coast. In spots, the road hugged the edges of the rocky palisades before it led downward toward the two towns nestled at the base of the harbor.

He helped her put away the food that remained and fold up the blanket. Once everything was carefully stowed in the trunk, Elizabeth got back behind the wheel of the car and he slipped in beside her. As she started up the car, he said, "I had a nice time today."

Grinning broadly, she replied, "I did, too, but the day's not over yet. You're going to love the views on the road home."

He was kind of loving the view right now, he thought, but didn't say so. It would just embarrass her. Instead, he contented himself with watching her out of the corner of his eye as she steered onto the road and they began the downward trek along the coast.

It was as beautiful as she had said: the harsh imposing cliffs and rocks against the cerulean blue of the ocean and baby blue of the sky, Elizabeth in her pink a vibrant contrast in the foreground.

She handled the car well, maintaining a controlled pace along the downhill road with its constant curves, some of which came precariously close to the rocky edges of the cliffs. They were about halfway down the road, along a stretch that was a little straighter, when an SUV suddenly appeared behind them.

Aidan was a bit surprised he hadn't noticed the car before, or maybe it had just turned onto the road behind them. Something bothered him about the car. Okay, maybe more than one thing. The windows were tinted so darkly it was impossible to see inside. The black of its oversized hulk loomed behind them as it picked up speed, getting closer and closer.

Elizabeth had noticed the car, as well, and muttered, "Wonder where he's going at that speed. It gets kind of hairy up—"

She didn't get to finish as the SUV suddenly lurched forward and bumped them from behind. The Gaston swerved wildly as Elizabeth battled for control, but she quickly regained it and centered the car in her lane.

Aidan gripped the wooden dash with one hand, Elizabeth's seat with the other as he braced himself for another possible impact. He looked back and noticed that the SUV had fallen behind by at least a car length. Elizabeth had sped up to avoid the other vehicle.

But a second later, the black SUV hurtled forward like a battering ram, smashing into their back bumper once more. The sickening crunch of metal and tinkling of glass sounded. The impact whipped them back and forth within the car, which fishtailed once more with the blow.

Elizabeth, however, didn't panic. If anything, a determined glint came into her eyes. Her jaw set into a tight line. She expertly steered out of the fishtail and into the middle of the road. This time, she kept dead center, ignoring the white lines for the lanes as if to give herself room to maneuver.

Aidan looked back and out of the corner of his eye, noted Elizabeth using the rearview mirror to keep the SUV in sight while staying aware of the road ahead. A road that was veering sharply to the right. To the left—nothing but sky and sea. Not even a guard rail.

Shit, he thought, until Elizabeth—looking more like an Indy race-car driver than a chef—downshifted and hit the gas. Wheels squealed as they shot around the curve and created a few car lengths of good distance on the bulkier SUV, which barely managed to stay on the road.

Dirt kicked up as the driver of the other vehicle skirted the warning edge along the coast side of the road, but then they were into another short straightaway and the SUV picked up speed.

So did Elizabeth.

"Elizabeth," he called out to her, for the wind was rushing past them, noisy and wild.

"Hold on, Aidan," she screamed at him before she steered confidently through another curve, increasing the distance between them and the SUV, which fishtailed before coming through the curve more slowly.

But as before, on the straightaway the SUV made up some distance until it was nearly on their tail.

And then Elizabeth did the unexpected.

With another cliff-edged curve before them, Elizabeth pulled over hard to the right, did a one-eighty into a switch-back and stopped, tires skidding on the soft shoulder.

Surprised and unprepared, the SUV shot by them and then Elizabeth became the chase vehicle, pulling out and staying close to the SUV as it now tried to outrun them.

"Get the plate numbers," she called out to him, but the car in front had no plate.

As soon as she realized that, she dropped back, slowing down as their attacker increased the distance between and then finally, after one last barely controlled turn on a curve, the SUV sped out of view.

Elizabeth pulled over then. Her hands were fisted against the steering wheel, her knuckles white from the pressure. She was breathing roughly, as was he, he realized. "You okay?"

She nodded, obviously unable to speak.

"Would you like me to finish the drive?" he asked and she nodded, popping out of the driver's seat.

He got out of the car and met her halfway, at the back of the Gaston where she had stopped to look at the damage. Tears filled her eyes and she wrapped her arms around herself tightly.

Embracing her, he winced at the dented chrome bumper, scratched and bent trunk, and the jagged glass shards that remained of her taillights. Her father's pride and joy, he recalled, and trying to comfort her, said, "We can fix it."

She nodded brokenly and tears finally slipped down her face as she replied, "But it will never be the same."

Chapter 13

Aidan hated leaving her, but she insisted she was fine.

When he mentioned calling the local police to report the incident, she had grown agitated and insisted that it made no sense. They had no ID of the driver and no plate number.

All good reasons, except that any normal person would think that the police just might be interested in an attempted murder. But Elizabeth was clearly not a normal person, he thought as he walked back to the hotel and recalled the professional way she had handled herself at the wheel.

Back at the hotel, both Lucia and Walker were waiting for him.

Lucia jumped out of her seat and stalked over to him. She gesticulated wildly with her hands as she demanded, "Is there some reason you've been incommunicado all day?"

Aidan cursed and stopped her hands in midair. He reached into his jacket pocket for the earpiece that he had taken off when he'd realized they were beyond its range. Hoping he would get up close and personal with Elizabeth, he had not wanted to risk her seeing it. "Sorry. We were out of range."

"All day?" Walker asked and examined him carefully, anger darkening his normally blue eyes to a slate gray. "You look…confused."

Aidan plopped himself down on the couch. Lucia and Walker joined him, sitting on the chairs opposite him. "It was an odd day." He recounted what they had done, leaving out some key personal parts. Finally, he provided a detailed account of the SUV attack.

"Tinted windows. No plates. Sounds like someone was intentionally after you," Lucia said, and then added, "Any idea on the make?"

"Big. Relatively fast. Might have been a Hummer. It was dark and too much was happening too fast."

Lucia added her two cents. "I'll check through the island's DMV records and see what I can dig up."

"But there's more that's bothering you, isn't there?" Walker asked, leaning forward and resting his forearms on his thighs as he clasped his hands together. "Want to tell us what it is?"

Aidan slumped down into the cushions of the sofa and looked up at the ceiling, unable to meet Walker's discriminating gaze. Afraid the psychiatrist might see too much. "Everywhere we went, people were so happy to see her. She seemed to really take an interest in them." He then recounted the talk about the prince and after, the one about honor and still believing in it.

"But she refused to call in the police. She had something to hide," Lucia reminded him before Walker piped in with his opinion.

"The Sparrow is a stone-cold, remorseless killer. A pathological liar who is unable to form commitments of any type, but can fool people exceptionally well. Classic antisocial behavior."

"Elizabeth seems to have lots of commitments: her friends, all those people we met today." He didn't add that for a moment there, she seemed to have been getting committed to him.

"These kinds of killers are by nature glib and superficially charming. If it came down to it, the Sparrow would do as she pleased with little regard for that supposed friendship or affection," Walker reminded him.

"Like Mitch," he said out loud and finally met Walker's gaze.

"Or like you, Aidan. Don't let this woman trip you up with her charm and beauty," Walker warned.

"What made her like this?" he wondered aloud, still trying to reconcile what the Sparrow had done with the woman who was getting a little too close to his heart. Who threatened his mission.

"If she's a psychopath—nothing. She was born that way. But I think Elizabeth is likely a sociopath, slipping into this behavior due to the deaths of her parents."

Aidan recalled Elizabeth putting up the walls whenever talk turned to her parents. Her tears about the car came to mind. The tears hadn't been about crunched metal and broken glass. Certainly their deaths still plagued her. "You may be right about the why," he admitted. "She's still deeply affected by her parents' murders."

"You need to be careful around her," Lucia reminded, clearly concerned that he had lost perspective.

And maybe neither she nor Walker were all that wrong. Elizabeth was making him doubt who she was. Making him want to find a reason why she did what she did if she was indeed the Sparrow. A reason he could understand—like wanting revenge. He could comprehend that one well. It was what should have still been motivating him—avenging his friend's death.

He sat up and rubbed his hands along his thighs. "Lucia, were you able to get into the safe and the locker?"

She smiled emphatically. "Your little gadget worked like a charm. Broke right into both, only… There was no foot locker in the safe."

"She got it out of there without us seeing it? How?" he questioned sharply.

Shaking her head, Lucia answered, "There was nothing on

the cameras. I can't explain how she did it. And as for that secret pathway, it led into a series of tunnels which might take weeks to explore."

He turned his attention to Walker and suddenly recalled the evidence bag in his pocket. He tossed it to the other man. "Here's your foxglove. Maybe the DNA will match. Did the photos help at all?"

Walker admitted that they had, but motioned to the phone on the coffee table. "I think it's better that we get Xander on the line for this one."

Alexander Forrest, Xander to his friends and colleagues, was the Lazlo Group's DNA specialist and resident botanist. Lucia used her laptop to connect with Xander and his image filled the computer screen. After the preliminaries, he toggled the window on the monitor to display the photos Aidan had taken with his PDA.

"I assume you want a rundown on the Sparrow's flora," Xander said.

"Yes, please, Xander," Aidan confirmed and then the three of them settled back to listen and watch Xander's report. With swift strokes of his mouse, he instructed them on the assorted plants in Elizabeth's garden.

"The lady has a veritable pharmacy of poisons and medicines in her little gardens," he began. "These low-lying flowers are nasturtiums and completely edible."

He circled the bright orange and yellow flowers.

"But right next door and not so good—Lily of the Valley. Poisonous to cats, dogs, goats and, of course, humans. Next and a little further back, delphiniums. Likewise poisonous. But again, mixed in with this, there's some chamomile— good for stomach upsets. And some…"

Aidan listened and watched as the screen was slowly filled by Xander's strokes as he identified one plant or another. When that screen was filled, he went to the next shot and likewise detailed a number of other edible, poisonous or medicinal plants: calendula, valerian, echinaecea and peppermint.

Aidan had already been familiar with the latter since Elizabeth had shown him where he could get peppermint to use for drinks at the bar.

Last but not least, Xander flipped to the snapshot of what Aidan had suspected was the foxglove.

"*Digitalis purpurea* subspecies *mariana*. More commonly found in Portugal. Great choice for rocky areas prone to drought. Flowers are closer to rose than purple. But no matter how you use it—leaves or seeds—still deadly," Xander confirmed.

"So this garden—"

"Chock full of all kinds of plants that one could use for either good or bad," Xander interrupted.

Something went cold inside Aidan at Xander's words. Up until now, Elizabeth's actions had almost had him convinced that she wasn't what he suspected. That she might not be the Sparrow. But now…this was just one other thing to add to the ever-growing list of evidence against her.

First, her obvious presence in so many of the areas where the Sparrow had had a kill attributed to her.

Her physical condition and martial arts skills, not to mention her driving abilities.

Now the deadly garden plants. As he remembered his first day in the kitchen, he recalled her nimble handling of the knife. A killer's way with a knife.

If Elizabeth wasn't the Sparrow…

"Walker's got some leaves I snipped off the plants. Will you be able to do anything with that?"

Suddenly Xander's face filled the screen again. He held up a test tube. "I've already done the PCR testing on the sample our crew lifted off the prince's marble coffee table. Seems that's where he decided to do the lines of coke."

"So we were able to get more evidence at the crime scene?" Lucia asked her colleague.

Walker was the one who answered. "Our unit collected some remnants of coke, but no fingerprints, hair or fiber other than the prince's."

"What about fluids?" he asked, interested in a perverse and decidedly personal kind of way in whether the prince had shared himself with the Sparrow before biting the dust.

Walker looked at him and saw past the professional reason for the question. "No fluids at the scene," he replied, concern lacing his words.

"What about on the body?" he pressed.

"No indication of sexual activity," Xander advised over the speaker and Aidan glanced at Walker.

"What about good ol' saliva? I can't imagine that the prince would have had someone as attractive as the Sparrow in his room and not have traded spit."

Walker glared at him coldly. "Is that opinion based on personal knowledge?"

He stood, tired of Walker's and now Lucia's scrutiny. "You expect me to crack the Sparrow. That isn't going to happen unless I use everything at my disposal. Everything."

With that comment he started to walk from the room, but as he neared his door, he paused and faced Walker. "And may I remind everyone that I'm the lead agent on this assignment. While I appreciate your concerns, I need to do what I think is right to crack the Sparrow."

With that, he grabbed hold of the knob, but as he opened the door, Walker said to Xander, "Make sure we've got swabs of the prince's mouth. And if we don't, get them pronto."

Chapter 14

As usual, Elizabeth was up bright and early, flitting around the garden like a beautiful butterfly or a vicious little bee. Snipping here and there. Filling her basket with murder and mayhem, Aidan thought.

It was a trifle early for him to go to work, but there was little reason for him to hang out in the hotel room. Grabbing the special surveillance equipment Lucia had used to crack the safe and locker, Aidan stepped out into the suite where, as ever, Lucia vigilantly perused the monitors while typing away on her laptop.

"Anything?"

"Just the Sparrow's typical morning routine." Noticing that he was dressed and holding the equipment, she asked, "Where are you going?"

"Figured I'd take a look in those tunnels. See what I can make of them."

Lucia gave him a heads up. "FYI— You'll find my footprints—size nine—for the first few feet in the main tunnel and then in the path to the right. Once I saw that way branched out into multiple tunnels, I stopped."

"Good job. Just keep an eye on Elizabeth and let me know if I've been compromised." When she returned to her busy pecking on the keys, he asked, "What else are you up to?"

"Hacking the Silvershire DMV."

"Why hack? We're on the government payroll," he began, but then he remembered Walker's earlier concern about the *Quiz* and their source for information. "I get it. You don't trust whomever we have to ask."

"Too much leakage of vital details. If there's a mole, I don't want them knowing what we're up to," she confirmed.

He patted her on the back, but as he walked away, Lucia called out to him. He stopped, turned.

She seemed hesitant to speak. Unusual for the normally feisty operative. "You and the Sparrow. It's just business, right? Because if it isn't—"

A sharp slice of his hand silenced her. "The Sparrow or Elizabeth. So far, we've got lots of things linking them, but nothing definitive."

"You're right. But it's hard to ignore everything we do have, isn't it?"

Aidan agreed despite his unease. "I still want definitive, Lucia. I want to solve this case. I want it for Mitch."

He didn't add that he wanted it for himself, because he was too conflicted. But Lucia knew. She might specialize in talking to machines, but she had great people sense, as well.

"Just watch your back," she noted.

"You help watch it for me." He motioned to the monitors and with a wave, headed for Elizabeth's cellar.

He had dressed in sweats. The gym bag he held contained assorted workout gear and the special surveillance equipment he had developed.

Elizabeth was in the front garden when he arrived, picking

things from the garden, presumably herbs for what she would cook that day. He waved and called out, "Good morning."

She walked over, examining him as she did so. "Working out?"

He pointed to the restaurant. "You did say we could use the equipment in the gym before the patrons arrived."

"I did." She nervously grasped and ungrasped the handles of her garden basket. "You were right yesterday," she blurted out.

"Right? About what?"

"The police. I called them this morning and filed a report. Called the insurance company, as well. An adjuster is coming in a few days to check out the damage."

Another decision that didn't make sense if she was the Sparrow.

Then he remembered her words to him about how things could never be the same and tried to reassure her, to work his way into her confidence. "Once it's fixed, it'll be like new."

"Right. Like new," she repeated, although she was clearly not on board.

"Right. So, I'm heading to the cellar. Unless you need help with something." Or unless you want to pick up where we left off on the bluff, he thought, wondering if that was possibly the way to the truth.

"No, no. I'm fine. I've got to decide on the day's menu. Prep a few things," she advised and turned toward the door.

He walked beside her and they entered the kitchen. It was empty, but she had clearly already been at work there. A number of bowls and items were laid out in anticipation of the day's meals. Tomatoes, basil and other herbs, fresh picked from her garden. He could smell their aroma as soon as they entered the room.

When she headed to her prep table, he peeled off and rushed down the cellar stairs. Just to be convincing, he decided to start on the boxing bag first. Grabbing the wrist wraps from his gym bag, he wound them snugly around his hands and wrists, and then began his routine on the bag.

Punch after punch. An assortment of kicks that would send noise up to the kitchen above. He wanted to make sure Elizabeth was aware of what he was doing. Afterward, he unwound the wraps and tossed them beside the bag. Hitting the center of the mat, he did crunch after crunch. As he'd expected, the sudden drop in noise drew her attention.

From his prone position on the mat, he was able to see the door to the cellar open. Her feet—petite feet he made a point to note, thanks to Lucia's earlier comment—were visible as were her toned calves, but not much else.

She was checking on him, and, seeming satisfied that he was up to just what he'd said, she closed the door.

Perfect. He quickly laid out some of the free weights on the mat, just in case she checked on him again. He needed to be able to grab one of the weights immediately as a cover. "Red Rover, I'm going in," he advised.

"All's clear. She's working in the kitchen."

He headed to the locker and with the combination Lucia had secured earlier, opened the lock and removed it.

Inside the locker it was much as he had expected. A sweat-shirt and sneakers. He picked up the sneakers and noted the size—a six. A T-shirt lay tossed onto the floor above the sneakers. He held it up to his nose, but there was no scent. No fragrance.

Elizabeth didn't wear any perfume, just the hand lotion. A hint of plumeria, Kate had said when he had bought the jar. A jar he'd passed on for chemical review with the evidence from the crime scene.

There was no hint of plumeria. Actually, there was just a fresh-laundered smell that said the shirt hadn't been worn. He placed it back where he had got it, trying his best to rearrange it in the exact same position.

Leaning toward the back, he realized it would be a tight fit for him to go through the locker, unlike the Sparrow and Lucia, who were more petite. Tight, but doable.

The back of the locker appeared to be plain metal like any

other gym locker. He ran his hands along the edges of the
metal and down at the bottom right-hand corner, behind the
sneakers and beneath the T-shirt, he discovered a tiny button,
right where Lucia had told him it would be. Barely the size
of a pencil eraser.

He pushed.

The back of the locker swung smoothly inward into the
tunnel.

Here goes, he thought, and wedged himself through the
space into the opening.

His shoulder scraped against the metal and once he was in
the passageway, he had to crouch to walk. It had definitely
not been intended for a man his size. But a woman a few
inches shorter, like Elizabeth, would have no problem moving
about the tunnels freely.

The passage had been carved out of the dirt some time ago.
Well before Elizabeth's time. Long-term water seepage had
stained the walls a darker brown in spots or had calcified on
them from mineral deposits. That might make the whole
network of tunnels unstable. The tunnel was dimly lit by a
series of light bulbs strung from wire at odd intervals along
the earthen walls. There was enough light for him to see the
footprints. Larger ones, likely Lucia's, moving straight ahead.
Interspersed with them, both coming and going, a much more
diminutive set. Elizabeth's? he wondered.

He bent and guesstimated the second set of footprints to
be a size six, like the sneakers in the locker. For confirmation,
he located two sets of prints adjacent to one another, laid
down a coin for reference and snapped off a picture with his
PDA.

Shoving the PDA into his pocket, he moved further into
the tunnel. He heard a crackle in his ear and worried that he
was losing the signal. "Red Rover. Copy, can you hear me?"

"Copy, Mixmaster. Not as strong as before though."

Conscious of that, he crept forward until he was at the spot
where the tunnel branched. As Lucia had mentioned, her

prints were clear in the sand of the passage to the right. Since she had already gone that route only to find it led to multiple tunnels, he chose the path to the left.

Careful not to compromise any evidence, he stepped cautiously, preserving the earlier footprints, hoping the Sparrow wouldn't be looking for his. As he moved deeper into the earthen corridor, he once again hailed Lucia. "Red Rover. Copy, Red Rover."

A snap, crackle and even a pop as she answered. "Barely…hear…you." Her words were punctuated by static.

"Copy, Red Rover." Up ahead, the path dipped downward, sloping lower below ground level. For sure the signal would be lost up ahead. He wondered how long he'd have to explore before Elizabeth would check on what he was up to in the cellar again. Without the connection to Lucia, he risked discovery…

"You may lose me in a moment," he advised and plowed forward, needing to determine what was up ahead. Where the tunnel led.

Nothing but earthen walls and bare bulbs. It was cooler though and for a moment he thought he heard something. He closed his eyes to eliminate any extraneous sensation from interrupting.

The ocean—it sounded like he was stuck in the middle of a giant shell. Another noise. The scuffle of a shoe?

He held his breath and there it was again. Louder. Definitely a footfall in the tunnel ahead of him. Elizabeth?

No word from Lucia, but then again, maybe he had finally lost her signal. And if he could hear the Sparrow's footsteps, he had to remain silent.

He held his breath and slowly inched back a yard or so toward a spot in the tunnel where a jagged outcropping of rock sprang from the earthen wall. Not very large, but enough for him to partially hide behind it. As he tucked himself tight to the outcropping, a faint and incontinuous signal came across his wire.

"…move…lost…beach," was all he could make out, and he tried to fill in the blanks.

The Sparrow was on the move and I lost her on the beach.

The beach being possibly straight down the passageway judging from the sound of the sea. He waited and listened for yet another footstep.

Nothing. Had the Sparrow realized he was there and run?

He cursed again beneath his breath. If he forged ahead, he might smack straight into her and if he did…

Proof positive that Elizabeth was the elusive assassin?

He didn't want to guess at why that thought now bothered him.

Another crackle of static and some scattered words pierced his ear. "Back…cellar…hurry…"

With a frustrated sigh, Aidan made the call and turned.

A sudden blur of movement caught his eye, but before he could register who or what it was, blinding pain smacked him in the middle of his solar plexus, doubling him up. It was immediately followed by a hard, swift kick to his head.

The force of that sent him flying against the wall, where his head connected roughly. As he dropped to the ground and his gaze darkened, all he could see before him were a pair of feet. Petite women's feet encased in running shoes.

Then everything went black.

"Aidan? Aidan?" Elizabeth repeated and wiped the damp towel over his forehead and the side of his face.

His eyelids flickered for a moment, and then he was instantly alert and in action.

He grabbed hold of her hands and shoved her down hard onto the mat, pinning her there with his greater force and strength. "What did you do to me?"

"What the hell's the matter with you?" she said and pushed at him, trying to loosen his grip.

He seemed disoriented for a second, looking around the cellar as if thinking he was elsewhere. When he realized where he was, he released her and sat back onto the mat, a puzzled look on his face.

Natalie came running down the cellar stairs at that moment, a bag filled with ice in her hand. "Here it is, Lizzy," she said and stopped short as she realized something was up.

Elizabeth rose from the mat, walked over to Natalie and took the bag of ice. She approached Aidan, who was looking a little dazed, probably from the blow that had put the bruise on the side of his face.

Not wanting to risk that in his current state he would take her down again, she paused well before reaching him and held out the ice bag. "Here. This might help."

Confusion reigned on his face again, finally forcing her to kneel before him and place the ice bag gently above the injury. He winced as she did so and roughly asked, "What the hell happened?"

She shrugged and Natalie piped in from behind her. "When you didn't come up for a while, Lizzy came down to see what you were doing."

"You were lying on the mat with one of the free weights beside you," she said and motioned to the equipment off to the side of the mat. "You were out cold, so I ran up to get some damp towels and asked Natalie to make an ice bag."

"Oh," he said and grasped the ice bag from her hand. As he held it to the injury, he winced again.

"Do you need to see a doctor?" she asked and Natalie broke into the conversation once more.

"You're not going to sue, right? After all, it was your fault the weights hit you," she said nervously, clearly concerned on her employer's behalf.

Elizabeth gritted her teeth. She knew Natalie meant well, but she wasn't helping the situation at all. While still kneeling before Aidan, she said, "Nat. Aidan is not going to sue—"

"You know how litigious these Americans are," her friend worried out loud, wringing her hands like an anxious old maid.

If it wasn't so serious, it would be laughable, Elizabeth thought. Trying to calm her assistant, she gave Natalie instructions that would remove her from the cellar. "Please finish up the prep work while I see to Aidan. I'll be up shortly."

Natalie seemed about to argue with her, but Aidan clinched it with, "I'm not going to sue. It was an accident. I think the weight slipped from my hand."

With that, Natalie scurried up the stairs, leaving the two of them alone.

She examined him again, reached out and eased the ice bag from the side of his face to take another peek. "There's a bruise already."

Aidan wanted to say, "Well, hello, duh. You kicked the shit out of me," but her look of concern was so real, it was hard to imagine she could fake it. "I'll be fine," he reassured, although a whopper of a headache was rapidly growing behind his eyes.

She dropped her hands to her thighs and rubbed them there nervously. "You scared me. I thought you were really hurt."

Again, apprehension, seemingly real and unpracticed, flashed across her face on his behalf. "I'm fine. And I know you have to get to work. I'm going to head back to my place to rest."

"That's not a good idea. You were out for a while. You could have a concussion."

She was probably right, because he was sure that at any moment, his head might split open. When he moved it too quickly, nausea set in along with a wave of dizziness. "So what do you propose, Lizzy?"

"Let's get you to the cottage. You can sack out there so I can check on you." As she said that, she slipped an arm beneath his shoulder, helped him to rise and then to navigate the stairs.

He appreciated her assistance, especially since his knees were wobbly. If it hadn't been for her support, he might not have made it to the ground floor. By the time they reached the door to the cottage, a fine cold sweat had erupted on his skin.

She must either have seen or sensed his discomfort since she asked, "Are you okay?"

"I need to sit down." No lie on his part. He worried he might keel over at any second.

She helped him to the sofa where she urged him to lie down and adjusted the pillows beneath his head until he was comfortable. When she examined him again, she said, "You look pale."

He wanted to upchuck, but manly man that he was, he forced it down. "Fine," was all he could manage, and he closed his eyes, hoping to make it clear that the one thing he wanted was to be left alone.

He sensed her continued presence by his side for a moment before she finally left.

Normally, he would have taken advantage of the opportunity to investigate the cottage at his leisure. Only now, he wasn't up to it.

And come to think of it, he hadn't heard a peep of any kind from Lucia. Reaching up to his ear, which was the side of his head that had taken the initial brunt of the kick, he dislodged the earpiece. It had tightly jammed into his ear canal from the force of the blow. It had also been accidentally shut off. Powering it back up, he slipped it into his ear and said, "Copy, Red Rover."

Chapter 15

Aidan maintained his prone position on the couch, his head pounding too badly to consider moving right at that moment. Even the slight crackle from the earpiece seemed overly loud as he waited for a response from Lucia. While he lay there, he recalled Elizabeth's concern for him. It troubled him. Had it been his imagination, or had he seen caring on her expressive face before he had closed his eyes against the pain? Could she be that good an actress?

He cursed under his breath as Lucia's voice finally came across the earpiece, too loudly. Pain stabbed through his temples from the sound of it. "What happened, Blender Boy?"

He wished he knew. He had no explanation for how Elizabeth had managed to elude him in the tunnel, nor how it was possible that Natalie thought Elizabeth had been with her in the kitchen the whole time.

Maybe because it was someone else who nearly took your head off?

"I don't know what happened. I heard someone and then they knocked me out."

"You should return to base," Lucia suggested, dragging a harsh chuckle from him.

"If I could, I would. Did *you* see anything?" He tried to keep his tone neutral, but even he could hear the pain and annoyance behind his words.

"Nothing. Someone jammed the signal," Lucia replied.

Damn. That was not so good, he thought and again it occurred to him that it would have been difficult for Elizabeth to do the jamming. It would take some sophisticated equipment and software to break into the encrypted signal and decode it. Not to mention jam it—or worse—listen in. Hopefully they weren't jacked into their current transmissions. For the moment, he had no way of knowing, however.

"Where was Elizabeth when I was decked? Did the jamming begin at the same time?"

"As far as I know she was up in the kitchen until I lost the signal. I don't know how that fits into when you were attacked," Lucia answered. In the background he could hear her fingers flying across the keys. She was likely loading up images from all the various cameras just to make sure.

"Great. So someone knows how to jam us," he said with a tired sigh.

"Have we been compromised?"

Aidan shook his head, but then winced from the movement. His voice was tight as he held the ice bag to his face and replied. "Don't know. Easy to jam. Harder to break in."

"Don't know if this is proof that Ms. Moore is the Sparrow or that it's someone else."

Proof? Someone had attacked him and jammed the signal, but as far as they knew, Lizzy had been in the kitchen at the same time. But then again, maybe Lizzy had slipped away without Natalie noticing, Aidan thought. Again conflicting emotions rose up and he told himself it was possible that someone else had attacked him and done the jamming. As it was, he was already torn about how the kind, gentle and seemingly honest woman he had come to know could be an assassin.

"We need concrete proof, Lucia. Not just circumstantial evidence."

"That knock on your head do some damage, Aidan?" Lucia responded with some puzzlement in her voice.

"No damage, only… It just doesn't feel right. My gut tells me we're missing something here."

"Copy. When are you returning to base?"

"Give me half an hour or so. First I need to check on Lizzy in the kitchen," he answered, closing his eyes and shifting the ice bag on the side of his face.

He intended to take a good part of that half an hour to consider everything that had just happened and try to regain perspective. That, and let the pain behind his eyes recede.

Then he intended to track Lizzy down and try to find out just what was going on.

Chapter 16

Elizabeth didn't head straight back to the kitchen. She sat on the stone wall between the cottage and restaurant to take a moment to calm the shaking of her hands. To settle the knot in her stomach as she thought about what had happened to Aidan.

He could have been badly hurt. As it was, he seemed to be in pretty rough shape.

Maybe she should call a doctor. Make sure the nasty-looking injury wasn't serious. And, as Natalie's words came back to her, maybe she should make sure she did everything she needed to in case he did sue.

Americans *were* a litigious lot after all.

But Aidan wouldn't sue because she trusted him to honor his promise, she told herself. No matter that he was a nomadic man, she had the sense that he was true to his word.

She shot a glance at her watch. Only a few minutes had gone by since he had lain down. She'd give him half an hour or so and then go back and see how he was doing.

Rising, she walked to the kitchen where Natalie was assigning jobs to their two kitchen assistants. Satisfied everything was under control, she grabbed the list she had been working on earlier and reviewed the menu she'd devised for the daily specials.

It was going to be a hot day today according to the weatherman, so she wanted to keep the day's specials light.

Broiled hake served with a side of homemade tagliatelle covered with fresh pesto. She and Natalie would have to get to work on making the pasta soon. Next, fresh *haricots vert* tossed with a citrus vinaigrette and toasted almonds as well as a spicy gazpacho as first courses. For dessert she had a collection of wonderful fresh-picked berries. They would be great either alone, with some zabaglione, or around a scoop of fresh sorbet. Maybe mango, she thought and realized the sorbet would need to be prepped shortly for it to be set in time for dinner.

Satisfied with the specials, she returned to the prep table where Natalie was busy slicing what looked like morels. A basic, although pricier ingredient, for one of their staple dishes—a pan-seared duck breast in a red wine and morel reduction. But as she approached, she realized something didn't look quite right.

"Hold up, Nat," she called out and her sous chef's knife paused in mid stroke.

"Something wrong?" Natalie asked.

Elizabeth stood next to her and gazed down at the morels Natalie had been cutting. "These came in our regular delivery?" Even as she was asking, she plucked two slightly different-looking morels from the basket and laid them out side by side on the cutting board.

She grabbed a paring knife from a knife holder and carefully split each morel in half. "Damn," she muttered under her breath.

"Something up?" she heard and turned.

Aidan was at the end of the table, watching them intently, ice bag pressed to the injured side of his face.

"You are obviously. Are you sure that's wise?" she asked, concerned since he appeared a little too pale for her tastes.

"I'm feeling better. I just wanted to drop in and let you know I'd be back later," he said and walked directly over to where she was standing. "So, what's up?" he asked again and motioned with his head to the morels. He immediately grimaced, the action obviously painful.

He should have rested some more, she thought, annoyed that he was possibly making his injury worse. But first, she had to deal with the problem sitting before her on the cutting board.

She motioned down to the morel pieces. "The delivery we received this morning was tainted."

Was it her imagination or did Aidan's face harden at her words? She carefully explained to Nat, so that she would know for the next time. "See the differences between the two mushrooms here? The cap on this one is only connected at the top and the inside of the stem isn't hollow. That's a false morel."

"And that would be a problem because?" Aidan asked.

"It's poisonous. Not as poisonous as the aminita mushrooms, but definitely deadly," she replied.

His eyes turned cold, the lighter flecks of blue becoming like shards of ice. "You seem to know a lot about things like that," he challenged.

She twirled the sharp paring knife around once in her fingers before spiking it into the cutting board so that it stood upright, tip embedded in the wood. Expertly and efficiently. "It's my job to know things like that," she responded, angry with him on a variety of levels, including that he seemed to be questioning her expertise on culinary matters.

"I bet it is," he replied gruffly, tossed the ice bag to her, and walked out the door without a backward glance at the two of them.

"What's with him?" Natalie asked as she followed his stiff retreating back.

Elizabeth shrugged. "For the life of me, I don't know."

* * *

Her job. Yeah, right. World-renowned assassin. Aidan's head was pounding with all the facts running around in his mind and the conflicting emotions they raised.

He'd had his doubts about Lizzy, but with each passing minute, there was yet more and more evidence piling up against her. The tunnels. Shoe size. The attack. Those damn poisonous mushrooms and of course, the too-vivid reminder of her adroitness with a knife.

Back at the hotel, a concerned Lucia hovered over him like a hummingbird, inspecting the blow to his head.

He brushed her off with a weak swipe of his arm. "I'm okay. Really."

"Really?" she asked and examined his face, sensing that his anger was about a multitude of things beyond his injury. "Well, then I guess we can call Xander and hear what else he has to report."

In a way, it was almost the last thing he wanted to hear since he suspected that the DNA test would clinch the determination that Lizzy was indeed the Sparrow. But maybe it was better that way. Maybe that would allow him to regain full objectivity about her and complete a mission that was turning out to be more than he had expected. With a nod that brought fresh waves of pain and nausea, he sat down by Lucia's laptop and the speakerphone.

Lucia dialed Xander and he answered a moment later. "Alexander Forrest here."

"Xander. It's Lucia and Aidan," she advised.

"I was waiting for your call," he replied, an eager tone in his voice that told him that the younger man had good news.

Or bad depending on which camp you were in.

"Get on with it then," Aidan said grumpily.

"Whew. Wrong side of bed this morning," Xander said and after a short pause, his image filled Lucia's screen. The young man winced and with a chuckle said, "Or maybe the wrong side of someone's fist?"

Lucia was quick to explain. "I think it was a roundhouse kick judging from—"

"Enough," Aidan barked and regretted it as the word echoed painfully in his skull. "Get to the important stuff, Xander," he added more softly.

Xander shuffled some papers prior to beginning his report. "You were right about the prince not being able to resist the Sparrow. And may I say that I, too, find her babealicious."

"Xander," Lucia warned, heading him off before Aidan could admonish the young specialist.

"Okay, okay. On to the good stuff. Swabs from the prince's mouth yielded two sets of DNA. I did the PCR test and ran the unknown sample against some blood that Ms. Moore had donated during Silvershire's annual blood drive."

"When was that?' Lucia questioned and Aidan was thankful for her intercession, since his head throbbed so painfully, even speaking hurt.

"About two months ago."

"And? Do we have a match?" he finally asked.

"That's the strange thing," Xander said and immediately began flipping through his papers again. "We had a clean sample from Elizabeth. The one taken from the prince—well, it should have been fairly good."

"You're doubting the integrity of the evidence you were given?" Lucia pressed and shot a worried look at Aidan, obviously not liking where this was going. Too much information had already leaked from an inside source. To think that the same source could manipulate the evidence…

"There's nothing to say it was tampered with, only… It's not a complete match, but it's not far enough apart for it not to have come from the same person."

"What?" Aidan snarled in low tones. "What do you mean?" After he spoke, he leaned closer to the laptop to get a better view of Xander's face as he explained.

"About seventy-five percent of the DNA matched in the specimen from the prince and Ms. Moore's blood. But not all, which is weird. Unless the sample was compromised some-how or…" Xander chortled before continuing, "…unless Ms. Moore has an evil twin out there somewhere."

"You think the DNA can belong to someone other than Elizabeth Moore?" he pressed.

"Yes. Identical twins have identical DNA. Fraternal twins share fifty percent of the same DNA," Xander answered.

Aidan cursed under his breath. "But you said we had a sev-enty-five-percent match. So where does that leave us?"

"There's a theory about a third type of twin—polar body twins. Basically, the polar body is a remnant near the egg. Normally it dies, but if it should grow as large as the egg, it can be fertilized," Xander explained.

"Which means that both the egg and the polar body have the identical DNA from the ovum, but fertilization by differ-ent sperm causes the difference in the DNA," Aidan contin-ued for him.

"And that results in what?" Lucia jumped in.

"In theory, twins that are nearly identical, but not quite. Of course, this is just a theory and some say that even if it is possible, it is quite unusual. Very, very rare."

Aidan glanced at Lucia, and, as he met her gaze, it was obvious what she was thinking. "This is getting to be a night-mare, isn't it?"

At her nod, he snapped at Xander. "Run the tests again."

"I can do that, only—"

"Xander. Just run the tests again," he repeated gruffly.

The young man nodded and signed off.

"Odds are the tests are going to come out the same way," Lucia advised.

Aidan shook his head, but regretted the action since it brought pain. In fact, his headache had been steadily growing during the entire conference. "She really nailed me."

"She did. *Elizabeth* did. Not some rare or nonexistent evil twin."

He hated to admit it, but the twin thing was a farfetched

idea. Nothing in the personal history suggested Lizzy had a sibling. But personal histories could be altered. The Lazlo Group did it all the time to protect its operatives and their families. It kept the cases away from their private lives. Or at least, that's what they tried to do.

The Sparrow, if she wasn't Elizabeth, could have done the same in an attempt to protect her twin.

"Aidan?" Lucia questioned, since he hadn't answered her earlier question.

"Your Lazlo bio says you're an only child. Are you?"

When she didn't reply, Aidan had his answer. "I'll try tonight to get more info from Elizabeth about her family."

"You plan on going to work? Do you feel well enough?"

"It's what I have to do," he replied and walked away, intending to get some rest. He planned on going to the restaurant, but laying low. He needed Lizzy to worry. He needed her to make the first move. If he did the approaching, it might seem too pushy, create a blip on her radar if she truly was the Sparrow.

Which, once again, he was unsure about.

Why? he asked himself. Maybe because Xander's report had only created doubt. He couldn't see her knocking him out in the tunnel and then faking the whole concern thing so well. Until he remembered the expert way she had handled that little paring knife and her knowledge regarding the poisonous mushrooms.

He was dumbfounded. Again.

But that's what she does. She creates the persona you think you know and then…the reasonable voice in his head reminded. It's what he was doing, except that he was finding it hard to reconcile all her many facets. In fact, he was fascinated by all her layers.

Somehow tonight, he'd find a way to reach her. To get more answers about her, because if they were on the track of the wrong woman…the real Sparrow was still out there. As deadly and dangerous as ever.

Chapter 17

Restlessness kept her awake. A restlessness created by all that had happened in the past few days.

First, that crazy-ass driver on the coast road the other night.

Second, Aidan nearly killing himself in the gym this morning.

And last, but probably highest on the list, her feelings for Aidan, a man about whom she knew so little. A man whom she couldn't figure out. During their picnic the other day, she'd thought they had connected, but this afternoon he'd seemed…angry. Ready to attack. Maybe it had been the blow to the head, because later that night, he was a changed man. Alone and distant.

She had wanted to approach him, see if everything was okay, but it had been impossible thanks to an unusually busy Tuesday night and a party that lingered later than normal. She had hoped he would wait around after his shift, but he hadn't.

Maybe she had misread his interest the other day. Her radar was obviously off, which was to be expected. It had been so long since she'd played this man-woman game. Too long maybe. A reason to stay out of the game, the annoying voice in her head urged, even while she thought: nothing ventured, nothing gained.

Those dueling emotions were the reason for the unsettling feeling that her life had taken an unexpected turn thanks to this man. An unwelcome turn that wouldn't necessarily take her where she wanted to go. Especially since Aidan was just passing through. He had bluntly told her that the day he'd come back, trying to convince her to hire him.

She hadn't made a mistake with the decision to hire him. He had turned out to be a competent bartender. And a most competent kisser.

However, losing control with him had possibly been not such a wise decision.

She suddenly needed to take back the control she considered so necessary. It was what she had done her entire life. First, when her parents had been killed. Next, when Dani had left.

It was what she planned on doing now.

Changing out of her pajamas, she slipped on a pair of black jeans and grabbed the first shirt she laid her hands on— a black tank top sitting atop the clean laundry pile. She didn't bother with a bra. No one would be out on the beach at this hour and besides, she wasn't all that big anyway.

She tied up her hair with the pink scarf once more and slipped down the stairs barefoot, pausing at the door a moment to glance around her living room. She held her breath as she listened for the sounds of someone else, since the hairs on the back of her neck tingled as if she was being watched.

Only the susurrus of the ocean. It called to her and she listened.

She was on the move again, Aidan realized from the video feed on his PDA. He had been watching her for at least an hour or more. For the better part of that time, she had been standing by her bedroom window, looking out to sea. One arm wrapped around her midsection while the other hung down at her side. Occasionally she would reach up, rake back her shoulder-length hair or rest her hand at her mouth pensively.

Lizzy was clearly troubled. He wondered if he had even made the list of what she was worried about. He had tried to be distant tonight and it had worked. He had noticed her watching him, possibly interested in approaching, but it had not been possible. Too many restaurant patrons far too late into the night. And he couldn't just hang out and wait for her. It would be too obvious. So he had left. Tuned into the broadcast on his PDA of Elizabeth in her room.

Despite the late hour she'd returned home, Lizzy had obviously not been tired. She puttered around the cottage and then her room. After, she went to the window to stand until she abruptly sprang into action, changing into the black clothes and moving downstairs.

She waited at the door and cautiously looked around.

Aidan stood, yanked on his jacket as he watched her. Did she sense the surveillance? Was her assassin's radar that acute?

When she walked out the door, he rushed out of his room and nearly collided with Lucia.

"I was on my way to get you," she explained and he held up his PDA.

"I've been monitoring her."

She shot him a condemning look, apparently convinced that his interest had been anything but work-related.

"It's not what you think," he defended, even as he grabbed the binoculars and hurried to the windows.

Lucia said nothing, but instead joined him at the windows with her own set of binoculars. "She's headed for the beach again."

Aidan tracked Elizabeth's flight down the cottage path and along the rocky trail to the shoreline. "I'm going after her," he said and turned, but as he did so, some other activity on one of the monitors caught his eye.

He raced back to the table, certain he'd seen someone in black in the cellar of Lizzy's restaurant, but when he reached the monitor, nothing. It must have been his imagination.

"I thought you were leaving?" Lucia asked and craned her head over his shoulder while he kept his eyes trained on the feed from the cellar.

"Thought I saw something here." He pointed to the screen.

Lucia shook her head. "Not possible. We both know the Sparrow's on the beach."

"Right," he answered and yet his instinct told him something was off. Straightening, he motioned to the monitor as he hurried toward the door. "Keep an eye on that one," he said.

Lucia looked from him to the monitor, but, realizing he was serious, she confirmed, "Whatever you say, Blender Boy."

With a nod, he rushed out the door to chase the elusive Sparrow.

The sea at night could be so many things.

On some nights she sat and watched its movement and thought about how big it was. It made her feel insignificant and yet connected to it and the multitude of life deep within. It brought peace when she was troubled, as she was tonight.

On other nights, when a storm would kick up the waves, she would revel in its wildness and energy, imagining that buried within her there was more still to be explored. That she had the strength to do whatever was necessary.

As she walked along the moonlit water's edge tonight, the ocean was relatively calm, although there was the hint of a storm on the breeze blowing into shore. It matched the maelstrom of her emotions, seemingly calm on the outside, but within, restless.

She strolled for a bit further and was almost at the edge of town when she noticed the lone figure coming down one of the public-access ramps to the beach. It was too dark to see the person's face and yet she knew who it was.

Aidan.

Funny how in a few short days he had become familiar enough that she could pick him out even from a distance.

He strolled onto the sand, but then just stood there, staring out to sea, hands tucked into his jeans pockets. Eventually, he plopped down before one small dune to watch the ocean.

She had a choice to make: turn around or keep on walking. It took her but a moment to make the decision.

Chapter 18

"The Sparrow's at nine o'clock and approaching slowly," Lucia advised, but Aidan dared not move. Better not to let her know he was aware of her presence.

Instead, he whispered, "I'm going incommunicado, Red Rover."

Lucia's response came immediately, but he curtly advised, "I can't think personal knowing you're in my head, over."

With that, he removed the earpiece, turned it off and stuck it into the back pocket of his jeans. The front one would be too obvious if they got down to doing what he wanted to be doing.

Solely on a business level, he reminded himself.

The sand masked the sound of her approach. When her bright-pink-painted toenails were directly to the left of him, he finally looked up.

She stared at him intently, as if trying to solve a puzzle,

before she said, "If I didn't know better, I'd say you were following me."

Not quite what a normal woman would say, and a reinforcement of his colleagues' suspicions about her true identity. Playing coy, he glanced over his shoulder behind her and then up to the public-access ramp he'd descended to reach the beach. Finally meeting her gaze directly, but with an easy smile on his face, he replied, "Seems to me I'm the one who's sitting near his tiny pay-by-the-night room at the somewhat dubious Leonia Inn, while you, on the other hand, are quite a distance away from your cottage. So, who's following who?"

She chuckled while shaking her head. "Touché." Without waiting or asking she plopped down next to him and mimicked his stance, knees drawn up to her chest, arms wrapped around them. "What are you doing here?"

Playing it cool, he thought, but instead responded, "Watching the moon and stars and the ocean. And now, sitting beside a beautiful woman."

Snorting inelegantly, she bumped his shoulder with hers. "You are such a liar."

Pot calling the kettle black. "And you? What are you doing here?"

A long pause followed his question. He was unprepared when she said, "Wondering what it would be like to kiss you again."

Barely containing his groan, he sneaked a peek at her. Despite her audacious words, she was staring straight ahead, a blush so bright on her cheeks that not even the indistinct light of the moon could hide it.

"Okay, so you're right that I'm a liar," he said and shifted slightly so that he might face her. As he did so, his butt sank a little deeper into the sand and his knee brushed her side.

She turned so that she might also be able to see him better and studied him intently. "So I'm *not* beautiful?"

Balls. The lady had them in spades and he liked it. Possibly too much. Cradling the side of her face, he ran his thumb along the blush of color. Was it his imagination or was her skin hotter? "That's not what I lied about."

She arched her perfectly waxed brow upward. It only emphasized her sexy girl-next-door look. "Really? So what—"

He slipped his thumb over her lips, silencing her. "I wasn't just watching the ocean and the stars. I was thinking of how nice it would be to kiss you, too."

"Liar," she repeated again, taking him aback.

"Huh?

"You were thinking about doing more than kissing and duh, so was I," she confessed, took his thumb between her teeth and gave a little love bite.

This time he did groan. When she licked the bite, it was impossible to ignore her offer.

He reached out and scooped her up into his lap, her knees splayed around his waist. He was totally hard and she couldn't fail to notice. He didn't rush it though, letting her get settled in a comfortable position. Bringing his hands to the middle of her back to slowly urge her forward until the tips of her breasts grazed his T-shirt front.

"You know that we might both regret this in the morning?" he tossed out for reflection.

"Possibly." Behind her words was a big hanging question. So he asked it, "But?"

"We might regret not doing it more."

The time for action was there. Right before him. Literally in his lap. It's what he had wanted—to break past the Sparrow's barriers.

And if she's not the Sparrow? the voice of his conscience warned.

"Lizzy—and I can call you Lizzy considering where this is likely to lead, can't I?"

Was he testing her or giving her one last out? Impossible to tell or at least that's what she told herself. That made it easier to push away her common sense and give into the desire she had been feeling since the other day. The desire that had given her the strength to brave taking a chance.

"Lizzy. I like the way it sounds coming from you," she confessed.

"Lizzy," he repeated and leaned forward, nuzzling her nose with his since in this position, they were face to face. "I want to take this slow, Lizzy."

His voice was soft and low. Slightly rough with want. His bedroom voice, only she didn't think she could wait to get to a bedroom. Returning the caress and shifting forward, she whispered in his ear, "How slow, Aidan?"

His breath hitched for a moment and she tugged on his earlobe with her teeth. "Aidan?"

He urged her the last little distance, licked the edge of her earlobe. "I want to touch you," he said, but made no motion to do so.

Her nipple was already hard and she wanted what he wanted. Wanted the promise in his voice. Nuzzling the side of his face with her nose, she brushed a kiss against his cheek. Against her lips, his beard was rough with evening growth.

She cupped the hard muscle of his chest and grasped his nipple between her thumb and forefinger. "I want you to do this," she admitted as she caressed him through the insubstantial fabric of his T-shirt.

His harsh exhalation was warm against the side of her face. He said nothing, only complied with her request, bringing up both his hands and rolling the taut nubs of her nipples between his thumbs and forefingers.

A sharp mew of pleasure escaped her. She kissed the side of his face again and shifted her hand downward to his side where she eased it beneath his jacket and ran it up and down along his lean muscled flank. Needing more, she pulled his T-shirt out of his pants and slipped her hand beneath the edge of his shirt.

His skin was warm. Smooth. She imagined what it would feel like against her. Wanted it. Soon.

She worked her mouth to the edge of his lips, traced their outline before kissing him again.

He opened his mouth against hers, apparently as hungry as she for a greater intimacy. She granted it to him, opening her mouth and meeting his tongue with her own. Sucking and biting until there was a tight ball of need inside her from his hands caressing her, a little more roughly now, and the feel of his tongue making love to her mouth.

When she broke away from him, they were both breathing heavily. Their bodies trembled as they strained toward one another.

"Aidan?" she half asked as she cradled his head in her hands and lovingly kissed the side of his face. The side he had injured that morning.

He must have misread her actions since he said, "Do you want to stop?"

She chuckled sexily and dropped a quick kiss on his lips. "No. I want to go somewhere more…private."

He looked back at the public beach ramp, chagrin on his face. "My place—"

"Let's go back to the cottage," she offered and he nodded, smiled.

Somehow they untangled themselves and rose. He took her hand and they started walking, but somehow, it wasn't quick enough for the need pulling at her. Shooting him a half glance, she said, "Race you back?"

A boyish grin erupted on his face, his teeth white against his tanned skin. "And the prize is?"

It took her only a second to consider what she wanted and to answer. "Winner gets to be on top."

With that, she dropped his hand and took off down the beach.

Lizzy broke into a run, her long legs quickly eating up ground. He could have watched her run, the elegance and fluidity of it, but he was much too competitive to just let her win the challenge.

He dashed after her, trying to make up the ground that he had lost, although it did occur to him that even if he did lose it would still be a pleasurable experience. Lizzy on top, he thought, and stumbled for a moment.

Dashing that thought from his mind because it was too distracting and the blood was shifting to places that weren't conducive to speed, he slowly closed the gap between them as Lizzy kicked up the sand before him.

He reached the cottage just paces behind her. Heard Lizzy's delighted laughter at the door as she said, "I win."

"Why don't I feel like I lost?" he said, his voice tinged with humor and sex because all he could think about was making love with her.

Lizzy shot him a suddenly shy smile, but threw the door open and backpedaled into the room, all the time motioning to him that he should follow.

He did and plastered himself to her as they paused for just a moment in their headlong flight toward what he hoped was Lizzy's bedroom.

As she gazed up at him, there was a look in her eyes that said she truly cared for him.

Normally he would have banked money on knowing that look was real.

But lately, and particularly around Lizzy, he no longer could be certain. His gut, however, was telling him that nothing wrong was going on right now. That he should have no fear. No concern.

He hoped it was right.

Chapter 19

Great, Lucia thought as she flipped from one camera feed to the next and realized that someone was jamming the signal. And with Aidan deciding to go incommunicado, she had no idea whether or not he was in any kind of trouble.

Over and over she tried to restore the signal, but the cameras were unresponsive. Whatever was screwing up the transmission was pretty powerful. Which meant that she might be able to track its location and shut it down.

But first…

She rose from the table and snatched her binoculars from the tabletop. Hurrying to the windows, she searched the beach, but there was no sign of Aidan or Ms. Moore. Shifting downward, she noticed the lights were on in the cottage. Through the window, she was able to pick out Aidan and Lizzy as they…

Well. It sure didn't look like Aidan was in any kind of trouble. Well, at least not of the physical kind.

Emotionally… That was a whole 'nother issue. She had

sensed his indecision during this assignment. Realized that he was either unwilling or unable to get past his attraction to the Sparrow.

There was more going on than just the mission. That was not good. And as for what was about to happen in the cottage...

Lucia walked back to the table holding her laptop and the surveillance monitors. She needed to find what was jamming the cameras and how Elizabeth had managed to activate it with Aidan literally at her side the whole time.

She would give the Sparrow credit. She sure seemed to know her spy stuff.

Let's hope Aidan realizes that, Lucia thought.

Aidan wrapped his arms around Lizzy's waist and dragged her close. Her shirt accidentally rode up with the action and his forearm brushed along her bare back. It was slightly damp, probably from their mad dash up the beach.

It was happening so fast. Too fast, he thought, doubting he had the patience to finish this upstairs in her bedroom.

As she eased her hand beneath his jacket and under the hem of his T-shirt, he knew he couldn't wait.

He gripped her to him tightly and bending his head, he laid his forehead against hers, brushed a kiss there before moving lower to meet her lips in a kiss.

Opening his mouth against hers, he tasted her, savored the slick slide of her tongue along his. Imagined it sliding along...

He groaned and pulled away, his breathing rough. "Lizzy, I can't—"

She placed a finger on his mouth, a sexy smile on her face. "I won't let you run from me now, Aidan." She didn't wait for his answer, choosing instead to stand on tiptoe and run her tongue along his jaw and then down to the side of his neck, to the sensitive hollow close to his shoulder where she gave another lick before a bite.

He cradled the back of her head in his hand and she gave another quick bite before licking and sucking at the spot.

He hadn't gotten a hickey since high school. He had forgotten how good it felt. How wonderful it was to put the bite on her, he realized as he brought his face to the hollow between her neck and shoulder. Bit and sucked and licked until they were both moaning and clutching each other.

They finally eased away from one another. Breathing heavily. Bodies tense with need.

He was certain of one thing. It was going to be…

Wild, he thought as she hopped up and wrapped her legs around him, bringing herself hard against erection. "Lizzy?"

"Touch me, Aidan. Like you did before," she urged, her hands locked behind his head, drawing him close.

He kept one hand at her back while he jammed the other under the edge of her tank top, moved it upward until he was cupping her breast. Her nipple was a tight peak in the center of his palm. He gripped it between his thumb and forefinger, rotated the peak and she let out a little gasp of pleasure, tightened her legs around his waist.

In the back of his mind came the thought that this was wrong. That Lucia would be watching and hoped she knew the meaning of discretion and shut off the cameras because…

He wanted to hear more. Feel more. Taste more. Smell more: he wanted everything with her.

Somehow he bared that breast to his gaze. Her nipple was a sweet caramel color against the cream of her skin. As he brushed his lips against it, Lizzy let out another little gasp and his erection tightened painfully at that sound.

He needed to be inside her. Hearing her pleasure spill from her lips as he moved within.

But first, he had to taste her again.

He licked the tip of her. Sweet. Hard against his mouth as he closed his lips around her nipple and sucked.

She gripped his head to her with one hand. Eased the other one under his shirt. Her palm was soft against his skin. Warm.

He didn't know how it happened, but they were suddenly on the edge of the large sofa in the middle of the room. She was leaning back against the soft, welcoming cushions, her legs open. He was immediately there, drawing himself against her as he continued caressing her breast.

She held him close, and he moved his mouth on her. Sucking. Biting.

He wanted her to do the same. All over him. Which meant they had way too much clothing on.

Elizabeth must have felt the same way since she eagerly reached for the hem of her tank top and ripped it off, revealing herself.

It distracted him for a moment. He sat back on his heels and looked his fill. Placed his hands on her midsection and traced the indentations in her abs. Slowly shifted upward until he was holding her breasts in his hands. Rubbing his thumbs across the distended tips of her nipples.

She surged forward, slipped her hands beneath his jacket and eased it off.

His T-shirt followed quickly as he removed it and knelt before her again. She ran her palms all along his skin and he leaned close, shifted his hands to her back to bring her nearer.

She did the same, but encountered the hard ridges of scar as she did so.

He sensed her hesitation and immediately reminded, "Shrapnel. Army, remember?"

With an accepting bob of her head, she traced the edges of his scars with her fingers, as if to soothe, although the hurt was long gone, Aidan thought.

A shudder ripped through his body at her actions and he gripped her tight, buried his head against her neck.

Her comforting brought a change in what had been happening between them. A banking of the fires for the moment as they held one another, drawing succor from the embrace.

Finally he eased away, reached up and brushed a lock of her hair back from her face. "You're…beautiful."

She smiled. A slow, comfortable smile that did something funny to his insides. "Thank you."

He brought his hand down to her shoulder, where he traced the straight line of it. Moved down a little further and ran his thumb along the classically defined edge of her collarbone.

He bent his head, ran his lips along that strong line before urging her upward so that he could kiss her breasts again. Lick her nipples before sucking on them gently.

She cradled his head to her and kissed it. Urged him on with soft cries that told him how much she liked what he was doing. When she leaned back onto the cushions of the sofa, he took the moment once again to admire the strength in her, the lean muscles along her midsection that were impossible to resist.

He laid his hands there, running his finger along the ridges before replacing his hands with his mouth. He paused to kiss the tempting indentation of her navel before reaching the edge of her low-rise black jeans. She shifted her hips up then, and he smiled against her belly.

"Impatient, Lizzy. That's not a good—"

She silenced him with a kiss that rocked him with its intensity. When she pulled away and sat on the edge of her couch, her sherry-brown eyes were liquid heat. Warm as her gaze, her hands ran down his body while he kneeled before her. They felt even hotter as she eased her fingers beneath the waistband of his jeans before she undid the snap and dragged the zipper down the nearly painful length of his erection.

He was so hard, he immediately sprang out once he released the zipper. She wasted no time in wrapping her hand around him.

"Very impatient," she confessed.

Almost lightheaded from the surge of desire, he somehow managed to kick off his pants and tightie whities while leaving his wallet, with his condoms, within easy reach.

He was standing before her, ready to kneel again when she leaned forward and kissed the tip of his jutting erection. It trapped his breath somewhere in the middle of his chest, but then she took him into his mouth and his breath disappeared completely.

She was amazing, he thought as he held her head to him. Her mouth was hot and eager as she sucked on him and then withdrew to lick the tip. She bit around the head of his penis while with one hand, she cupped his balls.

His knees nearly buckled and it took all his control not to come right then. Somehow, he mustered his strength, reached for her and urged her to stand. He undid the zipper on her jeans, parted them and slipped his hand beneath to encounter nothing but sleek warm skin.

He was so on the edge, he couldn't waste the time to take off her pants. Easing his hand downward, he found the center of her. Applied pressure to the bud nestled between her damp lips. He stroked her until she was clinging to him, her breasts against his chest. Her hand stroking up and down the length of him, wet from her mouth.

He met her gaze again and saw her need. Saw her indecision, as well. At least he wasn't alone in what he was feeling.

She grabbed hold of his shoulders and he finally eased a finger inside her. That action dragged her eyes closed. He didn't know why, but he needed her to see him. He needed to see what she was experiencing through those amazingly expressive eyes.

"Open your eyes, Lizzy," he said in soft tones.

It was a battle to do what Aidan asked. It wasn't just the pleasure she was experiencing from the way he was moving his fingers inside her, or the way her breasts brushed against his smooth chest. Maybe it was that she might give up too much of herself if she did so. Too much of what she was feeling. Hoping for.

"Lizzy, please," he urged, and in his voice there was something that said she wasn't alone in her yearnings or her fears.

She did as he asked. Those gorgeous eyes of his were a fusion of lighter and darker blues, like the ocean during a storm, revealing to her as much she had feared.

Cradling the side of his face, she traced the line of his cheek and then shifted downward to the edge of his lips. She moved her thumb across them and he bit down on it, which created a tsunami of desire that swamped her senses.

"Lizzy?" he questioned, his gaze searching her face. Making it impossible for her to do anything other than tell him the truth.

"I want you to kiss me…there."

Aidan groaned, but hastily removed her jeans.

She sank onto the giving cushions of the sofa, opening her legs as he knelt before her. He rubbed his hands up and down her thighs nervously and his gaze as it skittered up to hers was equally tense.

"Aidan?" she asked and cradled the side of his face.

"You're like no one I've ever met," he confessed and dropped a kiss on the palm of her hand.

"I hope that's a good thing," she said, feeling exposed on too many levels.

"It is, only… I might not be able to stop after this."

She laid her hands over his to still the motion of his hands as he moved them on her thighs.

"Who said we had to stop?"

His hands trembled hands beneath hers.

He looked up, his gaze intense. Compelling. Troubled.

She suspected that she knew the reason why. Leaning forward, she cradled the back of his head and kissed him. A reassuring kiss. One that said, no matter what happens, it's okay.

And it was.

When he finally parted her with a hesitant kiss and then licked the swollen bud of her clitoris, she nearly jumped out of her skin. It had been too long and Aidan…Aidan knew just what to do even before she thought it, much less gave voice to it. He slowly licked until she was pressing toward him. Then he sucked and slipped first one finger inside, followed by a second.

She was writhing on the couch, holding his head to her when he bit down on that nub and sent her over the edge.

"Aidan."

She cried his name out and he rose, was suddenly poised

at her entrance. Somehow he'd managed to get a condom on. She couldn't recall when or how. Come to think of it, she couldn't remember anything other than how wonderful he was with his hands and mouth.

And although she had just had one of the most satisfying orgasms of her life—even if her experience was limited—she was suddenly on the edge again, wanting him to enter her and ride her to another.

She met his gaze, her breathing still shaky. Reaching for him so that he could join with her, she was surprised when he inched away a bit and shook his head. But when he grinned, she realized with relief that it wasn't about stopping.

"You won the race, remember?" he said, and, with that, he lay down on the floor and pillowed his head in his hands.

The race? Puzzlement turned to amusement. Ah, yes, the race. The win that guaranteed her position…at least for this time.

She eased off the couch and knelt beside him as he lay exposed to her. That long sculpted body within reach and absolutely impossible to ignore. Almost as impossible to ignore as the long, equally impressive state of his erection.

A pool of damp drenched her as she imagined what would happen soon.

But first, she had to touch.

Chapter 20

Lucia cursed as the signals from the cameras continued to be nothing more than static. She hadn't been able to end the jamming. But she had been able to pinpoint the general source of the transmission—a spot right behind the cottage where she had seen Aidan enter with the Sparrow.

She could head there, but by doing so, she risked compromising Aidan's assignment. Given what she had seen of what was going on…

Aidan was physically safe. His heart, however, was another matter. And the assignment…possibly already compromised if what she suspected was happening was actually happening.

Lucia had heard what he said about it being just about the job. But behind those tones, her women's intuition had picked up on his attraction to the Sparrow.

Glancing at her watch, she realized Aidan had been incommunicado for just over twenty minutes. That's all it took, she joked with herself, but realized she couldn't rush in just yet. She would get in gear, get prepared and give it just a little while longer before she went in search of the jamming device.

Alone. She knew that broke with procedure, but calling in Walker now was sure to cause problems and, as the lead, Aidan would not take it well.

They'd had enough problems without creating another.

Aidan lay watching Lizzy as, in turn, she looked at him. Her sherry-colored eyes had darkened to that cognac color he'd seen the other day. Her gaze was so rich with the heady promise of what was to come, that he nearly grew dizzy from it.

"Lizzy?" he questioned at her delay.

"Just...admiring," she answered and laid her hand in the middle of his chest. Shifted it over to caress his pec. Run it along the hard edge of his nipple.

He wanted to do the same, and he reached up, cupped her breast. Took her nipple between his fingers and gently twisted it.

Her eyes half closed for a moment and her breath hitched slightly. She liked that. A lot. But so did he.

He needed her closer, so he placed his hands on her hips, exerted gentle pressure so that she would straddle him, the center of her just above his erection, her soft hairs teasing the sensitive skin at the edge, just below the condom's reach. Then he reached up once more, cradled both her breasts and pleasured her as she slowly explored him.

She placed her hands on his chest and loitered for a moment before inching them down his body, investigating every hollow and plane. Her palms were smooth against his skin, warm and slightly damp.

When she met his gaze, her pupils were open wide. Her lips must have been dry because she licked them nervously.

And suddenly he wanted to lick them too.

He surged up, captured the back of her head in his hand and kissed her. Slipped his tongue into her mouth and sucked on it. When he pulled back a bit and their gazes collided, they both knew it was time.

He didn't lie back down. He needed to see her eyes. Be close to her as she took him in.

She shifted the final inch, raised her hips and hesitated for just a second, poised above him. Would she take him hard and fast or…

Slowly, Elizabeth thought.

The tip of him just breached her entrance. She lowered her hips, lingering over every inch of him as she moved downward. Her breath was held prisoner in her chest and his face filled her vision as he stretched her.

When she finally had taken all of him in, she paused as the sensation nearly overwhelmed her. "Aidan?" she said and licked her lips.

He picked up one hand and cupped the side of her face. The other was supporting him, allowing him to be close to her as she rode him. "Sweet Lizzy. This is…amazing."

She couldn't argue. His length tucked inside her was creating a jumble of sensations. Heat. Wet. A clenching of her insides that demanded she do more to satisfy the knot of need somewhere inside her. Was it down there and just sexual? Or was it in her heart? she wondered, but then she flexed her hips and moved upward, languidly.

The friction of it made her moan and close her eyes.

Aidan didn't press her then and she was glad for it. She wanted to focus on the pleasure of him next to her. In her. On the delicious sensations that came from moving on him, slowly at first, but then faster and faster as she sought her satisfaction.

He urged her on with soft encouraging words. With the lick of his tongue at the sensitive spot on her neck that he had sucked before. At her breasts as he caressed them with his hand.

At some point, he finally lay back down and brought his hands to her hips to help guide her.

With her hands leaning on his chest and her hips pumping against him, she was near the edge. Her breath was rough in her chest. Her body was trembling. It would only take a little more, she thought, aware that she was near release.

He must have sensed it, as well; for he exhorted her onward, and when she was poised at the edge, he leaned up just enough to suck at the tip of one breast, then bit it gently.

It pushed her over the edge.

She drove down on him hard, called out his name as her body shuddered and trembled with her climax. But he was still hard within her and even as he soothed her with his hands, she could feel her hunger coming back to life.

Aidan sensed her renewed need even as he marveled at it. She had pleasured herself with him, but the pleasure hadn't been all hers. The feel of her around him, of her breasts and legs and skin…of all of her, was so enticing that he didn't want it ever to end.

But already her renewed desire was dragging him toward his own climax. He was barely keeping control despite his wish to be with her.

Somehow he managed to get her on her back without breaking away from her. He would have rather died than lose that contact with her, he thought.

She looked up at him, wide-eyed and vulnerable. Almost disbelieving the passion sizzling between them. Afraid. "I'm feeling it too, Lizzy."

"It's…scary," she confessed, creating a spot in his heart for her he didn't want to have.

Leaning down, he brushed a kiss on her lips and said, "Don't be scared. I would never hurt you."

Although he knew he would, because there was no good way for this to end between them. If she wasn't the Sparrow, he'd still have to leave at the end of the day. He'd already warned her he wasn't a stay-at-home kind of guy.

And if she *was* the Sparrow…

He was doomed for sure, he thought, as he moved in her and brought them both to the edge again before they slipped over together.

Afterward, when they were finally breathing and their legs could hold them, they slowly walked upstairs to her bedroom and climbed into bed.

He held her cradled to his side, knowing they would make love again. It had been too amazing for them not to. But before then…

He had a mission. That was why he was here. Liar, the little voice in his head yelled, but he ignored it and pressed forward with his assignment.

"What was it like growing up here? Always being in one place?" he began, in part because he needed to discuss her family, but also because a part of him actually did wonder what such a life was like, having never had such stability during his younger years.

She ran her hand across his chest, the gesture soothing, one of connection rather than desire.

"Nice at times. Annoying at others. In a town as tiny as Leonia, everyone knows everyone. Everyone knows everything about you."

"Hmm," he said and rubbed his hand up and down her arm, but didn't say anything else. He didn't want to press too hard and arouse suspicions.

"And you? What was it like always moving around?"

Aidan's answer came quickly, too much so, he feared. "When I was younger, it was hard. I would just get used to the place and make friends and we would get our next assignment."

"And later? When you were older?" she asked and snuggled closer to him, her body plastered along his side, one thigh tossed over his legs beneath the sheets.

His arm was tucked under her and he eased his hand over the curve of her waist to hold her close. "When I was older? I stopped trying to make friends. It made it easier," he confessed.

She was quiet for a long time before she said, "I had my friends and family. And all the aunts and uncles and cousins, not to mention the neighbors and the milkman…" She stopped with a chuckle and he joined in her amusement.

"It must have been nice. I just had my family."

"And Mitch," she added.

Involuntarily, he stiffened at the mention of his friend's name. Especially coming from her. But she was right. He'd had Mitch. "Mitch was…like a brother."

"Did they ever find out—"

"Why he was killed. No," he answered tightly, since at the reference to his friend, the headache he'd had that morning had begun to return.

"I'm sorry. I didn't want to bring up anything painful." She sat up then and the sheet fell away, revealing all of her to him.

"Headache's back?" she added quickly. He must have been making a face of some sort for her to notice.

When he affirmed it, she straddled his legs so that she might have a better position and began a slow and careful massage along his temples. "Close your eyes," she said.

He did, not only because she asked, but because the sight and feel of her was arousing him again and he had other things that needed to get settled first.

"Was it hard for you? After your mom and dad—"

"I'd rather not talk about that time. It was…difficult."

He slowly opened his eyes, inspected her face. The hurt was there for the world to see. "Didn't your other family help out?"

Lizzy stopped her massage and dropped her hands to her sides. Of course there had been family to help out, she thought, but that hadn't made it any easier. Especially when the person closest to you, the one you knew you could always count on, had as good as lost it.

Dani had been inconsolable for days and then the grief had turned to anger. Anger at the police who couldn't find the killers and later, at all the bureaucrats who had seemed so intent on covering up anything to do with her parents' deaths. Maybe even anger at herself for not being there to stop it, Lizzy thought.

"Lizzy?" Aidan asked and placed his fist beneath her chin, applying gentle pressure so that he could read her face.

"Sometimes you're alone even when you're surrounded by people."

He cursed beneath his breath, slipped his hand to the nape of her neck to draw her close for a kiss. "I'm sorry," he whispered afterward. "For everything," he said and Lizzy got the weird sense he wasn't just talking about her parents.

Chapter 21

He didn't know how many times they made love that night. He had run out of condoms and Lizzy had supplied some more.

Enough times that he was sore. Dead tired. Exhausted.

Thoroughly satisfied. Totally confused.

Rolling onto his side, he propped his head up with one hand and glanced at her as she lay sprawled on her back beside him. A rumbly and all too regular noise came from her.

She was a snorer.

How long had it been since he'd spent enough time with a woman to know something like that?

Too long.

That had to be the explanation for his abandon. For the feelings he was having toward her. Walker could surely explain how it was transference or some other such psychological issue.

It certainly couldn't be love.

Her eyelids drifted open slowly and as she saw him there, a broad welcoming smile erupted on her face. "G'mornin'," she said, her voice husky.

He shifted over, dropped a quick kiss on her lips. "G'mornin'. Do you have any plans for today?"

A tired sigh escaped her. "Some errands to run in town before work. And you?"

"I'm supposed to meet a friend," he lied since he couldn't risk her going with him. Not when he had to report in and possibly go back to investigating her. Back to proving she was a killer.

She glanced at her wristwatch and grimaced. "I guess we should get going."

"I guess we should," he replied, but made no motion other than to shift closer, until he could lay his hand beneath the sheets on the indentation between her hip and waist.

"That's not going to get me moving."

"No? Then how about this?" He slipped his hand downward, parted her thighs and found the tender bud tucked between them.

"Oh. O-o-h. That might work," she answered and gripped his shoulders with her hands, urging him over her.

"I thought so."

Inside the hotel suite, Walker and Lucia were waiting for him.

He shot a quick look at his watch. Barely eight o'clock. "What's up?" he asked as he strolled in and then plopped himself on the couch next to Lucia.

"Besides you? All night?" Lucia teased and Aidan blushed as it occurred to him what Lucia might have seen during her surveillance.

Walker silenced her banter with a harsh glare and a sharp slash of his hand.

"Is this mission compromised, Spaulding?" Walker asked, clearly all about business this morning.

Aidan was not about to let the other man dictate to him as he seemed so fond of doing. He had always found Walker to be a fairly easygoing kind of guy, but he'd been anything but

during this assignment. Not to mention that Walker chastis-
ing him for his arguably less than professional interest in
Lizzy was kind of hypocritical to the max.

"Jealous? Not getting any from the doc?" Aidan shot back,
referring to Walker's ongoing affair with the royal physician.

Walker was on his feet in a second, fists clenched at his
sides. When he took a step toward him, Aidan rose, picked
up his chin and stepped right up to him, spoiling for a fight.

They were of a like height and similar build. He knew he
could hold his own, but this little show was accomplishing
nothing. "I did what I had to for information," he said from
behind gritted teeth, trying to defuse the situation.

"Was that the only reason?" Walker wondered aloud and
arched a sandy-colored eyebrow to emphasize his point.

Lucia seemed to think it best to intervene, since she
stepped between them and laid a hand on each of their chests.
"Down boys. I'm overdosing on all the testosterone."

After a final exchange of glares, they all sat down again,
an uneasy silence filling the room.

"Report, Spaulding. What did you learn during your midnight
escapade that we can tell the duke? He is expecting us to find
the *prince's* killer." Walker pressed and stared at him intently.

He had to give the other man credit. He had perfected the
whole bushy-eyebrow, give-you-guilt look. And it worked. He
was unable to meet his gaze as he said, "Nothing."

At least nothing that he would share. Like that Lizzy was
an aggressively passionate lover. One who pleased as much
as she liked being pleased. And that she snored...

He smiled at that last recollection. The seemingly perfect
woman had at least one flaw.

Besides being an assassin? the voice in his head questioned snidely.

"The *Quiz* plans on going to press tomorrow with a story
on the prince. It seems they've got more information than we
do." After he spoke, Walker clasped his hands together and
laid them across his midsection. It was a pose that seemed

comfortable at first glance, but was anything but if you looked closely at the tight set of his jaw.

"We've got this," Lucia said and tossed something small, black and plastic on the coffee table before him.

Aidan picked up the object and examined it. He recognized it immediately. He had designed his share of jamming devices. This one was compact and well-made. Besides the on/off switch, there was a dial, he suspected for modulating the strength of the signal. It called to memory a similar device he had seen. "Where did you get this? It looks like MI6 issue."

"In the reeds behind Ms. Moore's cottage. It was on for the earlier part of the night until I was able to home in on its signal and retrieve it."

His relief that his time with Lizzy hadn't been monitored was short-lived. He inspected the device again and racked his brains for any moment he wasn't with Lizzy, trying to figure out when she could have planted the device. Nothing came to mind. "When did—"

"I don't know when she put it there. As far as I could tell, she was with you the whole time," Lucia admitted, but then pressed onward. "What I can tell you is that there were no prints, but there was DNA. She must have had it on a belt clip or something else that rode against her skin."

"And?" Walker asked, leaning forward intently now as he awaited her answer.

Lucia weakly motioned with her hands. "Xander is running the PCR tests as we speak. We'll have the results later today."

"We need more."

Aidan glanced at Walker after those words. "And how do you propose we get more?"

"As far as I'm concerned, you've jeopardized your position, Aidan. There's no sense in not coming clean with Ms. Moore."

He pictured telling her. If she was the Sparrow, he would be prepared to deal with the reaction. If she wasn't…

"I'm not sure—"

"Be sure," Walker jumped in. "The *Quiz* hits the streets tomorrow with whatever information they have. Real or imagined, we'd better have something to tell the duke so that he knows his money is being well-spent."

Risking a glance at Lucia, he realized she was as uncomfortable as he was. "What do you think, Lucia?"

"I don't like being rushed. If Ms. Moore is the Sparrow, I don't think she's going to give herself up just because you admit you're an agent for the Lazlo Group. She has no reason to fear us."

Walker confirmed his agreement with a quick nod. "You're right. But if she isn't the Sparrow—"

"She'll be afraid? I don't think you know Lizzy. She doesn't strike me as the type to be afraid."

"Lizzy, huh?" Walker said in low tones before shifting to the edge of his seat and leaning forward to emphasize his point.

"Be ready to deal with her if she's the Sparrow. Lucia and I will have your back."

He met Walker's gaze and surprisingly saw commiseration there. After all, the other man had fallen for the royal doctor during his assignment. He knew what it was like to mix pleasure and business. The difference was, Aidan could see no happy ending in his mission.

"Let me get cleaned up. Liz…Ms. Moore said she would be running some errands in town. If I can't find her there, I'll head for the restaurant."

Lucia rose and said, "We'll be there when you need us."

Aidan had no doubt they would be. Only, if Lizzy wasn't the Sparrow, the kind of support they could offer would do little to help the situation.

Less than half an hour later, he was back in the main part of the hotel suite, watching Lizzy in the monitors. Like him, she had showered. He wondered if, like him, she had thought of him as she'd run her hands over parts kissed during the night.

The reaction of his body was unwelcome right now given what he would shortly have to do. He muttered an expletive beneath his breath, drawing Lucia's attention at a nearby monitor.

"You ready?" she tossed over her shoulder as her hands flew over the keys on her laptop.

He wondered what she was working on so intently and approached. "What's up?"

"You got me thinking yesterday when you mentioned how our histories were altered. I've been trying to track down more info on Ms. Moore. Old info. Pre-alteration, if something like that occurred."

He leaned his hand on her shoulder and peered at the screen. It was a listing of past students from the Leonia High School Alumni Association. "Looks normal," he replied.

"It does, but I want to dig deeper. See if I can't hack into the server and check out their other files," she advised and chanced another glance at him. "You ready to go?"

He motioned with his head in Walker's direction. "What about him?"

She shrugged while typing. "Some kind of urgent call from Corbett. Said for you to go ahead and he would be ready whenever you needed."

Which was fine by him. He didn't need Walker to watch his tail. He was perfectly capable of taking care of himself. Besides, first he had to meet up with Lizzy.

Returning to the far monitor, he realized she was no longer in her room. Flipping from one camera shot to the other, it became obvious that she was nowhere on the premises of either the restaurant or the cottage. Accessing the earlier images stored on the hard drive, he realized Lizzy had left the cottage. Picking up his binoculars, he scoped out the beach front and then tried to see if he could pick her out along the streets of Leonia.

Damn. Nothing. Time for him to hit the bricks.

"I'm out of here. The code word if I need assistance is…"

He stopped dead, wondering what they might be discussing in those moments after he made his revelation. Lucia turned to face him as he considered it. But it suddenly occurred to him there was one last thing he wanted the Sparrow to hear if that's how it played out. "The code word is *Mitch*."

She uneasily acknowledged it with a nod and he was out the door, hurrying down the stairs and onto the main street. Where might Lizzy be headed this morning? The docks and markets for food? One of her friends' places or the WAC?

He was closest to the latter and so he drifted by there, seemingly to check out what the WAC would be offering. The doors were closed as was the ticket office. Still, he lingered by the posted schedule, checking it out as any normal patron might. Anything to lessen attention.

After a few minutes, he ambled back in the direction of town, hands tucked into his jacket pockets. The reassuring weight of his HK Mark 23 dragged at one shoulder. At his ankle, the Glock 36 rubbed his pant leg.

He was ready for battle.

Once on the main street, he opted for Samantha's shop, which was closest. Inside the store, calm reigned, unlike the other day during the sale. Unfortunately, Samantha had taken the morning off, her sales clerk advised.

As he stepped out of the store, he wondered if Samantha had taken the time to be with Lizzy. If so, would Kate also be in on the outing?

Hurrying up the block to the next shop, he noticed a familiar figure up ahead on the opposite side of the street. Lizzy. Dressed in black jeans with a black leather jacket covering a figure-hugging white T-shirt. She looked stunning. Not at all tired. He called out to her, but she seemed not to hear.

Raising a hand and giving a wave, he once again yelled her name.

She finally noticed and looked his way, but acted as if she didn't even recognize him. Puzzled for a moment, his delay allowed her to turn down the side street before he could react.

Fixated on following her, he jumped into the street, but stopped short at the strident blare of a horn. He glared at the driver who had nearly hit him and who shook a fist at him angrily.

Aidan ignored the driver and continued across the street, past the traffic in the opposite lane and onward to the corner of the block onto which Lizzy had turned.

No Lizzy anywhere on the street. There were a number of shops, however, and so he walked down the block, pausing at the shop windows to peer within searching for her, but she was nowhere to be found. At the end of the street, which had turned out to be a dead end, he paused, wondering where she could have gone when Lucia came on over the wire.

"Blender Boy. The Sparrow's returned to her nest."

He examined the street, unable to determine how she had eluded him. "Confirm, Red Rover. Cottage or restaurant?"

"Cottage."

"I'm on it," he said, and foregoing any further exploration of the dead end, he rushed back to the main road and then to the restaurant. Once he was within sight of the low stone wall for the building, he said, "Red Rover. What's your ETA?"

"Walker and I are already in position about ten yards behind the cottage along the shore. Just say the word."

Mitch, he thought, a second before confirming Lucia's communication. Funny how after nearly two years of searching, his goal was within his grasp, but it gave him no satisfaction. No relief.

Entering through the gate to the restaurant, he cut across the front yard, straight to the back patio and the granite stepping stones that led to Lizzy's cottage. At the door, he hesitated and took a deep breath.

No matter the outcome of this confrontation, whatever was going on between him and Lizzy would never be the same.

Chapter 22

The knock at the door surprised her. She hadn't been expecting anyone, only possibly hoping for…

She smiled as she opened the door and her hope was fulfilled. A fierce and all too serious look marred his face. One that warned trouble was ahead. "You okay?"

"May I come in?" he asked and motioned to her front parlor. The parlor where, the night before, they had done wonderful things both to and with each other. She suspected that wouldn't be the case this morning.

"Sure," she said and extended her arm in invitation.

He walked in, but didn't sit. Just stood there, obviously awkward.

"You okay?" she asked again as she closed the door and went to stand before him.

He shrugged and the movement pulled the front of his jacket open slightly, revealing a quick glimpse of something at his side a moment before the black leather dropped down again, hiding it from sight.

"Saw you in town. Waved to you." A puzzled look crossed his features. "You were dressed differently."

Town? She'd been in and around the house and restaurant all morning. "I've been here," she said, but then it occurred to her what might have happened.

"Dani. She must have come home as a surprise." Joy swept over her at the prospect of seeing her sister.

"Dani? Who's Dani?" he asked, another quizzical look on his face.

"Dani's my twin sister. She must have—"

Aidan raised his hands and waved them while shaking his head vehemently. "You don't have a twin, Lizzy. Look, if you're having any kind of mental problems—"

Now it was her turn to silence him with a slash of her hand. "If anyone's gone mental, it's you. How the hell do you presume to know—"

She abruptly stopped when Aidan took out some official-looking badge from beneath his jacket and the movement also revealed the gun tucked into the holster. She realized then it was what she had spied before.

Barely glancing at the badge, her gaze snared by the weapon, she said in soft tones, "Who the hell are you?"

He hesitated, clearly troubled, before slipping the badge back into his pocket. "Aidan Spaulding. I work for the Lazlo Group. We've been hired to track down Prince Reginald's killer."

"You lied to me," she said and stepped close to him, wanting to see his eyes as he answered.

"I had to. I—"

She slapped him, hard enough to snap his head back. "You prick. You've been lying to me the whole time. You were lying to me when…"

She went for him again, but this time he snared her hand in midair. "Don't," he warned.

"Or what?" Anger drove her to taunt him.

"You have no twin. Nothing in the files supports that," he advised and released her.

She let out a harsh laugh. "Your files are wrong, Aidan. Danielle Elizabeth Moore is my twin sister. My older sister by half an hour."

Aidan examined her features carefully, but the lady was either an amazing liar, telling the truth, or totally demented. He didn't know which of the three possibilities he preferred. But two of them could be easily eliminated.

"Prove it," he said.

Lizzy immediately sprang into action. Striding to the bookcase at one side of the room, she knelt before it and rummaged through some of the books before saying, "It's gone."

He stood behind her and asked, "What's gone?"

She was shaking her head and flipping through the books once more. "Our high-school yearbook. Weird. But it doesn't matter. There's pictures in here."

She yanked a photo album from one of the shelves and flipped it open. As she balanced it on her thighs, she turned one page after another, her movements becoming more agitated as page after page failed to reveal anything other than pictures of her and her parents.

Her hands shook as she tossed that album aside and reached for another, repeated her search, her actions more frantic with each page of photos until finally she had gone through every album with no satisfaction. After she tossed aside the last one, she glanced up at him.

The look on her face had him leaning toward the demented possibility.

"I don't understand," she said, her tone uncertain, as if she was beginning to doubt her own sanity.

He bent down until he was face to face with her, reached out and cupped her cheek. "Lizzy—"

She batted away his hand. "Don't you dare ever call me that again."

He nodded, but pressed onward. "I can get help to cure this delusion."

"I'm not crazy." She enunciated each word carefully and with determination. It only worried him more.

A second later, she popped up and said, "I know where there's proof."

She hurried to the door and Aidan whispered into the wire, "Stay put, Red Rover. This isn't going the way I envisioned."

"I so totally copy that, Blender Boy," Lucia advised as he followed Lizzy to the restaurant and then down into the cellar. She purposefully strode to the safe, spun the lock and popped open the door.

He stepped beside her, recollecting the view he'd had of the safe just days earlier. It appeared the same except...

"There was a foot locker down at the bottom." He motioned to the glaring emptiness of the bottom shelf.

"Dani's foot locker. She must have come by to get it," Lizzy explained and grabbed a smaller box from another shelf. Working the lock on that box, she opened it and, as before, unsuccessfully rummaged through the papers there.

Every line of her body reflected her dejection. Her surprise. "I don't get it."

"Look, we have a doctor who can deal with this kind of thing," he said and laid a reassuring hand on her shoulder.

She shook off his touch. Her words were clipped, laced with anger. "I am *not* crazy."

With that she was in action again, heading back to the cottage and up the stairs to her bedroom, where she began tossing things out of the drawers at the desk in the corner of her room, clearly searching for something. Anything, apparently.

Aidan just stood watching until it became clear she would find nothing to justify her delusion. Turning his attention to the rest of the room, he examined it more carefully and something on the nightstand beside her bed caught his eye.

He walked over slowly, disbelievingly, until he got closer and closer and there was no denying what he was seeing.

Picking up the frame, he ran his fingers over the photo of the two women standing before the Spanish Steps in Rome.

Two identical women. No delusion could have fabricated this, he realized.

"Red Rover. Come in, Red Rover," he said and turned to face Lizzy.

She must have realized what he was holding, for her earlier anger and confusion fled from her face. She smiled, crossed her arms over her chest and said, "I told you I wasn't crazy."

He acknowledged it, but then Lucia finally responded.

"Come in. Walker wants to know if you have proof of the Sparrow's allegations?"

"I'm holding it, Lucia. I think you two need to get here so we can all discuss this."

As he spoke he looked at Elizabeth, who immediately said, "You're damn right that we'd better discuss this. My sister—"

"Is the Sparrow. She's a world-renowned assassin. We think she murdered the prince."

"And I should believe that because your information has been reliable so far?"

She didn't wait for his answer but turned on her heel and headed downstairs.

He watched her go and confessed to admiration at her spunk. He only hoped it would last past the interview with Walker and Lucia.

Elizabeth waited patiently for Aidan's colleagues to arrive. Or at least, she hoped she looked patient, since she was anything but. Her emotions were a jumble from the revelations that Aidan suspected her sister was a cold-blooded killer and that Aidan himself had been deceiving her. He had lied his way into her bed. Into her heart.

The former concerned her more since she knew he was wrong about Dani. Her sister could never do what he claimed. The latter...she couldn't begin to deal with the latter. With her poor judgment.

It took just five minutes or so after his call for a knock to come at the door. During those minutes, she and Aidan stared at one another awkwardly.

He looked guilty and upset. Good, the bastard deserved major angst after what he had done.

She picked up her chin and glared at him, conveying her rage as he walked to the door to allow his colleagues to enter.

Another man, one very similar in size and looks to Aidan, and an attractive coffee-color-skinned woman walked through the door. Aidan motioned them in the direction of the couch where she was sitting. "Elizabeth Moore," he offered in explanation.

Elizabeth rose slowly.

The tall sandy-haired man held out his hand. "Dr. Walker Shaw."

The woman was next. "Lucia Cordez."

She noticed that the woman had a laptop in her other hand and Elizabeth motioned to it. "Is that where you have your proof?"

"No sense delaying, is there?" Shaw said and held out his hand, inviting her to sit once more.

She did, and the woman and Shaw bracketed either side of her. Aidan took a seat across the way, obviously having no need to see the proof.

Lucia powered up the laptop and, once it was running, assisted Shaw as he detailed their evidence that Dani was the Sparrow.

Elizabeth listened. Looked. The dates and facts for certain times she could personally confirm. Dates like the one that fell during the week that she and Dani had met in Rome.

Thinking back on it now, Dani had been so happy for the first few days and had even hinted at a new man in her life. One with whom she could get serious. But then, something had happened. Dani wouldn't say what, but her sister had been a changed woman by the end of the week.

And then there was the weekend for the cooking expo in the town near Prince Reginald's estate.

Dani had been home that weekend. A surprise trip, she had

said. She had even gone by the expo to see Elizabeth, although she hadn't come home until very late that night.

The night the prince had been murdered.

As each fact seemed to point to the possibility that her sister was what they said, Elizabeth scrambled to find an explanation for why she wasn't. Why they were wrong.

The explanations were hard to find.

"She couldn't have done all these things that you say," she countered weakly.

"These things were murders, Ms. Moore. Cold-blooded, for-hire assassinations," Shaw said.

The woman was a little more sympathetic. She laid a well-manicured hand over hers and squeezed reassuringly. "Look, my sister… She got into trouble, too. But I was able to help her."

"Help her? Like maybe we can do an intervention? Or maybe there's an anti-assassin patch that'll curb her need to kill?" Anger laced her words, mostly because despite the proof before her, she couldn't believe her sister was what they said.

"Maybe there's a reason why she did this," Aidan offered from across the way.

She picked up her head and shot him a glare. "A reason? How about that maybe you're wrong?"

"Maybe what happened to your parents pushed her over the edge," Shaw piped in.

Out of the corner of her eye, she examined the man beside her. Attractive, if you liked the Nordic type, which she obviously did since she'd given it up to Aidan. But his eyes weren't as clear a blue and his hair not as blond. And she could sense the tension between him and Aidan.

Although right now he was trying to be sympathetic. Caring. Possibly open to her pleas about Dani. "When Ma and Da were killed, Dani lost it. She felt guilty that she hadn't gone with them that morning. We had both slept in after a school dance."

"Did you feel the guilt?" Shaw asked.

"Wouldn't you?" she shot back quickly.

"If you'd gone, maybe you'd both be dead right now," Aidan said.

She met his gaze. "Maybe. It didn't make it any easier then. Not even now. You always wonder about the what if."

"What if that's what made Dani do this?" Lucia said and once again, squeezed her hand.

She considered it for only a moment. "Afterward…Dani wasn't quite the same. She had always been a protector and after, it was even more extreme. She became everyone's champion. Always there to right a wrong."

"Maybe that's how she justified all these kills. Except for Mitch, every one of these men were involved in nasty things. Seemingly above the law—"

"But not beyond the Sparrow's own brand of justice," Aidan finished for Shaw.

Even with that explanation, Elizabeth still couldn't believe it and shook her head. "You're wrong," she reiterated.

"And if we're not?" Shaw pressed, but Elizabeth didn't get to answer as all three of their cell phones went off at the same time, creating a noisy cacophony in her front parlor.

Shaw was quickest on the draw and, as the other two waited, he listened quietly. His expression grew darker with each second that passed. When he hung up and slipped the phone back into its holder, he shot an uneasy glance between Aidan and Lucia.

"We've got major problems. Lord Southgate will brief us back at the hotel, Lucia. Aidan, I think it's wiser for you to stay here. If the Sparrow's back in town—"

"She's bound to turn up around here. Brief me once you know more," he said and rose, walked the other two to the door. Once they had left, he faced Elizabeth and said, "You're not telling us everything about Dani."

"What?" she said, uncertain of what information Aidan thought she might have. "I've told you everything I know."

He strode over and suddenly loomed before her, his arms on either side of her on the back of the couch, effectively trapping her. "No, you haven't."

She tried to bat his arms away, but he held firm. With a sigh, she said, "What else could I possibly tell you?"

He knelt before her until there was no way she could avoid looking at him. Finally he said, "You can start by telling me where Dani is."

Chapter 23

Dani hurried along the coast road, intent on reaching the cottage. She had to find out who the man was making moves on her sister.

She thought she had seen him today, after she had dropped by Kate's to get the scoop on what was up. Kate was always the one in the know and things hadn't changed. Their old friend had been able to tell Dani about Mr. Tall, Blond and Dangerous who had appeared in town right after Lizzy's bartender had deserted her. A man who had made his attraction to Lizzy clear.

An attraction that even Kate had noticed was reciprocated by her younger sister.

Dani knew that well from what she had seen the night before from outside Lizzie's cottage.

Now she had to figure out who he was and what he wanted. Even more importantly, for whom he worked. Not, she hoped, the man who had hired her to kill the prince. If that was the case, Lizzy might be in danger and Dani had to make sure her sister was safe.

She hurried up the central road until she was past the docks. Then she cut down a shallow footpath through the dunes and grasses. The tall grasses hid her at times, but could also camouflage someone else along the path. She moved along with caution, therefore.

The path dipped toward the beach, and, once there, she hastened her pace, breaking into a slow jog so that she could reach her grandparents' cottage and start searching for more information on Mr. Aidan Rawlings.

That was the name Kate had provided, although Dani had no doubt it was an alias. Still, there were ways to get around that and secure more information.

Didn't she know it. She'd gone from Danielle Elizabeth Moore to Elizabeth Cavanaugh and most traces of her existence had been blotted out from official papers and computer databases. She had even been excised from the high-school yearbook that the Leonia Public Library kept as a record of every graduating class.

She was a ghost now. Nonexistent except to those people who knew her personally, and of course, to her sister.

Her sister who might be in danger, she thought and hurried onward.

About half a mile up the shore, there was another footpath leading to the base of the bluffs where her maternal grandparents had a cottage—her safehouse. The climb up this path was more arduous as it inclined sharply from the rocks and beach below to the start of the bluffs.

She was slightly out of breath from the climb as she entered the cottage and flipped on the light.

"So good to see you again," she heard from behind her and whirled, reaching for her gun.

A blow like an iron fist struck her, powerful enough to send her reeling backward. Searing pain erupted through her midsection. Her legs failed to cooperate, buckling beneath her.

She fell back heavily onto the couch in the middle of the room.

The pain was like a white-hot poker driving deep into her. She could barely breathe. When she finally did, her breath was shallow. Almost inconsequential.

This wasn't possible, she thought as the man approached, his voice and shape familiar from the night he had hired her to kill the prince. From the night they had fought on the docks when he'd failed to provide her the promised information on her parents' killers.

"Such a shame," he said as he finally stood before her, his face protected by a black ski mask. A slimy smile slicked across his lips as he trained his gun on her. "The Sparrow won't elude this trap."

Dani tried to go for her weapon, but her body wasn't responding. Still, the man wasn't taking any chances. He reached under her jacket and removed her gun from its holster.

She had the Sigma tucked behind her. Could feel its presence against her spine, but knew she would be unable to draw that weapon.

He inspected the HK and smiled. "Nice piece. Seems a shame to waste it, don't you think?"

He tucked it into his belt with one hand and raised his gun with the other. Pointing the barrel at her head, he sighted the shot.

Dani met his cold eyes along the matte black of the barrel and stared him down. If she was going to die, it wasn't going to be like a coward, pleading and begging for her life.

His hand trembled for a moment and she mustered enough breath to say, "What's...matter? Not man enough to do it while...I watch?"

He laughed harshly, his dark eyes glittering through the slits of the black ski mask. "Actually, no. Just taking time to appreciate that you broke your own rules. You let yourself get distracted. A fatal mistake, wouldn't you say?"

Dani gritted her teeth against the pain and struggled for another breath. He was right. She had been so worried about

Lizzy, she hadn't noticed that the fine wire she had rigged on the door to the cottage had fallen off, as it should have if the area was compromised.

And he was also right about another thing—she was dying. She could tell from the way the warmth was fleeing from her fingers and toes. Trying to pull into the center of her as her body battled to hold onto life.

She risked a glance downward. So much blood. Oozing down the front of her shirt. Too much.

"That's right, my dear. You're dying. And of course, I could spare you the pain and end it now, only…" He laughed with malice once again. "You've caused me too many problems. Better you should suffer a little before you go."

"Bastard," she spat out with a rough breath.

"Payback's a bitch, isn't it, Sparrow? And guess what? Little sis is next. Never leave anyone behind who can come in your place."

She tried to speak, causing a swirl of blackness to cloud her sight before she blessedly passed out.

There was no way Elizabeth was going to help him find her sister. Using more force than before, she broke past one of his arms, rose and braced herself for action. "Even if I did know, there's no way that I'd—"

He was on her before she knew it, his hands gripping her arms tightly. She reacted out of anger and out of frustration. Freeing one arm, she turned, dropped a little before flexing with her hip and sending him flying over her shoulder.

He landed with a satisfying thud, but not before upending an end table by the sofa and sending a lamp and some knick-knacks flying. As he lay there, recapturing the breath driven out of him by the fall, he muttered, "Learn that from big sis?"

"Yes. After…she insisted we take self-defense classes. In case they came back for us."

"She protected you then. Don't you think it makes sense to protect her now?" he posed, and in her mind's eye it was unfortunately too easy to see a full-scale manhunt for her sister. One in which Dani could be injured or killed.

She glared at him, hands on her hips and asked, "Promise you'll give Dani a chance to explain?"

He leaned up on his elbows, considered her proposition and agreed to her request with a nod. "Promise. Do you know where she is?"

With a hesitant hunch of her shoulders, she admitted, "My grandparents had a seaside cottage about a mile and a half away. Dani always loved going there to think things through."

He did a little jump/flip she had to admire and was immediately on his feet before her. "Let's go get a car."

She shook her head. "It's faster on foot. The coast road makes too many turns near the bluffs."

Without waiting for his reply, she whirled and raced out the door, alternately eager to see her sister and worried that Dani would not have an explanation for Aidan's allegations. She didn't hesitate, however, for she was sure about one thing: better they find Dani and not someone else.

Her steps were quick, nearly a jog as she hurried through the garden and up the path to the main road. She never paused to look behind her, sensing he was near as a tingle of fear grew swiftly. Gripped her. Urged her to rush.

Something was wrong with her twin. She was certain of it now as surely as she suddenly knew Dani would be at the cottage.

Increasing her pace, she weaved in and out by the pedestrians at the docks. She was at the farthest end of the wharf when she first noticed the car bearing down on them, racing along the coast road. There was something familiar about…

Loud pops, like those from a large firecracker, peppered the air before Aidan tackled her from behind. She hit the ground hard, his weight covering her protectively for just a moment.

Then he was on his feet, more gunfire shattering the stillness of the afternoon air as he returned fire.

She rolled onto her side. The car—it was a big black Hummer—fishtailed as it sped away from them. "That's the same car from the other day."

Aidan held his free hand out to her to help her rise. "It sure is."

In his other hand was a large black gun which he holstered in order to grab his PDA. "Come in, Red Rover."

"Copy, Blender Boy. We heard the noise. What's up?" she asked over the walkie-talkie, making the conversation audible to Elizabeth.

"Same perp in the Hummer. Can you get the locals to put out an APB?"

"I'm on it. Do you need backup at the cottage?"

Aidan glanced at Elizabeth for a second, hesitated, but kept his earlier promise. "That's a negative, Lucia. I think we can handle it for now."

A long silence filled the air before Lucia came back on. "Aidan. You need to hurry. The shit's hit the fan here."

"Copy, Lucia." With that, he popped the PDA back onto his belt and looked at Elizabeth.

Her gaze skipped away from his knowing one since there was no denying it any longer. Whoever was in the van was likely after her sister and had mistaken her for Dani. There could be only one explanation for why so many people were after her.

Cold settled inside her. And the fear that something else was wrong returned, even stronger than before. Aidan was still holding her hand, and he must have sensed the change that came over her.

"Lizzy? Are you okay?"

She finally met his gaze. His concern for her was clear. Heartwrenching since they were on opposite sides right now. "We have to hurry. Something's wrong with Dani."

He didn't question her. Just inclined his head in the direction of the path down to the beach. "This way?"

She nodded and they raced down the path together, hands still joined.

Chapter 24

The cottage, its outline stark against the skyline at the top of the cliff, was not as large as Lizzy's. Tall grasses almost hid it from sight as they approached, but then it was there, a lonely dark silhouette in the fading light of dusk.

There were no signs of life. No movement besides those of the grasses as they approached the door.

Aidan pulled out his gun and, standing to one side, motioned Lizzy to the other.

"Call her name," he mouthed and Lizzy did so. "Dani? It's Lizzy Bee. Are you home?"

At the silence, Aidan reached out and threw open the door.

Nothing happened, but he wasn't about to risk either himself or Lizzy. And above all, he didn't want to trade fire with her sister. He crouched down and cautiously stepped inside the doorway, hit the switch.

Lights flared to life inside the cottage.

On a sofa in the middle of the room, Lizzy's twin lay

slumped. The front of her white T-shirt from her midsection down was soaked in blood. The T-shirt, jacket and jeans were those he had seen that morning on the woman he had called to. That had been Dani and not Lizzy, he realized as he lowered his gun.

Lizzy stepped inside and, seeing Dani, exploded from his side to that of her sister.

"Dani," she said as she took hold of her twin's limp, blood-stained hand and stroked a lock of hair back from Dani's ghostly face.

Dani's eyelids fluttered open. She smiled weakly. "Lizzy Bee. I didn't think…" She stopped and grimaced, but fought back the pain to finish. "I wanted to see you."

Lizzy stroked Dani's hair once more and smiled tearily. "I'm here, Dani. I'm here. You'll be okay, Dani. I know you will."

Dani nodded, but shot a look at Aidan as he approached and stood watching. A look that told him she knew she was dying. Not if he could help it. He picked up his PDA and called Lucia with the walkie-talkie. "We need EMTs, stat. A cottage on the coast road about a mile and a half up and off toward the bluffs."

"Got your location already with the GPS chip. I'm on it," she acknowledged, and with that, he sprang into action, pulling a tea towel from a nearby caddy. He kneeled beside the sofa, folded the towel and applied it to Dani's wound—a gunshot. Fairly large caliber and close range based on the damage done. He applied pressure to staunch the blood still pouring profusely from the wound. The blood was a dark color, causing him to suspect the shot had caught her liver. Not good. She might bleed out before help arrived.

Dani moaned, closed her eyes, and ground her teeth as he applied the pressure.

"Sorry, but—"

"S'okay," she said, her voice weaker than it had been just moments earlier.

"Why did you do it?" He needed to know not only to accomplish his mission, but to also to protect Lizzy from whoever had tried to kill her. From whoever had shot Dani.

Lizzy glared at him. "Shut up, Aidan."

"S'okay, Lizzy Bee. It's not what you think," Dani offered, each word more frail than the one before.

"You didn't kill the prince?" he pressed, hating that he might be ruining Lizzy's last moments with her sister, but having little choice.

"I dangled…" she began, but squeezed her eyes shut against the pain before continuing, each word expelled with a rough breath. "The bait. Left…coke on…table."

"And Mr. Party Boy swallowed the bait," he finished for her. "Who hired you?"

Dani's gaze fixed on her sister as she said, "Let…personal interfere with…job." Every word was a struggle.

"What job, Dani?" Lizzy asked and comforted Dani by stroking the side of her sister's face lovingly.

"My…job. Made a…mistake," her eyes rolled back in her head and she sagged against the cushions of the sofa.

"Dani," Lizzy said and shook Dani's hand, trying to revive her. When she didn't rouse, she repeated her name again, more urgently.

Aidan continued to apply pressure to the wound in Dani's midsection, but with his free hand, he felt for a pulse along her neck. Weak. Too weak. He didn't have much time left to get the complete story from the Sparrow.

"Dani," he urged and stroked the side of her face gently, a face so much like Lizzy's that it hurt.

Once more Dani's eyelids fluttered open, her gaze slightly unfocused for a moment while she struggled to regain consciousness.

When she was with them again, Aidan forged ahead, time too short for delay. "Who hired you?"

"Man named Donovan." Each word was laced with anguish and fear. Each breath more shallow. Less substantial. "Said Reginald…not…true prince."

Lizzy looked up at him, her gaze as confused as he was. As far as he knew, Reginald was the one and only heir to the throne, but that question was for another day.

"Is that why you did it?"

She shook her head with more force than he thought her capable of. "Donovan…pictures." She paused, fighting for a breath. Trying to hold onto consciousness.

Winning the battle for the moment, she continued. "Reginald with drug dealers… The ones who killed Ma…Da." As she finished, she stared at her sister and tears slipped unbidden down her cheeks. "Did it for them."

"I understand, Dani," Lizzy said and leaned forward, slipping an arm around her sister to hold her close. She kissed the side of Dani's face and in soft tones repeated, "I understand."

"What did Donovan look like?"

"Mask…didn't see. Nothing else…distinguishable."

Her eyelids drifted downward again as she battled for awareness.

Aidan checked her pulse once more. Thready and barely noticeable. He had to act fast. "Lizzy, give me your hand."

She released her sister's hand and he took hold of Lizzy's, placed it over the blood-soaked towel. "Keep pressure on here. Hard pressure. Understand?"

"Aidan?" she questioned and he stroked the side of her face.

"I'm going to check on that help."

Elizabeth watched as he stepped away, grabbed his PDA and once again called someone.

"Lizzy?" her sister said and her voice seemed stronger than before, giving her hope that Dani would be all right.

She bent close to her, stroked the side of her face with her free hand. "I'm here, Dani. I'll always be here for you no matter what."

Dani's eyes, a greener shade than her own, darkened with dismay. "The prince—"

"Chose his own poison. I know," she said and leaned her forehead against his sister's. "But the rest—"

"It's not what it seems…." Dani began, but immediately began to struggle for air.

"Dani?" She applied more pressure and wrapped her one arm around her sister's shoulders, trying to comfort her. "Hang on, Dani. Please. Just a little longer."

Dani bit her lip, drawing blood. She gulped in a breath, forced a rush of words out with her exhalation. "Doing a job… Not what they think… Didn't kill…"

Aidan stepped over then, crouched down so Dani could look into his face.

"Mitch? Why did you kill Mitch?" he asked, needing to understand why his friend had died by her hand.

Tears blurred Elizabeth's vision as she pulled away from her sister. She still held Dani in her arms while she was applying pressure, but beneath the palm of her hand, the warmth of her sister's blood was too real a reminder that these might be her last moments.

"Aidan, please," she pleaded, but Dani whispered, "Oh, God. Mitch."

Tears flowed harder from Dani then and her gaze was unfocused as she stared ahead, labored for another breath, a hesitant, almost nonexistent one, and yet she somehow managed to whisper, "Didn't…kill. Loved Mitch."

A breath came. Like the hiss of air escaping a balloon. A last breath. Her body went limp and her eyes lost their life before they closed.

Elizabeth continued to hold her as Aidan searched for a pulse.

"Shit," he cursed and called Lucia again. "Damn it. What's the ETA on those EMTs?"

"Two minutes."

"Shit," he cursed again. When his gaze met hers, she finally understood Dani was gone.

"No," she said softly, but then it grew into a wail as she repeated it over and over, and cradled Dani in her arms, rocking her lifeless body back and forth.

Aidan couldn't just stand there, watching Lizzy's heart

break. Knowing that with every second that passed, there was less and less possibility of bringing Dani back.

"Lizzy, please. Give me room."

He slipped his one arm between Lizzy and her sister, pried Lizzy away so he could pick up Dani and carry her over to a free spot on the floor. Laying her out, he knelt beside her and began to do CPR. Lizzy knelt opposite him and took hold of Dani's slack hand.

He kept up the CPR for what seemed like hours until the wail of a siren grew closer and closer.

The EMTs arrived barely a minute later and urged them to the side so they could immediately get to work on Dani. Walker was with them, but as he observed from afar, Aidan could see in the other man's eyes that Dani's condition was not improving.

The EMTs were still working on her as they wheeled the gurney from the room. Lizzy went to go with them, but Walker shot out his arm and blocked her way. "I'm sorry, but that won't be possible."

"What?" Aidan shouted and advanced on the other man, grabbed his arm and yanked it down, but Walker immediately blocked their way once more when Aidan would have led Lizzy to the ambulance.

"Get out of the way, Walker. Lizzy should be with her sister."

Walker shook his head and faced Lizzy. "I'm sorry, Ms. Moore. But given who your sister is—"

"The Sparrow," Lizzy said weakly, her arms wrapped around herself as she gazed beyond Walker to the ambulance outside as it pulled away from the cottage.

Walker nodded stiffly. "Yes, the Sparrow. She's being taken to a secure location where she can be treated. If she should survive—"

"You cold-hearted prick," Aidan said and forcefully shoved Walker out of the way. "Let's go, Lizzy."

She laid a hand on his arm. A hand that was cold and covered with her sister's blood. Despite that, she was calm.

Much calmer than he. He finally realized his anger on her behalf was only causing her even more grief. He reached out and dragged her into his arms. "I'm sorry, Lizzy. I really am."

"I'm...okay. Now."

He stepped away, but not before he caressed the side of her face and said, "She'll be okay."

Lizzy confronted Walker. "When can I see her?"

Walker seemed truly uncomfortable about his answer, which made Aidan only a little less angry. Maybe he wasn't as big a prick as he seemed. "I'm not sure, Ms. Moore. Things are a bit...unsettled right now. If we all return to our hotel, I'll be able to tell you more and we can wait for news on your sister's...condition."

With a gracious nod, Lizzy walked out the door, her arms wrapped around herself once again as if that grip was all that was keeping her from breaking into pieces.

Walker was about to follow her out, when Aidan snared his arm.

The other man stopped, looked down at Aidan's hold and then up to his face. "You've let this get way too personal."

"You bet I have. You get Corbett on the line. You tell him that this business about a secure location is a load of crap."

"I'll do one better, Spaulding. I'll get him on the line so you can tell him yourself."

Chapter 25

Elizabeth sat on the couch in the hotel room that Aidan's crew used as their base of operations. Not the Leonia Inn as Aidan had mentioned, but the more upscale Lion's Heart Lodge.

A series of tables lined one wall, their surfaces littered with monitors and other surveillance equipment, computers and assorted phones.

Aidan and Lucia were huddled over one computer, intently reviewing something that had been sent to them by Lord Southgate, the Duke of Carrington. The man who would be king now that Prince Reginald was dead. As Aidan bent over the monitor, the holster with his gun dangled between his body and outstretched arm.

A gun.

If she had one in her hands right now, she could see herself killing the man who had hurt Dani. She understood better how her sister had taken a dark path on her way to avenging their parents.

Her sister the assassin. Or so the Lazlo Group claimed.

It had been nearly an hour without word, but she could sense Dani still. It gave her hope that her twin was hanging on.

She rubbed her arms against the chill from the air conditioning in the room. It was set on high, probably to deal with all the equipment within. As she did so, she roused the smell of blood.

Holding her hands out in front of her, she realized her sister's blood still clung to one hand. Glancing downward, she noted it on her shirtfront, as well from when she had cradled Dani in her arms.

"Lizzy?" Aidan questioned and took hold of her blood-stained hand with his own. "I'm sorry. I should have thought to get us cleaned up."

His hand also bore the remnants of Dani's blood as did his shirt from when he had carried her to the floor. "Thank you," she said and raked back a lock of his hair with her clean hand.

A puzzled look came to his face. "For what?"

"For keeping your promise. For helping Dani."

His eyes hardened. "I'm sorry I couldn't stop whoever shot her, Lizzy. But I promise—"

"Don't. Not that I don't want him dead, but… It just brings more death. More violence, doesn't it?"

"Yes. It does," he said and she could see in his eyes that he was thinking about Mitch.

Mitch, who Dani had said she'd loved. The pieces of part of the puzzle fell into place. "When Dani and I were in Rome, she told me she had met someone special. She was so happy for the first few days."

"Mitch, as well," Aidan admitted as he knelt before her.

"Then she came home one night… She was crying. Almost as inconsolable as when our parents had died. I figured Mr. Wonderful had broken it off with her."

"Maybe he did, but not for the reasons she thought. Maybe he was dead," he said.

"She loved him," she said and Aidan inclined his head in agreement.

"I think he loved her, only… The kind of lives we lead don't hold out many promises for happily ever after, Lizzy."

She hadn't needed him to tell her. Maybe it was his way of reminding her that he, too, had that kind of life. That he was a wanderin' man in a dangerous job who would move on as soon as this assignment was over. A man who one day, might end up like Mitch.

She wouldn't say, like Dani. No, not like Dani. Dani was still alive. Still with her, Lizzy believed with all her heart.

The door opened then and Walker Shaw stepped in, the planes of his face like granite. His blue eyes shuttered until he looked her way and said, "I'm sorry, Ms. Moore."

They were the last words she heard as Aidan caught her in his arms.

A tender touch skimmed the skin along her cheek, rousing her.

She opened her eyes and Aidan was there. "I'm sorry," he said and once again stroked his finger across her cheek.

Shaking her head, she said, "Dani's not dead."

"Lizzy—"

"She's not," she insisted and popped up. She realized someone had changed her shirt and cleaned her hands. It defused the situation immediately. "Did you do this?"

He nodded and took hold of her hand. "Are you okay?"

She would be better if she could see Dani. See for herself that Dani was dead since her twin instinct was telling her otherwise. "I want to see Dani. Say goodbye."

He rose and held out his hand to help her up. "I'm told that's not possible."

"Make it possible," she insisted as she went to his side.

With a nod, he said, "We can talk to Walker about it."

"Walker? I get the sense the two of you don't get along," she remarked, recalling the men's earlier confrontations.

Aidan shrugged away her concern. "That's what happens

when you put two alpha males to work on the same assignment. He's actually not such a bad guy."

"Let's hope so."

She walked out of the bedroom, Aidan following behind her, his hand riding at the small of her back. In the suite outside, Lucia and Walker sat at the monitors once more, but at her approach, they rose.

"Ms. Moore. I'm sorry for your loss," Walker offered and Lucia echoed his sentiments.

Elizabeth picked her head up a notch. "I want to see Dani. I want to say goodbye to my sister."

Walker's gaze skittered from her back to Aidan. "Didn't you tell her?"

"I did, but I can't agree with the decision. Elizabeth should be able to see her sister," Aidan replied.

"It's not possible," Lucia jumped in and came to stand before Lizzy. "I know this must be hard—"

"What do you know about how hard this is for me?" Elizabeth snapped. "You tell me my sister's dead, but you won't let me see her body. Won't let me say goodbye."

Walker also took a step toward her. "Ms. Moore—"

"Save it, Dr. Shaw. If you can't make it happen, get someone on the phone who can."

Walker looked back toward Aidan, as if to ask him to intercede. But as she risked a glance over her shoulder, Aidan just shrugged at the other man. "She's right on this. We all know it. It's what we'd all want if…"

An uneasy silence followed his words. A silence shattered by the ringing of the phone. Walker was the one who hurried over to pick it up. A one-sided conversation ensued, occasionally punctuated by Walker's yes sirs and no sirs. Finally there appeared to be a break and Walker said, "Mr. Lazlo. Ms. Moore has a request for you."

There was the static of a reply and then Walker moved to the table holding a speakerphone and hit a button. "Mr. Lazlo?" he said.

A crackle rent the air before a man's resonant voice said, "Ms. Moore. My sympathies are with you at your loss."

She walked closer to the speaker, leaned toward it so she would be clearly heard. "If you truly meant those words, Mr. Lazlo, you would let me see my sister."

"Unfortunately, the body—"

"My sister, Mr. Lazlo. Not just a body," she emphasized, her hands clenched on the surface of the table.

"Of course, Ms. Moore. Your sister. Unfortunately—"

"You're sounding like a broken record, Mr. Lazlo. And so far, I haven't heard a single reason why I can't see Dani one last time."

Aidan came up behind her and placed a hand on her shoulder. Leaning past her, he spoke into the speakerphone. "Corbett, it's not an unreasonable request."

"Mr. Spaulding. There are some things over which even I have no control," Lazlo responded, his tone bordering on sympathetic.

"Please, Mr. Lazlo. I'm sure a man with your connections can make the arrangements," Elizabeth added.

Lazlo stammered for a moment. "Yes, well. Of course, Ms. Moore. I shall endeavor to see about a last visit."

A last visit. The words made her knees go weak again, but luckily Aidan was behind her. He eased an arm around her waist and steadied her. "Thank you, Mr. Lazlo."

The sound of the dial tone filled the room for a second before Walker reached over and cut the connection. As she glanced over at him, he saluted. "Ms. Moore, you've just played one of the world's greatest players. My hat's off to you."

She was about to respond when a machine on another of the tables began to beep and spit out paper.

Lucia reacted immediately, heading over to pick up the sheet the machine spewed out. Her hands trembled for a moment as she read the document. When she finished she faced them and offered the fax to Walker, who also perused it quickly.

"What is it?" Elizabeth asked, seeing the look on the psychiatrist's face go hard once again.

"It's an advance copy of the *Quiz,* courtesy of Lord Southgate." He picked up the piece of paper and held it up for them to see.

The headline read: The Prince of Fake: Reginald's False Claim to Throne Revealed.

Chapter 26

The Lazlo Group clearly had a problem on their hands. A problem that needed their coordination with the royal family as soon as possible.

But she had her own problems, as well.

The restaurant would be in full swing by now, even if it was midweek. Natalie would be crazed, wondering where Elizabeth was, since she had never missed a day without notice. Calls had to be made.

After Aidan had instructed Lucia to print out the entire article and also the materials Lord Southgate had sent over earlier for their review, he turned to her. "I need to deal with this," he said, his tones apologetic.

"There are things I need to address, as well, Aidan. Arrangements for Dani—"

"Once Corbett tells us we can."

Anger boiled up inside of her and she moved close. So close her nose brushed the edge of his jaw. "No one decides what to do about Dani except me."

"Lizzy—"

"No one, Aidan." Her tone conveyed her emotions quite clearly.

"I understand. I'll do what I can. In the meantime—"

"I need to call Nat. She's probably frantic by now."

Aidan gave a resigned nod. "You'll need to stay here until we know more about Dani's assailant. For now, we should keep any information regarding Dani's death to ourselves."

She walked over to a phone and dialed the restaurant. When the hostess answered, she asked for Natalie.

"Lizzy Bee! Thank God. We were so worried about you," Natalie immediately said as she answered.

"I'm okay, Nat, but Dani… She's been hurt. Bad. I'll need to stay with her for a little while so please close the restaurant for a few days," she explained, all the time looking at Aidan to make sure she didn't give out any more information than was necessary.

"Will she be okay?" Natalie asked and tears came to Lizzy's eyes.

She bit back the tears, but her voice was tight as she answered. "I'm not sure, Nat. I'll keep you posted."

"Lizzy. If you need anything, absolutely anything—"

"I know, Nat. Please tell Kate and Samantha. I'll keep you posted, okay?" she said, but didn't wait for an answer as the tears came more furiously.

Aidan reached out and pulled her into his embrace. "You need to get some rest, Lizzy."

"I'm not sure I can," she mumbled against his chest.

He tightened his hold and rubbed one hand up and down her back in a soothing gesture. As he did so, he called out, "Guys, I just need some time."

"Aidan," she protested, but he silenced her by gently placing a finger against her lips.

"Don't argue on this, Lizzy. The next few days may be rough. You need to be ready to deal with them."

With that, he slipped his hands to her shoulders and applied light pressure, guiding her in the direction of the room she had been in earlier. Once inside, he led her to the bed and made her climb in. As he tucked the sheets in around her, she laid her head on the pillow and smelled his scent.

"Is this your room?"

He confirmed it with a shrug. "Is that a problem?"

"No. Thank you."

It was so awkward between them when just last night…

"Was any of it true? The army? The moving around?" she asked, peering up at him as he stood by the side of the bed.

He stroked her hair. "It was all true, Lizzy."

She looked away to the edge of the sheet, afraid to ask about the rest. About his feelings for her. Despite that, he must have known what she was thinking.

"Lizzy. What happened…it was real. I never meant to hurt you. Believe that, please."

If she'd had any doubts, they vanished in that moment. The sincerity in his voice quashed any qualms about his true feelings. "I believe you, Aidan. But it doesn't change anything does it?"

His lips thinned into a harsh line. "No. It doesn't. I'll go and let you rest now."

He pushed away from the bed. She didn't look up until she heard the solid thunk of the door closing.

Then and only then did she give in to the tears she had been holding back. Tears for her sister and the man she'd loved. Tears for herself, selfish as they were.

Aidan heard her sobs even through the thick wood of the door. It made him want to return to the room and comfort her, only that would be a bad move all around.

Lizzy was strong. She would deal with whatever came in the days ahead. Without him.

He forced his attentions to the mission that still needed to be completed. Lucia and Walker were sitting around the coffee table in the middle of the suite, reviewing the assorted papers sent to them today.

When he approached, Lucia handed him a set to peruse and he plopped down on the sofa and got to work.

The news article from the *Quiz* detailed how Prince Reginald was not the biological son of King Weston and the queen. But other than going into detail about the DNA tests that had proven it, the story was basically a rehash of past speculation about the prince's recreational habits and the possible suspects in his killing. The *Quiz* even went so far as to bring up the months-old speculation that it was quite convenient that Lord Southgate, the next in line, had immediately stepped in and married the prince's betrothed.

Aidan tossed it aside, finding nothing of interest in the article other than the claims regarding Reginald's paternity. Dani had mentioned the same assertion.

He tossed that out for consideration by his colleagues. "The Sparrow indicated that the man who had hired her claimed to be doing it so that the true prince might inherit the throne."

"Who hired her?" Lucia asked.

"He said his name was Donovan," he advised, earning the interest of both his colleagues. "Yeah, I thought the same thing. Nikolas Donovan and his Union for Democracy are making trouble and the Sparrow's employer has the same name."

"Could be someone wants to cause trouble for Donovan, as well," Walker tossed out.

"Could be. If you discredit Donovan and the Union for Democracy, the royals get a free pass to choose whomever they want to be king," Lucia hypothesized.

"The royals being Lord Southgate." Aidan picked up the faxed copy of the *Quiz* article. "Pretty much says the same in this tabloid."

"So far they've gotten more information than we have," Walker said irately before flipping through the other papers that had been sent over earlier. "Not to mention that after weeks of trying to open this vault—"

"All you get is a fingerprint and a lock of hair once you break in. Is Xander working on it already?" Aidan asked.

Lucia nodded. "He thinks he'll have an answer for us in the morning."

Tired and frustrated, Aidan tossed the papers onto the coffee table. "I'm calling it a night, then. We'll pick up where we left off in the morning?"

Walker rose and stretched his long frame. "Let's all get some rest. I think that when this story hits the stands tomorrow, we'll need all the energy we've got."

With a wave at his two colleagues, Aidan walked to the door to his room, but hesitated at the entrance. Pressing his ear to the wood, he listened intently.

Silence.

He breathed a cowardly sigh of relief. He didn't think he had the strength to deal with her tears. But he couldn't leave her alone, either.

Entering, he trod softly so as not to wake her. She was asleep on her back and snoring. It yanked a smile to his face as it brought a recollection of their one and only night together.

He pictured himself sleeping with her again. Making love with her.

She stirred and caught him spying on her. He hoped his emotions weren't obvious.

"Did Mr. Lazlo call about Dani?" she asked and sat up.

He walked over to the bed and settled himself beside her. "Not yet."

With a slow nod, she leaned back against the wooden headboard and crossed her arms. "I can feel her still. I know that you say she's dead, but…she's still here with me."

He pointed to a spot right above his heart. "It's because Dani will always be with you. In here."

Lizzy peered at him. She wondered who stayed in his heart. Whether she might be there. "Is Mitch there with you?"

"Sometimes," he admitted immediately.

"That's good," she said.

A furrow appeared between his brows as he mused about her statement. "Why?"

"Because I don't like to think of you being alone," she confessed.

He closed his eyes, shook his head and expelled a harsh breath. When he opened them, the look in his eyes was intense. Devouring. There was no denying what he wanted any more than she could deny she wanted the same.

"If we do this tonight—"

"It will be for all the wrong reasons, wouldn't it?" she finished for him.

"I think I should leave, Lizzy," he said and rose from the bed, but she reached out and grabbed hold of his arm.

"I don't want to be alone tonight, Aidan. I just want you to… Just hold me."

He obviously couldn't resist her plea. He toed off his sneakers, slipped onto the bed beside her and wrapped an arm around her shoulders.

She went willingly, settling into his side, one hand laid over his heart. He placed his hand over hers, rubbed it as if to warm it. Not that he could. A deep chill had established its hold over her core earlier—when she had heard Walker say Dani was dead.

"I feel…cold inside. Numb," she admitted.

"It'll go away," he replied and rubbed a little harder.

"When?" she wondered aloud and snuggled closer, the warmth of his body calling to her.

He sighed heavily. "When Mitch was killed… It took a while."

Nodding, she eased back a bit so she could examine his face. There was a closed look about it. His jaw was set tightly and his eyes were hard. Frigid. Like the ice of an arctic glacier. She knew then that the cold…the pain it represented…never really went away.

"I won't believe she's dead until I see her, Aidan. Until I can hold her hand one last time. Kiss her goodbye so she knows someone cared."

He cursed before gripping her arms tightly, so tightly she

suspected she would have bruises in the morning. "She knows you cared, Lizzy. You were with her when… She knows, damn it."

Somehow she knew his anger was about more. She reached up and caressed his cheek. Ran her finger along his lips before inching up slowly and brushing a kiss there. "Mitch knew it also, Aidan."

He expelled a harsh breath and cursed again. "Close your eyes, Lizzy. Try to get some rest."

She inclined her head in agreement, but kissed him again lightly before relaxing against him and shutting her eyes.

He moved his hand to the small of her back, slipped it beneath the hem of her shirt, as if needing the contact with her skin.

She welcomed it, craving his touch. Wanting to feel anything besides the numbness inside.

"Aidan?" she said and glanced up at him.

"What is it, Lizzy?" he asked and cupped her cheek with his free hand.

"I don't care that it's for all the wrong reasons."

Chapter 27

A shudder ripped through him at her words.

He didn't care, either.

Bending his head, he kissed her. Gently at first, wanting to push away the thoughts of what had happened today. Wanting to ease her pain, if only for the night, since in the morning…

He opened his mouth, invited her to join him and she did, easing her tongue inside his mouth. Tasting him.

He cradled her face as if it was a precious work of art. Tracing the lines and shape of it with his hands as he kissed her, he remembered that somewhere on an ice-cold slab, a woman with an identical face lay dead.

It tempered his passion, turned it into something…deeper. More intense.

She must have sensed the change in him. She withdrew from him so she could see his face. Running her hands over it so as to soothe what she saw, she whispered, "It's okay, Aidan. I understand this doesn't change anything."

It already had, he thought, bending his head to kiss her again. He might be unable to voice his thoughts since the emotion was too strong, but he could show her. Let her feel it as he made love to her.

He kissed her over and over while he moved his hands down, and then cupped her breasts. A little hitch in her breath told him she liked it. Wanted him to continue.

He did, barely brushing his fingers over the tips until they hardened into tight peaks. Taking those peaks between his fingers, he kneaded them until her breath came uneven against his lips and her hands gripped his shoulders, pulling him close.

He slid his hands beneath the hem of her borrowed shirt, moved it up and over her head to reveal her to him. The cream-colored bra she wore was trimmed with lace. A front clasp. He undid it and her breasts spilled free.

Bending, he replaced his hands with his mouth, skimming his lips against the tips until she was straining toward him. Finally taking one hard peak into his mouth, he sucked as she cradled his head to her.

Elizabeth sighed at the heat of his mouth on her nipple. She took a hesitant breath when he sucked and then circled it with his tongue.

She held his head to her, urged him on. The feelings he roused…they chased away the chill. The deadness inside of her, but not Dani.

No matter what anyone said, Dani was still there.

As Aidan would be even after he was long gone.

And that made her need more of him. She needed it to remember a bit longer what it was like to be loved so much.

She urged him up and kissed him. Deeply, never wavering as she told him with her lips and mouth how much she needed him. Never hesitating as she pulled on his shirt and dragged it over his head. She reached down and undid the zipper on his jeans, freed him.

He groaned when she held him and broke away from her

kiss. Leaning his forehead against hers, he whispered, "I want you so badly, but…not so fast."

"Not fast," she repeated. "Only, I want you next to me. Making me warm."

He smiled and cradled her face. "I want it, too."

With those words and a smile, they both quickly undressed and then slipped beneath the sheets together. Bodies naked, warm, as skin met skin.

"That feels…good," she said and ran a hand along the muscles of his chest.

"Really good?" he teased and ran his hand along her breasts, rousing her again.

She savored it. The light caress of the back of his hand, hardly touching her.

Easing her thigh between his legs, she shifted so they were closer. At her belly, his erection nestled contentedly, which was perfect. She wanted so much more right now.

She laid her hands on his shoulders and kissed him, made love to him with her mouth. Opening his mouth with her tongue to slip inside, she danced it beside his tongue before withdrawing it to trace the edges of his lips, eager to memorize the shape of them, the feel, so that once he was gone, she could still remember them.

When that memory was imprinted on her brain, she shifted her mouth to his jaw, kissed along the line of it. Moved up to the shell of his ear and his lobe, which she bit gently, sending a shudder through his body.

He moved his hands to her back and pulled her close until their bodies were pressed together. Her breasts against the hardness of chest. His hardness jutting into her belly.

He moved his mouth to her ear and then lower, to the juncture of her neck and shoulder and the spot that was still sensitive from the night before. When he brushed his lips there, it awakened her within and her insides clenched.

She butted her hips against him, but he whispered, "I feel it, too, Lizzy. Touch me."

She did, reaching between their bodies to wrap her hand around him while she moved her mouth to the side of his neck. There was a purple spot she'd put there. Her love bite. She covered that same spot, sucked gently and he moaned. His erection jumped in her hand.

But she still took it slowly, sucking on his neck while gently caressing him with her hand.

He lowered his head, kissed her breasts over and over before moving one hand downward and parting her. He eased his hand over the center of her, already damp and hot from his caresses. "You feel so warm," he whispered.

She wanted another part of him to feel it and eased her thigh over his, shifted her hips and guided him with her hand until he was nestled between her thighs. His erection pressed along the length of her.

He groaned, rubbed himself along her while she held him to her with her hand. He was breathing hard, gripping her shoulders to control himself. "I wish I could be inside you. Feel the heat. The wet, but…"

She wanted it, too, but knew they couldn't do it without the protection that was just a few feet away in the nightstand. "Just feel this for now," she urged, moving her hips to rub along his shaft. She dampened him with her desire, warmed him with the heat of her.

He was breathing roughly, barely in control when he finally reached for a condom from the nightstand. His hands were shaking so badly, he couldn't open the foil packet, and so she reached up, did it for him. Took out the condom and gently unrolled it over his erection.

He groaned again as she did so, and then he was between her legs and pressing into her. The width of him stretching her. Slowly, he eased in until she no longer could focus on anything other than the way him being inside rocked her. Hot and so hard.

When he flexed his hips, she brought her hand to the small of his back and stilled his motion.

He met her gaze and seemed to know what she wanted, for he pressed forward just a bit more, causing her breath to leave her sharply. After, he met her lips in a kiss and for the longest time, that was all they did.

Just kiss with him buried inside her.

When that was no longer enough, he bent and sucked her nipples. Teethed the tips until her insides clenched around him. She knew he felt it because he groaned against her breasts.

"Do you like that?" she asked, and he looked up from her breasts.

"Yes," he said, but then immediately bit the tip of her breast, yanking a mew of pleasure from her. "Like you like this," he teased and did it again.

She held his head to her and tightened on him. It seemed as though he grew even larger within her, grew hotter, and she continued moving her muscles on him that way while enjoying his mouth on her breasts until it too wasn't enough.

With the flex of her hips, she rolled him onto his back and straddled him. Drove him even deeper, which she hadn't thought possible. She stilled for a moment, savoring the sensation. Relishing the warmth of him that was finally beginning to dispel the chill within.

And as temporary a feeling as that was, she strove for it. Shifted her hips and rode him to build the heat until her body was shaking and, beneath her, he was likewise trembling.

She met his gaze, joined her hands with his as the passion built even more as she pumped away on him faster and faster until, finally, her body clenched around him tightly. He pushed up into her to send her over the edge and he called out his own completion.

She dropped down onto him, breathing roughly, her body damp with sweat.

He pulled the sheet up to keep her warm and wrapped his arms around her. She snuggled against him and laid her head on his chest. The strong, if somewhat erratic, beat of his heart reminded her they were still alive.

It was that beat and the warmth of him that finally lulled her to sleep.

Chapter 28

Lucia had been kind enough to retrieve some of Elizabeth's own clothes while she showered. So now she sat, refreshed and clean, waiting for a call from Corbett Lazlo.

Despite that, she jumped when the phone rang.

Someone had run a longer cord so that the phone now sat on the coffee table in front of the couch where she and Aidan were seated. Opposite them, Walker and Lucia waited in matching wing chairs.

It was Lucia who caught her gaze for a moment before reaching over and picking up the phone. "Lucia Cordez," she answered and a second later, she said, "Yes, of course, Mr. Lazlo."

She reached over again, this time to engage the speaker. "Can you hear us, Mr. Lazlo?"

"Yes, thank you, Lucia. Ms. Moore, are you there?"

As if she'd be somewhere else, she thought, but didn't voice. "Yes, I am. Do you have any news for me?"

"I'm sorry, Ms. Moore. I spoke to the various authorities, but you must understand—"

"All I understand is that you say my sister is dead, Mr. Lazlo, but you refuse to let me see her," she interjected, pain and annoyance coloring the tones of her voice.

"That won't be possible, Ms. Moore. I have the CIA, MI6, even Interpol who all want their time with the bod…with your sister. They all want their experts to gather the evidence they need to close their cases."

The cold returned full force. She swallowed, her throat tight with emotion. Struggling for control, she nevertheless managed to say, "I don't want Dani's body butchered, Mr. Lazlo."

Aidan reached over then, grabbed hold of her hand to offer support. She latched onto him, needing the stability.

"I assure you she'll be treated with the utmost respect."

His promise did little to calm her fears. "I want to bury her here. With our parents. When can I…"

She couldn't finish. Couldn't picture laying Dani in the ground alongside her Ma and Da. She was too young to be dead. Her presence still too alive with Lizzy for her to believe it possible.

"I'm sorry, Ms. Moore, but that may take some time. You must understand that the Sparrow… Well, there's a lot of work that needs to be done," Lazlo blustered uneasily.

It was Aidan who jumped in on her behalf. "She needs closure, Corbett. Let her see Dani and then let the experts do what they need to. It's the humane thing to do, damn it."

"Mr. Spaulding. I would have thought that you more than anyone would appreciate how important it is to get the evidence we need. You do want to confirm who killed Agent Lama, don't you."

Aidan was about to protest again, but she squeezed his hand. An unlikely defender rose up, however. "I imagine that by now you already have the Sparrow's fingerprints and DNA. What more could you need?" Walker challenged.

A sigh that was part annoyance, part fatigue came across

the speakerphone. "Dr. Shaw, et tu? This discussion is concluded. When the various agencies are done, I promise you, Ms. Moore, that the Lazlo Group will make the finest of arrangements for your sister."

"Thank you, Mr. Lazlo," she replied, but had no sooner finished when Lazlo continued.

"As for DNA, it's time we got to business. Lord Southgate is on his way and I'm afraid we have some rather disturbing news for him."

Elizabeth shot a look at Aidan to question whether she should leave, but he shook his head and leaned over. "Stay and I'll walk you back to your cottage."

She nodded, sat back and prepared herself for the report that was to follow, fearing yet more negative things about Dani.

"Xander, here. We've matched the Sparrow's DNA to that at the scene, but that's not the news for the day," he reported in a too-cheerful tone.

"Mr. Forrest. Decorum, please. What news do you have?" Lazlo admonished.

"Lord Southgate provided the fingerprints and DNA retrieved from the vault located by Doctors Shaw and Smith. I got a match on the fingerprints from the Silvershire police archives."

Lucia inched to the edge of her chair and shifted toward the speaker. "Xander, please make this long story short."

"The fingerprints belong to Nikolas Donovan and the DNA from the hair links its donor to King Weston. Short enough?" His loud guffaw followed the bluntly worded report.

"Donovan?" Elizabeth said aloud. "As in the same man who hired Dani?"

"And if the prints belong to him, what are the odds that the DNA doesn't?" Walker added and shook his head.

"Lord Southgate—"

"Isn't going to like this one bit," came from the doorway. Everyone jumped to their feet and stood awkwardly, except for Elizabeth. She immediately dipped into a curtsy. "Your Grace."

Lord Russell Southgate, Duke of Carrington and soon to

be king, waved off her display, clearly uncomfortable. "Please, Ms. Moore. Rise, and also accept my sympathies for your recent loss."

"Thank you, Your Grace," she responded and watched as the duke sauntered in and stood before the group.

"Mr. Lazlo, are you there?" he asked the speakerphone.

"I am, Your Grace, and I apologize about the manner in which this information came to you," Corbett Lazlo replied, obviously annoyed.

"That's fine, but…Mr. Xander. Are you sure about the results?"

Xander hesitated and in the background, the sound of rustling papers came across the line before the young agent finally responded. "Yes, sir. No doubt about the match on the prints or the DNA. If we find the donor of the hair, you've found Weston's real son."

"And you believe that would be Nikolas Donovan?" the duke pressed.

"Yes. It's only logical that since the prints and hair were the only things in the vault, there's a connection," Lazlo offered up for his technician.

"And easy enough to confirm if you can get a sample. Some more hair, preferably with the root or some skin. Saliva or some other body fluid," Xander said calmly.

Elizabeth had been listening intently and almost failed to notice that the duke had now turned his attention to her and Aidan. When he spoke, it was directed to them.

"I understand that the Sparrow identified a man named Donovan as the one who hired her to eliminate Reginald."

Aidan quickly added, "We also suspect that Donovan was the one who shot the Sparrow."

Lord Southgate paced back and forth for a second before advising, "Although Nikolas served in the military, I find it hard to believe that he could locate and kill someone that various international agencies have been unsuccessfully chasing for years."

"He had information the Sparrow wanted. That might have made her vulnerable," Aidan offered and Elizabeth chimed in with, "Donovan told my sister that he possessed information on who murdered our parents."

Again Southgate paused to digest that statement. Finally he asked, "And Reginald was somehow connected to their murder?

"Apparently, Reginald was using cocaine he purchased from the men responsible for the murders. I know killing him was wrong, but Reginald and those men should have been punished for what they did," she urged.

The duke shocked her by agreeing. "Punishment delayed is punishment denied. Nevertheless, Donovan's reasons for Reginald's murder would seem to be for personal gain. Highly unlike the Nikolas Donovan I know."

"I would suggest that we track him down and get not only the sample, but question him about his whereabouts the last few days. We could also do a GSR test to confirm whether he's fired a weapon recently," Aidan suggested.

"Sounds like a plan, but… Nikolas and I know each other. Quite well, actually."

"We can provide backup, Your Grace, if I understand that what you'd like to do is approach him first," Lazlo offered.

Lord Southgate ratified that was his intent with a regal motion of his head. "That's exactly what I'd like to do."

"Lucia and I will go along, Mr. Lazlo. Agent Spaulding needs to keep an eye on Ms. Moore until we ascertain whether she's still in danger," Walker indicated and rose from his chair.

After a flurry of goodbyes, only Aidan and Elizabeth remained, standing before each other awkwardly. "I guess I should walk you back to the cottage. Make sure the surveillance and other things are still intact so I can keep an eye on you."

"You know that's really not necessary. The watching. Once Lord Southgate talks to Donovan—"

"I understand, Lizzy. I don't have to be the one watching." With those words, he stepped away and made a call. He was speaking too low for her to hear. When he returned, however, he said, "I've arranged for a detail to watch your grounds. This way you can try and get things back to normal."

Elizabeth couldn't imagine things being normal. At least not for awhile. First she had to call family and friends, tell them about Dani's death. After that, she'd arrange for a memorial until the Lazlo Group released her body and after that…maybe after that…

Who was she kidding? Even after that things wouldn't be normal. Her sister was dead and Aidan…

Aidan would be gone. "I need to go. I've got a lot to handle," she said.

He walked with her all the way back to her cottage. As they neared her home, the door opened and Nat, Kate and Samantha stepped out.

"I called them earlier," he said. "Figured you could use the support."

Tears came to her eyes at this thoughtfulness. "Thank you."

She faced him and swiped at the tears. "I guess this is…goodbye."

Aidan stuffed his fingertips into his jeans pockets. A familiar pose. One which dragged a smile to her face despite the sadness of the moment.

He rocked back and forth on his heels for a second and then finally said, "I'll be around for a little while. If you need me."

"Right. Take care of yourself, Aidan," she said and whirled, hurried from him and toward the women anxiously waiting at the door to the cottage.

They circled her and herded her inside, but not before looking his way and shooting him looks that warned him to go away and stay away. He couldn't blame them in a way. He'd hurt her. Nothing was going to change that.

But in time, she would forget him.

In time, he was certain he would forget her, as well.

It was part of who he was. What he was. What he had done since he was a child and become used to a wandering life.

Nothing was going to change that, especially not a woman like Elizabeth who needed stability and a place to call home. Those things were not in his game plan. Ever.

Chapter 29

Nikolas Donovan had disappeared.

Lord Southgate had tried every location he knew. Called every friend they had in common. None had any idea where Donovan had gone.

Donovan had run like the guilty man he might be, Aidan thought as he reviewed the report Lazlo had e-mailed that morning about Donovan's disappearance.

From the looks of it, Donovan had left some time close to when Dani had been shot. Now, days later, the only clue they had was a report that he had been spotted in France.

Which meant that for the moment, Lizzy was safe.

The cell phone on his PDA rang and he pulled it off his belt, answered. "Spaulding here."

"Mr. Spaulding. Lazlo here."

As if he wouldn't recognize his boss's voice after seven years. "Mr. Lazlo. I was just getting ready to call. It would appear it's time to give Ms. Moore back her privacy."

"Do it then, Aidan. Remove the surveillance equipment and the detail guarding her, but after…Lord Southgate has asked us to track down Nikolas Donovan."

Donovan. He wanted him found and punished almost as much as he had wanted vengeance on the Sparrow. Maybe even more. "What will it entail?"

"I've called in Rhia de Hayes to track down Donovan."

Aidan couldn't hold back his disbelief. "Rhia? Doesn't she normally specialize in more…youthful targets?"

Lazlo also allowed himself a chuckle. "Yes, she does. In fact, Rhia is rather amused by this assignment. She's currently finishing up a case and will be available in a few days to get on Donovan's trail."

Aidan appreciated being kept in the loop, but wondered about it since it wasn't standard operating procedure. Which could only mean one thing… "Do you need something else from me, Corbett? Or do you have my next assignment already?"

"How badly do you want Donovan?"

He should have known he couldn't fool Corbett. "Badly. He killed Liz…Ms. Moore's sister."

"Then I guess you wouldn't mind being backup for Rhia. It would mean leaving in a few days to meet her in Paris," Lazlo advised.

Leaving Leonia. Leaving Lizzy.

"I understand, Corbett. Let me finish up here. Clean up everything. Get things settled." It would give him a few more days of seeing Lizzy. A few more days to work up the courage to say a proper goodbye. Not the hurried and angered one they had shared days earlier.

"You sound…hesitant, Mr. Spaulding."

He wondered how the man could be so intuitive across a telephone line. "I just need to straighten out a few things here before I go."

"Get it done quickly, Mr. Spaulding. Rhia could use your help."

With that, Aidan hung up, but immediately contacted the

four agents who he had assigned to keep an eye on Lizzy while he…

While he kept an eye on her, his PDA tuned into the various channels as he watched her with friends and family when they came by to pay their condolences. Worried as she stood by the window at night, staring out at the ocean. So alone. So wounded.

He wished her relief from her pain. Hungered to see her back at what she did best—tending to her gardens, her hands skimming over the flowers and herbs as she selected what she would need for one of her fabulous dishes.

Only, it was too soon since Dani's death. The restaurant had been closed for days and would remain closed until Dani's memorial service. It was scheduled for tomorrow and he, along with Lucia and Walker, planned on attending.

After that, Lucia would pack up and head back to New York to await another assignment. Walker had resigned his position with the Lazlo Group to stay with Dr. Zara Smith, the royal physician. As for him…

The assignment with Rhia seemed the right thing to do. Not that he normally cared, but Silvershire was in an uproar and finding Donovan would help calm things down. On a personal level, Lazlo had been right that finding and dealing with Donovan would give him great satisfaction.

And possibly bring some closure for Lizzy to know that her sister's killer had been apprehended.

The lead agent on the detail watching Lizzy called to confirm that all four men were returning to the hotel. Now it was up to him to remove the surveillance equipment only…

Lizzy was likely preparing for Dani's memorial service. He didn't want to intrude in that fashion at such a difficult time.

Removing the cameras could wait another day…or two.

Lizzy smoothed her fingers over the photo she had chosen for the service later that day. It was the one of Dani and her taken in Rome two years earlier. Both of them were smiling brilliantly, the happiness apparent to anyone who viewed the picture.

It was the way she wanted to remember Dani. Full of life. Full of love for her and for Mitch.

Inside the restaurant, Nat, Kate and Samantha were setting up chairs for those coming to the memorial service. On the mantel above the fireplace was an enlargement of the Rome photo.

Out back, she'd had her staff set up tables and chairs for a cold buffet she planned on serving her guests. A simple meal, mostly prepared by Nat. She couldn't face going into the kitchen or out into the gardens.

Guilt swamped her that she was alive when Dani was dead.

And in the back of her mind, she kept on hoping it was all a mistake. That Dani would walk through her door at any moment, because inside her, Dani's presence niggled at her, begging to be acknowledged.

A knock came at the door and her heart sped up. She'd seen the agents leaving earlier. Could that mean Dani's killer had been caught? Could it be Aidan coming by with news?

She hurried to the door, but it was only a boy from a few houses down with an armful of flowers for her. "Mum says you might want some for the service."

"Thank you, Billy. Thank your mother, as well." she said to the ten-year-old as she took the flowers from him and cradled them to her chest.

Billy seemed satisfied with her response since he gave her a spontaneous hug and dashed off.

She buried her nose in the large bouquet of flowers and inhaled deeply. Their fragrance was heavenly. Billy's mum always had the nicest garden in town and was quite particular about her blooms. That she would cut so many flowers from it for Dani...

Her throat tightened and she decided to walk the bouquet over to the restaurant, complete the preparations for the memorial.

Inside the restaurant, Samantha and Kate had finished setting up the chairs and were now placing the hostess's podium at the front of the room for those who wanted to speak. Elizabeth hadn't wanted anything too formal or religious. Dani had sworn off religion after their parents had died.

As she walked through the door with the flowers, her friends rushed over to take them from her.

"These are lovely," Kate said and smelled them.

"Mrs. Sanders?" Samantha asked.

"Yes and yes. Can I help with anything?"

Kate placed her hands on her hips and looked around. "We're pretty much done. Maybe Nat needs some help in the kitchen?"

"Subtle, Kate. Really subtle," Samantha chided and elbowed Kate in the side.

"I'm not..." Elizabeth was going to say she wasn't ready, but stopped short. When had she ever not wanted to cook? In the months after her parents had died, cooking for her and Dani had helped numb the pain. Later, working at the health food restaurant had done more than just provide money for the assorted things she and Dani needed. The joy of creating something tasty had driven away her sadness. Brought happiness back into her life.

Meeting her friends' gazes, she nodded and said, "I'll go see if Nat needs my help."

She was in the kitchen, cooking. Flitting from the prep table to the stove where she hovered by one of the chef's assistants as they worked on something. From the stove back to the prep table where another of the assistants was busy assembling a large salad.

Finally, she walked over to the ovens where Natalie was checking on a large pastry of some kind. Lizzy stood next to Nat and the two women seemed to confer about the pastry before easing it back into the oven. After, Lizzy turned to Nat and embraced the younger woman tightly, the emotion clear on the faces of the two women.

Emotion that he had no right to be spying on.

He shut down his PDA and looked at his watch. Another hour until the memorial service. Another hour until he saw her, up close and personal.

What would he say? That he was sorry about Dani? He was, but that sorrow was tempered by the anger surrounding Mitch's death and a sense of incompleteness when he thought that maybe, just maybe, Dani hadn't been the one responsible.

And of course, Dani's death had just created another wrong to be righted. He considered whether he would be the one to take up that wrong and see it avenged, whether leaving here and going on that quest would bring him peace. Or was it just another windmill he was tilting at?

Nagging doubt chased him as he showered and dressed for the service. He met Lucia and Walker down in the lobby and they paused at a flower shop on the way to purchase a mixed bouquet, one filled with the colors and flowers he recalled from Lizzy's garden.

Funny how vividly the memory was of those things Lizzy. The flowers. The food. The way she looked jogging along the shore and how she could pound the hell out of the heavy bag down in her cellar. The slight, but noticeable aroma of plumeria that clung to her at night, after she had finished in the kitchen and indulged in the luxury of moisturizing her hands with the lotion from Kate's shop.

It was crazy to be here, he thought as he reached the entry to the restaurant grounds. He hesitated at the stone wall, wondering if it was wise to come here, to invade her space at such a personal time.

"Aidan?" Lucia asked and laid a hand on the arm of his dark charcoal-gray suit, the one he had worn to convince Lizzy to hire him. The one that had unfortunately already seen another funeral. "What's the matter?"

"I'm not sure I—"

"She would want you here," Walker added and grasped his shoulder in a reassuring gesture.

"It's the right thing to do," he said out loud, almost as if to convince himself. It *was* the right thing, but also the painful thing. The thing that would add yet another memory that he could dredge up whenever…

He missed her.

With a deep sigh, he pushed forward, walked through the open door of the restaurant and to the back of the room so as to not call attention to himself.

Lizzy was at the front, bending down and talking to two blue-haired ladies in the first row. She was dressed all in black, in a simple dress that hung loose on her body. She seemed to have lost weight in just a few days.

Dark smudges beneath her eyes were a stark contrast to the paleness of her face. Her rich brown hair, shot through with auburn and blond highlights, was pulled back from her face with a black scarf. Her smile when it came, was forced. A toothless slash of her lips into a thin line. A brittle smile that looked ready to shatter.

He winced for her, knowing how hard it must be.

A few more people straggled in and a priest sitting in the front row rose and motioned for everyone to take their seats. He was young, barely older than Lizzy. A fact that was confirmed when he began his speech.

"I want to thank you all for coming to celebrate Dani's life. Lizzy asked me to speak first since, at one time, I fancied myself marrying Dani before I got an offer from someone else," he said, prompting a round of chuckles.

He went on to describe the Dani he knew. A vibrant, loving woman who was quick to anger, but equally as quick to apologize. A woman who stood up for what she believed to be right and wasn't afraid to take action when necessary.

After he finished, he asked others to share their memories and one by one, a myriad of people came up to the podium. The one common element was that Dani had been their friend and their champion. The one everyone could speak to. The one they turned to when a wrong needed to be righted, when someone needed protection.

It matched what Lizzy had told him about her sister. Lizzy, who sat there flanked by Kate and Samantha on either side and Natalie behind her, but sitting on the edge of her chair with her hand on Lizzy's shoulder. As he examined the crowd, he noted other familiar faces—Addy and others from the hedge veg adventure. Some people he recalled serving drinks to at the restaurant.

He had no doubt she would be well taken care of by her friends, family and the assorted neighbors and townspeople who had filled the restaurant to capacity. As he looked toward the door, he realized there was a crowd of people there, as well, and that the back wall and sides of the dining area were standing room only.

Dani had apparently been well-liked and respected. It made him wonder about Lizzy's sister and what she really was—a champion or a cold-blooded killer?

Finally it was Lizzy's turn. As she rose, he thought she wavered for a moment. Kate reached out and offered a steadying hand and Lizzy took it, let Kate help her up to the podium.

Once there, she hesitated and even from this far, the glint of tears was visible as she took note of everyone who was in attendance. "Thank you all for coming. I appreciate it. I know Dani does, as well."

She struggled for composure and he wanted to rush up there, found himself beginning to rise when Walker laid a hand on his arm. "What can you offer, Aidan? You'll be long gone in a few days," he whispered.

He hated that Walker was right. He dejectedly dropped back down into his seat and waited for Lizzy to go on.

"After my parents died, it was hard for Dani. She missed them terribly. She wanted justice for them." Again she paused, as if reconsidering where she was going, but then she charged onward. "Dani always stood up for what she believed in.

Always was there to help if someone asked. She was everyone's champion. She was *my* champion. My best friend. A sister who I will miss every day of my life, but who will always be alive in here," she said and motioned to a spot above her heart.

"I know Dani is okay and in a better place. One where she's with her loved ones. One where she's happy. Because of that, I can't grieve for long."

The tears finally came, spilling over to run down her cheeks, but she didn't wipe them away. Instead, she took a shuddering breath and said, "Thank you all for your kind words and support. For those of you who wish to stay a bit longer, please step into the back garden for some refreshments."

Moving from behind the podium, she stepped into the crowd of well-wishers, moving from one to the next to give her personal thanks. Embrace one person or the other and motion them in the direction of the side door that led to the back patio.

Aidan waited alongside his colleagues until the room was almost empty and they were some of the last people standing there. Lizzy finally seemed to notice them. A guarded smile came to her face.

She walked over, embraced Lucia and shook Walker's hand. They both offered their condolences and then with a sidelong glance at him, excused themselves.

Lizzy stood before him, her hands clasped together. Her body language sending the clear signal that she was uncomfortable. That whatever he did, he shouldn't touch.

He broke the ice first by holding out the bouquet. "I came to say how sorry I am. I know how hard this is for you."

"Thank you. I really do appreciate all you've done on behalf of Dani," she said, but made no motion to embrace him or even shake his hand as she had with Walker. She seemed too fragile to do so. When she took the flowers, she cradled them tightly to her body. So tightly that a petal fell off one stem and fluttered to the ground.

"Well, I'll be going soon. In the meantime, I was going to drop by tomorrow and remove our surveillance equipment," he explained and motioned to the room around them.

A stain of color came to her cheeks at his words. "You bugged my restaurant? What about my house? Did people see what—?"

"No, they didn't. Dani jammed the signal. I'm sorry. It was what we had to do to catch—"

She silenced him with a tense wave of her hand. "Don't. Dani said it wasn't what we thought. That's what I want to believe."

Given what he had heard from person after person during the memorial service, he could understand why she wanted to hold onto that belief. So many people couldn't be wrong. It made him wonder yet again what Dani had meant when she had said she'd been doing a job. That it hadn't been what it seemed.

"I understand, and again, I'm sorry. About everything."

She said nothing and for a moment, he thought the rigor might leave her body, but it didn't. Despite that, he embraced her awkwardly, needing that last touch since he had decided that tomorrow he would send the men from the guard detail to remove the equipment.

It would be better that way, he thought as he stepped away and raced out the door, eager to put some distance between them.

Lizzy roused too many feelings, some of them threatening to the way he lived his life—carefree, exciting and without any attachments.

It was the way it had been all his life.

He wasn't about to allow one woman to change it all.

Chapter 30

Days had passed since the Lazlo Group technicians had come to retrieve their equipment, removing cameras from every room in the restaurant, the gardens and even her front parlor.

She assumed Aidan was long gone, as well, moving onto his next assignment. Did he ever look back? she wondered. Did he think about the job he had just finished and the people he had met?

The people he'd slept with and lied to? People whose lives he had irrevocably changed?

Rubbing her temples to quell her growing headache, she stared out her bedroom window. The ocean was calm tonight. Totally unlike the way she was feeling. Restless. Angry. Lonely.

Even though Dani had been gone often, there had always been the prospect of seeing her. That would never happen again. Ever.

Just as she would never see Aidan again. Ever. He and Dani had had so much in common. They were both warriors and wanderers. She only hoped that Aidan's life didn't end like Dani's. Or like his friend Mitch's.

If there was any consolation in either of their deaths, it was that neither had died alone. She and Aidan had been at Dani's side. Aidan had been with his friend.

And one day, Aidan would…

She shook her head and drove that thought away.

She wanted to wedge any remnants of him from her mind. Best to forget what had happened between them. It would only bring continued pain since, like Dani, Aidan was gone from her life forever.

Unable to stay in her room for another second since it brought too many reminders of what she had shared with him, she rushed from the cottage and out onto the beachfront.

A breeze, strong and brisk, washed over her. As she walked along the shore, she wished for it to wash away memories of him. To cleanse her spirit and bring peace to her heart, a heart battered by the loss of two people she had loved.

Dani and Aidan. Both lost to her. One never to return. The other…

He had given them the location of every camera except one. He'd known it was wrong, but convinced himself that he'd done it for her sake. So that he might keep an eye on her just in case Donovan returned. Just in case she needed him.

Her image filled his laptop screen. The smallish picture on the PDA didn't quite satisfy his need.

Lizzy was at the window facing the ocean. A familiar stance for her lately. She had been at the window every night since he had brought her home after Dani's death.

Unlike those other nights when he had watched her in silence, his observation was interrupted by the shrill ring of his cell phone. "Spaulding."

"Aidan. Ms. de Hayes has advised that she should be arriving in Paris in two days. Are you prepared to meet her?"

Was he? he wondered. When Corbett had mentioned continuing with the next part of this assignment, he'd been eager. After all, it entailed tracking down Dani's killer and someone who might be a possible threat to Lizzy.

A good reason to leave Leonia and Lizzy. Or so he'd thought.

But faced with the prospect of it now...

"Aidan? You have terminated your surveillance of Ms. Moore, haven't you?" Corbett asked and Aidan sensed that the other man somehow knew about the remaining camera.

He didn't have it in him to lie. "No, sir. But..."

He could have said that he'd remove it immediately, but he couldn't. He needed that connection to her. Hell, he needed her.

For days he had been telling himself otherwise. Trying to convince himself that staying in Leonia would be as boring as shit. That there was nothing there to keep his interest.

Except Lizzy. And some really nice people. Her crazy friends. Some fine fishing and surfing areas. Beautiful gardens and cute little homes along the road and the stunning coast and beachfront.

"Aidan?" Corbett prompted again and this time, Aidan knew exactly what to say.

"While working with Rhia would be quite an experience, I've decided that it's time I resigned my position with the Lazlo Group."

"Are you sure about this?" Corbett asked, and Aidan shot another peek at his laptop.

Was he?

The answer came immediately.

"I'm sure, Corbett."

The other man chuckled, surprising him. "This is getting to be a costly operation for my group. First Walker resigns and now you."

"I'm sorry if this leaves you in a lurch."

"Not to worry, Aidan. Rhia can probably handle this job on her own for the moment. Despite the Sparrow's deathbed information, I can't see Nikolas Donovan as her killer," Corbett advised, confusing Aidan with the statement.

"What? Donovan's Union for Democracy has splintered into two factions, one of them violent. What makes you believe Donovan isn't responsible for that violent bent and Dani's death?" Aidan questioned.

"Lord Southgate is quite familiar with Nikolas Donovan. He believes him innocent in Reginald's death and also in that of the Sparrow."

Aidan wasn't quite as convinced. "If Rhia needs backup, I'm there," he said, guilt driving him. He liked the woman, who had an adventurous streak and could be a refreshing smart ass at times.

"I appreciate the offer, but if I'm right, we won't be needing your muscle on this one," Corbett advised and then quickly added, "And you, Mr. Spaulding, have a lady to contact."

He peeked at the laptop and cursed beneath his breath when he saw her room was empty. But he knew where she would go. Where she always went when she was troubled. "Goodbye, Corbett. It's been a pleasure."

"Not goodbye, Aidan. I do expect an invitation to the wedding."

He chuckled at the other man's audacity. "You'll get it," he said, not that Corbett Lazlo would show. In the seven years that he had worked for the man, he had never met him.

But that was for another day. First he had to get the lady in question to agree to marry him.

Grabbing his jacket, he raced out of the hotel and down the public-access ramp to the beach. Much as he had expected, she was walking down the beach, headed in his direction. When she noticed him, she paused and wrapped her arms around herself, waited there for a moment before continuing toward him.

No coward, his Lizzy.

He didn't wait. He hopped down onto the sand and raced in her direction. When they finally stood facing one another, barely a foot apart, he said, "Lizzy."

Duh. Totally stupid. Inane.

"Aidan. I would have thought that you'd be gone by now." Her arms remained wrapped around herself and she rubbed her hands up and down in a telling gesture.

He reached out, laid his hands over hers to still that motion. "I would have thought so, too, only...I couldn't imagine leaving you, Lizzy."

Elizabeth's breath caught in her throat with his words. Was she imagining this? She shook her head in disbelief. "I don't understand, Aidan."

He smiled and his blue eyes glittered with joy as he said, "I don't understand, either. Maybe it's because I've found an adventure more compelling than any other."

"An adventure," she repeated, unsure of what he meant.

"Yes. You. And if you'll have me, I can't imagine a more interesting and challenging way to spend my life," he said and took hold of her hands, dropped to one knee.

"Marry me, Lizzy."

This was insane. Totally outrageous. And yes, possibly an adventure. One she was willing to risk with the man kneeling before her. "On one condition."

"Just one? As I recall, you had quite a few that night," he teased, raising one sandy brow playfully.

She laughed and embraced him, urged him to rise. "Do you think you could be happy here in little ol' Leonia?"

"I can be happy anywhere you are, Lizzy," he answered and as she searched his features, she recognized the truth of his statement.

She trailed her hands down and twined her fingers with his. "Can you be happy being my bartender?"

Aidan grimaced. "That may take a little ... No, make that a long while. Unless I can develop something," he said and pulled out his PDA, began explaining to her how he had managed to survive behind the bar.

"So let me get this," she began as he sketched his idea for a new bar area filled with electronic gadgets with the stylus of his PDA. "You're ex-military. An MIT grad in electronics. Anything else I should know?"

"That I love you. Totally and completely love you. All the rest, you can learn in the years to come," he said and, grabbing hold of her hand, gave it a playful shake. "So, will you marry me?"

"When you put it that way, how can a girl refuse?"

Epilogue

The stone-and-bronze marker matched the one laid over a decade earlier for her parents.

Elizabeth knelt and ran her hands over the words engraved in the bronze.

Danielle Elizabeth Moore. September 10, 1980— August 22, 2006. She was everyone's champion.

She wondered who had decided to add the last. Corbett Lazlo possibly?

"Lizzy, you okay?" Aidan asked and knelt beside her. In his hand he held a bouquet of flowers she had cut from the garden earlier that morning.

"I'm okay."

"There's a big 'except' there, Lizzy. What is it?" he asked and laid his free hand over hers as it rested on Dani's grave marker. The sun caught the gold band on his ring finger. It glinted brightly against the darker color of the bronze and the even deeper brown of the freshly turned earth.

"I've been waiting for months for Dani to come home. I thought it would bring closure."

"But?" he pressed.

"I can feel her, Aidan. As if she was still alive. Still with me," she urged; for in the many months since Dani had been carried away in the ambulance, her sister's presence remained strong.

"Lizzy, I can't begin to understand this twin thing. But I do understand you. If you believe this, I won't argue with you."

She smiled, leaned close and kissed the side of his face. "How like a husband, you sound. Indulging me in this even if you don't believe."

Aidan laid the bouquet of flowers along the top of the grave marker and then cradled her face in his hands. "I will always be at your side. Stand by whatever you believe, Lizzy. Believe that."

The amazing thing was that she did. She trusted Aidan as she had no else before, except for Dani. But unlike Dani, Aidan had shown her he was here to stay.

It might have started off as just another mission for him, but now it was more. He was her champion. She was his home. It couldn't be any more perfect than that.

* * * * *

THE REBEL KING

BY
KATHLEEN CREIGHTON

Kathleen Creighton has roots deep in the California soil but has relocated to South Carolina. As a child, she enjoyed listening to old-timers' tales, and her fascination with the past only deepened as she grew older. Today she says she is interested in everything—art, music, gardening, zoology, anthropology and history, but people are at the top of her list. She also has a lifelong passion for writing, and now combines her two loves in romance novels.

This book is dedicated to the victims and heroes
of Hurricane Katrina, to those who lost so much,
and to those who've given so much in an ongoing
effort to bring aid, comfort and hope to the devastated.
I am in awe of you all.

Chapter 1

He'd always been a little in love with Paris. She was the village eccentric, that mysterious lady reputed to possess a past both lurid and glorious. True, she was a bit blowsy now, not terribly clean and beginning to show her age, but beautiful still. And while she may have been mistrusted and reviled—and secretly envied—by her more conventional neighbors, one knew she was always ready to welcome a lad in need of refuge with open arms.

And there had never been a lad more in need of a refuge than Nikolas Donovan. His life had recently gone careening out of control with the dizzying speed of a sports car traveling down a steep and winding mountain road without brakes. It seemed to him a ride that could end only one way: with a calamitous plunge off a cliff.

Though at the moment, he had to admit, all the turmoil of the past several months seemed far away. It was an early September evening in Paris. Rain was expected later, but now the air was warm and soft with humidity. The trees were still green, with only a few leaves, harbingers of the autumn avalanche to come, tumbling and skittering like playful kittens under the flying feet of the children playing soccer among the chestnut trees in the Tuillerie Gardens. He felt pangs of envy as he watched them and listened to their grunts and scufflings of effort. He envied them this time, this age when a boy's only concern was whether he could kick the football between the makeshift goalposts before darkness and his mother's voice calling him to supper put an end to the game.

As he turned reluctantly back toward the flat he'd been calling home for the past few days, he was conscious of a certain irony in the fact that innocent children's games should be played in this spot where so much blood had been shed during France's chaotic march through history. It occurred to him that maybe there was a parallel, too, between those bumps and unexpected turns that were a natural part of growing children into adulthood, and the war, violence and turmoil countries seemed destined to endure on the way to becoming peaceful, democratic nations.

Certainly, in the past several months, Silvershire, the island country of his birth and of his heart, had experienced more than its share of that violence—murder, blackmail, attempted murder, conspiracy, terrorist bombings and assassination plots against the ruling family. Acts of violence in which he, Nikolas Donovan, had been suspected, if not openly accused, of complicity. Now the country seemed poised on the brink of outright rebellion—a rebellion Nikolas was assuredly guilty, at least in part, of fomenting.

He hadn't wanted rebellion.

Change, yes. He'd worked all his life for change. But not by violence. Never by violence.

But now change had come, and with a vengeance. Catastrophic change. Just not quite the way he'd expected.

The temporary lightness of heart he'd enjoyed while

watching the soccer game sifted away, and he felt it again—the cringing coldness in his chest, the hollow tapping of a pulse deep in his belly—the symptoms that came to him now whenever he remembered his life had been turned upside down.

Dusk had fallen. Lights were winking on in the trees and bridges and on the tour boats cruising up and down the river, and lovers were strolling the pathways along the riverbank hand in hand, taking advantage of the lovely late-summer evening. Paris would always be a city for lovers. Feeling more alienated and alone than ever, Nikolas quickened his steps toward home.

On a quiet tree-lined street not far from the Eiffel Tower he paused to look up at the third-floor windows of the borrowed flat that was his temporary refuge now. He wasn't sure what made him do that—perhaps a habit of caution learned from his life as a rebel with a cause, accustomed to watching his own back. Or maybe simply stealing a moment to appreciate the charm of the grand old buildings with their balconies and tall mullioned windows framed by creeping vines. Whatever the reason for that quick, casual glance, the move that followed it was launched by pure instinct, and it was not in the least casual. He slipped into the shadows between trees and parked cars and became utterly and completely still while he studied the window of his supposedly empty apartment where, a moment before, he was absolutely certain he'd seen something move.

The movement didn't come again, but never for a moment did he believe it had been a trick of the eye. Unlikely as it seemed, someone or something had just entered his flat through the balcony window.

All his senses were on full alert as he quickly crossed the street and let himself into the building. Inside he paused again to listen, but it was quiet as a mausoleum; most Parisians would still be out and about this early on such an evening, at least until the forecast rain arrived.

The quaint old staircase with its ornate wrought-iron balusters and railings that spiraled up through the center of the building seemed to hang unsupported above him in the shadows as he curled his fingers into a fist around the keys and began to climb. His heart was pounding, sweat trickling coldly down his back, and not from the exertion of the climb. Nikolas made a point of keeping himself in shape. He was no adrenaline junky, but with everything that had been happening in Silvershire lately, a certain amount of paranoia seemed not only healthy, but prudent—perhaps even vital.

He mounted the last flight of stairs on tiptoe and moved soundlessly down the hallway, footsteps swallowed by the carpet runner. At the door to his flat he paused one last time to consider the situation, which was, the way he saw it, as follows: Someone had entered the flat through the balcony window. That someone either was or was not still in the flat. If not, he'd have a little mystery to solve at his leisure. On the other hand, if someone *was* in the flat, odds seemed against whoever it was being there for friendly purposes.

It had been a good eight years since his military service and commando training, but he was gratified to feel his mind and body shifting gears, settling into that particular state of quiet readiness he thought he'd forgotten. He could almost hear the hum of his heightened senses as he took hold of the doorknob and silently turned it.

The flat was in shadows, the darkness not yet complete. He'd left no light burning, but everything seemed as he'd left it. Aware that the slightly brighter backdrop of the hallway must cast him in silhouette, he stepped quickly into the room and closed the door behind him, checking as he did so for a body that may have been flattened against the wall behind it. Then he paused again, the old-fashioned metal key gripped in his hand like a weapon, and sniffed the air.

The room was empty now, he could feel it. But moments ago *someone* had been here, someone who had left traces, a faint aura…a scent too delicate and ephemeral to be aftershave or perfume.

Something about that scent jolted him with an untimely sense of déjà vu. But before the feeling could coalesce into thought, he received a different kind of jolt entirely—a shock-wave of pure adrenaline.

There—a movement. Swift and furtive, just on the edges of his field of vision. The window curtain, stirring where no breezes blew.

Nikolas was naturally athletic and very quick for a big man. Moving swiftly and soundlessly, like a creature of the night himself, he crossed the room and slipped through the open casement window onto the balcony. In the fast-fading twilight he could see a figure dressed in black standing frozen beside the balcony railing. He heard a sound…saw a hand come up and extend toward him…and before the sound could become speech or the hand activate whatever death-dealing object it may have been holding, he launched himself toward the intruder, going in low, aiming for the knees.

He was a little surprised at how easy it was. There was no resistance at all, in fact, just a soft gasp when he drove his shoulder into a surprisingly slim midsection, then a somewhat louder *"Oof!"* as his momentum carried both him and the intruder to the balcony's plaster floor. With that slender body pinned half under him, Nikolas caught both wrists and jerked them roughly to the small of the intruder's back.

It was over just that quickly—so quickly, in fact, that it took another second or two for Nikolas's senses to catch up with his reactions, and for him to realize that, A. his would-be as-sailant carried no weapon, and B. wasn't a "he" at all. Wrists that slender, a bottom so nicely rounded and fitting so sweetly against his belly, that elusive scent…those could only belong to a woman.

The revelation didn't induce him to relax his vigilance or ease his grip, however. If there was anything he'd learned from the recent events in his homeland, it was that assassins came in all sizes and both genders. And that no one—*no one*—could be trusted.

"I expected someone with a bit more in the way of fighting skills," he said through gritted teeth, his face half-buried in the woman's warm, humid nape. The smell of her hair made his head swim.

That scent…I know it…from somewhere.

"I have skills…you can't even imagine," his prisoner replied in a breathless, constricted voice. "Just didn't think… it'd be smart…to kick a future king…where it'd hurt the most. Not exactly…a brilliant career move, you know? Plus… there's that little matter…of you being required to produce an heir…"

That remark, as well as the fact that the woman's accent was distinctly of the American South, barely registered. "Who are you? Who sent you? Was it Weston? Carrington? *Who,* damn you?"

"Neither. Well…sort of— Look, if you'll get off me and let me up so I can get to my ID…"

"Not a chance." An ingrained habit of courtesy under similar physical circumstances did induce him to take some of his weight off the woman—a concession he made sure to compensate for by tightening his grip on her wrists. She wasn't showing much inclination to resist, but he wasn't ready to take anything for granted. "I'll get it. Where is it?"

She gave an irritable-sounding snort. "Oh for God's sake. It's in my jacket—inside pocket. Left side. Just don't—"

He was already in the process of shifting both himself and his prisoner onto their sides so he could slip his hand inside her jacket, which was leather and as far as he could tell, fitted her like her own skin. It closed with a zipper which was pulled all the way up, almost to her chin. "Don't…what?" He found the tab and jerked it down, impatient with it and with his own senses for noticing and passing on to him at such an inopportune moment how supple and buttery soft the leather was, almost indistinguishable from her skin, in fact…and how warm and fragrant her hair…*and what was that damn scent, anyway?*

He thrust his hand inside the jacket opening…and froze.

"Never mind." A rich chuckle—hers—seemed to ripple down the length of his body as his hand closed—entirely of its own volition, he'd swear—over a breast of unanticipated voluptuousness. Furthermore, the only barrier between his hand and that seductive bounty was something silky, lacy and, he felt certain, incredibly thin. A chemise? It seemed to him an unlikely choice of attire for an assassin.

And the nipple nested in his palm was already hardening, nudging the nerve-rich hollow of his hand with each of her quickened breaths in a way that seemed almost playful. As if, he thought, she were deliberately taunting him. Testing his self-control.

A growl of desperation and fury vibrated deep in his throat. He tried again to shift his weight to give his hand more room to maneuver inside the jacket and only succeeded in bringing her bottom into even closer contact with the part of his own anatomy least subject to his will.

"You're not going to have much luck finding it where you're looking," she remarked, her voice bumpy with what he was sure must be suppressed laughter.

"I'm so glad you're finding this entertaining," he said in his stuffiest, British old-school tone, feeling more sweaty and flustered than he had since his own schoolboy years in that country. "Forgive me if I don't share your amusement… These days I don't consider— *Ah!*" With a sense of profound relief, he withdrew his hand from its enticing prison, a thin leather folder captured triumphantly between two fingers. "Yes—*here* we are."

"How are you going to look at it? It's dark out here." The woman pinned beneath him now seemed as overheated and winded as he, and her body heat was merging with his in steamy intimacy that should have been unwelcome between two strangers—or, he thought, at the very least, unsettling. Exotic. Instead there was that odd familiarity, as if he'd been in this exact same place, with this same woman, before.

The situation was becoming intolerable. Nikolas levered himself to his feet, hauling his unwelcome visitor with him. "Come on—inside. Now." His natural bent toward gallantry deserted him as he hauled her none too gently through the casement window.

"This really isn't necessary," she panted, and he was grimly pleased to note there was no laughter, suppressed or otherwise, in her voice now. "If I'd wanted to leave we wouldn't be having this conversation."

"Yes, and then the question becomes, why are you here at all, doesn't it?" He quick-marched her across the shadowy room to the light switch beside the front door, and flipped it on, filling the room with the soft light from an art deco chandelier. "Now then, let's see who… Ah—the Lazlo Group. I say—I'm impressed. And you are—" And he halted, the ID in his hand forgotten…or irrelevant.

That face.

The face he'd half convinced himself must be a fantasy.

She was the fantasy every heterosexual male past the age of awareness must have entertained at least once. The impossibly beautiful woman who came from out of nowhere to land—almost literally—in his lap, proceeded to make passionate love to him and then…vanished without a trace.

The summer between his second and third years at Oxford…

Nikolas was interning with Silvershire's diplomatic mission to Paris. He'd been to a reception at the embassy in honor of the newly appointed ambassador from Spain, where the wine had flowed rather freely. He returned to his hotel in a not entirely unpleasant state of fuzzy-headedness. The weather had turned hot and muggy, and that combined with his mild intoxication had made him too warm to sleep, so, in the hope of clearing his head and cooling his body, he'd stepped out onto the balcony.

He was leaning on the railing, enjoying a breathtaking nighttime view of the Eiffel Tower and contemplating the possible sobering effects of a cold shower when it happened. Someone—a body—a woman's body—clad all in black and lithe and supple as a cat's, seemed to fall right out of the night sky. Fell on top of him and knocked him flat.

Perhaps it was the wine he'd drunk, but he didn't feel terribly alarmed by this odd occurrence. Merely—understandably—a bit surprised. As he lay on his back gazing up into what he was certain was the most beautiful face he'd ever seen in his life—rather feline, like the rest of her, he decided, with wide cheekbones and pointed chin, and exotically tilted eyes— the woman placed her finger against his lips and whispered, "Shhh..." Then she lowered her head and kissed him.

Not a casual brushing of the lips, meant to be an expression of thanks for breaking her fall, perhaps, or even a droll bit of teasing. No—this was the kiss of fantasy; deep and warm and lush, it seemed to vault right over all those bothersome—to a young lad's way of thinking—preliminary stages of intimacy, and plunge straight to the heart and soul of the matter: Sex! And the lithe and supple body squirming into even more intimate alignment with his seemed to second that idea most heartily.

Nikolas's state of shock-induced paralysis didn't last long; his was not a passive nature. But as his body was flaring to life like a gas burner under a lighted match, he heard a preemptory masculine voice somewhere above his head say loudly, "Excuse me, you didn't happen to see— Oh, I say!"

Opening his eyes and aiming them—as much as was possible under the circumstances—in the direction of the voice, Nikolas saw a man's head hovering atop the half wall that separated his balcony from the one next to it.

"Terribly sorry—excuse the intrusion—Pardon, Monsieur..." The head disappeared, and the string of apologies died to an annoyed but unintelligible mutter on the other side of the wall.

It was several more enjoyable—and volatile—seconds before the woman detached her mouth from his, and even that process she managed to turn into a sensual adventure. With her lips separated from his only by their warm mingled breath, she murmured a pleased and rather surprised, "Hmm..." And then she lowered her mouth again.

He suspected she meant it to be a briefer kiss this time, a sweet, perhaps regretful, farewell peck. But Nikolas had had enough of games, at least the way this one was being played—according to her *rules. Before she knew what he was about, he tightened his arms around her and rolled her under him, and knew a fierce, hot shaft of pleasure at her gasp of surprise.*

"Who are you? What the hell is this?" he asked in a rasping whisper. He could feel her heart beating a wild tattoo against his chest.

And her catlike eyes narrowed and tilted with her smile as she whispered back, "Serendipity."

"Rhia de Hayes," Rhia said, eyeing her assignment as she might a tiger who'd stopped suddenly in midspring and begun instead to purr and rub his head against her legs. The smile that had flared so unexpectedly in his fierce gray eyes to spread like sunlight over his rather austere features was intriguing, for sure, and she had to admit she liked it a lot better than the frown. But she didn't trust it for a moment. What it reminded her of was a limerick she'd heard somewhere, about a young lady who'd smiled as she went for a ride on a tiger. As Rhia recalled the limerick, when they'd returned from that ride the lady was inside, and the smile was on the face of the tiger.

What is *he smiling about? As if he knows something...as if he knows* me. *But we've never met before. Have we?*

Uncertainty wasn't a condition Rhia suffered often, or well. But so far this whole assignment hadn't gone as expected, and that had her feeling off balance. She liked losing control of situations even less than she liked being unsure of herself, and she meant to remedy that state of affairs as quickly as possible. Rhia de Hayes had never failed to complete an assignment successfully, and she wasn't about to sully that record now.

Of course, none of her previous assignments had been quite like this one. Her specialty within the Lazlo Group was retrieving lost children of the rich, royal or famous, and while it was true that this was undoubtedly the offspring of a man who could claim to be all three of those things, there was nothing even remotely childlike about Nikolas Donovan.

Except for that damn smile. There's mischief in that smile. Reminds me of a kid hiding a big ol' bullfrog behind his back.

"So, Rhia de Hayes…they've sent you to 'bring me in,' I expect," he said as he handed back her ID. His eyes were veiled now, and his voice was that languid upper-class vaguely British drawl she'd always found so annoying. "What were you planning to do, conk me on the head, heave me over your shoulder and haul me back to Silvershire?"

"I was *plannin'* on checkin' the place while you were gone," Rhia said, leaning heavily on the nasal Cajun twang of her childhood; she could out-drawl just about anybody on the planet, if that was the way he was going to be. She glared at him as she tucked the ID back in her inside jacket pocket, inadvertently allowing him another glimpse of the silk chemise that had apparently so unnerved him before. And she reveled in the spark of response that flared in his cool gray eyes. Veiling the triumph in hers, she said accusingly, "You came back early. I figured you'd be havin' supper out."

"It was going to rain," Nikolas said with a dismissive shrug, "and I didn't have an umbrella. So, what was it you hoped to find hidden away amongst my socks and tightie whities? Guns, knives, explosives? Leaflets inciting the violent overthrow of the monarchy? Evidence of what a dangerous fellow I am?"

"Oh, I think I know what a dangerous fellow you are," Rhia said, and instantly wanted to bite off her tongue. Not only was it an inappropriate comment to make to a royal heir, but the voice that uttered it had turned low and husky, become almost a growl. It wasn't as though she'd never heard such a sound coming from her own throat before—on…certain occasions, yes, but never under these circumstances. Not while on a job, put it that way.

She wasn't sure which surprised her most, that or the small vibration that had begun to hum somewhere deep inside her chest.

Half angry with herself, she tore away the clip that had held her hair clubbed tightly to the back of her head and shook the thick dark waves down to her shoulders.

"You could easily have beat a hasty retreat when you heard me at the door," Nikolas remarked in a relaxed, conversational tone. "I assume you had an escape route planned. Why didn't you use it?" As he spoke, his gaze followed the motions of her hand and hair, his gray eyes heavy-lidded and amused, as if he knew exactly the effect he was having on her.

Of course he knows, dummy. Rhia repressed a shiver as she became intensely conscious of the cool silk of her chemise licking across her hardened nipples. How could he not know, when the evidence was right here in front of his face?

But to zip up her jacket now would be an admission of awareness she wasn't willing to make, and besides, she'd never been shy about her body. If it was going to go shivery and shameless over Nik Donovan, well…so be it. It wouldn't affect her ability to do the job she'd come to do.

And, if it came to that, she was also well aware of the effect her body had on members of the opposite sex, and she wasn't above using it to distract an opponent, if the occasion demanded.

When did the assignment become my opponent?

She faced this one unflinchingly and inhaled deeply, and smiled at the slight but unmistakable hitch she detected in his breathing. "I'd planned on coming back and knocking on your door. Talking to you—you know, like a civilized human being, one to another? Figured since I was already here I might as well save some time, see if I could persuade you to do the right thing and come back with me voluntarily."

Nikolas folded his arms on his chest. He was smiling too, now, a lazy, arrogant smile that caused an immediate and automatic elevation of her hackles. "And if that didn't work?"

She gave her head an airy toss and broadened her smile to a 'gator grin. "I planned to conk you on the head, throw you over my shoulder and haul you back to Silvershire."

He laughed, briefly but out loud, something she suspected he didn't do often. He made no comment, though, as the promised rain chose that moment to announce its arrival with a rush of cool wind that set the curtains to dancing and carried a mist of droplets into the room. Nikolas straightened and strode quickly to the balcony doors. He closed and latched them and twitched the curtains across the black rain-spangled glass, then turned to give her a leisurely up-and-down appraisal.

"It would appear you also are without an umbrella," he said mildly, lifting one eyebrow—an ability she lacked, and coveted. "I seriously doubt you'll find a taxi just now. Since I suppose this means you'll be staying for dinner, may I offer you a glass of wine?"

She shook her head, both in bemusement and in refusal of the offer of wine—she had no intention of letting anything slow her reflexes or cloud her judgment, not with this man. And although he seemed completely at ease, now, and was being effortlessly charming, she thought again of the smiling tiger.

She decided it wouldn't be necessary to tell him she had no intention of calling a taxi, or, in fact, of leaving him at all. Fact was, she wasn't about to let Nikolas Donovan out of her sight until she had delivered him safely into the arms of his father, the king of Silvershire.

Chapter 2

Rhia stood in the entrance to the apartment's tiny kitchen and watched the recently discovered "lost" heir to the throne of Silvershire take a stoppered bottle of wine out of the tiny refrigerator.

He turned to make an offering gesture toward her with the bottle. "Are you quite certain you won't join me? It's rather nice for a rosé, actually. Fellow who lent me this flat comes from a wine-making family down in Provence—he's left an apparently bottomless supply."

She shook her head, and he responded with a shrug that seemed to her more French than British. It was what came of growing up in an island kingdom located halfway between those two countries, she thought, as she watched him pour himself a half glassful and lift it to his lips. She couldn't imagine why observing that mundane activity should make her mouth water; she wasn't terribly fond of wine. She seldom drank at all, but when she did, she preferred bourbon whiskey. Straight.

His eyes, meeting hers above the rim of his glass, crinkled suddenly. He lowered the glass. "Oh, hell—of course, you're on the job, aren't you? Do forgive me. Perhaps a glass of water? Cup of tea?"

"I'm from South Louisiana," Rhia said drily. "We Cajuns aren't all that much for tea." Well, hell, if he was going to play the British fop again—badly overplaying it, in her opinion, and she didn't know what his game was or whether to be amused by it or annoyed—she figured her trailer-park Cajun could trump his Oxford Brit any day of the week.

"Ah, yes—coffee would be your drink of choice, I imagine. Made with—what's that other…" He snapped his fingers impatiently.

"Chicory," she grudgingly supplied, then tilted her head. "How'd you come to know a thing like that?"

His chuckle was dry, his smile sardonic. "I know a little about a great many things, my dear." He waved the wineglass in a sweeping gesture. "My education has been…shall we say, eclectic? Wide-ranging?"

"An education fit for a man who would be king," Rhia said softly.

He snorted—a most unprincely sound. "An education attained courtesy of some very good scholarships and a lot of hellish hard work, which I doubt could be said of most royals." He paused, and his lips curled with disdain he made no effort to hide. "Not the one I knew personally, at any rate."

"Reginald, you mean. Yes, you two were at Eton together, weren't you?"

"And Oxford." Nikolas gazed at his wine as if it had gone sour. "Look, I am sorry he's dead—God knows I wouldn't wish for anyone to be murdered that way—poisoned, I mean—but the man was an arrogant, insufferable prick, if you want to know. And not fit to govern a frat house, much less a country."

"Ah," said Rhia, smiling slightly, "but he never got the

chance, did he? And, as it turns out, he wasn't even the prince after all."

Instead of answering, he took a quick gulp of wine and set his glass down with a careless clank. Turning abruptly, he opened a cupboard door and took out an espresso maker which he placed on the countertop, plugged into a wall outlet and set about filling with an ease and efficiency that spoke of some degree of familiarity with the process.

Watching the movements of his hands, Rhia felt again that odd little quiver beneath her breastbone. His glossy dark hair might be in need of a trim, and a day's growth of beard might be shadowing his jaw, but there was no denying the grace in the lines of his body, the power in the breadth of his shoulders, the authority in the set of his chin, the intelligence in those intense gray eyes. And all of it, she thought, completely natural to him.

It must be in his genes. Even here, in this little bitty kitchen, making coffee for uninvited company, he looks like he was born to be a king.

"You can come in and sit down—I promise not to bite you." He threw the brittle invitation over his shoulder as he worked, and Rhia gave a guilty start, as if his long list of royal attributes might include the ability to read minds.

She shook her head and smiled, but stayed where she was. Prince or not, the kitchen was too small a space to hold two people who weren't already on intimate terms.

Intimate. The word sprang into her head from out of nowhere and sat pulsing in her brain like the neon lights on a Mississippi River casino boat.

"Tell me something." He gave her another look, this one as sharp and keen as any scrutiny she'd ever received from Walker Shaw, the shrink who'd done her psych evaluation when she joined the Lazlo Group. "How does a nice American girl from Louisiana come to be working for Corbett Lazlo?"

She gave him back a smile she knew would dazzle but tell him nothing. "Ah, that's a long story."

Still his gaze lingered, intent enough to kick-start that hum in her chest again, and, as they often did when she felt ill at ease, her fingers went of their own volition to the small silver charm that hung from a narrow chain around her neck, nestled in the hollow at the base of her throat. She rubbed it idly as she watched Nikolas shrug and go back to measuring dark roasted coffee beans into the grinder.

He switched it on, and for the next few seconds the racket made conversation impossible. The grinding completed, Nikolas poured water into the espresso machine, closed and secured the lid and punched a button. He turned back to her, then, and picked up his glass of wine and the thread of conversation he'd temporarily put aside.

"Might I ask what your specialty is with the Lazlo Group? You do seem an unlikely choice of field agent to send after a notorious suspected terrorist." This time a smile crinkled the corners of the eyes studying her across the rim of the wineglass, though it didn't diminish their intensity one bit.

"My specialty?" Her smile was small and wicked. "I locate and retrieve lost children."

Caught in mid swallow, Nikolas gave a sputter of laughter and quickly lowered his glass. He touched the back of his hand to his mouth and managed to say in a choked voice, "A lot of call for that, is there?"

"Unfortunately, yes." She wasn't smiling now.

"I'm well aware of the sad state of the world," Nikolas said, matching the new seriousness of her tone as he stared at the contents of his glass. He'd been enjoying himself entirely too much, he realized, given the fact that it was this woman's intention to fetch him back to Silvershire whether he wanted to go or not. That he could enjoy himself at all, under any circumstances, was surprising in itself. It had been rather a long time since he'd found anything in his life amusing. "I meant in the context of the Lazlo Group, of course. Isn't their clientele pretty much limited to the rich, royal or famous?"

"Theirs is," she replied shortly. "Mine isn't."

"Meaning?"

"Meaning, the ability to take cases pro bono when it suits me is one of the conditions of my…shall we say, employment agreement."

"I'm impressed." He was, too. He hadn't thought there was anybody on the planet who could dictate terms to Corbett Lazlo, and that included royalty. He sipped wine while he studied the woman lounging with easy grace in his kitchen doorway. Tall and lithe, but curvy as well—truly an amazing body, as he had ample reason to know, and he really did need to discipline his mind past those recent memories of her. Under the circumstances, they were proving entirely too distracting. He couldn't afford to be distracted with this one; he had a feeling if she'd intended to take him by force he'd already be hog-tied and on a plane bound for Silvershire, so it was a safe bet she must have something else up her sleeve. "I gather, then, that you're quite good at what you do. Might I ask how you go about it—this business of finding lost children?"

She smiled, the enigmatic little Mona Lisa smile he'd seen before. "Oh, the Lazlo Group has resources you can't even imagine." The smile vanished again—fascinating, the way it came and went, like the sun playing hide-and-seek with clouds. Something he couldn't identify flickered in her eyes, and her hand went again to whatever it was she wore on that silver chain around her neck. He couldn't quite make out what it was—something oddly shaped but familiar as well—and it was beginning to intrigue him.

"And then," she went on in an entirely different kind of voice, "I suppose I probably just have the knack."

"The knack?"

She shifted, as if the door frame against her back had grown uncomfortable. "Instinct. You know—a sixth sense. I just always have been good at finding people. Particularly kids."

"Ah. You mean, like second sight?"

She gave him a brief, hard look. Suspected him of mocking her, he imagined. Which he wasn't; he'd seen too much of the world and of things in it that defied logical explanation to scoff at the unknown and unproven. When it came to the mysteries of the human mind, he preferred to keep his open.

The espresso machine chose that moment to erupt with a gurgling, hissing cloud of fragrant steam, and the last thing he saw before he turned to attend to it was Rhia's lush pink lips tightening and her long slender throat rippling as she bit back and swallowed whatever it was she'd been about to say.

Second sight? Yeah, that was what Mama called it. Her gift to me. Now it's the only thing I have of her, except my music and my memories. And this necklace.

Rhia fingered it briefly as she watched her assignment— and host—pour steaming black liquid into a tiny cup and place it on the table along with a spoon and a bowl filled with sugar cubes, and was thankful for the lifelong habit of self-control that made her keep those thoughts inside.

"I don't suppose you'd have any hot milk?" She kept her voice as bland as the request.

He lifted that damned eyebrow. "Milk? Sorry."

"That's okay, I'm adaptable." She pushed away from the door frame. It was only two short steps to the kitchen table, but her pulse quickened as if it was a tiger's den she'd entered.

She sat in the nearest of the two chairs and shifted it so the small arched window and its rain-blurred view of the Paris lights was at her back. She stirred a sinful amount of sugar into the espresso—she hated cubed sugar because it always seemed as though someone might be keeping count. *How many, dear, one lump, or two? Yeah, right. How about...ten?* Then she settled back with one elbow propped on the tabletop to watch the future king of Silvershire take eggs and a variety of other things out of the fridge and scatter them across the sink and countertop with the reckless abandon of a gourmet chef.

The future king… How remote and unreal that seemed to her now, with her pulse tap-tapping away and that strange little vibration humming somewhere deep inside her chest and an intense awareness of silk slithering over her naked skin—because what, after all, could be more of a turn-on to a woman than watching a smolderingly handsome and mysterious man cook dinner for her?

She took a cautious sip of the potent coffee—though Lord knew she didn't need any more stimulation—and tried to coax her mind into placing the man presently whacking merrily away at a pile of mushrooms into his proper setting, one that included his royal peers—the Grimaldis of Monaco…the DuPonts of Gastonia…the Dutch and the British royals. But her rebellious mind kept returning, like a drunk to his bottle, to the memory of what his body had felt like, out there on the balcony, lying full-length on top of hers.

And why did that memory kindle another, one that flared bright for frustratingly brief moments, then before she could grasp it, vanished into the darkness of her mind like a lightning bug in a bayou summer night?

"I'd give a lot more than a penny to know what you're thinking right now."

Rhia blinked the heir to Silvershire's crown into focus and found him studying her with—naturally—one eyebrow a notch higher than the other, and a similar tilt to his smile.

"It would take more than you've got to find out," she retorted, and gave up, for the moment, trying to think of him as royalty. After all, she reminded herself, at the moment he was merely Nikolas Donovan, college professor, rabble-rouser, rebel and fugitive, and she was the special agent hired to bring him in. "But," she added after a moment, "since

you're cooking me dinner, I guess I can give you one for free."
She paused. "You have to know I feel a little odd about that—
you fixing me dinner. Considering you're the future—"

"Look," he interrupted, before she could say the K-word
again, "You're here, it's time to eat—what did you expect me
to do?" A smile slashed crookedly across his austere features
again. "Ask *you* to do the cooking?"

"I've known men who would," Rhia said drily.

"Ah. Well." He watched his hands maneuver the knife
across the chopping board. "Since I grew up without benefit
of a mum, I suppose I never acquired the prevailing attitude
that a woman's primary purpose is to serve a man."

"Oh, wow," she said in an awed tone. "You really are a rev-
olutionary, aren't you? My mama would have loved you."

He glanced at her, his eyes unexpectedly gentle. "*Would*
have. She's gone, then, your mum?"

She nodded, and found to her surprise and dismay that it
was the only answer she was capable of giving him just then.
Where had it come from, she wondered, this bright shaft of
pain and loss, like a lightning strike out of a clear blue sky?

Nikolas watched her struggle with it, soft mouth and
pointed chin gone vulnerable as a child's, those exotic golden
eyes fierce as a tiger's, and her fingers once again fondling
the tiny silver charm at her throat. Something shivered through
him, a new awareness, a magnetic tugging he was pretty sure
had nothing to do with sex.

"Sorry to hear that," he said, careful not to let too much
softness into his voice, suspecting it wouldn't take much in
the way of sympathy to send her scurrying for cover. "When
did she die?"

"When I was eighteen."

"Ah—well—" he broke an egg and plopped it into a bowl
"— at least you had a chance to know her."

He heard her take a breath, sharp and deep. He knew she
had herself in hand again when she said with a soft, breathy

chuckle, "What I remember most about my mama is her laugh, you know? She had this great big laugh, and when she laughed, her eyes sparkled. She laughed a lot, too. My mama did know how to have a good time."

He broke a few more eggs into the bowl. "You had a happy childhood, then." He glanced up when she gave a bitter-sounding snort.

"Yeah, I did. Until my father came and took me away from it."

Before Nikolas could reply, she rose abruptly, frowning. If she had been a cat, he thought, her tail would surely have been twitching.

"Mind if I use your…what do you Silvershirers call it? The loo?"

"Do you mean the bathroom?" He said it with the deadpan courtesy of a butler he'd once known and gestured with the whisk in his hand. "It's that way—next to the bedroom."

She slipped from the room like a cat through fog, and left him with a bowlful of eggs on which to beat off his bemusement and frustration.

"You're a pretty good cook, Donovan, even if you don't have any Tabasco," Rhia remarked, studying the last bite of her omelette before popping it into her mouth. As she chewed, her expression grew thoughtful. "Not that that surprises me— you cooking, I mean, not the Tabasco. I imagine you're good at whatever you take a mind to do."

"Thank you," Nikolas said, with only a hint of a smile. He was glad to see she'd recovered her aplomb, since he'd found she was a much nicer person when she felt she had the upper hand.

"Tell you what does surprise me, though," she went on as if he hadn't spoken. "I never would've taken you for a coward."

It took some doing, but he kept his expression bland. "A coward, you say. Really."

To his further bemusement, she wiggled in her chair and said in a testy tone, "Oh, stop it. I hate it when you do that."

"Do what?" The woman did have a way of keeping him hopping off balance. He didn't know whether he found it amusing or demoralizing.

She waved her finger in a circling motion. "That…that *thing* with your eyebrow."

"My *eyebrow?*"

"Yes. It goes up. Just one. The other doesn't. It's damned annoying, if you want to know."

"Really." He leaned back in his chair and gazed at her, trying his best not to elevate any of his facial features. "I had no idea. Well, I shall endeavor to keep my various body parts under better control, if it offends you. Now, what was it you were saying about me being a coward?"

She returned his gaze with a narrow stare of her own, as if she suspected him again of mocking her. Then she gave a shrug and pushed back her plate. "Well, you did run away."

"Ah. Yes. There is that." He scrubbed a hand over his face, as if doing so could rub away the tiredness and confusion that were like a veil of cobwebs over his brain at times. Then he tried a sardonic smile. "I prefer to think of it as a strategic retreat."

"Look—Nikolas—"

He held up a hand to stop her there. "Miss de Hayes—Rhia. Try and put yourself in my shoes. Six months ago the heir to the throne of Silvershire is found dead in his mountain retreat—murdered. So who do you suppose shot directly to the top of the list of probable suspects? Right you are—an organization bent on doing away with that very same monarchy, an organization known as the Union for Democracy, of which I happen to be founder and de facto head."

"Yes," Rhia said, frowning, "but your group was considered an unlikely candidate for Reginald's murder, since it's well-known you've never advocated the use of violence."

"Ah, but that didn't stop the rumors, did it? Especially

after the king's collapse due to the grief and strain of his son's death. There were rumors Reginald was being blackmailed, rumors of terrorism, of hostile invasion or violent revolution. Rumors of a split in the UFD, with a violent faction taking over control. Even after I met with Russell—Lord Carrington—to reassure him—"

"Just because they're called rumors doesn't mean they can't be true," Rhia said quietly.

Nikolas looked at her for a moment in silence. Then he pushed his plate aside and leaned back in his chair with a careless wave of his hand. "It's true there've been some… things going on in the UFD I'm not happy about. There've always been members of the group who are somewhat…shall we say, less than patient with the slow-grinding wheels of change, which is what we've advocated up to now. That faction seems to be growing of late. But I see that as a *result* of the unrest surrounding the monarchy, rather than the *cause* of it."

"Sort of a We-should-strike-while-the-iron's-hot attitude?"

His smile was brief and wry. "Something like that."

"How did you get involved with the organization?" She asked this in a conversational way, leaning forward with an expression of great interest, though Nikolas was fairly certain whatever dossier the Lazlo Group had on him would have included that bit of information.

Still, she was a treat to look at and fun to spar with, and he didn't mind playing along once again. So he settled back, outwardly relaxed but inwardly alert, and replied, "When I was in college, actually. That's when we got organized. Before that, my uncle Silas—the man who raised me—had already gotten me interested in the idea of bringing about an end to monarchy in Silvershire."

"You say…your uncle. That would be…"

"My father's brother."

"Ah," she said, those feline eyes of hers intent again, "but now we know he couldn't have been your father's brother, could he?"

An expected surge of anger hardened his voice. "So *you* say. So *they* say. If you ask me, it's all ridiculous nonsense." *Please, God, let it be so.*

This is hard for him, she thought. *His whole life, who he is, his perspective—everything has changed.*

She knew how that felt. She'd had only a few short years to be Rhia de Hayes in a Louisiana trailer park with her mama and her big laugh and sparkling eyes, where there was always music and dancing and good things to eat and she could run barefoot all summer long. Then one day everything had changed, her world and everything in it—her home, her school, her friends, her clothes, even her name had changed. As everything would change for this man.

She wondered if he was thinking now, Who the hell is Nikolas Donovan? Who am I?

She said gently, "I'm afraid it's not nonsense. You are the biological offspring of King Henry Weston and his late wife, Queen Alexis. DNA proves that, and DNA doesn't lie, Nikolas."

He said nothing, only burned her with his smoldering eyes.

"I'm curious, though. What did your—uh, Silas Donovan—tell you about your parents? That they were dead, I assume, but what was supposed to have happened to them?"

His mouth hardened. "My parents were patriots—some would say traitors, I suppose. Insurgents—anti-royal activists—call them what you will, it was Weston's people that had them killed. It was supposed to have been a road accident. Their car was forced off the road—went over the cliffs near Leonia into the sea. Their bodies were never found."

"Oh, ouch." Rhia winced. "So you were pretty much programmed to hate King Weston from birth, weren't you?"

"I don't hate the man." He rose abruptly, swept up her plate along with his and carried them the two short steps to the sink.

No...I don't think you have it in you to hate. Rhia studied him thoughtfully, quivering inside again with that strange sense of recognition. *But where do I know you from, Dono-van? I know we've met before. I know it.*

"I don't even think he's that bad a king," he said with his back to her, and she could see the tension in his neck and shoulders, hear it in his voice. "I just don't think something as important as running a country should be determined by an accident of birth. Can you imagine Silvershire in the hands of that spoiled, selfish twit, *Reginald?*"

"Well, it didn't happen, did it?" said Rhia. "Someone made sure of that. What do you think of the current regent, Lord Russell Carrington, by the way? I know you've met with him. He seems to be doing a decent job filling in for the king while he's been out of commission."

"Carrington's a decent man. Probably make a decent head of state as well." He jerked around, eyes gone dark and fierce, and she was aware once again of how small the kitchen was, and how big Nikolas Donovan seemed standing in it. "Look—that's not the point. No man should have the right to rule without the consent of the people he's ruling. This is the twenty-first century. The people—"

Rhia held up both hands in mock surrender. "Hey, you don't have to explain democracy to me—I'm an American, remember? Anyway, back to the issue at hand. You're going to have to face this sooner or later, Nikolas. You do know that, don't you?"

"Of course, I do." He was silent again, staring past her at the rain-splashed window glass. She waited, and after a moment he drew a breath and shook his head. "It came at me too damn fast. I needed to think a bit." Another pause, and then he drilled her with his intent gray eyes. "I went to ask Silas, you know. It was the first thing I did when I heard the…rumors. I suppose I wanted him to explain, or some such thing." His eyes went bleak.

"And?"

He shrugged, and his mouth twisted and settled into

hard, angry lines. "Couldn't find him. Wasn't at his apartment in Dunford, hadn't been to his job at the college in days. Don't know where he's got to. I know I want to hear it from him, and until I do, as far as I'm concerned it's just that—rumors."

It was Rhia's turn to be silent and thoughtful as she watched Silvershire's reluctant prince run hot water and scrub egg off frying pan and dinner plates. She was remembering the rich, velvety voice on the phone that was her only contact with her boss, the founder and head of the Lazlo Group.

Nikolas Donovan can be a hard man. Never forget that. He's also intelligent, resourceful, charming and suave.

I've heard he's something of a fanatic, Rhia had said.

Not a fanatic, Corbett Lazlo had responded after a brief pause. *He's too intelligent for that kind of insanity. Donovan's a reasonable man. Focused, yes. Passionate...but capable of iron self-control. It would be a grave mistake to underestimate him.*

Wonderful, Rhia had thought then. *Just what I need—another powerful, bullheaded man determined to have his way.*

A small shiver passed through her body now, as she gazed at the broad and powerful shoulders, the rich sable hair curling slightly on the back of a smooth sun-bronzed neck. So far she'd seen the suave sophisticate, the smiling charmer, the intelligent man, the hard man. She wondered what the passionate man would be like...and what it would take to test his iron will.

"Lord Carrington was ready to arrest you," she remarked. "I assume you knew that when you ran. Were you aware that Danielle Cavanaugh—the assassin known as the Sparrow—named *you,* before she died, as the man who hired her to kill Reginald?"

His laugh was brief and harsh. "Nothing much surprises me these days, you know." He turned, drying his hands on a dishtowel. "Considering what's happened in Silvershire over the past few months." He held up a clenched fist, one finger extended, a sardonic smile curving his lips. "One—the crown prince gets murdered practically on the eve of his marriage to the princess of Gastonia and his ascent to the throne, thus saving Silvershire—*and* the princess—from unimaginable disaster." Up went another finger, along with the errant eyebrow. "Two—the reigning king collapses from shock and grief, and Lord Russell Carrington, off in Gastonia to escort the bride-to-be to her nuptials, rushes home to assume the king's duties—but not before falling in love with and ultimately marrying Reginald's erstwhile intended, the lovely Princess Amelia."

His smile was all teeth. "How'm I doing so far?"

"You must read the *Quiz,*" Rhia murmured. "You're certainly up on all the royal gossip."

"Hmm, yes, well, I do try to keep informed. Particularly when my name is being bandied about as the most likely candidate for royal murderer."

"You haven't mentioned the part where it's discovered during the royal autopsy—through routine blood typing, I assume—that Reginald could not possibly have been the biological child of either King Henry or Queen Alexis."

He gave her a quelling look. "Hush. I was coming to that."

He held up a third finger. "The plot thickens. Scandal follows mystery, follows intrigue. We learn Reginald has an illegitimate child by the illegitimate daughter of the prince of Naessa—ah, those randy royals!" The fourth finger shot up. "Next, we have a bloody great explosion right next to where the king is lying in a coma. He's not injured, thank God, but I understand the same can't be said for his personal physician. I'm told the lady—Dr. Smith, is it? Something exotic—Zara, I believe—was rather badly injured."

Rhia nodded. "She was. A head injury. She had amnesia for a while. Fully recovered, now, though, and marrying the psychologist for the Lazlo Group who helped bring her back. Walker Shaw—I know him personally. He's a good man." She paused. "She's the one who discovered the vault, you know."

Nikolas gave her a sidelong look, narrowed and wary. "Vault?"

"Oh, mah goodness," Rhia said in her sweetest Southern, "I thought for sure you'd know 'bout that. That's where the DNA evidence came from that proves—"

Nikolas's teeth snapped shut. He closed his fist and punched the air with it as his voice raised to override hers. "Yes, and then we have *the Sparrow*. An assassin by trade. This woman makes a deathbed confession *you* say, in which she names me—"

"Donovan." Her voice was quiet, now, but firm. "She said she was hired by someone named Donovan." She paused while he stared at her, hot-eyed. "There's more than one Donovan in this story, Nikolas."

"Silas…" It hissed from him on an exhaled breath as he leaned back again against the counter. He shook his head. "Yes, and what could he possibly have to do with any of this?" He pressed the heels of his hands hard against his eyes as if they burned even him, but when he looked at her again his eyes were cold. And hard. "They'd have arrested me anyway, wouldn't they." It wasn't a question. "And they sent you to find me."

"Well, my Lord, what did you expect? Look, there are questions that need answering. And naturally the king wants to meet you—since you appear to be his long-lost son and all. Carrington has questions…doubts…suspicions, maybe, but you've met him, talked with him, you know he's a fair man. If you're innocent—"

"Carrington *is* a good man—and I *am* innocent."

"Then why," Rhia said on a gust of exasperation, "won't you come back with me and prove it?"

He passed a big, strong-boned hand over his eyes again, and this time when they emerged from cover they were no longer hard. They looked tired, she thought. Wounded. Still, when he spoke his voice held the ring of cold steel.

"I have questions of my own that need answers. When I have them, I'll go back. Not until then."

"Well, then," Rhia said briskly, getting to her feet, "I hope you have a comfortable couch and a spare bath towel or two, because my orders are not to come back without you. And since I'm not about to let you out of my sight now that I've found you, I'm afraid I'm going to be staying right here until you're ready to go home."

Chapter 3

"What happened to throwing me over your shoulder and hauling me off to see the king?"

Instead of being annoyed by her announcement, Nikolas's voice and smile betrayed amusement, and even his eyes had lost their steely glitter. Rhia wondered if that was simply more evidence of his legendary self-control. For all she knew—could only hope—the man was seething inside.

"Sorry to disappoint you," she said tartly, annoyed herself at the hum that had come again from nowhere to warm her chest and quicken her pulse.

"You have, actually," he said in a faintly surprised tone. "I was rather looking forward to the experience."

"Oh, don't worry, it may still come to that. For right now…" She shrugged and turned away to hide the heat she could feel rising to her throat…her face. *His* face was entirely too attractive when he smiled at her with that rakish charm, his eyes heavy-lidded and gone unexpectedly soft… "The fact is, I have a little leeway—not much, but a little. You say you need some time, I'm willing to give it to you—to a point." Faking a huge yawn, she paused in the kitchen doorway to lift her arms over her head in a sinuous catlike stretch, knowing that motion would lift her jacket as well, and reveal a good bit of silky chemise and the skin on the small of her back, and hint…just hint…at everything below that.

Two could play the subtle tease, she thought.

"Hmm—pardon me. It's been rather a long day for me," she murmured huskily. "If you don't mind, I think I'd like to take that couch, now. If you'll just throw me a blanket and maybe a pillow…"

"Nonsense," Nikolas said grandly, "what kind of host would I be? You shall have the bed, of course. I'll take the sofa." He slipped past her with the quickness that seemed so unexpected in a big man, touching—apparently casually—her waist as he did so. The sensation of his warm hand on her bare skin sent an entirely involuntary shudder of pleasure coursing through her. "After all—" for a moment his eyes, bright with laughter, stared straight into hers, and for that moment her brain seemed to cease all function "—I do have a certain reputation to maintain…as a gentleman, that is."

My God, she thought, what's the matter with me? I was warned about this man!

"Hold it." Recovering quickly, she caught up with him as he crossed the living room with his long-legged athlete's stride and tapped him on the shoulder. "Not so fast, Your Highness. Don't think for one minute you're going to stick me off in a bedroom behind a closed door and leave you free to slip out and away the second I nod off. This couch right here will do me fine, thank you very much."

Nikolas tilted his head and gazed thoughtfully past her. "Slip out…and away…do you know, it's a pity the idea hadn't occurred to me."

Yes, he was enjoying himself again, but that fact no longer

bemused him. He was growing accustomed to the realization that this woman, Corbett Lazlo's crack bounty hunter, stirred his juices as no one had been able to in a very long time. Maybe ever. Since there seemed to be no use fighting it, he reasoned, what else *could* he do but enjoy it?

"I do see your point. I suppose comfort and good manners must occasionally be sacrificed to duty. All right," he said briskly, "so it's the sofa for you, then. I'll just get that blanket...." He stepped toward the bedroom, then paused and turned back to her, one eyebrow lifted deliberately toward his hairline. "I suppose you're going to tell me you're a light sleeper as well."

She narrowed her eyes, watching him the way he imagined a cat might eye a mouse weighing the merits of a suicide dash across open floor. "Very light."

"Ah. So...there's not much chance I could slip past you in the middle of the night, then, is there?"

She smiled, and it was the same smile he'd seen once before, hovering a warm breath above his, just before she whispered the word, *Serendipity*.

"Not a chance," she purred.

"Huh." Pasting on a frown to contain the grin he could feel quivering dangerously through his facial muscles, Nikolas went to fetch his unexpected houseguest a pillow and a blanket.

The next few hours, he thought, promised to be entertaining indeed.

Rhia lay awake in the shadowy darkness, listening to the sounds the rain made in the night. For a time there had been the noises Nikolas made as he prepared for bed—footsteps and scufflings, the gush of water running through pipes, and doors opening and closing—but now there was only the rain, swooshing down the window glass, pattering on the balcony floor, rustling in the vines that covered the apartment building's outside walls.

It should have been a recipe for instant slumber, but instead she was wide awake, tense…restless. Not because the couch wasn't comfortable, but because it was. It was *too* comfortable, that was the problem. She couldn't let herself relax for fear she'd fall asleep. In spite of her arrogant claims, in her exhausted state she was afraid she might sleep soundly enough to allow Donovan to slip away from her. She hadn't been exaggerating when she'd said it had been a long day for her; she'd left the Lazlo Group's headquarters long before dawn that morning—only minutes, in fact, after verification of her target's location had come in around 2:00 a.m. Rhia didn't like delays. Once she had the information she needed, she moved and moved quickly. It was just her way.

She needed rest, and badly; she had a feeling it was going to take all her resources, mental and physical, to keep even one step ahead of Nikolas Donovan.

But she couldn't risk letting him escape while she slept. What she needed, she realized, was some kind of alarm.

She threw back the down comforter Nikolas had generously provided and rose from the couch. Ignoring the robe he'd also given her—nice of him, she thought with a wicked inner smile—she felt in the darkness for the belt she always wore on assignments like this one. Her fingers quickly located the pouch containing the items she needed—nail clippers and a small roll of nylon fishing line, nearly invisible, yet strong enough to land a thousand-pound marlin…so useful in so many ways.

By this time her eyes were well adjusted to the semi-darkness. Working without a flashlight and almost soundlessly, she tied a loop of the fishing line around the front door handle, then threaded it carefully around the leg of a small table nearby. It wouldn't go undetected in full light, but if Donovan decided to run, she doubted he'd be turning on any lamps. She did the same to the balcony doors and then, confident nobody was going to exit or enter the apartment without her knowing about it, Rhia lay down once again on the couch and pulled the comforter over herself with a satisfied sigh.

Nikolas, who had been monitoring this activity from the bedroom, heard the sigh and smiled to himself in the darkness. She hasn't lost her resourcefulness, he thought, as his mind flashed back yet again to his first encounter with her on that Paris hotel balcony. Or her sex appeal, his mind wryly added as his body responded predictably to the memory.

She was a worthy adversary. It was going to be fun outwitting her.

Rhia woke up shuddering with sexual arousal, her body scalded, pulses pounding. *My God, what a dream. Was it… Nikolas? No—surely not. Somebody who reminds me of Nikolas, though, or—no, wait…I think I remember…*

But it was too late, the dream was already slipping away. She remembered a balcony…maybe? Though hazy, it was all she could recall. That, and the same nagging sense of déjà vu that had been bothering her all evening.

Exasperated, she once again threw back the comforter and rose, this time putting on the robe her reluctant host had left lying over the arm of the couch. It felt cool and slick on her skin, and smelled of aftershave and masculinity. Just what her overheated senses needed. Like using gasoline to douse a fire, she thought as she made her way through the shadowed room that was already becoming familiar to her.

The rain had stopped. In the quiet even her bare footsteps on the thin carpet seemed loud, but she made no effort to tiptoe. *I hope I do wake him,* she thought, cranky and jangled from her own interrupted sleep. *Serve him right.* Though just what it would serve him right *for* she didn't try to figure out.

In the kitchen she opened the refrigerator and stared hot-eyed into its depths. Where was that damn wine? Ah—yes. She reached for the bottle of rosé, now barely a third full, and plucked out the stopper with an audible pop. She raised the bottle to her lips, tilted her head back and swigged down what was left of the wine in noisy unladylike gulps. With a violent

shudder—she really did not care for wine—she set the empty
bottle and stopper in the sink and made her way back to the
couch, managing to stub her toe only once.

She was about to reach for the comforter once more when
it occurred to her that perhaps she would be wise to use the WC
before settling in. To do so, of course, meant she would have
to pass Nikolas's door, which she'd noticed he'd left partly ajar.
Figures, she thought. *He trusts me about as much as I trust him.*

It seemed to her rather like sneaking past the cage of a
sleeping tiger—and this time she *did* tiptoe. Having just gotten
her libido calmed down, the last thing she needed was a
middle-of-the-night run-in with the man who for some reason
appeared to be the cause of its recent rampage.

So, when a voice like the deep-chested growl of a tiger
came rumbling out of the bedroom just as she was passing the
half-open doorway on her return from the bathroom, it was a
miracle she didn't jump right out of her skin.

"Trouble sleeping?"

With one hand braced against the wall for support and the
other against her chest to keep the adrenaline surge from
forcing her heart through her ribs, Rhia managed to make her
voice sound almost normal. "No trouble—I'm just…"

"A light sleeper—I know." The voice was a velvety purr,
fairly oozing sympathy. "Are you sure you won't change your
mind about the bed?" Light flared warm and golden, splash-
ing across the carpeted floor.

Although she tried her best to stop them, her eyes darted like
curious children to the door opening. In the rectangle of soft
light from the lamp he'd just switched on, she could see Nikolas
reclining gracefully on his side with his upper half raised,
propped on one elbow. That same half, the only part of him she
could see—sculpted muscles of chest, torso, shoulders and
arms—wore nothing but smooth tawny skin with an appealing
masculine patterning of ink-black hair. His face wore a knowing
smile, and one eyebrow raised in deliberate challenge.

A challenge? That was all Rhia needed. It was a bucketful of cold water in the face, that eyebrow—a clarion call to battle. A slug of Jack Daniel's, neat.

Icy calm settled over her as she pushed the door wide open and leaned, with arms casually folded, against the door frame, her focus so narrow now, she barely noticed—or cared—that the lower half of that magnificent body was modestly covered by a blanket.

"No, I haven't changed my mind. The couch is quite comfortable." Her sultry smile changed to a grimace. "If you must know, I was having a rather unpleasant dream." She paused before adding wickedly, "You were in it."

"Really!" She was ridiculously pleased at the genuine surprise in his voice.

"Yes—not all that hard to figure, really, considering you've been pretty much the whole focus of my existence for the past few days. Plus…" She hesitated, frowned, then reluctantly gave in, wondering whether she was going to regret putting these particular cards on the table. She let it out with an exasperated gust of breath. "Plus, I've been trying all evening to think who you remind me of, dammit. Or where I've met you before. Because I'm sure I have, and it's driving me crazy—" She stopped and straightened up, eyes narrowing; his eyes had a suspicious sparkle in them, like someone with a bad poker face and a secret ace up his sleeve. "Okay, wait. You *know*, don't you? We *have* met before, and you know where."

His satisfied chuckle confirmed it. Inwardly grinding her teeth and wearing her most winning smile, she took a cajoling step toward him, her role as his captor and keeper temporarily put aside. "Come on, you have to tell me. I can't believe I wouldn't have remembered you…."

"Hmm…flattering," Nikolas murmured. His eyes had softened with laughter…and something else she couldn't name. His smile grew downright seductive. "I won't *tell* you…but if you'll come here a minute, I'll give you a hint."

"A hint?" She paused, thinking of the limerick again. She really did not trust that tiger-smile.

"Yes, luv, a hint. But you'll have to come closer than that." He shifted, lying back on the pillows, and patted the blanket beside him. "Come, come—what are you afraid of? Surely you don't think a future king would stoop to ravishing an unwilling lady."

"From all I hear, Reginald would have," Rhia said darkly.

"Ah. Yes. But I'm not Reginald. Nor a future king, either, actually, so that's not much help, is it?" His eyebrow rose, his mouth tilted wryly, and his voice deepened with an unmistakable note of mockery. "Miss de Hayes. I never would have taken you for a coward."

She stood where she was, studying him, the challenge ringing in her head. She was far from a coward, and confident enough of that fact not to feel a need to prove it. So why the quickening pulse and heightened senses, the thrum of excitement pounding deep in her belly and shivering across her skin? *This is crazy. Definitely against the rules. Possibly even dangerous.*

Why? Because she'd always loved risk. And hated rules.

Hands thrust deep in the pockets of the borrowed robe, she resumed her unhurried stroll toward the bed and its infuriating and intriguing occupant and stopped an arm's length from both. "Okay, let's have it. The hint."

He shook his head, eyelids half-closed. *Sleepy tiger...* "Sorry, that still won't do, I'm afraid. In fact, you're going to have to come quite a *lot* closer." He patted the blanket again.

"Oh, you can't be serious," Rhia said. "You can't actually think I'm going to get into bed with you."

"Not *into* bed, darling—appealing as the idea may be. Just *on* will do. On *me,* actually. On top of the covers, of course— I did promise not to ravish you."

"No, you didn't."

"Didn't I? Oh, well, all right then, I do now. No ravishing— cross my heart." He drew an *X* over one firm and dusky pec, then said drily, "Anyway, I like to think if I were of a mind to ravish someone, I could manage to do so without resorting to such an idiotic plot."

"Being ravished," Rhia said darkly, "is hardly my greatest fear, at the moment."

"Really? How refreshing. What is, then?"

"Being made a fool of. I don't like being mocked, Donovan."

His eyes and smile softened instantly. "Oh, my dear, that's the last thing I'd want to do to you, believe me. No—you wanted to know where we've met before, and I said I'd give you a hint. I'm about to do so, if you'll allow me, but you're going to have to trust me."

"Trust you?" Rhia said that with a shivery little laugh. But she sat down on the edge of the bed—rather abruptly due to the fact that her legs were feeling uncommonly weak. Grumpy because of that, she muttered, "Oh, why don't you just tell me? Save all this trouble."

Nikolas chuckled. "I could, I suppose, but this is so much more enjoyable. Now—if you could bring yourself to stretch out here…."

In spite of that weakness in her knees and a giddy, fluttery sensation in her stomach, Rhia had to admit she was enjoying herself, too. She didn't like to imagine what her handlers at the Lazlo Group would make of all this, but the truth was, she always had been allowed a considerable amount of latitude when it came to choosing her methods of operation. So long as those methods resulted in a successful mission, that is. If playing the lighthearted seduction game with Nikolas Donovan was what it took to get him back to Silvershire and into the arms of his royal biological father, then she was willing to make the sacrifice.

The odd thing was, she *did* trust him. Probably more than she trusted herself.

"On top of you, you said?" She turned, arranging herself first beside the long blanket-covered mound that was Nik's body, trying not to think about the part of that body that wasn't covered, the part that was giving off the intoxicating scent and sultry warmth of a clean, healthy man in waves that made her head swim. Catching and holding a breath, she eased her body carefully over and onto the mound. She lifted her head and looked down into those dusky gray eyes, and it was like looking into a very deep well. Fighting an unaccustomed wave of vertigo, she unstuck her tongue from the roof of her mouth and mumbled in a shivery voice, "Like this?"

"Hmm…perfect. Lovely." His voice vibrated against her chest. "Now, then…are the bells ringing?"

Rhia uncrossed her eyes and shook her head. "No…"

His sigh lifted her gently, and she felt an urge to grab hold of something and hold on. Something…like *him.*

"Then I'm afraid you're going to have to kiss me."

Her head rocked back, clearing instantly. She let go a gust of breath. "*Kiss* you! What are you trying—"

Nikolas lifted his head from the pillows and held his arms out wide. "Look—I promised, crossed my heart. No ravishing, see? Arms way out here. I won't even—"

"Oh, just shut up," Rhia said recklessly. She ducked her head and kissed him hard on the mouth. After a moment—a very brief moment—she raised her head and glared at him. "Well? I still don't hear any bells."

He gave a soft, dry snort. "Yes, well, small wonder, with a peck like that. Try it again, luv, and this time put some… hmm, how shall I put it?…some *sex* into it."

She closed her eyes; her heart thumped heavily against the place where her chest met his. "Oh, God—please don't tell me we had a one-night stand. That's impossible. I know I'd have remembered—"

"As someone recently said, do shut up." He lifted his head and his mouth found hers even before she knew she was bringing it down to his once more.

She had no idea how long it was before she raised her head

again; she lost all sense of time. She lost all sense of space, too. She felt the world whirl around her; she was floating, weightless. She needed desperately to hold onto something, or better yet, to have something—strong, masculine arms— holding her. Electricity skated along her nerves; her hands clenched, fisted in the blanket, gathering it in greedy handfuls. Her heart rocked her body with each beat, like hammer blows.

Desperate for breath, she pulled away, finally, and found that her eyes now refused to focus. In a drunken voice she managed to mutter, "What the hell was *that?*"

Nikolas's smile swam into her blurred line of vision, and his breath was soft on her lips as he whispered, "Serendipity."

She opened her mouth and a gasp burst from her throat, but that was all she had time for as his arms came around her and, with one deft and powerful twist of his body, he rolled her under him. Stunned, she looked up at the face suspended above her, the face filling up all her world with its chiseled jaw and patrician nose, its dark brow and brooding eyes, its beautifully sculpted mouth. *That face. That mouth...*

Memories flickered like lightning flashes; a clap of thunder shuddered through her. She whispered, "Oh, my God, was that *you?*"

She'd never forgotten him, the man who'd saved her career that night. Possibly her life. She remembered every detail of the encounter, from the moment she'd vaulted over that balcony wall, not knowing what she'd find on the other side, knowing only it was bound to be better than staying where she was. The legitimate occupant of the room she'd been searching was known to be a dangerous man—and was evidently unpredictable, too. She hadn't expected him back for another fifteen minutes, at least.

When she heard the key card slick in and out of its slot, she hurled herself through the sliding door and onto the balcony, knowing it was only a temporary refuge. Even a blind man or a complete idiot would be able to tell in seconds the room had been searched—and Clive Harrington was no fool. A wife-beater, a child-stealer, a cheat, a liar and a mean-as-a-snake SOB, for sure, but not stupid. The balcony was the first place he'd look.

Rhia figured she had three choices: She could go up, down, or sideways. Since the balcony was fifteen floors up and she lacked both wings and climbing gear, that left only one choice, and she took it without hesitation. In roughly two seconds time she was pulling herself over the six-foot wall between her assignment's balcony and the one next door and dropping down on the other side…

…Right on top of the unfortunate and unsuspecting person enjoying the view of the lights of Paris and the cool night air.

She didn't know what made her do it. She remembered looking down into his face—the face of a man, a young man…and handsome. More than handsome, if she'd had time to think about it. But…she remembered hearing the muffled cry of fury from the room next door, and realizing she had only seconds in which to save herself. And then she was kissing the strange man lying half-stunned beneath her, kissing him as if she'd done it…oh, many times before.

She remembered hearing Harrington's voice asking about her, then apologizing for the interruption, and feeling exhilarated…smug…clever. Somehow she'd done it—pulled it off. She was free and clear!

But…there was this…man she was lying on…kissing. And his mouth tasted good, tasted faintly of wine…and felt warm and firm and enthusiastic, and—after the first shocked seconds—oh, so skillful. Still tangled with his, her lips formed a smile.

Then, slowly, even a bit reluctantly, she separated her mouth from his and gazed down at him, searching for the words to tell him how grateful she was. Searching for a way to say thank you. And good-bye.

But…when she lowered her head to touch his lips again in sweet farewell, she felt his body grow hard and quiver with

*wiry strength...and his arms were around her now, and she
felt his head lift and his muscles surge and a moment later she
was lying on her back and his weight was pressing down on
her and his face was filling the sky above her, blotting out the
pale Paris night. She felt his arms tight around her and his
heartbeat thumping off-beat against hers. And she thought...*

Foolish Rhia! Stupid—stupid to play with fire this way!

*Her panic lasted only a moment. She was still in control—
of course she was. She could stop this any time she chose. The
arms holding her prisoner were masterful but not brutal; the
eyes burning down into hers were angry, yes, but bright with
questions rather than lust.*

What was that? What the hell do you call that? *she heard
him demand in a croaking, unexpectedly young voice.*

*And somewhere deep inside her she felt a smile shiver free
and bubble up through her chest and emerge with a whispered
sigh:* Serendipity.

*He gave a brief huff that might have been wonder or merely
acknowledgment, then lowered his mouth to hers for one
quick, hard kiss, a kiss that left her with throbbing lips and
racing heart and a strange humming in her chest. Then he
rolled his weight off of her to lie on his back with one arm
across his eyes. She felt his body shake with silent laughter.*

*For one insane moment she thought of staying right there.
Wondered what a kiss like that might possibly lead to, and who
this young man was who could have a strange woman drop
on him from out of the sky and not only keep his cool and play
along in her game with life-and-death stakes, but laugh about
it afterward. But Harrington was a few yards away in the next
room, undoubtedly on the phone to the French police and the
British embassy at that very moment. She couldn't count on
her good luck holding forever. She didn't know how Corbett
Lazlo felt about bailing his agents out of jail—in her case, a
second time—but she didn't care to find out, not on her first
solo assignment.*

She sat up, patted her savior's shoulder and breathlessly muttered, Thanks—I don't know who you are, but I definitely owe you one. *Then she rose, stepped over his body and slipped through the balcony door, moving quickly and nimbly as she always did...moving as if her legs weren't shaky and her stomach jittering with the aftereffects of a kiss she knew even then she was never going to forget....*

"You did say you owed me one," Nikolas said, his voice an amused rumble against her chest. "Although I've never been quite clear on what for, exactly."

"Oh, nothing much," Rhia said grudgingly. "Just possibly my life. Definitely my career."

"Ah—I see. Then I would be correct in surmising that what you were doing in that hotel room was something similar to what I found you doing in mine this evening?"

She tried to squirm, then thought better of it. "Well...yes. I guess you could say that." She focused her eyes on the lock of dark hair that swept across his brow like a blackbird's wing. Studying the silky, glossy blackness of it, she found herself smiling. "But somehow...I don't think that gentleman would have cooked me supper and offered me his bed."

"Hmm...foolish man."

The lock of hair brushed her forehead like a whispered command, and obediently her eyelids fluttered closed. She felt the warmth of his breath flow over her lips, and her heart gave a crazy leap, gave a foolish, giddy leap, like a smitten schoolgirl's. Her breath caught; unable to help herself, she lifted to him, searching again for that clever, clever mouth. He chuckled; his lips hovered...brushed...nipped...teased. Her stomach dropped sickeningly as she felt herself lifted on a wave of desire, like a roller coaster when it shoots up...up...up to the crest...just before it begins its heart-stopping plunge back down. Down...toward certain disaster.

But, as she teetered there, waiting for the plunge, breathless with exhilaration, trembling with desire, she felt a heartbeat thumping against her palm. And she realized that, without any recollection of having done so, she'd placed her hand against his chest like a barrier.

Roller-coastering emotions bumped and careened over realizations and fears and screeched to a halt just short of panic. *My God, what am I doing? I can't...*

"Nikolas—wait," she gasped. "I can't...do this."

"Mmm...why not?" The soft words tickled her lips and his tongue lightly soothed them. "It's not like we haven't done this before."

"That was...different. There was a reason...circumstances." *And I was young, then. Reckless!* Her voice went breathy with panic. "And I didn't know...who you were."

His laughter was dry with irony. "So...it's okay to kiss a stranger, but not a prince? And you wonder why I'm not exactly thrilled at the thought of being one?"

And he rolled away from her, leaving her just as jangled and shaky as she had been on that memorable night so long ago.

He jerked the tangled blanket aside and got up, and she barely had time to register the fact that he was wearing a pair of black silk boxers that rode low on narrow hips, before he leaned down to brush her forehead with his lips. "Don't get up, luv. I'll take the couch."

He was walking away from her when she fought her way free of the half of the blanket that still cocooned her. "No way. Dammit, I'm not letting—"

He turned back, put his hands on her shoulders and gently but firmly pushed her down onto the bed, clucking to her as he did so like a mother hen to a wayward chick. "Don't get excited. I promise I won't run off while you're sleeping. In fact, I give you my word on it—how's that?"

She eyed him warily, not trusting that smile or the gleam in those pewter-gray eyes, not for a second. "Word of a king?"

His smile vanished. "No," he said coldly as he straightened up, "Word of honor. *My* honor."

He turned and strode from the room. And in that moment, in her opinion—boxers and all—had never looked more like a king.

Chapter 4

Word of honor. My *honor.*

Nikolas lay awake, listening to those words whisper in his mind like ghost voices in an empty castle. The words had meant something, once. So had the words of the man who raised him, the man who had been like a father to him. The man who had taught him all he knew about honor. About duty. About love of country.

And hatred of tyrants. Hatred of kings in particular, and of one king, Henry Weston of Silvershire, specifically.

Silas Donovan. The man's face flashed before his mind's eye like a slide show on fast forward, in all the ways he'd come to know it in his thirty years. True, it was a hard face in many ways, austere and forbidding, with a mouth that seldom smiled and eyes that often glittered with the light of fanaticism. The man Nik had called simply Uncle had never been warm or affectionate, or even particularly kind. And yet, in his way, he'd been good to Nikolas. Among many other things, Silas had taught him strength, discipline and a willingness to sacrifice and dedicate his life to a cause greater than himself. He had taught him so well, in fact, that Nikolas couldn't remember a time in his life when he'd ever been free of the burden of responsibility Silas had placed on his shoulders. A time when he'd been allowed to be just a lad: young, carefree, with a whole world of bright possibilities to explore.

Word of honor. My *honor.*

But what value could there be in either his word or his honor when the basis for both was a lie?

It was hard for Nikolas to explain, even to himself, why he wasn't yet ready to return to Silvershire to deal with the catastrophic changes in his life. There was a part of him that still clung desperately to the hope that it was all an awful mistake, that at the very least there was some kind of explanation for how his DNA and Henry Weston's could be a close match—distant relatives, perhaps? But in his heart, he knew there was no mistake; as Rhia had pointed out, DNA doesn't lie. The only thing left for him to do now was accept this new reality, and try to think how it affected his future, both immediate and long range.

No small task.

For one thing, there were the questions looping through his mind, flitting in and out among the images of Silas Donovan's face, most of which he couldn't even pin down, much less find answers to.

He needed time. Just a bit more time.

Nikolas turned his head toward the small pile of clothing that had been left carelessly draped over the back of the couch, only a shadowy wrinkle in the darkness, but he caught a whiff of that faint feminine aura that seemed so familiar to him. After a moment he reached out a hand and idly stroked the butter-soft leather jacket with a finger, and smiled grimly to himself in the darkness. *Sorry, luv. I hope you'll understand...one day.*

* * *

Rhia had never considered herself a particularly sensual person, and certainly not indolent. Yet, when she came slowly awake in a feather-soft bed to the smell of coffee and the sweet and gentle warmth of a hand caressing her forehead, she wanted only to snuggle down and wallow in the pleasure of it, like a cat in a puddle of sunshine.

He's here. He kept his word. She told herself she'd never doubted he would.

Two things happened then. Memories of the events of the night before hit in an all-out sensory barrage, and at almost the same moment, she felt firm, velvety lips brush hers. Her breath hitched and her lips parted, almost without her knowing, and then she was sinking…helplessly drowning in a deep, intoxicating whirlpool of desire.

She couldn't help herself…her body wasn't hers to govern. Of its own volition it arched and curled and lifted…outposts like fingers and toes tingled as blood abandoned them to rush to more exciting, throbbing places. Her hands ventured from their blanket-cocoon…reached…found his…and her fingers spread wide to allow the erotic slide of his fingers between hers—even those ordinary places now suddenly so sensitized his touch there made her moan.

He lifted his head, and hers lifted, too, following his mouth, not wanting to let it go. His chuckle stopped her—and the fact that his hands were holding her captive, pressed into the pillow above her head. She collapsed back into the pillow, panting slightly, trying to focus her eyes, and finally mumbled, "What in the hell was *that?*"

His lips pressed a smile to hers. "What, haven't you ever been kissed awake before?"

"Not by a prince." She smiled lazily at him through the curtain of her lashes…knowing she shouldn't. Knowing full well she was flirting with a smiling tiger.

She became aware, all at once, of the strength in the hands

that imprisoned hers. She squirmed in a testing way and murmured, "Do I smell coffee?"

His eyes rested on her, dark and benign…and so close she could see the twin images of her own tiny self reflected in them. "You do. I've brought you a tray—breakfast, actually."

She watched him narrowly, while her heartbeat rocked her breasts against his chest, against the crisp white shirt he wore. "You didn't have to do that. I need to get up anyway."

"Well, luv, that's not quite true. You see—" he lowered his mouth to hers, and she responded to him as she had before, opened to him even as her mind's sleeping sentinels were finally waking up and sounding the first confused alarms "—you aren't going to be going anywhere for a while, I'm afraid."

She uttered a muffled howl of outrage and began to squirm and writhe in earnest, but the alarms had come too late. Helpless against his greater strength, she felt cold steel around her wrist, and heard a sound she knew all too well—the click of handcuffs locking. She gave her imprisoned arm one furious yank, an entirely futile move, since the other end of the handcuffs was securely fastened to the iron framework of the bed. She lay still, then, seething and glaring up at Nikolas, who was sitting beside her now, placidly smiling—though still holding her uncuffed wrist as a precaution, she surmised, in case she tried to claw his eyes out.

"Please tell me," she said through tightly clenched teeth, "those aren't *my* handcuffs?"

He shrugged, grinned—had the nerve to try to look endearing. And almost pulled it off, having that unmistakable just-showered and -shaved look she normally found irresistible. And dammit, he did smell so good….

"Well, they were *there,* you see—that's quite an interesting belt you have, by the way—most enlightening, really—and since it didn't seem likely you'd be using them in the near future…well, how could I resist?"

"Fine," she said, glowering at him as she twisted her un-cuffed wrist experimentally in his grasp, "you've had your fun, now get this thing off me."

His smile would have been devastatingly attractive if it hadn't been so damn—there was no other word for it—*smug*. He made scolding noises with his tongue. "Now, now, clever girl that you are, I'm quite certain you know that isn't going to happen. Not right away, at any rate. I did try to tell you I needed a bit more time before I'd be ready to go back to Silvershire. I know you have your job to do as well. This seemed the best way to solve the problem—from my perspective, at least."

"You can't seriously be thinking of just *leaving* me here. Like this. You wouldn't." Sheer disbelief kept any traces of fear out of her voice. The implications, the possibilities didn't bear thinking about.

Nikolas looked genuinely shocked. "No, of course I wouldn't. Well—not indefinitely. Not even for very long, actually. Just until the cleaning lady shows up." He shot the shirtsleeve cuff on his free arm and glanced at his watch. "Should be here in about…two hours, I imagine. When she arrives, tell her the key to the handcuffs is on the kitchen table. That should give me enough of a headstart, I think. Well, sorry, luv, but I must be off."

He started to get up—then, almost as an afterthought, leaned down and kissed her instead. Not a quick farewell smack, either, but a long…leisurely…lingering…completely devastating reminder of how lovely his lips felt, how talented his tongue was, how completely powerless she was to prevent her body from responding to their touch. She tingled and tickled and burned in all her most vulnerable places. She wanted to sob with frustration, to scream with fury. But when he released her from that terrible torture and rose at last, she was so shaken that for a moment she couldn't utter a sound.

"*Au revoir*—enjoy your breakfast," he said softly, and left.

She sucked in air and found her voice. "*Nikolas—damn*

you!" She held her breath and listened so hard her head hummed, but all she heard was his retreating footsteps. "Okay, I'm not allowed to kill you," she screamed after him, "but I promise you I will find a hundred ways to make your life a bloody living *hell!"*

The only reply she heard was the soft closing of the door.

Nikolas dropped a heavy bunch of dusty red grapes into his bucket and straightened up, removing the wide-brimmed hat he was wearing and wiping away sweat with a forearm. "What?" he asked in response to the voice from the next row over that was now swearing softly in French.

"Here comes another bloody tourist," his friend Phillipe replied in English. "Wanting to help with the *vendange,* I expect, like it's an entertainment we put on for them. More trouble than they're worth, most of them, but good for business in the long run, I suppose. The winery benefits a little, anyway."

Nikolas turned his head to follow the progress of the tall figure striding briskly up the dusty lane between vineyards already beginning to shimmer with the heat of the rapidly climbing sun. A woman, he saw now, wearing a backpack and carrying a black oblong case of some kind. As she walked, he could see her head moving from side to side, and he wondered if her eyes, shielded by the dark glasses she wore, were searching among the heads bobbing up and down between the rows—all that was visible of the army of hardworking pickers—searching for one head in particular.

He couldn't help himself; a wry smile tugged at his lips and he chuckled. "That's no tourist, I'm afraid."

There was a rustling sound and Phillipe's dark, interested eyes peered at him through the bronze-tipped leaves of the grapevine separating them. "It is her, then, the woman who chased you out of my apartment in Paris? The one who wants to take you back to Silvershire to become a king? And she has found you so quickly? *Mon dieu,* my friend, you must be losing your touch."

"So it would appear," Nikolas said absently. He was trying to decide whether the odd sensation quivering up through his belly and into his chest was indicative of dismay or delight.

"Would you like to hide under here? She'll never find you among all these vines." Phillipe's teeth gleamed white among the grape leaves. "How is this? I will go and tell her you've gone away to…I don't know where. I'll make up something—something far away. Brazil, maybe?"

"Very funny. You don't know this woman. She wouldn't be fooled for a second. And besides—it would be much too undignified to be discovered crouching under a bush. Here—take my bucket, will you? I suppose I'd better go and face the music—sooner rather than later."

"I'm coming, too—it is, after all, my vineyard. I think I should give a personal welcome to the woman who brought Nik Donovan to his knees, don't you think?" Grinning unforgivably, Phillipe stuck his hand in the air and shouted *"La hutte!"*

A moment later a large cone-shaped basket came bobbing down the row, borne on the back of a wizened fellow with a face like ancient parchment and a grin that displayed several missing teeth. Phillipe bantered jovially with the man in French as he emptied his bucket into the basket, then took the bucket Nik passed over to him and emptied it as well. After waving *la hutte* and its carrier on their way, the two men set off down their respective rows on a course to rendezvous with the visitor coming up the road.

"I am curious," Phillipe said, quickening his pace to match Nik's, "what is this 'music' you face? I know most of your English expressions and quite a few American ones as well, but this one…? Am I correct in assuming this particular music will not be pleasing to the ears?"

"You could assume that, yes," said Nikolas drily. "The last time I saw the lady she threatened me with a hundred fates worse than death."

Phillipe made scolding noises. "You really must work on

your people skills, my friend. Especially if you are to be a king one day. You know—" He broke off with a chuckle as Nikolas threw a fat ripe grape at him and missed.

To Nikolas's bemusement, he felt his heartbeat accelerate as he stepped from the rows of grapevines onto the dusty road. A few dozen yards away, Rhia had come to a halt. Her expression was impossible to read from that distance, particularly with her eyes hidden from view, but he felt safe in assuming it wouldn't be pleasant. The odd thing, though, was the warm little nugget of pleasure he felt forming way down in his belly at the sight of her.

Not that anyone would fault him for that; she was, after all, a sight to warm any man's loins. She wore jeans that sat low on her hips, and a tank top that brought to mind vivid memories of the chemise she'd been wearing the last time he'd seen her…not to mention the circumstances in which he'd left her. Then, her thick, wavy dark hair had been in a sultry tangle tumbling onto her bare shoulders. Now it was caught back by a bandana handkerchief folded into a triangle and tied at the nape of her neck, and the tawny skin of her arms and chest and throat wore a golden slick of sweat.

Without saying a word, she lowered the oblong case to the ground between her feet and took a water bottle from its holder on her belt.

"Mother of God, what do you suppose is in that case? Please tell me she's not come armed."

Nikolas barely heard and didn't acknowledge Phillipe's remark, made in a droll undertone out of one side of his mouth. Rhia had removed her sunglasses, and those cool green eyes had found his, found them and snared them with an intent and unreadable gaze, and his world, his awareness had narrowed until it only had room for her. Phillipe, the vineyards, the army of pickers, the barrel-laden wagons and the tractors pulling them, all faded into background noise, like the busy hum of bees on a summer's day.

She drank long and deeply from the water bottle and returned it to her belt. Watching her, he felt his own throat go dry. Her eyes never left his as he closed the distance between them, though oddly, they seemed to him more puzzled than angry.

He paused a double arm's length away from her and nudged his hat to the back of his head. "That was fast," he said, offering her a smile as a hopeful peace offering. "What did you do, hide a tracking device in my shoes?"

She snorted and said, "I wish I had." But he could tell her heart wasn't in it. She seemed distracted, he thought, as if her mind was on something else entirely. "No, I told you—I just have a knack for finding people."

"Huh. A 'knack,' you say. So…you just *knew* where I'd be? So you *are* psychic."

She shifted her shoulders in an impatient way—again, as though the discussion was interrupting something far more important. "No, I…you'd mentioned your friend, the one whose apartment you were staying in in Paris. You said he had family in Provence. A winery. It seemed like a good bet." She put on her sunglasses, then lifted one shoulder in a dismissive way. "It was where I'd go."

"Ah," said Nikolas. "Empathy."

She'd bent over to pick up the oblong case at her feet. Her shielded eyes came back to him as she straightened. "Empathy?"

"Your 'knack'—that's what it is, you know. Empathy. The ability to put yourself in another person's shoes. To think like he does. Feel what he feels. I can see where that would come in handy in your line of work. Here—let me take that for you."

He reached for the case and she surrendered it to him without an argument, which he thought was a pretty good clue that it wasn't, as Phillipe had suggested, a weapon. He hefted the case. "What's in here? And by the way, whatever possessed you to have the cabby drop you at the bottom of the hill when you had all this to carry? You could have had him take you straight up to the house, you know."

She cut her eyes at him, and her smile was wry. "I thought I'd sneak up on you—in case you took a notion to run again. But I have to tell you, I never expected you'd be out in the vineyards picking grapes." Above the dark lenses of her glasses her forehead crinkled in a frown.

And I sure didn't expect my heart to go nuts at the sight of you, damn you.

Rhia studied her assignment moodily from the shelter of her sunglasses. Today he was wearing a pair of blue dungarees and a white shirt made of some kind of loosely woven material, with long sleeves rolled to the elbows. No collar. His neck was deeply tanned and gleaming with sweat, and looked sleek and powerful as that of some dominant male animal— a stag, perhaps, or a stallion. *Or a king?*

Why did you have to be so damned attractive? Why didn't I stick to finding lost children? They weren't nearly so complicated.

His lips took on a sardonic tilt. "Not quite the occupation one expects of a prince? No—I suppose not. Though I've picked many a grape in my life—make of that what you will. Come." He took her elbow, and Rhia felt a small electric shock where his fingers touched her bare skin. The dryness of the air, she told herself. Static electricity. And somehow she found herself walking beside him up the dusty road, and they were walking together in casual intimacy, like lovers out for a stroll.

"Let me introduce you to Phillipe. This is his vineyard— or his family's, as I'm sure you already know. Phillipe—come and meet the woman who has promised me the punishments of a hundred hells. Rhia, this is Phillipe, one of my oldest and most tolerant friends. Phillipe—say hello to Rhia de Hayes, bounty hunter."

Nikolas's companion, who'd been waiting for them at a discreet distance, flicked away the cigarette he'd been smoking, removed his hat with a sweeping gesture and placed it over his heart. His hair was a mass of sweat-damp curls, lighter than

Nik's, a rich warm brown that matched his eyes. He had extraordinarily nice eyes. He was, in fact, every bit as attractive as Nikolas Donovan, and his smile was just as charming.

Then why was it, she wondered, that when he murmured, *"Enchanté, ma belle,"* and lifted her hand to his lips, she felt no little shock of awareness, no tingling warmth where his lips touched, no hollow flip-flopping sensation in her stomach, no humming sensation in her chest?

"I am in complete sympathy with you, mademoiselle—it is high time someone gave this man the treatment he deserves," Phillipe said solemnly, still holding her hand. "I can only hope I may be allowed to watch."

Rhia burst out laughing—he was so outrageous she couldn't help it. Phillipe grinned irrepressibly and kissed her hand once more before releasing it.

"Nik, my friend. Take this lovely lady up to the house and make her welcome. We'll be stopping for lunch soon—we're about finished for the day anyway. Tell Elana to make up Maman's room for our guest—she won't be back from Monte Carlo until the *vendange* is finished, I'm sure. That is—unless you would like her to sleep in your room, Nik?"

Rhia didn't have to look at him to know Nikolas was grinning. "Please don't bother," she said smoothly. "I won't be staying long. As it happens, Nikolas and I have an important engagement in Silvershire." She turned her head, then, and gave him a long, deliberate stare. He gazed back at her with cool gray eyes, arms casually crossed on his chest.

Phillipe made a gesture that was extravagantly—almost comically—French. "Oh, but you must stay! At least until the *vendange* is finished. I cannot possibly spare this man at the moment. And for you, mademoiselle, it will be an enjoyment. *Vendange* in Provence is like one big party—like your Mardi Gras. A moveable feast. A few more days, eh? What can it matter?"

She shot Nikolas a dark look. He held out his hands in one

of those half-French, half-British gestures of his. "I swear, I did not put him up to it."

She gave in with a put-upon sigh, and didn't tell him she'd planned to give him several days, anyway. A few more days of freedom....

"Don't think you've won this battle," she said as she and Nikolas resumed their leisurely stroll up the gravelly dirt road toward the oasis of dark green trees that shaded the stone-and-stucco house—not touching, now, and she refused to admit to herself she was sorry. "I just don't want to leave your friend short-handed for his damned *vendange*—what is that, by the way?"

"*Vendange?* That's the grape harvest. Happens every year around this time."

Other than shooting him a quelling glance, she ignored the facetious remark. "I can't believe the vineyard owner is out here picking grapes like a field hand. Is that part of the tradition?"

"It is, actually. Among the small growers, anyway. Most of the pickers you see here are neighbors and other small farm owners from around the area. They all come together to help each other with the harvest, moving from farm to farm, vineyard to vineyard until the job's done."

"A 'moveable feast'?"

Nik smiled. "Partly. You'll see soon enough. You heard him say they'll be breaking for 'lunch' soon? I'm afraid the word *lunch* doesn't come close to describing it. All the farmers sort of compete with each other to see who can put on the biggest and best noonday spread. The wine and local hooch—which is called *marc,* by the way, and unless you've a cast-iron stomach, I don't recommend you try it—will be flowing freely as well."

"In the middle of the day? How does anyone work afterward?"

"They don't. You heard him say they were about done for the day. He meant that."

"Nice short workday," Rhia remarked.

"Like hell it is. When it's hot like this we start at three in the morning."

She threw him a look of horror. "Why?"

"Because the grapes don't like it when you take them out of the nice warm sunshine and toss them into a cooler. It sends them into shock, or some such thing." His easy smile made something inside her chest wallow. As if her heart really had turned over.

Because the implications of that didn't bear thinking about, she said crossly, "You talk about grapes as if they're…I don't know—alive."

His eyebrow went up, and she repressed a shudder. "Really? I suppose I do. You hang around vintners very long and it rubs off on you."

"You spend a lot of time here, then?"

His smile went crooked. "*Spent,* not spend. When I was at university, mostly. Spent most of my holidays here, when my…when Silas was off somewhere."

"Doing…?"

"Whatever it is he does, I suppose. Fomenting rebellion, rousing the rabble." He shrugged and looked off across the vineyards for a moment. "I didn't mind, actually. Phillipe and his family were…like family. His *maman* was pretty much the only mum I ever had." He threw her his lopsided smile, and she felt the most astonishing sensation—an aching pressure at the base of her throat. "I probably have her to thank for civilizing me, at any rate."

Rhia cleared gravel from her throat. "You were happy here."

"I was, yes. At one time I actually considered making a career of it—grape-growing…wine-making. There's a region in my country I've always thought— Have you been to Silvershire?"

"Only to the capital—Silverton."

"Ah—yes, well, it's southwest of there. Carrington's ancestral lands. The climate is quite similar to this—perfect for growing wine grapes."

"Why didn't you? Make a career of it?"

The crooked smile flickered again. "It wasn't quite what Silas had in mind for me. Or fate either, as it turns out."

Nik's stomach went hollow suddenly. Hefting the case he was carrying, he said, "What the devil's in this, by the way? Not, as Phil suggested, some sort of weapon, I hope?"

Her lips didn't smile, and he wondered what her eyes would tell him if it weren't for the damned sunglasses. "Nope," she said, "just a saxophone."

He gave a bark of surprised laughter. "A…*what?*"

"You know…jazz, the blues…it's a horn…you blow it…"

He hadn't thought anything she could do would surprise him, but obviously he'd underestimated her. Again. *Serendipity…* A strange little shiver ran down his spine. How could she have known he'd always had a particular fondness for American jazz? "Don't tell me you know how to play it."

"No, of course not," she replied in a frosty tone, "I just have a really eccentric taste in accessories."

"A bit cranky, are we?" he remarked evenly, hiding all traces of his inner delight.

"That's how people get when they're left handcuffed to a bed," she replied, and he could almost hear her teeth grinding. "Particularly without access to a *bathroom.*"

"Ah. That." He stopped in the middle of the road to look at her. Realizing his eyebrows were doing that thing that annoyed her so, he made a conscious effort to stop them— also to contain his grin—before he walked on. "I really had hoped you'd gotten over that."

"Not a chance, Donovan." He could feel her eyes on him, dark as a threat.

He glanced at her and made scolding noises with his tongue. "Oh, come now, you aren't the type to carry a grudge, surely?"

There was something hypnotic about her eyes… "My mother always claimed one of her grandmothers was

Creole—a voodoo priestess," she said, and hissed the last word like a curse. "It's in my blood."

He wanted to laugh, but the tingle of excitement rushing beneath his skin didn't feel like amusement. He could feel heat and heartbeat intensifying in places they shouldn't have been, not at high noon in the middle of a French vineyard. Not in response to a woman whose avowed mission was to take him into custody and return him to a place he had no desire to go. But…really—*Creole? Voodoo?*

He was mulling over this interesting new tidbit of information about his adversary's background when the convoy of tractors pulling trailers laden with barrels and people began to stream past them. Phillipe shouted and waved from the midst of the crowd on the last one, and it halted in the road beside them. Nikolas looked at Rhia and made an offering gesture. She threw him a challenging look, then took the helping hands reaching out to her from the crowd on the wagon and allowed herself to be hoisted aboard. Nikolas passed the oblong case containing her saxophone up to her as she settled into the midst of the boisterous crowd, then levered himself onto the back of the flatbed. Someone gave a shout and the tractor began to move forward again. Someone began to sing, and most of the passengers on the trailer joined in. And Nikolas, for no reason he could think of, found himself smiling.

Chapter 5

For the second morning in a very few days, Rhia wallowed her way to consciousness to the smell of coffee, and to find Nikolas Donovan sitting on the bed beside her. This time, instead of gently caressing her face, he was shaking her. Not the least bit gently.

"Rise and shine, luv—time to get up." His voice sounded obscenely cheerful.

She pried open one eye and said, "It's *dark!*" in an outraged tone. And then gasped, cringed and covered her eyes with her hand as light stabbed them cruelly from the lamp on the table beside the bed.

"There," Nikolas said without sympathy. "It's not dark anymore. Come on—get up. I've brought you coffee. We've got about fifteen minutes before the trailers leave."

"Leave? For where, in God's name? At this hour—" Oh, God, was she whining? She struggled to sit up, and Nikolas helpfully drew back the light blanket that covered her. She pulled it back up to her chin and glared in his direction without focusing. "What hour is it, by the way?"

"Two forty-five—well, actually—" he glanced at his watch "—it's two forty-eight, now. I suggest you hurry if you want time to drink that coffee."

She closed her eyes and rubbed at her temples, which did absolutely nothing to diminish the pounding behind them. To make matters worse, when she opened her eyes again Nikolas was still there, and, once she had him in focus, looking sinfully handsome and smiling at her like a beneficent saint. She regarded him for a moment with loathing, then said, "Are you being deliberately cruel, or is this an aspect of your personality I wasn't briefed about?"

His laugh sent involuntary ripples of pleasure through her. It was like rubbing against fur. "My dear, you did say you wanted to pick grapes with the crew this morning."

She gave him a sideways look of stark disbelief. "Impossible."

"Sorry to have to tell you this, but I heard you with my own ears. So did Phillipe and most of the crew."

"I couldn't have...could I? *When?*"

"Hmm...let's see. It was after your third glass of *marc,* I believe—or perhaps it was the fourth—I'm afraid I lost track. Anyway, the crew was very much impressed with you. If you back out now, you're going to suffer an enormous loss of face."

Rhia groaned and collapsed back on the pillows, closing her eyes. "Oh, God. Father Matthew was right."

"Father Matthew?" Nik's voice was vibrant with rather poorly suppressed emotions—laughter, she was sure. And something else. Something that sounded a lot like—oddly—affection.

"Yeah—he was the priest in the Catholic girls' school I went to in Florida. He always told me I'd go to hell. I think this must be it."

He made a smothered sound—definitely laughter. "Oh, come now—it's not so bad once you get outside. Rather nice, actually." There was a pause, and she felt the touch of something cool and soothing on her aching head—something that warmed almost instantly and became Nikolas's fingers. "You're really not a night person, are you?" he said tenderly. "Who knew?"

She opened her eyes and tried to glare at him, but found that her eyelids had grown inexplicably heavy. "It's not night," she mumbled, "it's morning. Dark, pitch-dark morning." Her tongue felt heavy, too, and her lips seemed to have swollen. She had a powerful desire, now, to press them into the nice warm palm that was cradling the side of her face. "I've always been a night person, actually. My nights have only become an ordeal since I met you."

"It doesn't have to be that way, you know." The pad of his thumb brushed gently across her swollen lips, but instead of soothing them, set them on fire. The heat and heaviness began to spread…like melting molasses…into her arms…her legs…her body. Her breasts felt tight, and even the kiss of silk and lace was more than her sensitized nipples could bear.

"You do know," Nikolas murmured, "if it weren't for this unfortunate hang-up you have about my allegedly royal blood, you and I would be lovers by now."

Her heart stuttered and her stomach wallowed drunkenly—roughly the way those parts of her had behaved the first time she'd jumped out of an airplane during her training for the Lazlo Group job. Now, as then, pride made her catch a breath and fight valiantly against the panic. "You're awfully sure of yourself, aren't you?" *There*…tart, and not *too* breathless.

His reply was wordless. He simply leaned down and kissed her.

In some buried, weakened part of herself, had she been expecting it? In that same part of herself she'd definitely wanted it. When she felt his warm lips pillow against hers, she uttered a single whimpering cry…and opened to him.

And then she was in free fall, the wind rushing so hard against her face she couldn't breathe. Fear gripped her, and then exhilaration. *I've got to stop this! I have to stop...*

But she couldn't stop. And in the end, after she thought she must surely have passed the point of no return, it was Nikolas who pulled the ripcord. "Yes," he murmured, with his lips still touching hers, "I am."

His lips moved, then...along her jawline, riding on the velvety cushion of his sweet, warm breath. Her breasts grew heavier, each breath lifting them intolerably against the chafing fabric of the silk-and-lace camisole she'd slept in, making them yearn for the touch of his fingers instead.

Fighting it, she said in a desperate rush, "It's not just your ancestry—it's my job...Nik. My job—oh, damn."

His mouth found the hollow below her jaw, slid, hot and open, along the side of her neck. She moved her head—didn't want to...couldn't help it—moved it to give him better access to the sensitive places there, the places where her pulses thumpety-thumped like the jazz beat pouring from a Bourbon Street bar. Her fingers ached with the struggle to keep from burying themselves in his hair.

"Your job doesn't need to know what happens between us here," he whispered against her singing flesh.

"*I'll* know." It came on a gasp...or maybe a sob.

Nikolas let go of a breath and fought his way out of the whirlpool of desire like a diver struggling toward the light. He knew he had no business being angry—and he wasn't. He'd had no business doing this in the first place—he knew that, too. At least, not now. Although...someday, someday soon...

He pulled away from her swiftly, the way he'd tear off a bandage or pull out a tooth—because it was less painful that way. Brushing her warm, moist cheek with the backs of his fingers, he said lightly, "You're unusually dedicated to your job, aren't you?" *Or is it your employer you feel such loyalty to?* He wanted to say it, but didn't. He wasn't a jealous man—

or never had been. So why was it he felt a sudden urge to strangle a man he'd never met?

"I am," Rhia said in a voice that was flat and slightly thickened. She sat up and drove both hands, fingers spread wide, into her hair. Holding her head between her hands, she uttered a small and somewhat surprised, "Ow."

"Hangover?" Nikolas inquired, feeling like a wretch.

She nodded carefully. "A wee one, yeah." And he could see her girding herself, and her willpower marching out to do battle with her human frailties. After a moment she drew herself up, pinched the bridge of her nose between a thumb and forefinger, pulled in a long breath and opened her eyes. She reached for the cup of coffee he'd placed on the bedside table, sipped, than lifted her head and leveled a determined look at him. A steady green look from under thick black lashes. "I owe Corbett Lazlo a lot. I'd hate like hell to let him down."

"Ah," Nikolas said. "I see."

She shook her head and set the coffee back on the table. "No, I don't think you do." Throwing back the bedclothes, she pulled her knees up and swiveled them past him so that, for one heart-stopping moment, she was sitting beside him on the bed, with her smooth, sleek thigh touching his, and her body's warmth and musky feminine scent wafting over him, clouding his senses.

While he was still fighting the effects of her nearness, she rose and walked unselfconsciously to the bathroom, and his gut clenched as his gaze followed her. Buttocks…firm and rounded, solid muscle under a delicate veneer of feminine softness, scarcely disguised at all by the skimpy panties she wore. Long, taut legs and a stride of confidence and an athlete's unstudied grace. When the bathroom door closed behind her, he released a breath he didn't know he'd been holding, then laughed silently at himself for his heart-pounding, sweaty schoolboy's lust.

When she emerged from the bathroom moments later, he

had himself in hand…somewhat. It helped that she looked like a well-scrubbed teenager, with her hair in damp strands around her face and her eyes struggling to focus. She didn't look at him as she went straight to the backpack she'd left lying on the floor near the foot of the bed.

"I probably owe Corbett Lazlo my life," she said in a matter-of-fact tone as she hefted the backpack onto the bed and unzipped it. "I definitely owe him for the fact that I'm not in jail right now." And she lifted both hands and clasped them together above her head in a long sinuous stretch that bared a good bit of her lean and supple torso and momentarily robbed Nikolas of his breath.

When he had it back again, he said drily, "Nice try, luv, but you're not going to distract me that way. You can't suppose I'd let that remark go without explanation."

She threw him a look over her shoulder, a look of vague innocence he didn't buy for a minute. "There's not that much to explain, really." She gave him a sleepy-eyed smile, and he remembered the way she'd evaded the question about her association with the Lazlo Group when he'd asked it in Phillipe's kitchen a few days ago in Paris, evaded it with a smile, then, too, and the same subtle little seductions.

He said nothing…watched her take a rolled-up T-shirt and jeans out of her backpack and put them on over the wisps of underwear she'd slept in. Her movements were brisk and efficient, slightly jerky, without any hint of awareness or seduction, now. Socks and a yellow bandana handkerchief came from the depths of the backpack next. She tied the kerchief around her hair the way she'd worn it the day before, then zipped up the backpack, picked up the socks and turned to look for her shoes. He snaked out a hand and caught her wrist.

She went utterly still. Her eyes met his and seemed to shimmer in the lamplight, the way the sea does when the sun strikes it through a hole in the clouds. He felt her wiry strength, and the pulse tap-tapping against his grip, and they both knew very well she could have broken free at any time and done him considerable damage in the process. Instead, for reasons he couldn't imagine, she stood quietly, her hand relaxed in his grasp, and waited.

"It's quite unfair, you know. You know so much about me," he said softly. "And I know so little about you."

He thought he saw something flicker behind her eyes, and for a moment her mouth…her face seemed to blur…become younger. Become vulnerable. Her lips parted, and he held his breath. But instead of words, he heard the reedy beep of a tractor's horn.

"They're here," she said breathlessly. Reaching for the coffee he'd brought her, she gulped down half of it, then bent down and scooped up her shoes from the floor beside the bed. "You'd better have something for me to eat out there somewhere," she threw darkly over her shoulder as she marched barefooted out of the room. "I don't pick grapes on an empty stomach—not even for a prince."

It felt good to have the last word, but it was a hollow victory. As she sang out good-mornings to the work crew and allowed reaching hands to pull her onto the wagon, Rhia's stomach was still jittering with the aftereffects of too much *marc,* and the awareness of how close she'd come to opening up to Nikolas Donovan—emotionally *and* sexually. *My God, Rhee, what were you thinking?*

The picture that flashed instantly into her mind was graphic and unequivocal: Herself…Nik…gloriously entwined. Heartbeats bumping against each other in sultry, syncopated rhythms…sweat-slick bodies gliding together… melding in sweet and perfect harmony…. *Rhee, oh, Rhee— you're not seriously thinking of going to bed with him, are you?*

Someone handed her a fresh sweet roll and she bit into it without tasting it, unable to swallow, unable to think or respond to the friendly babble of voices around her. Unable to hear anything at all but the chorus of happy voices inside her head crying, *Yes! Oh, please, yes!*

The morning went by faster than Rhia had imagined it would. And Nikolas was right—it wasn't so bad once she was out in the fresh cool darkness of the early morning. Floodlights set up at intervals along the road cast long mysterious shadows as the pickers fanned out through the rows of grapevines, men, women and teenagers, all joking and jostling and calling challenges to one another. Competition was fierce among them to see who could fill a bucket the fastest. Fierce, but good-natured.

Rhia was given a bucket and a pair of clippers—secateurs—and shown how to snip each bunch of grapes from the vine and drop it into her bucket. After that she was on her own. She quickly lost track of Nikolas, which was probably a good thing, as she found herself becoming caught up in the friendly competition, too, not wanting to be the last one to fill *her* bucket. She worked as quickly as everyone else did, squatting down to reach the lower vines, snip-snip-snipping until all the bunches had been picked, then rising and moving on to the next vine. In spite of the coolness of the morning air, she was soon sweating, and glad of the bandana she wore which helped keep not only the dust and leaves out of her hair, but the sweat out of her eyes.

She learned to shout *"La hutte!"* as the others did, when her bucket was full, then wait for the person with the cone basket strapped to his back to come down the row so she could empty her bucket into the basket. When the basket was full, it would be carried back to the wagons and dumped into a barrel through a large funnel with a hand grinder, which would break up the grapes, partly crushing them.

It was hard work, but it made the time go quickly, and Rhia was surprised when she discovered that the darkness had thinned to pale lavender, and the hum of the generators that had powered the floodlights was replaced by the chatter and warble of birdsong, and the distant crow of a rooster. She paused to watch, entranced, while the sky became rosy pink, then salmon, then scarlet, and the sun lifted a molten eye above the purple hills and turned them a rich golden brown. The sun's touch felt like a warm hand laid lightly on her shoulders.

She saw that Nikolas, two rows over, had also stopped to watch the sunrise. As if he felt the touch of her eyes, he looked at her and smiled, and she felt a swelling inside, and the in-explicable prickle of tears.

But she refused to let herself ponder the meaning of such unfamiliar feelings, and instead brushed away a runnel of sweat with the back of her hand, pushed her hair impatiently over her shoulder and Nikolas Donovan from her mind and went back to snipping bunches of grapes from vines now sparkling with a diamond dusting of morning dew.

By midmorning, though, she was starving, and her head-ache had returned with a vengeance under the late-summer sun. She could feel it pounding like a hammer and anvil behind her temples as she reached the end of her row and straightened stiffly, rubbing at the small of her back. Her bucket was nearly full—might as well empty it before starting a new row, she thought.

She was looking around for *la hutte* when she spotted Nikolas over by the wagons, leaning against the tailgate, talking with Phillipe and drinking from a bottle of water. And keeping an eye on her, apparently, because when he saw her looking his way he motioned her over. It was her contrary nature that made her defy the happy little lifting sensation inside her chest and first pause to take off and unhurriedly retie her headscarf...take her own water bottle from her belt and drink...rearrange the grapes in her bucket—completely unnecessarily—before joining him. That made her refuse to look at him, lounging there with unconscious elegance in spite of the sweat that made Rhia feel itchy and dirty but only made his dusky skin gleam like polished wood and his black hair curve in wet spikes over his forehead. Made her refuse to admire the way he managed to look regal in spite of the open-neck shirt and jeans he wore, and the red scarf tied rakishly at his throat like a buccaneer's.

As she approached the two men, she saw Nikolas say something to Phillipe, who clapped him on the shoulder, blew Rhia a kiss, then sauntered off. She hesitated, then walked on, knowing the heat in her face and body wasn't all from the warmth of the sun. She was acutely aware of every inch of her body, the way it moved inside her clothes, the chafe of fabric against her sensitive places, because of the way his eyes watched her…eyes full of knowledge, confidence, and promise. *We would be lovers by now…*

"Taking a coffee break?" she said caustically, furious with the way her nipples hardened and rubbed against the lace that covered them, the way her pulses throbbed in all the wrong places. The way her chest hummed at just the sight, the nearness of the man.

"Nope—quitting time." Nikolas took her bucket from her and motioned with his head. "Job's all done."

She saw then that the other pickers were drifting in from the vineyard, laughing, chattering, teasing one another as they passed their laden buckets up to someone on the wagons to be dumped into the grinders mounted on barrels. Phillipe was there in the midst of it all, bantering and exchanging back-slaps with the men, kisses with the women, as they removed hats and scarves, wiped necks and brows, lit cigarettes or drank from water bottles.

"So, what now?" Rhia closed one eye, squinted up at the sun and added hopefully, "Lunch?"

His smile kindled, and she felt herself responding to it even though she very much did not want to. "If you mean like yesterday's bacchanalia, sorry to disappoint you, luv, but no.

No *marc* for you today, I'm afraid. Everybody'll be heading on home, I should imagine. They've chores of their own to take care of, after all. Things to do…"

"So, tomorrow you all move on to another farm, is that the way it works?"

"Not tomorrow, it's Sunday. Nobody picks on Sunday." He made a scolding noise with his tongue. "Shame on you—nice Catholic girl, you should know that."

Rhia gave him a look as she lifted a hand and pulled the scarf from her head, gave it a shake to let what breeze there was move through her sweat-damp hair. She was too hot and tired to banter with him. And hungry. "Right now, all I know is, I need a sandwich and a shower—not necessarily in that order."

"I think I can arrange that." His lashes lowered, his smile grew lazy and his movements unhurried as he casually reached out and fingered a damply curling lock of her hair off her neck and guided it over her shoulder.

Somewhere, far, far away, bees were humming, birds were singing, people were laughing…and Rhia heard none of it. She heard only the pounding of her heart, felt only the sizzle of the sunlight on her cheeks, and the shivery brush of Nikolas's fingers on her neck. She swayed slightly; she couldn't help it.

"Though…I must say, I like you this way—all wet and wild, hot-eyed and dusty. Rather like a gypsy."

He knew he shouldn't do it. Shouldn't touch her, shouldn't tease her—though it amounted to teasing himself more than anything. But he couldn't seem to help it. Somewhere along the line, his wanting had become need, and since he wasn't in the habit of allowing his physical and sexual needs to get in the way of his commitments and responsibilities, he wondered if he was allowing this particular need to blossom on purpose, as a distraction and a buffer from the chaos of his life.

As good an explanation as any, he thought. A tiny ember of alien emotions flared within him—anger, a touch of fear, touches of bitterness and bleak despair—and was quickly smothered. In a day or two he would face whatever the future had in store for him, but for now…for now, by damn, he would allow himself to enjoy whatever pleasures this beautiful, exotic, intriguing creature might offer him. No guilt, no regrets.

He'd devoted his life so far—his youth, certainly—to a cause, denied himself the comfort and fulfillment of relationships, settling instead for the temporary ease of casual affairs, the willing company of the type of woman that seemed to come his way in endless supply. He had no idea what he might be doing a week or a month from now, but for today, and perhaps tomorrow, there was this woman. Rhia. That the most beautiful and fascinating woman he'd ever met should have come into his life at such a time seemed to him more than chance. More, even, than serendipity. It almost…*almost*… made him believe in fate.

Fate. The thought jarred him back to awareness, where he discovered green cat's eyes gazing into his, hazy with confusion, and his hand resting on Rhia's neck, his thumb stroking up and down her sweat-slick throat, and a hot coal of desire in his belly that threatened to set him on fire.

Taking back his hand, he said, "Right, then, let's see what we can do about getting you your heart's desire…" Brisk was what he'd intended, and instead heard his voice emerge thick and furry as woolen mittens. He swiped his hand across the leg of his jeans—as if that could wipe the feel of her skin from his sensory memory—then walked the length of the wagon, checking the load of filled barrels. He paused beside the tractor to give Rhia a come-here gesture with his head and hand. "Here, this rig looks ready to go—come on, up you get."

He watched her eyes get that certain glow and her chin that particular little tilt that he was coming to know very well. It meant her independent nature was about to do battle with her feminine side. He felt a ridiculous surge of purely masculine triumph when she stepped forward and gave him her hand, allowing him to "help" her onto the tractor's high step. And a surge of something much more mysterious, a kind of exotic delight, when she gave him a sideways look as she did so, a look that clearly said, *I'm only doing this to humor your masculine ego, you know.*

She gave her head a toss as she seated herself on the high rear fender. Nik chuckled as he took the driver's seat and started up the tractor. He waved to Phillipe and the other pickers and pulled out of the line and onto the road, smiling to himself, all his senses, his nerves, his whole body sizzling with a particular excitement…alertness…expectancy. He remembered it well, that feeling, though it had been a good long while since he'd experienced it.

The thrill of the chase.

Chapter 6

The shower was primitive by American plumbing standards, obviously a late—though not recent—addition to the old stone farmhouse. It consisted, as so many European showers do, of a handheld device that had a tendency to snake out of control and spray tepid water in unintended directions, usually, Rhia found, when her eyes were tightly shut and her face covered with shampoo. So it wasn't the sensual pleasure of it that made her linger much longer than she should have.

She needed to think. She did some of her best thinking in the shower; something about the gentle drumming on her scalp, the relaxing massage and caress of the water, the shushing sounds that drowned out all distractions. Sometimes she thought it seemed as though the water actually loosened up her mind…washed away clutter…made things clearer. And she desperately needed to think clearly—about many things, but mostly about Nikolas Donovan.

Thoughts of Nikolas were dangerous. Even painful. But

she forced herself to think of him anyway, like pressing on a bruise to assure herself that it really did hurt. The attraction she felt for him that had seemed so entertaining at first—daring…a little wicked, but ultimately harmless—had begun to feel instead like being caught in a flood. The water had risen before she'd realized it, and now she was being swept away by the torrent. Sometimes swimming hard and still fighting it, true. Sometimes, for a moment, giving in and letting the current carry her. Those times, the giving-in times, the letting go of the struggle times, were beginning to feel like such a relief to her, and every second the temptation grew to simply…let go. Stop fighting it. Stop trying to cling to what remained of her sanity and good sense, which were as useless anyway against the rising tide of her feelings as grabbing for twigs in a flood.

She could not fall for Nikolas Donovan. *She could not.* She could see no good outcome for herself if she did.

He wasn't making it easy for her to resist him. Damn him. Of course, he would probably have been irresistible without one particle of effort on his part, but he seemed determined to indulge himself in this lighthearted pursuit of her, as if… as if, she thought, shivering with sudden anger under the shower's cooling spray, it were some sort of *game.*

Though actually, if it were a game she could probably handle that; she'd played them herself, from time to time. Enjoyed them as much as anyone.

But what if it's not a game?

Oh, yeah, admit it, Rhee. That's what's really worrying you, isn't it? That this doesn't feel like a game. Not to you, anyway. Games don't make you feel like you're riding a torrent. Like you're not in control.

Rhia really hated not being in control, which was probably why she'd never allowed herself to fall in love before. But suppose…just suppose…that was what was happening to her now?

The thought caused a swooping sensation in her midsection, which in turn made her drop the shower wand for the sixth or seventh time. She picked it up and aimed the spray full in her face, head bowed, eyes closed and breathing hard through her mouth, and after a moment was able to make herself face the awful possibility that she might be falling in love with Nikolas Donovan.

Falling in love with a prince. The heir to the crown of Silvershire.

Okay. Suppose she was. The way she saw it, there were two possible outcomes.

One, it's just a game to Nikolas, and Rhia completes her mission, delivers him to his father the king and returns to her job with the Lazlo Group with a few bruises on her heart. Not a happy prospect, but she'd survive.

Or two, it's not a game for Nikolas, either. But the prospect of that didn't bear thinking about.

She emerged from the shower physically refreshed and more emotionally exhausted than when she'd stepped into it. She hurriedly toweled her hair and left it to dry in its own way, dressed in the only clean clothes she had in her backpack—khaki walking shorts and a red tank top—and slipped on her dusty running shoes and went to find Nikolas and, she hoped, some food.

She found both waiting for her in the small shaded courtyard off the kitchen. And something else.

"What's this?" she asked, nodding at the bright yellow scooter standing at the ready between Nikolas's outstretched jeans-clad legs.

His eyebrow lifted. "This? Strangely, it's a Honda—evidently, they're quite the thing in Europe these days. Phillipe's, not mine. He's been kind enough to lend it to me, though. Hop on—I want to show you something."

She sauntered toward him, arms folded across her middle, where her stomach had begun to growl uncontrollably. "Is there food in there?" She nodded at the cooler lashed to a small metal ledge on the back of the scooter.

"There is. A repast fit for a—do pardon the expression— king." He held out his hand, waiting with supreme and annoying confidence and a smile tugging irresistibly at his lips.

How *could* she resist? But she did, finger-combing her damp hair back from her face as she replied coolly, "Only if I get to drive."

His smile blossomed and his eyes grew smoky behind sleepy black lashes. Bracing the scooter with his feet, he pushed himself back and up onto the pillion seat and lifted his hands from the handlebars. "She's all yours," he murmured, laughing softly.

"'There was a young lady from Niger…who smiled as she rode with a tiger…'" Rhia muttered under her breath as she settled onto the front part of the seat. A seat which seemed very small, suddenly, altogether too small for two people to sit on at the same time. At least, not without a great deal of body contact.

"What's that?" His voice was a furry growl so close to the nape of her neck that it made shivers cascade in rivers down her back.

"Nothing," she breathed. She tested the reach and the foot pedals, then started up the motor and clicked into gear.

"That's right, you do like to be on top, don't you?" Nikolas murmured in her ear as she guided the scooter skillfully out of the courtyard. "I'll have to keep that in mind."

What had she been thinking? Thoughts that made her scalp sizzle. With him sitting so close behind her, she felt as if she'd been wrapped in a Nikolas-cocoon, steeped in Essence of Donovan. His heartbeat thumped against her back, his body heat melded with hers, his scent filled her head with sultry, sweaty images of tangled bodies…hers and his in wicked disarray….

Her jaws locked and her eyes squinted as she fought to keep her attention focused on the operation of the scooter as it grumbled impatiently through the farmhouse grounds. It whined with excitement as she accelerated down the lane, and came to a purring stop where the dirt lane met the paved road. "Where to?" she asked in a voice that held strange vibrations not caused by the scooter.

"Left," Nikolas said.

"Right," she said, and pushed off, accelerating into the turn. And felt his arms come around her and hold on tight.

"Watch it," she muttered desperately between clenched teeth. "Do you want us to have an accident?"

His laughter rippled down her spine. "My love, it's precisely in anticipation of that possibility that I'm hanging on to you for dear life."

"That had better not be a criticism of my driving, Donovan." With a grim smile she shifted gears and the scooter leaped forward. The wind snatched the breath from her lungs and forced Nikolas to reply in a shout.

"Not at all. I'm more than impressed, actually."

"I had one of these things when I was in high school," she shouted back. "Well, not a Honda—a Vespa, oddly enough. My father bought it for me for my sixteenth birthday. Oh, hell—" She broke off as her rapidly drying hair began to whip in the wind, lashing her neck and, she was sure, Nikolas's face as well.

Good—serves him right, she thought as she slowed the scooter for an approaching crossroads. *Serves him right...for what? Being too damned attractive? You're the one who insisted on driving.*

She let go of one handlebar to try to corral her hair, and felt his hands there already. Felt his hands, both of them, gather her hair and gently twist it...lift it away from her neck.

"Mmm, your hair smells good," he murmured. Something—his lips, his mouth, his breath—brushed her nape.

Her spine contracted involuntarily; shivers shot through her like Fourth of July sparks. And to her embarrassment, the scooter's idling engine chose that moment to sputter and die.

"Dammit, Nik." She'd intended more anger, more force behind it. Why did it have to sound so feeble?

For a long moment, Nikolas didn't reply. Something in her voice… How could he have made this confident, capable woman sound so desperate? So vulnerable? What was driving him, lately, that he kept behaving in ways so out of character for him—or, for the Nikolas Donovan he'd always thought himself to be?

Blame it on my bad angel, I guess.

The thought made him smile. It was what Phillipe's maman had called it, on those rare occasions when he'd gotten into mischief during his stays with Phillipe's family. *You have been listening to your Bad Angel, Nikki. You must not listen to him. Listen only to your Good Angel. He will never make you do things you will later regret.*

He let out a short gust of laughter and lifted his arms away from Rhia, shifted so there was space between his body and hers. As if he'd released a switch of some kind, the scooter's engine immediately snarled to life, and as it shot forward, this time he held on to the scooter instead of its driver.

Listening to his good angel, he managed to maintain the distance and keep his hands away from Rhia for the rest of the trip, leaning close only to make his voice heard as he guided her along the familiar route. Strange, though…the more space he put between his body and hers, the more he felt himself drawn to her, compelled by that same odd magnetism he'd felt first in the kitchen of Phillipe's flat in Paris. An attraction he felt certain even now had very little to do with sex—although it did affect him in some of the same ways….

At Nik's direction, Rhia turned the scooter off the paved road and onto a dirt lane that soon dwindled to a rock-studded track. The track wound downhill through thickets of oak trees and pines and around and between outcroppings of granite boulders through which, now and then, she caught glimpses of a meandering river. Finally, obeying another tap on the shoulder and hand gesture from Nikolas, she pulled the scooter into a little clearing of hard-packed earth and turned off the motor.

Still straddling the bike and trying without much success to finger-comb her hair into order, she said, "What is this, the local make-out spot?" It was very quiet, and in the stillness she could hear no sounds of people or vehicles, only the rush and chatter of the river.

Nikolas, who was unbuckling the cooler from the rear of the scooter, didn't look up but merely smiled. "Patience, luv. You'll see in a minute." He lifted the cooler and beckoned with his head. "Coming?"

She drew a shuddering breath, pocketed the key and followed him. Her shoes crunched over a carpet of oak leaves, acorns and pine needles. The air was warm and smelled of pine and earth and...something else. Something that tugged dusty memories from half-forgotten shelves. *River bottoms... bayous...hot sticky summers.*

She nudged the memories to the back of her mind and kept her eyes on Nikolas as he walked ahead of her down the bumpy but well-trodden path. It gave her such pleasure to watch him. He moved with the effortless grace of a leopard—a black leopard, she thought, as the wisp of a breeze lifted and toyed with his glossy black hair. A strange excitement shimmered all through her, and at the same time there was a heaviness in her heart. Which, she reflected, was the way she always felt now, being around him—or even just thinking about him—this terrible mixture of joy and despair, pleasure and pain. And she thought that if this was what falling in love was like, she was glad she'd managed to avoid it for so long.

Up ahead where the path curved around a pile of boulders, Nikolas had paused to wait for her, smiling with a touch of an odd eagerness and endearing self-consciousness. As she caught up with him he tilted his head toward the vista that had come into view just beyond the rocks.

The question hovering on her lips died there, and she said, "Oh, wow," instead.

Ahead of them the river ran wide and shallow, chuckling over rocky patches and lying quiet and leaf-dappled beneath trailing branches of the weeping willows that lined its banks. It would have been a lovely spot even without the towering structure that spanned the river's width a hundred yards or so upstream—a stone bridge, it appeared to be, consisting of two tiers of magnificent arches.

"It's Roman, of course—not as impressive as the *Pont du Gard*," Nikolas said with a modest shrug as he led the way down to the water's edge. "But also not as well-known, and therefore—" he smiled in a way that made her heart quicken "—less apt to be overrun with tourists."

"It looks as if it enjoys its share of visitors, though," Rhia said, glancing around at the hard-packed pathways and areas worn bare of grass by picnickers. Or lovers?

"Kayakers and fishermen, mostly." He nodded toward a small group of the former farther up the river beyond the bridge's arches, their brightly colored kayaks looking, from that distance, like petals of gaudy tropical flowers strewn on the waters. He glanced at Rhia and his smile tilted. "And lovers, of course."

"And which of those were you?" She asked it lightly, her heart tappity-tapping behind her ribs as she followed Nikolas across boulders and through thickets of trees and shrubs, following a pathway only he could see.

"What's that?" He paused to look back at her. "Oh—you mean, when I've come here before? All of the above, I suppose, over the years. Though more of the first two than the third, I'm afraid," he added wryly.

"Oh, come now."

"Sad, but true. I was a studious lad, you see. No time for

the lassies." He held out his hand to help her down the last treacherous steps, and his grin, as he looked up at her, seemed to belie that claim. It might have been only because she knew from his dossier that the words were in fact true that Rhia was able to find the regret in his cool gray eyes.

Thinking of that Nikolas, the quiet, studious, lonely schoolboy Nikolas, she put her hand in his. The warmth of it seemed to spread all through her body. She felt his hand tighten around hers as she slipped on a gravelly patch and for a second pulled hard against the strength in his taut muscles. Then, as she regained her footing, instead of releasing her he drew her to him in a motion as fluid and easy as a dance movement between longtime partners.

For Rhia, time seemed to stand still in that moment before he kissed her. All her perceptions seemed heightened...honed. She heard music all around her, in the trickle and chatter of the water and in the songs of birds calling to each other in the trees, in the whisper of leaves falling and the hum of insects, and even in the bass growl of a vehicle of some sort passing on a nearby road. She saw sunlight sparkling on wet rocks and the edges of leaves turning gold and a spider's web hanging between two trees, catching the light and shining like spun silk. She felt the warm breeze on her bare arms and legs, her cheeks and hair like a gentle caress...and it all felt to her like summer saying good-bye. The beauty of that moment seemed unbearably sweet to her, achingly sweet, as though she knew it would never come again, not in just this way, and she knew she would leave a piece of herself behind in this moment forever.

She felt the kiss before he kissed her, as if all the nerves and cells in her body were springing eagerly to meet him. And she knew then that she'd been wanting this, needing this, and that it had been inevitable from the moment he'd lunged for her across a Paris balcony and she'd stood unmoving and let him take her down when she could so easily have eluded him.

When his lips met hers she lifted a wondering hand and

touched his face, and the textures—his textures—on her fingertips…the softness of skin contrasted with the roughness
of emerging beard, the delicate play of muscles over the granite hardness of jawbone…the incredible intimacy of that…
made it intensely *real.*

And at the same time it seemed an impossible forbidden
miracle, and the pain of that contradiction made her lips
tremble and tears etch the backs of her eyes.

She felt his hand on her back, firm between her shoulderblades, and another on the nape of her neck, fingers spread
wide to burrow through her sweat-damp hair as he brought
his mouth to hers, took her lips with a tenderness that made
her ache. It was a giving, not a taking kiss, and she held herself still, breath suspended, and let it fill her with all the sweetness and goodness and light and joy she could possibly hold,
until she quivered with the surfeit of those things, utterly
overwhelmed.

He withdrew from her slowly, still holding her, and she let
her head lie in the cradle of his hand as she gazed up at him,
seeing him through a haze of light, like fog lit by sunshine.
He seemed impossibly beautiful to her then. His hard features
had blurred edges and his keen eyes a soft sheen of confusion,
and the lock of hair curving down across his forehead made
him look like a gentle saint.

His forehead creased suddenly with a frown, and he said
in a voice gravelly with awe, "My God, Rhee, I can't believe
how desperately I want to make love to you. It's quite extraordinary. Unprecedented, really."

Thus did Nikolas, feeling himself teetering on the edge
of a vast unknown, manage once again to pull himself back
just in time.

There was a suspenseful moment, though, before she began
to laugh, to his profound relief—and laughed until tears glistened in her eyes like tiny jewels. At least, he hoped they were
laughter's tears….

"Unprecedented?" she sputtered, wiping her eyes. "That's as bad as *Serendipity!*"

"Yes, I suppose it is." He caught a lifting breath and turned her neatly into the curve of one arm while every muscle and nerve in his body cramped in disappointed protest, then picked up the cooler and hiked it under the other arm. "I don't do my best work on an empty stomach, I'm afraid." He let his glance skim over her hair, the glossy strands so close to his cheek he could smell its elusive but familiar fragrance, and added lightly, "The sentiment's dead-on, though." And quickly, before she could respond, took his arm from her shoulders and caught up her hand instead. "Come—let me show you my private rock."

"If that's a variation on 'Come see my etchings,' I'd say you get honorable mention for originality, at least," Rhia muttered drily.

He chuckled, and after a moment began to sing lustily the line of a song that had been taunting him for the past twenty-four hours or so. *"'Come let's be lovers…'"*

"Simon and Garfunkel," he said when she looked at him curiously. "Come, come—you should know them, they're American. Very popular in the sixties—your mum's era, probably."

She was watching her feet, but he caught the wry tilt to her smile anyway. "During the sixties I think my 'mum' was more into John Coltrane and Cannonball Adderly."

"Ah," he said, "of course. Jazz saxophonists, both of them, right?"

"Right." He felt her head turn and her sharp green gaze touch his face. "Is there *anything* that wide-ranging education of yours didn't cover?"

"I doubt it," he said, striving for lightness but somehow unable to keep an edge of bitterness out of his voice.

What *had* it all been for, he wondered, that education of his? Had he been lied to and groomed all his life for…*this?* To become the one thing he despised above all others? *A king?*

What a joke that would be, he thought, if it were true.

They ate sitting on a flat rock that jutted out over the water, in the dappled, constantly moving shade of the giant weeping willows nearby. The meal Nik had prepared for them was simple—crusty bread drizzled with olive oil and sprinkled with garlic and herbs, topped with a delicious mixture of ripe tomatoes, olives, eggplant, anchovies and capers; a variety of goat cheeses, and wine—rosé, of course.

He cut a slice of the bread and showed her the proper way to anoint it with olive oil and toppings, then offered it to her with a reticence that bordered on shyness and seemed to her almost unbearably sweet. This was a new side of Nikolas Donovan, one the Lazlo Group's extensive dossier had evidently overlooked, and she didn't know what to do with the feelings it roused in her. Tender, nurturing feelings, alien to her nature. Or so she had always believed.

Was that why, instead of taking the piece of bread from him, she opened her mouth and let him feed her the first succulent bite, knowing what a seductive and dangerous thing it was? Or was she simply caught in the golden web of that magical afternoon, and unable—or unwilling—to claw her way out?

So she laughed self-consciously when bits of the vegetable topping escaped and fell onto her shirtfront, and the seasoned oil oozed onto her lips and down her chin. And when Nik flicked away the crumbs, she let herself wallow shamelessly in the pleasure of that casual touch. When his finger deftly caught the riverlet of oil, before she even thought about it, she licked it from his fingers.

His touch was like some sort of magic wand that turned her skin to shimmering fire in an instant. Something thumped in the bottom of her stomach, and her eyes opened wide and looked straight into his. And she wondered if the soft haze of confusion she saw there was only a reflection of what he saw in *her* eyes. She licked her lips and waited, tense and heavy with wanting, for him to kiss her again, and was bitterly disappointed when he leaned away from her instead, and picked up the loaf of bread, whittled off a slice and handed it to her with a smile, then cut another for himself.

And so they ate, sitting at angles across from each other, almost but not quite facing, almost but not quite touching, making little in the way of conversation beyond murmurs of pleasure and muttered requests to pass something or other. A pair of doves fluttered down and waddled shyly about on the fringes of the picnic, hoping for handouts which both Rhia and Nikolas readily provided. The sun came and went, burning hot on their faces sometimes, playing peekaboo with the waving branches of the willows on its slow descent into evening.

When she had eaten all she could hold, Rhia brushed off her hands, picked up her wineglass and gave herself up to the sheer pleasure of watching the man beside her…and wondered how and when it had come to this, that just the sight of him could make her ache with that terrible combination of joy and sadness.

He was sitting relaxed now, one leg outstretched, one arm propped on a drawn-up knee, lips curved in a little half smile as he tossed bits of bread crusts to the doves. As if he'd felt her eyes on him, he spoke for the first time in a while. "This was one of my favorite places when I was growing up, I'm sure you've guessed. Still is, I suppose."

"I never would've guessed that," Rhia said drily, not letting him hear a trace of softness in her voice.

He gave a short, gentle laugh that reminded her of the chuckling sound of the river. "I always felt good here, you see—didn't seem to matter what I was doing or who I was with—fishing with Phillipe, canoeing with a bunch of his friends, or…"

"Necking with a girl?"

"Once or twice." He flicked her a glance, then shrugged. "First time I've been here with a woman, though."

"Oh, my," Rhia murmured, "should I be honored?"

"Oh, definitely," he said, and his smile grew in a slow and sensual way. "After all, I've brought you to my special place."

She studied him for a long, simmering moment before asking, with solemn curiosity, "Why did you, Nikolas?"

His forehead crinkled in that puzzled little frown that told her he was about to tease her again, which she was beginning to realize was his way of easing back when things threatened to become too intense.

"I'm not quite sure, actually. I suppose there's something primitive involved—caveman-ish, you know? Some sort of male imperative where I show you, the female of my choice…" he trailed a finger lightly down her bare thigh as his eyes drifted over her face "…that I am capable of providing you with a safe, secure and lovely place in which to consummate—*what?*" She was laughing and shaking her head.

What else could she do?

His eyes slipped downward to study the movement of his finger on her thigh, as if fascinated by the goose bumps its stroking had raised there. When they lifted again to hers there was a softness in them, like the sky before it rains. "We *are* going to be lovers," he said softly. "I know it, and so do you."

She turned her head quickly to hide the tears that had sprung unexpectedly to her eyes. Her throat ached.

"The idea doesn't appear to make you happy. Why is that, Rhee?"

She swallowed…shook her head, tried to laugh. Then, instead of answering him, heard herself say in a husky Cajun accent, "I had a place like this when I was growing up. A place where I always felt good, no matter what I was doing or who I was with."

He didn't speak, and his hand lay quiet on her thigh, waiting…as if he knew there was more to what she was telling him than reminiscence.

Chapter 7

"My cousins—well, they were my mama's cousins, actually—had this place down in the bayous." He wondered if she even realized she'd lapsed into the cadences of her childhood. "We used to go down there and visit, now and again…sit and fish, play music, eat…just generally have fun, you know? We Cajuns are good at havin' fun." She flashed him a smile, and the wave of tenderness that rose inside him when he saw the pain in it stunned him to utter silence.

"It was the nighttime I loved best," she went on after a moment. "When the darkness came down, you couldn't see the squalor, the poverty, all you could see was the moonlight dancin' on the water, and lightnin' bugs twinklin' out in the trees, and the soft yellow light from the porch where the grown-ups were sittin', playin' music. One of the cousins— or maybe his daddy—played the mouth organ—harmonica, you know? Played it so it would just about make you cry without you even knowing you were sad. Mama, she could play just about anything, but she liked alto sax best. And there was always a fiddle and a banjo, and maybe some spoons…I don't know what all else, but together they made a beautiful sound. It just sort of filled in the spaces between the frog and cricket sounds and the slap of the water against the pilings, and the 'gators bellowin' off in the swamps. And the air was so soft and wet it seemed like it got inside your skin…made you feel gentle all over, like nothing could ever rile or upset you and you'd just stay this happy for always and forever."

"But you didn't stay that way, did you?" Nikolas said softly when she paused. "Because your father came and took you away."

Her head jerked around and she stared at him with wide startled eyes. "How did you—"

"You told me—in Phillipe's kitchen, in Paris—remember?" For no other reason except that he desperately needed to touch her, he reached out and with one finger guided a stray lock of her hair away from her cheek and nudged it behind her ear. Her skin felt like warm satin against his fingertip, and he ached to feel its softness on his palms…his lips…with every part of him.

His fingers, trailing wistfully down the side of her neck, snagged on the thin silver chain he'd noticed the day she'd arrived in Phillipe's Paris flat. He hooked it and drew the tiny silver charm from its nest between her breasts. He watched it swing from his extended finger for a moment, then lifted his eyes to hers. "A saxophone," he said softly. "I get it now."

He relinquished the charm as her fingers closed protectively around it. "My mother gave it to me," she said in a thickened voice. "For my twelfth birthday. She told me it was to remind me that no matter what happened, I'd always have music. That was right before my father came for me. That's why—" She stopped, shook her head and looked away.

"I didn't ask you to tell me about that in Paris," Nikolas said, watching his fingers skim lightly over her shoulder. "I barely knew you, then. I thought I hadn't the right. But now that we know we're going to be lovers…" He took his gaze from the place where his finger touched her skin to meet her somber green eyes…and smiled.

Her eyes darkened as he watched. "I'll tell you," she said gravely, not returning his smile, "so maybe you'll understand why that notion doesn't make me happy. But—" her lashes quivered and fell and she caught a quick breath "—it would be a whole lot easier to talk about this if you wouldn't touch me."

He felt a surprising stab of pain, but lightly said, "I'll give it a try." He lifted his hand from her shoulder and stretched out sideways, propped himself on one elbow and gave her a go-ahead nod.

She looked at him warily along her shoulder as she drew up her knees and wrapped her arms around them, and it seemed to him she was building a fortress around herself—a fortress meant for one purpose: to keep him out.

"Mama was working in a jazz joint on Bourbon Street when she met my father—playing music, mostly, but between sets she'd serve drinks…tend bar. My…father—" her mouth and even the tone of her voice changed shape when she said that word "—was in the real estate business—in a big way. Like—think Donald Trump, okay? Only Southern-style—based in Miami. He was in New Orleans for a couple of months getting some new project going, and one night he happened to walk into the place where my mama worked." She paused to give him a sideways look, lifted a shoulder and tried to smile. "I guess he liked her looks and her music—she for sure liked his looks and his money…. Anyway, sparks flew. By the time he was ready to leave New Orleans I was well on the way. He did marry her—I'll give him credit for that. And he took her home with him to Miami. That's where I was born."

She was silent for a while, but he didn't prompt her, just listened to the river sounds and watched the setting sun paint her hair with reddish light. The wistfulness in her face as she gazed into her past made his own throat tighten with a sadness he didn't quite understand. Nostalgia, maybe? Thinking of— and lonesome for—a past he'd never had?

She let go a soft, sighing breath. "She was miserable in Miami—wasn't happy with *him*. No big mystery why—she was warm-hearted and a free spirit, and he was a cold-hearted control freak. Anyway, when I was about two, she took me and ran off—went back home to her folks in New Orleans. Naturally, he followed her, not because he loved her—or me— so much, I'm sure. He's not capable of that. It was because he just couldn't stand that she'd left him. And worse, because she'd taken something that belonged to him, *he* thought. Me."

She lifted her head and shook her hair back and glared at him, and there was an angry fire in her eyes. "He was rich and powerful. In a custody fight you'd think my mama wouldn't have stood a chance, right? But you'd be wrong. She was no dummy, she filed for divorce in Louisiana, and a Louisiana judge—a Cajun judge—gave her full custody of me. My father had to go back to Miami empty-handed, and for ten years, Mama and I were as happy as could be."

She fell silent again, and this time Nikolas didn't wait for her to pick up the thread. He shifted restlessly and sat up. "Ten years…and then he came and got you? What did he do, take your mother back to court? Why did he wait so long to do it?"

In the golden light he could see a bitter little half smile, her only answer—then—to his second question. "Nope, just showed up one day in his Mercedes and took me."

"*Took* you? As in…kidnapped? My God. What did your mother do? Didn't she—"

"Mama wasn't home at the time. I think—" Her voice went high and then broke, startling them both. She waited a moment, fingering the little gold saxophone. "I think she knew he was coming. I think she made sure she wasn't there when he showed up."

Nikolas just stared at her, The question—*Why?*—in his mind so deafening he couldn't even say it.

She stared defiantly back at him and answered it anyway. "Hey, I was twelve. And growing up fast, if you know what I mean." She hunched one shoulder in a shrug that reminded him of a wounded bird. "Maybe she felt like she wouldn't be able to handle me. Maybe she decided she wanted her freedom—who knows? I don't know if she contacted him or he contacted her, but I'm positive they made some kind of deal. Anyway—" her lips spasmed briefly, then firmed "—he came and got me, and I went to live with him in Miami. I wasn't given a choice. End of story."

He cleared his throat and said harshly, "Oh, I seriously doubt that. More like the end of a single chapter, and I can't wait to hear the rest. But I'm already beginning to get the gist, I think. You said you were telling me this now to explain why you aren't happy about the otherwise delightful prospect of making love with me, so I must assume it's because of this complete jackass of a father, right? He's turned you against men, or some such bilge?"

"Not all men," she corrected. "Just…very rich and powerful men."

"Ah," said Nikolas.

"And who is richer and more powerful…"

"…than a king. Yes, I see."

Silence and purple twilight wrapped them in its gentle cocoon.

Hunched and wretched, Rhia watched Nikolas lean away from her to open the cooler. Reaching for the wine, she thought, wishing there was something a good bit stronger in that cooler—Jack Daniel's maybe. But instead he took out a shallow crockery bowl covered in plastic, and then a short fat glass jar containing something thickly liquid and amber in color. In silence, and with almost ceremonial reverence, he uncovered the bowl and opened the jar, then selected a cut section of ripe fig from the bowl and dipped it in the contents of the jar. He turned it to corral the drips, then held it out to her.

"Come 'ere," he said softly when she looked at him askance. "I want you to taste this."

"What is it?"

"Dessert. Open up."

"Oh, Nik. I don't think I can eat another bite…" Not because she was full, but because her throat was so tight, and aching like sin. But she opened her mouth anyway, because when he smiled at her that gentle way, she'd have done anything he asked. She let him place the sticky morsel on her tongue. An incredible sweetness burst inside her mouth, figs and honey flavored with lavender and…orange blossoms. "Oh, my God," she murmured. "It's delicious…heaven." *No—this is sin. Decadent…sensual…*

He was already leaning toward her. He had only to lean a little farther to kiss her, and at first she could hardly distinguish the sweetness of his mouth from the honey already clinging to her lips. Then there was a blending of the two sweetnesses that seemed to turn liquid and run into every part of her, filling her to bursting with a sweetness so intense she couldn't bear it. She felt a building pressure inside her chest, a rising whimper…and just when she thought she wouldn't be able to hold it in another second, he pulled back from her, wiped his essence and the stickiness of honey from her lips with his thumb and murmured, "I'm just a man, Rhee. Not rich, not powerful. I'm a rebel, I suppose. But definitely not a king."

"But," she whispered, "you will be."

"Unless I choose not to be." His eyes were grave and very close to hers.

She stared back at him. Her lips felt chilled and bereft without his, with all the sweetness gone and her stomach doing cold flip-flops under her ribs. At the same time her heart was quivering eagerly, doing happy-puppy dances and crowing, *Yes, oh yes! Choose not to go back! We'll run away to-*

gether—or stay right here in this sunny valley among the vineyards. I will even learn to like wine!

While her head, heavy with the weight of duty and responsibility, sternly chided, *Are you insane? It's your job to take him back. You must take him back. His country needs him.*

Then he kissed her again, and both of those voices went silent, the only sound inside her head now the hushed and daring love words she knew she could never say.

With one hand between her shoulderblades and the other cradling her head, he slowly laid her back. His mouth followed her down, and then his body, as his hands lifted her to meet him, bringing her hard against him, and somewhere amidst the shock waves of pleasure rippling through her came the realization that it was the first time she'd felt the full strength and warmth of his body like this, touching, pressing all along the length of hers, without blankets or layers of clothing between.

The first time? Then why did her skin seem to know his touch already? She felt his hand slip under her top, slide rough and warm over her skin, pushing the soft, giving fabric ahead of it until it found and nested one tight and aching breast. Her breast felt so good in his hand…and so familiar…so right. She let her head drop back, baring her throat to him, offering him that and any other vulnerable part of her he cared to conquer. Complete and unconditional surrender.

Her breast lifted eagerly into his palm, and when she felt his mouth encapsule the tender tip and his tongue begin its exquisite torture, waves of desire all but overwhelmed her. She felt like a fragile shell around a liquid center…her inside sweet and melting, like honey in the sun.

She heard herself whisper—whimper—his name. Her fingers were tangled in his hair.

He took his mouth from her breast, pressed his lips briefly, warmly against hers and whispered back, "I know…I know, luv. But not here."

She was dazed with arousal, shivering with wanting… wanting to do anything to keep from stopping this…sick with knowing it had to stop. "Do you really think," she asked, her voice bumpy from the shivers, "anybody's going to come along?"

"Probably not." Laughing softly, he kissed the tip of her nose, then her chin, then each eyelid. "But I know you like to be on top, and I'd hate to think what this rock would do to my tender bum."

Then she was laughing, too, pushing furiously at him, clinging helplessly to him, tears seeping between her lashes. Wondering how she could still laugh when she was about to charge headlong into sure disaster.

The house was quiet and dark when they returned. Nikolas had expected it would be; Phillipe would be out carousing with his friends on a Saturday night and unlikely to return before morning, celebrating the end of *vendange*. Maman wasn't due back from Monte Carlo until tomorrow.

He dropped Rhia off in the courtyard near the kitchen door, then returned the scooter to the garage. When he came back to the house he found her standing in the hallway, looking uncharacteristically uncertain. She watched him as he came to her, and her eyes followed his as he cupped her cheek in his hand and tenderly asked, "So…is it still yes?"

She smiled then, her lashes dropping across her eyes with what might have been relief, and huskily replied as she swayed into him, "Against every ounce of good sense and judgment…it's still yes. I guess I'm my mother's daughter after all."

A fierce little jet of protective anger spurted through him and hardened his voice. "You may well be, but I'm bloody well sure I'm not like your father."

Her lips parted with an almost inaudible gasp, and he caught whatever response she might have made with his own mouth. He kissed her without restraint, knowing there was no reason now to hold anything back, and found that he was hungrier for her than he'd thought, hungrier than he'd thought he could be. His need for her was a fist in his belly, a burning weight in his loins, and something else the exact location and nature of which were far less easy to define. He knew he'd never felt its like before with any woman. It emptied his head of all coherent thought and filled him instead with feelings too vast and complex to articulate, so that when he lifted his mouth from hers at last he could only gasp and hold her close to him, like a dazed shipwreck survivor finding a raft to cling to.

So it was left to her to mumble, her words a moist warmth on his throat, "My place or yours?"

Cobbling his scrambled wits together, he gave a shaken laugh. "Well, since technically yours belongs to Phillipe's maman, I think I'd prefer mine, if that's all right with you."

She tipped her head back, searching for his mouth, and managed to get as far as, "Fine with—" before he gave her what they both wanted.

He never did know quite how they got from there to his bedroom, or how long the journey took. It might have been seconds or uncounted hours. He remembered shutting the door at last, closing them into the quiet embracing darkness of his bedroom, and after that his only reality was the woman in his arms, the taste of her mouth, the shape of her breasts pillowed against his chest, the firm round weight of her buttocks in his hands…her hands pushing under his shirt, their warm thrusts impatient on his skin…yet no more impatient than he was for her touch.

He'd never felt such a hunger, such impatience before. Lovemaking, liaisons, sex…had always been simple for him. A lighthearted—sometimes intense—experience, no more complicated than the enjoyment of a good meal or a fine wine, indulged in whenever he'd felt the need of relief from the pressures and demands of school, work, *the cause*. One or two had been…memorable; none had ever consumed him. None had ever obliterated thought, overridden judgment. None had made him consider, even for a moment, shirking his duty to his country or abandoning the task he'd set for himself of releasing Silvershire from the burden of medieval monarchy and guiding her kicking and screaming into the twenty-first century.

But he wasn't thinking of any of that now. What was he thinking? He wasn't thinking. He only *wanted…felt…needed.*

With greedy hands he pulled her against him, and was shocked to discover that at some point he—or she—had divested her of her clothes—most of them, all but the thin scrap of nylon that still stood as a barrier to her most vulnerable and guarded places. Her nakedness in his arms was both a delight and a torment, his need to bury himself in her like a vast and terrible thirst.

And yet, though his skin felt feverish and his clothing an intolerable abrasion, though pulses hammered in every part of his body, he felt himself holding back. *Why?*

It stunned him to realize that it was *she* who was the brakes on his runaway passion—her need, her desire, her vulnerability. He understood that he wanted the same things for her that he wanted—needed—for himself, and he wanted to be the one to give them to her. Wanted to watch her face light with joy and her eyes grow hazy with sated passion, her lips curve with a smile of feminine mystery.

This, too, was something new—not that he cared for his partner's pleasure; he'd always made that a priority, and available evidence suggested he'd done it rather well. But this was different—he wasn't sure how, exactly, only that it was.

So he slowed himself down, even though there was urgency in his every heartbeat, and touched her with tenderness, even though his own skin felt on fire. He whispered to her passion words he didn't recognize and wouldn't remember, even though his own need was a screaming pressure behind his eyes. He held her gently from him while her clever hands stripped him naked and then traced patterns across his skin that left him all but blind and quivering like an infant.

It was then that he laid them both down. He ran his hands over her powder-soft skin, dipped them under the lacy edges of the last nylon barrier and pushed it away, and her gasp when his exploring fingers found her warm, protected places made him swell with a fierce masculine triumph, and at the same time, something like…awe.

He regretted, then, that he hadn't turned on the lights so he could see her, too. Regretted, but only a little. His senses were already on overload with the taste, the smell, the feel of her; adding sight to the feast would have been gluttony.

Besides, he already knew she was beautiful—though at the moment, strangely, that didn't seem important to him at all.

Sound, too, was muted, limited to breath sounds and sighs, and those passion-whispers that aren't really words. Both of them were lost in the wonder of discovery like small children on Christmas morning.

The rhythmic push of her body against his hand…the sweet, soft powder-scent of her breast, the bud-like tip blossoming in the warmth of his mouth…her quick lifting breaths, the momentary stopping of them when his fingers found her hidden depths…it all seemed new to him somehow. Her body in his arms, sleek and lithe as an otter's, her hands weaving pleasure-spells over his skin, her lips murmuring love words she probably didn't realize she was saying…it all seemed like a miracle to him, and at the same time as natural as the sounds of the river running along its bed.

It felt natural, too, when passion had obliterated thought, when murmurs had become whimpers of desperate demand, that he should bring her to *him,* drape her over him so that her long, supple body covered his from chest to toes. Natural that her legs should move apart and her knees come up to straddle him, and her hair slip forward and fall around his face and hers like a curtain…natural as the rain falling.

He felt her body shaking as she lifted her head to look down at him in the darkness. "You really did mean it, didn't you?" She leaned down to him again, but it was her forehead that touched his lips and it was then he realized with a surge of dazed delight that she was laughing. Laughing in the broken, breathless way of someone overwhelmed. "About me being on top…"

"Always…" His tongue could barely form words. They were whispers, mere puffs of air. "You have the power…but I think…if you don't plan to let me inside you now…you should just kill me at once…put me out of my misery."

He heard her breath catch…felt her body shift…her hand gently encircle him…the first exquisite giving of her tenderest places. He gasped when he felt resistance. "Rhia—luv—are you—" But she silenced him with a quick, breathless kiss, and slowly, slowly her warm body accepted…adjusted…enfolded…welcomed him.

She drew a shuddering breath and whispered, "Are you still in misery?"

His hands held her hips as he set himself more deeply inside her, and his silent laughter jolted him…and her. "Misery? No…but did you kill me after all? Because I think…this must be Paradise."

Her shaken laughter joined his and then was extinguished in their merging mouths…in hungry, questing, greedy, heedless kisses. His arms encircled her, brought her down to him, held her as close to him as he dared—and then, almost before he knew what she was doing, she was leaning back, bringing him with her so that they were both sitting upright, still holding each other, still together, still entwined. She wrapped her legs around him and he felt himself nested deep inside her, as deep as he could possibly go. And he felt her mouth blossom into a smile.

"Now…neither one of us is on top," she murmured, teasing his moistened lips with the words. "That's the best way, isn't it?"

"The best way possible," he agreed, and bringing one hand up to cradle her head, brought her mouth deeply to his again.

She began to move then, a smooth undulation of spine and muscles, a sensuous rocking that stroked every part of him at once, and he was dizzy with the pleasure of it…lost in desire. He felt his mind leave him, aware only of building pressure, an urgency like nothing he'd ever known before. His hands moved over her back and his body thrust against her rocking, hard…and harder…and her breaths became frantic whimpers. She tore her mouth from his at last and he buried his face in the hollow of her throat and pressed his mouth against the leaping pulse there while her back arched and tightened like a bowstring.

He said something to her…he didn't know what. She gave a little sobbing cry and he felt the tension inside her break and her body ripple with the shock waves, waves that caught him up and carried him with her, helpless as a rag doll in a flood.

When his mind came back to him he was in a quiet, peaceful place, dazed and battered but exhilarated, too.

He lay back slowly, bringing her with him. Her body was still wracked with shivers, so he reached for the edge of the comforter that was folded across the foot of his bed and flipped it over them both, wrapping her in its warmth and his arms. Then he lay silently holding her. Unknown emotions were swelling inside him, making it impossible for him to speak. He wondered about her silence, wondered if it was because she felt the same emotions, and what she would call them if he asked. Knowing he wouldn't ever ask.

Finally, when her body had stopped quaking and the comforter's warmth became too much, he folded a corner of it back and kissed her damp forehead, and she stirred and slipped to one side, leaving her head pillowed on his shoulder, her arm across his torso and one leg companionably tucked between his.

"Sorry, luv," he murmured as he stroked a hand idly up and down her back, "I hate to say it, but…I'm afraid the word that comes to mind, once again, is…unprecedented."

Her body rippled with laughter. "Works for me," she said in a sleepy purr that made him think, for the first time in a while, of a cat.

He woke to find himself alone, the comforter smoothed and tucked against his side where Rhia's body had been. He realized, though, that it wasn't her absence but a sound that had awakened him, a sound that came from somewhere far off, like a cry in the night. That's what he thought it was, at first—someone crying. Then he realized it was music, and he thought it was the most beautiful and at the same time the saddest sound he'd ever heard.

He knew he wasn't dreaming it; certain demands and discomforts of his body left him no doubt that he was fully awake. Throwing back the comforter, he got up and walked naked to the bathroom he shared with Phillipe, noting as he did that Phillipe's bedroom door was still open a few inches, indicating he hadn't, as Nikolas had expected, returned from his evening's celebrations. Nikolas quickly took care of the demands and discomforts, washed himself and put on a bathrobe, then went in search of the music, and Rhia. He was certain he'd find both in the same place, and he did.

She was in the courtyard, sitting on a low semicircular stone wall that skirted the base of a fountain set into the courtyard wall. The fountain wasn't running at that time of night, and the water lay still and dark at her feet, reflecting the moonlight in turgid undulations. She was wearing a light robe that must have been Maman's that hung open to reveal the scrap of lace she called panties and a sleeveless top like the undershirts some men wear. It hugged her breasts and slender torso like skin only slightly paler than her own. Her back was propped against the courtyard wall and her bare legs were drawn up, cross-legged under her. Moonlight lay around her like spilled milk and glinted subtly on the instrument in her hands.

He stood in the kitchen doorway and listened to the saxophone's mournful wail, not wanting to interrupt her, letting himself fill up with a sweet melancholy, the kind only a sad song could make him feel.

He must have made some movement, or maybe she only sensed him there. In any case, she let the music die to a whisper, then lowered the saxophone and sat waiting for him, her head back and resting against the wall.

Unable to read her expression and not knowing why she was out here in the courtyard playing the blues alone in the moonlight, he went to her slowly, hands in the pockets of his bathrobe to keep from reaching for her.

"Regrets, luv?" he asked softly, a sharp little pain lodging near his heart.

She shook her head. Reaching out a hand, she caught the belt tie of his robe and pulled him closer. Then, instead of lifting her face for his kiss, she simply leaned her head against him. Unfathomably moved, he stroked her hair for a moment, then sat behind her on the fountain's base and settled her against him. With his arms wrapped around her and his lips against her hair, he murmured, "Then why the sad song?"

"It's called the blues," she said with a hint of a smile in her voice. "You don't need to be sad to play the blues."

He kissed the top of her head, closed his eyes and inhaled the sweet fragrance of her hair. "But you are, aren't you." It was a statement, not a question.

She let out a breath, and it was a minute or two before she answered, in a voice that was husky and soft. "Yeah, I guess I am. A little."

"Why, luv?"

"I don't know. I think—" He felt her body strain as she hauled in another breath, as if she had vast spaces inside that air couldn't reach. "I came here to bring you back. It's my job to bring you back. You are the crown prince of Silvershire. It's your duty to go back. But…" her voice became a breaking whisper "…dammit, I can't help it. I don't want you to go."

He tightened his arms around her and rested his cheek on her head. "I don't want to go either."

"But you're going to…aren't you." She didn't make it a question.

He let out a breath, and it was a long time before he answered, "Yes, I guess I am. I think…I must."

She turned her face into the hollow of his neck. "Yeah. That's why you're going to make one helluva great king, you know that, don't you?"

He was shocked to feel a warm wetness on her face that could only have been tears.

Chapter 8

The Lazlo Group's sleek black helicopter churned across the waters of the channel on the morning sun's glistening path. Rhia, watching the wakes of ships and the Channel Islands—Alderney, Guernsey, Jersey—drift by below, thought it was like being the lone traveler on a broad superhighway paved in gold.

She tore her gaze from the sparkling vista and glanced again at the man sitting silently beside her, narrowed eyes focused intently on the hazy outline just coming into view on the horizon. A cold little frisson of misery rippled through her. This morning there was no sign of the Nikolas Donovan she'd come to know, the cynical charmer from the Paris apartment, the carefree, flirtatious grape picker—somewhat more earthy than expected. The skillful and incredibly tender lover. This, she thought, must be the man Corbett Lazlo had warned her about, the hard man, the rebel who for years had organized and led a powerful and dedicated opposition to the monarchy in Silvershire. A man both respected and feared.

The man who'd made love to her, made her feel things she'd never felt before, the man who'd made her laugh...and cry, was a stranger to her now.

She was glad the clatter of the chopper's rotors and the headphones they both wore made conversation difficult, if not impossible. What would they have talked about? Impersonal things, probably, fit for the ears of the chopper pilot—an unnecessary recap of plans for the coming reunion with Nikolas's father, King Weston, perhaps. It was to be a private meeting, held in strictest secrecy, not at the royal palace in Silverton, or even at the official royal retreat in Carringtonshire, but at a little-known hunting lodge in the Lodan Mountains in the province of Chamberlain, the king's ancestral home. Those present at the historic meeting would include King Weston, Nikolas, Rhia and a few trusted members of the king's security staff. Those were the terms both the king and Nikolas had agreed upon. The details had been left to Rhia and other representatives of the Lazlo Group to work out.

And after the reunion...what then? Rhia's job would be done, another difficult assignment successfully completed. And Nikolas...what would become of him?

Bleakly, she watched a muscle work in the side of his jaw, his steely gray eyes fixed on the approaching coastline. Would he accept the charge that had been taken from him at birth and assume the crown he'd always despised? Become king...and thus forever beyond her reach? Would she ever again feel his hands on her body, taste his mouth, smell his skin?

Pain knifed through her and she drew a sharp, gasping breath, just as the chopper swept over the lacy edge where the lapping Channel waves met the rocky shores of Silvershire.

The helicopter's route brought them into Silvershire's airspace just north of the town of Dunford, in Danebyshire. As they crossed the gleaming ribbon of the Dane River, Nikolas nudged Rhia with his elbow and pointed; she nodded in reply. It was an acknowledgment, nothing more. He knew it wasn't necessary for him to tell her Dunford was where he'd lived and worked for the past five years, teaching history at Dunford College of Liberal and Fine Arts. She would have learned that fact, and just about everything else there was to know about his life, from the Lazlo Group's dossier. Though right now, looking down at the slate roofs and church spires of the town and the campus, he felt as disconnected from that life in spirit as in body.

That was his past. No matter what happened at the coming meeting, he had to accept that he could never go back to the way things had been.

Though he stared out his side of the chopper, watching its shadow flit across the forested landscape below, he was intensely aware of the woman sitting beside him. She was dressed once again in the black pants and leather jacket she'd worn for breaking and entering Phillipe's flat in Paris, though the chemise had been replaced by a black pullover embroidered just above her left breast with the green-and-gold plaited pentagram that was the Lazlo Group's logo.

Rather ironic, he thought, that she should be the one bright spot for him in all of this, when she was the one who'd yanked him out of his former life and pitched him kicking and screaming into this new one he'd never dreamed of nor wanted. In any case it would have been idiotic to blame her for it, and he didn't. She'd only been doing her job. And as for what had happened between them, he acknowledged that was more his doing than hers, and furthermore, in his selfishness he'd caused her some degree of pain.

Still, he couldn't bring himself to regret what had happened…making love with her. Or to contemplate the possibility that it might never happen again.

To block that thought, he turned his mind instead to the coming meeting. Another irony, that was. He'd tried so many times, as head of the Union for Democracy, to arrange a meeting with His Majesty, to discuss his plan for phasing out the centuries-old and outdated monarchy and ushering in a form of democratic government based—in his opinion quite reasonably—on that of their neighbor, Great Britain's responsible monarchy. In the past, he'd never gotten past Weston's advisors—not hard to understand their diligence, perhaps, since most of their jobs no doubt depended on keeping the status quo. And now…here he was, on his way to a private, one-on-one meeting with the king at his secret mountain hideaway. But not to discuss politics.

What, he wondered, as his heart lurched and a pulse began tap-tap-tapping in his belly, does a man say to a long-lost father who is not only his sworn adversary, but his king?

The chopper churned on across the Dunford Wood, the province of Perthegon, and crossed the Kairn River into Chamberlain. *My father's lands. I suppose that makes them my lands, too?*

His mouth curved in a sardonic little smile as the chopper banked sharply south over the Lodan Mountains.

The helicopter settled onto the grassy clearing, a little meadow surrounded by pine trees not far from the lodge. As the rotors slowed to a lazy swishing, Nikolas opened the door and stepped down onto the yellowing grass. He paused to wait for Rhia to do the same, and then they both hurried at a half crouch through the turbulence to meet their welcoming committee.

Three people had emerged from the woods on the edge of the clearing. Two were men, obviously security guards, resplendent in the king's livery and looking gloriously out of place in that rustic setting. The third person, Rhia was startled to see, was a woman, casually dressed in slacks and a windbreaker. Her auburn hair was pulled back in a ponytail, and it was a moment before Rhia recognized the king's personal physician, Dr. Zara Smith—or was it Shaw, now? she wondered. Lady Zara had recently become the wife of Dr. Walker Shaw, the Lazlo Group's chief psychologist and an old friend of Rhia's.

While the two guards stood stiffly at attention, Lady Zara, whom Rhia had met only briefly at her wedding reception, greeted her with a smile and a brisk handshake. "Hello, Rhia, it's good to see you again."

"Likewise, Lady Zara," Rhia said, returning the smile. "Good to see you looking so great. Married life must be good for you."

"Walker is good for me," Lady Zara replied, with the soft eyes and satisfied smile of a woman deeply in love, and Rhia couldn't help feeling a small, treacherous stab of envy.

"I'm surprised to see you here," she said. "I thought you were still on your honeymoon."

Lady Zara's forehead creased momentarily with a tiny frown. "Lord Southgate suggested I be here for the meeting," she said in an undertone. "He is…concerned. But it was His Majesty who insisted on it."

She turned curious, champagne-colored eyes on Nikolas and offered him her hand. "Mr. Donovan, I must tell you that I have strongly advised against this meeting."

"I imagine you have," Nikolas said drily as he shook her hand. "You, and I'm sure many others as well, considering I'm suspected of murder for hire—among other things."

"That's for others to determine," Lady Zara said without smiling. "My concerns are for His Majesty's health. The king is still recovering from his recent illness, as you know. He is still not entirely himself, which is to be expected given the series of shocks he's had to deal with. His son—ah, Reginald's death, then surgery for a brain tumor, and the hospital bombing and his subsequent coma on top of it. The news that Reginald wasn't the king and queen's biological son, and the fact that he was murdered…and now…" she shook her head "…learning his biological son and the true heir to his crown is none other than the man who's been trying to take it from him—" She broke off, realizing, perhaps, that she'd been a bit too frank.

Nikolas said with a touch of impatience, "Of course. I'll try not to say or do anything that might upset His Majesty."

Rhia winced at the note of sarcasm, but the doctor only said mildly, "Your presence alone will upset him quite enough, I expect. If you will come this way, please. He's been waiting for you—somewhat on edge, as you can imagine."

She turned and led the way to a broad pathway that wound through the pine forest. One of the guards fell in behind them while the other took up a sentry's position at the edge of the meadow—to keep an eye on the helicopter and its pilot, Rhia guessed. She turned once to look back at the chopper, sitting motionless now, like a great black insect, the pilot leaning relaxed against the Lazlo Group logo on its door.

The path beneath her feet was spongy with pine needles, the air pungent with the scent of the pines and the dusty earth. She breathed deeply as she walked, filling her lungs with that warm dry air, hoping it might help to quell the butterflies rampaging through her middle. Wondering whether Nikolas had butterflies, too.

If he does, no one would ever know it, she thought, stealing glances at him as they made their way along the pine-carpeted path. His eyes were cool as rain, his face might have been chiseled from the earth itself. There was only the tiny muscle working in the side of his jaw to tell her of the turmoil inside.

Oh, yeah. He definitely has butterflies.

Was this what Nikolas would call empathy, she wondered? Or was it only her newborn feelings for him that made her feel his turmoil too, and ache to take his hand?

The mountain setting was idyllic and beautiful, no doubt a perfect place for healing both body and soul, if Nikolas had taken notice of it. But he had gone far away for the moment, retreating inside the chilly isolation of his analytical mind. It was where he often took refuge from the chaos of his emotions or circumstances beyond his control. The meeting ahead, the current upheaval in Silvershire, the unanswered questions, even his new and unsettling feelings for the woman walking silently beside him, all these things were manageable, he believed, if he could simply reduce them to problems to be solved.

Focus, he ordered himself sternly, as his mind whirred dizzily through a blizzard of thoughts, unable to see any of them clearly. *One thing at a time. First things first.*

Get through this meeting first. After that…who knows where I'll be? In prison, maybe.

You will naturally conduct yourself with dignity, he told himself.

Yes, he would be courteous. But not cordial. Weston was the sovereign ruler of his country and as such, deserving of respect, no matter how Nikolas might feel about the monarchy itself.

But no amount of DNA will ever make the man my father.

And, he reminded himself, Weston no doubt had the same reservations about him. After all, the man had raised that twit Reginald as his son and heir for thirty years, and undoubtedly felt a father's love for the blighter in spite of his rather considerable shortcomings. That sort of feeling didn't disappear because of a few mismatching strands of double helixes.

Nikolas told himself he wouldn't expect a thing from this one-on-one meeting with His Majesty, except maybe a chance to begin to clear his name of those insane suspicions of murder and mayhem. No, all that would happen today was that he and Weston would take each other's measure, ask and answer whatever questions might occur to them, and that would be that.

He just wished he could do something about the bloody butterfly convention taking place in his stomach.

He stole a glance at the woman beside him, sleek and lithe in her uniform black, silent and intent as a hunting cat, green eyes focused on their guide up ahead as if she were some fascinating species of mouse. He wondered what she was thinking—feeling—right now, and whether she had butterflies, too.

He wished he could reach over and take her hand.

* * *

The Weston family's so-called hunting lodge was in fact a sizeable manor house built in the Georgian style out of natural stone. It was only two stories in height, with leaded windows, a slate-tile roof and towering chimneys, a large one at either end and several smaller ones scattered between. Rhia, who'd been picturing something more on the order of a log cabin, or maybe a Swiss-style chalet, thought that if this was what royals called a modest hunting lodge, she couldn't wait to see the palace.

The house seemed oddly out-of-place here, tucked among the towering pines. Such an imposing house, Rhia thought, deserved a proper setting, with sweeping lawns and curving driveways and magnificent formal gardens. Here, it reminded her of Sleeping Beauty's castle under the spell of the evil fairy, left at the mercy of creeping vines and rampant vegetation…neglected, abandoned, forgotten.

However, any signs of neglect—real or imagined—ended at the mansion's front door. Their approach had evidently been observed, because as they mounted the wide stone steps, the massive double doors were opened and held for them by two more of the security guards in full dress uniforms. Lady Zara, being accustomed to the trappings of wealth and position, swept through the doorway without a glance or a pause; Rhia and Nikolas followed, with their escort bringing up the rear.

The doors swung shut behind them with a quiet thump, and they found themselves in a great hall with a high vaulted ceiling, paneled in gleaming wood and lit by the soft glow of lamps tucked in alcoves along the walls and recessed high up near the ceiling. The atmosphere was peaceful, filled with the scent of wood polish and pine and an indefinable aura of elegance.

They were given no time to admire the portraits, tapestries and carved-wood panels along the walls, however. Their escort led them on at a brisk pace, her footsteps tapping on the parquet floor and instantly swallowed up in the vastness of the hall. Around them the house seemed deserted, and eerily still.

Lady Zara paused in front of a door near the far end of the hall. With her hand on the doorknob, she looked over her shoulder at Nikolas. He nodded almost imperceptibly, and she lifted one hand to knock while opening the door with the other. "Your Majesty," she said quietly, "Mr. Donovan is here."

She stood aside, then, and gestured for Nikolas and Rhia to enter ahead of her.

Neither the room nor its sole occupant were what Rhia had expected.

The king had elected to meet his son in what was obviously a private retreat, with none of the trappings or ceremony of royalty. The room was informal, even cluttered. The walls were lined with cabinets—cupboards below, and above them shelves filled with books that had obviously been read, not selected for the elegance of their bindings. The chairs arranged in casual groupings looked comfortable, even a little shabby, and there were reading lamps conveniently situated beside each one. There was a large cluttered desk, a comfortable couch, several small tables and ottomans, and in one corner, incongruously, a stationary exercise bicycle in gleaming chrome. There was a fireplace—unlit—and flanking it, twin French doors that stood open in invitation to the pine-scented breeze.

In front of the doors and the fireplace, with his hands resting on the back of a large leather chair, a tall but frail-looking man stood waiting.

She'd been prepared, but even so the king's appearance shocked her. In tapes she'd seen of his last public appearances before Reginald's death and his own surgery and subsequent collapse, Henry Weston had been a robust and vigorous man, much younger-looking than his age, which she seemed to recall was somewhere in his late sixties, with strong, handsome features, silver hair and fierce dark eyes, and the same regal bearing she'd seen in Nikolas. Now, his face was much thinner, those still-magnificent eyes were sunk deep in shadowed sockets. Although he was plainly making an effort to stand erect, he appeared to have aged a decade in less than six months.

Lady Zara closed the door, then hurried to her patient's side. "Your Majesty, please. You must—"

But the king waved her aside with a regal gesture and came around the chair, leaving one hand on its back for support. Rhia found herself stepping quietly aside and leaving Nikolas to go forward and face his father alone.

For a long moment there was absolute silence in the room, while the two men took each other's measure. Then His Majesty, King Weston of Silvershire, spoke in a soft and rasping voice:

"By God, it's true. You have your mother's eyes."

Looking back on it later, Nikolas was able to recall very little of what was said in those first moments. He felt…not so much numb as insulated. As if his mind and emotions had been carefully packed in cotton wool. He remembered being shocked, on some level that didn't involve his emotions, at the king's appearance; even knowing of Weston's illness, he hadn't been prepared to see the powerful monarch he'd considered his adversary looking frail and old.

He remembered hearing the words, …*your mother's eyes*… and seeing Weston's mouth spasm with emotion and the sudden glaze of moisture in the fierce dark eyes. He remembered hearing Rhia's soft intake of breath, as if she'd felt a stab of unexpected pain. But he himself felt no reaction whatsoever. Weston might have been referring to someone Nikolas didn't even know.

There must have been awkward moments—there was no rush of prodigal son to his father's welcoming arms, for one, and…did one offer to shake hands with a king? But if there were, he was immune to self-consciousness. He did recall introducing Rhia, and requesting that she be allowed to stay, and being formally introduced in turn to the Lady Zara. He remembered Weston seating himself, at his physician's urging, and he and Rhia being invited to do the same. He even allowed himself to acknowledge the pride and strength of will that had compelled the man, in spite of his obvious physical weakness, to insist on standing to greet this long-lost son who was also, possibly, his enemy. But he didn't allow any of it to touch his emotions.

Not then.

"I know how difficult this all must be for you—as it is for me," King Weston said when they were seated and Lady Zara had left to arrange for tea. He lifted a hand, and only the slightest tremor betrayed the emotional and physical strain Rhia knew he must be under. "I am aware of your…political position, you know—and of your…activities during the past decade." He lowered his head and aimed a scowl of mock sternness at Nikolas. "They tell me you want to do away with my crown, Mr. Donovan." And then, to Rhia's amusement and delight, the king arched an eyebrow. *One only.* "How ironic it must be to find now that you are destined to wear that crown yourself, one day." His lips twitched, and there was a gleam of humor in his eyes.

"Ironic…yes, I suppose it is," Nikolas replied coolly, and Rhia marveled again at his calm, his iron self-control. "Whether or not that is my destiny is another matter."

King Weston merely chuckled. He regarded Nikolas intently for a moment. "I didn't want to believe it myself, you know, when they told me. I know, I know—" he waved a hand impatiently "—DNA doesn't lie. However, I had to see for myself. I felt—I believed, you see, that I would know my own son even if I had never set eyes on him before. And I was right…I was right." His face seemed to spasm, then stiffen with its effort to contain what must have been overwhelming emotions. He coughed, then added gruffly, "You *are* the image of your mother, you see."

Nikolas didn't reply. He sat in utter silence, and only Rhia could see the tiny muscle working in the side of his jaw.

King Weston placed his hands on the arms of his chair and pushed himself to his feet. Both Nikolas and Rhia rose immediately, as royal protocol demanded, but the king waved Rhia back to her seat. "No, no, my dear, don't get up. Nikolas, my boy, walk with me for a moment, if you will—while my doctor isn't here to forbid it." He added the last with a sly smile and arched eyebrow for Rhia, as he held out his hand to his son.

After a moment's hesitation and a quick, questioning glance at Rhia, Nikolas offered his father his arm. As the two men moved slowly to the open French doors, Rhia could see that the king was making an effort to walk erect, leaning only slightly on that support.

Watching them, she felt some unknown emotion ripple through her and emerge in a silent, quivering laugh. *My God,* she thought, *how alike they are: proud, iron-willed, both of them...born to be kings.*

As he and Weston stepped through the French doors onto a small terrace of shade-dappled slate, Nikolas could feel his protective cloak wearing thin. It was one thing to keep a man at arm's length in the abstract, or while listening to his voice and watching his face from half a room away. It was quite another when the man's hand was resting on one's arm and one knew that the warm blood pumping beneath the thin, age-spotted skin was the same blood that ran through one's own veins.

The whole insane thing was in danger of becoming real to him. He wasn't at all certain he was ready for that.

Beyond the terrace, a path thick with bark mulch and pine needles wound through a garden of perennials and shrubs in an autumn state of blowsy disarray, rose hips and berries of various shades clinging to sparsely-leafed branches, a few sturdy asters and chrysanthemums still blooming among the browning stalks of last summer's lilies. They strolled slowly along the meandering path, the king evidently in no hurry to disclose his purpose in requesting this moment of privacy, Nikolas mentally bracing for whatever might come.

Weston paused finally, plucked an autumn rose from an overgrown bush and tucked it almost absentmindedly in the breast pocket of his jacket. "First, I must tell you," he said, in a voice that seemed to have regained much of its power and authority, "that most of my advisors were strongly opposed to my meeting you alone like this." He gave Nikolas a glance along his shoulder, one eyebrow arched. "Seemed to think I might be in some danger."

Nikolas, distracted by the eyebrow—*So that's what she was talking about. Strange, I don't seem to find it quite as annoying as she did*—frowned and muttered, "I can imagine." He drew a quick breath and pulled himself back to the moment. "I hope you don't believe me capable of murder, as so many others seem ready to do," he said, narrowing his eyes.

"Carrington—Lord Southgate—seems to think you are a man of principle and honor. He trusts you, and I trust him. Which is why…" Weston paused and turned to face Nikolas, meeting his eyes with his intent black stare. "Why I must ask a favor of you, Mr. Donovan—one I suspect you will not be happy to grant me."

Startled and a bit wary, Nikolas began a murmured protest. Weston lifted a hand to silence him.

"I want you to know…Nikolas…that I've learned a great deal about you since this whole incredible affair was revealed to me. By all accounts, Carrington's evaluation of your character is on the mark." His frown turned fierce, his voice gruff. "In fact, my boy, I think you are everything a man might wish for in a son, and I will be proud to call you that one day, when we've both had some time to get used to the idea. I suspect your mother would have been proud as well." He paused to clear his throat loudly, while Nikolas squinted intently into the woods and swallowed hard several times.

"However," Weston went on after a moment, with a quiver of anger in his voice, "in spite of his shortcomings, I raised and loved Reginald as my son for thirty years. Nothing he did could have changed that—as I hope you will find out for yourself one day, a father's love is unconditional. But…blood will tell, evidently. And it did concern me, as the time approached for him to assume my crown, that he hadn't matured and, er…hmm… settled down to the degree I had hoped he would. Nevertheless, I believed…" He shook that off, and when he turned once again to face Nikolas, his face had hardened.

"Someone murdered him, Nikolas. Someone did this—to him, to you, to me. Someone has plotted against me for more than thirty years. Thirty years ago, someone took you from me and put that poor boy in your place, a child ill-equipped for the life he'd been thrust into, thus dooming him to failure, to a lifetime of expectations he wasn't equipped to meet, and, ultimately, to a terrible and much too early death. Someone robbed him of his life, me of my true son, and you of your father. Your mother, the queen, God rest her—" He broke off, shaking his head.

He took the rose from his pocket and regarded it for a moment with such unfathomable sadness that Nikolas felt his own throat tighten. Then Weston crushed the petals in his fingers and placed his closed fist on Nikolas's arm. When he spoke again his voice was strong and vibrant, like that of an orator. "This is the favor I ask. I ask it of you as my son, as my heir, as the future king. Find the person or persons responsible for these heinous acts. Find out who has done these things to you, to me, to Reginald…to Lady Zara—yes, she was nearly killed, as well, you know. I want the wretch found and brought to justice. I want this…this cloud that has hung over Silvershire since Reginald's death lifted. Will you do this for me, Nikolas…my son?"

Chapter 9

*M*y son.

Nikolas was surprised by a contrary surge of resentment—contrary, because he knew hearing the words should be a cause for joy, not anger. And he did feel anger, though not with Weston, not even for such a blatant assault on his emotions—perhaps even deliberate manipulation. He was angry with himself for the way his heart kicked when those two words replayed in his mind. For the way they'd arrowed right through his protective shields and found the hidden desires of his soul.

"I'll be happy to do as you ask, sire," he said evenly. "Or at least try. Not, however, as your heir, and definitely not as 'future king.' Understand this—I don't want anything from you, least of all your crown."

Weston inclined his head slightly. His eyes were shielded, but his lips had twitched into what wasn't *quite* a smile. "I must accept that, I suppose—for now. Why, then?"

"Because I was planning to do so anyway, for one thing. And then—" he smiled sardonically, making a valiant effort to keep his eyebrows level as he made a little mocking bow "—there is the small fact that you are my king, and as such, your wish is my command."

Weston's features spasmed briefly, as if he'd felt a twinge of annoyance, or maybe pain. He made a dismissive gesture with his hand and said gruffly, "When I give you a command, Nikolas, you will know it. However…" He drew a breath and straightened his spine. "Whatever your reasons for accepting this charge, I thank you for it. And now, there is something I would like—" He turned as if to retrace their steps, then halted when he saw Nikolas had remained in place, feet firmly planted in the thick layer of garden mulch. "Yes? Is there something more you wish to discuss?"

"Two things," Nikolas said bluntly, folding his arms on his chest. "First, I'd like to have Rhia—uh, Agent de Hayes—the woman who came with me today—working with me on this. And second…" He hitched in a breath. "I'd like to see the evidence—the 'proof'—whatever it is that makes you so certain all this is true—that I am, in fact, this missing heir."

Weston's eyebrow shot up. "Proof—other than your appearance, you mean?" His smile tilted, and his strong bony hand closed on Nikolas's elbow. "That 'proof' is what I am about to show you. Come.

"Of course," he added grandly as they strolled back through the overgrown garden, "you may have whoever and whatever you need to assist you in solving this mystery of ours—the resources of my kingdom are at your disposal."

They walked on, footsteps crunching on garden debris and pine straw, releasing earthy scents into the warm autumn air. "This agent of Corbett Lazlo's…de Hayes. She seems like a capable young woman. A competent agent, I assume?"

Nikolas kept his expression and tone neutral. "More than competent."

"Yes, yes…I suppose she must be, if Lazlo chose her to find and bring you back." Nikolas didn't reply. Their footsteps crunched slowly on, keeping step. Weston threw him a sideways glance, and his tone became…could it be *sly?* "She is also, I observe, an extraordinarily attractive young woman."

Nikolas opened his mouth, then closed it again. He was almost certain, above the crackle and scuffle of footfalls, that he heard King Weston chuckle.

"Don't you wish you were a little bee out there in that garden right now?"

Despite its softness, Lady Zara's voice startled Rhia. She was standing beside the open French door, so intent on watching the two men outside that she hadn't realized anyone was behind her. She gave a little spurt of laughter and placed a hand over her quickened heartbeat. "Oh—I didn't hear you come in. Sorry."

"That's okay—I can see you have…someone else on your mind." Zara's smile and sympathetic eyes left no doubt as to her meaning.

Rhia closed her eyes and sagged against the draperies. "God…is it that obvious?"

Lady Zara laughed. "I'm a newlywed, remember? I know how it feels—and what it looks like, too. I get to see it every day in my husband's eyes."

"Great," Rhia muttered on an exhalation. "That's all I need." Her eyes returned to the two figures in the garden as if pulled by forces beyond her control. "I can't let him know," she added bleakly.

"He doesn't feel the same way?" Lady Zara's voice was half-curious, half-sympathetic.

Rhia gave her head an impatient shake. "It's not that—well, actually, to tell you the truth, I don't really know whether he does or not. But…it wouldn't matter if he did. In fact, I think that would make it worse."

Lady Zara's forehead creased in a physician's concerned frown. "I can't imagine why."

The ache in Rhia's throat kept her silent for a moment. Down at the far end of the garden, Nikolas and the king were facing each other, deep in what was obviously a tense, even passionate conversation. "Look at them," she said at last, and left it there as that were explanation enough.

Following her gaze, Lady Zara nodded. "They *are* very much alike, aren't they? Anyone seeing them together like this would know them for father and son, without a doubt."

The ache spread into Rhia's chest. "He's born to be king—will be, one day," she whispered, then laughed and said flatly, "And I for sure am not ever going to be anyone's queen."

Lady Zara's mouth opened—in surprise, perhaps—then closed and curved into a knowing smile. "Oh, Rhia. Never say never. If there's anything I've learned from all that's happened in the past few months, it's that *anything* is possible. Anything. Trust me on this."

Rhia didn't bother to argue, or to explain to Lady Zara, daughter of a duke, whose husband had just been made a baron, that it was *she,* Rhia de Hayes, daughter of a blues musician who'd grown up barefooted in a Louisiana trailer park, who wanted no part of royalty. Instead she remained silent, her gaze focused once more on the two men in the garden. They had turned and started back toward the house, now walking side by side like old friends out for a Sunday stroll.

Lady Zara, watching them, too, spoke softly. "What *does* a man say to a son who was stolen from him, after thirty long years?"

Rhia touched away a single silent tear. "Or a son to a father he's been taught to despise?"

The other woman placed a gentle hand on her arm. "They'll be back here in a minute, but…a word of advice—from one who's been there? The man himself will probably be too dense to notice—it's everyone else you have to worry about."

She tapped the pocket of Rhia's jacket and smiled. "With those eyes…I suggest you wear your sunglasses, darling—at all times."

Rhia and Dr. Smith appeared to be comfortably settled in a pair of matching tapestry armchairs when Nikolas and the king reentered Weston's study. The women were drinking tea—and they might present the very picture of genteel ladies, Nikolas thought in some amusement, were it not for Rhia's sleek black leather, and the fact that he recalled her saying once that she didn't care much for tea. When his eyes had adjusted to the indoor light, though, he could see they were both smiling, and that their eyes were bright with laughter, and he felt a momentary twinge of envy for that lightness of spirit.

Both women instantly put down their teacups and popped to their feet when the king entered the room, but as before, Weston gestured impatiently for them to be seated. He touched Nikolas's arm. "Mr. Donovan, if you would please…open that door over there and ask the gentleman standing outside to bring in the chest—he'll know what I mean. Then come have some tea—Zara, my dear, if you would pour, please…"

While Nikolas went to comply with his king's request, Weston lowered himself heavily into the big leather armchair, then immediately leaned forward to accept a steaming cup from the doctor's steady hand. "Ah, yes…thank you, my dear. And do stay," he added, when she stood up and turned as if to leave the room. "You are the one who found it, after all. I'm sure Nikolas will have questions."

Weston waited while Nikolas returned and took his seat in the chair he indicated—a twin to his own brown leather, set beside and at a slight angle to it. Then he took a sip of tea and grimaced at the heat, placed the cup and its saucer on the table beside his chair and turned his keen black eyes on Rhia. "Miss de Hayes, I must ask you to forgive me."

Nikolas saw her give a small start, like a wool-gathering

student called upon unexpectedly by the teacher. She hastily lowered her teacup and produced a hoarse, "Your Majesty?"

Weston smiled, although his eyes remained intent. "I haven't thanked you for finding my son and bringing him back to me— although thanks alone don't seem adequate for what you've given me. If there is anything I can offer you in return…"

Rhia's cheeks turned dusky pink beneath her tan. She muttered, "Oh—no—sire…I was just doing my job." Then she reached to put her cup and saucer on the table and added in a dry tone more like her own, "And I didn't 'bring' him." Her eyes flicked toward Nikolas but didn't quite make it all the way. "Nikolas—Mr. Donovan agreed to come. Entirely on his own."

"Yes, yes, I'm sure he did." Weston sounded amused, and with the chuckle he'd heard in the garden still fresh in his mind, Nikolas felt an inclination to squirm. "Nevertheless," Weston went on "I am grateful to you for whatever part you may have played in influencing his decision—which," he added, with a glance at Nikolas, "if my son is anywhere near as headstrong as I think he is, I imagine was considerable." He inclined his head in a gesture of honor. "Thank you, my dear, from the bottom of this father's heart."

During an awkward pause filled with throat clearings and rustlings and birdsong from the garden outside, Nikolas became conscious of an odd stiffness in his jaws, and at the same time a restlessness…an edgy sense of isolation…an unaccustomed need to make contact, to touch or lock eyes with another human being.

With one specific human being. Rhia.

But she was too far away to touch and seemed to be avoiding his gaze, and it came to him that the cramping in his jaws was tension, and that its source was the frustration he felt at being denied what he wanted. Needed.

I need her.

The thought was so new to him, so shocking, he was barely aware of the knock on the door…of the door opening to admit one of the uniformed guards—rather incongruously wearing latex gloves—carrying a medium-sized wooden chest. Still half dazed, he watched the guard march across the room and place the chest on the oriental rug between Weston's feet and Nikolas's. The guard then saluted, did a crisp about-face, and left the room.

As he blinked the chest into clearer focus, Nikolas felt a strange prickling in his scalp. Then a chill flooded him from head to toe, and the room and everyone in it receded, leaving him alone in a whirling vortex. Memories came at him like flying debris, and voices from his past filled his head, blocking thought:

Nikolas, it's past your bedtime. Put your toys away this minute.

Do I have to, Uncle?

Nikolas, are you still reading, boy? Put that book away and lights out. Tomorrow's a school day.

Yes, Uncle.

Nikolas, how do you think you'll do at Eton if you persist in playing games instead of studying?

I'm putting it away now, Uncle.

He became conscious of a choking sensation in his throat, and his lips moved as he silently said the only clear thought in his mind: *Impossible.*

It was very quiet in the room as King Weston took a key from his jacket pocket and inserted it into what appeared to be a new and very efficient lock. Everyone's eyes were focused intently on the chest—everyone's eyes but Rhia's.

At that moment hers were on Nikolas, which was why she was probably the only one in the room who saw his face drain of all color, his body jerk almost imperceptibly before going still as stone. She was the only one aware that the knuckles of the hands gripping the arms of his chair were bone-white… and that the eyes staring into the chest had gone glassy with shock.

In her concern, she almost…*almost* spoke to him, said his

name aloud. Instead, with her pulses pounding in her ears, she swallowed hard and shifted her gaze to the chest, forcing herself to think about it, focus on it, catalog every detail in her mind as she'd been trained to do.

In spite of some dirt and wear, it was actually quite attractive, she thought. And obviously very old. Rhia, who had a fondness for old things for their history and character, beautiful or not, felt a strong desire to explore it with all her senses...run her fingers over the smooth wood—cedar, perhaps?—and brass fittings...smell the old-wood-and-dampness smell that always reminded her of the French Quarter in New Orleans. An innocuous, innocent-looking little chest, to contain the cause of so much turmoil...so much grief.

"Where did you find it?"

Nikolas's calm voice startled her. Her eyes jerked back to his face, and she could hardly believe it was the same one they had been focused on a moment ago. His eyes, resting on Lady Zara, were merely curious, now, his face completely composed. Only a hint of white around his mouth and the muscle working near the hinge of his jaw gave evidence—and to her alone—that he'd just received yet another emotional body blow.

Lady Zara glanced at King Weston. "In a moment, Mr. Donovan. I think you should see whatever is in the chest first—don't you agree, Your Majesty?"

King Weston didn't reply. His eyes were shielded, his jaw intent as he leaned over, turned the key and opened the padlock, then removed it from the chest and placed it in his jacket pocket. He lifted the lid, which gave an obligingly gothic creak.

Then the only sounds were the incongruously joyful warble of a bird outside in the garden, and some faint rustlings as the king carefully lifted something wrapped in tissue from the chest.

"Before I show you these things, Nikolas, I must explain," the king said. "Naturally, the essential items of evidence are in Lord Southgate's custody, locked safely away in a forensics lab somewhere. I will tell you that they consist of a lock of hair, and a baby's, er…nurser—uh, bottle—from which they were able to obtain both fingerprints and DNA."

"But that doesn't—" Nikolas all but exploded.

The king lifted a hand to silence his protest. "The fingerprints on the bottle," he said patiently, "though an infant's, are a verified match to yours—" his lips twitched "—which I regret to say are on file with our police department, as well as national security. Your DNA is not. However, since the DNA recovered from the bottle, as well as from the hair follicles, is a close match to mine, it was considered necessary to obtain a sample immediately. Which Mr. Lazlo's agents—" he gave Rhia an acknowledging nod "—were able to do quite easily, from materials found in your office at Dunford College."

Nikolas stiffened and threw Rhia a look that stung. "You… broke into—"

"I did no such thing," she shot back, more calmly than she felt. "The dean was more than glad to—"

"Be that as it may," King Weston said, in a crackling voice that instantly reclaimed everyone's attention, "Your DNA was obtained, Nikolas, and it, too, was found to match the samples from this chest. But there is more." He took a breath, and his voice wavered and lost some of its volume. "There were…two items which I withheld from the forensics scientists. Lord Southgate—the Duke of Carrington—and I—and one forensics expert sworn to absolute secrecy—are the only ones who know of their existence." Almost reverently, he lifted the tissue-wrapped object he'd held concealed in his hands and folded back the paper to reveal a small silver box, quite tarnished but exquisitely carved. "And now…the three of you."

He opened the lid to reveal, nestled in a bed of royal purple velvet, a baby's silver cup, the kind once given to every newborn infant by doting aunts and uncles, engraved with the child's name or initials and date of birth. King Weston removed the cup from its velvet nest and held it up for all to see, turning it so the monogram HRW—Henry Reginald Weston—was plainly visible. Then he rotated the cup.

"This," he said softly, tapping the engraved crest on the other side with one index finger, "is the royal crest of my predecessor, King Dunford. This cup was given to my parents by His Royal Majesty on the event of my birth. I, in turn, gave it to my son, on the day of *his* birth. This—" with hands that shook slightly he held up the second item—a black-and-white photograph in a gilt oval frame "—is a photograph taken on that day." He handed it to Nikolas, quickly, as if it burned his fingers, and went on in a breaking voice, "That is your mother, Queen Alexis. This was taken just two days before she died— I know, because I took it myself—she would have no one else except the doctors see her. She thought—" He smiled slightly. "She didn't like the way she looked, you see. However, I thought she looked quite beautiful, as always, and I convinced her to let me take this one photograph. The babe in her arms, Nikolas, is you. And the cup you see in the picture, here— your mother was holding it for you—is this one." He held up the silver cup with an air of triumph. "This very same one."

The ringing voice seemed to hang in the air…in the ears… like the tolling of a bell. Nikolas shook his head to dispel the echoes and stared narrow-eyed at the photograph in his hands. Through the clouded glass he could see a gaunt, exhausted-looking woman with heavily lashed light gray eyes, her dark hair hastily arranged in a style he recognized as having been popular in the 1970s. She was propped on a massive pile of pillows, smiling bravely and holding what seemed to him an uncommonly ugly baby with a smashed-in face and puffy, slitted eyes. The child's most remarkable feature was a shock of jet-black hair.

In a harsh voice very unlike his own, he asked, "What makes you so sure I'm the child in this picture? He looks— it could be anyone."

Weston smiled gently. "I am sure, my boy. Absolutely

certain, even without the DNA. Do you see in the photograph, the way the infant's hand is open and touching—holding, one could almost say—the cup? When I saw the photograph I asked Lord Southgate to have the cup tested for fingerprints. Remarkable as it seems, they were able to match the prints left on this cup by that tiny hand…to yours, Nikolas. *To yours*."

Dazed and fighting for control, Nikolas cleared his throat and handed the photograph over to Lady Zara. Ignoring her faint gasp as she looked at it, he croaked, "How could—how did this happen? Didn't you—didn't anybody notice it wasn't the same kid?"

It was brutal, but he was beyond caring. Sometime during the past ten minutes or so, the relentless assault on his emotions had evidently achieved what all the scientific evidence in the world could not. Nikolas was no longer speaking to a king; he was merely a son like so many other sons, having heated words with his father.

Weston leaned back in his chair with a sigh. "Ah, yes. I assure you, I have asked myself that a thousand times since…all this came to light." He shot Nikolas a fierce glare. "I am certain it would not have been possible if your mother had been alive. She would have known her own child. But…" His face spasmed with that same terrible grief, and he closed his eyes and shook his head. "But, shortly after I took that picture, she…there were complications. She was rushed into surgery, but she lapsed into a coma. Two days later, she was dead, and I—I'm afraid that in the days that followed I wasn't aware of much of anything. It was days—God help me, maybe even weeks—before I saw you—before I saw my son again. If I noticed changes, I wouldn't have thought anything of it—children change from one day to the next at that age."

"What about…I don't know—nurses, nannies?"

Weston's face hardened. "I imagine at least one of them had to be part of it, but they're all long gone, I'm afraid. Anyone who might have known about the switch is dead…" He paused and aimed his black stare at Nikolas. "Good God. You don't think—"

"I think," Nikolas said softly, "it's time Lady Zara answered my question. I'll ask it again. Where did you find the chest? And how?"

Mystifyingly, she blushed. Clearing her throat, she replied, "I'd rather not say *how* I found it. It's complicated, and... somewhat personal. Suffice to say, Walker—Dr. Shaw—and I found it in a vault under the collapsed ruins of an old pavilion on the grounds of an abandoned estate. The estate..." she glanced at the king and drew a steadying breath "...belongs—belonged—to Benton Vladimir, the Duke of Perthegon."

"Vladimir!" Nikolas exclaimed. "But...he's been—"

"Missing, yes—exiled, vanished," Weston said grimly. He waited a beat before adding in a deliberate tone, "For thirty years."

"Perthegon..." Nikolas shook his head, which was swimming with implications, with possibilities, with scenarios he didn't want to think about or look at too closely. Not now. *Not now.*

"Uh, excuse me," Rhia said, holding up her hand like a shy child in a classroom, "can somebody take pity on the ignorant American in the crowd and explain what all this means?" She knew quite a bit about recent developments in Silvershire, of course, and the name Vladimir sounded familiar, but she still felt like the only one in the crowd who didn't know the people being gossiped about.

Lady Zara gave a little spurt of laughter. Weston arched an eyebrow at Nikolas. "I believe we have time for a short history lesson. Professor Donovan, will you do the honors?"

She felt his reluctance like a stiffening in her own muscles as he turned toward her, and a shiver went down her spine at the hard, set look of his mouth, the cold glitter of anger in his eyes.

Empathy. Remember, it's not you he's angry with.

"The Duke of Perthegon—Lord Benton Vladimir," Nikolas

began in a voice that grated with poorly disguised impatience, "was supposed to have succeeded Pritchett Dunford as king of Silvershire." He acknowledged his father the king with a formal little nod. "When Lord Henry Weston, Earl of Chamberlain, was chosen instead, this country was very nearly plunged into civil war." He paused to take a gulp of tea. When he continued he seemed to have relaxed a little, as if finding some small refuge from his rampaging emotions in the familiar role of teacher.

"The trouble began when King Dunford and his wife, Queen Eloise, were unable to produce an heir to succeed him on the throne. You know, of course—"

"A *male* heir, I assume you mean?"

"*Any* heir…actually," King Weston said, looking mildly amused at the interruption, as if Rhia had been a favorite child guilty of some minor misbehavior. "King Dunford and Queen Eloise had no children. If they had had, perhaps the issue of female succession would not have had to wait until this past decade to be resolved."

It was a moment before the meaning of that statement caught up with her. "You mean, a woman can—"

"Oh, yes, a princess can succeed to the throne," Lady Zara put in, glancing at the king with a smile of apology and sympathy. "It hasn't happened yet, but it will. Someday." She looked at Rhia…and *winked*.

"To return to our history lesson," Nikolas said, tapping a finger on the arm of his chair and looking stern. "In the Charter of Lodan, which was adopted in the thirteenth century following the Battle of Lodan—in the two centuries prior to that, you see, Silvershire's nobles had been trying their level best to annihilate one another—the rules of succession were set forth. One rather unique article states that the heir shall succeed to the throne on his thirtieth birthday, rather than waiting for the current ruler to kick off—thus, it was hoped, preventing the possibility of an interminable reign by a tyrannical or doddering monarch. And also, I imagine," he added drily, "reducing the temptation on the part of an impatient heir to hurry his predecessor's departure along.

"In any event, the system has worked quite well for a good many centuries—I will give it that." Nikolas aimed a fierce glare at his father. "But times do change. The world has changed. It's high time Silvershire entered the twenty-first—"

"That may be," King Weston interrupted gently. "However, my reign is at an end, and that, my boy…is an issue for my successor to decide. Now, if you will, please continue…"

Nikolas cleared his throat. "Of course. Forgive me. Anyway, as I said, King Dunford had produced no heir. The Charter provides, in that event, for the king to chose a successor from among his nobles. In this case there were two candidates—cousins, very near in age—Lord Vladimir and Lord Weston. Vladimir, by virtue of being two months the elder of the two, and from a slightly more exalted lineage—" Nikolas's mouth tilted sardonically "—was the obvious choice to inherit the crown."

King Weston nodded and picked up the narrative. "I had always assumed that would be the case, even though King Dunford made it a point to include me in his royal tutorials with Benton—Lord Vladimir. He wanted us both to have as much knowledge as possible about the running of the kingdom, you see, assuming that I would serve the kingdom in some position or other." He paused to rub his eyes, as if, perhaps, he had a headache, and Lady Zara gave him a look of concerned appraisal.

Ignoring her, the king went on, with a wave of his hand, "Unfortunately, Vladimir felt threatened by King Dunford's insistence in involving me at every level. Perhaps he believed the king was considering me for the crown instead of him… who knows?" Again the king paused. To Rhia, he looked like a man carrying a heavy burden of sadness.

"The sad thing is," King Weston said at last in a musing tone, "the circumstance that finally pushed Benton into acting as he did had nothing whatsoever to do with the succession. My father was dying, you see. He didn't wish that fact to cast a shadow over the coming coronation ceremony and the attendant festivities, so he had asked that his illness be kept secret. Only my mother and I and the king and queen knew the truth. It was, naturally, a difficult time for me, and I often sought my king's counsel.

"But Benton—Lord Vladimir—misunderstood these private meetings, and incorrectly assumed King Dunford had changed his mind about whom he would choose to succeed him. Fearing he was about to lose his chance to become king, Lord Vladimir—" King Weston made a grimace of distaste and an abrupt dismissive gesture with his hand. "I dislike speaking of it, even now. Suffice to say, Lord Vladimir made an attempt to discredit me by framing me for acts of high treason. Reprehensible acts. Thankfully, his plan was discovered before it could be carried out. I was chosen by His Majesty, King Dunford, to succeed him as King of Silvershire, and the Duke of Perthegon, just as he was about to be imprisoned and prosecuted for his crimes, vanished into thin air. He has neither been seen nor heard from in the thirty years since. It has always been assumed he fled the country. Now…I am not so sure."

Rhia, who had been listening intently to the king's story, stiffened to attention. "Are you suggesting he—the exiled Lord Vladimir—is behind these recent acts of violence and sabotage? And that it was he who switched the babies— replaced Nikolas—uh, the prince with an impostor?"

Again the king rubbed a hand over tired eyes. "I can think of no one else who would do such a thing. And," he added with a wry smile, "he did vow to make me pay for robbing him of his 'birthright.'"

The smile vanished and he brought his closed fist down hard on the arm of his chair. "God help me, though—I am at a loss to see how he could have done it! If he did not leave this island, if in fact he's been living right here among us all this time, how in blazes has he managed to do it? How has he managed to come and go at will, even invade the heart of the palace itself, without being seen? *Where is he? How has he hidden himself? Who is he now?*"

King Weston clutched the chair's arms and pushed himself to his feet. Lady Zara went instantly to his side, but he shook off her help. Holding himself tall and erect, he lifted a hand that shook only slightly, and when he spoke his voice held the vibrant timbre Rhia remembered from his television appearances. "This, Nikolas—and you, my dear—this is the task with which I now charge the two of you. *Find that blackguard Vladimir.* Wherever he is, whoever he is pretending to be, the wretch…must…be…found!"

Chapter 10

"Nikolas…" Rhia halted in the middle of the path and touched his arm. "Hold up a minute."

The two of them were alone, for the moment, making their way unescorted through the sun-dappled forest to the meadow where the helicopter waited. Lady Zara had stayed behind to see her exhausted patient to his chambers, and the security guard who had accompanied them on their arrival had returned to his regular post. The hunting lodge had been swallowed by the woods behind them and up ahead the meadow was still only glimpses of gold between dark trunks of trees.

Nikolas paused and turned his head toward her. His eyes were crinkled in a questioning frown, but their focus was on something only he could see.

"We have to talk." She spoke in a low voice, though there was no one to hear her. Her heart had begun to beat hard and fast, and she didn't know why, only that something was dreadfully wrong. "Now. Here—before we get back to the chopper." She heard him exhale, and his gaze lifted and slid past her head. She could feel the tension vibrating through the muscles in his arm, radiating up through her fingers like a low-voltage current of electricity. She gripped his wrist harder, and the urgency she felt was in her voice, now. "What the hell happened back there? Something about that box—that chest—hit you like a ton of bricks. I saw it, so don't try and deny it. And unless I misunderstood him completely, His Majesty just asked me to work with you to find this guy, this…Vladimir. Look—if I'm going to do that, I'm going to have to know what's going on. *Everything,* Donovan. I don't go into a job blindfolded."

She was completely unprepared when he pulled her to him and wrapped her in a bone-crushing embrace. Unprepared…but her flesh responded to his like thirsty earth to a sudden shower of rain. She felt her blood rise beneath her skin, felt the heat of it and the pressure, and she thought she might burst from it. She gave a sharp gasp that turned into a whimper when his mouth covered hers.

His mouth was hard, the kiss deep, demanding; there was a kind of desperation in it, and an unfathomable hunger. Pressed tightly against his body, she could feel the rapid thud of his heart and the tension quivering in his muscles. Overwhelmed herself, she could only cling to him while her pulses rocketed into warp speed and the earth beneath her feet ceased to exist. She felt her legs buckle and might have fallen if she hadn't been wrapped so tightly in his arms.

He ended the kiss as abruptly as he'd begun it, tearing his mouth from hers with a gasp that was like a small explosion, an escape of passionate and powerful emotions held prisoner too long. Heedless of clips and fastenings, he clutched a handful of her hair in one big hand and buried his face in the curve of her neck. He groaned softly. "Ah…Rhee. You have no idea how much I've needed to do that."

"Yes…I do." Her lips felt numb; she could hardly get the

words out. "Because I've needed it, too. Dammit." She could feel herself trembling. Furious with herself for her inability to stop it, she pounded the hard, ungiving muscle of his arm with her fist. "But don't think this is going to distract me, Donovan. I still want to know what it was about that box that upset you. Tell me, dammit. Or—"

He cut her off with another kiss, this one almost playful. "God, I love it when you're assertive," he said huskily against her mouth, sounding like the Nikolas she knew. "It's such a turn-on." He kissed her again, long and slow and deep. Her insides went liquid and warm and she could feel a moan rising dangerously in her throat.

Then he drew back and looked down at her, and his eyes were shadowed and grave. "I wish I could, but I can't. Not now. Not yet. I don't know myself…there's something I need—" He broke off, dropped a kiss on the tip of her nose and said firmly, "I need you to trust me, luv, okay? And…I need your chopper. D'you think Corbett Lazlo would mind if we kept it just a bit longer?"

"It's yours to command," Rhia said, but her voice was bumpy as he turned her and pulled her against his side. He held her close with one arm while they continued along the path.

"Good—let's go wake up our pilot, shall we?" His tone was light again, but his eyes were hard, and she could see the tiny muscle working in his jaw.

"The old Perthegon Estate? Sure, yeah, I know where it is. No problem." The helicopter pilot, whose name was Elliot, spoke with an American accent—from New York or thereabouts, Nikolas guessed. The pilot tucked the wrapper from a package of cream-filled cupcakes into the pocket of his uniform shirt and levered himself nimbly up from his lounging position in the doorway of the chopper. "Hop in and buckle up. I can have you there in a jiff."

Nikolas waited for Rhia to climb aboard, then followed.

She took the jump seat opposite the door, leaving the seat beside the pilot for him. The chopper's rotors began to spin while he was still strapping himself in.

"That old place is pretty much a ruin, now, but from what I hear it used to be somethin' else," Elliot shouted above the noise of the chopper's turbine engine. "Ever been there?"

Nikolas shook his head. "Seen pictures—that's about it."

"Real showplace, I guess it was like something out of Disneyland."

"Yeah," Nikolas said.

Disneyland…yeah, that's what this whole thing is like— some kind of fairy tale. Not the happy, chirpy, singing-mice kind, though. The scary kind with wicked stepparents and evil villains and all sorts of blood and gore.

Elliot spoke into his radio and the helicopter lifted into the air. Nikolas's stomach and the golden meadow dropped away, and in minutes the forest had vanished into cloud haze.

As they left the mountains behind, the clouds thickened, becoming patchy fog as they neared the capital city. Situated as it was, on the Kairn River plain just thirty kilometers or so inland from Kairn Bay and the Port of Perth, Silverton was frequently blanketed by the marine layer as it crept inland following the low river valley like a crooked, beckoning finger. Elliot spoke often into his radio mike now, in constant touch with the tower at Silvershire International.

Once across the river and out of the city's busy airspace, Elliot keyed off the mike and jerked a thumb back over his shoulder. "Gonna need to gas this thing up—we're runnin' on fumes. After I drop you guys off at the castle, I'm gonna head on back here to the airport and refuel."

Nikolas nodded. Rhia leaned forward and tapped him on the shoulder.

"Tell him to bring us back some burgers and fries—I'm starving."

He gave a little laugh half of surprise, half chagrin. He

was hungry, too, and hadn't realized it. He'd been too tense, his stomach tied in too many knots to feel anything so mundane as hunger.

As if awakened by the power of suggestion, or out of pure contrariness, his stomach gave a loud growl.

Elliot did another thumb-jerk. "Got a buncha stuff back there in my duffel—keep it handy for times like this when I don't get to make a pit stop. Help yourselves—in fact, take it with you if you want. I can grab a bite at the airport."

"What kind of stuff?" Rhia was already reaching for the duffel.

Elliot grinned. "Junk, mostly. Chips, chocolate bars…stuff like that."

"Yum," said Rhia happily.

The helicopter banked sharply and plunged down through a hole in the clouds.

Elliot deposited them in a field of waving grass plumes and fading meadow flowers on the back side of the house—or castle, more like—and immediately took off again. Holding her hair with one hand against the chopper's turbulence, Rhia turned in a slow circle and said, "Wow."

Nikolas didn't reply. He took off his sunglasses and tucked them in his jacket pocket, then stood gazing at the castle—Perth Castle, ancestral home of Lord Benton Vladimir, the Duke of Perthegon. He didn't know what he'd expected—some kind of blinding revelation, maybe? A vision? At the very least, a clue that would help provide answers to the questions swirling inside his head. Instead there was the same restless stirring all through his body, that had been with him since he'd boarded the Lazlo Group's helicopter in Paris. And at the same time a cold hollow feeling of dread.

The day, it seemed, had turned to match his mood. Tendrils of gray-white fog were coiling up from the river, wrapping themselves around the castle's stone turrets and cupolas and blotting out what was left of the sun. A damp chilly breeze touched the back of his neck like ghost-fingers.

"I don't know about Disneyland," Rhia said, gazing up at the castle, head back, thumbs hooked in her belt. "I'm thinking more along the lines of Dracula."

"The fog does lend it a certain atmosphere," Nikolas said absently. He nodded toward some scaffolding that could be seen climbing the wall far off to their right. "Looks like someone's been doing a bit of work on the place, at least."

"Doesn't appear to be a soul around at the moment, though." There was a pause, and then: "Are you going to tell me now just what it is we're doing here? Because whatever it is, I vote we explore whatever's in that goody bag of Elliot's before we do anything else."

He let go of a breath he didn't know he'd been holding, and to his surprise, a laugh came with it. Peeling his gaze away from the castle, he looked at Rhia instead, and felt the knots in his stomach begin to loosen. Her tilted green eyes were studying him intently, and he had the feeling that if she'd had a tail it would have been twitching. Laughing softly, he reached for her with one arm and pulled her against his side.

"That's not what I'd like to explore," he murmured into her hair. His hand crept around her waist and flattened over her stomach…then inched its way upward under her jacket to cradle and measure the weight of one firm round breast.

She socked him smartly on one of his pecs—though her nipple had already hardened treasonously beneath his palm.

"Ow. That's hardly the response I was hoping for, luv." But he'd felt a shudder ripple through her body—just before she twisted away and out of his reach.

"Stop trying to distract me, damn you. I told you, that's not going to get you off the hook with me. I want to know what

we're doing here. What is it you're looking for? If you'd tell
me, maybe I could help you find it."

"That would be somewhat difficult," Nikolas said in a
musing tone, "considering I haven't got a clue myself."

He turned his back on the castle and gazed out across the
meadow, which lay like a messy bed coverlet on the gentle
slope. Farther down, closer to the river, it was dotted with
copses of trees that almost hid the marshes and the island
where the pavilion had once stood, the ruined pavilion where
Zara said she and Walker Shaw had found the chest.

The pavilion had been demolished and the vault beneath
it filled in, Zara had told him. There was nothing left there
now. And in any case, he wasn't keen on the idea of wading
through a swamp just to look at an empty ruin, and was pretty
sure Rhia wouldn't be, either.

"There's nothing out here," he said, turning back to the
castle. "I need to get inside. D'you suppose it's locked?"

Rhia looked over at him and her lips curved in a kitty-cat
smile. "Shall we go and see?"

She set off up the hill toward the castle, moving ahead of
him with her long athlete's stride. He didn't try to catch up
with her; the view from where he was was far too enjoyable.

Their circuit of the castle confirmed Nikolas's fears: All the
windows were either locked from the inside or firmly painted
shut, and the doors were sporting what appeared to be new
and very effective padlocks.

"Well, that's that, I suppose," he said, having given the lock
on the massive front doors a fruitless yank. He stepped back
and craned his neck to study the upper-story windows. "I
guess we can try the scaffold, see if any of the upstairs windows—what are you doing?"

Rhia had taken a small black leather case from her belt and
was unzipping it. As he watched with dawning apprehension,
she selected several small metal objects from the assortment
laid out inside, then tucked the case in her pocket and stepped

forward. "Excuse me," she murmured, picking up the lock in one hand and weighing it appraisingly, "this might take me a minute. It's been awhile…"

He said in flat disbelief, "Rhee…those aren't *lock picks?*"

"Yep." She was intent on the task now, the tip of her tongue clamped between her teeth, eyes narrowed in concentration.

It was hard to tell whether the strange shimmery feeling inside him was wonder or dismay. Stifling laughter, he managed to choke out, "Rhee…luv…are you insane?"

"Shh! Be quiet. Almost…*there.*" She gave the lock a tug and it opened in her hands. She straightened and threw him a triumphant look—a bit of a smug one, too.

He gave an incredulous snort. "Where did you—did Lazlo teach you that?"

She was suddenly very busy returning her tools to their case and not looking at him, but he saw when her smile slipped awry. "No, not hardly—though he did provide me with this nice set of tools." She gave him a sideways look from under her lashes. "Guess I forgot to tell you—I used to be a cat burglar in my former life."

"Come on…seriously." He'd given up trying to stop the laughter, though a cold little breath of unease was wafting across the back of his neck. Or was it only the fog?

"He thinks I'm kidding," Rhia muttered to the brass lion's head on the door.

She pushed the door open all the way, then leaned her back against it and watched him as she waited for him to pass through it ahead of her, chin lifted in unspoken challenge.

He hesitated…almost reached for her…almost touched her. Almost asked the questions he knew she expected, with that look of defiance that couldn't quite hide the vulnerability underneath. But then something—the chill stale wash of air from the closed-up castle, the musty smell of abandonment, perhaps—reminded him of where he was and why he'd come there, and the questions floated away like cobwebs to the back rooms of his mind.

Rhia pushed away from the door and closed it carefully
behind her, enclosing them in gloomy darkness that was
only slightly diluted by the pale light slipping through the
cracks in dusty draperies and the panes of stained glass high
in the stone wall above the entrance doors. Feeling vaguely
abandoned, she tucked her hands in her jacket pockets and
ambled unhurriedly after Nikolas, who was working his way
down the vast hall, jerking doors open and looking briefly
into rooms.

"What are we looking for?" she asked when she caught up
with him, peering over his shoulder at a gray darkness filled
with the ghostly shapes of shrouded furniture.

"You remind me of a small child on a long road trip," he
said tartly, narrowed eyes still studying what appeared to be
a lady's sitting room. He pulled the door shut, shot her a look
and mimicked a child's falsetto: "Are we there yet?"

"Oh, very amusing." She folded her arms on her chest
and gave him a quelling look. "However, I ask because we
are trespassing, and our ride is going to be coming back to
pick us up soon, and whatever it is we're here to do, I
suggest we get it done quickly. Oh, yeah—and did I
mention I'm starving? And that I tend to get bitchy when
I'm hungry?"

His soft laughter reached for her in the gloom, then his arms
and his warm mouth. "Sorry, luv…" The words of remorse
brushed her cheek like a caress, and she melted inside. Her
arms found their way around his waist all by themselves. His
arms crisscrossed her back and he wrapped her close against
him so that she felt the slight jerking of his body when he
laughed. "I'm a pig…an absolute prick. I forgot. Of course we
should eat something. Where did I leave the bloody duffel?"

"It's back there…by the door." Her reply was muffled
against his shoulder, and she released a long, uneven breath
that snuggled her even more comfortably against him. Hunger
forgotten for the moment, she felt a strange reluctance to let

go, a premonition, perhaps, of a future she dreaded and didn't want to acknowledge. A future without him. A shudder rippled through her, and tears burned the backs of her eyes.

Low blood sugar, she told herself. With clenched teeth and willpower, she pulled herself away from him and half ran back across the hall to retrieve the duffel bag from where Nikolas had thoughtlessly dropped it on a huge mirrored hall tree just inside the entrance.

When she returned with the bag, Nikolas had seated himself on a step about halfway up one side of a matched pair of curving staircases that rose like gracefully spread wings to a second-floor landing. As she mounted the stairs to join him, she could feel his eyes drawing her in, almost like a guiding hand. Her eyes had adjusted to the dimness, and in that shadowy light his face looked grave and bleak.

She halted a few steps below him, her eyes on a level with his and a cold, undefined fear coiling in her stomach. "Nik, what—"

"Shh…" He took the duffel bag from her and patted the stairstep beside him. "Food first. Questions later. Let's see what sort of goodies our Elliot has squirreled away."

"You want to eat *here?*" She was eying the dusty steps.

Nikolas had the bag open and was sorting through its contents. "Good a spot as any. The whole place is dust and cobwebs… Ah—look what we have here. Something called… Cheese Doodles. D'you suppose they actually have cheese in them? That would be protein, I suppose."

"Gimme." Rhia snatched the bag from his hands and plunked herself down on the step below his, squeamishness and premonitions both, for the moment, forgotten. "Oh, my God," she breathed as she tore open the bag and inhaled the familiar smell, "do you have any idea how long it's been since I've eaten a Cheese Doodle?"

"None whatsoever," he murmured as she popped a handful of the dusty orange crunchies into her mouth. She closed her eyes as she chewed, shutting out his expression of horrified fascination.

She opened her eyes and dusted her fingers on her pants, leaving orange-ish streaks. "Mmm-mmm—that was tasty— I used to love these things. What else is there?"

"What? Oh—yes, of course…" Tearing his gaze from her mouth, he dug once more into the bag. "Well, okay, here's something else for you, peanut butter crackers."

"Mmf—hand 'em over. I love peanut butter."

"Of course you do. You're an American. Ah—here's something for me—crisps! That's chips to you, I suppose. Hmm… onion-flavored—not my favorite, but beggars can't be choosers, can they? Oh, and look—the fellow has a sweet tooth, it seems. Here's a tin of biscuits."

"Biscuits? Oh—right. You mean cookies. Goody—hand 'em over." She licked her lips, wiped more orange Cheese Doodle dust on her pants leg and reached for the red plaid tin of Scottish shortbread cookies. Wonder of wonders—they were dipped in chocolate.

He laughed and held the cookies out of her reach. "You are a little glutton, aren't you? Sorry—no dessert until you've had your dinner…" He leaned down and kissed her, just in time to catch her mouth opening in protest.

She felt the kiss all the way down to her toes. Had she ever craved a man's touch so much? If she had, she couldn't recall it. Her head fell back and the world tilted….

Nikolas lifted his head, licked his lips and said thoughtfully, "Hmm…I believe I'm actually acquiring a taste for Cheese Doodles. Let me just see…"

He lowered his mouth to hers again, his hand gentle on her arched throat, lips and tongue firm and clever as they tasted the cheese dust clinging to her lips in teasing nibbles. It tickled, but she felt no desire to laugh. She wanted him with a boundless yearning that made those unfamiliar tears prick at her eyelids again, and helpless anger rise quivering into her chest. And what was this *crying* thing all of a sudden? She wasn't a crier—never had been. She'd been eighteen years old the last time she'd cried.

A chuckle jerked beneath the hand she'd placed, without realizing it, against his chest. Words whispered softly across her lips. "Mmm...lovely. Wonder if it works with peanut butter as well..."

She pushed hard against his chest, contrary to her heart's desire. Laughing, she scolded in a voice that tried hard to be stern, "Sorry—no dessert until you've eaten your supper," and turned her face away so he couldn't see how desperately she wanted him to kiss her again...and again...and never stop.

"Ah—yes, I suppose you're right." He drew back, wearing a look of mock seriousness, though a grin of appreciation tugged at his lips and his gray eyes were alight with laughter.

Gazing at him, watching him pop open the bag of potato chips, Rhia felt bedazzled. She thought, *If he wasn't born to be a head of state, he could be one anyway. With that charm, that charisma, in America he could be a movie star.* Hungrily, she watched him put a chip in his mouth and chew, then lick the salt and crumbs from his lips, and she understood the impulse that had made him kiss her.

"You know," he said between munches, giving her an appraising, sideways look, "I must say I'm surprised. I never would have taken you for a junk-food junkie."

She swallowed a mouthful of Cheese Doodles and licked her fingers, then picked up the package of peanut butter crackers. She gave her head a little throwaway toss and said lightly, casually, "I'm not, anymore. Used to be, though. A bad habit I picked up in juvie."

"Juvie?"

"Juvenile detention—you know, jail for kids?" This moment had been inevitable from the beginning, she realized now, but that didn't mean she was prepared for it. She felt her heart racing, her nerves twitching, urging her to jump up and run away from it. Foolish thought; there was no running away from destiny.

"You're kidding."

She shook her head and concentrated on opening the package so she wouldn't have to see his face while she told him. "Nope. That's where I spent a good part of my teenage years, actually."

"What on earth for?"

"Truancy, running away, shoplifting—that sort of thing. I wasn't a good person, Nik. I ran away for the first time about…oh…three days after I got to my dad's house in Palm Beach. Got as far as the bus depot in Miami, that first time, before his security guys picked me up. After that he bribed me to stay—first it was a bicycle, then a wave runner…a scooter…you name it, I had it. I still ran away, though—every chance I got. So, eventually, I wound up in juvie." She shrugged and popped a cracker into her mouth, though her mouth was too dry already.

"And…the shoplifting?" His voice was gentle. She risked a glance at him and wished she hadn't; the sympathy and kindness in his eyes were almost her undoing.

She swallowed the bite of cracker, then took a breath that hurt her chest. "Ah. That. Well…when the running away didn't seem to be working, I thought I'd become a big enough pain in his ass that he'd be glad to get rid of me." She laughed harshly and threw him a bitter smile. "Didn't work, of course. That would have been admitting failure. My dad didn't believe in failure. So…" she wrapped up the remaining cracker in its cellophane packaging paper and began systematically crushing it to smithereens "…on the day I turned eighteen I left for good. Left everything—took some clothes and enough money for a bus ticket to Louisiana and to eat on until I could start earning a living, and that was all. I told my father I was an adult, and if he tried to stop me or come after me I'd get a restraining order." She dropped the pulverized cracker into the duffel bag and leaned back on her elbows, tilting her head back to glare up at him. "And, I know what you're thinking."

His eyebrow shot up. "*Do* you now?"

Guilt made a hard lump in her chest; rejection of the guilt made her breathlessly angry. "Yeah. You're thinking I was too hard on him—my dad. After all, he didn't abuse me, he gave me presents, put up with all my crap, and I was a spoiled, thankless brat. Well…you'd be right. But there are two things—two…things, okay? One, I was just a kid. And two… he robbed me of my mama. *My mother.* I can't forgive him for that. I won't forgive him for that."

She was shaking, suddenly too angry to sit still. She would have jumped up, paced up the stairs, run down them…anything to release the pent-up emotions…the rage and the sorrow. But Nikolas's hands were resting on her shoulders, massaging, kneading, compelling…keeping her firmly anchored. And so she gave in to their gentle prompting and leaned her head against his thigh instead, and sighed and closed her eyes. And it felt so good…*so safe* there…the tears that had been threatening all day came seeping through and puddled beneath her lashes.

"And did you find her?" Nikolas asked softly, his fingers lightly stroking. "Your mum?"

"How did you know—"

"Hush—" a chuckle stirred through her hair, like a sweet warm breeze "—d'you think you're the only one with empathy? Obviously you went to find her. It's what I'd do."

"I did." Her whole body ached now with the memory… memories of the last time she'd cried. She gave a liquid, hiccupping laugh. "I guess you could say it was…my first missing persons case. And my first failure. Because I was too late. Mama was gone. She died just a few months before I got there. She'd left me…" she drew a shuddering breath "…her saxophone. It's all I have of her now."

Nikolas stared at the stained-glass window at the opposite

end of the great hall until his eyes burned dry in their sockets. He asked himself when the conviction had come to him that what he felt for the woman sitting quietly nestled against him, her head resting on his thigh, her soft hair wafting like a baby's breath over his hands…that what he felt for this woman, perhaps the sexiest and most desirable woman he'd ever known…wasn't at all about sex. Well, at least, not *all* about sex.

Had it ever been?

He thought about that magical long-ago encounter on the balcony of a Paris hotel, and the events that had brought that fantasy creature back into his life, this time as a very real, very human, flesh-and-blood woman. Was she a part of it, this destiny with which he seemed to be on a collision course?

His mouth tightened and a little quiver of resolve skated down his spine. She *would* be a part of his future. He would make sure of that.

With that resolve came emotion, emotion so powerful he didn't know what to do with it, except wrap the cause of it tightly in his arms and bury his face in the soft curve of her neck, close his eyes and breathe the sweet scent of her into his lungs, let her warmth seep into his pores and the shape of her body and the texture of her skin imprint themselves eternally on his mind and his senses, make her his in every way he possibly could. *In every way…*

The wave of desire that hit him then was unlike anything he'd ever known. It grew out of those overwhelming emotions like a tsunami out of an earthquake…a natural force, impossible to ignore or defend against or deny.

"Memories," he said, and she turned her face up to him, eyes tear-glazed and questioning. He touched her face…cradled her cheek in his hand and answered in a thickened voice, barely able to get the words out, "Memories of your mother— the ones you told me about. You have them, too." *At least you have those…*

But he didn't say that aloud.

Chapter 11

Rhia stared at him, stared at him so hard her eyes burned, as if his image were being laser-printed on her retinas. *Memories...* Her whole body ached with the thought: *That's all I will have of you, too, one day...soon.*

And then, through the blur of unshed tears, she saw the pain in his shadowed eyes. She hadn't believed it possible to hurt more than she already did, but in that moment her own sense of grief felt as if it had doubled. *Oh, selfish Rhee! Thinking only of your own loss. Talking about your own past. What about his? This day, this trip, this time—it's for him, not you!*

She placed her hand over the bigger one that lay warm on her cheek and whispered brokenly, "I do have memories. But you don't. You don't have anything of your—"

"Hush..." His voice sounded harsh, even angry. "Can't miss what you've never had."

They both knew it was a lie.

She started to say something—to tell him so, maybe—but

his mouth came down and she let it take hers, so desperately, achingly glad to have him touching her that nothing else mattered. *I'll have this, at least,* she thought, and as she opened her mouth to him she gathered the memory up and tucked it away in her heart like a greedy child hiding candy.

Was it just her natural gift of empathy that made her respond to his kiss like dry tinder to a match, Nikolas wondered, or could she possibly be as hungry for him as he for her?

What did it matter? He only felt the burn of it, the heat of her body colliding with his as she turned in his arms and reached for him…the sting and sizzle of her fingers on his skin as she half lay across his lap, her mouth surging up to his, meeting the rhythmic thrusts of his tongue with little whimpering pulses of her own. Desire—his need of her—ripped through his body with cruel force, doubling him over like a bad cramp. A groan slipped unguarded from his throat.

Rhia tore her mouth from his and gasped, "Nik, what—"

But he caught her to him, hid her face against his throat and whispered hoarsely, "Nothing…nothing, my love. I just want you so badly…." It wasn't what he wanted to say.

She could feel his body shaking with silent, rueful laughter. "I want you, too," she whispered back, shaking, too, though not with laughter.

"This is insane…" But his hand dove under her jacket, plucked her shirt free from the waistband of her pants, and then his fingers were thrusting beneath it and spreading urgently over her flesh…and the abrasion felt so sweet and good it made her want to weep. "I feel like a bloody teenager."

"Nik, we're on the damn *stairs.* We'd prob'ly kill ourselves." She was laughing now, clinging to him, spotting his shirtfront with her tears.

"And I, for one, would die blissfully happy."

"And…Elliot's going to be back any minute."

A heavy groan rumbled from his chest. "Woman, you are entirely too practical-minded for my—" He stopped.

As tuned to his moods as she was, she felt the change in him instantly. She tensed and drew back to look at him. "What? Nikolas?"

He was looking over her head, his expression a study in conflicting emotions. His eyes flicked down at her and he smiled, if somewhat crookedly. "I don't think Elliot's going to be coming for a while." He nodded toward the front of the hall.

She lay back in his arms and turned her head reluctantly to follow his gaze. "What…"

"Look at the stained-glass window. The light's gone."

"It can't be that late." She was struggling to sit up.

"It isn't, dear heart. We appear to be fogbound."

"You're kidding." She was squirming in his embrace, trying to reach the cell phone on her belt.

"Trust me," he said, "if there's one thing I know about, it's fog." There was a cryptic note of irony in his voice.

She paused…stared at him, thinking she should feel dismay, trying hard not to grin, understanding fully the ambiguous look on *his* face. "So…" she said in a low voice, thoughtfully weighing the slender device in her hand, "you're saying we're stuck here? As in…stranded?"

He gave her a sideways look and nodded. "Uh-huh. For the night, at least."

"Bummer," she said somberly. And deliberately tucked the phone back into its case.

He caught her to him, taking her breath away, his laughter gusting into her hair. Then, for a few minutes they simply held each other, rocking slightly, laughing in wonder at the unexpected gift they'd been given. A gift of time, Rhia thought… like happening upon a lovely little tropical island in a sea of chaos.

When the laughter died, finally, they drew back and looked at each other. Just…looked. Nikolas let his fingers trail down the side of her face, tracing the curve of her cheek…the velvety line of her jaw…the incredibly, impossibly perfect shape of her mouth. And he shook his head, dazed to silence by the enormity of what he felt inside.

"What?" She was gazing at him, her eyes as guarded as he knew his must be.

"Nothing," he murmured. "It's just that you're so damned beautiful."

She gave a tiny squeak of laughter, and laid her fingertips against his lips, reverently, the way people do when they petition a saint. "I think you're beautiful, too."

He closed his eyes and exhaled gustily. "*God,* I want to kiss you so badly. But if I do, I'm absolutely certain I won't stop, and intriguing as the idea of making love to you on the stairs of Vladimir's castle might be…I think we'd better find a place to spend the night while we can still see our hands before our faces."

There was a long pause during which neither of them moved. Nikolas kissed her nose and said tenderly, "Rhee— my dearest—I need you to be strong and get up, because I don't think I can bring myself to let go of you otherwise."

"Me! What makes you think I'm stronger than you are?" Her eyes narrowed. "What about that legendary willpower of yours?"

He snorted. "Evidently I have none whatsoever where you're concerned. All right, then—we'll do this together. Ready? One…two…"

Separating from him left her feeling cold, as if she'd gotten thoroughly chilled and would never be completely warm again. And shaky…hideously vulnerable—an appalling weakness she tried to hide from Nikolas by pretending not to notice the helping hand he offered, busying herself gathering up snack papers and brushing off cracker crumbs instead. Fooling no one. Wondering, as she handed him the unopened tin of shortbread cookies and the half-eaten bag of Cheese Doodles, what had happened to her appetite. Now, she was hungry for nothing at all except him.

It grew lighter as they climbed the stairs, pale gray light from curtainless windows spilling from open doorways all along the landing. In the large common rooms nearest the stairs, Rhia caught glimpses of stepladders and draping drop-cloths, and smelled the faint but unmistakable odor of fresh paint. Farther down the landing, though, shadowy hallways led to wings that housed the private rooms, where the work of renovation hadn't commenced yet. They poked their heads into all of them, while Nikolas provided commentary and hurried them from one to the next like a tour guide in desperate need of a bathroom break.

"Bedroom…bedroom…hmm, with adjoining sitting room, I see—*and* a dressing room as well… Lovely. This would be the nursery, I suppose. And a schoolroom—what fun. Hmm… bathrooms seem to be in rather short supply, don't they? Ah—what do we have here?"

He had opened the last door, which seemed to be wider than the rest. As Rhia caught up with him, he pushed it back and strode into the room like the returning lord of the manor. "The master suite, I believe. What do you think, my love? Will this do?" He turned to smile at her, a strange tense smile that showed his teeth but didn't reach his eyes.

"Do? This room is bigger than my whole apartment," Rhia muttered as she wandered past him, threading her way among the shrouded furniture shapes to the tall multipaned windows that graced two adjoining walls. A corner room, obviously. The view would be breathtaking, she thought, without the fog.

She heard a thump behind her, and turned to see that Nikolas had dropped the duffel bag onto a sheet-draped chair. Before she could stop him, he had energetically whisked the dust sheets off the bed—typical man!—sending a small dust blizzard into the air. They both erupted in laughing, coughing fits, and Rhia was about to choke out a teasing remark of some kind—*Good job, Donovan!*—when he suddenly went still. Simply froze, with the back of one hand touching his mouth and his eyes staring over it at something she couldn't see. Something near the foot of the bed.

"What is it?" She pushed her way back to him through the shapeless mounds of furniture, heart already quickening, nerves and senses snapping to full attention.

The shocked and frozen look on his face was the same one she'd seen there when the king's guard had carried in the chest that held the proof of his identity.

She touched his hand—not surprised to find it cold as ice—and said softly, "Nik, what's wrong?"

Instead of answering, he moved slowly toward the foot of the bed, which was the old-fashioned kind, small in width by modern standards, but so high it would require steps to get in and out of easily, with four tall posts and a canopy frame soaring toward the shadowed ceiling. It was made of some kind of dark wood, maybe mahogany? And in a style Rhia—no expert—thought might be Queen Anne. At the foot of the bed was a large chest, made of different wood than the bed—cedar, surely—and studded and bound with brass, probably meant to store blankets and comforters during the warm summer months. It was much bigger than the chest King Weston had shown them, the chest that held the proof of Nikolas's identity. But even Rhia could see that it had been crafted by the same hands.

Slowly, as if it were some sort of alien and possibly dangerous artifact, Nikolas reached out his hand to touch the chest's vaulted lid. "I thought maybe…I had hoped…" he murmured as he watched his fingers brush settling dust from the intricately inlaid wood. A smile tugged painfully and unsuccessfully at his lips, and he finally just shook his head. "I thought there was a chance, at least…that it could have been someone else who put it there, in the old pavilion. Someone who simply happened by and thought it would make a convenient hiding place…" He looked at her then, and the pain in his eyes struck her like a blow. "You know?"

She shook her head, bewildered and obscurely frightened. "No, I don't," she said flatly, folding her arms to keep them from reaching for him, tapping her foot like an angry wife. "I don't know because you haven't told me, Nikolas. What *is* it, dammit? What was it about that chest—and now this one— that has you looking like...like...I don't know—like you've seen a *ghost?*"

He exhaled, drew a hand over his face and slowly lowered himself onto the chest. "A ghost? Maybe I have, at that." Again, he tried to smile. "Except...I don't think inanimate objects can have ghosts, can they?"

"Dammit, Donovan—"

"Rhee...my love." He reached for her hands and drew her to him, guiding her between his knees as his eyes roamed her face with a tenderness that made her ache. "Don't you know, it's not because I want to keep this from you that I haven't told you. It's just...difficult for me to talk about it at all, you see. I think...because saying it out loud...saying the words...makes it real." His eyes held hers as his legs pressed inward, locking her hips between them. His hands slipped under her jacket and skimmed upward along the sides of her waist. "Then, once I've said it, I can't keep dodging around it any longer. Do you understand?"

When she nodded, he released a breath that sounded like a pressure valve letting go, closed his eyes and drew her close. And he seemed to relax then...like someone walking into his home after a long hard day. She stared past him into the deepening twilight until her eyes burned, fighting a powerful desire to weave her fingers through his hair and cradle his head against her breasts. Instead, she gripped his shoulders hard and said very softly, "Do *you* understand that if you don't tell me this instant, I *will* strangle you?"

He drew back from her, laughing, sounding like himself again, as if holding her for just those short minutes had recharged him. "Ah—my little pit bull terrier. Yes. All right then." He caught a quick, exaggerated breath and said with a lightness that didn't fool her a bit, "The reason seeing the chest sent me into a bit of a tailspin is because I'd seen it before."

"What?"

"Or one like it, I should say. *Almost* like it."

"But, Nikolas, that's not—"

"Hush." He silenced her with a finger pressed gently to her lips. "Let me explain. When I saw this one, I knew. They were obviously made as a set, identical except for the size. This is the largest, I would think, the one Weston has would be the smallest, unless, of course, there are more than three. Mine—the one I saw—is a size between the two. They must have been meant to nest inside one another, do you see? Like Chinese boxes."

Rhia nodded automatically…then shook her head, because she didn't see at all. "But why should that upset you? So, they're a set—even I could see they're the same. So what? Where did you see this other one? Are you sure it's even the same?"

His lips curved in an odd, bitter smile. "Oh, yes. I'm absolutely sure. It was mine, you see. Or rather, my uncle's. When I was a child, growing up, I kept my 'stuff' in it—my bits and pieces. My favorite toys, books, the odd treasure I'd found. So I could hardly mistake it, could I?"

He watched her face as he said it, amazed at how easy it was to utter the words after all, and how swiftly the unthinkable became reasonable and logical when shared with someone else. And how relieved he felt, as if a great burden had been lifted from his shoulders.

He saw her eyes narrow slightly and take on a kind of glow, like a hunting tiger's. "So…your uncle must have been working for Lord Vladimir—he had to be." Her voice was hushed, vibrant with excitement. "He was probably someone very close to him, too—a valet, maybe. His right-hand man. Someone he trusted with *your* care and upbringing, anyway. You know what that means? It means…"

Nikolas nodded. "If anyone knows where the bounder is…"

"It's Silas Donovan. We have to talk to him, Nik."

For a long moment they simply looked at each other, her

hands tense on his shoulders, his on her sides, his fingers curving around her slender torso, his head tipped slightly back. And as he gazed at her shimmering eyes and raptly parted lips the thought finally came clear to him like a gentle explosion, the pop and sizzle of a Chinese fireworks candle, to sear itself forever into his consciousness: *I love this woman.*

The pain that had twisted like a knife in his belly for weeks was gone. Now, instead of dread when he thought about the future, he felt full of optimism, even excitement. If his becoming king was what it was going to take to bring democracy to Silvershire, he'd do it, by God—as long as Rhia de Hayes consented to be his queen. With her by his side, he could face any challenge, defeat any foe. Never mind the fog outside the windows, the growing darkness in the room; in Nikolas's soul the sun had come from behind the clouds and was shining warm and bright.

"Nik?"

"Yes, luv?"

"Do you know where he is—Silas—" Her voice seemed to snag on a breath. "Why are you looking at me like that?"

"I'm bedazzled. It's merely one of the hazards of being this close to you—another is that I keep getting this dangerous desire to make love to you on the spot." He saw a lovely pink flush creep across her cheeks and thought of soft, sweet things…like kittens and rose petals.

"I do know where we might find him," he said softly as he moved his hands stealthily upward under her jacket. "But there's nothing we can do tonight…not until Elliot gets back with the chopper. And in the meantime…didn't we leave something rather important unfinished?"

"You mean…supper?" Her lips curved with her kitty-cat smile.

He laughed and said huskily, "No…dessert."

Inside the jacket her body was warm and humid, and her breasts seemed to swell when his hands covered them, to make a perfect fit. He watched her eyes as he spread his fingers slowly, absorbing her softness, learning the shape of her, rejoicing at the eager leap of her nipples into the cups of his palms, and the way her eyelids grew heavy with desire.

Rhia felt herself sway into him, though her hands were stubbornly braced on his shoulders, and she'd told herself she couldn't possibly think of sex right now, that her mind should be occupied with the search for Vladimir, and her feelings caught up in the tangled skein of Nikolas's emotions. But her body wasn't buying it. Instead, it did impossible things: her heart turned over, the bottom dropped out of her stomach, her knees turned to water.

"How do you do that?" she asked in a thickened voice.

"This?" Catching an erect nipple between each thumb and forefinger, he teased them gently…then harder, his lips slowly curving into a smile as he watched her eyes.

She gasped; sensation, sharp, bright and fierce, arrowed straight down through her body and converged on the pulse-spot between her thighs. "No—I mean…how do you just… forget it? Put it all aside? How can you think of sex with all that's— Oh…my g—*Nik*—"

"It's my Y chromosome," he said softly. "We men can compartmentalize. For example…right now…" His fingers were doing incredible things to her breasts, things she felt with every exclusively female nerve ending in her body. "Right now…the only thought in this awful male brain of mine is how much I want to put my mouth here…feel your softness on my tongue…taste you…"

She couldn't think…couldn't see. And she gripped his shoulders now, not to fend him off, but to keep herself from toppling over.

"My sweet Rhia…tell me—are you thinking of sex right now?"

Her laugh was almost desperate. She barely managed to produce a whisper. "You know the answer to that."

"Then...will you take this off for me? Please, my love..."
Holding her eyes with his, he brought his hands upward under
the two halves of her jacket and moved them apart...peeled
them slowly back...pushed them over her shoulders. The soft
leather whispered as it slid to the floor. "And this?" He teased
her pullover up just far enough to bare a wide strip of her torso
to his warm, exploring hands, leaving it for her to take from
there. He closed his eyes and drew a rapt breath. "Ah...luv...
you feel so good to me."

A shudder of desire jolted her as she pulled her sweater
over her head. He murmured something soothing and moved
his hands around and spread them wide across her back to
support her as he brought his mouth to her unguarded breast.
Freed of clothing, her arms settled like wings around him, and
a fine velvety warmth enveloped one nipple...then the other,
leaving the abandoned one cold and bereft, and hardening
painfully against the moistened lace of her bra. A moan
slipped from her lips almost unnoticed.

His wandering fingers found the clasp of her bra. "And this,
my love...will you take this off, too?" His face swam before
her in deepening shadows...his voice was a low, hypnotic
murmur, almost felt rather than heard. It seemed to weave a
web of enchantment over her, leaving her powerless to speak
or to move.

But not to think.

My love...my sweet: *does he even realize he's saying
those words?*

His fingers slipped under the straps of her bra and eased
them down her arms, turning even that into a caress so tender
and erotic it made her stomach quiver. And when, on their return
journey, those same fingers traced a new path along the undercurve of her breasts, and his mouth, exploring...tasting... discovered a bared nipple chilled and longing for its return embrace,
she felt pressure swell in distant nerve-rich places...and her
neck muscles melt and her eyelids drift down like velvet curtains.

And if he does realize it…does he mean them, or are they just…words?

She swayed dizzily…her fingers burrowed deep in his hair while his parted lips feathered downward over her stomach and his clever fingers released the buckle on her belt.

"I want to see you…taste you…touch you…all of you. Will you let me, sweet Rhia? Do you want that, too?"

"Yes…oh—please…"

His fingers…magic fingers…eased the zipper down… slipped between flesh and fabric and shucked away the last of her barriers, and in the same swift motion, claimed what he'd uncovered for his own. She stepped out of her clothes, clinging to his shoulders for support, and felt his knee push between her trembling legs.

He tilted his head back to look at her and whispered hoarsely, "Kiss me, now, my dearest Rhia…come to me, love."

And if he does mean them? Oh…what if he does mean it…?

She remembered, then, what she'd said to Zara. *Was it just this morning? I told her it would be worse if he did…and it is…oh, it is!*

She gave a shaken, whimpering cry; had she ever made such a sound before? Blindly, she lowered her mouth to his, and it was a little like hurling herself into a bottomless sea. Immersed…lost…she scarcely felt it when a second knee pressed between her thighs, barely knew when her trembling legs gave way and his strong hands guided her down and settled her naked onto his lap.

While she waited in quivering anticipation, legs apart, her feminine places open like a blossoming flower, exposed and vulnerable to his clever, questing fingers, his hands moved unhurriedly, almost lazily over her body, scattering hot-cold shivers across her skin wherever they touched. The rough fabric of his shirt abraded her tender nipples, and her hands gathered it convulsively across his shoulders, tugged at it in frustration, wanting only his naked skin touching her. Anything else was torture.

And his mouth…his mouth consumed her. His tongue slid rhythmically over the sensitive surfaces of her mouth, venturing deeper, filling her, blotting out thought. There was only *feeling,* searing sensation…and Nikolas, his mouth, his hands, his body.

And a desperate need. A terrible emptiness waiting to be filled. She *wanted,* with an urgency unlike anything she'd ever known before. And yet *asking* for what she wanted… needed…seemed beyond her. She seemed capable only of tiny breathless whimpers.

Then…even that was stilled. Her breath stopped as his fingers found her swollen petals at last, and with incredible gentleness slipped between them…then inside her. Just a little, at first…then deeper…filling the emptiness…filling her with a fierce dark heat that drove the breath from her body in a shuddering gasp. She tore her mouth from his as her spine convulsed and her body arched back, and she uttered his name in a sharp, piercing cry.

Instantly, his arm came across her back, strong as steel, protective as a bird's wing, shielding her, supporting her. His hand came to cradle the back of her head, bringing her face into the comforting hollow of his neck and shoulder, and he held her there, held her in warmth and safety while his fingers moved rhythmically inside her and the throbbing pressure built to its inevitable breaking point.

"Nik—" Her voice was silvery with panic, her breath like a knife in her throat.

Instantly, his whispered words were there, cooling the damp hair above her ear. "Too much, sweetheart? Shall I stop?"

"No! But I can't…I—" …*can't say I love you!* "I need you to…hold me. Please…"

"I am, my love. This is me, holding you. I've got you…it's okay…it's *okay…*"

And for that moment, as she finally let go of reason and tumbled headlong into the vortex, she let herself believe it could be…

I've got you... But Nikolas wondered for a time, as he felt the strongest, most capable woman he'd ever known tremble like a frightened fawn in his arms, just who was holding whom. The cataclysms he felt rippling like small earthquakes through her body were only echoes of the shock waves tearing through his soul.

I love you, Rhia de Hayes. The thought came, not with fireworks now, but as a steady drumbeat deep in his heart, a pulse that would be a part of his life force from this day forward for as long as he lived.

While he was holding her, tightly...tenderly...and her hot and swollen flesh still throbbed in his hand, darkness came at last and settled over them both like a chilling mist. He felt Rhia shiver as the passion-heat subsided, but when he shifted her slightly and gently withdrew his hand from her body, she gave a tiny cry of protest and shuddered convulsively, as if trying to burrow closer to his warmth.

He knew how she felt. He hated to let go of her, as well, even though he knew that, in order to find relief from the growing discomfort in his nether regions, he was going to have somehow to find a way to extricate himself from his clothes.

"Forgive me, my love," he whispered to the sweet-scented dampness of her hair. "Poor planning on my part, I know, but...in my defense, I simply couldn't wait another minute to have you... We need to find a better place for this. Warmer...at least."

From the hollow of his neck her voice came, a muffled and unsteady version of his own British accent. "Ahem...I seem to recall seeing a perfectly lovely bed around here somewhere. Seems a pity not to use it..."

He started to laugh, then winced. "Ow. Dearest...before I do myself permanent injury, d'you think..."

"Don't worry," she said as she lifted her head, sounding both husky and giddy at the same time, seemingly caught up in a strange half-dazed euphoria, "if you do, I shall kiss it and make it well."

Laughter gusted from him as the same lightness of being washed over him, too. He kissed her and then, holding her tightly still, managed to get both of them to their feet.

He was relieved to discover the chest he'd been sitting on wasn't locked. As he'd hoped it might, it yielded up a treasure trove of feather bedding, relatively dust-free and reeking of cedar. Uncounted seconds later, he and Rhia were up on that high old-fashioned bed, both wrapped in one great cloud-soft comforter, naked and breathless, laughing and shivering like naughty children.

The laughing and the shivering died quickly and together as the passion-wave engulfed them again. And like a tsunami's second wave, it was just as devastating as the first—more so, since there were no barriers left in its way, nothing at all to slow it down. Hands and mouths were free to roam where they pleased, and they did, taking and giving pleasure in equally greedy measures. Sensation layered upon sensation until the heat, the pressure, the passion became something like agony.

"Darling…I—" Nikolas couldn't say more. He was on fire, in pain, stretched to the stinging point.

From somewhere in the nest of feather bedding came a fat, smug little chuckle—the Rhia he'd first come to know and adore, pleased, he imagined, to be back on top and in control, with him completely at *her* mercy. Then all thought fled, as her lithe, warm body slithered upward over his in one excruciating all-over caress.

Yes!

He caught her legs and drew them upward along his sides and lifted his head and shoulders to meet her, joy and the anticipation of sweet relief making starbursts of heat in his belly and chest. Her fingers tangled in his hair as her mouth found his and took possession of it, breathtaking as hot, honeyed brandy. He slid his hands along the back of her thighs to grasp her firm round buttocks, one breath away from sinking his aching flesh into her sweet softness….

But it wasn't to be, not yet. Her hands clutched at his shoulders, and she murmured something against his mouth he couldn't hear. Her legs tightened around him and her body tensed…and he thought: *Of course.* Remembering the way she'd positioned them before—neither one on top— *The best way…*

Only, this time he felt her body tighten and twist…and a moment later, in a move that reminded him of the way he'd turned the tables on her the first time he'd ever held her in his arms, that long-ago night on a Paris hotel balcony, he found himself above her, looking down at her face in the darkness.

She didn't say a word, but there was tenderness in the way her hands reached up to touch his face, and he could feel her body trembling with some vast unknown emotion. Moved himself without fully understanding why, he braced himself on his elbows and cradled her face between his hands, and when he brushed her cheeks with his thumbs, found them damp with tears. He kissed her, then, lightly at first, then deeply, as her arms and legs…her whole body embraced him, and wordlessly invited him in.

As before, penetration wasn't easy, though he knew she was moistened and ready for him. And, as before, he could feel her body brace for the invasion, determined, in her passion, both to ignore and to hide from him any pain he might cause her. But he was just as determined as she was; no matter how urgently he wanted to be inside her he was determined *not* to cause her pain. And, she had given him the control.

So, when she opened to him, he introduced himself into her body only a little, until he felt the slightest resistance…then held himself back, though his arms, his whole body quivered with the strain. When she pushed against him, he lowered his head and whispered, "Relax, my love…let me take it slow…okay?"

"But I—" Gasping.

"Shh…" He kissed her, then, deeply, rhythmically…penetrated her with his tongue, made her mouth hot and slick with his essence…drove his tongue into her until she whimpered… until her mind abandoned her, and her body, left unguarded, warmed and softened and bloomed around his aching flesh. He slipped into her smooth, sweet depths with a sigh that became a duet, her breath and his, woven together in perfect harmony.

And his release, when it came, was like a crescendo of the same song, one she joined to make a climax that, though soul-stirring, was only a part of their own beautiful music.

Rhia woke to find light streaming through the multipaned windows, and Nikolas's chuckle stirring warm across her lips.

"Rise and shine, my sweet…"

As the notes of a blues song, achingly sad and lovely, slipped rapidly from her dream memory, she lifted her arms around his neck and sighing, tilted her mouth to his kiss.

"Mmm…love, don't tempt me. Fog's lifting—you can see the river. I expect our friend Elliot will be arriving shortly, and—" he dropped a delicate kiss onto the tip of her nose "—not that *I* mind, but I thought you might prefer not to have your colleague catch you in such an…ah…exposed, albeit delectable—"

"All right, already…I'm up, I'm up…okay?" She opened her eyes, sat up and threw back the comforter, trying hard to scowl, but the image that filled her sleep-fogged vision made her smile blissfully instead. Nikolas…elegant as ever, even when wearing nothing but a day's growth of dark beard stubble. His body was so lean and lithe and beautiful…her heart stumbled, and her body's tender places tingled to wakefulness. Well-being filled her, and she lifted her arms over her head in a glorious stretch, like a cat in a pool of sunshine.

"Stop that, you shameless minx!" Nikolas thrust one arm around her waist and the other under her knees and hauled her, laughing, into his arms. He kissed her once, hard, then lowered her feet to the floor. "Get dressed—*now.*"

Muttering dark Creole curses under her breath, Rhia

obeyed. And as she did, she felt the sunshine fade and a chilly little cloud come to darken her heart instead. *If only...*

If only it could be like this for us always. If only it didn't have to end.

But it did. She knew that. The night just past had been an enchantment...a fantasy interlude...a day at Disneyland. Time now to wake up and return to the real world beyond the gates. And as before, she grieved secretly for the end of the dream...the loss of something wonderful she knew would not come again.

Once up and awake, she dressed with her usual efficiency—inspired, no doubt, by the need to find a bathroom as quickly as possible. While she did that, Nikolas, who had finished dressing even before she, folded the bedding and returned it to the chest, then turned out the contents of Elliot's duffel bag. They were wolfing down chocolate-dipped Danish butter cookies and bottled water when they heard the distant clack of a chopper's rotors.

Hastily stuffing what was left of the snack goodies back in the bag, they gathered it up along with their jackets and ran. Rhia, a few steps ahead of Nikolas, was halfway down the curving staircase before she realized he wasn't following. She stopped, gripping the banister railing, and looked back.

Up on the landing, Nikolas was standing absolutely still, frozen in place, like someone caught in a tractor beam.

"Nik?" She started back up the stairs, her heart already beginning to pound, though she didn't yet know the reason.

Light from the window at the far end of the landing had flooded across the wall directly in front of him, bringing into full glory the gilt-framed portraits hanging there. As she came closer, she could see that Nikolas was staring, apparently transfixed, at one portrait in particular. It was a large dark portrait—of one of the previous lords of the castle, she assumed—probably from the Victorian Era, judging from the gentleman's severe clothing, longish hair and full beard and

mustache. His only visible features were a knife-bridged patrician nose, and eyes of a fierce and steely blue that glared
frostily down at them from under thick, bushy eyebrows.

"Who's that?" Rhia asked sharply. "One of the former
Lord Vladimirs, surely."

Without taking his eyes from the portrait, Nikolas shook
his head slowly. Words came, barely audible, whispering from
lips that might have been carved from stone.

"It's Silas."

Chapter 12

"I don't understand. If Lord Vladimir *is* Silas Donovan, how could he just…slip on a whole new identity and for thirty years live right here in Silvershire, in plain sight, and not leave any kind of trail?"

"People do it," Nikolas said grimly. "All the time."

"Not to us," Rhia said, gritting her teeth as she clutched at the dashboard of Nikolas's middle-aged Opal. "The Lazlo Group's resources aren't that easy to outwit."

He threw her a glance, then brought his narrowed gaze back to the road ahead—a great relief to her, since their speed had been hovering somewhere between suicidal and insane ever since they'd left Nik's apartment in Dunford. At the moment, they were careening along an almost deserted highway that followed the rugged coastline from the town of Dunford to the northeasternmost tip of the island kingdom. It would probably be a spectacular drive, she thought, under calmer circumstances. Walls of white that were a smaller version of the famed White Cliffs of Dover towered above the road on one side and on the other, dizzying drop-offs plunged to rocky shores and crashing surf. At the moment, however, she was too busy careening back and forth between nausea and fear of imminent death to appreciate the view.

She could see the muscle working rapidly in the hinge of Nikolas's jaw. Sympathy for him tugged at her like a child begging for attention. Ignoring it, she said impatiently, "Dammit, Nik, people know what Vladimir looks like!"

"Do you?" he asked, without looking at her.

"Do I…what? Know what Lord Vladimir looks like? Of course I do—what he used to look like, anyway. I've seen pictures."

"Okay, describe him for me."

She stared straight ahead, concentrating on the pictures in her head and trying not to think about the precipice hurtling by a few feet from the car's tires. "All right, let's see. Tall—over six feet, if I remember right. Strong build. Bald head…blue eyes…aristocratic features—thin lips, high-bridged nose, hollow cheeks, prominent jaw—" She let the words trail off into nothing as the portrait of Vladimir's hirsute ancestor floated into her mind. She turned her head slowly to look at Nikolas. He was nodding, lips curved in a grim little smile.

"It didn't occur to me until I saw that picture. I don't know whether Vladimir was naturally bald or shaved his head, but all he'd have had to do to disguise himself was acquire hair—his own or a wig—and grow a full beard. The rest would be a matter of stance—changing his walk, stooping instead of standing tall. Things like that." He paused, and the smile tilted wryly. "My uncle always stooped. And he walked with a pronounced limp—from an old boating injury, he told me."

Rhia was silent. Her mind was racing madly, trying to take it all in. There'd been no time, until now, to talk about it, work out all the implications, make sense of it. Immediately after Nikolas's stunning announcement, they'd had to dash to meet the chopper. Conversation had, of course, been next to impossible during the short flight to Dunford, and at Nikolas's apartment they'd taken time only to shower and refuel themselves on canned soup and crackers from his meager larder before heading up the coast to a destination he had yet to reveal.

"I take it you know where he is—your, uh…Silas?" Rhia had asked him as they were leaving, trying to curb her annoyance at being left in the dark, hating the distance he'd put between them, the distracted way he spoke to her, the way he carefully avoided her eyes as he replied.

"I believe I know where he might have gone, yes."

They would take his car, he said, rather than the helicopter, which Elliot had told them was at their service for as long as they needed it. He offered no more explanation, and Rhia, looking at his stony jaw and cold-steel eyes, had decided not to argue the issue.

Now, she rather wished she had.

She also wished she'd insisted on acquiring a weapon.

Rhia seldom carried a gun, although she was skilled in the use of firearms and fully licensed to carry concealed. Naturally, bringing a weapon of any sort along on this particular assignment—accompanying Silvershire's crown prince to a clandestine meeting with his father the king—had been out of the question.

She'd asked Nikolas before they'd left his apartment if he was bringing a gun along—it seemed a reasonable question to her, considering they were heading off to confront a possible kidnapper and murderer. He'd told her flatly that he didn't own one. Sorry.

She wished now she'd taken the time to insist on getting herself one. But they'd been in such a hurry….

"There's something else I don't understand," she said, again striving for distraction after a particularly hairy turn had caused her stomach to lodge itself temporarily in her throat. "Lazlo has a pretty extensive dossier on Silas Donovan, including family history. The information goes back a good long way—generations, in fact. A couple of hundred years' worth. How is it that an imposter can come along and insert himself into the Donovan family tree, and nobody be the wiser? What about kinfolk? Neighbors?"

His smile broadened, though there was no more humor in it than before. "Patience, my love," he said softly, the first words of endearment he'd spoken to her since they'd left Vladimir's castle. "All will become clear in due time, I promise. Very soon now, in fact…"

Except for one sharp exhalation, by clenching her teeth and counting silently to ten Rhia managed to keep her seething impatience locked inside.

The car sped on, hurtling around corners on a road that wound steadily downward, ever closer to the foaming surf… then climbed steeply up again, arrowed through a cut in the shallow cliffside to emerge at last onto a barren plain. The plain, studded with scrubby vegetation, stretched ahead to a cloudless blue sky and ended in a rocky point that jutted like an arrowhead into a churning sea. At the tip of the arrowhead, a lone structure rose like a stubby white candle from a gray stone holder.

"It's a lighthouse," Rhia said, with a little hiccup of surprised laughter, and then went silent as Nikolas pulled the car to the side of the road and stopped, leaving the motor running.

He'd had to stop. For a minute. His heart was racing and his hands were cold and sweaty on the steering wheel. Though, at least his voice seemed gratifyingly normal as he said conversationally, "It's called the Daneby Light. A few centuries ago, wreckers made a pretty good living here, using lanterns to lure unwary sailors onto those rocks. The crown put an end to that activity sometime in the mid nineteenth century when they built this lighthouse and appointed someone as full-time keeper. Someone named Donovan, I believe."

Beside him, Rhia was staring at the lighthouse, slowly shaking her head. "My God, Nikolas…*this* is where you grew up? You must have been—" her voice slipped away from her and she snatched it back with a hard, hurting breath "—so *lonely.*"

She turned her head to look at him, and he saw her throat ripple and the intense shine of her eyes beneath sooty lashes, and he felt something hard and cold inside him soften and warm. For the first time since they'd left Perth Castle, he smiled a real smile. "Darling," he said softly, stroking her cheek with the back of his finger, "your empathy is showing."

He shifted gears abruptly and pulled back onto the road. He felt renewed…strengthened, suddenly, all the tension and dread in him gone. "Actually, it wasn't all that bad. You don't really need chums, you know, when you're just a little tyke. And then, I had all this as my backyard. Silas used to take me out on the moors, or along the beach, or exploring the tide pools, and he'd teach me the names of everything we found. And at night, when it was clear, there were the stars—he taught me their names, too. On a moonless night…you wouldn't believe the stars—there aren't any lights out here to compete with them, you see. Can't say I was fond of the storms, though. Or the fog."

"This is what you meant when you said if there's anything you know about, it's—"

"—fog," Nikolas joined in, wryly. "Yeah…I did have my fill of that. But then…I went off to school." He paused, looking back, then let out a breath. "*That* was the only time I was really lonely, I think. The first year was rough, but at least I had the solace of company. There was a lot of sniffling that went on in the first-term's dormitory after lights out, I can tell you. But…it got better. And later on I met Phillipe and started spending summers and holidays with him, and after that I didn't come back here much at all, actually."

"But…wait." She tilted her head, frowning. "Silas doesn't still live out here, does he? According to his file, he lives and works in Dunford. At the college."

"He does. He moved to Dunford when they closed down the lighthouse—or automated it, which amounts to the same thing. That happened when I was at Oxford. After I started teaching at the college, I got him a job there as a custodian." He gave a sharp bark of laughter as it struck him. "My God—can you imagine it? The Duke of Perthegon—working as a *janitor?*" He paused, then said in a voice with no humor in it whatsoever, "He's been AWOL from his job, and he's not at his apartment in Dunford, either. Believe me, the first thing I did when I heard about…all this, was go looking for him. Figured he owed me some sort of an explanation. Didn't think of it then, but it has occurred to me that he might…just possibly…have come here to hide out. He'd done it once before."

They were both silent for a moment, watching the lighthouse loom steadily larger in the car's windshield. Then Rhia said slowly, "Okay, I get how Vladimir could have disguised himself as the old lighthouse keeper and escaped notice all these years—I mean, living way out here, no neighbors—especially if he hadn't any family. There's just one thing I don't understand." He felt her head swivel toward him…felt the burn of her eyes. Felt a chill wash over him before she even asked the question.

"What happened to the *real* Silas Donovan?"

He turned his head and met her eyes—briefly—but couldn't say the words. He knew he didn't have to.

She closed her eyes, let out a hissing breath. "*God,* I wish I had a gun."

The feeling of lightness and optimism left him as quickly as it had come. "Silas would never hurt me," he said stiffly, and felt her eyes turn on him again.

"Nik, the man is very probably a sociopath—you do know that, don't you? He has no feelings, for you or any other human being. People only matter to him if he can use them. Otherwise, they're disposable. He used you—"

He hit the steering wheel with the palm of his hand, surprising himself as much as her. It was a child's anger, stubborn and irrational. He knew that, but it made no difference. "*Dammit,* Rhee! The man was a father to me!"

"He *stole* you from your father. And raised you, groomed you, planned to use you to fulfill his own sick agenda for revenge. You think you know him? How can you know what he'll do?"

He stared bleakly through the windshield. He didn't want to quarrel with Rhia; quarreling with her made him feel cold and sick inside. But he couldn't let himself agree with her. He couldn't. "He was both mother and father to me," he said in a voice that hurt his throat. "The only parent I ever had. I can't forget that."

She didn't reply.

The car topped the last rise and began the long gradual descent toward the tip of the arrowhead. And although outside the sun continued to beat down from a cloudless sky, inside the car Nikolas felt the way he had as a child when the fog rolled in from the channel and shrouded the lighthouse and its two lone occupants in a blanket of white—chilled, isolated...*alone.*

It seemed fitting, somehow.

"Doesn't look like anyone's here. I don't see a car," Rhia said in a low voice that was a measure of how tense she was rather than fear of being heard by anyone outside the vehicle.

Nikolas had parked the Opal nose-in to a row of white-painted rocks separating a bare gravel parking area from an overgrown garden. He was staring through the windshield at what had once been a charming lightkeeper's cottage, built of white-painted stone with a slate-tile roof to withstand the buffeting of storm and sea. Now, wind and rain had scoured away most of the paint, so that the cottage seemed almost to be trying to return to the rock that surrounded it. Windows set deep in the thick stone walls were clouded with cobwebs and salt spray, and wooden shutters bearing slivers of blue paint hung crookedly from rusting hinges.

"There's a garage around the back," he said absently. "If he's been living here for a while and doesn't want that fact known, I expect he'd keep his car in out of sight."

She nodded, but didn't reply. Her throat felt clogged with emotions she couldn't express...words she couldn't say. Oh, how she wanted to reach out to him...touch his cheek...take his hand. *What are you feeling now, Nikolas, my love? This must be so hard...and you are so far away from me.*

He turned his head to give her a lopsided smile. "I must say, the place has gone to ruin a bit since I saw it last. A pity, really. A lot of history here..."

She cleared her throat and returned the smile. "I think it definitely ought to be preserved. When you're king, you should turn it into a museum, or a national monument." Nikolas snorted and reached for the door handle. "Sure," she said as she followed suit, "you know, turn it into a tourist attraction, like they do the childhood homes of presidents back in the States. You could—" The rest froze solid in her throat.

The door of the cottage had opened partway—no more than a foot or so. Through the crack came a pair of arms holding a rifle, and a voice that was cold and hard as steel.

"Ye have 'til I count ten to get back into your car and drive away. On the count of eleven, I start shooting. One..."

"Nik—" *I knew it—I should have insisted on bringing a gun.*

"Shh—it's all right." He pushed the door open and called cheerfully, "Don't shoot, Uncle—it's me, Nik."

The rifle barrel wavered, but didn't withdraw. "Show yourselves—the both o' ye," the voice commanded. "And keep your hands where I can see them."

Rhia eased herself out of the car slowly, hands on the top edge of the door but keeping most of the rest of herself barricaded behind it. Nikolas, meanwhile, stood up boldly, unconcernedly slammed his door and held his hands out to his sides.

"Come on, Silas, what are you doing? This is a fine welcome. For God's sake, put that thing away."

While Rhia held her breath, the gun slowly lowered, then abruptly disappeared. The door opened wider, and a man emerged, scowling into the sunshine. He was tall, but stooped and gaunt—a big-framed man losing flesh to age, though he looked strong and wiry still. He was wearing olive-green wool trousers tucked into knee-high boots, a black knit long-sleeved sweater and an open brown leather vest. He also wore a black wool fisherman's cap over long graying brown hair that had been pulled back into a clubbed ponytail. His beard, moustache and bushy eyebrows were almost entirely gray, and what visible skin he had was weathered as old leather.

"Nikolas, me boy—is that you? Ah—" he made a gesture of impatience with his hand "—forgive an old man. I don't see as well as I used to." As if daring her to challenge the statement, eyes as sharp and blue as steel knives flicked at Rhia before returning to Nikolas, and she winced involuntarily, to her inner fury, as if stung by a lash.

"Thought you'd be Weston's men, come to arrest me for trespassing in me own house," Silas Donovan went on, thin lips drawn into a sneer. Then he laughed—a single harsh sound, like the crack of a whip. "But I hear that's who ye be, ain't it? Weston's man? Henry Weston's whelp, so they're saying. Who'd've thought it, eh, boy? If I'd known who ye were when I found ye on me doorstep thirty years ago, I'd've drowned ye like a runt pup, I would." Baring strong teeth in a wolfish grin, he clasped Nikolas's hand and pulled him into a hard embrace. The two men thumped each other soundly on the back for a moment or two, then Silas turned and aimed his fierce glare at Rhia. "And who is this ye have with ye?" And he bowed his head and doffed his cap in an oddly charming gesture. "Aye, I must be getting old indeed, me lass, to have mistaken ye for Weston's, or any sort of *man.*"

Rhia was rarely tongue-tied, but the bombardment of conflicting thoughts and impressions she was experiencing had her reeling. It was all she could manage just to mutter her own name as she placed her hand in Silas Donovan's leathery grip.

Who is this man? Can this crusty old seadog possibly be the exiled Duke of Perthegon, cousin to King Weston and erstwhile heir to Silvershire's throne? This is the man who raised Nikolas, nurtured him as an infant, was both teacher and companion to him when he was a little boy. Can this be the same sociopath who plotted against the crown for more than thirty years, kidnapped an infant prince, arranged one murder and committed another...and who knows how many more?

Could we...could Nikolas...be wrong? What is a picture, after all—a portrait painted more than a century ago? A couple of chests made by the same craftsman? Can it have been as this man says? Was he only a lonely lighthouse keeper who chose to raise the foundling infant left on his doorstep?

"...a friend of mine," Nikolas was saying.

She felt the brush of whiskers and warm breath on the back of her hand, and a shiver ran down her spine. She lifted her eyes, seeking Nikolas's, and found them resting on her, their gray gaze calm and reassuring.

"Well, come in, come in," Silas said, straightening with a beckoning gesture. "I've just put the kettle on—about to have me tea and a bite, I was. You're welcome to join me, if ye don't mind tinned meat and a bit of bread."

"Nothing to eat, thanks," Nikolas said. "I wouldn't mind tea, though. Rhia?"

She mumbled something in acquiescence, feeling a little like Alice in Wonderland as she followed him into the cottage. And she took care to note, as she did, that the rifle was propped against the wall beside the door.

The front door of the cottage opened directly into a large room that was all but bare of furniture, although a large stone fireplace at one end still held the remnants of a recent fire. It was dim inside; the only light was that seeping in through the small, dirt- and salt-encrusted windows. The place smelled of stale ashes and abandonment.

"I stay mostly in here in the kitchen," Silas said as he led the way with a sprightly step across the room and through a doorway opposite the fireplace, his boots making echoing footsteps on the dusty wood-plank floor. "Make me fire in there at night, when ye canna see the smoke." He swept off his cap and favored them with his wolfish smile as he gestured toward a wooden table and chairs. "Rather not advertise me presence here, if ye take me meaning."

"Why *are* you here, Uncle?" Nikolas sounded merely curious. He pulled out a chair and sat down, leaving Rhia to do the same while Silas turned his attention to the teakettle steaming on a portable gas camping stove that had been placed on the warped linoleum-covered countertop. "I've been looking all over the map for you, since I found out I'm not who I thought I was."

Silas nodded without looking away from his task. "Aye, ye'd be wanting answers, I'll warrant." He spooned tea leaves into a pot and poured boiling water over them. "Ask your questions, lad, and be done with it. We have important things to talk about, ye and me."

"Is that how it happened?" Nikolas asked, and though his voice was quiet, something in it made Rhia feel chilled. "You just…found me abandoned on your doorstep?"

The old man gave his whip-crack laugh. "You think the likes o' me crept into the royal palace one fine eve and stole the royal babe from its mother's arms? Am I a ghost, then? A will-o'-the-wisp?"

"No, not a ghost," Nikolas said softly.

Silas seemed not to hear that as he carried the teapot and three crockery cups to the table and set them down with a thump. His eyes were aglow with a feverish light. "And what does it matter to ye now, eh? That's in the past and done with. *This* is the time that matters. It's *our* time now, boy—everything we've worked for, planned for—it's here now—" he made a fist with one hard bony hand and shook it in front of Nikolas's nose "—right here in our hands. Not quite the way I'd planned it…but either way, that conniving thief Weston's done. Silvershire's ours, Nikolas—*ours. At last…*"

The countryman's lilt had disappeared from his voice, Rhia noticed. He spoke now in the clipped accent of Silvershire's upper class—British, only more so. She reached unnoticed for the heavy crockery cup, weighing it in her hands, assessing its possibilities as a weapon.

Nikolas leaned casually back in his chair. "*Ours,* Uncle? Exactly how is Silvershire 'ours'? I thought we were working to build a new democracy here."

Silas straightened and drew back, his eyes suddenly wary and his smile more fox, now, than wolf. "Why, that's what I meant, lad…what did you think? Democracy, aye, that's what we've been about, ye and me, t'be sure 'tis."

"Is it?" Nikolas's voice had gone deadly quiet. His eyes, Rhia noticed, were iron-hard, and were fixed unwaveringly on the other man's face. "I know what *I've* been working for, but somehow I don't think we've had quite the same goal in mind…*Lord Vladimir.*"

For the space of a half dozen heartbeats, everything stopped—all sound, all movement…even breath. The air itself seemed to freeze solid.

The older man broke the stillness first, cracking it like a stone thrown onto an ice-covered pond. But before his harsh croak of denial could form into words, it was overridden by Nikolas's cold and implacable voice.

"Don't. I've just come from Perth Castle. I've seen the proof with my own eyes." He leaned forward and placed his hands on the tabletop, and to Rhia, watching with suspended breath, he seemed almost to grow taller…broader. *Every inch a king…* "The only thing I want to know, Lord Vladimir, is how you did it. And *why.* Was it all about revenge?"

"Revenge?" Every muscle in Rhia's body tensed as Vladimir swooped down like a hunting hawk, eyes fiery with rage, fingers curved into talons. Hers clenched around the crockery teacup, relaxing only slightly when he grabbed hold of the table's edge. She could see droplets of spittle on his lips, shining like tiny diamonds. "You call it revenge? *I* call it justice! *I* was King Dunford's choice! *I* was supposed to inherit his crown. That weasel…Henry Weston…he plotted behind my back…poisoned the king's mind against me. He took what was mine! Took my crown, my life…left me with *nothing!*"

On the last word he pushed back from the table, and Rhia started to breathe again, though she kept her eyes riveted on the man's face the same way she would a coiled-up rattlesnake. *He's insane,* she thought, watching his glittering eyes. *Completely mad.*

Why, then, does he seem so familiar to me?

Vladimir drew himself up and glared down at them from his full height with the haughty bearing of an emperor. "So, I took what was his—I took his son. Is that not *justice?*"

"Brilliant," Nikolas murmured, studying him with thoughtfully narrowed eyes. "How on earth did you manage it? Must have had help from inside the palace, I imagine."

"Help? Pah—never needed it." His face took on a crafty look, and his eyes shifted to a distant place only he could see. "I have my ways…come and go from the palace any time I please, yes, I do…and no one the wiser. Took the babe from under their noses…" He laughed—a thin, gleeful snicker. "Raised the boy to despise his father, too…taught him to hate everything the man stands for…educated him…" His gaze snapped back to Nikolas, sharp and bright again. "Oh, and you were a fine boy, a clever boy, Nikolas. Blood will always tell. That was my one mistake you know—that brat I put in your place. Low-class genes…should have known better…"

"Who was he—Prince Reginald?" Nikolas asked softly.

A sneer curved Vladimir's lips. "Bought him. Didn't cost

me much—mother was a prostitute and a drug addict. She was glad to get the bit I offered her."

"What happened to her? Did you have her killed, too?"

"Didn't have to," said Vladimir with a disdainful sniff, looking as if he'd gotten something foul on his hands. "Naturally, the bitch took the money I paid her and bought drugs—too much, as it turned out. Just as well—saved me the trouble of getting rid of her."

He seemed so pleased with himself, seemed not to realize how damning his boasting was. Rhia wondered whether he didn't care if they heard his confession—and the implications of that were chilling—or whether he was simply relieved after so many years of silence finally to be able to let the world know how clever he'd been.

"Wait," Nikolas said, shifting forward in his chair like an interested student at the feet of the master, "I don't understand. If you can get into the palace whenever you want, why didn't you just kill Weston and be done with it?"

Vladimir grimaced. "You disappoint me, boy. Think— what would that have gained me? If the king dies, the crown passes to a child—Reginald, and the power to a regent. I'd have my revenge, yes, but not the rest that I'm entitled to. The *power,* lad." He clenched a fist as if plucking that elusive commodity from the air. *"The power that should have been mine."*

"So…what was your plan? And why kill Reginald, after all those years? I thought he was your ticket to the power."

Vladimir snorted. There was a pause while he picked up the teapot and lifted the lid to inspect the brew. "Why, indeed. As I said, the boy was a lowlife, and stupid in the bargain. I'd kept the proof of your identity, of course—hidden safely away until I had need of it. I meant to use it to blackmail Reginald into doing my bidding—he'd inherit the crown, but I'd be the real ruler of Silvershire—the power behind the throne. But alas, the twit got a bit too big for his britches— tried to have me killed, if you can believe it! Stupidly, too—

fortunately for me, I suppose." He leveled a glare at Nikolas from under bristling eyebrows. "Well, after that, what could I do? The nitwit left me no choice. Ah…but this is so much the better. We can have it *all* now, Nikolas, my boy, don't you see?" He was smiling again, that wild, insane light glittering in his eyes.

He seemed to have forgotten Rhia, who sat rigid in her chair, fighting a disgust so intense she could feel her nails biting into the palms of her hands.

She looked at Nikolas, caught his eye…and the instant flash of communion between them was like electricity in a dark night, a beautiful light flooding her soul. The message in his eyes was plain as spoken words, calming as a touch.

She cleared her throat…pushed her chair back. "I'm afraid that's not going to happen, your lordship, or…whatever. You see, I'm a licensed bounty hunter with the Lazlo Group. I've been commissioned by His Majesty King Henry Weston and his regent, Lord Russell, Duke of Carrington, to take you into custody and return you to Silverton to answer charges of kidnapping, extortion, murder, attempted murder, treason…let's see, what else? Oh, a bunch of things. Anyway, now—" she rose, hitched in a breath "—I'm going to have to ask you to put your hands behind your head—"

Vladimir's whip-crack laugh cut off the rest. "*You?* Think you can arrest *me?* Tell me, *wench,* how you mean to do that, precisely." His sneer was almost audible. "You don't even have a weapon!"

Rage sizzled behind her eyes…twisted cold in her belly. But it was the flash of recognition that took her breath away… turned her body to stone. *My God…that's who he reminds me of. Except for the madness, he's my father.*

Nikolas was smiling without a shred of humor. "Trust me, Vlad," he drawled, "the lady doesn't need one. Make a move on her, and you'll find that out soon enough. I'd do as she says, if I were you. And, by the way…" His voice took on an edge of steel.

"In the unlikely event she *should* need an extra set of hands, she's got me. It's been awhile, but I've found that my commando training does come back to me when I need it. I don't think you'd get far against the two—" That was as far as he got.

Rhia had quietly slipped her handcuffs from the back of her belt where they'd been hidden by her leather jacket. She was bringing them into view when Vladimir, shrieking curses, hurled the teapot full of scalding hot tea at her face and bolted from the room.

Chapter 13

Rhia's scream cut through Nikolas like a bolt of lightning, deafening him to everything else. As he dove for her he didn't hear his own bellow of rage or the crash of his chair hitting the floor or the tinkle of shattering crockery. Silas/Vladimir vanished from his mind like a puff of smoke.

Then his hands were touching her…fearfully…feathering over her cheeks, her hair, the sleeve of her leather jacket, slick now with already-cooling tea. Shaken to the core, he whispered, "God…Rhee—are you…"

"Dammit…*dammit!*" Her eyes blazed at him with rage and pain as she tried to shake him off. "*Go!* He's getting away— I'm *fine,* dammit—leave me—just go—don't let him—"

"Let him go." His voice was jerky, uneven. "It's an is-land—how far can he get? And you're *not* fine, you were drenched with boiling water. How bad…" He had to stop; he felt light-headed, all of a sudden. He drew an unsteady hand across his brow, wiping away ice-cold sweat. "My God…I'm sorry…I knew he'd never hurt me, it just never occurred to me he'd go for you instead…" *Because you are a part of me now.*

"I really am fine," she said in a tight voice that was itself proof positive of the lie. She was bent forward at the waist, breathing shallowly, one hand braced on the table, the other holding her black knit pullover away from her body. "Did he…does he have the gun?"

Nikolas nodded absently; he had himself in hand again, his attention focused now on getting Rhia's leather jacket off her without causing more damage. "He went out the front, so I'm guessing he's taken it with him. Can you let me have your hand for a minute, love? That's got it…now the other one… there's a good girl." He eased the jacket away from her and tossed it onto a chair, then took her by the arms and turned her gently to face him. "Which is another reason why I don't want you haring madly after him, my darling. He's got the gun, we haven't. There's only one way out of here, and we'll be on his trail soon enough. First, I want to see—"

They both jerked as a shot rang out—then quickly, before either of them could react, two more.

"What—"

He felt her muscles tense under his hands and tightened his grip. "No, you don't—you stay right here. *Don't…move.*" He set her firmly aside and in two strides was at the window, flattened against the wall beside it. He leaned over for a quick peek, then sucked in a breath. "Bloody *hell.*"

"What?"

"He's shot out our tires. I heard three shots, so it's nice of him to leave us one, I suppose." He said it with a jauntiness he was far from feeling. He knew better than anyone just how isolated they were.

And he didn't know, yet, how badly Rhia was injured.

"Guess that means he's got a car," she said, slurring her words a little.

They both froze once more as an engine roared to life

somewhere nearby. Tires squealed and spat gravel. Nikolas watched through the grimy window as a nondescript gray hatchback of unknown vintage raced away on the windswept highway, trailing a plume of smoky exhaust.

"Which is another thing he has and we haven't," he said lightly as he returned to Rhia, hoping his face wouldn't give away the helplessness and frustration he felt…the crushing sense of self-blame. The anger—at Vladimir, of course, but mostly at himself.

He was shaking inside as he took her face between his hands…frowned tenderly while he studied it feature by feature for damage. His knees went weak and he let out a breath of profound thanksgiving when he found it apparently untouched. Her skin was definitely paler, though, than her usual vivid coloring, and when he kissed her forehead, it felt clammy and cool to his lips.

"Sweetheart," he said huskily, "I am so sorry. This is my fault—I underestimated him. You were right. I was still thinking of him as my father—the man who raised me…."

Her head jerked quickly from side to side—she was beginning to shake all over, now. Through chattering teeth, she mumbled, "No, no—I was distracted, too. I let him get to me. Wasn't on my guard. He…just reminded me so much of someone…"

Startled enough by that to tear his eyes away from his examination of her neck and throat, he said, "Really? Who?"

"Dammit, Nik." She hauled in a breath and her eyes flared hot, bringing some of the color back into her cheeks. "Except for being totally insane, I swear the sonofabitch is just like *my* father. Cold, arrogant, supercilious…so bloody insufferably *certain* every thought in his head is gospel, his every opinion a *fact.* Stop it, damn you, I'm not joking!"

He was shaking with silent laughter. "Rhee, my love, I'm not laughing about your father—believe me, I'm not. Just… hearing a Louisiana Cajun swear like a Brit…got to me.

Sorry." He touched his lips to hers and said tenderly, "I want to hold you so badly, but I'm afraid I'll hurt you. Will you let me have a look at the damage?"

She closed her eyes and gave a shivery laugh as she swayed slightly toward him. "I'm almost afraid to look. It hurts like such bloody *hell*."

"I hate to say it, but…that's probably a good thing. Third-degree burns don't hurt—the nerves are destroyed." And she would never know, from the blithe way he said the words, that he was half-dizzy with nausea at the thought of the destruction of even the smallest part of her. "So, tell me, dear heart, at the risk of cliché…where does it hurt?"

"I got my arm up in time to keep the teapot from hitting me in the head…deflected most of the water away from my face, at least." Her teeth were chattering again, and her nipples stood out in sharp relief under the wet—now cold—pullover. Naturally, his ignorant body, oblivious to anything but that familiar signal, insisted on reacting to it in the usual way as he slipped his hands under the bottom edge of her shirt. "I think…the jacket may have protected me, too," Rhia said. "Some went down inside…down my front. That's where it hurts the most."

Her breath hissed sharply between her teeth as he pulled the clinging fabric away from her skin. He had to hold his own breath to keep it from doing the same when he drew the shirt slowly and carefully up and over her head and saw the splash of angry red welts across her chest and the tops of her breasts, down the valley between and on to her stomach. He looked away, swearing viciously.

"This, too," she said in a choked voice, tugging at the front of her bra where it met scalded skin.

With unsteady fingers he unsnapped the front clasp and eased the two halves apart, then slipped the straps over her shoulders, all the while keeping his gaze focused on the little silver replica of a saxophone hanging from its thin chain nestled between her breasts, lifting slightly with each muted breath. Rage stung his eyes and the saxophone seemed to shimmer as if in agreement.

"Anywhere else?" His voice sounded cold; he had to make it so in order to maintain even a small measure of control.

She shook her head. "Just a little bit in my scalp…not too bad. Nik…" He lifted his eyes to her face, and they felt like deadweights. She was gazing at him, eyes soft…the color of whiskey. Her fingers touched his face.

A tremor shook him. He said harshly, "I can't remember— what the devil is first aid for burns?"

Her lips trembled into a smile. "Cold water…antibiotics…something to make it stop hurting…" She leaned in and touched his mouth with her smile. Her lips were cold…he felt them warm and soften against his, and juices pooled at the back of his throat as if he'd tasted something unbearably sweet. "There," she whispered against his lips, "that's the best painkiller there is…"

An easing breath poured silently from him as he took her head between his two hands. Holding it like a priceless treasure, he closed his eyes and let his mouth find its way to hers again…sank into it, and felt it begin to heal his wounded soul.

But even without touching her body he could feel her shivering. She was cold, hurt, possibly in shock, and his muscles ached to hold her close, to warm, protect and nourish her, make her all right again. The fact that he couldn't do any of those things brought the rage simmering inside him to a boil again. He'd been a believer in nonviolence all his life; it astonished him that he could feel such a powerful urge to kill.

He left the sweet solace of her mouth reluctantly, pressed his lips to her forehead instead. "My love, you're shivering. There's a blanket in my car, I think. Not much of a heater, though. You're better off staying here while I go and see what I can find. Here—sit down. Maybe see if you can raise Elliot on your cell phone." He pressed his lips to her forehead. "Back in a flash."

He let go of her and strode jerkily from the room, only then discovering how badly shaken he was.

Outside, he retrieved the blanket from the car's boot—dusty and smelling damp—and confirmed his suspicion that the tires were indeed casualties of war. He shook out the blanket as best he could, then wadded it up and headed back to the kitchen. "Here, luv—not terribly clean, but at least it's warm. I'm going to see if there's anything in the garage to patch a tire—" He halted. Rhia wasn't sitting where he'd left her, but was standing beside the window, frowning at the cell phone in her hand. "What is it? No signal?"

She shook her head and made a little grimace of annoyance. "Not even a smidgen."

Nikolas pulled in a careful breath and tried to make his tone light. "Then I'm afraid we're—pardon the expression—royally screwed. This place has been shut down for years—no power, no telephone…I suppose I might try building a fire, perhaps send up a few smoke signals…."

"You can…" Rhia paused, biting her lower lip in concentration as she tugged at something on the back of her belt "…I guess, if you have a really strong desire to practice your Boy Scout merit-badge skills. Or, we can use this." She held up a little black box about the size of a deck of playing cards.

"Don't—" he did a double take and stared at the thing sideways "—tell me that's a—"

"Yep—emergency radio beacon. All we have to do is open it like this—" she was demonstrating as she spoke "—and hit this little button right here…and we're in business." Her valiant efforts to hold back a gleeful smile produced a dimple he'd never seen before, and her eyes had the glow of aged brandy.

He could only gaze at her and slowly shake his head. "A man could easily develop one hell of an inferiority complex hanging around you—you know that, don't you?"

"Donovan, I doubt you're in danger of ever having an inferior anything." The sultry look she gave him from under her eyelashes quickened his pulse and reminded him graphically of the fact that she was naked from the waist up—something *she'd* apparently forgotten. "Anyway," she said with a shrug, "I can't take the credit. It's standard issue for all Lazlo's agents. First time I've ever used mine—I've always considered it kind of a nuisance, to tell you the truth. Just one more thing to carry."

She looked around at the thick stone walls. "I suppose we ought to take it outside. I don't know exactly what the range is, but I'm sure the less interference the better."

She was on her way to the door, looking like an artist's rendition of Athena off to the hunt, when Nikolas cleared his throat and said, "Uh…sweetheart…aren't you forgetting something?"

She paused to throw him a questioning look over one bare shoulder, saw the direction of his gaze and glanced down at herself. "Oh," she said. "That. So what? There's nobody around for miles."

"*I'm* around," he pointed out as he picked up her jacket and draped it carefully over her shoulders. He stroked a strand of damp hair away from her ear and with his lips almost touching its delicate shell, murmured, "Have a little pity, love. You have no idea how rotten it makes me feel, having lusty thoughts about you when you're injured and in pain." It wasn't the time, he knew, to tell her how far beyond lust—light-years beyond—his thoughts about her had gone.

She leaned against him, her head bumping onto his shoulder, her body's curves seeking his. "But I told you—a little lust is like an all-over shot of morphine."

"Rhee, I adore you," he said, laughing weakly, his lips in her hair and her scent, lightly flavored with tea, filling his senses. "But…forgive me, sweetheart, I don't know where to put my hands."

She groped for and found the windowsill, set the transmitter box on it and reached for his hands. She placed them on her hips and covered them with hers, her fingers warmly stroking the backs of his as she turned her face to his neck and whispered, "Anywhere below the waist seems to be fine…"

He groaned. Her warm, firm flesh taunted him, safely protected from his lascivious touch beneath layers of fabric and a belt like something medieval knights put on their women when they went off to war. "My love, you're killing me, you know. You can't possibly—oh…g—" His breath hissed between his teeth as her hands reached behind her, slipped between her backside and his front side to stroke the growing bulge behind his zipper.

"Tell me you don't just want me for my medicinal qualities," he said in a grating voice. Holding himself rigidly still, aware that she was trembling, now. Not the tight shivers that meant she was cold, or breathless ripples of passion, but shudders of overwhelming emotion that racked her body from head to toe.

"I don't…just want you…for your medicinal qualities. I want you…for *all* your qualities."

"So, you do want me, then…"

"Yes…oh, yes…more than want. I think…I need you. I need—" She broke off with a dry sob. Nikolas caught her tightly to him with one arm across her waist, and with the other pressed her head into the curve of his neck and shoulder.

"It's okay," he crooned as he rocked her, "it's okay…"

"Dammit, Nik. Dammit, dammit, dammit…"

"I know…I know."

"I want to kill him. Seriously. I…want…to…kill…him. If I'd had a gun…"

"It's probably a good thing you didn't." He kissed her temple. "Have you ever killed anyone, my love?"

She shook her head. Sniffed. "No. Have you?"

"No." He rocked her silently for a moment. "But I have an idea it's not an easy thing for a good person to do."

She sniffed again, a longer one this time, more an indrawn breath. "No, I suppose not."

She stirred in his arms, and when he let her go she pulled away from him, raking the fastenings from her hair, combing it with her fingers—carefully, because of her scalded scalp. "I'm okay now—really," she said, sounding breathless. "I'm sorry, Nik. I hope I didn't—I mean…" She made an embarrassed little gesture. Avoiding his eyes.

"I may be crippled for life," he said somberly. Her eyes flashed at him, bright with dismay. He smiled and brushed her cheek with the back of his finger. "I'm kidding, my dearest. Contrary to what most adolescent males would have you believe, I don't know of any documented evidence of permanent damage caused by unfulfilled lust." He nodded toward the window. "Let's get our little Mayday box outside where someone might actually hear it, shall we?"

"I think somebody has," Rhia said in an odd voice, going motionless with her head cocked at a listening angle.

Then Nikolas heard it, too—the steady thump of a helicopter's rotors. "Well, well. I suppose that's Elliot?" He lifted one eyebrow. "Lazlo does take good care of his people, doesn't he? I must say, though, I'm rather glad the cavalry didn't arrive a few minutes earlier, aren't you?"

"Sorry I didn't get here sooner," Elliot shouted as Rhia took the hand he offered. "I was outside taking a—uh…sorry—taking care of…uh, personal business—didn't catch the signal." He glanced at but didn't comment on the way she held her jacket together loosely with one hand when she let him help her into the chopper. As she settled into the jump seat, he yelled over one shoulder, "Don't tell Lazlo, okay? He'll have my head. I had strict orders not to take my eyes off your six."

She reassured him with a smile, the best one she could manage with her teeth clamped together. The pain raking down the front of her body no longer made her nauseated, at least. Now, it just stung like bloody hell.

Nikolas's tall form filled the doorway of the chopper. She

watched him toss in Elliot's duffel bag and the other odds and ends he'd brought from the car, then grip the sides of the opening and lever himself gracefully through. His eyes found hers immediately, asking if she was okay, telling her everything would be all right. And as he slipped past her and into the shotgun seat beside Elliot, he let his hand lie for one brief moment on the top of her head.

She felt the warmth of it slide all the way down through her pain-wracked body. An ache filled her throat and she closed her eyes...wishing. *Wish his touch didn't feel so damn good. Wish I didn't love him so much...*

"You must have been pretty close by," Nikolas said to Elliot as he belted himself in. "How'd you know where to find us? Didn't we leave you at the airport in Dunford?"

"I've been on your tail pretty much since you left Dunford. Like I said, I had orders from the man himself—s'posed to stick to you guys like glue." The chopper swooped upward, lifting a swirl of fine sand into the air with it. "I was hunkered down a couple miles from here—didn't want to get too close, 'fraid I might spook the target." Elliot jerked his head toward Rhia. "Looks like I missed some action."

Nikolas nodded his head. Rhia could see the side of his jaw twitch with his wry smile. "Little bit."

"She okay?"

"She will be."

"The target?"

"Got away."

"Ah. Figured that when I saw that oil-burner hightailin' it down the road," Elliot said with a small headshake. "Maybe I should've gone after 'im, but like I said, I had my orders."

Rhia didn't hear Nikolas's reply. Exhausted by pain and emotional turmoil, she closed her eyes and let her head fall back against the headrest. Inexplicably, as a new wave of anger rippled through her, the image imprinted on the backs of her eyelids wasn't the murderous Lord Vladimir's. It was her father's.

* * *

Later that evening, in Nikolas's seaside apartment in the college town of Dunford, Rhia lay in his bed propped up on a pile of pillows, wearing only a pair of his black silk boxers. As she listened to the sounds coming from the adjoining bathroom—the hum of an electric shaver…the rush of water in the shower…the thump of a dropped bar of soap—she was in serious danger of engaging in what for her was a rare sin: self-pity.

And why not? She was entitled, dammit. She couldn't have a shower…couldn't wash her hair. Her chest and stomach hurt; so did her scalp, in places, so she couldn't even give her hair a decent brushing. And the burns looked awful. Sickening, she thought as she lifted her head to look at the angry blisters one more time. Yes—truly ugly. Blood would have been better.

Scowling, she reached for the tube of antibiotic cream lying on the table beside the bed and unscrewed the cap.

The bathroom door opened. Nikolas emerged, freshly shaved, water-spangled, black hair falling in damp commas across his forehead, a towel loosely knotted around lean hips…and every cranky negative thought flew right out of her head. Something warm and sweet enveloped her, like delicious perfume carried on a soft summer wind. She felt her face being taken over by a smile she knew was besotted, even goofy, and there seemed to be nothing she could do to make it leave. In a daze, she watched him come toward her, and felt herself filling up with a tingly, effervescent joy.

"Hello, you," he said as he sat on the edge of the bed beside her, smiling with such undisguised tenderness it made her throat quiver. Warmth radiated from his still-damp body, along with the scents of aftershave and soap. He took the tube of cream from her and sniffed it. Lifted one eyebrow. "This the stuff the doctor gave you?"

She nodded; speech was beyond her just then.

He squeezed a bit of the cream onto his finger and touched

it gently to a welt just above her collarbone. "Shh…" he said when she winced. And then, to distract her, she suspected: "Did you get all reported in?"

She nodded, then countered in a tightly controlled voice, "Did you get through to the palace?"

"I did." He was watching his fingers, intent on his task. Gazing down at him, she forgot about pain…thought how utterly beautiful his lashes were…thick and black and long. *A woman would kill for those lashes…* "Spoke with Russell— Lord Carrington—himself, actually. He's increased security…put the palace on high alert."

"Do you really think Vladimir's going after the king?" He was so near…she had to clutch the sheet in handfuls to keep from touching him. She wanted so badly to touch him…to smooth away the frown of concern that had gathered between his eyebrows.

But if she touched him, she wouldn't stop there, and that wouldn't be fair to him. She squirmed inwardly, thinking of the way she'd behaved earlier, in the lighthouse cottage. She wouldn't do that do him again.

He flashed her a look and a wry smile. "You were a wee bit preoccupied, so you probably didn't hear what Vlad was screaming when he tore out of the cottage. It was all pretty insane, but I did hear some dire threats against the king's person." The smile faded. "It wouldn't surprise me, since all his plans have fallen apart anyway, if he's decided to go out with a bang and take the man he blames for his misfortune along with him."

"I don't see how he could get to him. He'd have to get past the palace security, which I'd think would have a difficulty factor along the lines of…oh, I don't know, breaking into Fort Knox or stealing the British crown jewels."

"He's done it before," Nikolas said grimly.

Rhia watched the tiny muscle working in the side of his jaw, and after a moment said softly, "You're worried about him, aren't you? King Weston, I mean. You really do care about him."

He lifted a shoulder, watching his fingers tap cream onto a blistered patch of her chest with the delicacy of a watchmaker. "Of course I care. He's the king. His murder would be a national tragedy."

"A personal one, too, I think. You haven't even had a chance to get to know him yet—your *father*." She caught a breath, trying so hard not to flinch. "He's a good man, Nik. And you're very much like him, you know. You should be there with him. If we leave now, we could—"

"Tomorrow's soon enough."

"But—"

He leaned over and kissed her, just thoroughly enough to make her tingle all the way down to her toes. Then he pulled back just far enough to murmur, "Do shut up and relax, won't you? Right now, all I want to do is make you feel better. Let's see…didn't you tell me this is what works best?" His lips, firm and warm, the texture of satin, slid across hers…nibbled at their sensitive insides. He caught the lower one between his teeth when she pouted and sucked it gently, laughing low in his throat.

Her hands fisted in the sheets. Freeing her mouth from that exquisite torment, she whispered, "You're supposed to kiss the owie. But I don't think I could stand…"

He lowered his head, and his hair, cool and damp from the shower, tickled her throat. "Hmm…how about if I kiss it close to the owie? Like…here? Would that hurt?" And she felt the warm, liquid laving of his tongue on her neck…then a hot, drawing pressure.

"Oh—" She drew a shuddering gasp. Then, faintly whispered, "No…" How had her hands escaped from the knotted sheets and found their way to his hair, touching it half fearfully, as if it were soap bubbles, or thistledown?

"Hmm…how about here, then?" And again…the gentle stroking, first, then the heat. She felt it in her breasts, the soles of her feet, and between her thighs. "And here…" It was all she could do not to moan. "And...this lovely little nipple seems quite untouched..."

Same thing—tongue caress...gentle sucking—but this time the sensation that arrowed through her to the swelling, heating place between her legs was sharp and raw, and the gasp slipped from her throat before she knew. The muscles in her back and legs contracted. Her chest rose and fell with her quickening breaths, lifting her distended breast to him, pushing her nipple deeper into his mouth. Pain was forgotten completely; she clutched at his shoulders, wanting him...on her... inside her...everywhere. Never mind the blisters. Nothing else mattered.

He lifted his head...his hair in silky feathers on his forehead, eyes full of a shimmering softness...and smiled at her with such—the word that came into her mind, like the lyrics to a well-loved song, was *sweetness*. And she giggled— couldn't help it—because it seemed such an unlikely word to apply to the next king of Silvershire.

"Ah, feeling better already, are we?" His voice was a husky growl that only fed the fire inside her.

"You're a very good doctor," she whispered, threading her fingers through the longish hair on the back of his neck.

"Hmm...and I've always wanted to play doctor." The angelic smile tried hard to turn itself into a leer.

"You have a very nice bedside manner, but I think... you've left some of my injuries...oh—" Her voice hitched to a new octave as he lowered his mouth to the hollow below her rib cage. She sucked in air and her stomach muscles tensed.

"Relax, my love..." His breath flowed like warm oil over her taut skin. His hands moved slowly down her sides, stroking...gentling...following the curve of her waist and hips... then retreated to the waistband of the boxers. His fingers hooked into the elastic and drew them down, baring her belly to his questing mouth.

She held his head in her hands, glorying in the silken flow of his hair over her fingers. Her eyes closed…her eyelids felt heavy and warm, as if the sun was shining brightly on her face. She felt her whole body swell and ripen…and her heart did, too, until she felt it would surely burst inside her, and all the love she felt for him come pouring out. *I can't…I can't. Can't let him know…* She bit down on her lip, fighting to keep the words inside. And focused intently…fiercely…on the physical sensations that were nearly tearing her apart.

She scarcely felt it when he slipped the boxers off. Her legs, obeying his gentle command, parted as easily, as naturally as a flower opening at the behest of the sun. It felt like the sun's touch, too, the way his hands seemed to heat all of her skin at once…a sizzling heat that spread over her body…her stomach, her legs and her buttocks. She arched and stretched in the lovely warmth, sensuously, like a cat.

And then his mouth found her center…moved to claim it for his own. His tongue licked over her…into her…and the heat coalesced into a searing white-hot ball that exploded through her like a supernova. Time ceased; she lost all sense of place… didn't hear herself cry out as her body rocketed through a pulsing void, completely out of control…

…until she felt herself gathered in, held fast in powerful arms, felt her back cuddled against a strong chest and her whole body rocked by a steadily thumping heart. Satin lips touched words of reassurance to her temple and the sweat-damp place behind her ear. She felt safe and warm and loved. Why, then, were her cheeks wet with tears?

She lay quietly in the grip of a dream, content to let the happiness she knew was ephemeral as a rainbow bathe her in its lovely light…until it dawned on her that the hard male body pressed against her back was no longer swathed in a towel. She moved her bottom experimentally. Yep, definitely Nikolas and nothing whatsoever else.

He stirred restlessly, one rock-hard leg hooking around hers to hold her still. The muscles in the arm supporting her head bunched under her cheek as he lifted his hand to caress her hair. "It's all right, my love…go to sleep."

"But—you—"

"Shh… You've been injured, you need to rest."

"But…don't you want—Nik, I can feel—"

"Don't worry about me. I'll be perfectly fine…if you'll just stop doing that…"

"You mean…this?"

"Dar—" breath hissed between his teeth "—stop that this instant, minx—I mean it."

"Or…what?"

"Or…" His tongue licked into her ear and she went limp, every inch of her skin spangled with goose bumps. He drew his hot, open mouth down along the side of her neck and chuckled when she gasped…squirmed closer, fitting her buttocks into the nest of his body. He raised himself on one elbow and leaned down to ask in a growling whisper, "Are you sure, my love?"

She nodded, already beyond speech. His lips pressed against her temple as his hand reached around to cup the mound of damp curls between her thighs. Finding her moist and ready, he slipped his hand under her leg and lifted it. She shifted, adjusted, making it easy for him…and he slid into her body slowly, like the sweetest of homecomings…filled her body with heat and her heart and mind with an aching joy.

His hands were strong and sure, holding her steady against his rocking thrusts, his fingers gentle as they stole between her swollen petals and found the sensitive place hidden there. Sensation bolted through her once more; she whimpered… gasped…cried out…and hurtled headlong into climax.

It was every bit as intense as the first orgasm had been, but instead of a terrifying void, she felt surrounded in love and warmth; instead of aloneness, a deep communion. She did feel

lost…as if her *self*, her heart and soul, had become inextrica-
bly joined with his, and she would never be the same Rhia
again. Somewhere in her fractured self was the thought that
this should be a frightening thing…but it wasn't.

Tears of overwhelming love and joy sprang to her eyes
when she felt his release follow hers, and afterward she floated
into sleep, still blissfully wrapped in Nikolas's arms.

Chapter 14

He watched her come awake, and was steeped in the same sense of wonder with which he'd once observed, as a very small boy, the emergence of a butterfly from its leafy chrysalis. First, the delicate flutter of eyelids…a hint of green sparkling through dark lashes…a tiny frown gathered between bird's-wing brows…the quivering of rose-petal lips on the verge of a yawn…and once again, as then, he couldn't resist reaching out to touch the miracle with an unsteady finger.

She twitched her nose…brushed at her cheek where he'd touched it. Then her eyes opened and looked directly into his, and he thought no sunrise had ever been so beautiful.

"Whazza matter?" she mumbled, her eyes crossing slightly in their effort to focus on his face. "What're you doing?"

"Just looking at you, my love," he said tenderly, stroking her hair back from her forehead. "Watching you sleep."

She rolled her eyes and gave a husky laugh. "Oh, *that* must have been lovely."

"It was, actually. I was going to do the whole Prince Charming thing and awaken you with my kiss, but you seemed about to return to life without it, so I've enjoyed watching the process. Quite fascinating."

"Oh, God…" She put a hand over her eyes, then scrubbed it across her face and glared at him—or tried her best to. "At least you didn't handcuff me to the bed this time." But he could see the smile and the answer to his deepest wishes shimmering in her eyes.

"Never again," he whispered, and leaned down to kiss her. Then he drew back and added thoughtfully, "Not without your permission, at least."

"Seriously…how come you're all dressed already?" Too early in the morning for humor, evidently. She frowned, yawned hugely as she pushed herself up higher on the pillows, then winced and sucked in her chest when the sheet dragged across her burns. "I must look like bloody hell. Feels like I haven't showered in *days*. Can't imagine what you must be thinking…"

Smiling at her grumpiness, he hooked a finger in the sheet and lifted it away from her breasts. "Actually, I was thinking how very much I should like to see your face on my pillows every morning when I wake up."

Yes, and I should love to see your face grow rosy and your body plump with my child. I want to watch our sons and daughters suckling at your lovely breasts. I want to watch the joys and sorrows we share etch lines in your face, my love, and your skin grow ever softer, more fragile and even more beautiful in old age.

Those things he thought but didn't say. And because he was too steeped in love and his own fantasy, he failed to notice that Rhia's eyes had gone wide and dark with dismay.

"Marry me, sweetheart." The words slipped from him without thought. He didn't feel them pass his lips; it was as if they had simply gone straight from his heart into the air.

And her response came back the same way—a recoil that pierced him like an arrow. *"What?"*

Too soon, you imbecile! But that realization came too late; the words were out there, hanging suspended between them, and could not be unsaid.

"Yes. Marry me." Nothing to do now but forge ahead. Leaning casually on one elbow to hide the crazy pounding of his heart, he looked into her horrified eyes and smiled. "You must know I adore you—I've hardly made a secret of that. I intend to spend the rest of my life with you, anyhow, and quite frankly, I can't think of any reason why we couldn't...shouldn't make it legal."

"Oh, I can think of at least one really good one." Her voice was dark and soft.

"You don't love me..." He was sure enough of her feelings to say the words, but they quivered in his throat regardless. "Is that it, sweetheart?" He lightly stroked the soft white undercurve of her breast with the back of one finger.

"No!" She batted his hand away...hitched in a breath. "You know that's not...it." Another breath, and she gathered the sheet to cover her nakedness again. "You're about to become king. Or have you forgotten? You can't marry me."

"Why not?" He sat up suddenly, and swiveled to face her. "Oh, wait—don't tell me it's because you're a 'commoner'? Good God, woman, this is the twenty-first century—didn't that crap get done away with somewhere along in the twentieth? Besides, if you come down to it, I'm a commoner myself, in everything but blood. No, love—sorry, that excuse won't wash. The people of Silvershire are going to fall for you as madly as I have. They're going to think you're an absolutely smashing queen."

She stared back at him in stony-eyed silence for a moment. Then swallowed, and said in a voice to match her eyes, "Yes, I'm sure the good people of Silvershire would be positively thrilled to have a convicted felon as their queen."

He shook his head and gazed at her indulgently, laughing. "What on earth are you talking about?"

"I told you, but you didn't believe me. If you had—"

"Told me what? When? You mean, about your juvenile record? Don't they seal those?"

"No. Not that. Back at the castle. When I was picking the lock. I told you I used to be a burglar, but you just laughed."

"Now, wait a minute—"

"See? You're doing it again. Maybe if you'd taken me seriously the first time, you wouldn't be entertaining crazy ideas about something that just ain't—gonna—happen." She was scrambling off the bed, still clutching the sheet. He could feel her body trembling as she slid past him.

"Okay, hold it right there." He shook his head again, no longer feeling the least bit like laughing. "Good God—I think you *are* serious. Do you mean to tell me you actually were a burglar? Convicted? As in…jail?"

She nodded, chin lifted, arms folded across the wadded-up sheet she was holding to her chest.

"Does Lazlo know? Okay—foolish question—of course he'd know—he knows everything."

Her mouth tilted wryly. "Where do you think he found me? I don't know how, but he got me released—paroled into his custody, actually. He convinced me there were better uses for my talents than stealing rich people's jewelry…made me clean up my act, get healthy, get in shape. Sent me to college, trained me, gave me a job—one I happen to love, by the way. One I…don't want to lose."

She watched his face change as it hit him. The pain.

Though none of it showed in his voice as he said softly, almost gently, "That's it, isn't it? Not that I can't marry you. It's that you don't want to marry me."

"Not you! Don't you understand? I don't want to marry a *king*." She paced angrily, dragging the sheet like an oversized toga, furious with him for being hurt, with herself for hurting him, and with him again for making it necessary, for bringing up the subject she'd been dreading, trying so hard not to think about. "Look—to you, being king is a simple matter of obliga-tion. Of duty. Not to mention the opportunity to fulfill your lifelong dream for your people. But for me…my God, Nik—" she whirled, trembling, to face him "—the idea of being queen, being married to a king—it would be like being trapped. Put in a cage. I know what royals' lives are like— I've seen it firsthand, in my job. They're *on,* all the time. They have no privacy, no personal freedom. I couldn't live like that. I'm sorry, I just couldn't." She gave a desperate, hiccup-ping laugh. "And, I know the romantic thing is supposed to be, all for love, right? Well, I've seen how that works out first-hand, too. Up close and personal. My mother gave up every-thing to marry my father, and look what happened. She was miserable. In the end, she messed up both her life and mine. It doesn't work, Nikolas!"

He'd watched her diatribe in patient silence, with set ex-pression and glittering eyes. Now, he lifted one shoulder and said stonily, "Then I won't be king."

She gave another helpless, hurting laugh and stared past him for a few moments, fighting for control. When she was sure she had it, she drew a breath and said in a low, husky voice, "Yes, you will. You know you will. You have a duty to your country, your father…maybe even to destiny." She laughed again, lightly, this time. "You'll go down in history, Nikolas…the father of Silvershire's democracy. Future generations of schoolchildren will be required to memorize your birthday."

"Rubbish," Nikolas snapped, then got restlessly to his feet. "Okay, you're right. I suppose I'll have to be king, but not forever. Just long enough to bring about free elections. Then my duty's done. I'll be free—"

"Elections? Free? Are you kidding me? In any election you'd win in a landslide. With your charisma, King Weston's long-lost son, the kidnapped prince? If you didn't run, they'd write you in. Probably proclaim you king by acclamation!"

"Okay, fine—" he folded his arms on his impressive

chest and drew himself up to his equally impressive height "—if I'm the king, I can bloody well choose who I want to be my queen."

"Listen to you!" She threw up her hands in exasperation, then had to grab hastily for the sheet. "My God, you sound like a king already!"

"What's that supposed to mean?"

"It's all about power, Nikolas. When men have power, they think they can have everything their way. Just like my father."

"Oh, okay—that's what this is all about, isn't it?" It was his turn to throw up his arms. "Your father. You're still mad at the jerk for taking you away from your mother. Well, let me ask you something, sweetheart. Where do you think you'd be, if he hadn't done that? If you'd stayed in that trailer park with your mum—what would you be doing right now? Working as a cocktail waitress, playing blues in some New Orleans pub? Do you think you'd have gone to college? Would you be working for the Lazlo Group? How many abducted kids do you think you'd have saved? Would you have met me?"

She could only stare at him, holding herself rigid while furious unreasoning tears gathered in her throat.

"Think about it." He reached out to brush her cheek with the backs of his fingers. "Ask yourself if you like your life the way it's turned out. Then, ask yourself if you'd have anything you have now if your father hadn't come for you and taken you back to Florida. Ask yourself if you'd have anything different, if you could go back and change it. Think about how mad you are at your father for giving you this life." He let his hand drop away from her, and his voice hardened. "Think about it, Rhia. Then get over it."

She gave a gasp of rage, whirled and made for the bathroom—an exit that would probably have been much more satisfying if she hadn't first had to untangle her legs from the sheet.

In the sanctuary of the bathroom, she gripped the edge of the sink and leaned on her hands, staring blindly down at them and breathing hard, teeth clenched. Refusing to let the tears come. Thinking, *I'm right, dammit—I know I'm right!*

While hovering anxiously over her, another Rhia—a heart-broken Rhia—was wailing, *What are you doing, you silly fool? The last thing you wanted to do this morning—the last thing you'd ever want to do—is fight with Nikolas!*

The angry Rhia, self-righteous Rhia, turned her back on the sink and the mirror and squeezed her eyes tightly shut. *Dammit, Nikolas. Damn you. Why did you have to go and ruin things? Why did you have to ask me to marry you?*

I can't...just can't. I don't want to be a queen. It would never work, no matter how much I love you.

With that thought the heartbroken Rhia and the angry Rhia coalesced into one, with a shaft of pain so intense it doubled her over. *Oh, Nikolas, I do love you. I do...* She rocked herself, arms folded over her breasts like broken wings, heedless of her unhealed burns, refusing to allow herself the solace of tears. *Maybe it's just as well. Yes—it's good this happened now, while I'm still strong enough to say no.*

She sniffed, and slowly, experimentally, unfolded herself. Discovering that she felt stronger, quieter inside, she washed her face and dressed in the clothes she'd worn the day before and washed out last night in Nikolas's sink. Except for the bra—no way could she wear that. She'd have to do without. The pullover was still damp, but the coolness felt good on her burns.

When she opened the door, Nikolas was just disconnecting the telephone. He glanced at her and said, in a voice as neutral as his expression, "I've summoned a cab. Rang Elliot on his handy, as well—he's warming up the chopper. All right with you if we grab coffee and a bite at the airport?"

"Sure, that's fine. Coffee's all I want, anyway." She wasn't hungry; Nikolas had fed her well the night before...in more ways than one. But the memories that tried to sneak into her mind through that door were too fresh, too raw, and she slammed it firmly shut on the beginning ripples of pain.

She picked up her utility belt, which, along with her leather jacket, she'd left draped across a chair. She buckled it on over her pullover, then reached for her jacket. Taking a nine-millimeter Walther from the holster built into the jacket's lining, she proceeded to check the weapon over thoroughly and with the efficiency of long practice. She'd asked Elliot to get her a weapon, and he'd given her his own backup piece. It was a little lighter than she was used to, but it would do the job.

She slapped the magazine back into place and looked up to find Nikolas watching her, eyes darkly intent. A sardonic little smile tugged at the corners of her mouth as she imagined the struggle being waged behind his carefully controlled features. She knew what he was thinking…what he wanted to ask her…

You're going to visit a palace, Rhee—the royal palace, home of kings, the most beautiful and elegant building in all of Silvershire, one of the most beautiful in the world—and you're wearing that?

But he didn't ask it. Probably he'd already realized what it meant even to think it, and stopped himself in time.

Instead, he nodded at the gun and said mildly, "Do you think they'll let you take that into the palace?"

On that safe ground, she allowed her smile to bloom into full irony. "Nik. I have a permit and my Lazlo Group credentials. With those I could probably take a weapon into *Buckingham* Palace."

He said nothing, only nodded. She felt his gaze following her every move as she returned the gun to its holster, picked up the jacket and slipped it on…shrugged it into a more comfortable fit on her shoulders and tugged down the sleeves. Thus armored, she looked up at last and met those hooded, pain-filled eyes.

"This is who I am," she said softly.

From the street below came the beep of the taxicab's horn, saving him the necessity of a reply.

* * *

Rhia's reaction to her first glimpse of the royal palace was everything Nikolas could have hoped for. One word that pretty much said it all:

"Wow."

He smiled wryly and didn't reply, but the words *gilded cage* slipped unbidden into his mind as the car swept up the long drive toward the sentry boxes at the main front gates.

Beyond the heavy wrought-iron gates and the concrete security barriers, he could see the graceful stone spires of the palace outlined against a clear blue autumn sky, the yellow painted walls gleaming like gold in the morning sun. He'd been to the palace—the public part of it—more than once, the first time as a very small child, brought there by his "uncle" Silas Donovan to see where the man who'd murdered his parents lived. He'd tried, then and on each subsequent visit, to feel the anger and disdain he knew his uncle expected, but deep inside, even as a child he'd thought it must surely be the most beautiful place in the world. Now, for the first time in his life he allowed his throat to swell with a lump of pride.

The unmarked limousine that had brought them from the airport had tinted windows, an amenity Nikolas was profoundly thankful for when he saw the reporters and paparazzi staked out along both sides of the drive.

"Do you suppose it's always like this? The media, I mean?" Rhia had torn her gaze from the palace to look at them, too.

"I have an idea there are always a few lurking about. With all that's happened in and around the palace lately, though, it's probably to be expected there'd be a crowd."

"Especially since the rumors broke about the existence of a long-lost prince," Rhia said drily. "Good thing they can't see who's in here. We'd probably have a riot on our hands."

"Oh, come now," Nikolas said, laughing uneasily, "I think you're exaggerating my popular appeal. Not so very long ago, they were sure I was guilty of murdering the crown prince."

"And, now they know you're not. Care to put your 'popular appeal' to the test?" Even in the shadowed car, he could see her kitty-cat smile. "Go ahead—stop the car, get out and introduce yourself."

He snorted and said, "No thanks." But deep inside he felt a small shudder, and the same voice that had spoken of gilded cages now whispered, *Are you sure you're ready for this?*

He'd thought he was ready…had even looked forward to the challenges of running a country. That had been when he'd let himself dream that he'd be doing so with Rhia at his side. Now… He'd do it, of course, because it was his duty. His country needed him. But it loomed as a lonely and daunting task.

As soon as the limo had cleared the security checkpoint, Rhia ran her window down—partly so she could gawk unhindered as the car wound its way through the magnificent grounds, but also because she was finding Nikolas's silence oppressive. She knew the silence probably had nothing to do with the fact they'd quarreled; Nikolas wasn't the type of man to sulk. She had an idea it was finally beginning to hit him— the enormity of what had happened to him, and the changes that were coming. And the overwhelming responsibility. But still…the silence, the tight, thin line of his mouth, the muscle working in his jaw…were all reminders to her of the way she'd hurt him, like a toothache that wouldn't go away.

The limousine prowled past the palace's magnificent formal entrance, with its three-tiered sweep of gleaming marble steps leading up to the wide double doors that had been hand-carved from ebony and inlaid with silver and ivory, and the grand balcony above from which generations of Silvershire's monarchs had greeted their loyal subjects. Rhia would have liked to have taken a tour of the great halls and public rooms she'd heard so much about, but that would have to wait for another day. A day when there was no longer a madman on the loose. A madman with a chilling ability, it seemed, to enter and leave the most secure parts of the palace at will. She wasn't here as a tourist, she reminded herself, or even as a friend of the prodigal prince. She was here as an agent of the Lazlo Group, the most exclusive and highly regarded private security organization in the world. And her job was to catch a killer—before he killed again.

After what seemed to Nikolas enough twists and turns to have brought them back to where they'd started, the limo slipped beneath a beautiful stone portico and rolled to a stop in front of the entrance to the royal family's private wing. Standing at parade rest on either side of the doors were a matched set of uniformed guards armed with two-way radios and automatic rifles. As the limo driver got out to open the door, a fit-looking silver-haired man in a dark gray business suit with the royal crest emblazoned on the jacket pocket came briskly down the shallow steps to meet them. He took Rhia's hand to help her from the car, then stood stiffly at attention as Nikolas followed.

"Maximillian, chief of palace security, at your service, sir," the man said, addressing the air to the right of Nikolas's ear.

Nikolas held out his hand. "Hi—I'm Nik Donovan, and this is Agent Rhia de Hayes."

There was a sound that may have been smothered laughter from the limo driver, then a moment of startled silence before Maximillian, looking faintly bemused, took Nikolas's hand, bowed over it with a muttered, "Your Highness." When he looked up, his eyes met Nikolas's and his lips twitched into a smile. "Welcome home, sir. His Majesty is waiting for you in the Bourbon Rose Garden. I can take you there now, if you wish. Or," he added, with a pointed look at Rhia's militant black leather, "to your quarters, if you would prefer to, er... freshen up first."

"We'll see the king straight away, if you don't mind," Nikolas said with what he hoped was an absolutely blank face, still trying to get over the shock of hearing himself addressed as "Your Highness." Taking Rhia's arm, he met her mutinous look with an elevated eyebrow, and she snapped her mouth shut on whatever indignant retort she'd been about to make.

"Bourbon roses? Did I hear that right?" she said in a stage whisper out of the side of her mouth as they followed Maximillian through elegantly appointed rooms with high ceilings and walls covered with gleaming carved wood paneling or murals painted in soft pastels.

Nikolas smiled. "I doubt that means what you're thinking, love."

Maximillian had heard the exchange, and answered over his shoulder in the chatty but rather formal manner of a docent. "Bourbon roses are named for their place of origin, not the alcoholic beverage, Agent de Hayes. They were developed on the Ile Bourbon, an island in the Indian Ocean now known as Réunion. They're quite old—from early in the nineteenth century, I believe." He paused to unhook a velvet-covered chain barrier and waved them through, then followed, replacing it behind him. "The palace's rose garden originated in the 1860s, when Bourbons had become quite the thing in Paris."

"This is the first I've heard of it," Nikolas said. "I gather it's not part of the public tour?"

"No, Your Highness. In the first place, it is located in the oldest part of the palace, which, although having undergone some renovation in recent years, is still not considered safe. A regular maze, dark and confusing passages...not quite the place you'd want tourists wandering about. Then, there's the fact that His Majesty likes to spend time there." He paused again, this time to throw Nikolas a look of apology. "Since the queen passed, God rest her soul, he's the only one who does. It's been let go a bit, I'm afraid."

The security chief had been leading them at a brisk pace through increasingly dim and dusty corridors festooned with cobwebs and rank with the smell of damp and decay. Now, he preceded them down a short flight of stone steps to a small vestibule, where a thick and ancient wooden door stood open to the courtyard beyond. Here, too, a pair of uniformed guards equipped with two-way radios and automatic weapons stood at ease in the rectangle of brilliant autumn sunshine, and snapped to attention when they heard footsteps on the vestibule's stone floor. They saluted the captain, flashed curious surreptitious glances at Rhia as they bowed to Nikolas, then stepped aside to let them pass.

The first thing Rhia noticed was the smell. Not roses, which she'd expected—something darker, earthier, more mysterious...but to her every bit as sweet. So sweet, and so achingly, wrenchingly familiar it brought a soft gasp to her lips and an unexpected stinging to her eyes. For the second time in the past week she found herself inundated with memories of her childhood, of the bayous...of slow-moving water and thick black mud...of rotting leaves and moss and all manner of growing things. It must be the river—the Kairn, she thought, Silvershire's largest and most important river, which she knew flowed right through the heart of the capital city. Quite nearby, too, perhaps just beyond the thick courtyard walls. But even standing in that sunlit rose garden, she felt that if she only closed her eyes she would feel the soft humidity on her skin... hear the frogs and cicadas singing their shrill duets...see fireflies winking against the blackness of her eyelids.

The pressure of Nikolas's fingers on her arm as he guided her around the arched and swaying branch of a gigantic climbing rosebush dragged her out of the past, back to the present. And it hit her then—the thing he'd tried in his own way to tell her earlier that morning. The bayous *were* her past. *This*—old roses in a palace courtyard...the familiar weight of a nine-millimeter handgun against her side...Nikolas, close to her...touching her, holding her hand—this was her *now*. Like the river beyond the walls, her life flowed on...always and only onward; it could never go back. And childhood had been left behind long ago.

The ache in her throat felt like a whispered good-bye.

King Weston was waiting for them at the far end of the courtyard, in a shaded alcove created by two stone arches and a tangle of nearly leafless rose canes. Beneath the thicket of canes, two carved stone benches had been placed facing each other. The benches were thickly upholstered with leaves and the fallen petals of a scattering of autumn blooms, evidence the king had not been making use of them before they arrived. As he came to greet them, leaning only slightly on an ivory-handled ebony cane, the bouquet of densely petaled blossoms in his hand—and several more spilling from the pockets of his jacket—gave a hint as to how he'd been occupying his time.

As before, Rhia found herself hanging back to observe the reunion between royal father and son, keeping a distance—a physical one, at least. Impossible, though, not to feel the pressure of colliding, conflicting emotions as she watched the two men greet each other with a typically awkward masculine embrace. Impossible not to feel her heart flutter when both men turned to her wearing the same unbelievably appealing smile. Impossible not to feel shivers all through her body—shivers of love—when she thought how beautiful Nikolas was, and how good. Yes—he was a *good* man. He would be a good king, too. Like his father, good to the core.

Unlike *her* father.

…I'm bloody well not like your father.

"Rhia, my dear!" King Weston held out his arms, cane in one hand, roses in the other, and to her utter astonishment—and Nikolas's obvious amusement—embraced her and kissed her soundly on one cheek. "So very sorry to hear about your injuries," the king said, drawing back to study her with a concerned frown. "I trust you'll heal quickly, my dear. That blackguard Perthegon must be caught! And soon—before he does any more harm."

"Yes, uh, sire—er, Your Majesty…" *Damn.* She was all but

stammering. She took a breath and felt the calming press of the Walther against her ribs. "We're doing our best."

"Yes," the king said, with a wry and glittering look at Nikolas, "I expect you are—and everyone else as well. I feel as if I'm a prisoner in my own home—a prisoner on…what do they call it? Huh—lockdown, I believe. Yes. Anyway, I came out here to get away from it all. For a breath of freedom. And fresh air." He waved the rose bouquet in a sweeping gesture. "How do you like my rose garden?"

Rhia coughed. "Uh…it's…beautiful."

King Weston laughed. "You lie rather badly, my dear. It's a neglected mess." His eyes creased in a squint of sadness as he gazed around him. "This was the queen's favorite spot, you see. After she died, I'm afraid I let it go to ruin. Lately, I've begun to think about putting it right again. This one here—" he held up a blossom of rich rose-pink, sniffed it, then pointed it at the tangle of canes overhead "—was her favorite. Zepherine Drouhin, it's called. It has no thorns, you see. That's why she liked it—she loved roses, but was always pricking herself on the thorns." He touched the blossom to his lips, and to Rhia's complete bemusement, presented the rest of the bouquet to her. "These are for you, my dear. Welcome to the palace.

"And now," he said, taking Rhia's arm and turning to walk a few slow steps back toward the vestibule, "I expect you'd like to see the rest of the place."

"Uh, yes," she said, clearing her throat in a valiant effort to pull herself out of the Disney movie she seemed to have wandered into. "As a matter of fact, I'd like to go over security arrangements—"

The king waggled his cane. "No need for that. Between my own palace guard and the extra security forces Corbett Lazlo has provided, everything has been well taken care of, I assure you. We are all safe here."

Safe as a babe in his mother's arms? Rhia glanced at Nikolas and suppressed a shiver. His gray eyes were glittering as he looked back at her, and she wondered if he'd had the same thought.

"Forgive me," he said, in a tone that was probably a bit more abrupt than should have been used to address a king, "but Vladimir—Lord...Vladimir—has gotten into the palace before."

King Weston nodded. "Through the old tunnels, yes. But that's all been taken care of now. The tunnels have been closed off or filled in. At any rate," he said firmly, drawing himself up and gesturing again with his cane, as if it were an eraser, "*you,* my dear girl, are here as my guest, not my bodyguard. Nikolas—have Max get someone to give her the grand tour, won't you? And show you to your rooms. Then later on I should like it very much if you would both join me for dinner in my chambers."

Rhia could actually feel herself blushing. "Oh—but...Your Majesty...I'm not—I'm honored, but...I didn't exactly..." Oh God, and stammering, again, too. She didn't dare look at Nikolas; if he was grinning, she'd have no choice but to kill him. *I can't believe this,* she thought. *I can't believe I'm going to say it...* "Your Majesty, I'm sorry, but I don't have anything to wear!"

King Weston halted and turned to her with smiling eyes. "Quite frankly, I think you look smashing just as you are." He lifted her hand to his lips and kissed it. "However, I do know all women like to dress up, put on fancy things now and then. Don't worry, Miss de Hayes, I shall see to it that you have something to wear."

He turned to Nikolas and clasped his hand. His voice seemed to deepen and grow husky. "My boy, I'm glad you're here at last. I shall look forward to our visit this evening—perhaps we can begin to get to know one another. I'll send someone to escort you to my chambers—shall we say...five o'clock?"

Nikolas murmured, "Yes, of course. That will be fine."

The king waved them on, then pivoted and returned to his roses.

"Will someone please just kill me now?" Rhia ground out

between clenched teeth, as she and Nikolas made their way back across the courtyard. "Could I possibly *be* more embarrassed? And don't you *dare* laugh, or I swear I will kill you."

"I'm not laughing," Nikolas insisted, while doing exactly that. Then he shrugged, and the grin faded. "I'm not even going to claim credit for 'I told you so,' because I didn't."

"No, but you thought it. God, I hate it when you're right..." They were almost to the vestibule. She caught his arm to stop him and whispered, "Nik—am I insane, or did the king—your father—just flirt with me?"

"Oh, you're not insane," he said drily. "Although I may be—with jealousy."

She shot him a sideways look, pretending disgust. "Now I know where you get it from. You can't help it—it's in your genes."

Chapter 15

"**M**y God," Rhia whispered, "I can't believe I'm actually wearing a Givenchy. Me—the former Miss Trailer Park of New Orleans."

Nikolas didn't comment; he knew how sappy he'd sound if he told her the truth, which was that in his opinion no queen or empress had ever looked more regal. Besides which, if he told her *that,* he was fairly certain it would only make her mad.

Although, to be truthful, lately he couldn't be certain of anything where Rhia was concerned. Since they'd arrived at the palace, she'd seemed…different. Edgy, nervous…lacking her usual poise and self-confidence.

"Are you sure I look okay in this thing? It's not too…*you* know…"

He didn't know what to make of her. It was the first time he'd ever known her to be insecure about her appearance. It was also the first time he'd seen her wearing a dress and high heels, and he did know what he'd *like* to make of that. Take them right off her again, as soon as he could possibly manage it.

He let his gaze slide over her—quickly, which was as much as his libido could stand. "No, love," he said gently, "it's not too…anything. It's just exactly right."

"I don't know…it *is* from the nineteen sixties, after all." She heaved in a breath, twisting and turning in front of the window in a way that made his mouth go dry as she tried to catch a glimpse of her reflection in the dark glass. She paused to throw him a look of bemusement. "I still can't believe he let me wear his wife's—Queen Alexis's—your mother's clothes. I'm amazed he'd even still have them."

"Yes, well I suppose it would be rather difficult to dispose of something like a queen's wardrobe," Nikolas said drily, and to remove himself as far as possible from temptation, paced to the opposite end of the informal reception room in the king's private chambers, where they'd been left to await his majesty's pleasure. "It's not as though one can simply drop everything off at the Oxfam shop. I should imagine some will eventually go to a museum."

She gave a breathy little laugh. "In the meantime, I'm wearing Givenchy. I feel like…who is it?" She snapped her fingers. "Audrey Hepburn—*Breakfast at Tiffany's*. You know—the little black dress?"

He folded his arms on his chest and pretended to give her a critical once-over. Truth was, she did look a little like Audrey Hepburn—from the neck up: Dark hair piled high on her head, exotic eyes and luscious mouth…long, elegant neck. But from there down…from what he could recall, for all her grace and beauty, Audrey on her best day had never had curves like that.

Avoiding the issue, he frowned at his watch, then glanced at the doors that led to the king's inner sanctum. "Wonder what's keeping our royal host?"

Her eyes jerked to his and her lips parted. The look that came over her face was one he'd never seen before—frightened, even confused. His heart began to pound as he asked hoarsely, "What? Rhia, what's wrong?"

She shook her head—a quick, erasing motion—and pivoted away from him. "Nik—it's nothing. I…"

He was at her side in an instant, gripping her arms and turning her to face him. "It's obviously not nothing. Tell me."

She gazed at him…opened her mouth. But the words wouldn't come. *It's hard…I don't think I can…I'm sorry.* She'd never tried to put it into words before—*the feeling.* The sizzling under her skin, like static electricity…the flashes of *something* just on the edges of her consciousness that never came into focus…the hum in her head that wasn't quite sound.

She swallowed…took a breath. "I know this is going to sound…weird. I thought it was just nerves—you know, I'm wearing this dress, having dinner with the king, for God's sake. Anyway, I've been feeling it ever since we came in here. And then, when you mentioned him, I *knew* what it was. It's…"

"Your sixth sense," he said quietly. Not mocking, not questioning. The relief that flooded her almost made her knees buckle. And she knew she'd never loved him more than at that moment.

She nodded and clutched at his arms. "Something's wrong, Nik. Don't ask me how I know, I just do." She twisted to throw an anguished look at the closed door to the king's private rooms. "We can't just go barging in there—he's the *king.* What—"

"Who says we can't?" Nikolas crossed the room in long strides and gripped the ornate brass door handle. He pushed it, then looked at Rhia, who was right behind him. "It's unlocked. Do you think that's normal?"

"I don't know," she murmured through rigid jaws. The sizzling was more of a crackling now; she could feel it running along her scalp, lifting her hair. Her chest was tight with the certainty that she needed to get through that door. "But I think we should find out."

He nodded grimly. "I'll go first—"

"Like hell you will. I'm the one with the training here."

"Look, you don't even have your gun. If anything—"

"Who says I don't?" She lifted up her skirt to show him the Walther strapped snugly against her thigh. "Now—are we going to stand here and debate, or open this door?"

He shook his head wonderingly. "Have I mentioned you're giving me an inferiority complex? Okay…you first, but go low. I'll cover your back. And…maybe you should leave the gun where it is until we know…"

"Right. Ready…let's go."

Adrenaline surged into her veins as Nikolas pushed down on the handle and silently opened the door; she scarcely felt her feet touching the floor as she slipped through. She was a breath of wind, nothing more. A wide paneled hallway stretched ahead of her…empty. She moved swiftly along it, glancing into open doorways as she went, aware that Nikolas was right behind her, and that what she was looking for was somewhere ahead of her…somewhere close.

And so was danger. She could feel it lurking, like something watching from beyond the firelight….

The Walther lay heavy against her flexing thigh muscle as she crept closer to the end of the hallway. There was only one door left, the one door that wasn't standing open. She approached it like a cat stalking her prey…took her position to the right of the door. Nikolas moved silently to the left side, facing her.

On her nod, he lifted a hand, knocked sharply on the door panel and called out, "Your Majesty, it's Nikolas. Are you all right in there?"

They waited, frozen, listening to the pounding of their own hearts.

Rhia held up three fingers, and he nodded, then pointed to her skirt and lifted one eyebrow. She shook her head; something told her it wasn't yet time to reveal her hidden ace. She held up one finger, then two, then three.

Again Nikolas gripped the handle and pushed open the door, but this time he managed to slip through before her, effectively shielding her from whatever might be waiting for them on the other side. The irresistible force that was her adrenaline-charged body collided with the immovable object that was his, and as the resulting explosion burst from her lungs in a gasp of helpless fury, she heard a cold, quiet voice.

Vladimir's.

"Come in," he said pleasantly. "I've been wondering when you two would decide to join us."

Nikolas barely heard the words. For those first seconds he seemed to be swathed in a gauzy film that muffled sound, paralyzed muscle and cloaked vision so that he saw the impossible scene before him through a reddish fog: Henry Weston, his father, sitting in an upholstered Queen Anne chair that had been positioned to face the door. Behind him, Lord Vladimir, clean-shaven now, and dressed in black fatigues and beret, holding a handgun with the barrel pressed to the king's temple.

Nik came abruptly back to the moment when he felt Rhia try to slip past him. Catching her arm, he pulled her against his side and stretched his lips in a smile. "Silas…"

"How did you get in here?" Rhia's voice could have etched glass.

King Weston's smile was wry. "It appears not quite all of those tunnels have been found and disposed of, after all. The blackguard came right through the wall in my library, if you can believe—"

Nikolas felt Rhia jerk as Vladimir's whip-crack laugh slashed across the last word. "Believe it, *pretender*. You can't keep me out. I know this palace better than you do—better than anyone does. And why shouldn't I? It's *mine*."

Holding himself in a grip of steel, Nikolas said, "What do you want, Silas?"

"My name is *Vladimir*," the intruder thundered, grasping Weston's arm and jerking him to his feet. "*Lord* Vladimir—

Duke of Perthegon! I want what is *mine*—what was stolen from me. Nothing more, nothing less. And I shall have it—or die. But if I die, before I do, this—this *thief* will die, too!"

"Lord Vladimir," Rhia said quietly, "you must know it's over. Your secret is out—you can't possibly get what you want now. But if you give yourself up, you will have a chance to tell your story, get it out there for the people to hear, so everyone will know what was done to you."

Nikolas edged closer, still holding on to Rhia and trying his best to keep himself between her and the madman with the gun. He could feel her muscles vibrating and bunching under his fingers. It would be just like her, he thought, to do something unthinkable—like go for her weapon, or put herself in front of Vladimir's gun to save him or the king.

Vladimir's glittering eyes flicked at Rhia like the tongue of a snake. "Give myself up? So they can put me in a cage? What, *wench,* do you think I'm stupid enough to barter my freedom for my story? No—I'll die first, and die a happy man, so long as *this*—" he gave Weston's arm a vicious yank "—dies first. And before he dies…he will know the worst pain a father can feel." A terrible smile stretched his lips. The barrel of the gun slowly shifted.

Nikolas went cold. He felt Rhia's muscles gather under his fingers.

But before anyone could move or speak, there came a thunderous booming from the far end of the hall. From the reception area. Someone was pounding on the outer door.

Vladimir froze, teeth bared in a grimace of madness. He looked quickly one way, then the other, like a cornered animal, and then began backing in a tight circle toward the door to the sitting room Nik and Rhia had just come through, dragging Weston with him, the gun once more pressed tightly against the king's temple.

Henry Weston's face was pasty gray, but his eyes were calm as they met Nikolas's.

Nik didn't think. He just let go of Rhia's arm and stepped forward, hands out to his sides. Heard himself say harshly, "Let him go. Take me with you."

"No!" Color flooded back into the king's face as it contorted with anguish. "I'm the one he wants. I'm old, my reign is over. You're my son, Nikolas. You mean more to me than my crown. More than my life…"

The pounding was louder, now. A preemptory voice was shouting, "Maximillian—security. Your Majesty, is everything all right in there?"

Vladimir's eyes flicked from side to side, then narrowed. "This way—all of you," he hissed. Gesturing with the gun, he herded them through the door and into the hallway. "In there—hurry!" He pointed toward the first open door on the left.

Nikolas pulled Rhia with him into what was obviously the king's private study. Like his mountain lodge, the room contained floor-to-ceiling bookcases filled with obviously well-read books. Vladimir shoved Weston in after them and followed, slamming the door behind him just as a loud bang and running footsteps were heard in the reception room down at the far end of the hallway.

"Don't move—any of you," he snarled, "or I kill him now." He backed across the room, still holding the gun on Weston, then let go of him long enough to grasp the carved molding that framed one of the bookcases and give it a mighty yank. Ancient gears creaked as the section of shelves slowly began to move.

To Rhia, it seemed that an eternity passed before the gap in the wall of shelves widened enough for a body to squeeze through. Everything, even her heartbeat, seemed to be moving in slow motion. Beyond the library door she could hear voices and running footsteps, but their rescuers, too, it seemed, were coming at the speed of growing grass. Meanwhile, she needed only a moment to go for her weapon, but it had to be the right moment. She didn't dare risk it as long as Vladimir had his gun to the king's head. She had to wait for her chance. Maybe, once they were in the tunnel, in the darkness...

But her chance didn't come—not then. Vladimir shoved her through the opening first, then Nikolas, then the king, with the gun jammed ruthlessly against the base of his skull. Once they were all crammed into the small dusty space behind the wall, Vladimir activated some sort of mechanism that reversed the door. Then, while there was still light coming through the opening, he took a battery-operated torch from a niche in the stone wall, turned it on and thrust it at Nikolas.

"Here—take this. She's going first—your lady friend. Keep the light pointed at her back. Don't move it, or I shoot her first." He didn't sound mad, now, only terrifyingly purposeful. Efficient. Like a stone-cold killer. "That way. Go on—move."

With a final groan, the panel clicked shut. In a darkness alive with jumping shadows and the sounds of breathing, Rhia moved forward, the Walther like a hot brick against her thigh.

The passageway seemed endless, following a bewildering succession of twists and turns, short ups and downs, until she had lost all sense of direction. Finally, at the end of a short stretch of passageway, she came to a flight of stone steps that seemed to disappear into the darkness beyond the glow of the flashlight. The steps led...not down, but *up*.

"So that's it." Nikolas's musing voice came from close behind her. "They found all the underground tunnels, but nobody thought to look up."

"Shut up," Vladimir hissed. "Climb."

"Just out of curiosity," Nikolas said in a conversational tone, as Rhia started up the steps, trailing one hand along the wall of ancient stone, "where does this go? To the roof, I assume? What do you do after that—fly?"

"You'll learn soon enough," Vladimir said with a sneer that didn't have to be seen. "Keep moving."

At least it's not a tunnel, Rhia thought with a shudder as she climbed steadily upward into the leaping shadows. The air was close, but reasonably cool, and smelled of ancient dust and rat droppings rather than mildew and damp. But she was worried about the king. How much more stress could he take?

I have to find a way to stop this. I have to get to my gun. Maybe…when we get to the roof…

Nikolas watched the flashlight beam dance across Rhia's slender back, swaying skirt and well-muscled legs. As he followed her up the stairs, he thought he could almost see the gun strapped to her thigh. It was within reach of his hand. Maybe…if they were to pause for a moment…if he could get to it…

I have to find a way to stop this. I don't know how much more my father can take. Maybe…when we get to the roof…

"This seems to be as far as I can go." Rhia's voice came drifting down from the shadows above him. "What now?"

"It's a trapdoor," Vladimir snapped. "There's a latch. Find it. Open it."

Nikolas moved the light higher and heard a grunt. "Ah— I see it. Okay…" There was a loud creak, then a thump, and a rectangle of starlit sky appeared overhead.

"I trust you will remember that I'm holding a gun, and that I will kill Nikolas first if you do anything I don't like," Vladimir said coldly. "With that in mind, please…ladies first. Nikolas, keep the light on her so I can see her clearly, or I will shoot this old man in the leg."

They emerged, one after the other, into the fresh air, like survivors creeping out of a bomb shelter. The night was chilly and clear—and where was the bloody fog when you needed it? Nikolas wondered, as a brisk autumn breeze penetrated the silk fabric of his evening jacket.

They were on a flat surface, stone, from the feel of it, not slate. He could see the lights of the old town, Silverton-upon-Kairn, twinkling festively just across the river, looking almost close enough to touch. He could smell the river, too, and hear the murmur of it as he turned in a slow circle, trying to get his bearings. How could the river be so close—almost beneath his feet, from the sound of it? And the spires of the Renaissance part of the palace so far away?

"Douse the light," Vladimir ordered. "Move on—down there. Go on…"

It came to him, then. This was the old part of the palace, the part built on the ruins of a medieval abbey. He remembered the docent on one of the tours he'd taken telling about the original structure, which had included a stone footbridge connecting the abbey to the market town of Kairn across the river. The bridge had long since crumbled and fallen into the river, leaving only the ruins of an ancient guard tower in one corner of the thick stone walls of the abbey courtyard. They had emerged from the passageway, he realized, not onto the roof, but the top of the six-foot-thick wall itself. Behind them was the king's special refuge, the Bourbon Rose Garden. Straight ahead, the remnants of the old bridge jutted out over the glittering water.

"Looks like a dead end to me," Nikolas said, holding his hands out to his sides. "Come on, give it up. There's no place to go. It's over."

"It's not over!" Vladimir was panting, his voice shrill with fury. "We can still do it—I can kill him for you—right here. It's what you always wanted—Weston dead. The people—they'll know it was me—they'll follow you, Nikolas. I have a boat—"

"It's over," Nikolas said softly. "Let him go."

"No!" It was like the roar of an enraged lion. "I'm taking him with me—he's my way out. If you try and stop me, I'll kill you *and* the woman. Maybe…" He paused, breathing audibly. "Maybe I *will* kill you—you betrayed me, boy. I raised you! I taught you! And you went back to this—"

"That's enough, Benton." Weston's quiet voice cut through the shrill babble like a knife. "Kill me, if you wish—I've lived my life. Nikolas, my son…I'm grateful to have had a chance to meet you. My only regret is that we didn't have

more time. You will be a good king. Come, Lord Vladimir—
leave them, and let's be gone."

"No!" Nikolas shouted, his voice shaking. "Father—"

While Weston had been talking, Vladimir's head had swiveled toward Nikolas; he could see the glitter of hatred in his
foster parent's eyes. Now, those eyes flicked at Weston, and
his lips pulled back in a smile. When the eyes returned to
Nikolas, the barrel of the gun came with them.

"My son…" Vladimir said in a sneering voice, and laughed
his whip-crack laugh. "Yes—this *is* a more fitting revenge, I
think. Weston, say good-bye to your precious *son*. I took him
from you once—now I do so again—forever!"

Nikolas never saw it coming. He heard a cry of pure
anguish, a bellow of rage…threw up his hands in an instinc-
tive and futile attempt to hold back the inevitable. Instead,
something flashed into his line of sight from out of nowhere,
hit him hard. He felt himself falling.

Even as his mind was screaming *Rhia… No!* he heard two
shots, one after the other. And then he was lying on his back
on the cold stones with Rhia half on top of him, and her gun
was slowly drooping, falling from her limp hand.

Dazed, he lifted his head, straining to see beyond her
inert body. And his heart stopped. A few yards away, Vladimir was crouched, swaying, blood dripping from one
hand. The other still held the gun, which he brought slowly
around until it was pointed directly at Rhia. Nikolas could
see his teeth gleaming in a grimace of pure malice. And all
he could do was fold himself over her body and brace himself once again, waiting to feel the impact of bullets tearing
into his flesh.

Once again, that particular horror was spared him. Instead,
he was forced to watch in dreadful slow motion as King Weston, summoning all his reserves of strength, lashed out and
struck the gun from Vladimir's hand, then crumpled slowly
to the ground. He had to watch helplessly as Vladimir, blind

with rage and pain, swooped down on the helpless man, his fingers curved into eagle's talons, going for the king's throat.

"Nik…"

He almost didn't hear the whisper.

"Nik…take it. My gun…here…I can't…"

Moving as if in a dream, he picked up Rhia's gun from where it had fallen…found it sticky with her blood…aimed and squeezed the trigger.

Vladimir jerked as the first bullet hit him. Spun around and staggered backward with the second. With the third, he toppled slowly over the edge of the ruined bridge and disappeared into the dark water far below.

The silence that followed was like a blanket of ice. Nikolas could feel it encasing his body, his mind, his soul. He wondered if this was what death was like. The death of all hope and love and joy.

He didn't feel the gun slip from his hand. He was folding Rhia in his arms, holding her close and rocking her, trying desperately to force his own life-forces into her still, still body. Praying.

Stay with me, Rhee…stay here, my love. I need you. I love you. You don't have to be queen…I don't want to be king, not without you…

Again, he almost didn't hear her whisper.

"Nik…" Her fingers were touching his face, wiping something from his cheeks. "I'm not going to die."

"You'd bloody well better not," he said fiercely, brokenly. "You're going to marry me. I'll give up the crown. We'll go and raise grapes in Provence, if that's what you want. Just… don't leave me."

"You…don't have to give up the crown." She drew a rasping breath that sent cold ripples of fear through his body. "I'll marry you…one condition…"

"What, my dearest? Anything."

"I get…to keep my job. The…pro bono stuff…at least."

Nikolas was laughing helplessly, unable to speak, when he realized, suddenly, that he wasn't alone. That someone was there beside him, helping him support Rhia's body, lending them both his warmth and courage and strength.

"I believe that can be arranged," King Weston said.

Maximillian and an army of palace guards found them there a few minutes later, the three of them so tightly entwined they made a single silhouette against the sparkling lights of the city.

Epilogue

I.
Royal Palace, Silvershire, one month later

"Do stop checking your tiara, my love."

His Majesty, Nikolas the First, newly crowned King of
Silvershire, spoke to his wife of three weeks and queen of
scarcely three hours out of one side of his mouth as they
made their way slowly along the royal purple carpet that
stretched the entire length of the great reception hall, smiling,
nodding and waving at the glittering crowd of specially
invited guests. "I've been assured that it is firmly attached.
It's not going to come loose and tumble over one eye. And
if it does," he added tenderly, patting the gloved fingers
curved around the crook of his elbow, "heads will most certainly roll."

"Don't joke," Rhia snapped. "I can't believe I let you talk
me into wearing it."

"I'm rather surprised about that, myself, actually. I imagine the chief of protocol was greatly relieved, and I know the citizens of Silvershire—your loyal subjects—loved it."

"I didn't do it for them," she muttered darkly behind a rigid smile. "I did it for you and nobody else. This is our first public appearance together. I didn't want you to be ashamed of me."

The king's chest fluttered with emotions he was still trying to get used to as he let his gaze rest briefly on his bride…his queen. Sometimes the miracle of her was almost more than he could bear, especially when he thought how near he'd come to losing her. It had only been a month since Vladimir's bullet had ripped into her chest, collapsing her lung and narrowly missing an artery. And scarcely three weeks since he'd married her in a small—very small, very private—ceremony in the newly renovated royal suite in the palace's medical facility. Only Lady Zara, Lord Shaw and King Weston had been present as witnesses. Lord Russell Carrington, in his capacity as regent and acting head of state, had performed the ceremony. Immediately afterward, Nikolas had taken his wife off to the south of France for rest, recuperation and TLC. *Lots* of TLC. Which seemed to have done the trick, he was pleased to note. The vibrant color had returned to her cheeks, and the kitty-cat glow to her eyes.

"I'm touched, my darling, but there is no way on earth you could possibly shame me. I'm insanely proud of you, you know. Not to mention madly in love."

"Yes, well…just wait until the paparazzi catch me climbing up someone's balcony—oh, look, there's Zara and Walker. I haven't seen them since we got back from Provence. We really must invite them over for dinner soon, Nik."

"Don't try to distract me, minx. If you think I'm going to let that outrageous remark go by…" He aimed a kingly smile over her head, while his eyes burned down at her from under his lashes with a husband's stern authority. "There will be no more balcony-climbing for you. Not for the next several months, at least. The doctor said—"

She gave a soft gasp. "Hush! Don't you dare tell anyone. Not yet. You know I want to keep it secret, at least for the first few months. I hate it when people start counting the months."

"They'll do that anyway, you know. And if you intend to keep our secret, you're going to have to do something about that glow…."

They reached the end of the reception line at last. The orchestra struck up a waltz, the carpet was rolled up and carried away. Nikolas turned to Rhia and bowed over her hand.

"My queen…my dearest love…may I have this dance?"

Her heart fluttered and tears pricked—she was still a little weak from her injuries, she supposed. But to be truthful, in spite of her griping and grumbling—which they both knew was all for show—as she allowed herself to be swept away in her husband's arms, she felt as though she were waltzing on clouds.

How did this happen? How did I get so lucky? Look at them—all the crowned heads and dignitaries of the entire world—watching me—me!—dance with the most beautiful, wonderful man in the world, and all of them—the women, at least—envying me in their hearts…

And then, in that glittering sea of faces…one jumped out at her. Familiar. *Impossible.*

A shaft of cold stabbed through her. She gasped…stumbled. Nikolas's arms tightened around her, and his concerned whisper touched her ear. "What is it? Are you in pain?"

"I—no. No, I'm fine. I just…thought I saw…someone. Never mind." *Impossible.*

The waltz ended and another began. Nikolas tucked her hand in the bend of his arm and led her to the sidelines, as behind them other couples began to drift out onto the dance floor. They moved together through the throng, accepting congratulations and well wishes, greeting friends and dignitaries…until Rhia suddenly halted, her fingers tightening on Nikolas's arm.

"Nik, who is that man—the silver-haired one talking to

King Weston? I can't tell who it is, from the back, but I feel as if I should know him." Her voice was breathless. The still-healing surgical scar on her chest tingled and burned like fire.

"Let's go and see," her husband said, in an expressionless voice that was a dead giveaway in itself.

But she let him lead her through the crowd anyway, her feet moving of their own volition, it seemed. Her heartbeat pounded mercilessly against her aching chest.

And then…the man turned. The shaft of ice stabbed through her again, then melted instantly in the heat of fury. "Bloody hell. What's he doing here?" she hissed, turning her face to Nikolas's shoulder. "Who invited him?"

"I did," he said, smiling crookedly and lifting an eyebrow as he looked down at her. "I know you're angry, dearest, but I also know you will forgive me, in time." His eyes softened, and the smile faded. He lifted her hand to his lips. "My wedding gift to you, my love. You gave me back my father. Now, I return the favor."

He turned, keeping a firm hand on her elbow, to greet King Weston and his companion.

The tall, tanned, silver-haired man shifted his flute of champagne hastily to his other hand in order to shake the one Nikolas offered him, but his vivid green eyes came right back to Rhia. He looked slightly dazed, and, to her utter amazement, uncertain as he shook his head and said wryly, "Well, Rhee, looks like you've grown up a bit since I saw you last."

She drew an uneven breath. She could feel her husband's hand, strong and steady on her elbow, feel his warmth and love all around her…enfolding her. She could hear his words, telling her what she'd needed for so long to hear. She took another breath, and felt the tension inside her ease.

"Hello, Dad," she said, and walked into her father's arms.

II.
University Medical Center, Silverton

Zara, Duchess of Perthegon, and her husband, Lord Walker Shaw, stepped past the security guards at the door and advanced into the room on tiptoe, eyes shining, faces wreathed in smiles. Dr. Shaw shook Nikolas's hand while Zara, being a creature of tradition, dropped him a quick curtsey before she bent to kiss Rhia's cheek.

"Dear, you look absolutely beautiful. And so does this little angel." Her voice had dropped to a whisper in deference to the newborn princess sleeping soundly in her father's arms.

"She is beautiful, isn't she?" Rhia hadn't been able to take her eyes off of her daughter from the first moment she'd laid eyes on her. "I think she looks like her daddy, don't you?"

"Oh, no," said the King of Silvershire, gazing down at his daughter with a besotted grin. "She's absolutely the image of her mother—thank God."

"I don't think I've ever seen so many flowers," Zara said, gazing around at the room, which had begun to look more like a hothouse than a hospital room. "Who are they all from?"

"Oh, everyone—those over there are from Prince Charles and the Duchess…that obscenely huge one is from my father, naturally." Rhia rolled her eyes. "He seems to think money spent equals love."

"For some people, it does," Dr. Shaw remarked.

"Well…anyway. Those little pink rosebuds are from Chase and Sydney—they were here earlier. Sydney's baby is beautiful, too, isn't she?"

Zara nodded. "We saw them as were coming in. Yes, she's just adorable. Whatever else you can say about Reginald, he was a very handsome man."

Her husband gave a warning cough. Rhia rushed on, "Oh—and these right here are from Russell and Amelia—oops, I mean, Their Royal Majesties, the King and Queen of Gastonia." She grimaced apologetically; she was still getting used to the protocol of titles. "They're coming for the christening, by the way."

"Did you check the bouquet for rubber snakes?" Zara asked tartly, and her husband chuckled.

"She's still ticked because Lord Carrington got her with a water balloon the last time he was here. Personally, I think it's great that even a king can have an inner child."

"Well," Zara said, touching a finger to the sleeping baby's downy head, "we'll leave you three alone—we just stopped by to say hello and greet the new arrival. We're on our way to the opening of the Alzheimer's and Dementia Center at Perth Castle. King Weston is supposed to cut the ribbon. I hope—"

Nikolas nodded. "He's been here already. Stopped by on his way to the ceremony as well."

"Oh, good. Okay, then, I guess we'll see you at the christening." Zara dipped another curtsey as she turned to go, then paused in the doorway. "Speaking of which, have you two decided on a name yet?"

Rhia and Nikolas looked at each other. Nikolas nodded.

"Yes, we have," Rhia said, drawing a breath that quivered with happiness. "It's…Sarah."

Zara looked startled for a moment, then brightened. "Oh— *Sarah*. That's lovely. Is it *for* anyone in particular?"

Rhia looked into her husband's eyes and smiled. "For serendipity," she whispered.

Author's Note

In addition to abolishing by royal decree the restrictions of gender on the laws of primogeniture governing inheritance of property and titles, in the first year of his reign, King Nikolas the First established Silvershire's first democratically elected parliament. He also appointed a special committee to draft a new constitution for the country, to include articles providing for the future of the monarchy. Popular opinion being in favor of retaining Silvershire's monarchy as a cherished part of its history and traditions, provisions are being considered whereby future rulers may be chosen or deposed according to the will of the people.

* * * * *

By Request

RELIVE THE ROMANCE WITH THE BEST OF THE BEST

My wish list for next month's titles...

In stores from 20th April 2012:

❏ Marrying the Italian – Melanie Milburne, Caroline Anderson & Margaret McDonagh

❏ Rocky Mountain Brides – Patricia Thayer

3 stories in each book - only £5.99!

In stores from 4th May 2012:

❏ The Mistresses – Katherine Garbera

Available at WHSmith, Tesco, Asda, Eason, Amazon and Apple

Just can't wait?

Visit us Online — You can buy our books online a month before they hit the shops! **www.millsandboon.co.uk**

0412/05

Book of the Month

We love this book because...

Rafe St Alban is the most dark-hearted, sinfully attractive rake in London. So get ready for fireworks when he sweeps prim Miss Henrietta Markham off her feet in Marguerite Kaye's compellingly sensual story of redemption!

On sale 4th May

Visit us Online

Find out more at
www.millsandboon.co.uk/BOTM

0412/BOTM

MILLS & BOON

Special Offers

Every month we put together collections and longer reads written by your favourite authors.

Here are some of next month's highlights— and don't miss our fabulous discount online!

On sale 20th April

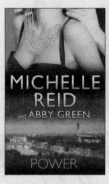

On sale 20th April

On sale 20th April

Save 20%
on all Special Releases

Find out more at
www.millsandboon.co.uk/specialreleases

Visit us Online

0412/ST/MB369